GLINDA

GLINDA: The GOOD Witch

A Novel by

R.W. ADAMS

Standard Paperback Edition
ISBN: 978-1-9191662-7-8
Printed in the United Kingdom

Cover Design & Visual Direction by R.W. Adams
Published by Blueprint Publishing Group.

Oz

DREADHOLLOW
MOUNTAIN

ZILLIGOON
LAKE

UGABU
TRIBE

DRAETH MOR

GLINDA'S
CASTLE

WINKIE MARKET

FEATHERED
WYRM

W I N K I E   C O U N T R Y

DEADMAN'S
CEMETARY

VALLAS
TRIBE

GOATEEY
GANEE
TRIBE

OZIAN FOREST
CAMP

ZINKWATER
LAKE

N

W   E

S

LORD OBSCURO
CASTLE

SILVERSWILL
LAKE

QUADLIN
CITY

QUADLIN

The Land of Oz

GILLIKIN FOREST

GILLIKIN MAIN

MT. VELLADINE

MT. LURLINE

GILLIKIN COUNTRY

YELLOW BRICK ROAD

NOTTICA FARM

OZ UNIVERSITY

THE INN

GILLIKIN MARKET

RAVENTHORNE FARM

MUNCHKINLAND

EMERALD CITY

POPPY FIELDS

MUNCHKIN CAPITAL

OZ BANK

YELLOW BRICK ROAD

PRYZM ROAD

LITTLE MAN'S BRIDGE

ENCHANTED FOREST

UPPER UPLANDS

FAIRMOOR CASTLE

VEILFORGE CASTLE

SILVERCREST ACADEMY

WILLOW-WOOD HILLS ACADEMY

LANDS

SOLAR TEMPLE

MID UPLANDS

COUNTRY

WATERFALL GARDEN

LOWLANDS

DEADLY DESERT

To Ami, thank you for being the best Sister in the world,
sitting on my bed listening to me read whenever I finished a chapter.

"Beware those who proclaim themselves good,
and cherish those who dare to admit they are wicked."

Contents

I *Before*

II *Change*

III *Undone*

Prologue

The smoke danced. A curl into the violet sky as the firewood crackled, carrying the scent of scorched thistle and sweet moss. At the campfire, seven children in velvet cloaks huddled for warmth from the burning **Kindling** and each other's company.

"Can you tell us the story?" asked the smallest child, curling her knees to her chest. "The one—"

"You always ask for stories," muttered the tall boy, though he grinned all the same.

"Which one?" asked The Storyteller, their voice low and honey-thick. The Storyteller leaned closer to the fire, its light gilding their features in amber, eyes catching gold. "The girl who fell from the stars and crushed the witch beneath her house? Or the green one, with the hooked nose and terrible laugh?"

"No," the smallest one growled. "Not the Wicked Witch. Not the girl with the dog. The *Good* one. The one with the bubbles!"

"Ah," The Storyteller gasped, drawing a hush from the circle. Even the trees seemed to pause.

"The one with the name soft as a lullaby."

"Glinda," one child whispered.

"The Good Witch of the *North*," another breathed.

"No! You're wrong, she was the Good Witch of the South."

"No, she wasn't," a boy rebutted.

The children turned wide-eyed to The Storyteller who remained silent as they quarrelled.

The Storyteller gave a knowing smile, letting the kindling burn fill the pause as it transformed, curling at the edges like burnt paper.

"You are all amiss. See, that's not the version I know, because she wasn't as good as you all believe her to be."

One of the children pulled their cloak tighter. Another stared into the fire and whispered, "I don't think I want to know the truth anymore…"

The Storyteller looked up at the sky, almost like someone or something was watching from above. "But what I will tell you, is the absolute truth. Because the Fates see all and know all and this they have accounted for."

"So, tell us! If we have it completely wrong, then—how can she not be good when it is in her name?"

"Names lie," said The Storyteller. The children leaned in.

"She was different," The Storyteller continued. "And in Oz, *different* is dangerous. They say she made herself good. Learned to wear it like perfume. Learned that smiles and silk could hide almost anything. But what if… she was just as wicked as the green one?"

"But she *helped* Dorothy," the tall boy protested. "She gave her the slippers!"

"She was beautiful," said another. "How could she be as wicked as the Witch of the West?"

A log snapped, and sparks rose like fireflies into the dark.

"Then you too are part of the misled," The Storyteller murmured.

"They say the Wicked Witch was her sister," someone whispered.

"They say they were more than that," said another.

"They say Glinda was the real witch."

"No," a girl scoffed. "She had no magic at all. Her power was people."

The children turned toward The Storyteller, breath held.

"What do you say?"

The Storyteller's eyes gleamed.

"I say Oz has always told the same story—history written by the ones who remain. They needed someone to name as good so they could name another as wicked."

The Storyteller paused. Their gaze lifted skyward once more.

"But now… I'll tell you the whole truth. Not as I've heard it—"

Their voice fell to a whisper.

"—but as I *know* it."

A hush.

The fire popped. A single spark flared bright pink—then vanished. A wind stirred the clearing, gentle but sudden, brushing their faces like breath.

"The Fates," the smallest one murmured.

No one else spoke but The Storyteller.

"This is Oz as it was. Not as it is remembered. But as it truly was."

This tale has been spun in many ways, each telling veiled in half-truths, each world spinning its own version. But now, let the *Fates* reveal to you, the ***Absolute Truth***.

BEFORE

Before

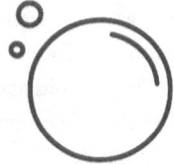

CHAPTER 1

Somewhere Over the Rainbow

long time ago, Somewhere Over the Rainbow, as the saying goes, there lived a girl, perched higher than most, in the loftiest part of the South of Oz. Glinda was her name as I'm sure you're aware; it is most *popular* on this edge of town and across worlds. In this part of the world though, such a name has the familiarity of a lullaby, repeated often, hummed in polite circles, woven into the fabric of aristocratic expectation.

She was fair of skin, blonde-ish of hair, and born to parents of immense wealth. Not the sort of wealth that simply *buys* things, but the kind that *inherits* things: influence, reputation, a legacy polished so relentlessly that its gleam could blind even those who had no wish to look upon it. They lived atop the highest mountain, a place so elevated it made all the rest of Oz seem like a sunken world. From this vantage point, Esmelda and Dainhurst Fairmoor—Glinda's parents, if one could call them that, surveyed the land below with a kind of detached curiosity, as if observing a colony of ants scurrying about their inconsequential concerns.

Esmelda, blonder than blonde itself, had eyes the colour of melted emeralds and a smattering of freckles, as if she had been lightly dusted with cinnamon by an indecisive *Gohd*. Dainhurst, similarly golden-haired, bore the only meaningful distinction in the household: a robust, self-satisfied moustache that bristled with its own silent authority. But more on them later.

Today was a *special* day.

The sun rose from the West, as it did every morning, because in Oz, the sun does not bother itself with *Otherworldly* conventions, the Fairmoors made their way to the highest tower of their castle. This was their morning ritual: to take their breakfast in the west wing, where they could see munchkinland and enjoy the distant commotion of the munchkinlanders below. A touch uncivilized, those munchkins, but entertaining in their own way, like watching fireflies in a jar.

The morning's repast consisted of honeybee tea and a freshly baked cream tart, the preferred delicacies of the insufferably well-bred. It would not do to begin the day without them.

BEFORE

Glinda was not alone in this castle of alabaster and glass. There was an older sister, Gisella, three years older and fairer still—so fair, in fact, that the sun itself seemed to dim in her presence, as if conceding defeat. It was said that her beauty rivalled the stars in the sky. And if you found that hard to believe, well, you had only to ask Esmelda and Dainhurst. They would assure you that it was absolutely true.

But today was not Gisella's day. Today belonged to the newborn Glinda, whose *Moonshine Coronation* was at hand.

The household bustled in barely restrained chaos, though the Fairmoors themselves moved at their usual unhurried pace, descending the grand staircase while servants scrambled to prepare the infant for her first great entrance into Ozian society. Outside, the stable boy ensured that the *Golden Goose* carriage was properly polished, while the footman packed spare shoes, because the very notion of mid-Upland dirt being tracked into their **home** was simply *unthinkable*.

By Morn-Mid Oz'Clock, equivalent to 12pm in the *Otherworld*, the grand gates swung open. Lady Esmelda, Sir Dainhurst, and Gisella stepped into their carriage with effortless grace, while maid Zelena followed, cradling baby Glinda in one arm beneath her bosom and dragging an enormous suitcase in the other. The Fairmoors did not believe in *surprises*. It was best to be prepared for anything, whether it be an impromptu rainstorm or an inconveniently timed aristocratic funeral.

With heads high and noses higher, the Fairmoors set off toward the Solar Temple.

By Sir Dainhurst's standards, the journey was agonizingly long, twenty Oz'mins at least, though the *Pryzm Road*, a path made of crystals reserved for the distinguished, could shorten the trip to fifteen. Even so, it was an eternity to endure the indignity of travel. He spent the ride huffing and sighing at various inconsequential irritations, while Esmelda gazed listlessly at the passing scenery, and Gisella examined her reflection in a handheld mirror, making imperceptible adjustments to her already flawless visage.

As for baby Glinda, well.

Dainhurst had not looked at her. Not *really*. There was something about the child that unsettled him. Perhaps it was the shade of her hair—three shades darker than it should have been. Or perhaps it was the peculiar tilt of her nose, an eerie echo of some long-forgotten ancestor whose portrait had been discreetly tucked away in the Family History room, where unpleasant features went to be forgotten.

But it did not matter. The ceremony was an obligation, and obligations were to be met.

Upon arrival at the temple gates, the footman swiftly exchanged their shoes, one could not *possibly* touch Mid-Upland dirt with Upper Upland shoes. The Fairmoors were promptly led inside by Wise Sage escorts.

The Solar Temple, true to its name, shimmered with refracted light. The chandelier that looked like droplets of enchanted water hung suspended from the ceiling, catching the sun's rays and scattering them across the monastery in dazzling patterns. The floor, composed of rare Winkie Country milkglass, gleamed beneath their feet. The benches, carved from dragon scales sourced from the Southern Midlands, lent the space an air of ancient, rustic grandeur.

Dainhurst gave a derisive sniff.

"Cheap oak."

Esmelda, distracted by the unfamiliar thickness of the air—*was the oxygen denser here?*—paid him no mind

A harp and drum orchestra accompanied their procession, though the Fairmoors appeared utterly unmoved. Esmelda carried Glinda in the most perfunctory manner possible, ensuring she appeared maternal *enough*. Dainhurst, with an air of weary efficiency, led them toward a private chamber.

The door was ajar.

"Welcome, my Fairmoors," came a deep voice, reverberating from the empty room.

Gisella's eyes darted about, searching for its source. Moments later, a figure materialized, a nearly hairless man in pristine white robes, carrying a stack of papers with the practiced ease of one who dealt in bureaucracy.

This was the Grand Sage, Barbarus.

He smiled, spreading his arms in greeting.

"We welcome another day at the temple with a new ray of sunshine to coronate," he declared.

Dainhurst exhaled sharply. "We can only thank Goodness, Barbarus."

Barbarus chuckled. "Ah, the famous Fairmoor punctuality. 'A Fairmoor always arrives on time', isn't that what they say?" He laughed as though he had uttered the cleverest remark ever to pass a munchkin's lips.

Esmelda, still fixated on the atmospheric conditions, remained unimpressed. Dainhurst, meanwhile, ran a skeptical hand along the surface of Barbarus' imported willow desk, testing its authenticity.

With a flourish, Barbarus produced two sheets of parchment.

"Same as last time?" Dainhurst inquired.

"A slight upcharge," Barbarus admitted cheerfully. "It's all in the fine print."

Dainhurst, unfazed, withdrew a *Silverwinkle* fountain pen and signed both documents with mechanical precision. Business concluded, it was time to begin the coronation, then to make their way back ***home***, where the air was always right and perfect.

The Fairmoors followed the Wise Sage, Barbarus, as he exited the room with haste.

"We should ring the bells now and begin the ceremony, don't you think? The sun is already burning at its brightest," Barbarus suggested.

"Yes, Barbarus. We can begin as soon as possible," replied Dainhurst, his voice betraying a sense of impatience as if eager to get the task over with.

BEFORE

Outside, the temple bells rang, a signal to the waiting nobility, empresses, dukes, and gentry (all of whom, by sheer coincidence, were blonde or platinum-haired) to take their places upon the dragon-scale benches.

The choir began to hum the *Day Songbird* melody, its sacred notes swirling through the chamber like invisible threads of salvation. It was said this song had the power to purify even the darkest of souls.

Not that such a thing was *needed* here.

The final note hung in the air, delicate and trembling. The applause was graceful. Then it grew louder because the Fairmoors had taken their place.

And the ceremony was about to begin.

Barbarus, having perfected the art of pronouncement, took a preparatory breath, his voice a rolling thunder across the temple's marble expanse.

"We are gathered," he intoned, with the same reverence he might use to inaugurate a new star in the heavens, "to mark the birth of a kindling. To bear witness. To introduce—"

He hesitated, a momentary pause that might have passed for dramatic flair if not for the sidelong glance he shot Esmelda, who in turn, blinked as though woken from a pleasant, if irrelevant, dream.

"Gli—Glinda," she murmured, tasting the name as if it were an unfamiliar dish she had once encountered at a noblewoman's banquet and had been too polite to refuse.

Barbarus recovered seamlessly. "To introduce to you the kindling, Glinda. May she always be Good."

The response came in unison, a choir of devotion or obligation, difficult to tell. "May she always be Good."

With the assuredness of someone who had lifted a hundred infants to the light and received only applause in return, Barbarus took the child from Esmelda's limp grasp and hoisted her aloft.

A hush.

Not the anticipatory hush of awe, nor even the indulgent silence afforded to noble newborns, but something else, something more akin to doubt.

A rustle of silk, a clearing of throats, a faint, stifled gasp. The audience, each a curator of generational perfection, took in the child's attributes: the hair, three shades too dark; the nose, unmistakably reminiscent of an ancestor who had been, at best, a quiet embarrassment and, at worst, a scandal. The whispers swelled, then subsided, as the weight of decorum pressed them into silence.

Barbarus studied the child for the first time. There was something unsettling about her, no, not unsettling, just... ugly. But he was not paid to ponder. He was paid to proceed.

"Now, let us see what the future holds for this kindling," he declared, his voice booming with forced normalcy. "Bring forth the Raindrop Gemz!"

From the wings, a veiled woman glided forward, bearing a tray that seemed to hum with its own inner radiance. Eight stones, each a jewel of impossible clarity, pulsed in hues of red, orange, yellow, green, blue, indigo, violet, and pink. The child would choose one, and in doing so, her destiny would be sealed.

A tense whisper slithered from Esmelda to Dainhurst. "Which do you think she'll pick?"

"She had better pick green or yellow," he muttered, his eyes locked on the tray as though willing fate itself into obedience. "Like everyone else in the family."

"If she knows what's good for her," Esmelda murmured in return.

The child's fingers, chubby with infancy, wavered over the stones. A collective inhalation.

Then—

Pink.

Gasps. A maid fainted. A noblewoman clutched her husband's arm as if the ground had become unstable beneath her feet. Dainhurst stiffened, his spine a rod of fury barely contained. Esmelda swayed, momentarily unmoored, and clutched at her husband's sleeve.

Barbarus swallowed. He had not prepared for this. He gestured for water.

Dainhurst's voice was strangled with outrage, though he contained it. He let out a little laugh then found his words at last. "This is ridiculous, certainly you made a mistake. Redo it."

Barbarus, ever the pacifier, raised a conciliatory palm. "The Ozma's decree is clear: the chosen stone is final."

"No," Dainhurst said, his voice like iron dragged over gravel. "Not this time."

The crowd stirred, murmurs rising into a chant. "Redo. Redo."

Barbarus hesitated. But he was nothing if not pragmatic. "Very well. But only this once."

He cleared his throat, voice lowering. "It is known that no kindling has chosen the pink stone in three hundred and thirty-three years. Not since Seraphina: The Forsaken Witch."

A voice from the crowd shrieked, "How dare you mention her name in here!".

Ignoring the protest, Barbarus continued, "This redo will be final. The stone she chooses will determine her fate."

A second attempt. Then a third. A fourth.

Each time, the same result. The small, unassuming fingers drifted inevitably, inexplicably, to the pink gem.

The sun passed its zenith. The other stones dulled. Only one still glowed.

Barbarus exhaled, the weight of inevitability pressing down upon him. "I'm sorry," he murmured, but to whom, it was unclear.

BEFORE

Dainhurst moved. In a blur of suppressed fury made manifest, he wrenched the child from Barbarus' hands, snatched the pink gem from the tray, and cast it to the marble floor.

A silence deeper than reverence, deeper than horror, settled upon the temple.

The nobility watched, their lips pursed, their minds already turning.

Glinda, still cradled in the arms of an ashen-faced Esmelda, stared at the empty space where the gem had lain. And without a word, Dainhurst stormed out of the temple, with Esmelda, Gisella and Glinda trailing behind, leaving the gathered nobility in stunned silence.

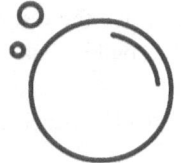

CHAPTER 2

There's No Place Like Home

The Fairmoors located their carriage with the precision of those accustomed to grand departures, Dainhurst barking a final instruction to the footman, Esmelda smoothing the hem of her gown as she stepped inside, and Gisella, oblivious to the tense undercurrent, dangling her feet over the edge of the step before climbing in.

The hush that settled over them as the wheels found purchase on the *Pryzm Road* was thick, almost suffocating. Esmelda, ever attuned to atmospheres both social and meteorological, noted that the air inside the gilded compartment felt significantly denser than it had been in the Mid-Uplands, though whether it was the fault of the cramped quarters or the weight of unspoken grievances, she could not be sure. But perhaps it was best to say nothing until they were in the confines of their castle. After all, there was no place like *home*.

Gisella, in her usual way, cared for none of it. She pressed her nose against the glass, naming the bluebirds flying way up high, as if bestowing a title upon a creature might grant it some permanence in the world.

It was Dainhurst, of course, who finally ruptured the silence. He let out exaggerated sighs, hoping someone would acknowledge him, and when no one did, he huffed louder.

"Why call it a Moonshine Coronation if it's all about the sun?" he groused, arms folded. "The deception of it! The audacity! Ever since I acquired fifty percent of the Mid-Uplands estate, they've taken every opportunity to make a fool of me. But I won't stand for it."

Esmelda made a sound of agreement, soothing his ire with a gentle nod—one of her more practiced gestures.

"We won't stand for it, Dainhurst," she echoed, though her words, unlike his, were featherlight, meant to placate rather than enflame.

But Dainhurst's attentions had already shifted. His gaze, sharp as a blade, landed on the sleeping form of his youngest daughter, Glinda, her tiny hands curled against her chest.

"Why is this kindling determined to ruin me?" he muttered. "Why couldn't she have chosen green or yellow like the rest of us? Even a lesser colour, something dull, something agreeable! But pink? Pink has no place, Esmelda. Am I being unreasonable?"

"No, my darling, not at all," Esmelda assured him, her voice as smooth as a diplomat's.

And so, he turned to Gisella instead, running his fingers through her golden hair, so silken, so obediently correct in its shimmer. Here, at least, was a daughter he could take pride in.

But as the carriage approached the towering silhouette of their castle, his composure faltered once more. His eyes flicked back to Glinda, still sleeping, blissfully ignorant of the disappointment she embodied.

"If it had to be an off-colour, why not red?" he murmured, as if the baby might answer. "I don't care much for other Quadlings, but at least red would've sufficed. I am a reasonable man, but now you're the only baby in Oz without a tribe."

The carriage jerked to a halt. The footman swung the door open, and standing just beyond the threshold was Zelena, hands folded, prepared to take the child inside for her evening feeding. Behind her, the castle loomed, its high arches and burnished spires reflecting the last of the day's light. They'd been out for hours, and the sky was already beginning to darken, stretched wide and indifferent, a muted violet bruising at the edges. Glinda looked weary and hungry, though nothing a warm bottle of *Moss-Dew* couldn't fix. Perhaps a *Tulip Gumdrop*, too, something to lull her back to sleep.

◇

The following day, Dainhurst summoned their personal physician, Dr. Thistle. The matter, after all, could not be ignored. Something had to account for the absurdity of it, the pink, the peculiar nose, the utter disregard for heredity. Surely, there was a medical explanation.

Was she mentally unstable? Diseased? Special in all the wrong ways?

Dr. Thistle arrived promptly at noon, his assistant in tow, with a trolley full of medical equipment and *giZmos*, just as Dainhurst had instructed. The doctor made his way up the long hallways and into Dainhurst's office, where they discussed the purpose of the visit.

The doctor, a small man with a severe expression, listened as Dainhurst laid out his concerns with the gravity of a man revealing a terrible national secret. As the assistant finished setting up in the grand hall, Glinda, swaddled in lace, was placed upon the examination table like an offering to the gods of logic and genetics. The doctor circled her with academic curiosity, making little notes in a leather-bound journal. Dainhurst, eager for answers, tried to remain patient, though the tension in the room was as sharp as an *Ozian Guillotine*. Esmelda, growing increasingly paranoid, couldn't hold back any longer.

"So, what is it?" she demanded, half rising from her chair. "What disease does she have?"

Dr. Thistle paused, his pencil tapping against his chin. "No disease, ma-lady."

Esmelda's expression hardened.

Dainhurst frowned.

They had never questioned the expertise of Dr. Thistle before, but this time, something didn't sit right. If there was no disease and no malady, that meant there was nothing to blame as to why Glinda decided to inherit her destitute ancestor's weird nose and chosen the pink gem.

"Are you sure?" Dainhurst asked, his voice strained. "Perhaps you should use one of your *giZmos* and look again."

"I suggest," Dr. Thistle replied, with the placid air of a man stating the obvious, "that the child suffers from an overwhelming case of normality."

Silence.

Dainhurst sank into his chair, rubbing his temple as if he might massage the facts into something more palatable. Esmelda, unwilling to let the matter rest, pressed on.

"But look at her," she insisted, gesturing at Glinda. "That nose. And the pink. The pink, Thistle. Are you sure I did nothing wrong? I knew I shouldn't have taken that Pondicherry Juice you prescribed while I was carrying her."

Dr. Thistle quickly cut her off.

"This is not a side effect of the juice, Esmelda. Her face may not fit the typical features of your people, but that doesn't make her sick. I have another appointment soon so if that is all?"

Frustrated, Esmelda waved her hand dismissively.

"Fine, fine. If that's all, then go."

With that, the doctor closed his journal, snapped his bag shut, and took his leave.

The house, for a moment, was utterly still. Then Esmelda waved for Zelena to take Glinda away to bathe her, to feed her, to carry on as though nothing had happened. She called for a *lemon-water* bath to ease her nerves, while Dainhurst retreated to his study, where he could drown his frustrations in ledgers and estate records.

Glinda, blissfully unaware of the discussions surrounding her existence, was carried off by Zelena, who hummed softly as she cradled the child.

Zelena, unlike the Fairmoors, did not see an aberration when she looked at Glinda. She saw something softer, something unguarded, something that might, in time, grow into something remarkable. There was something about Glinda that reminded her of her own childhood, as though caring for the child was like taking care of the younger her, who too had to make do with the limited love of her parents. Although separated by blood and class, it felt like the *Fates* had gifted her, her very own little sister.

Zelena would sing to baby Glinda and tell stories of the old days in Oz, trying to weave goodness into Glinda's soul, even though the child was too young to understand.

But Glinda *did* understand, even as she seemed oblivious to the world around her. She felt the way her mother held her tentatively, at a slight distance away from her body, and that neither of her parents smiled at her happily but instead stole quick, concerned glances at her face, rife with unease.

Meanwhile, Gisella with her radiant smile and energy kept the castle from sinking entirely into its own melancholy. Every morning, before school, she would sing, though croaky, it served as Dainhurst's natural alarm clock, like a *Chickengoose* crowing at dawn. After getting dressed, she would rush to see her little sister to play and sing with her. After school, she did the same. The once-silent halls and rooms now echoed with something dangerously close to joy, and soon enough, the two sisters were inseparable.

The light they brought was palpable, and even Dainhurst and Esmelda noticed the sisterly love Glinda brought out in Gisella, which was the only thing that softened their perception of her, just a little.

◇

And as the years quickly passed, as Glinda grew, the matter of her schooling could no longer be ignored.

Eight years old. That was the expectation. A *kindling* must be sent to school, must be taught the history and must bond with their tribe.

Except Glinda had no tribe.

Esmelda and Dainhurst could no longer hide Glinda in that mesmerising castle of theirs, hidden and locked away for much longer.

And so, with the weight of obligation pressing upon them, the Fairmoors enrolled her, however reluctantly, into *SilverCrest Academy*.

CHAPTER 3

SilverCrest Academy

S chool was to be an adventure, and Glinda was prepared to meet it with bright-eyed enthusiasm. Though, she wondered if the other children would be kind, would the teachers, like her governess, smell of starch and old books? The uncertainty only heightened the anticipation.

The Fairmoors set out early, as was their custom, for Glinda's appointment with the headmistress. Gisella, in an untroubled display of sibling unity, walked beside her sister toward the *Golden Goose* carriage, their bags slung over their backs—Glinda's pink, Gisella's green.

Their parents, by contrast, were uncharacteristically subdued. There was no languid tea-sipping from the castle towers, no wry remarks at the expense of the munchkins below. Dainhurst, usually so grand in his blustering opinions, sat with the rigid silence of a man bracing for bad news. Esmelda, ever the dutiful wife, matched his silence with a graceful melancholy.

The only disruption came from the coachman, who was fond of Glinda in the way that people often are of well-meaning, oblivious creatures.

"Alas! We're here, sire!" he declared with an enthusiasm that might have bordered on mockery if it weren't so sincere.

Glinda barely noticed.

The schoolyard was alive with the buzzing energy of children, a cacophony of voices blending with the creak of swings and the metallic clang of the *Slydes*. It was, at last, the moment she had long awaited: a world populated by potential friends.

She wasn't entirely sure what friendship entailed, but she was determined to find out.

As the carriage doors opened, a desert of children in colourful uniforms poured across the grounds. Every colour of the rainbow was accounted for.

Except pink.

Which of course, did not fit the rainbow.

Gisella, spotting her companions, veered off toward the playground, leaving Glinda to trail behind her parents toward the entrance. There, waiting with the patience of someone who has long since exhausted her supply, stood the headmistress.

"Mrz. Thornegraves, Headmistress of SilverCrest Academy," she intoned, extending a hand in a perfunctory greeting.

Inside her office, she slid two crisp sheets of parchment across the desk. Dainhurst, with the air of a man signing a treaty he did not entirely approve of, produced his *Silverwinkle* fountain pen and scrawled his name.

Formalities complete, Mrz. Thornegraves led them into the hall.

The Fairmoors, whose nerves had been uncharacteristically frayed all morning, maintained a silence that bordered on the unnatural. Ordinarily, their social standing ensured that matters proceeded in their favour without complication. But Glinda, with her infernal pink, had a way of complicating things.

Instead, the headmistress prattled on about school policies, recounting details that were, at best, ornamental. The Fairmoors, already well acquainted with SilverCrest from Gisella's tenure, endured the tour with a strained politeness. The tour dragged on for thirty Oz'mins.

Glinda, much like her father, was impatient. But her eagerness came from excitement, she couldn't wait to meet the other children and play.

At last, the bell rang.

Children gathered in a semi-circle at the entrance, the beginning of the school day.

Glinda's classroom was just ahead. As students hurried inside, Mrz. Thornegraves called for the teacher.

"This is Glinda Fairmo—" she began, and then faltered.

Something in her gaze flickered. A hesitation, a calculation.

She swallowed hard, then turned to Mz. Everburn, the red-haired instructor with startlingly blue eyes.

"Mz. Everburn, this is Glinda Fairmoor of the Uplands. She's your n-new student, so... take care of her."

There was something unsaid in the way her voice caught. A hurried aside followed:

"They're paying large sums. I warn you, tread carefully with this kindling."

Mz. Everburn frowned slightly, confused. Surely, treading carefully was the very nature of education?

Returning to the Fairmoors, she crouched slightly to meet Glinda's gaze, her smile warm. Glinda, who had yet to learn caution in the face of kindness, beamed back, her grin wide and gummy with all the optimism of the untested.

And then, just like that, the Fairmoors turned and walked away.

None of them looked back.

Glinda hesitated at the threshold of the classroom, suddenly uncertain.

Mz. Everburn guided her forward. "Come now, there's nothing to worry about."

The moment she entered, however, the shift in atmosphere was palpable.

Whispers. Stares.

She could feel the scrutiny prickling against her skin.

Her nose. Her hair. Her uniform.

She could hear the unspoken questions.

She shrank under their collective gaze.

Mz. Everburn, unfazed, introduced her to the class. It did little to soften the response.

Still, the lesson began. Today's topic was *Zeography*, the study of Oz's environments.

"Who can tell me what this is?" Mz. Everburn pointed to a projection on the board.

Hands shot up.

A skinny boy with golden curls and emerald eyes named Ominson answered confidently, "That's the Magic Waterfall here in Quadling Country!"

"Correct. And what does it do?"

"It makes you forget!"

"Well done. Can anyone tell me why it makes you forget?"

The room fell silent.

Then, a single hand, hesitant.

Mz. Everburn's gaze softened.

"Glinda?"

She hesitated, then found her voice.

"The waterfall's properties were altered centuries ago by Seraphina the Forsaken Witch," she said, voice small but steady. "She tried to create a raincloud that would make people forget who they were so she could rule Oz. But the first Wizard of Oz stopped her. Ever since, the waterfall has been restricted."

Silence.

The children were not merely stunned by her knowledge.

They were stunned by *her*.

Pink.

Just like Seraphina.

One by one, their expressions changed.

Suspicion.

Mz. Everburn, noting the shift, carried on. But Glinda felt it. The weight of it.

She lowered her head, heels clicking anxiously beneath her desk.

At last, the bell rang.

As the students hurried outside, Mz. Everburn called her forward.

BEFORE

"I was very impressed by your answer, Glinda," she said warmly. "How do you know so much about the waterfall? That's quite advanced for someone your age."

Glinda hesitated, then murmured, "My father has a big library. When my sister's at school, I spend hourz reading alone."

Mz. Everburn's smile remained warm, but there was something else beneath it now, a flicker of recognition, a delicate calculation running behind her eyes. She hesitated, smoothing an imagined crease from her sleeve, before speaking again, her tone light but measured.

"Are you…" a pause, deliberate, careful, "the kindling who chose the pink gem eight Sun-Moons ago?"

A stillness settled over Glinda.

"Yes."

The single word escaped her lips, barely more than breath, and yet it seemed to ripple outward. Shame crept into her posture, coiling like a vine around her shoulders, pulling her inward.

Mz. Everburn straightened, brushing imaginary dust from Glinda's uniform, then pressed a reassuring hand to the child's shoulder.

"Thank you for sharing, Glinda," she said, her voice as soft as spun sugar. "Go outside and enjoy your break. Come see me after school, alright?"

Glinda nodded, an ember of comfort kindling in her chest. She liked Mz. Everburn—the first person in this place to offer her kindness unaccompanied by scrutiny.

The playground was a sea of shifting colours, jewel-toned uniforms swirling in the wind like a field of enchanted wildflowers. Before stepping out, Glinda inhaled deeply, summoning what little *courage* she still possessed.

She crossed the threshold, and the world seemed to contract.

Where once there had been movement, now there was only stillness.

The children, once laughing, playing, bickering—paused. One by one, heads turned, feet shuffled, backs stiffened.

The sea of colour parted before her, a natural, instinctual recoil as if she carried some airborne contagion like *limepox*.

She walked the length of the parting, each step heavier than the last.

The castle had been lonely, yes, but it had been a solitude she understood. This—this was worse. This was a kind of *not-belonging* that settled in the marrow of her bones.

Tears burned at the corners of her eyes, but she refused them the satisfaction of falling. She would not stop, not turn, not run. She would walk forward, even if she did not know where she was headed.

And then, through the blur of shame and unshed tears, she saw her sister.
Gisella.

The familiar green uniform. The golden hair, brighter beneath the sun. A figure solid, unwavering, unafraid.

Glinda barely had time to register her before she was enveloped.

The embrace was immediate, absolute—arms wrapping around her with the kind of quiet authority that needed no declaration.

Glinda did not hesitate. She melted into it, pressing her face against the safety of her sister's shoulder, allowing the tears to flow freely.

The spell of silence broke.

Whispers rippled outward, hushed voices carrying on the wind.

Gisella, princess of the court, did not yet turn to address them. First, she was a sister. She shielded Glinda with her body, allowing her a moment to gather herself.

Then, at last, she whispered, "Are you alright?"

Glinda nodded.

It was a lie, but a necessary one.

Gisella took a slow, measured breath, then turned, straightening. She cleared her throat, deliberate, pointed.

"Whoever wishes to remain friends with me must be kind to Glinda, my *sister.*"

The crowd inhaled as one.

"Sister?"

"I didn't know she had a sister."

Their eyes flickered between the two girls, recalibrating.

The children of the court, sharp-eyed, quick-witted, ever attuned to the shifting sands of social hierarchy, sat with this revelation. And after a moment's careful deliberation, they reached a conclusion:

If Gisella endorsed her, she would be tolerated.

For now.

They told themselves it was fine. They could permit this *creature* in their midst, so long as she did not enchant them, so long as she did not poison their minds with magic water or spells that would make them forget.

Not that it would matter.

Even if she *did*, they reasoned, in the dark, private places of their minds, they would never forget that face.

But Glinda, for all she had learned that day, knew only this:

As long as Gisella was there, she would be alright.

◇

The school day ended, and Glinda had a promise to keep.

At Mz. Everburn's request, she returned.

The classroom was quiet now, the frantic energy of the day drained from its walls. At her desk, Mz. Everburn sat waiting, offering the same unshaken smile she had worn all day.

"Follow me," she said.

Then, without preamble, she took off down the corridor.

Glinda hesitated only a moment before hurrying after her, her small legs struggling to match the teacher's long strides. She stumbled once, but before she could fall, a hand reached out, catching hers, steadying her.

Together, they reached the end of the corridor, where a dim, unmarked door waited like a forgotten secret.

Mz. Everburn pulled a tarnished key from her pocket, slid it into the lock, and turned.

The door groaned open.

Inside—darkness. The scent of aged parchment and candle wax. A room untouched by time.

With a graceful flick of her fingers, Mz. Everburn summoned *firelight* in her palm, and the shadows scattered, revealing rows upon rows of bookshelves stretching into the gloom.

Glinda gasped, whether at the magic or at the sheer impossibility of the hidden library, she did not know.

"You... you have magic?" she gasped, her excitement bubbling over.

Mz. Everburn knelt, her gaze steady.

"I do."

A pause.

"But you must keep it a secret."

Glinda nodded, pulse quickening. It was not just secrecy, it was trust.

"Good girl," Mz. Everburn said, leading Glinda deeper into the library.

It was the first time someone had entrusted her with something that mattered.

But a thought prickled at the edges of her mind. A question.

"Why would anyone want to hide their magic?"

Mz. Everburn smiled, but there was something else in it now, something weightier, something edged.

"*Becoz*, Glinda," she murmured, "people fear what they do not understand, and even more what they cannot control."

Her fingers twitched, and with an elegant flick of her wrist, she sent a row of books into the air. They twirled, hovering, before settling back onto the shelves.

Glinda's mouth fell open.

"You can *do* that too?"

The teacher chuckled.

"Yes, but it's not just for show. Magic is a gift. It's something you're born with, not everyone has it, in its raw form anyway. Today, magic is rare and feared."

"But the Wizard has magic," Glinda pointed out. "People aren't afraid of him."

Mz. Everburn's expression shifted.

"The Wizard? He doesn't have real magic, Glinda. He puts on a spectacle, illusions, and the people really do love when you put on a show," she said, using her body to jolt, making Glinda giggle.

"But real magic, raw magic, like Seraphina's…" Mz. Everburn's voice grew softer. "People still fear it *becoz* of what happened. You've heard the stories, haven't you?"

Glinda nodded but replied firmly, "I don't believe them."

"Smart girl," her teacher said with a proud smile. She gestured, and a single book floated down from a high shelf, landing gently in her hands. The cover read: *Piottor's Collection of Ozian Magical Artifacts.*

"This was my favourite when I was your age," Mz. Everburn said, handing it to Glinda. "Take it. But be careful, don't let your father see it."

Glinda cradled the book like a treasure, her **heart** racing. "Thank you!" she exclaimed before racing out of the library, faster than she ever thought she could run.

At the gates, the *Golden Goose* carriage gleamed in the fading light, its lacquered sides polished to a blinding shine, its gilded trim an unnecessary reminder of their status. Already half inside, Gisella turned, her golden curls bouncing with the movement.

"Hurry, Glinda!" she called, her voice light, unburdened, as if the day had not carried the weight of rejection.

Glinda climbed aboard, careful not to let her eagerness betray her.

◇

By the time they arrived at the castle, dusk had set the Uplands aglow, the sky burnished with pinks and golds that would have made lesser poets weep. The moment the carriage halted, Glinda was out, her legs burning with urgency, darting past the sculpted hedges, the opalescent fountains, the ornamental nonsense of her father's wealth.

"Glinda—wait!" Gisella's voice trailed behind her, concerned, but Glinda would not wait. She tore through the halls, her feet slipping on the polished floors—left, then up the stairs, another right, another right—until she reached the sanctuary of her bedroom, collapsing onto the rose-silk coverlet as if the journey had been far greater than a sprint through their palatial **home.**

Gisella entered a moment later, panting, leaning against the doorframe, studying her. There was curiosity in her eyes, but also a flicker of something else, concern, perhaps, or the ghost of a question she didn't know how to ask.

Glinda hesitated. Then, she made a choice.

"I found this book," she whispered, peeling it from her embrace like some illicit treasure. "It's about magical artifacts."

Gisella stiffened, glancing toward the door as if it might have ears.

"Glinda," she breathed, "you know Father hates magic."

"I know," Glinda replied, just as soft, just as weighted. "Promise you won't tell?"

Gisella's hesitation was brief. "I promise."

"Do you want to see it with me?"

Before the words had fully settled in the air, Gisella was already beside her, so close their shoulders brushed, the familiarity of her presence easing something fragile within Glinda's chest. Together, they cracked open the tome. A plume of dust rose between them, and they coughed in unison before dissolving into quiet laughter.

The pages turned, and they travelled, without moving, to places neither had seen:

The Emerald Shard, the alleged source of Emerald City's perpetual glow.

Fiora's Magical Hairbrush, whispered to weave hairstyles that could ensnare hearts.

The Raindrop Gemz—ah, these they knew, especially Glinda, she knew all too well.

And then, a turn of the page—

Seraphina's Magic Wand.

The room felt colder.

Glinda's **heart** clattered against her ribs. She looked at Gisella, whose expression had changed, shadowed with something unreadable. Glinda searched for words, but before she could speak, footsteps echoed in the hallway, deliberate, heavy.

Then—

"Gisella? Where are you?" A booming voice, and then, more absurdly: "Popsicle has a present for you!"

"Quick, hide the book!" Gisella hissed.

Glinda slammed it shut, shoving it under the bed just as the door swung open.

Dainhurst entered, his imposing frame casting long shadows across the pink-tinged walls. His gaze skimmed the room, landing on Gisella with something resembling warmth.

"Gisella, what are you doing in here?"

"Talking to Glinda," she answered easily, as if it were nothing.

Dainhurst waved the explanation away. "No matter. How was school today?"

Gisella, wisely, ignored the question. Her focus had shifted to the large box in his hands, her curiosity piqued. "What's that, Popsicle?"

Dainhurst smiled, an unusual occurrence, and for that, all the more unsettling. "Open it and see."

The box, half her size, was wrapped with an ostentation that suggested excess rather than affection. But Gisella had always been adept at tearing through artifice. Within moments, the ribbons, the locks, the layers of extravagance had been discarded.

And then—

A gasp.

Inside, nestled in velvet, was a crystal necklace, clear as water yet sharp as a dagger, its frame adorned with delicate spikes that caught the candlelight and fractured it into rainbows.

Both Glinda and Gisella's eyes widened like they were seeing for the first time. The necklace shimmered in the light and a piece like this must have cost a fortune, and it wasn't even her *Born-Day*. And even though Dainhurst spared no expense, this purchase was out of his usual range for Gisella's usual spontaneous gifts. Probably the price of three *Golden Goose* carriages. Gisella, giddy, got off Glinda's bed and hugged her father.

"Thank you, Popsie."

Glinda still in awe of the necklace was entranced but quickly snapped out of its hypnosis as she noticed a slight chip on it but remained quiet because, truly and deeply, she was very happy for her sister. If there was anyone, she knew who deserved this, it was Gisella.

"It's one of a kind, only one ever made, do you like it?" Dainhurst asked. "*Becoz* if you don't I get you the *Sunspell Stone* instead".

Gisella, still transfixed, shook her head. "No, it's perfect." She turned to Glinda with a knowing grin, breaking the moment's strangeness. "Tell me I look pretty with it on."

Glinda, smiling despite herself, said, "You're pretty, Gisella."

Silence followed. Gisella, perhaps sensing it too, clutched the necklace to her chest and announced, "I'm going to show Mumsy."

And just like that, she was gone.

Now alone, Glinda watched as Dainhurst's gaze swept the room.

"It's dusty in here," he remarked, voice absent of real concern. "You should clean up, and maybe take a cue from your sister. Her room is always spotless."

Glinda bit the inside of her cheek, resisting the obvious reply: that Gisella's room was cleaned daily by Zelena, their maid, whereas Glinda's remained untouched. She couldn't imagine asking Zelena to do the same for her. To Glinda, it somehow felt insulting to ask someone she viewed as a sister to do her dirty work.

Dainhurst did not wait for an answer. He turned and left.

Glinda exhaled. The room settled.

She waited a moment longer, then reached under the bed, fingers brushing against the rough spine of the book.

She pulled it out.

And then, just as before, she turned the page.

CHAPTER 4

GOODness

There it was.

Seraphina's wand.

The very instrument wielded by the woman who had unravelled the fabric of Oz, who had sown discord with every flick of her wrist, who had, if the stories were true, warped the very nature of magic itself. And yet, at first glance, the wand hardly seemed the harbinger of destruction it was claimed to be. It was elegant, almost delicate, gleaming with a soft iridescence that suggested purity rather than peril.

Glinda, a girl who had spent her young life distinguishing the beautiful from the unbeautiful, knew at once that this wand did not belong in the latter category.

And yet, how deceptive beauty could be.

She studied the etching below its image in the book, the script carved with the solemnity of a tombstone inscription:

"This is the magic wand of Seraphina: The Forsaken Witch. This infamous relic was used to threaten Oz and brutalise those who defied her. Immensely powerful and dangerous, it is preserved at an undisclosed location but exists only to serve as a reminder of the Evillest witch to ever live."

Evillest.

The word sat uneasily in Glinda's mind. She had, once upon a time, considered herself immune to fairy tales of monstrous witches and noble heroes. But the certainty with which people spoke of Seraphina's wickedness, it had a way of seeping into the cracks of her scepticism. Could so many voices be wrong?

Still, there was the pink gem. The stone had chosen, the same as Seraphina. The coincidence gnawed at her.

She snapped the book shut and exhaled sharply, as if trying to push the thought away with her breath. Lying back on her bed, she stared at the ceiling, willing it to give her an answer. Was she wicked and simply unaware of it? Was she doomed, like Seraphina, to be forsaken?

Three hundred and thirty-three years had passed since another child had selected that cursed gem. Surely, that meant something.

She needed answers.

The castle was vast, and Glinda knew its every corner. Zelena was the wisest person she knew. If anyone could explain what all this meant, it would be her.

The little girl walked down the stairs to the kitchen to look for Zelena; she was always there cooking. But today the kitchen was empty. So, she checked the library in case she was cleaning. Empty too. She checked the gardens, the twenty-two bedrooms, the studies, dining room, the eighteen bathrooms, and even the stables that smelled of warm hay and damp leather. The only thing left to check was the grand hall. She approached the door, the fireplace already burning in the hearth, expecting Zelena but there was no one in there except for her mother.

"Mother," Glinda began, her voice measured, "have you seen Zelena?"

"No," answered Esmelda bluntly, a glass in her hand as she absorbed *The Daily Oz*.

"Oh, okay," Glinda said, lingering, uncertain whether to press further.

"What do you need her for? There are fifteen other maids in this castle."

"I had a question."

Esmelda turned a page. "She's not here," and with a swift shift of attention, she went back to reading her *NewZPapr*.

Glinda chewed her lip. "Can I ask you the question, then?"

This time, Esmelda did look up. Barely. "What is it?"

Glinda exhaled, her fingers tightening around the hem of her sleeve. "Mother… do you think I'm evil?"

Esmelda's expression shifted, briefly, before she caught herself.

"What gave you that idea?"

"Well, I am the only one that picked the pink gem in centuries besides Seraphina, the—"

"Do not speak that name in this house," Esmelda's voice was sharp, a blade against stone. Then, after a beat, she softened, just a fraction. "Come here."

Glinda obeyed, dragging her feet, her **heart** clenching with anticipation.

Her mother regarded her carefully, then spoke. "People aren't good by nature. They do good things, and that makes them good."

Glinda blinked. "Really?"

"Yes." Esmelda's attention returned to the *NewZPapr*, her answer final.

This was the first mother and daughter talk they'd had in years, and this was the first piece of advice her mother gave her. Glinda figured she was right, and it made sense. Though, Zelena had a better way of explaining things that didn't make her second guess herself.

✧

Glinda went back to her room, opened the book she was reading, and took another look at Seraphina's wand. This time, her **heart** was at ease. Then beat a little faster. As long as she chose to do good things, she wouldn't ever be compared or suffer the same fate as *Seraphina, The Forsaken Witch of Oz.*

◇

The very next day Glinda knew what her mission was, and she was going to accomplish it by any means necessary. When going into the *Golden Goose* carriage with Gisella, who was still wearing her crystal necklace, determined to never take it off, Glinda decided to do her first good thing. She opened the carriage door for her sister, closed it herself and made sure that everyone around saw her do it.

They arrived at school early, as always. More time to be good. More time to be seen being good.

When Glinda stepped out of the carriage, the eyes of her peers followed. They always did. But she felt no fear, Gisella was with her, and Gisella was safe.

She had time before class. Enough time to prove herself.

She needed a friend. A proper one.

She tried to catch someone's eye and then make a move, but when she thought she'd caught someone looking at her, they diverted their gaze.

She made her decision to approach a random person.

Glinda scoured around with her eyes, recognised a boy from her class. Ominson, the skinny blonde boy from the day before. Glinda took her strides carefully trying to be as non-threatening as possible so he would not run away. She walked slower than usual and relaxed her face.

Ominson was facing backward, speaking with his friends, so he didn't see Glinda approaching. As she neared, the others saw her coming. And like birds startled from a tree, they scattered.

She swallowed her nerves and spoke with practiced calm. "Hello. My name is Glinda."

Ominson offered a lopsided, uneasy smile. "I know."

A silence stretched between them.

What next? She had not planned this far. Gisella hadn't taught her how she made her friends.

Panic seized her.

"Will you be my friend?"

A chorus of snickers erupted from Ominson's friends, watching from a safe distance.

But Glinda ignored them.

She would not let anything ruin this. Not today.

"Oh—erm."

Ominson hesitated. He tilted his head, scrutinizing Glinda's face, up close now, much closer than he had ever dared to before.

Wait.

She wasn't actually horrifying to look at. Not if one really looked. If one stripped away the things whispered in hallways, the instinctive recoil. If one considered her as just a girl, then—well.

He considered.

"Yes," he decided at last, extending a hand with great formality. "I think we can be friends."

A contract sealed; a matter settled.

For a moment, Glinda could scarcely believe it. Ominson's friends could scarcely believe it either.

Then, with the certainty of a boy who had just upended a natural law, Ominson took Glinda's hand—actually took it—and led her toward his group. The others, having watched this act of social mutiny with hushed fascination, now regarded her in kind.

They saw what Ominson did not. The wrongness of her.

Yet here she was, first endorsed by the princess of the court, Gisella, and now by its prince, Ominson.

And while Ominson was normally a jester, prone to mischief and chaos, today he was solemn in his allegiance. The others, sensing this, granted Glinda what could be considered an embrace, if only in the way an oyster embraces a pearl—tight-lipped and with great reluctance.

But no matter.

If she had not made friends, she had made a friend. And that was, for the moment, enough.

As the Glowblossoms unfurled in the garden, signifying the transition from idle morning chatter to the more structured rhythms of school life, the students arranged themselves into a semi-circle. Ominson took Glinda's hand once more, this time fully, her small fingers swallowed in his grip, and pulled her beside him.

It was a small thing. And yet, to Glinda, it felt like she had been given the world.

Then, as the grand doors groaned open, they filed into the school and into their respective seats.

Mz. Everburn, their instructor, moved between the desks, distributing books with meticulous care. Glinda noted, with a kind of private amusement, that the woman could have easily levitated the books into place with a flick of her wrist. In fact, as she reached Glinda's desk, she winked, as if to confirm: *Yes, I could.*

Today's lesson: Ozian History. A subject Glinda adored with a fervour that most reserve for sweets or starlight.

"Turn to page two hundred and one," Mz. Everburn instructed, "and read about the Impassable Desert."

The rustle of pages filled the air as the students obeyed. When they had finished, Mz. Everburn straightened and surveyed the room.

"Now," she said, with the knowing expression of someone setting a trap, "this book is known to be *confusifying*. But tell me, why do we have the Impassable Desert?"

Only one hand lifted.

Glinda's.

No one else dared. The text was too advanced. Yet Glinda had inspired Mz. Everburn to push the curriculum further, to challenge her students more. And so, while they muttered about how unfair it all was, they also knew who was to blame.

Mz. Everburn, reluctant to make the lesson revolve around a single student, let the silence stretch. But as no other hands rose, she sighed and gestured.

"Glinda?"

Glinda folded her hands primly over her book and recited, "The Impassable Desert was once an ordinary desert, a place where travellers came and went, bringing new cultures, knowledge, and trade to Oz. But the constant flow of outsiders weakened the land's defences. In time, Oz was vulnerable. Exposed. And so, the first Wizard of Oz cast a spell upon the sands, enchanting them so that anyone who set foot upon them would turn to dust. Since then, the only person to enter Oz was the second Wizard, from the skies."

A breath.

"Very good, Glinda. Well done."

Her answer, though drawn from the book, carried an expertise beyond her years, the kind found in texts that had been deemed *not for children*.

A quiet venom filled the air.

Who does she think she is? Does she think she's *better* than us? Oh, look at *Smart Glinda*, with her *insanely rich family* and *perfect sister*.

Something had to be done about that.

Yet, as resentment curled its way through the room, there was one voice that cut through it.

"Well done," Ominson whispered, turning in his seat, his smile genuine.

That small kindness made her **heart** soar.

The scorn of the others was *disgustifying*, yes. But it paled in comparison to the warmth she felt at that moment.

For now, at least, her friend liked her.

And for now, that was enough.

CHAPTER 5

A Friend

The bell tolled its dismissal, and like floodgates unlatched, students spilled into the courtyard in a slow-moving current, seeking their usual haunts and alliances. Glinda was among the first to step outside, not because she wished to rush ahead, but because it was easier than dawdling behind, where conversations might begin without her. She crossed the playground with practiced purpose, arriving at the *Swyngs*, two curved seats suspended from iron chains. Here, she waited.

The others, her friends, or at least the girls she was expected to call such— had wandered to a different corner of the grounds, debating the merit of one game over another. They had not invited her to weigh in, nor had they sought her out. Perhaps they had assumed she would follow, as she always did. But today, she hesitated.

Ominson had not yet emerged.

And if she was being honest, brutally honest in the way one rarely dared to be with oneself, Glinda would admit that the absence of Ominson made her own presence feel like a half-finished spell, unravelling at the edges.

At last, he appeared, stepping into the light like an afterthought. He scanned the crowd, eyes flicking past his usual companions. He did not find Glinda among them. Instead, he found her here, perched upon a Swyng, the chains creaking softly as she rocked back and forth, her heels clicking and the tips of her shoes tapping against the ground in a steady, measured rhythm.

Without a word, he claimed the empty Swyng beside her.

"If we're going to be friends," he said, as though the matter had already been settled, "I need to know more about you."

Glinda stiffened. "How do you mean?" she asked, *dumbfoundified*, feeling at once interrogated and chosen.

Ominson grinned, leaning back, allowing the Swyng to lift him slightly before gravity pulled him forward again. "What's your favourite colour?"

"Green," she said without hesitation.

He raised a brow. "Oh? That was fast."

"I know what I like," she replied, as if it were the simplest thing in the world.

Ominson's grin deepened. "Can you guess mine?"

Glinda tilted her head, considering. "Violet?"

"Ha! How did you know?"

She smirked, nodding toward his uniform. "A lucky guess."

Ominson laughed, and Glinda found herself laughing too, really laughing, not the careful, practiced kind of giggle she gave to fit in, but something real.

"What's your favourite food?" she asked next, emboldened.

"Gooseberry pie and Ample Juice," he said, licking his lips as if conjuring the taste.

Glinda wrinkled her nose. "Yuck! Poppyloaf and Twister Tarts are way better."

"Poppyloaf?" Ominson recoiled in mock horror. "That's disgustifying."

The way Ominson's face churned at the thought of Poppyloaf sent them both into another fit of laughter, their debate playful but firm. Neither would concede defeat, but each secretly enjoyed the challenge of convincing the other.

Across the playground, Gisella was holding court, presiding over her subjects with the grace of an empress, until she realized that one subject was missing.

Glinda.

She turned, shading her eyes against the sun, scanning the courtyard. And there, where the light shone brightest, was her sister, engaged in deep conversation with the prince of the school.

Something in Gisella's chest tightened.

It was not jealousy, not quite. It was something stranger. Something unnameable.

With an urgency she barely understood, Gisella set off toward them, striding faster than she had even when rushing to show Mother her new necklace.

The playground took notice.

She arrived at the Swyngs and stood beside them, waiting.

And waiting.

And waiting.

For the first time in her life, she had to *announce* her presence.

"Glinda, is everything all right?" she asked, her voice clipped, her posture impeccable.

Glinda turned, startled. "Oh, hello, Gisella. Yes, I'm fine."

And then, horrifyingly, she turned back to Ominson, continuing their conversation without further acknowledgement.

Gisella's breath hitched.

She scoffed; a small sound meant to reclaim attention. It did not work.

Standing there a moment longer would be a humiliation beyond repair.

So, she turned, walking back to her circle, slower than a *Plodsnail*, every step an eternity.

Meanwhile, Ominson's usual companions stood in a cluster, waiting—watching.

Ominson was always the one who decided what game they played, the unspoken leader, the compass by which they navigated their free time.

Gisella had failed to separate them.

Someone else would have to try.

One of Ominson's friends stepped forward, approaching with a feigned air of casualness. "Oi, Ominson, when are you coming?"

Ominson, barely looking up, shrugged. "In a few Oz'mins."

A few Oz'mins stretched into many. The Glowblossoms had begun to bloom, an indisputable sign that break was ending.

And still, he remained with Glinda.

As they walked back to class together, grinning, trading whispered jokes, something between them had shifted.

It was undeniable.

Ominson's friends noticed.

The playground noticed.

And they did not like it.

Glinda was becoming a problem.

◇

The school day had dissolved into memory, the sun slanting lower in the sky, casting long shadows that threatened to stretch the hours into evening. Ominson, whose mind rarely idled in still waters, had a thought, perhaps not the brightest thought he had ever had, but certainly the most interesting one at that moment.

"Come to my castle," he blurted, as though the idea had struck him like an oncoming Cyclone.

Glinda hesitated. **A castle?** Well, of course it was a castle. He was an aristocrat, albeit of a slightly lesser strain. But *his* castle? *Today?* It wasn't as if she had plans, she never had plans, but that only made the prospect more terrifying.

She'd never been to anyone's **home** before, save for her grandparents' estate in the upper Uplands, where everything smelled like rosewater and reverence. But Ominson lived in the Mid Uplands. This was uncharted territory.

Her Golden Goose carriage was already waiting, polished and preened to a regal shine. Inside, Gisella sat poised beside their father, Dainhurst, who looked as though he had already endured a long evening before it had even begun.

Glinda approached him carefully. "Father?" She smoothed her skirts. "May I visit my friend Ominson's castle today?"

Dainhurst, having long since learned to ration his patience with his younger daughter, lifted a tired eyebrow. "Ominson?" He let the name roll off his tongue with practiced disdain. "*What kind of low-level name is that?*"

She pointed to Ominson, who stood a few paces behind her, waiting, fidgeting, aware that his fate hung on the whims of a man who likely saw him as little more than a transactional inconvenience.

Dainhurst followed her finger and squinted. Ah. *That* boy. A frail little thing, but familiar, yes, the son of an aristocrat with whom he had occasional business dealings.

This could be useful.

"Fine," he said, waving his hand as if granting clemency to a particularly dull criminal. "Just make sure they arrange a Ryde home for you."

Gisella watched the exchange, something shifting behind her eyes.

Glinda had *plans*. And most curious of all, those plans did not involve *her*.

As Ominson and Glinda walked off together, Gisella remained behind, the weight of unfamiliar exclusion settling around her like an ill-fitted cloak.

Ominson's *Wither-Swan* carriage arrived shortly after, a shimmering white and silver contraption that, while respectable, was decidedly less ostentatious than the Fairmoor's.

Glinda stepped inside, smoothing out invisible wrinkles in her dress; her nervous habit, while Ominson collapsed beside her, limbs sprawling like an untamed marionette.

The carriage set off, but the path was not the one Glinda knew by heart, the one that led **home** to endless etiquette lessons and ceilings so high they might as well have been the sky.

This was different.

The signs passing by the window read *Lunarville Pass… Bluebird Grove… Honeyhollow Road.*

She had read about these places in *Places to Visit in the South of Oz*, but seeing them in real life was something else entirely.

Ominson stole glances at her, perplexed.

She was staring at the scenery like a child seeing a *Magiklantern* show for the first time. *Had she never been here before?*

Even the poorest children in Oz had passed these roads at least once.

He thought to ask, but something in her expression—a quiet reverence, a silent wonder—made him hesitate.

The carriage rumbled beneath a rose archway, the scent of bloom and dusk filling the air as they approached the castle.

Ominson's castle was not as grand as the Fairmoor's, but it was striking in a way Glinda found unexpectedly lovely.

Inside, the floors were made of milkglass tiles, the walls shaped from *Frost-Stone*, the door handles shimmering sapphires that winked in the light.

"Do you want something to eat?" Ominson asked as they stepped further inside. Then, as if remembering something crucial, he added: "You can't be a *good* host if you don't ask your guest if they want something to eat."

Glinda made a mental note.

"Yes, I'm quite hungry," she admitted.

"Me too!" he grinned, as though he'd just made an extraordinary discovery.

The dining hall stretched before them, the table groaning under the weight of a feast so excessive it bordered on decadent.

There were *Chickduck wings, candied Emerald Apples, Cyclone Squash, Stromberry Truffles,* so many choices that for a moment, Glinda felt overwhelmed.

Ominson, however, zeroed in on his quarry immediately.

Gooseberry pie.

Slicing a generous piece, he thrust it toward her with the conviction of a prophet presenting sacred scripture.

"You haven't had proper Gooseberry pie until now," he insisted.

Her stomach clenched.

She had endured this battle before. Zelena, the best cook in the world, had tried and failed to convert her to its merits. What made *him* think he could?

But she was a guest. And a *good* guest.

With reluctant fingers, she took the fork, Ominson holding the plate with the eager expression of someone awaiting a divine revelation.

The fork entered her mouth.

Her body tensed.

Her face scrunched.

Her eyes squeezed shut.

Then, slowly, her expression eased.

It wasn't *bad.* It wasn't *good,* but it wasn't *bad.*

"Well?" Ominson pressed.

Glinda sighed, accepting defeat. "I like it."

"I *told* you!" Ominson cried, spinning triumphantly. He wished there was someone, anyone, to witness his victory.

He made a mental note to remind her of this moment the next time she doubted him.

Perhaps it was her family's fault. They loved their *Gooseberry pie* baked with *Grimwort* and *Scornleaf,* and whatever they ate was what she had available to her. Glinda had a second slice, before digging into the other confections on the table. She wanted to try everything, wondering what else she didn't like at **home** but loved at Ominson's.

"I can't even breathe, can you?" Ominson groaned.

"What do you think?" Glinda shot back.

They looked at each other, their faces smothered in grease and food stains.

And laughed.

"Stop making me laugh, my stomach hurts!"

"You stop making *me* laugh, *my* stomach hurts!"

Which, of course, only made them laugh harder.

They explored more of Ominson's castle and pulled a prank on the gardeners by throwing *Cobblefowl* eggs at them.

By the end, Ominson was already brewing another idea.

And this one—this one—would be even brighter.

Ominson turned to Glinda with a peculiar glint in his eye, something fragile, something reaching.

"Glinda," he began, his voice softer than his usual bravado would allow, "Can you promise me something?"

She tilted her head, intrigued. Promises were easy for Glinda; she could spin them like golden thread, make them shine and seem worth more than they were. She was good at making them and better at keeping them.

"Yes, sure," she replied, extending her hand in ceremonial fashion, as though sealing a business contract rather than a childhood pledge.

"Promise me we'll always be best friends."

Best friends? The phrase felt heavier than she expected, but not unpleasantly so. Wasn't it something of a relief, to have a role so clearly defined? Yes, best friends she could manage. She was good at roles.

"Yes," she said, shaking his hand with grave sincerity. "Best friends. Always."

And so, the deal was sealed.

The sky had darkened by then, the stars puncturing the indigo expanse like the shimmer of lost things. Her departure was inevitable. Ominson, never one for prolonged goodbyes, escorted her outside, his hand still curled in hers as if reluctant to let go. He barked an order to a coachman—"Take her home. And safely." The words were sharp, protective.

The Wither-Swan carriage, glinting under the first winks of moonlight, swallowed her whole. She peered through its window, waving until Ominson became a silhouette against the illuminated castle doors. Only when the sight of her had been fully devoured by the winding roads did he turn and shut the door.

The Ryde was long, though it barely felt like a journey at all, more like floating, untethered, carried by the afterglow of an inexplicable joy. She replayed the day in her mind like an old, beloved tune, each memory a note, swelling and tumbling. She had not only made a friend, but a best friend. Perhaps it was the best day of her life.

The golden gates of Fairmoor Castle loomed before her, and before the coachman could dismount, she had already burst forth with uncontainable glee. "Thank you!" she trilled, tossing the words over her shoulder as she bolted inside into her sister's room.

Gisella, lounging idly on her bed, looked up at her with mild surprise. "How was it?" she asked.

"Amazing," Glinda sighed, collapsing onto the mattress as though the weight of happiness itself had become too much to bear. "Who knew I liked Gooseberry Pie all along?"

Gisella snorted. "You hate Gooseberry Pie."

"I did," Glinda laughed, marvelling at her own apparent transformation. "We ate so much I'm wondering how I can still breathe. We explored Oz! Like, the places I only ever read about! And—" she hesitated for dramatic effect, before declaring triumphantly, "We even got in trouble throwing eggs at the gardeners!"

Silence.

Glinda, previously enthralled by her own storytelling, now noticed the shift in the air. Gisella had lowered her gaze, now fidgeting with the crystal necklace resting against her collarbone.

Glinda sat up, concerned. "How was your day, Gisella?"

Stumbling over an answer, Gisella mustered a too-bright, "Good!"—the forced enthusiasm too exaggerated to be real. "Popsicle bought me an emerald brooch." She dug into her drawer and produced the item, holding it up like a peace offering.

Glinda, ever the dutiful sister, made the appropriate noises of admiration. But inwardly, she puzzled. Gisella owned hundreds of brooches, some finer than this one. Why did this one matter? Why did she seem suddenly diminished?

She was too tired to puzzle it out. Besides, she had other things to think about. She bid her sister goodnight and left the room singing, an occurrence so rare that it sent a ripple of surprise through the household. Her voice, untrained but rich, pure as a cloud's sigh, drifted through the corridor.

◊

Morning arrived, and with it, a new purpose. There was no school, which meant Glinda had the luxury of choice, and she had already decided—she would share her Ozian Magical Artifacts book with her best friend.

She packed it carefully, as though it were a crown jewel rather than a battered old text, and summoned her Golden Goose carriage at dawn.

When she arrived at his castle, he was outside, kicking a rock with all the grandeur of someone with nothing better to do. But when he saw her, waving madly from the window before the carriage had even stopped, his face lit up, as if he'd been waiting for her all along.

She flung herself out of the carriage, barely taking the time to thank the coachman before enveloping Ominson in a hug. "I have something to show you!" she announced, nearly toppling him over in her excitement.

He had little time to object before she was dragging him inside, dropping her bag onto the floor with a theatrical thud. From it, she pulled the large tome, its pages thick and heavy with secrets.

The two of them sprawled onto the floor, elbows digging into the plush carpet, poring over the pages. Ominson's enthusiasm, however, was laced with hesitation. He knew the weight of magic in the South of Oz; it was not something one simply dabbled in. Magic was a sickness, a whisper that could unravel a family, a rumour that could lead to a quiet, permanent disappearance.

"Does your father know you have this?" he asked cautiously.

Her expression gave her away.

Ominson swallowed hard. "We can't read it here."

He took her by the hand and led her swiftly through the corridors, through passageways that only he knew existed, until they emerged in a secluded grove within the castle gardens.

There, on a weathered stone bench, they turned the pages together, their heads bent close, their fingers brushing against faded ink and forgotten lore.

Then they found it—the section on Seraphina.

Ominson's eyes flicked toward Glinda, mirroring the wary look Gisella had given her days before. But Glinda wasn't thinking about the old stories, or the Forsaken Witch, or any of it. Today, she wasn't troubled by the ways in which the world wanted to define her.

She was searching.

Her finger hovered over an illustration, tracing the shape of a waterfall, its waters swirling with an eerie luminescence.

"The Forgetting Magic Waterfall," she murmured.

Ominson, beside her, inhaled sharply.

"I want to go there," Glinda said, her voice firmer than usual. "I know it's restricted, but I want to see that place for myself and see if I can find anything."

Ominson sat back on his heels. The Forgetting Magic Waterfall. A place spoken of in hushed tones, referenced in old, brittle books, its existence little more than a myth whispered among scholars too frightened to investigate. No one had seen it in more than three hundred years.

But Ominson wasn't one to turn down an adventure. And as he was coming to learn, neither was Glinda.

"I'll help you," he said with an unsettling calm, as though he were merely agreeing to hold open a door rather than lead them both into a forgotten abyss. "But we'll have to go by Byke. If we take the carriage, my father will have me vanished, like those magic-wielders."

Glinda was a little confused.

Without another word, he strode back into the castle. She secured her book, slung her satchel over her shoulder, and followed him to the storage room where he kept his Bykes. There were four in total, each lined up like forgotten sentinels, their frames cloaked in dust. She hesitated only briefly before selecting the *Violet* one, something regal about its fading paint. He took the silver.

They rode.

Through twisting paths and crumbling roads, past fields of wild grass and ruins, Ominson, ever the pragmatist, had stolen a vintage map from his father's study, its edges browned with age. They rode for *HourZ*, following its inked paths, though their progress was slow, partly because Glinda, enchanted by the novelty of unfamiliar places, kept stopping to explore—and to buy *Candy Dream Drops*.

Ominson, for his part, was nearly undone by exhaustion.

The landscape grew harsher. The smooth roads disappeared into wild terrain, and before long, they arrived at the edge of a cliff.

"This should be it," Ominson murmured, scanning the empty expanse before them.

But there was nothing.

No waterfall. No landmark. No grand secret waiting to be uncovered.

Had they been fools? Gullible children chasing the echoes of a fairytale?

Ominson clenched his jaw.

Glinda, however, was unconvinced.

"It has to be here," she insisted. "It wouldn't be easy to find. Not if it's as dangerous as they say."

She pointed down the cliffside. "What if we ride down? Get a different vantage point?"

"Vantage point?" he asked.

"It means better view," Glinda replied.

It was as good a plan as any.

They descended carefully, the Bykes rattling beneath them as the terrain grew rougher. But at the bottom, they found nothing.

Now it was Glinda's turn to feel foolish.

Her ambition had led them on a useless errand, had dragged her best friend through heat and exhaustion for the sake of a place that may have never existed at all.

Ominson, ever her counterweight, merely shrugged. "I'm glad we came," he admitted. "I haven't seen half of these places since I was a kindling."

They sat on the ground, weary beyond words, and shared the last of Glinda's Sugardoughs in silence. The country air was thick with the scent of damp earth and distant rain, and for a while, that was enough.

Then, just as Glinda turned to mount her Byke, something caught her eye.

A glint of light.

It was small, nearly imperceptible, just a flicker of something bright against the dull stone beneath the cliff.

"Do you see that?" she whispered.

Ominson did. The light was emanating from a thin crack in the rock.

Glinda approached first, pressing her face close to the crevice, but moss blocked her vision. The stone was unmovable, at least for her small hands.

Ominson, master of breaking things apart, knew what to do.

He selected a sharp-edged rock, wedged it into the crack, and raised a flat stone high above his head. With one swift, deliberate motion, he brought it down.

The crack split, fracturing outward like lightning branching across the sky.

Glinda, breathless, placed her hands against the stone and gave the gentlest of nudges.

It all came tumbling down.

CHAPTER 6

The Waterfall

With the way now clear, Glinda and Ominson exchanged a hesitant glance. *Was this it?*

Hand in hand, they parted the dense veil of overgrown plants and stepped inside. Towering rock pillars surrounded them, their edges sharp enough to slice through careless skin. Before them lay an ethereal garden, a paradise alive with roses, pink tulips, and an array of otherworldly plants that looked deceptively edible. The grass shimmered with a green so vibrant it seemed unreal, and the waterfall flowed in perfect harmony, its crystalline waters unbroken by stagnation.

"Oh, Oz…" Glinda whispered, utterly breathless.

She pulled the book from her bag, flipping through its pages with trembling fingers. The scene matched the illustrations perfectly. Ominson stood wide-eyed beside her.

"We found it," he murmured.

The trek, every gruelling step of it, had been worth it. This was just the most beautiful place in Oz and perhaps in all the *Otherworlds*, beyond anything they could have imagined.

Too stunned to move, they lingered at the entrance until Ominson's curiosity finally won. He stepped onto the path of smooth stepping stones leading toward the waterfall, eager to explore. Glinda trailed behind, more cautious but equally captivated. Ominson, overcome with excitement, began to skip from stone to stone, his eyes darting around the vibrant paradise. Suddenly, his foot slipped. He teetered over the edge, dangerously close to the water.

"Guh! Be careful!" Glinda cried, grabbing his shirt just in time to pull him back.

Her voice was sharp, motherly in its urgency. "You almost lost your memory! You need to be more careful."

Ominson's face flushed with embarrassment.

"I—I wasn't thinking," he stammered, casting a wary glance at the inviting cascade.

Its transparency was almost hypnotic, as though one sip could cleanse every sin from his soul. Glinda sank onto the lush grass to steady herself, clutching the book in her lap.

Ominson joined her, stretching out on the impossibly soft grass.

"Thank you for coming with me, Ominson," she said, her voice tinged with gratitude.

"What are best friends for?" he replied, with a proud smirk.

Glinda hesitated, then confided, "I came here looking for answers. I can't stop thinking about Seraphina. I know we're different people, but I can't shake the thought... What if we're not?"

Ominson exhaled, his usual playfulness replaced by quiet seriousness. "I get it," he said.

"Sometimes I look in the mirror, and I see my father's face. I worry I'll become like him—selfish and incapable of love." His honesty startled even himself.

Glinda's **heart** swelled with understanding. For the first time, she didn't feel alone in her fears.

"Is that the only reason you came here? What answers are you trying to find?" Ominson asked, following whatever thought had popped into his mind.

"I thought I'd find out whatever happened here but also, I came to look for magic. I want magic so bad. Don't you?"

"No," Ominson replied swiftly.

Glinda was in shock. Why wouldn't anyone want magic? If only he could see Mz. Everburn use hers.

"I think it's the most beautiful thing in the world!" she said, now sighing at the thought of it. "Good magic, of course," she had to clarify; he was probably thinking she was referring to the Seraphina type of magic.

"It's not like you've ever seen magic, so how would you know? They're all the same."

Glinda didn't have magic, but she was so appalled and offended. Of course, she had seen magic and was going to tell him, but she remembered her promise. She held her tongue.

"How can you say that? The same way there are good and evil people, it's the same way there's good and evil magic. It's obvious. The Wizard has good magic."

"All I'm saying is that we're better off without it, it makes our lives much easier not dealing with all that kooky stuff."

"Well, Seraphina had magic and I'm the only other person that picked the pink gem, so would you think I was evil if I had magic too?"

"Do you? Do you have magic?"

"It's hypothetical," she replied quickly.

"Exactly! And besides I know you. You're a good person. No one can tell me otherwise."

Glinda began to smile but hid her face so he wouldn't see.

"Who knew you'd be so brazen about magic and your father is the one that leads the resistance?" Ominson said laughing so loud the entire waterfall garden echoed.

"What resistance?" Glinda asked, her eyebrow raised.

He stared at her, *dumbfoundified*. "You're jesting, right? The resistance against magic wielders. Your father's the one behind it."

The colour drained from Glinda's face. "What are you talking about?"

"You really don't know?" Ominson frowned. "People have been disappearing, Glinda. It's your father that's leading them. I mean only people like us know that, but he is the one that brought the proposal to root out anyone suspected of using magic."

Glinda's **heart** stopped.

She had been held hostage in that castle for so long that she knew nothing about the world. She didn't even know what life was like in Quadling Country let alone the rest of Oz. Glinda stood up, grabbed the book and mounted her byke. She didn't say a word, Ominson calling after her, but she kept on riding. The ryde **home** was a blur, her thoughts racing faster than her wheels.

Now, it made sense why Mz. Everburn was secretive about her magic, who would want to hide that part of themselves unless they had to. This revelation left a sour taste in her mouth, sourer than *Grimwort* and *Scornleaf* in her family's *Gooseberry Pie*.

When she reached the castle, she could barely stand. Exhaustion weighed her down, but fear pushed her forward. She went straight to the kitchen to look for Zelena, but she was not there. She asked one of the maids if they knew of her whereabouts, but no one had seen her for a week. Glinda was fearing the worst.

Where in Oz was Zelena?

She never left without telling Glinda.

Desperate for answers Glinda went to her sister's room.

"Where did you go today, Glinda? I haven't seen you all day!" Gisella said indifferently.

Glinda tried to reply but she didn't have the energy. She had to save her energy for something that mattered more.

"Gisella, have you heard of people disappearing around Quadling Country?"

Gisella paused and sighed. "Yes, why?"

"Ominson told me that Father is the reason why."

"And?" Gisella replied coldly.

Glinda stood rigid.

"How can you say that? People are being targeted for something they can't control. Worst of all, father is involved."

"You're so naïve," Gisella sneered. "Glinda, people like that shouldn't even breathe unless they are like us. Someone probably enchanted you as a babe and that's why you picked that pink stone. If you ask me, I think it was Barbarus that wanted to embarrass father at your coronation."

"Don't be ridiculous, Gisella" Glinda snapped.

"All this time, you've been an outcast *becoz* of that stupid gem," Gisella shot back. "You wouldn't be so lonely all the time if you had a tribe, but it was those glowing magic rocks that made you even more unlike all of us and you still defend it?"

Without another word, Glinda left the room, her knees trembling with exhaustion. Alone in her bed, she curled into herself, tears streaming down her face. Gisella's words echoed in her mind, not because of what she said, but because of how much it hurt to hear it from her. As her sobs subsided, Glinda drifted into a restless sleep, the weight of the day pressing heavily on her small, trembling frame.

The next morning was quieter than usual. At the breakfast table, Gisella avoided Glinda's gaze, focusing solely on her meal. Dainhurst preferred silence while eating—he believed it was the proper thing to do, but today Glinda had grown wings. She was ready to challenge her father.

"Father, I have a question," Glinda said, her tone blunt.

"No speaking whilst eating, Glinda," Esmelda snapped, clearly irritated.

But Glinda had a feeling her father was prepared for what she was going to ask. Nothing ever escaped Dainhurst's notice. Nothing. The wind had to inform him which direction it was going to blow beforehand.

"Let her, Esmelda," Dainhurst said calmly. "Speak, child."

Glinda swallowed the last of her *Yellow-Nectar*. She needed all the **courage** she could muster.

"Father, people are disappearing in town if they're caught with magic. Do you know anything about that?" Glinda asked, careful to keep her tone neutral, praying it was all a misunderstanding.

"Yes, Glinda," Dainhurst replied shortly, taking a deliberate sip of his *Crimson-Tonic*.

Glinda's **heart** skipped. "Father… are you the one taking them?"

"Yes," Dainhurst answered flatly, without hesitation, as if it were the simplest truth in the world.

Glinda felt a wave of nausea rise in her chest. The confession came so coldly, so casually, from the man who raised her. Gisella continued eating without looking up, and Esmelda turned a page in her *NewZPapr*, feigning indifference.

"Why, Father? What have these people done to you?" Glinda stood, her voice rising, her hands trembling with emotion. The maids froze mid-task but resumed their duties without a word.

"Glinda, sit down and act like a lady! If it is answers you want, then it is what you shall get!" Dainhurst's voice was sharp, but he didn't raise it.

Glinda sank back into her chair, dreading what he would say next.

"Glinda, I'm just doing all of Oz a favour," Dainhurst continued, sipping his *Crimson-Tonic* slowly.

"When you were born, and you chose the pink gem, do you know what I had to endure?"

Glinda shook her head, confused. *What did her birth have to do with the atrocities he was causing?*

"People were scared, Glinda; I was losing a lot of pull, money, status becoz of what you did. Picking the pink gem and looking the way you look did not help." He set his cup down, his gaze locking with hers.

"People believed you were Seraphina, reincarnated to get her revenge, and some going as far as trying to kill you as a kindling. But becoz you were born to two loving parents, we put a stop to you becoming a sacrifice."

Glinda's mind reeled, her **heart** sinking. Esmelda and Gisella exchanged looks.

Dainhurst continued, "So I took it upon myself to redirect their anger to the root problem: magic. Had I not argued at the temple that magic was a sickness that brings about only pain, just like Seraphina caused centuries ago, if I did not fight for its eradication, you would've been on a shrine and dismembered quicker than you could say 'Twister!'. So, before you sit there and judge me for what I had to do, for you to be able to go to the school you go to, the food you eat, the castle you live in, and most of all, saving your life, you better grovel at my feet and thank me! You hear?"

Glinda was horrified, and slowly the tears were filling in her eyes. She was so worried about magic wielders disappearing, but she had no idea that it was all her doing. People were paying the price just so she could live.

Glinda could not handle any more revelations that day. Her voice now trembling, she asked one final question. But first, she had to reason—it could not have been an easy decision for a parent to choose to save their child, despite the cost.

"How about Zelena? I'm worried about her, S-she's not been seen for a week, do you know where she is?"

Esmelda, looking at Dainhurst for his reply, was quiet, as if thinking and calculating. Dainhurst's cup, now refilled to the brim by one of the maids, was raised to his lips as he finally answered.

"I'll see what I can do."

Esmelda frowned slightly, then buried her nose back in the *NewZPapr* and continued reading.

Glinda knew she had just stepped into a whole new world, and things were not going to change. Deep down she wished she hadn't asked because she did not have the power to change anything and somehow knowing tormented her even more. The only thing she could do to even the bad things she was responsible for was to carry on being a *good* girl. To her parents and most of all the world.

In the Golden Goose carriage to school, Glinda opened the door for Gisella, but they barely talked the whole journey. Both sat on opposite sides of the carriage, staring out the window for bluebirds. When they arrived, Glinda went to her corner and Gisella went to hers. Ominson arrived later than Glinda did, so she waited patiently for him to arrive at the Swyngs. She had so much to tell him.

The Wither-Swan finally parked at the gate and the blonde skinny boy hopped out and approached the Swyngs when he saw his strawberry-blonde friend. He asked if she was doing well, and she did the same but what she wanted to discuss was not safe to do so in such an open space.

They made a pact to meet at their new spot, *The Waterfall*, when they got **home** after school. Both assuring each other not to mention or disclose its location to anyone.

The day passed very quickly, and it was time to put their plans into action but Mz. Everburn wanted to have a word with Glinda. The small girl was so nervous. What did Mz. Everburn need to ask her? Was her favourite teacher going to blame her for what was happening to magic individuals? It was partly her fault, she thought.

"How is your time at *SilverCrest* so far? Have you made any friends?" she asked even warmer than she usually was.

"Yes, I have" she answered, smiling.

"That's great. I had no doubt," Mz. Everburn said. "Have you finished that book I gave you?"

Glinda nodded, fighting the urge to look guilty. "I've read it four times over."

Mz. Everburn laughed, glad Glinda found the book just as interesting as she did when she was a child.

"Follow me."

And before they knew it, they were already at the library again. She waved her hands, lighting up the place.

"It's even dustier in here than last time, eh?" her teacher's eyes glistened in the firelight.

Glinda nodded silently, trying so hard to speak as little as possible.

"Alright" Mz. Everburn sighed, adjusting her posture.

Her teacher stretched out both hands this time and mumbled some words Glinda couldn't make out. They sounded like an ancient language, lost to time. Before long, the windows burst open, and all the dust swirled outside and into the wind. The room was now airy and fresh, and she could see all the books clearly. Glinda was in awe, much more than before. It seemed the more she was exposed to magic the more she wanted to have it.

"Mz., please," Glinda said. "Please teach me."

"Oh, Glinda," she said, now feeling responsible for getting Glinda's hopes high about magic.

But if she did not possess it naturally there was no way to teach her the type of magic she was interested in. Besides basic potions, and she doubted that was what she wanted to learn, even as a magic wielder, she didn't know much about potions and always found it boring. Mz. Everburn now gestured with a wave of her hands for another book to levitate forth, plucking it from the air.

"Glinda, if you had magic, it would be an honour to teach you everything I know, but you don't… do you?" her teacher asked gently.

Glinda shook her head.

"But you know what else has magic?" she said, now using her finger and pointing to Glinda's **brain** and **heart**. "If you always cherish those, you'll always have magic." She looked at the book in her hand. "And this is the spark."

She handed it to Glinda, the little girl carefully putting it into her bag. Glinda was smart, and she heeded what her teacher said, but not fully.

She wanted *real* magic.

Mz. Everburn was just trying to let her down softly, trying not to hurt her feelings. Nevertheless, she had a new book to read. She waved Ominson goodbye, reminding him of their secret meeting. The day was still young, but the weight of the new knowledge she'd gained felt heavier than she expected.

◊

Arriving at the Fairmoor castle took longer than expected, according to Glinda's standards. She waited for her family to get inside; they barely noticed when she was around, so that wasn't an issue. She mounted the Violet byke and rode to the waterfall. At this point, she figured out the shortcuts to get there; she could probably ride there blindfolded.

◊

They met at the waterfall, and this time Ominson remembered to steer clear of its waters.

Glinda assessed the atmosphere; it looked as though someone had been there since their last meeting. She was probably overthinking.

No one knew about the waterfall, besides them.

Glinda sat with her best friend on the grass to reveal what she had just learned. She felt like she had to confess that she was the reason why the people were disappearing.

"Ominson, I found something out this morning," Glinda said distraughtly.

"What?" Ominson said concernedly.

"I'm the reason why people are being taken."

"What makes you think that?"

"Well, my father said so himself," Glinda said, still in disbelief. "He said when I was a kindling, people tried to kill me becoz of Seraphina and the gem so, in order to save my life, he had to fight against people who had magic—"

"Listen, that was not your fault at all!" Ominson assured Glinda. "You didn't knowingly choose for this to happen, it's your father's fault. I never want to hear you blame yourself for what is happening."

Glinda didn't think anything could soothe her mind, but Ominson always knew what to say and how to say it.

"On a lighter note, when am I getting my byke back, Fairmoor?" Ominson furrowing his brow, "You just had to pick my favourite byke and ran with it."

"Hmm, I don't know; I'll have to think about it" Glinda laughed. "I'll return it to you."

"You know what, keep it." Ominson came to his decision rather quickly.

The two best friends sat by the waterfall in its serene beauty until the sun began to set in the east before veering off to their respective castles.

CHAPTER 7

The Missing Maid

The morning unfurled with the call of *Chickengeese*, an elegiac sound, nostalgic, almost mythic in its rarity these days. Glinda roused with an inexplicable stirring, an anticipation that quivered in her chest like a candle on the verge of extinguishing or flaring into something brilliant. She had always possessed an uncanny attunement to the tremors of fate, an inclination toward premonition, not the supernatural kind, but it was there nonetheless. And it seldom led her astray. Yet, this morning, the certainty of it wavered. The thought of Zelena pressed against her mind. *Where had she gone? What had she become?*

She had risen earlier than usual, a disruption to the pattern of her days. With nothing better to do, she wandered. There was always more castle than she had seen. Normally, the air would have been alive with the meticulous industry of the maids, their rhythmic sweeping of tiles already pristine, but today—nothing. The hush of inactivity struck her as curiously off-key. It was hunger this time, not curiosity, that redirected her steps to the kitchens. Breakfast loomed a good two *HourZ* away. That simply would not do. Zelena, ever the guardian of Glinda's whims, had kept a secret drawer for such occasions, a stash of honeyed oat biscuits and roasted cashews, a token of sisterly indulgence. But upon entering the kitchens, she was met with an unfamiliar tableau.

The maids, *all* of them, were gathered, standing as one. A rarity, as unusual as a silent sunrise. They never congregated like this. At best, two might be caught murmuring over a shared task, a hurried exchange of gossip before duty swept them apart. But now they huddled, shoulders drawn together, their bodies forming an unspoken barricade against the rest of the world. And against *her.*

Glinda hesitated, unwilling to intrude upon their clandestine murmurs. But her presence, when noted, caused a visible shift. They startled, stiffened—*then* softened. A breath of relief passed through them, dissipating like steam. They had mistaken her for a Fairmoor, and in realizing their error, let go of their fear. But the fear had been real. It had been guarding something.

GLINDA: The GOOD Witch

She took a step forward. They did not block her. They did not warn her away. If anything, they widened, retreating like a tide. *Inviting her.*

Her breath slowed. The universe held its breath with her.

Zelena.

Time ruptured. It lost its sequence. What was a moment? A second? An eternity? Glinda could not move, not yet. Her vision swam. She did not recognize her own sister—no, *she did*, but in a way, one recognizes an apparition: with disbelief first, with anguish second.

Zelena was diminished. Her frame, once proud, was carved down to something too slight, her skin etched with the history of suffering. Scars laced her limbs. And her hair, the envy of all who had once beheld it, was reduced to something unkempt, untended. Zelena, who had taught Glinda the sacred ritual of brushing one's hair, who had possessed the most resplendent locks in all the lands, had let them die.

Glinda collapsed. Her legs abandoned her, crumbling like sand beneath an unforgiving wave.

Zelena moved, not quickly, not easily, but with the last reserves of her strength. She pulled Glinda into her, held her as though the act alone could sustain them both. They wept, unguarded, unchecked, wetting each other's skin with sorrow. The maids, witnessing such intimacy, withdrew in reverence, as if the grief between sisters was a language too sacred for eavesdropping.

When at last Glinda surfaced from the depths of her sorrow, she gathered what little remained of herself. Sitting beside Zelena in the fragile light of morning, she took in the damage anew. A burn at the scalp, nearly reaching the bone, a wound that spoke of prolonged cruelty rather than momentary wrath.

"Who did this to you?" Glinda whispered.

"It doesn't matter," Zelena answered, her voice a shadow of itself. "The damage is done."

"It *does* matter, Zelena. Tell me who."

Zelena forced herself up, a ghost of her old self emerging. "Here," she said, moving toward the hidden drawer, reaching for food as if the mere act of caretaking could restore normalcy. But the effort was too great, and Glinda sprang up, catching her before she could stumble.

"Sit," Glinda begged. "Let *me* care for you."

Zelena did not argue. She was past that.

Glinda, feeling impossibly young in this moment, prepared a simple remedy—a cup of Moss-Dew with mint and honey, anything she thought would give Zelena some additional strength. Zelena drank.

The *Moss-Dew* was not enough. It was better to let Zelena collect herself and let her breathe before inquiring further, so Glinda helped Zelena to her quarters to get some sleep. Sleep claimed her swiftly and deeply, as if exhaustion had been waiting for permission. Glinda watched over her, studying the peaceful illusion of slumber against the rawness of her injuries. It was a cruel juxtaposition, this semblance of a fairy tale, this warped imitation of a sleeping beauty.

Glinda nearly wept again but swallowed it down. Sleep was the only gift she could give.

When she returned to her own chambers, she did not leave. She burrowed beneath her covers, the darkness beneath the fabric a welcome void. And there, unseen, unheard, she let the sorrow take her.

No one noticed her absence. Or if they did, no one cared.

Perhaps it was better this way. If Zelena's suffering had any thread that tied back to Glinda—if it was tangled in the knots of her own birth, the disappearances, the secrets—then she wasn't sure she could bear the weight of it.

She wasn't sure she *wanted* to survive another day.

◇

Glinda awoke from her cold slumber to the bleached hush of morning. She peeled herself from the tangle of silk and linen, slipping barefoot to the window that overlooked Zelena's quarters. A habit she had not quite decided was an act of care or one of cowardice. If Zelena was awake, she would be outside, arms crossed against the slight chill, indulging in the particular solitude that fresh country air provided.

But something was amiss.

Esmelda was awake before Dainhurst. That alone was an anomaly, as unnatural as a sun that set before the moon had the decency to rise. And she was making her way, no, *gliding* to Zelena's door.

Glinda stiffened; her breath still caught in the warm shallows of sleep.

Her mother did not do such things. It was beneath her, conversing with a maid, mingling among those whose hands knew the burden of labour. And yet, there she was, slipping inside Zelena's quarters without so much as a knock, without even the performative decency of hesitation. Esmelda cast a glance over her shoulder before disappearing into the dim room beyond.

Glinda knew her mother.

Her mother was up to something.

She knew the rigidity of Esmelda's spine when she was lying, the way her fingers twitched when she was withholding, the microscopic flinch when proximity to her own daughter became too close for comfort. Glinda had studied these mannerisms out of necessity; survival, after all, was a discipline.

And now, instinct reared itself. *No one* was permitted to get close to her Zelena without Glinda's explicit authorization.

The muscles in her legs ached from disuse, but urgency overruled frailty. She hadn't left her room in two days, but now, no hesitation. Her nightgown billowed behind her as she sprinted down the stairs. At Zelena's door, she found it already ajar. Esmelda stepped out, composed as ever…save for the flicker of surprise that darted across her face like a shadow when she saw Glinda standing there, defiant and waiting.

It was a rare thing to catch Esmelda off guard, and for a fleeting moment, Glinda savoured it.

Her mother recovered quickly.

"What are you doing here?" Esmelda asked, her voice clipped.

Glinda did not flinch. "I should ask *you* the same."

The words were out before she could temper them, and for a heartbeat, silence teetered between them.

Esmelda's lips pressed into a line. "Watch your mouth, you insolent child. Apologise. *Now.*"

Glinda clenched her teeth. "Sorry, Mother."

"Good girl."

The words were syrupy, poisonous. Esmelda smoothed her skirts, as if straightening her posture could restore her shattered pride. Then, with a careless flick of her fingers, she brushed Glinda aside as one might swipe away breadcrumbs on a table. She strode back toward the castle, the click of her heels punctuating the stillness.

Glinda barely allowed herself the luxury of watching her go. She had more pressing matters.

Zelena.

She hesitated only briefly before knocking.

Silence.

Then, the sound of something breaking apart, barely perceptible, a sniffle caught in the throat, a moment of weakness hastily swallowed.

Finally, a voice. Hoarse. Crooked.

"Come in."

The room was darker than it should have been, despite the full command of daylight beyond the window.

Zelena was turned away, shoulders curled inward, as though trying to make herself smaller, more difficult to notice. Glinda had known her long enough to see what others did not—the slight tremor in her fingers, the way she wiped at her cheeks too quickly, as if shame could be hidden in haste.

Glinda said nothing.

Instead, she crossed the room with slow, deliberate steps and reached out, brushing away the last traces of tears Zelena had failed to erase.

"Oh, Zelena."

The words were a whisper, an exhale of sympathy too quiet to be an intrusion.

Zelena managed a smile, small, fragile, but real. "Hope you had good sleep, hummingbug," she murmured before reaching out and tickling Glinda's side.

Glinda let out a shriek of laughter, twisting away. It was unexpected. Unforced. The kind of laughter that could unspool knots in the soul, even if only temporarily.

Zelena grinned, pleased with her success. "What do you want to eat? Churncakes or eggs?"

"No, *you* sit," Glinda said, wagging a finger in mock authority. "Today, *I* make *you* breakfast. I'm a *fantastic* cook, you know."

Zelena raised an eyebrow. "Hmmm. Remember the fish pie you tried to make like two moons ago?"

Glinda gasped. "I *thought* we agreed never to speak of that day again!"

They both dissolved into laughter, the room gradually warming.

Glinda turned to the kitchen in Zelena's quarters, retrieving ingredients with the confidence of a master chef, or, more accurately, the arrogance of the wildly overambitious. *Black-eyed pepper, Zalt, Sweetdust, munchkin Spice, Tornatyme, Winkroot.* She cracked two Chickengoose eggs, tossing them into the *oyled* pan with theatrical flair, seasoning them as though she were crafting a masterpiece.

Moments later, she proudly plated the meal, setting two steaming cups of warm milk beside their plates.

They took a bite.

Paused.

Locked eyes.

And spat it out.

Hysterical laughter overtook them both.

"I told you!" Zelena crowed triumphantly.

Glinda groaned, dramatic. "Shush, Zelly. Add this to the list of days we don't talk about when I decide to cook again."

"Noted."

Zelena, now in control of the kitchen, set about making proper Churncakes, salvaging what remained of their breakfast attempt. They ate by the window, watching the birds dance against the pale sky, the warmth between them more nourishing than the food itself.

Glinda studied Zelena quietly. She looked lighter, unburdened, if only for this moment. It would be wicked of her to bring up what had happened. The words ached on her tongue, but she swallowed them whole.

Some wounds needed time.

And sometimes, the kindest thing one could do for a loved one is to allow them the space to heal—unquestioned, undisturbed, and entirely in their own time.

"Are you doing anything today?" Glinda inquired, leaning in as though she were conspiring rather than simply asking.

Zelena sighed, already feeling the familiar weight of obligation settle on her shoulders. "Yes. Your mother has summoned me to begin my duties."

Glinda waved a hand as if swatting at an insect. "No, no, no. That won't do. I'll invent something academic. Research, perhaps—yes, research! I'll tell her I need a chaperone. You know how Mother stops listening at the mere mention of education."

A bubbling laughter overtook them, light and insistent.

"I'll go get ready," Glinda announced, twirling toward the door. "And you, you must dress, too!"

Before Zelena could muster an argument, Glinda was already gone, her retreating figure swallowed by the castle's opulent corridors. This was becoming a pattern—Glinda, full of schemes, slipping further into Ominson's influence.

Glinda's certainty was unshakable: she knew precisely where they needed to go, the one place that could coax the light back into Zelena's eyes. The audience with her mother had gone as expected, Esmelda heard the word *school* and lost all interest in further questioning.

So, when they set off, the Golden Goose carriage at their disposal, Glinda felt triumphant. She instructed the driver to leave them in town and return at sundown. The final stretch of their journey required secrecy, and secrecy demanded they travel on foot.

"Where are you taking me, Glinda?" Zelena's voice was laced with reluctant intrigue.

Glinda only grinned. "Patience."

Down the cliffside they went, weaving past jagged stone borders and pulling aside thick curtains of moss. And then—

"Oh Oz, Glinda—"

"I know," Glinda whispered, smiling.

"I-I don't know what to say, is this real?"

"Yes, beautiful, isn't it?"

"Beautiful? Are you a munchkin pulling a jest? This is remarkable!"

"I knew you'd like it," Glinda said, now stern, "Just don't touch the water."

"Why? Will I die or something?"

Glinda hesitated. "Something like that."

She led Zelena to a patch of grass so soft it could have been spun from clouds. They sat together in reverent silence, drinking in the tranquillity. For a moment, one fleeting, perfect moment, it seemed that no burden could find them here. No responsibilities, no expectations, from the world beyond.

And yet, the world always intruded.

A cough, deep, rattling, the sound of something buried trying to claw its way free.

Glinda glanced over, concern flickering across her face. "Zelly?"

Zelena waved her off. "It's nothing. Just dust."

But it was not just dust.

The coughing fit persisted, punctuating their once-quiet retreat with its ragged insistence. By sundown, Zelena's skin was damp with sweat, her eyes rimmed in fevered red.

Glinda would not tolerate resistance. "We're leaving."

Zelena, ever stubborn, attempted a protest, but her voice lacked its usual conviction.

They bordered up the hidden paradise, leaving it behind as they made their way back to the waiting Golden Goose carriage. No sooner had they settled inside than

Zelena succumbed to sleep, her head lolling against the seat, breath shallow but steady. Glinda watched her, **heart** heavy but resolute. Zelena had been the one to care for her since childhood. And now, it was Glinda's turn.

✧

Back at the castle, after settling Zelena into bed, Glinda found herself lingering in the hall. Passing Gisella's room, she felt the tension still thick in the air between them.

She knocked once, perfunctory, before slipping inside.

Gisella, lying in bed, refused to meet her gaze, but Glinda knew her well enough. She stepped forward, saying nothing, simply standing there, staring, waiting.

It was an old trick. One that worked.

Gisella cracked first.

"Oh, stop it," she groaned, rolling her eyes. "You're impossible."

The stiffness between them softened. A laugh escaped, grudging but real.

Then, in a rush, Gisella muttered, "I didn't mean what I said earlier."

Glinda arched a brow. "Didn't you?"

A pause.

"Okay," Gisella admitted, "maybe I did. But I didn't *mean* to mean it."

Glinda sighed, her expression unreadable. It was always the same, wasn't it? She was "the *other*." The one who didn't quite fit. But still—

Still.

She forgave her.

People made mistakes.

Glinda had made hers, too.

Like her own birth.

Gisella threw her arms around her, melting into something warmer, rekindling their love once more.

Evening had settled over the castle, but Glinda had no intention of letting the night go to waste.

She had an idea.

The gardens were off-limits after sundown, but she knew something equally as thrilling, something that required no permission, only cunning.

"Come," she whispered, leading Gisella down the winding halls. They descended into the kitchens, where Glinda approached a particular drawer.

Inside, treasures gleamed in the dim firelight—contraband delights from every corner of Oz.

Gisella gasped. "Oh, *Father* would be *furious* if he knew you had these!" Her eyes, wide and gleaming, never left the drawer. "How in Oz did you sneak them past him?"

Glinda smirked. "Zelena gets them for me. She travels, she brings me gifts."

Gisella, thoroughly uninterested in further explanation, reached greedily for the first treat within grasp. She had sampled some before, but *Mallowsnarts*, a forbidden confection from Gillikin, had never passed her lips. Their father, ever suspicious of the northern state, had made certain of that.

And yet, here they were.

The two sisters exchanged a glance, then they emptied the drawer, retreating back upstairs with armfuls of sweets.

Sitting cross-legged on the floor, they spread their plunder between them, devouring their bounty with gluttonous enthusiasm.

Gisella let out a satisfied groan. "If we get caught, we're doomed."

Glinda, mouth half-full, grinned.

"Then," she said, licking sugar from her fingers, "we simply mustn't get caught."

Between bites, Glinda asked, "Did you see Zelena since she got back?"

Gisella stiffened, her fingers freezing over the half-eaten pastry in her grasp. The lightness in her face vanished as if someone had pulled a curtain over it.

She didn't want to talk about *that maid*. Not now. Not ever. And certainly not while she was eating—knowing what that woman had done to their mother.

"No," she said curtly, focusing on the crumbs in her lap.

Glinda leaned back against the headboard, studying her sister through half-lidded eyes. "Don't you think it's strange? Father said he'd 'see what he could do,' and then she arrived the very next day. Have you seen her injuries?"

Gisella's face remained unreadable as Glinda spoke, no flicker of surprise, no wince at the mention of burns. Either she already knew, or she *didn't care*.

Glinda noticed. And because she noticed, she let the subject drop.

She finished her *Nutters-Bar* in silence, chewing as if the taste could wash away the conversation. It didn't.

The sisters stayed up late, laughter replacing words unspoken. They shared stories as if stacking bricks, building something sturdy between them again. Their lips were smudged with chocolate; their fingers sticky with caramel; their wrappers scattered like autumn leaves.

At some point, Glinda drifted under the covers beside Gisella, her first time in her sister's bed in years. She'd forgotten how soft it was, softer, perhaps, than even the moss-laden earth in the hidden waterfall gardens. The moment lingered, a relic from childhood, something fragile and fleeting.

They had school the next day. A trivial detail. Forgotten entirely.

Morning arrived *too soon*.

Not gently, but all at once, a groggy, bloated *awakening*, punctuated by the slow, dawning realization that their bodies had *betrayed* them.

Their stomachs churned in protest. Their limbs felt weighed down, sluggish from the excess of sweets.

Chocolate smears marred their faces, and the floor was still littered with the crinkled remains of their indulgence. It was as if a sugar-fuelled crime had been committed in the night, and now, in the cold clarity of morning, the evidence lay bare.

Gisella sat up abruptly.

"Oh, *Oz*, we're dead if Popsicle sees this."

Gisella didn't want to find out what it *felt* like to be scolded. More so, she didn't want to find out what it *felt* like to be Glinda.

They scrambled to clean up—hiding the wrappers under the bed, rubbing the chocolate from their faces with the sheets (an oversight that would later require a *very* strategic repositioning of pillows).

But it was *too late*.

The door creaked open, and there stood Dainhurst.

A man made of iron, if iron could arch a disapproving eyebrow.

His gaze flicked over the scene: the two dishevelled sisters, the suspiciously ruffled bedclothes, the faint, undeniable *reek* of sugar-stale breath.

He had expected distance between them, but here they were—reunited, if only by the mess they had made.

His lip curled in thought. "You're ill."

Glinda's breath hitched. "What?"

"Ill," he repeated, as if confirming it to himself. "The Floo, perhaps." He tilted his head, reconsidering. "Or maybe Zelena brought back something from wherever she disappeared to."

His tone carried the weight of suspicion, even as he made no outright accusation.

Gisella, sensing opportunity, clutched her stomach with a pitiful moan. Glinda followed suit.

Dainhurst exhaled sharply, making his judgment. "Stay home. I'll call the doctor to have a look at you both."

And just like that, *School* became an afterthought.

For Glinda, the day wasn't wasted.

Not entirely.

She had rekindled something with Gisella, something precarious but real. And despite the worries curling in the back of her mind like smoke, she felt a flicker of *hope* for the days ahead.

CHAPTER 8

Grim

D r. Thistle arrived the moment he was beckoned, the Fairmoors were among his most prestigious clients, and one did not rise in the medical profession by keeping the elite waiting. But if he were being honest (and, in his private thoughts, he always was), he had a particular fondness for *one* Fairmoor in particular.

Glinda.

She was an anomaly in his profession, a rare specimen of mischief wrapped in charm. Most children outgrew their theatrical impulses; Glinda honed hers like a craft. Even now, as he entered the room, he found her and Gisella nestled beneath the blankets, playing their roles with unwavering commitment—sickly children, fragile and pitiful.

Gisella's attempts were shallow and phlegmless. But Glinda's feigned drowsiness was impeccable. The droop of her eyelids, the languid tilt of her head, it was the sort of performance one might expect from an actress on her deathbed, milking her final scene for all it was worth.

Dr. Thistle laughed, setting up his instruments. He needn't have bothered. The girls were about as ill as a pair of kittens in a sunbeam.

Still, he played his part as well.

"Ah, yes," he declared, peering over his spectacles. "Nothing to worry about." His gaze flickered to Dainhurst, who loomed in the doorway, ever the skeptical patriarch. "Just a touch of the bogies. They'll be right as rain by morning."

Dainhurst exhaled, satisfied. His daughters had been cleared of whatever mysterious affliction Zelena might have dragged back from wherever she'd been *lurking*. He turned on his heel and disappeared down the corridor, leaving Dr. Thistle alone with the girls.

He packed up his tools. He should have left then.

But Glinda.

She had a way of making it impossible to refuse her.

BEFORE

Dr. Thistle had sworn, at the tender age of twenty-nine, never to involve himself in the personal squabbles of the ruling class. It led to complications, and complications led to—at best—displeased patrons, and at worst, exile.

And yet, here he was, following Glinda down the corridor toward the maid's quarters.

She had *pleaded*, not overtly, not desperately, but with those *large, earnest eyes*.

"Just look at her," she had said. "That's all I ask."

And now, he was here.

Zelena lay in her quarters, drenched in fever, her breaths slow and shallow. Dr. Thistle did not ask what had happened to her.

"I'll need privacy," he told Glinda, shutting the door before she could argue.

For thirty Oz'mins, he remained inside.

Glinda waited, her pulse hammering in her throat. *Thirty* was an eternity. Either he was treating something serious, or they were having an altogether *too good* a time.

She doubted it was the latter, she was too sick to partake in the exploring of Dr. Thistle's anatomy.

When the door creaked open, he did not offer her a diagnosis, only a slip of parchment with his cramped, unmistakable handwriting.

"This is what she needs," he said simply. "The sooner, the better."

Glinda tucked it into her pocket. She could have sent a maid. It was a task well below her station. But this felt personal.

She would go herself.

Gisella refused to accompany her, citing her own mysterious (entirely fabricated) illness.

Dainhurst had taken the Golden Goose carriage, which meant Glinda had no choice but to rely on the Violet byke.

The journey was long and tiring, but it was for a good cause. That was what she told herself as she gritted her teeth against the wind, as the wheels skidded treacherously on uneven cobblestones.

At last, she reached the Quadling City.

She purchased the medicine quickly, slipping it into her satchel. She was prepared to leave just as swiftly, but then—

Ominson.

Standing outside the tailor's shop, idly kicking pebbles, his hands stuffed into his pockets. His parents were inside, discussing fabrics and trims, an endless deliberation that likely felt like a lifetime to him.

When he saw her, he lit up like an oil lamp.

"Glinda!"

She crossed the street toward him, already smiling. "You look *miserable*."

"I *am* miserable," he groaned. "My parents insist on dragging me to these fittings. And if I have to hear another word about imported trims—" He made a strangled noise in his throat.

Glinda laughed.

He laughed, too, before shifting on his feet. "I've missed you," Ominson admitted. "My friends are still mad at me for spending too much time with you, they keep calling you my 'girlfriend,'" he said, rolling his eyes.

He could not understand what in Oz would give them that impression. It was just that Glinda was the only one that allowed him to be himself.

She had so much to tell him, but a conversation here, in the bustling streets, wouldn't do. "Meet me at the waterfall later?"

He shook his head. "Can't. We're at the tailor's becoz there's an event tonight. Something your father's organizing."

Something else she *hadn't* been told about.

There it was again, that peculiar tightening in her chest, that creeping unease.

Ominson's parents called for him, and with a final glance, he disappeared into the tailor's shop.

◇

Back at the castle, Esmelda was in the grand hall, standing on a dais as a seamstress fussed over the train of her gown. She did not have to *go* to a tailor's shop. She was the most important woman in Quadling Country.

Glinda watched for a moment, disinterested. This was, presumably, for the same event Ominson had mentioned. But she did not ask.

Instead, she handed the medicine to a passing maid, instructing her to administer it to Zelena at once.

There was still enough daylight left, and for the first time in weeks, she had *nothing* to do.

She turned to her bookshelf. There, collecting dust, was the book her teacher had given her. *Ozian Times: Past, Present & Future.*

She cracked open the tome, and a puff of dust curled into the air. The scent of old parchment filled her nose.

Her eyes skimmed over the chapters, until they landed on one title.

The Wizard of Oz.

Despite the wealth of knowledge stored in her father's library, *this* was a subject she knew surprisingly little about.

Curiosity piqued.

She turned the page.

And she read.

"Past:

From its inception, the Land of Oz had been ruled by a national Wizard—a magical individual entrusted with the monumental task of upholding the laws and the fair distribution of power. During the era when magic flowed freely and unrestrained, the first Wizard of Oz implemented strict regulations on its use, decreeing that only those who had received explicit permission from him could practice magic. Violators of this law were met with severe retribution—public execution by beheading.

*According to the Wizard's **Book of Records**, this policy had a profound effect on crime rates, establishing a fragile semblance of order. Magic became a centralized power, with the first Wizard acting as its sole practitioner for a time. But such control came at a steep cost—resentment festered among the families of those who had been executed. In secret, their descendants honed their own magical abilities, plotting to overthrow the Wizard in vengeance for their fallen kin.*

This undercurrent of defiance led to a brief but devastating civil war that ravaged Oz for three moons and three suns. When it ended, the land was left in ruins, and the first Wizard of Oz disappeared without a trace. Some claimed he had been assassinated by the very rebels he had sought to suppress. Others believed he had escaped to another realm, retreating beyond the Impassable Desert—possibly undoing the barrier spell on the sands temporarily and vanishing from the land forever.

*To restore order, a new law was instituted: magic could still be practiced, but only in private. Public displays of magic were strictly outlawed, and violators were sentenced to imprisonment in the notorious **Ozian Forest Camp**. Over time, the number of magic practitioners dwindled, and the land found stability once more. This shift was formally codified in the **Future of Oz Accord**, a decree that declared only the Wizard of Oz—the individual whose magical powers were said to come from a divine source, bestowed upon them by Ozma herself—could wield magic openly. As Ozma's appointed guardian, the Wizard was granted the responsibility of protecting the realm from heretics, evil witches, and any other forces that threatened the land's delicate balance.*

To this day, this law remains in effect.

Present:

*Exactly one century after the disappearance of the first Wizard, the Second Wizard of Oz descended from the heavens in a magical balloon. Ozma, as foretold in the sacred **Book of Ozma**, had promised that in Oz's darkest hour, a saviour with unparalleled power would arrive to restore justice. The prophecy spoke of one who would descend from the sky, referred to cryptically as the **"Green Wi——"** (the rest of the text remains redacted). Yet the context makes clear this saviour is the Green Wizard.*

The Second Wizard of Oz, who arrived in Oz draped entirely in green, established himself in the Emerald City. His reign has brought unprecedented stability to all corners of Oz: North, South, East, and West. Unlike his predecessor, this Wizard chose to relax the strict ban on magic, founding a university where magic is taught under his oversight. Though magic is rare today, this privilege is reserved for those who possess it and swear loyalty to the Wizard of Oz.

Future:
This chapter remains unwritten.

Glinda finished the chapter, and sat back in awe, her mind swirling. She hadn't realized how little she knew about the Wizards of Oz and the laws they established.

Mz. Everburn seemed to believe that the current Wizard did not have magical powers, but from what she read and people's testimonies, she might be wrong.

If magic wielders were the source of chaos in Oz, wouldn't a logical ruler want to control it for the *good* of the people? The thought made sense to Glinda. The Wizard wasn't just a leader; he was a symbol of goodness, a beacon of hope for everyone in Oz, including her. Closing the book, Glinda sighed.

Fresh air would do her some good, and perhaps it was time to check on Zelena. Surely, by now, it would be acceptable to visit.

She knocked gently on the maid's door and was granted permission to enter. Inside, Zelena stirred weakly, clearly expecting someone else.

"I told Dr. Thistle to tell you not to come in," Zelena croaked, her voice thin and strained.

Glinda's **heart** sank as she took in the sight. Zelena was far worse than she had imagined. Beads of sweat dripped from her forehead, her crimson-tinged eyes glassy and unfocused. Each breath was a laborious gasp.

"Have you been taking your medication?" Glinda asked, her voice trembling.

Zelena nodded faintly, but her body language spoke volumes. She didn't want Glinda to see her like this.

"I don't care how you look," Glinda said softly, moving closer. "We're practically sisters, and sisters take care of each other. That's what we do."

Zelena tried to smile but faltered. "Glinda, are you going to cry? Don't cry. If you cry, I'll cry too, and then we'll both be a mess."

Glinda bit her lip, holding back the tears that threatened to spill. "Are you going to be okay?" she asked, her voice breaking.

"Yes," Zelena rasped. "Dr. Thistle said so."

"Should I summon your family?" Glinda offered.

Zelena hesitated, her expression softening. "I don't have any family, Glinda. Apart from you. You are my family." She paused, her breath hitching. "And don't worry. I'll be fine soon. It's only a matter of time."

Glinda knelt by the bed. "Is there anything you need?"

"N-no," Zelena whispered. "Thank you, Glinda. I just... I just want to be alone right now, if that's okay."

Glinda nodded, though her **heart** ached to stay. She rose, determined to respect Zelena's wishes. "All right," she said softly. "Rest well."

As she reached the door, Zelena's voice called out one last time.

"Glinda... I love you so much."

Glinda froze, her hand on the doorframe. She smiled faintly, her chest tight with emotion. There was no need to go back inside and risk upsetting Zelena further.

She could tell her she loved her too—tomorrow. She stepped into the hallway, shutting the door quietly behind her.

As she walked away, her thoughts lingered on a book she had once read from her father's library: *How to Be Good to People*. It had cautioned against overstepping boundaries in the name of kindness. But even if she had crossed that line countless times, Glinda felt it was worth it. For Zelena, she would do it all again.

◇

The morning, eerily like the one just days ago, came with an unsettling quiet. The maids, usually bustling about in frantic, purposeful motions, seemed almost stagnant now. This too was becoming a strange new norm. The air hung heavy, thick with an oppressive stillness.

Glinda rose from her bed and dressed quickly, her steps echoing through the empty halls as she made her way down the corridor. There, she passed a maid who seemed to embody the bleakness of the day, her countenance grey and dark. Today, Glinda had school, and she had to be ready before the carriage arrived. A bath, followed by the crisp pink uniform the maids had prepared the night before, left her waiting for her family to be ready. Instead of staying in her room, she decided to go downstairs to the Fairmoor's grand hall.

Upon entering, she found Dr. Thistle already there, as reserved and focused as ever. He was signing papers with a practiced hand, the air around him thick with unspoken tension.

"Good morning, Dr. Thistle," Glinda said, her voice ringing clear in the otherwise silent space.

She seated herself in front of him.

He acknowledged her with a brief nod, but his attention remained fixed on the documents in front of him. Glinda didn't want to disturb him, so the room fell into an uneasy quiet. She clicked her heels softly, thinking about checking on Zelena later when the medicine's effect would finally show its results, so she continued clicking as her gaze shifted to Dr. Thistle. His eyes, though focused on his work, flickered up to study her. There was something in his expression that made her skin prickle with discomfort. He seemed to be assessing her, examining how she felt, perhaps waiting for her reaction to something unknown. His confusion was palpable, yet it felt intrusive, and it made her stomach twist uneasily.

Unable to bear it any longer, Glinda asked, "What are you doing?"

Dr. Thistle blinked, taken aback, as though he hadn't expected her question. His confusion deepened. *What else could he possibly be doing?* Before he could respond, Dainhurst appeared in the doorway, his expression unreadable, as always.

He cut their brief conversation short with a simple request: "Dr. Thistle, I need to speak with you privately, in my study."

As the two men left, Glinda was left alone in the hall.

Moments later, Gisella entered, hesitating before running toward Glinda. She wrapped her arms tightly around her, squeezing as if apologising for something unspeakable.

Glinda pulled back, startled. "What was that for?" she asked, her voice tight.

Gisella didn't answer immediately. Instead, she stared at her with a soft, sorrowful look. "Don't you know?"

A sigh escaped Glinda. She was always the last to know, it seemed. Even the maids, those invisible figures who flitted about her world, appeared to rank higher in the family's hierarchy.

"Glinda… Zelena… she's dead."

The words hit her like a sharp, jagged blow. The world spun around her, the air grew thicker with each breath, and eight-year-old Glinda struggled to breathe.

"No! No! You're lying!" Her voice cracked as she scrambled for some kind of certainty.

Gisella had played terrible pranks before, surely this was just another cruel joke. But something in Gisella's eyes, the raw sorrow told her this wasn't a joke.

Glinda bolted from the room, her small feet stumbling as she dashed down the hallway. She collided with a maid who gave her a look of quiet despair. Desperation seized her, and her voice rose, frantic.

"Where is Zelena? Where is she?" She shook the maid urgently.

"T-they're carrying her away from the castle," the maid stammered, her voice breaking. "I'm sorry."

The words hit Glinda like a fist. She ran straight for the stairs, out into the cold, still air of the courtyard.

There, outside, Dainhurst and Dr. Thistle stood in the distance, talking quietly, though their words were lost to her. Several men in black carried a stretcher on their shoulders.

The sight froze Glinda in place. Dr. Thistle's eyes widened as he saw her, panic flickering across his features, as though she shouldn't be there, shouldn't have seen this. Dainhurst, expressionless as always, watched her with clear disappointment.

"Who is that?!" Glinda shouted, her voice cracking. "Tell me this instant!" Her **heart** raced as fear, confusion, and anger twisted inside her.

Dainhurst's voice was sharp. "Lower your tone, Glinda!"

But she ignored him completely, her eyes locked on the men with the stretcher. "Stop," she ordered, her voice firm despite the trembling fear. "I need to see for myself."

The men hesitated, looking to Dainhurst for confirmation. He gave a quick nod, and they lowered the stretcher to Glinda's level.

Zelena lay there—cold, colourless, but almost peaceful. It didn't help. Not really. A strange calm passed over Glinda, then shattered. The tears came fast. Her vision blurred. Her chest heaved. Across from her, Dainhurst stood like stone. And when Dr. Thistle knelt beside her, trying to comfort her, she exploded. Rage surged up her throat. She turned on him with all the fury her tiny body could hold.

"You lied! You lied!" she screamed, her small fists pounding on his chest. The blows did no damage, but the rawness of her anger was tangible. "You said she would be okay! You're a bad person, you lied!"

Dainhurst, stunned by the ferocity of Glinda's outburst, moved to intervene, but he hesitated. He'd never seen Glinda like this. He had never witnessed such intense emotion, not from her.

Quickly, he tried to remove the body, to spare Glinda from seeing more, but the attempt was futile. Glinda's gaze was locked on the stretcher, her small body shaking with fury.

"You lied to me! You all lied!" she screamed; her voice hoarse. Her eyes burned with the sting of betrayal.

Dr. Thistle attempted to explain, his voice low. "Glinda, Zelena begged me to tell you she was going to make it. She knew from the moment I saw her that she wasn't going to survive. She didn't want you to hurt more than her death would cause."

The words only made it worse. Zelena had known? And yet, she kept it from her.

Zelena was just as cruel as Thistle. They both lied and lies were evil. The thought twisted in Glinda's chest, a searing ache that felt like it might tear her apart. She could have told her she loved her one last time—but that was impossible now.

Her *heart* couldn't bear the weight of it.

Too much. Too much for a child to endure. Her *heart* was tensing and physically hurting her like it was too big for her body.

Dr. Thistle could barely look at her, he simply removed his hat and bowed his head.

Glinda ran from the scene, away from the cold, lifeless body of her sister, and out of the castle gates.

The men and Dainhurst watched her go, but none followed. The men were too uncertain, too afraid of what this fragile girl might do next. Dainhurst turned to reassure them, muttering that it would be fine, that Glinda would calm in time.

But Glinda wasn't thinking of calming. She was running, driven by something primal, something deep within her that wanted to escape the suffocating weight of the loss.

She didn't know where to go. But the one place, the one memory that still clung to her mind, was the waterfall. The last place she visited with cruel Zelena. She ran, without thought, until she reached the stone-bordered entrance. And there, she stopped, as if she had arrived at the only place where her *heart* could finally break.

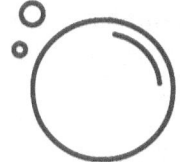

CHAPTER 9

Remembering to Forget

Glinda moved the stone borders with strength she didn't know she had, pushing aside the heavy, weathered rocks. The familiar space beyond them beckoned—Seraphina's Garden. A place that, until today, had always been a sanctuary. The waterfall beside her shimmered softly, its waters cascading with a quiet power. Glinda hoped it would cleanse her, heal the pain gnawing at her chest, but even its calming rhythm couldn't soothe the agony that clenched around her *heart*. She sank onto the cool grass, pulling her legs close to her chest. Tears welled up and spilled over like the very waterfall she was sitting by, yet they felt somehow distant, as if even her sorrow was too heavy to touch. Birds still sang. The water flowed. But nothing felt real, only the mocking clarity of the waterfall, too clean, too calm, for the grief inside her. Zelena was gone. And with her, so had the last piece of a love that felt unconditional, *unchanging.*

Glinda wiped her eyes and stood. The thought of remembering any longer felt like a burden. She no longer felt her memories were worth keeping. Losing them, losing herself—it seemed like mercy. She stepped closer to the waterfall, letting the cool mist spray her skin.

Closing her eyes, Glinda reached the edge of the stones that lined the river, feeling the steady flow of water beneath the rock. She took a deep breath, and then, with one last glance at the world around her, she leaned forward, letting her body fall toward the water.

She waited, the rush of water, the splash—she expected to feel it. But nothing came. No sound, no sensation. Her body remained still; her feet planted firmly on the stones.

She opened her eyes, confused.

Her feet were still on the edge of the water, but there was an invisible pull, a gentle tug at the back of her uniform. It was as though something, or someone, was holding her back. She paused, confused, disoriented, and for a moment, the world seemed to still.

Then, she heard a voice, soft, but unmistakable.

"Why are you trying to get wet?"

Glinda turned, her **heart** lurching in her chest. As she opened her eyes, a lingering speck of green shimmered into view. Standing there, her expression full of concern, was Gisella. Her sister.

"How did you find me?" Glinda asked, her voice cracking with disbelief.

She had kept this place a secret; only Ominson knew it.

Gisella smiled gently, stepping onto the stone beside her.

"You didn't think I'd let you wander off alone, did you? I knew you were hurting. And even though I didn't care much for that maid, I knew *you* did. So, I came. Just in case you needed your big sister."

Glinda thought it sounded like a plausible explanation. Her sister just saved her from doing something she would forever regret.

Glinda's **heart** clenched. Her sister had come.

She needn't say anything more; her tears had already answered.

The two sisters stood together sharing the same stone in the middle of the waterfall's flow. The world silent around them. Glinda collapsed into Gisella's arms, grasping at every sense of her warmth and comfort.

Gisella held her tight, stroking her hair. After a moment Glinda advised they move away from the water.

When they got to the grass, Gisella asked once more.

"Why were you trying to fall into that pool? You can't swim. In your uniform at that."

A little shaken, Glinda confessed.

"This is Seraphina's Garden." Glinda turned to the waterfall and pointed, "And that is the 'forgetting waterfall', I was trying to forget everything I was feeling but now I am a little better."

She paused, now able to breathe better than she could earlier.

"Does it make you forget your current emotion or—" Gisella asked.

"No. It makes you forget everything about yourself. It's like being a newborn *kindling*."

"Why would you ever try to do such a thing? Don't you ever try that again, otherwise I will make you wish you remembered."

Glinda laughed, not because she doubted Gisella. She didn't. She just forgot how territorial her sister could be. Gisella wrapped her arms around Glinda, holding her tighter and closer.

"Gisella, please don't tell anyone about this place. Only three people know about this." Gisella had taken Zelena's place in the secret. And somehow, Glinda didn't feel alone anymore.

"It's the only place I feel connected to, and I want to protect it."

"I promise!" Gisella assured.

They hurried back before anyone else could stumble on the waterfall's secret. The two sisters boarded up the entrance together and walked the long way back to the castle.

When they got *home* the Golden Goose carriage was still there and Dainhurst was not going to allow them to stay *home* for another day. School was non-negotiable. Dainhurst was paying dearly, and he intended to see his investment fulfilled. Glinda did the *good* thing—she didn't protest. She followed him to SilverCrest, despite half of the school day already being lost.

At school, the children were already in class completing their assignments. Glinda walked in without a care in the world. The skin beneath her eyes was pink from crying, her hair out of place. The day had taken a toll on her; worst of all Zelena was gone.

Too drained to pretend otherwise, Glinda sank into her seat and slumped forward, resting her head on the desk. Across the room, Ominson noticed her, his concern immediate. But he stayed in his seat, knowing she needed space, and that a classroom mid-assignment wasn't the time for heartfelt conversations.

Mz. Everburn approached Glinda gently and asked for a word outside the classroom. Though Glinda hated sharing her feelings, she believed no one truly cared, and that most people were either seeking gossip or a chance to boost their egos in trying to help—she told the truth.

Mz. Everburn listened, her compassion sincere, and led Glinda to the nurse's office. There, the nurse provided her with a place to rest, offering a cool drink and quiet supervision. Glinda didn't fight it. For once, she allowed herself to be cared for.

At the end of the day, Ominson found Glinda.

When he looked into her blue eyes, he could see they didn't have their usual sparkle. He hugged her and stayed silent. She was too tired to speak or explain herself. He helped her onto the steps of the Golden Goose, shut the door and waved her goodbye.

Glinda tried to shake the thought of Zelena, but she couldn't remember to forget. It was engraved into her *brain*. Zelena was lost. The image of her cold corpse kept replaying. She figured, her only escape was to go to sleep. She was only eight— taught facts, not how to survive a loss. That kind of knowledge came from living, and she never wanted it.

She thought *We*, **The Fates** would be merciful. But the *Fates* spare no one.

A soft knock echoed against Glinda's door. One of the maids stood there, cradling a box containing the few possessions Zelena had left behind.

Her voice was tentative as she asked, "Do you want to keep anything before they are discarded?"

Glinda hesitated, her gaze lingering on the box, but the weight of the moment was too much.

She wasn't *Unlimited*; she'd always known her limits very well.

BEFORE

"Store them in the castle's storage room," she instructed, her tone steady but distant. "Cover the box to keep it safe."

The maid offered a quiet expression of sympathy, murmured her condolences, and departed to carry out the task, leaving Glinda alone with her thoughts and the silence that now seemed so vast.

◇

Months passed, and the heaviness began to ease, bit by bit. Glinda started to resemble her old self, though she knew she'd never be quite the same. The loss had carved something permanent into her soul.

One thought plagued her, refusing to fade: *was Zelena evil for lying?*

She had always believed lying was a sin, a mark of wickedness. And yet, even after Zelly's deception, Glinda couldn't bring herself to see her as anything but good.

The contradiction gnawed at her. It was easy to categorize people as good or evil when their actions were clear-cut. But Zelena had shattered that simplicity. Despite her lie, Glinda's love for Zelena remained unshaken, perhaps even stronger. This realization consumed her. Most people weren't held to such impossible standards, but Glinda's legacy, intertwined with Seraphina's, demanded perfection. There was no room for shades of grey in her world. Only black and white. And yet, in her **heart**, she knew Zelly's memory would remain in the brightest part of her soul—flawed, yet beloved.

CHAPTER 10
Guh-linda

A year had passed, smoothing the edges of what once felt unbearable. Glinda, now nine, was advancing to the next class—a milestone that seemed mundane yet monumental in her young life. Gisella, three years her senior, was leaving *SilverCrest Academy* to begin at *Willow-Wood Hills*. The transition was bittersweet, marking the end of Gisella's tenure at SilverCrest and the start of Glinda's solo journey.

Dainhurst, ever the admirer of novelty, had purchased a new carriage, *The Golden Eagle*. Sleek and opulent, representing his love for the finest things. Each morning, Glinda and Gisella would part ways; Glinda boarded the familiar Golden Goose, Gisella stepping into the gleaming Golden Eagle. Two sisters heading in opposite directions, separate schools, and, it seemed, separate worlds.

Glinda couldn't shake her apprehension. The day loomed ahead, her first at school without Gisella. It had been weeks since she'd last seen Ominson, and she wondered if they would still share a class. Nervous didn't quite capture how she felt. But she convinced herself she was ready. She had to be.

At school, she made her way to the Swyngs. Glinda sat, waiting for Ominson, her thoughts tangled in hope and dread. When he finally arrived, later than her, as always—they eagerly compared schedules. The news hit harder than Glinda had braced for: not only were they in separate classes, but their break times didn't align. Their moments together would be fleeting, stolen glances in corridors or hurried exchanges on the way to class. She masked her disappointment. Perhaps this separation was an opportunity in disguise—a chance to forge new friendships.

The *Glowblossom* petals bloomed, and all the students unionised in their semi-circle and waited for their appointed teachers to escort them in. Even though Glinda was no longer in Mz. Everburn's class, they still retained their kinship. Both instinctively waving at each other.

Glinda's class was ushered in first, making their way past the labyrinthine corridors and up the stairs to the second floor. Glinda recognised some of Ominson's friends from the year before in her class. She tried to make conversation with them, but they didn't seem as enthusiastic as she was. This interaction was cut short when their new teacher, Mztr. Peasleton, stern and dry, shushed them, asking them to immediately pick a seat whilst he fixated on Glinda's face. He was a new teacher, so this was his first time seeing her. The seat at the back of the class was empty as usual. Almost as though it was saved for her. She took her place, hiding behind the other students. She had learned to seek refuge in the shadows, where she felt safest.

Mztr. Peasleton's lessons, much like his demeanour, were uninspiring. Glinda, who loved learning, found herself disengaged. She had already read much of the curriculum over the summer, but even the subjects she adored seemed lifeless in his hands. Around her, other students stifled yawns and fidgeted restlessly. Her teacher made it difficult for himself to become even one student's favourite teacher. His monotone voice and strict rules made it very difficult to warm up to him.

Determined to salvage the day, Glinda sought an ally. Her gaze fell on a blonde girl sitting to her right, whose boredom was evident in the way she propped her head on her hand. Summoning her **courage**, Glinda introduced herself. The girl's reaction was swift and cutting, her expression twisted into disdain, and she turned away without a word.

She got her confirmation; the girls wouldn't want to be anywhere near her. If she had any chance at a friend, her luck was better with the boys. The boy in front of her seemed like a friendly person. She couldn't bear another disappointment, but she took her chance. She tapped the boy on his shoulder to get his attention and he turned around. Before Glinda could speak, he looked her up and down and laughed in her face, slowly turning back round so she knew exactly that it was her appearance that prompted his reaction. It's like no matter what she did things just seemed to never go her way. Did she commit a sin she didn't know about and angered the *Fates*? She didn't know but she didn't want destiny to lead her down the path of Seraphina. Good deeds were sure to cleanse her from the *Original Sin* she was born with.

The day stretched on, heavy with loneliness, but Glinda resolved to endure. If fate was unkind, she would make her own way. Surely, somewhere in this vast, unfeeling world, a friend was waiting for her.

Somewhere. Someday.

When the bell rang for break, Glinda hesitated, dreading the hallway stares that followed her everywhere. Her classmates had grown accustomed to her appearance by now, but that didn't soften their contempt. She didn't belong here— just as she didn't belong at **home**. She didn't understand why people were being worse to her now than they were the previous year. It was not like she had sprouted a new nose or grown a penis in the past year. She was the same old Glinda. It didn't make sense. The realization struck her like a blow: Gisella wasn't here anymore. Gisella, who had shielded her from the worst of it, whose mere presence commanded others to mask their disdain.

Without her, the fragile buffer between Glinda and the cruelty of her peers had crumbled. Alone now, truly and utterly alone, she had no one to fend off the ghosts of their judgment. Unable to face the whispers and the pointed looks, Glinda slipped into the school lavatories. The hum of distant chatter and the muffled lessons of Mz. Everburn echoed faintly through the walls. In a building bursting with children,

64

Glinda had never felt so isolated. She stared at her reflection in an encrusted silver mirror to which she felt would crack if she kept staring at it. Her resolve flickered like a dying candle.

When the Golden Goose arrived, the little girl climbed aboard and made her way *"**home**."* She needed to be alone in her room so she could cultivate a plan that would make all of Oz love her. She wanted to make a detailed plan that would make her so renowned that even her mother would never forget her name again. She tossed her body on her bed and stared at the ceiling. The same way she always did when she was pondering deep subjects. Yet tonight, her thoughts felt scattered. The vision of who she wanted to be—admired, adored—seemed impossibly out of reach. The mirror was unkind, reflecting her perceived flaws. She didn't have to figure it all out at that moment, all she wanted was a start. The day will begin anew, and she will have another chance to put her plan into action to be liked, if not loved.

✧

The next morning, Glinda resolved to reinvent herself. Her smile was wide, practiced to perfection, and her strawberry-blonde hair cascaded freely down her shoulders for the first time in ages. It was an offering, a silent declaration: *I'm like you. Look past my differences.* She knew the stakes, one accidental grin that revealed too much of her hidden pain could betray her, exposing the darkness she fought to suppress. The Seraphina curse, they called it.

From the moment she walked into class, the children began to whisper secretly and laugh amongst themselves. The blonde girl that sat to her right was smiling at her and so did the boy who sat in front of her. Did it work? The whole time, was the key to *acceptance*: excessive smiling and her hair let down? Whatever the reason she was happy she was finally being seen for the good person she was. The day was ordinary like any other, even though people were smiling at her a lot more today, mostly laughing, she felt welcomed. Buoyed by this fragile sense of belonging, Glinda decided to take the boldest step yet: during break, she would try to make a friend. Again.

The time had come. All she had to do was step out that door and her future would change. Glinda sighed, practicing summoning up the **courage** to walk out those doors. She fixed her walk, straightened her posture, her head held high and swung the doors open.

The courtyard fell silent as she emerged, an eerie stillness that prickled her skin. Then came the shout: "Now!"

Her **heart** plummeted. Before she could react, the sky seemed to open above her, raining down an avalanche of rotting banana peels, soured milk, and half-eaten scraps. The smell was overwhelming, the humiliation suffocating. Drenched and stained, she let out an instinctive, guttural cry— "GUH!"—that only fuelled the crowd's hysterical laughter.

BEFORE

Glinda looked up, her tear-filled eyes meeting those of the two boys perched above, one of them the boy who sat in front of her in class. They were all in on it. Her classmates, the school, every single one of them. The tears of shame quickly turned to fury. Time moved slower, through her blurred vision, she spotted a rock on the ground, its jagged edges gleaming in the sunlight. She picked it up, her hands trembling with rage. The weight of it felt empowering, a means to strike back at the cruelty that surrounded her. Her mind raced as she scanned the crowd for a target, but they all blurred into the same hateful mass. It didn't matter who—anyone would do. She raised the rock, poised to throw, when a voice inside her broke through the storm of emotions.

If you do this, you'll become just like Seraphina. They'll see you as wicked, not wronged. You will forever be cemented to Seraphina, discarded and forsaken just as she was.

Her grip on the rock loosened, and it tumbled to the ground with a hollow thud. The laughter grew louder, more cutting, but Glinda remained frozen, broken. She was the joke right now, but perception was everything. For her to be seen as good she had to do good things always.

Glinda kept the incident to herself. She didn't think anyone would care, nor did she want to burden anyone with it. Her father had stopped coming to take her **home** ever since Gisella switched schools, and for that, she was grateful. Explaining what happened to them would've only made the wound deeper, a raw admission of her isolation. She cleaned herself up in her castle, slipped into her nightgown at midday, and sank into her bed, surrendering to sleep.

◇

The next day at school, the taunting began. The students jeered at her, chanting, "GUH! GUH!" over and over, their laughter echoing through the classroom. Glinda kept her chin high, a brittle attempt at bravery. She loved humour just as much as any munchkin, but this wasn't laughter she could join. The teachers, oblivious as ever, turned blind eyes to the cruelty. Children were adept at hiding their meanness when adults were near. Ominson, however, had heard the story in hushed whispers from his friends, who laughed at her expense. Later that day, as Glinda walked to her break and Ominson returned to class, they crossed paths. He offered his hand, a fleeting, quiet gesture of solidarity. She reached for it, their fingertips brushing briefly before they drifted apart. That touch, small as it was, reminded her of how much she needed a friend. But in her world, she felt encased in a bubble that no one seemed willing to pierce.

Despite her sensitivity, Glinda had a peculiar defiance. She refused to run from her fears as long as someone was watching. They mocked her, yes, but she was still the centre of their attention. She clung to the hope that if she showed no reaction, they might eventually stop. Above all, she wanted to be seen as a good sport—no one liked someone who couldn't take a joke.

GLINDA: The GOOD Witch

The day dragged on. Glinda dodged the small objects hurled her way, ignored the harsh words, and weathered the storm of laughter. The playground wasn't any kinder. Amid the chaos, a voice shouted, "Hey, Glinda! Look! GUH!"

Another chimed in, "Wait, wait! Maybe, we should call her, *Guh-linda!*"

Laughter erupted like wildfire, spreading from one corner of the yard to the next.

"Guhlinda! Hey, Guhlinda!" they cried.

Did they *really* think that was clever? Glinda hated how they stretched her name into something ugly. Guh-linda. The way they said it, she could feel every letter being dragged through mud. At that moment she did not know that a silly little joke would change the trajectory of her life *For Good.*

By the time she returned **home**, still clad in her pink uniform that seemed to lose a little of its brightness with each passing day, the weight of their words pressed on her chest. For a fleeting moment, she considered the Forgetting Waterfall—a place she knew she'd never truly go, but the thought of escape whispered to her like a siren song.

A soft knock sounded at the door and Gisella entered to check on her sister. Gisella knew when Glinda was having one of those days where she was fixated on her appearance. She had a bronze hand mirror, similar in design to Gisella's gold one, adjusting her hair, touching her face, desperately trying to convince herself she was beautiful. That the world was just misinterpreting her. Gisella, in her green uniform sat next to her in silence, moving herself into view of the mirror so her cheek pressed against Glinda's.

"Hmm… Pink and Green really are sisters you know," Gisella said softly, her eyes gleaming with certainty.

"Do you really think they go together?" Glinda asked, tilting her head with doubt.

"Without question. They were always meant to be."

For a moment, Glinda's **heart** softened. The thought of school still loomed over her, but her sister's quiet presence brought a sliver of calm.

As Gisella stood to leave, Glinda hesitated, she needed some advice, Gisella seemed to always have her emotions under control. "Gisella?" she asked.

Her sister paused at the door. "Yes?"

"What do I do if people keep calling me names?"

"Is it a specific name or many?"

"Many. But now they've decided on one."

"Is it harmful?"

Glinda considered this. "Not particularly."

"Then wear it as a badge of honour," Gisella said with a shrug. "My friends and I come up with nicknames all the time!"

Glinda pondered her words. If she was going to survive, maybe she *did* have to embrace the role they'd cast her in and if she acted unbothered, perhaps the name would lose its sting.

"Is that all, Glinda?" Gisella asked, one foot already out the door.

"It's Galinda," she corrected, her voice steady.

Gisella blinked, confused, but didn't question it. "Goodbye, Galinda," she said with a smile as she closed the door.

In the South of Oz, even names carried weight. A name could open doors— or close them forever. Left alone, Glinda turned to her mirror once more. She studied herself, the reflection of a girl on the verge of something new. Slowly, she whispered the name to herself, as though testing it out.

"Galinda. Galinda. Galinda."

It stuck, like a name on a WANTED poster. The name settled over her like a crown and a curse, both heavier and lighter than she'd expected. Glinda was no more.

Galinda got even more practice with her new name when the students kept regurgitating it. This time, she didn't show disdain for it. She embraced it, and the students noticed. The name once used for mockery had lost its sting over time. The teachers always forgot her name, so it was easy to convert them. She was now Galinda, and they couldn't tell the difference. There was one teacher though she didn't correct. Mz. Everburn. She was the only person that was allowed to remember the old her. She remembered her name, and even though she didn't feel a closeness to it anymore, she couldn't bring herself to kill the last ember of her previous existence that lived in Mz. Everburn.

◇

Galinda and Ominson planned to meet at their hideout, they hadn't caught up in a while. At the end of the school day when the Golden Goose arrived, she asked for the coachman to return whilst they took Ominson's Wither-Swan to cover half the distance before walking the rest of the way to the waterfall. Inside, again she had that strange feeling—like someone had already been there. She had no proof, but her intuition was yet to fail her. She knew things clandestinely.

"How have you been, Glinda?" Ominson asked with concern."

"I've been great," she replied, putting on a brave face. Then, she added with purpose, "Also, it's Galinda."

Ominson smirked. "I heard" but Galinda was serious, her face unchanged.

"How about you Omi?" she paused. "Can I call you that?" She giggled.

"Since we're using 'nicknames', I'll still call you Glinda and you can call me Omi?"

Galinda thought about it and reluctantly agreed.

"Great, I've been going through some things, if I'm honest. My father wants me more involved in politics, like the real politics but it's just not me."

"What kind of politics? Bad politics?"

"All politics is bad, Glinda; the Wizard is the only one that has managed to be a good leader."

Galinda hummed in thought. "I see..."

"He keeps saying that if I'm going to take over when I'm older, I need to start *now*—start watching, start learning. It's exhausting. And he's been spending more time with your father lately, which makes me even more suspicious."

He gave her a sideways glance. "No offence."

"None taken," Galinda shrugged.

The conversation shifted, lighter now, but no less significant.

"How are you holding up after the... Zelly incident?" Ominson asked gently.

Galinda hesitated. "As good as I can be, I guess. Some days, I'm fine. Other days, my ***brain*** pulls it out of the shadows and makes me sit with it until I forget again." She exhaled. "It's a cycle."

Ominson nodded, his voice quieter now. "I understand. It's like when I lost my dog."

Galinda blinked. "*Your dog?*"

A giggle bubbled up before she could stop it. Of all the comparisons, she thought he was about to mention **a person.**

Ominson shot her a look, but then, he started laughing too. He gave her a playful shove, and she toppled onto the grass. Before she could retaliate, he collapsed next to her, both of them breathless, hysterical, until the laughter faded into something softer.

Tears slipped down their faces, but neither of them said a word about it.

The Wither-Swan remained where they had left it, its white and silver exterior gleaming under the moonlight like polished diamonds. The coachman, steadfast and patient, waited silently by the carriage. Galinda stepped inside, grateful for the *ryde* back to her castle. She expressed her thanks openly, her words carrying an unmistakable undercurrent of pride. Gratitude was important to show, after all, it set her apart. Galinda would be better than *Glinda* ever was. She was determined to prove it, to herself and to everyone else.

This was Ominson's first time visiting her castle, though Galinda had been to his far too many times to count. She'd avoided bringing him here for one reason: her family. They had a way of leaving their mark on people, not with overt cruelty but with invisible stains that clung to a person's soul, growing darker and heavier with time. She didn't want that for Ominson. But tonight, he had insisted, and reluctantly, she relented.

"Do you mind if I come in?" he asked as the carriage stopped before the towering gates of her estate.

Galinda hesitated. It was late, and exhaustion tugged at her bones, but she owed him this much—a glimpse of her world.

"Fine," she said, offering a small smile. Her castle was a sprawling labyrinth of cold stone and looming towers, far larger than Ominson's modest estate. Yet, for all its grandeur, the atmosphere felt heavy, oppressive. She noticed his curious glances, the way his eyes roved over every detail as they moved through the halls. He was as nosy as she was, and though it irked her slightly, she understood.

She showed him the vast kitchens, the sprawling gardens, and even Zelena's vacant quarters, now steeped in quiet abandonment. Finally, they ascended the grand staircase to the first floor, where the grand hall and her father's study resided.

The study door was ajar ever so slightly, and the flickering glow of lamplight spilled into the hallway. Galinda froze when she heard voices inside. Her father was **home**, and he wasn't alone.

Ominson's eyes gleamed with mischief as he leaned closer. "What do you think they're talking about?" he whispered.

Galinda frowned. "Nothing good, I'm sure."

"Let's find out," Ominson suggested, already crouching beside the door.

Reluctantly, Galinda joined him, pressing her ear to the heavy oak. The voices were muffled but distinct enough to make out.

"Did you get the Wizard to sign the document?" an unfamiliar voice asked.

"Yes, and far quicker than I expected," Dainhurst replied, his tone laced with amusement. "Barely had to pitch it."

"I told you," The stranger said, a trace of smugness in his voice. "This is for the good of Oz. Criminals off the streets, children safe in their beds. Isn't that what we all want?"

"Of course," Dainhurst agreed smoothly. "That's the only reason we do anything, right?"

"Indeed!" the man chuckled, the sound sharp and grating.

Galinda felt a chill creep up her spine, but she kept listening.

"Besides, it doesn't benefit us having them around, does it? They're a problem, I once read in that book our Oscar Diggs gave us. Uh what was it?"

"You're thinking of *Society, Laws and Power*."

"YES! Remember the line he outlined in our copies: *If you ever wish to maintain your standing, you need to eliminate the enemy that have the power to oppose you.* But of course, you must know when to pick your allies."

"Of course," the man added whilst sipping a tonic from a glass.

"Those people were becoming too much of a problem, intentionally having more babies like we wouldn't notice. They're breathing becoz we allow it!" Dainhurst paused and leaned closer to the anonymous man and whispered, "Guess what?"

"Remember that time my tailor sent me the wrong colour suit for my rally you brought your boy to? I had him sent to the—"

Galinda strained to hear, but the words were lost to her. Instead, she heard the men laugh, a deep, cruel sound that made her stomach churn.

Ominson's face had gone pale. He looked at her, his expression mirroring the unease she felt. Whatever they had overheard, it was sinister, something they didn't fully understand but instinctively knew to fear.

GLINDA: The GOOD Witch

The study fell silent, and the two of them scrambled to stand. But before they could retreat, the door flew open with a sudden, violent force. They froze, staring up at the figures before them: Dainhurst and his shadowy guest, their expressions a mix of surprise and dark amusement.

CHAPTER 11

Family & Loyalty

The shadowy guest placed a firm hand on Ominson's shoulder, his piercing gaze locking onto the young man with unsettling intensity. Ominson shifted uneasily beneath the grip, his nerves taut. But no one in the room was more unsettled than Galinda, her wide eyes darting between the stranger and her father.

The guest tightened his grip on Ominson possessively, before turning to Dainhurst.

"You remember my boy, Ominson, don't you?" he said, his voice low and smooth, like the rumble of distant thunder.

Dainhurst inclined his head slightly. "I do." He made no move to introduce Galinda, nor did he intend to. Ominson's father already knew exactly who she was.

The guest's gaze flicked to Galinda, lingering just long enough to make her stomach churn. "Is this... that kindling?"

"Yes, Magnum," Dainhurst sighed, his tone heavy with resignation.

"Right, then. We'll be off." *Magnum Veilforge's* eyes swept over Galinda one last time, sharp as the edge of a blade. His lips curled into an almost mocking smile. "Goodnight."

Dainhurst waved him off without a word, watching as Magnum descended the castle stairs. The castle doors groaned shut behind them, the sound reverberating through the empty halls.

The moment they were gone, Dainhurst turned to Galinda, his face unreadable. "My study. Now."

Galinda followed without a word, her **heart** pounding. She slipped into one of the high-backed chairs in front of his imposing desk, her small frame dwarfed by the grandiose room. Dainhurst seated himself in his throne-like chair, leaning back as he studied her.

"Nosy little bug, aren't you?" he said, his voice sharp, cutting through the tension like a dagger.

Galinda shrank under his scrutiny, her cheeks flushing with guilt. "I-I wasn't—"

"What did you hear?" Dainhurst's tone hardened, his eyes narrowing.

"N-nothing!" she stammered, her voice barely above a whisper.

He leaned forward, the faint scent of his tonic reaching her. "Glinda," he said, his voice dangerously soft. "Do you like living in this castle?"

"Yes, Father," she replied quickly. "I do."

"Good." He nodded, his gaze piercing through her. "Becoz your father is on the verge of something monumental. Something that will change everything. And I cannot—*will not*—allow anything to get in the way of that."

Galinda nodded quickly.

"Whatever you heard, *if* you heard anything, you must keep it to yourself. You understand?" His voice dropped lower. "You wouldn't want what happened to Zelena to happen to Gisella, would you?"

"NO!" Galinda cried, her voice firm with sudden conviction.

Dainhurst's expression softened, a rare and unsettling sight.

"I thought so. You're such a good girl," he said, spreading his arms. "Come here. Give your father a hug."

Hesitant, Galinda stepped forward. She couldn't remember the last time he had embraced her, if he ever had. His arms were strong as they wrapped around her, holding her close. Being close to him in that way, for a moment felt like safety. Maybe the name change really did ease the curse that was placed on her.

When Dainhurst got tired of the hug he let go and dismissed her. His voice turned quiet but deliberate. "Loyalty to family is everything, Glinda. *Everything.* Never forget that."

"I won't, Father," she whispered.

As she turned to leave, she hesitated at the door. "Father?"

"Yes?"

"Can you… can you call me Galinda?"

Dainhurst gave the same curious look her sister Gisella had given her not long ago. "Galinda, hmm? It does have a certain sophistication to it..." He nodded slowly. "I like it. Galinda it is."

A smile spread across her face. "Goodnight, Father."

"Goodnight, Galinda." He winked.

As the door clicked shut behind her, Dainhurst leaned back in his chair, his lips curling into an amused smirk. "Galinda?" A soft chuckle escaped him, low and sardonic. "How ridiculous."

◇

The next day at the waterfall, Ominson and Galinda were quieter than usual. It was as though something in the air between them had shifted—not in their feelings for each other, but within their spirits. They spoke of everything except what had happened the evening before. Both knew where their loyalties lay, and that unspoken understanding hung heavily between them.

As the sun began to dip, Ominson mounted his Wither-Swan and departed, while Galinda returned to the castle atop her radiant Golden Goose. The *ryde home* was calm, but her thoughts buzzed, lingering on questions she dared not voice.

When Galinda entered her chambers, she found an elegant box waiting on her dressing table, tied with a delicate pink bow. She blinked in surprise. Gifts were a rarity, except on her *Born-Day*, and even then, they were modest. Galinda's hands fumbled with the stubborn ribbon until she gave up and sought professional help. Galinda went to Gisella's room, where her sister was busy at her gilded mirror, brushing her perfect golden hair as it formed gentle curls at the end.

"Gisella, can you help me with this box? I can't seem to get it open."

With a small, smug smile, Gisella set down her brush and opened the box with effortless precision. Inside was a magnificent golden hand mirror, its back engraved with a diamond-studded 'G.' The craftsmanship was exquisite, and the gift was accompanied by a card:

> To Galinda,
> I had this made Specially for you.
> From your Popsicle.

Galinda gasped, her cheeks flushing with excitement. The mirror gleamed in the late afternoon sunlight, its golden surface catching the light in a way that made it seem almost enchanted. She couldn't help but wonder what she had done to deserve such a treasure. Gisella, however, was less impressed. What was she going to do with a mirror so opulent? Honestly, with the way she looked she didn't need it. Gisella assumed it was a twisted joke her father was playing on Galinda.

"Gl-Galinda," Gisella stammered, forcing a smile. "That's lovely. I'm glad Father bought it for you. If he hadn't, I might have snatched it up myself. I think I saw one just like it… it was discounted… at the jeweller's."

But Galinda barely heard her. "It's beautiful! Look how it glistens!" She held the mirror up to the sunlight streaming through Gisella's window. Though the mirror was heavy in her hands, Galinda felt a strange sense of pride.

Gisella's smile faltered. Her mind raced; her confidence shaken. Was this some kind of punishment from their father? Galinda wasn't prettier than her—she would never be. Surely, he had made a mistake. Maybe he meant the gift for her instead. Both their names began with a 'G,' after all.

Feigning nonchalance, Gisella reached for her jewellery box. To regain some of her composure, she pulled out her prized crystal necklace and draped it around her neck, letting it rest perfectly against her collarbone. "Galinda," she said sweetly, "can you help me clasp this?"

Galinda obliged, fastening the necklace with care. As the giant crystal lay between her breasts, she further expanded her chest, repositioning her body so the light would reflect onto Galinda's eyes, blindingly so. The crystal almost blinded Galinda. That ought to show her, Gisella thought.

"Doesn't it look stunning?" Gisella asked, her voice syrupy.

Galinda was very smart but her lack of social interaction as a child affected her ability to pick up on social cues as well as behaving in society. Which is what heightened her awkwardness. But today, Galinda knew what Gisella was doing so, she *decided* to be a *good* younger sister and alleviated Gisella from her torment.

"That necklace never gets old, I just love it so much!" Galinda remarked as she touched it sharp spikes.

"You think so?"

"I would steal it but you're lucky you're my sister."

This made Gisella laugh uncontrollably. Galinda could be really funny sometimes, partly because she was such an odd duckling. Gisella felt ridiculous now. She shouldn't have felt threatened—it was only Galinda. She had been given her hand-me-downs since she was born, she deserved at least one extravagant gift, didn't she? Besides, a dozen mirrors could not match up to the cost of her necklace. At that moment, Gisella realised how much she couldn't wait for her eighteenth birthday. Dainhurst had promised her the *Fairmoor Crown*.

You see, the Dainhurst family descended from kings and queens until the first *Wizard of Oz* stripped the title to rule all of Oz by himself. The Fairmoor Crown cost more than the entire castle itself, so precious it was hidden somewhere within the castle where no one could find it. Not even Esmelda knew its hidden chamber. No mirror, no matter how fine, could compare.

Gisella straightened her shoulders, a satisfied smirk playing at her lips. Let Galinda enjoy her moment. Soon enough, she would have the world.

Galinda returned to her sanctuary still astonished by the mirror's beauty. For some unknown reason, she looked better in that particular mirror. Nothing about her appearance changed but she looked better in it. Galinda played with her reflection, posing and making different faces in the mirror. Galinda with her hair down, tossed it to the left then she tossed it to the right. This motion allowed her to feel the thick, silken texture of her hair. Although she lacked Gisella's blonde, there was elegance in the way her hair glowed with rich vibrancy in the sun. Its golden hue kissed with pink undertones, allowed her to find a glimpse of the beauty behind the beast. "Toss, Toss" she mocked herself repeatedly.

Galinda was finding peace within herself. Who knew the hidden power of a gold and diamond hand mirror? If *loyalty to her family* brought her gifts like this, how could she ever contest it. This was bliss. Being pampered like Gisella was intoxicating. No wonder Gisella stayed aloof; it served her well, it enhanced her charm. The new Galinda was going to be just like that. Just as nobody liked people who could not take a joke, no one liked an overly intelligent person. A *girl*, at least. It was on this very day, looking at herself in the mirror, that Galinda *decided* that she was going to adopt the Gisella gene and play the role of a *dumb-strawberry-blonde*.

BEFORE

She was going to master Gisella's art of a carefree ingénue.

Her thoughts drifted to the incident outside her father's study. Had she really heard anything damning that night? No, she must have misunderstood. Dainhurst should not have had a worry in the world, because, quite frankly, she didn't know what he was talking about with Magnum. It wasn't *good* to judge people or make assumptions, not until there was undeniable proof that her father was a wicked villain. He was innocent until **proven** guilty. It had been over a year since she heard about magic individuals disappearing from town. *It was all a misunderstanding.* Galinda had rationalised everything. What other reason did she have to not be loyal to her family?

The sound of Dainhurst's arrival snapped her from her reverie. Galinda rushed to the castle door, greeting him with a tight hug before throwing a sudden salute.

Dainhurst laughed.

She was proving her loyalty to him. She really was a funny odd duckling.

"I take it you liked your gift?" Dainhurst chuckled

"I love it, Father," Galinda replied earnestly.

"Good. Behave, and there will be even greater gifts," he said, planting a *kiss on her forehead.* As he ascended the grand staircase, he called over his shoulder, "Galinda, have one of the maids run me a hot bath."

Without hesitation, Galinda obeyed. He was a good man—her father, her protector, her anchor. And the *Wizard of Oz* himself trusted him. That alone was proof enough of his righteousness. Galinda felt a pang of shame for the times she had doubted him, for the moments she'd let others speak ill of him in her presence. Family was everything. Above all else.

Later, alone in her room, Galinda allowed herself to sing, her voice lilting and clear. She hadn't done that in a while despite her extraordinary voice. Feeling accepted or welcomed as part of the family seemed to bring that out of oneself.

Mz. Everburn had given her another book to read. They kept up their tradition even though she wasn't in her class anymore. Feeling buoyed by the moment, she turned to the old book: *The Ozma Prophetic Manuscripts.*

The book was practically falling apart—so neglected that one drop of water might turn it to dust. Galinda handled it with care, her pulse quickening as she read:

Ozma IV prophesied:

After the time of the Powerful Emerald Wi ——, there will come Another, chosen to lead Oz to its destiny. Descended from royalty with pure golden mane, the Good Witch born of the South shall reign as Oz's saviour in an age of despair. After the Emerald Wi——'s departure, When Oz is left broken, leaderless and in turmoil this prophecy shall come to pass.

It has been ordained. Blessed Be.

Galinda's breath caught. The description fit Gisella perfectly. It couldn't be Galinda—she wasn't blonde enough, nor was she magic-born. Was Gisella destined to take over the Wizard's role if he ever were to depart? Galinda needed a second opinion, so she went to Gisella to see what she thought.

"You have to see this," Galinda urged, handing her the passage.

Gisella, who did not like to read much, needed persuasion. Reluctantly, she agreed. As Gisella ran her finger across the frail sheet of paper her face began to beam, her smile becoming wider and wider. Gisella picked up the paper and made her way to her father's study. Galinda trailing behind her.

Dainhurst sat in his chair, glass in hand, when the door burst open. Nearly spilling his drink, he frowned. "What's this commotion?"

"Father, Father, look at this!" Gisella exclaimed, thrusting the book toward him. "Please read it," she requested once more, excitingly.

Dainhurst placed his glass on the table and scanned the page. His face was unchanged.

"Where did you get this?" Dainhurst asked, his tone sharp.

"It's Gli-, Galinda's" Gisella answered, rolling her eyes.

"Galinda, where did you find this? Who gave this to you?"

Galinda knew she couldn't reveal who gave her scripture, she was supposed to keep anything related to magic or Mz. Everburn a secret. Gisella was just too giddy and just had to show it to her father, didn't she?

"I found it in an old library" Galinda replied swiftly.

"Well, I'll hold on to it for now," Dainhurst answered whilst inserting it into his desk drawer and locking it definitively.

"But, Father," Gisella pleaded, clutching his arm. "Doesn't it sound like me? Oh, it *has* to be me!"

Gisella could not believe that there was a prophecy in that old text about her.

Dainhurst sighed, his voice softening. "Yes, it does. You weren't supposed to know until you turned sixteen." Dainhurst's eyes locked on Galinda. "Barbarus swore us to secrecy."

Galinda's chest tightened. Gisella really was born perfect!

"But Father," she blurted, "the prophecy says 'Witch' Gisella doesn't have magic."

"Don't be jealous, Galinda," Gisella said with a smirk.

"Yes, Magic often manifests by sixteen," Dainhurst explained, his tone measured but pointed. "If it doesn't, it never will. That's why Barbarus advised us to wait."

A knock at the door broke the tension. "Sir Dainhurst, your bath is ready," a maid announced before bowing and retreating.

"Girls, I know I keep asking you to keep many secrets," Dainhurst said, mainly directing his remark at Galinda. "But truly, you cannot mention this to anyone, becoz family is what?"

"Everything," Galinda answered, her voice hollow.

Gisella looked at Galinda in disbelief. Those words didn't sound familiar to her, and it seemed Dainhurst and Galinda were in sync.

The two girls exited the study and went to their separate havens.

BEFORE

✧

As Galinda lay in bed that night, staring at the ceiling, questions gnawed at her. Why did it seem that every book Mz. Everburn gave her had been orchestrated meticulously? Too deliberate, so perfectly timed. The thought sent a chill down her spine. Pulling the covers over her head, Galinda tried to shut out the whispers of doubt and the strange, *twisting fear* that something much larger was unfolding around her.

CHAPTER 12

Born-Day

Three years had passed, school became easier, and life was as good as it had ever been. Dainhurst was a better father and Esmelda did the best she could, though she had not been herself the past four years. Esmelda often took impromptu trips to Oz's countryside for some retreat. She would leave, seeking solace in the rolling green hills, and return either radiant and vibrant or silent and bedridden. Today, fortunately, was one of her brighter days. Galinda savoured these rare moments.

Today wasn't just another day, it was Galinda's 12th *Born-Day*. The castle bustled with preparations for the festivities, with platters of food being assembled and decorations hung high. But Galinda's mind was elsewhere. She was counting the minutes until her gifts arrived, and more importantly, until Ominson showed up.

Her **heart** raced at the thought of what her father might have planned. Dainhurst was the master of grand gestures, and though it had been three years since her last extravagant gift—the golden, diamond-encrusted mirror she adored—she hoped this year would rival the "Gisella treatment."

Gisella received three notable glamorous new gifts. A green ballgown, an emerald ring and crystal earrings to match her crystal necklace. Not to mention the platinum and diamond looking glass to replace the one she'd "accidentally" broken. Surely, this was her year to shine.

That morning, the family gathered at the table for breakfast. The scent of poached *Chickenduck* eggs filled the room, and sunlight streamed through the tall windows. Galinda fidgeted in her seat, anticipation bubbling under her skin.

Across the table, Gisella couldn't contain her excitement.

"Galinda," she said proudly, "I can't wait any longer! Here's your gift!" She slid a small velvet jewellery box across the table.

Curious and hopeful, Galinda opened it, only to find a green brooch she immediately recognized.

"You like it, don't you?" Gisella pressed, her smile wide.

Galinda hesitated. "It's… nice. But isn't this the one you got on your eighth Born-Day?"

Gisella faltered for a moment, then recovered. "Erm… yes! It's one of my favourites, of course. I had it polished for you this morning. Good as new!"

Galinda forced a smile. She remembered vividly how Gisella had called the brooch "gaudy and tacky" seven years ago. Still, she nodded. "I like it. Thank you, Gisella."

"Oh, and you can always have someone stain it pink if green isn't your colour," Gisella added with a tinkling laugh.

Esmelda placed a hand on Gisella's shoulder, nodding approvingly at her "selfless" gesture.

Galinda looked expectantly at her parents, hoping they'd offer their gifts next. But neither Dainhurst nor Esmelda made any move. Apparently, she would have to wait until the evening ceremony.

Dainhurst cleared his throat loudly, silencing the room. "I won't be back until later today," he declared, dabbing his mouth with a napkin.

"Why, darling?" Esmelda asked, clearly caught off guard.

"Meeting with the Wizard. Crucial business. I can't get into details," he replied gruffly.

"Is it about those despicable munchkins and their effort to be independent from the Oz state?"

"No, we settled that four moons ago. It's… something else."

"What about–" Esmelda rebutted.

"What did I just say?" Dainhurst's voice raised, "I said I can't get into details!"

The table was silent, and no one made a sound besides chewing and swallowing.

"Darling, I was asking what about the carriage? I am meeting the ladies later after your departure, we're going to Winkie Country for the jewel exhibit."

"And? What is it to me?" Dainhurst questioned curiously.

"I agreed to have the Golden Eagle take us, if you could take the Golden Goose instead?"

Dainhurst sighed heavily as he finished the last bite of his poached Chickenduck egg.

"Fine! I'll use the Golden Goose." Dainhurst looked to his *daughter*. Daughters, and said "When you're older and marry, you'd best hope your husband is as good as your father, sacrificing so much for his lady." Dainhurst reached for Esmelda's hand and kissed it, to complete his performance. "You hear?"

"Yes father." Gisella and Galinda answered in unison.

Dainhurst stood up to make his exit for his *top-secret* meeting.

"Good luck! Father." Galinda said softly, Dainhurst answering with a sideways smile.

"How do I look Gisella?" Dainhurst asked.

"Perfect! Wait!" Gisella stood from her seat and fixed the golden medal on his suit. Anything that glistened, she was an expert at it.

"Good luck, Father." Gisella added providing her sentiments.

Dainhurst kissed Gisella on the cheek and made his exit. He settled into the Golden Goose and went on his merry way, to see the *Wonderful Wizard of Oz*.

Shortly after, Esmelda also made her exit leaving but not without saying, "Be good, Galinda" and then ruffling Gisella's hair as if to remind herself of the sensation of Gisella's perfect silky-smooth hair. Esmelda climbed into the Golden Eagle and set on a journey to Winkie Country for new jewellery to buy.

There was no one left at the table, besides Gisella and Galinda the dining room felt cavernous. Her *Born-Day* was off to a good start, Galinda sarcastically thought to herself. But there was no use in making assumptions, it is probable that they wanted to personally go pick up her gift, maybe it was hidden in the castle already and they would be back in time for the ceremony. The day just started. In the meantime, she had her sister Gisella.

"Gisella," she began tentatively, "do you want to make Cream-Cones with me? Father and Mother aren't here, so we can have them for breakfast."

Gisella didn't even look up from her nails. "Oh, sorry, Galinda. Thelma and Veloria are coming to take me to the Ozian Fair. I'll bring you back a *Gooey-Buffo*, though. If you want?"

"That's... fine," Galinda replied, her voice trembling.

She excused herself and climbed the stairs to her bedroom, her **heart** heavy. By the time she reached her room, the sadness had turned to anger. Galinda slammed the door and started pacing in her bedroom, trying to get the anger to settle but the more she tried, the more tears kept falling down her face. When she spotted Gisella's carriage pulling away through the window, something inside her snapped. She grabbed whatever was in reach and hurled it across the room—pillows, books, even shoes. Her golden mirror, perched precariously on the edge of her bedside table, wobbled ominously.

"No!" Galinda screamed, lunging toward it. But she was too late. The hand mirror tipped over, tumbling toward the floor.

Her arm still stretched out; her eyes squeezed shut anticipating the sound of glass shattering. *Complete Silence.*

Galinda slowly opened her eyes scared to see what had become of her prized mirror. From that height it surely was broken. Just as she was today.

Galinda's eyes fully opened. The sight left her speechless. The golden mirror hung in the middle of the air. Paused in its descent. Galinda could not believe what she was seeing. How in all of Oz was the mirror not demolished? As it just hovered mid-air. Galinda stepped back, shaken and stumbling on the shoe she threw trying to understand what was happening. As her eyes remained focused on the mirror trying to catch her breath. The mirror began to slowly rise from its hovering mid-air position and floated forward turning gracefully until its glass faced her. Galinda's breath hitched.

The way the mirror moved, it almost felt sentient. The mirror moved closer and closer till Galinda's nose almost touched it, her breath leaving condensation on its surface. Galinda stomached her fear and reached slowly for the mirror plucking it from the air. She gulped as she closed her eyes and swallowed before looking at herself in the mirror. She was a mess, her hair was displaced from her tantrum, her weird nose was snotty and there were tears still on her face. She laughed weakly at her own mess of emotions, of ALL days and this was not the one for such things.

Galinda sat on the edge of her bed, the mirror beside her, staring at the wall in silence. *What just happened?* It made no sense. *Was the mirror magical?* Most likely not. It was made and sold in a shop in the South of Oz, where magical artifacts and people were ostracised greatly. Nobody would sell such a thing openly out of fear. *What if she? Did she? Was she?* Galinda sighed, looking at the hairbrush on her dresser, her eyes refusing to blink. She stretched out her hand, curling her fingers, expecting nothing but hoping for everything. The dresser began to shake dramatically, the ornaments on the dresser falling off the edges. Galinda stopped. Breathed in again and loosened her fingers. The hairbrush soon enough swept off the table and flew right into her hand. The hairbrush she had for years now looked brand new to her. She knew what happened but confused all the same. For the first time ever, Galinda had performed magic.

For a moment, she was frozen. Then, a smile spread across her face. Galinda elated began jumping on her bed, giggling and dancing. The one thing she always wanted she finally had and of all days, it was on her Born-Day. It felt like a dream, a daze, if so, it was too good that she never wanted to wake. Galinda flopped backwards onto her bed to stare at the ceiling and take in the moment. *What if it was temporary?* She had to try again. She sat up on the bed and focused on the shoe she threw, her arms stretched, and the shoe flew at lightning speed. Had she not ducked she probably would have been decapitated.

This was too good to be True.

♦

A sudden sound echoed from outside the castle, the unmistakable creak of the gates swinging open. Someone was either returning or arriving. Galinda rushed to the window, leaping. The Wither-Swan had arrived. Without hesitation, she flew down the stairs, eager to greet Ominson. She had something *special* to show him.

But when Ominson opened the castle door, he froze. Standing there impossibly close, was Galinda.

"What—What are you doing?" Ominson's eyebrows knit in confusion.

"I have something to show you. But not here," Galinda said, her gaze scanning the surroundings for privacy. "How about the waterfall?"

"Isn't today your Born-Day? If we go there, we won't be back in time."

"Do you see anyone here? No one's **home**."

"Then why are the maids hanging up ornaments and laying out platters of food?"

Galinda sighed, her voice a little defensive. "We do this every year. My family was supposed to be here, but… something more important came up. *Crucial Business.*" She fumbled for an excuse, but Ominson didn't need to hear more.

He paused, his gaze sharpening. "There's no one here to celebrate your Born-Day…"

"Let's go," Galinda urged. "If we're quick, we can catch the Wither-Swan before it leaves."

They sprinted out of the castle, laughing, chasing the retreating carriage. The Wither-Swan had already passed the gates, but the high-pitched cries of children startled the coachman, forcing him to halt.

When the carriage stopped on the outskirts, Galinda grabbed Ominson's arm and dashed toward the waterfall. Her little feet stumbled now and then, but nothing could slow her down. Ominson, dressed in his finest suit, was less thrilled about the sprint. Still, he couldn't help but smile at the sight of her joy.

By the time they reached the waterfall, Ominson was gasping for breath, but he managed to ask,

"What's all this about, Glinda?"

"Are you ready?" she asked, her voice vibrating with excitement.

"Ready for what? You're making me nervous."

"You might want to sit down for this," she said, her eyes gleaming with mischief.

Ominson, eager for rest, obliged. He sank onto the soft grass, leaning back on his hands and stretching out his legs. He let Galinda take centre stage.

Galinda's mind raced eager to impress, but also terrified of failure. *What if it didn't work? What if she looked like a fool?* She scanned the surroundings, looking for something that would amplify the spectacle. A few small pebbles lay nearby, but they weren't dramatic enough. She needed something bigger. Something that could demonstrate her power— but not so heavy that she couldn't lift it.

Her eyes landed on Ominson.

With a deep breath, she closed her eyes and imagined how Mz. Everburn had performed magic in the library. She raised both arms, her **heart** pounding, then locked eyes with Ominson. A surge of intent filled her as she willed the earth to obey her. Ominson's hands from behind his back began loosening off the ground, his feet lifted and soon his buttocks. Ominson was levitating.

"What is happening? Woah— WOAHHH!" Ominson yelped, flailing. Galinda couldn't hold back her laughter.

"Are you doing this?" he cried, his eyes wide with panic. "Glinda, put me down, NOW!" He shut his eyes tightly, not daring to look at the ground far below.

"Fine!" Galinda rolled her eyes but, not without a mischievous twist, spinning him around for her own amusement.

"GLINDA!" Ominson shouted as he floated, swaying from one side of the waterfall gardens to the other.

She slowly lowered her hands, easing him gently back down to the ground, watching as his feet touched the earth again.

"Never. Do. That. Again." Ominson gasped, trying to steady himself. "Woah."

Galinda, still grinning, wiped tears of laughter from her eyes. "I think I've got this down. I'm a quick study, even when it comes to magic apparently."

Ominson said nothing, still reeling from the experience. Galinda sat beside him, letting him regain his composure.

"You have magic?" Ominson murmured, his voice a mix of awe and disbelief. "Since when? How?"

"I discovered it just before you arrived at the castle," she explained quietly. "It's a long story, but I was upset, and suddenly, there it was."

"Woz! Guess you finally got what you wanted."

"I know! It still feels unreal. Pinch me."

Without missing a beat, Ominson complied, pinching her arm lightly.

"Ouch!" Galinda winced. "Want me to make you fly again?"

"No sirree." Ominson replied, shaking his head excessively.

They both burst into laughter, the tension evaporating.

"I remember, Zelena used to sing me this lullaby. There was one line that stuck with me: 'The dreams that you dare to dream really do come true.' I don't remember the rest of it, but that line always stayed with me."

"Why? Things don't just stick with us for no reason. It's probably becoz you hoped it was true?"

"I think so. Today, I was so upset, but I didn't stop to think about everything good I have. And now this, I dreamt of it for so long, and it actually happened. I know, I sound like a munchkin."

"Don't get all sappy on me, Glinda. You're turning soft."

"Shut up, Omi." She smirked, nudging him playfully.

"Alright, alright. But what else have you wished for that came true?"

"Well, when I started at SilverCrest, I wished for a friend. And here you are." She grinned at him, her eyes sparkling. "And I wished for Zelena to come back to me so badly, I wished on a star so hard every night and she came back. For a short while, but she still came back. And now this—my magic."

"Whoa. I've never wished for something, and it came true. Maybe becoz I don't really wish for things… or maybe it only works for people with actual magic."

"I think everyone has the ability to wish— but you have to be the right kind of person. If everyone's wishes came true, imagine the chaos."

"Yes, imagine if all of Gisella's dreams came true." Ominson joked, "Ooh shivers down my spine."

"Stop it," Galinda giggled, slapping his arm.

"What more will she even wish for? She already has everything." Ominson joked further.

The wind was soft and cool, the waterfall clearer than ever, its mist a calming presence in the quiet garden.

"Glinda…" Ominson's tone turned serious, ominous. "What are you going to do about your father? His stance on magic is clear, and now you have it. Need I remind you of what's happening to people who've been 'suspected' of using magic? You actually have it!"

"I know." Her voice faltered. "I don't know what to do. If he finds out, I'll be disowned—or worse. I was just starting to rebuild my relationship with him."

What had once felt like the greatest gift now felt like a curse. The weight of her magic suddenly seemed unbearable, as if the *Fates* were mocking her.

"What do I do, Omi?" Her voice cracked.

"I don't want to make this worse, but… you're the only person who chose the pink gem since Seraphina. Now you have magic. If people find out, I think they'll try to harm you. Badly."

"You're right." The fear in Galinda's chest tightened, her tears flowing again. "Oh, Oz… Ominson, I'm going to die. I don't want to die!" She cried, her words frantic. "My father fought so hard to outlaw magic for me. And now I have it. He'll never forgive me. People will think I'm Seraphina, returned to exact revenge."

Ominson acted instinctively, pulling her into his arms, holding her tightly as she cried. He didn't know the answers, but he knew he had to be there for her.

"I'll help you," he whispered. "But you need to do something, promise me."

"Anything."

"You can never use magic outside this garden. Never show it to anyone except me. I wish we knew someone with magic who could help."

In that moment, Galinda realised that she did indeed know someone who had magic, who was quite adept at concealing it for years.

Mz. Everburn.

If there was anyone in Quadling Country that could help, it was her.

Galinda stayed in Ominson's arms a little longer, needing his warmth, his reassurance. As dusk settled over the garden, they made their way back to Fairmoor Castle. Magnum had arranged for the Wither-Swan to bring Ominson *home*, cutting their time short, but it was enough for now. They would meet again.

"Wait!" Ominson called from the carriage window.

Galinda stopped, turning to look at him. Ominson stepped out, meeting her halfway.

"Yes?" she asked softly.

"I almost forgot." He reached into his pocket, pulling out a small velvet box. "Happy Born-Day."

Galinda's *heart* skipped a beat as she opened it. Inside was a silver necklace with a small heart-shaped pendant, the centre gem a rich violet.

"Violet, huh?" she said, smiling.

"Yes," Ominson replied, his voice a mix of nervousness and fondness.

"Your colour." She added, inspecting it smiling a little harder.

"Do you like it?"

"I love it!" Galinda lunged at Ominson, hugging him very tightly. She thought magic was the best gift she received all day, Ominson beat that by a mile.

Galinda turned around to make her way back into the castle but now it seemed she was the one that was forgetting something. She ran back to Omi and kissed him on the cheek. Before he could respond she was already inside the castle. Ominson stood there, his **heart** racing, his cheeks flushed with warmth. His colour was *Violet*, but his cheeks had turned bright *Pink*. As the carriage rolled away, he stuck his head out the window, feeling the Southern Oz breeze tousling his long, perfect hair.

"Wooooooh!" he yelled, laughing aloud. Today had been the best day of his life. And it would take something extraordinary to surpass it.

◇

Galinda climbed the winding staircase to her room, exhaustion weighing on her shoulders like a heavy cloak. Yet, as she passed Gisella's chambers, bursts of noise and muffled laughter spilled into the corridor. Galinda cracked the door open to investigate. Inside, chaos reigned. Gisella, Thelma, and Veloria were mid-pillow fight, feathers floating lazily to the ground as confectionary wrappers littered the floor. The girls shrieked with laughter, bouncing on the bed as though they were still children.

The moment Galinda stepped into the room, the raucous trio froze, Thelma and Veloria exchanging sly glances as they bit their lips to suppress laughter. Gisella, casually leaned against a post of her bed, her wild, blonde curls dusted with feathers.

"How was your Born-Day..." Gisella asked, looking at her friends, "Galinda?" the three girls clearly trying their hardest to hold the strongest laughter they'd ever have.

"Pretty great, actually," Galinda replied evenly, choosing not to rise to whatever bait Gisella was dangling.

"Really?" Gisella arched a brow, her tone as sugary as the Gooey-Buffos on her bed.

"Yes. Ominson gave me—" Galinda paused mid-sentence, her eyes narrowing as she spotted a half-empty bag of Gooey-Buffos crumpled among the chaos. "Wait... Are those Gooey-Buffos?"

"Yes," Gisella said dismissively, reaching for another pillow to hurl at Veloria. "We might've gotten carried away and eaten them all. Sorry."

There were clearly some left, but Galinda bit back the urge to argue.

"Can we *please* get back to this pillow fight?" Thelma huffed, rolling her eyes in irritation.

"Do you mind?" Gisella added with a flippant wave toward the door, signalling Galinda to leave.

Galinda's jaw tightened. She could've easily ended their little soirée with a flick of her wrist, levitating Thelma and Veloria off the bed and dumping them unceremoniously onto the floor. The idea was almost too tempting. But no, that wouldn't have been the *good* thing to do. So, instead, she turned on her heel and shut the door firmly behind her.

As she walked to her room, Galinda's thoughts churned. She'd almost told Gisella what had happened that day, how her magic had awakened, how she had levitated Ominson at the waterfall. But something held her back. She knew her sister too well. The last time she remotely shared something, she ran to Dainhurst and showed him the manuscripts.

Galinda lay on her bed, staring blankly at the ceiling. The prophecy lingered in her mind like an unwelcome guest. *A Witch from the South would one day rule all of Oz.* She frowned. Gisella had no magic, at least, none that anyone knew of, but Galinda did. Did that make her the witch in the prophecy? The word itself felt bitter and derogatory on her tongue. *Witch.* It carried centuries of fear and hatred, a label no one wanted.

Her gaze flicked to the window, where moonlight spilled across the stone floor. She closed her eyes, willing herself to silence the storm of questions in her mind. Whatever the prophecy said, it didn't matter. Not now. For the time being, her secret had to remain just that—a secret. Galinda took a deep breath, resolving to learn all she could about her magic in private. She would seek out Mz. Everburn, the only person she knew who had both magic and the wisdom to guide her. Until then, her path would be one of caution and quiet strength.

She pulled the covers over her shoulders, shutting her eyes. But even as sleep began to claim her, the words of the prophecy echoed faintly in the back of her mind, a whisper she couldn't quite silence.

CHAPTER 13

A Quick Study

In the three years that passed, Galinda and Ominson were finally in the same class at SilverCrest. Before class, Ominson turned to her, his voice a mere thread of sound between them.

"Do you remember our agreement?"

Galinda, adjusting the cuff of her uniform, did not look at him directly. "Yes."

"Tell it to me."

She hesitated. Then, lowering her voice to a whisper, she leaned in. "I can't use…" A pause, deliberate, a flick of the eyes toward the others in the room. "Magic."

"Good," he said, with a finality that buried the matter deep.

They both walked silently into class, neither too quick nor too slow, ensuring their movements did not betray the burden of something forbidden.

Galinda endured the drudgery of the school day with a quiet sort of impatience, willing time to obey her, to hurry along and deliver her to where she truly wished to be—downstairs, in the musty old library, in the confidence of Mz. Everburn.

The day mocked her, stretching itself long, teasing her with meaningless lessons and empty conversations. But eventually, as all things do, it ended. Galinda did not linger. She descended the stairs with a careful urgency, pausing just long enough to smooth the pleats of her skirt before knocking at Mz. Everburn's door.

The teacher barely glanced up from her desk, where she was sorting papers, a cup of half-drunk *Gizzleberry* tea perched at the edge. "Come in."

Galinda stepped inside, all brightness and poise. She could not contain the grin spreading across her face.

"Oh, hello, Galinda," Mz. Everburn greeted, her tone indulgent but distracted. "What can I do for you? Another book?"

The thought of a new book was enticing, delicious, even—but it was not the reason she was here.

"That's not why I came." She hesitated, then, glancing at the door, added, "Mz. Everburn… can we go somewhere more private?"

Mz. Everburn studied her for a moment, her head tilting, as though already suspecting what lay beneath Galinda's eager exterior.

"Of course. Just give me a moment. Let me finish my tea and put these away."

Tea finished; papers stacked. Then, as they always did, they made their way to the library.

Galinda nearly opened the door with her newfound power, but she held back. Not yet. Not until the moment was right. This moment required its due theatrics. She was a true *Show-Woman*.

Mz. Everburn, oblivious to the grand reveal in Galinda's mind, unlocked the door and ushered her inside. She flicked her wrist, and the lanterns inside flared to life, casting the space in their usual amber glow.

"So?" The teacher leaned against the nearest desk, arms crossed. "What's the big secret?"

Galinda wet her lips, drawing out the suspense. "You won't believe this."

Exhaling slowly, she raised her hand.

She *willed* it.

A book—just an ordinary one, nothing too heavy or ambitious—slipped from the shelf, floated in the air, and drifted toward her, settling neatly into her waiting palm.

Galinda turned, expectant.

Mz. Everburn's expression shifted, slowly at first, as if she had misinterpreted what she had seen. But realization dawned, and her hand flew to her mouth.

"Oh, Oz... Yes! *Finally!*"

"Finally?" Galinda repeated, the thrill of the moment dimming ever so slightly.

"I *knew* you had magic. The prophecy is true!"

"The *what?*"

But Mz. Everburn was already moving, already thinking, already calculating. "When did this start?"

Galinda recounted the events of her Born-Day, the first flicker of power, the sensation of something waking inside her.

Mz. Everburn was astonished, but not for the reason Galinda expected.

"I didn't think—" The teacher hesitated, tightening her lips together as though something had slipped.

"You didn't think *what?*" Galinda pressed.

Mz. Everburn studied her carefully, then sighed. "I didn't think it would come so soon. I thought I had more time to prepare."

"Prepare for *what?*"

A beat. Then, instead of an answer, another question. "Glinda," Mz. Everburn said carefully, "do you want me to teach you?"

Galinda blinked.

BEFORE

"I make an excellent teacher," the woman continued. "I can show you how to use it. How *not* to use it. Everything. Does that sound like something you'd be interested in?"

The question was unnecessary. The answer had been formed in her **heart** long before it had been asked.

"Yes," she said, breathless. "That would be *lovely*."

"How about your first lesson today?"

No reply was needed.

Mz. Everburn nodded approvingly. "You have advanced *shockingly* fast with levitation. I didn't achieve that level of precision until I was sixteen. But you lack control."

Galinda did not flinch as her teacher took her by the wrist, adjusting her stance.

"Estimate the weight of the object you want to move," Mz. Everburn instructed. "Relax your fingers. Make your intent *clear*. And then—"

Galinda moved her hand.

The table at the centre of the room scraped against the floor, shifting several inches before settling again.

"Perfect." Mz. Everburn grinned. "You learn quickly, don't you?"

Galinda giggled, delighted.

"One day, maybe you'll be able to move light objects with your eyes alone."

"Is that possible?"

"*Anything* is possible with magic," her teacher replied, a glint of something unspoken in her gaze. "But Glinda, don't tell anyone about your gift. I'm sure I don't need to tell you why."

"I won't say a word."

"Good. We can meet every day after school to practice. Would you like that?"

"Yes!"

By the time Galinda reached the waiting Golden Goose carriage, the sky had begun its slow descent into night. She climbed inside, the weight of the secret settling over her like a second skin.

The carriage rolled forward and to the castle they went.

In her bedroom, Galinda shut the curtains, for secrecy—still, no one in the house cared enough to check on her, let alone investigate the source of the intermittent thuds that rattled her bedroom floor. The curtains were also for *ambience*. Magic required the right atmosphere, didn't it?

She exhaled, turned her focus inward, and willed the dresser to rise. It did so, obediently, a wooden marionette to her invisible strings. She had suspected, and now she knew: the more she *practiced*, the stronger she became. The weight of the object no longer mattered, not truly—only the depth of her concentration.

But control, well… control was another matter entirely.

The moment she thought of setting the dresser down, it plummeted, landing with an ungraceful, resounding *thud*. Galinda winced, but only for form's sake. There was no reason to fear discovery.

◇

The next day, after school, Mz. Everburn led her not to the usual corner of the library but to the farthest wall, where the stones were bare and unadorned.

"We can't be near the books today," the teacher instructed.

"Why?"

"Becoz we're making *firelight*, and if the books catch fire—"

Fire! Of all things, fire! A true and tangible magic, something elemental—something *wicked*, even, if wielded wrong. Galinda had been waiting for this.

"Firelight?" Galinda's breath hitched. "Am I ready?"

Mz. Everburn gave her a measured look. "I think so."

They stood against the stone wall, and from the folds of her robe, Mz. Everburn retrieved a book, very different from the other tomes in the library. It was carved from oak, its spine and corners wrapped in gold, the edges of the pages glowing faintly in the dim light.

Galinda reached for it as if it were a gift she had been waiting for her entire life. "Is this a *spellbook*?"

"Yes."

The word was uttered simply, but its weight settled between them.

Galinda turned the first page with something approaching reverence. The second page, her destination, was lined with cramped script, the letters curling like vines around the margins. An illustration of a flame flickered to life under her gaze, the embers in its painted depths shifting as though breathing. Some of the words were written in a language she did not know, though she could feel them in her bones, sense the way they wanted to be spoken aloud.

Mz. Everburn cleared her throat. "Watch first."

She whispered the words, half-prayer, half-command:

Animo flara calidum flamma.

A flame bloomed in her open palm, frantic at first, erratic and flickering, but then it quieted, as if remembering itself, as if *obeying*. The light cast strange shadows over the stone wall, making the cracks seem deeper, the room itself older.

Galinda swallowed.

"Now you," Mz. Everburn instructed. "Repeat the words. Make your intent clear. Hold out your palm."

Galinda hesitated only for a moment. Then, with a breath that felt like stepping off the edge of a cliff, she lifted her hand and whispered the spell.

The fire erupted—too large, too wild, unbridled energy leaping from her hand like a thing with its own mind. Galinda gasped, instinctively recoiling, nearly flinging it away.

91

"Don't!" Mz. Everburn's voice was sharp, "It won't burn the caster! Stay calm. Command it to shrink. To *dilute*."

Dilute?

Galinda squeezed her eyes shut, her heartbeat hammering in her ears. The fire was warm—no, more than warm, it was *alive*. She clenched her fingers but did not close her palm, willing, *pleading* for it to shrink, to become *manageable*.

And it did.

The flame softened, curled inward, transformed from something monstrous into something gentle. Galinda exhaled.

"Yes," Mz. Everburn murmured, almost to herself. "*Yes.*"

The fire was no longer terrifying. It was, dare she think it? —*beautiful*.

"Well done! Well done!" Mz. Everburn clapped her hands together, breaking the tension. "Now, close your palm. *Intend* for it to cease."

Galinda obeyed, and the fire obeyed her. The flame dissipated. The warmth remained.

Mz. Everburn regarded Galinda with something like amusement, something like caution. The girl had taken to magic like a bird to the wind—instinctual, inevitable—but instinct alone was never enough.

"Magic isn't all practical," she said, pulling a weighty tome from her desk. "You have to understand theory."

She placed the book in Galinda's hands with deliberate reverence.

Magical Theory & History: Volume I.

The title was embossed in silver, its letters slightly worn from years of use, or perhaps disuse.

"Study this religiously," Mz. Everburn continued, as if magic were a doctrine to be obeyed rather than a skill to be honed. "I will test you on it."

A test. As if this were SilverCrest's arithmetic, as if magic could be reduced to pages and recitations.

Galinda, however, did not argue. She clutched the book to her chest and set off for ***home***, a quiet hum of satisfaction settling in her bones.

◇

Back at the castle, all she wanted to do was study the book her teacher gave her. The book lay sprawled across Galinda's bed, its weight a physical reminder of her newfound inheritance. It was only right that now that she possessed magic, she'd better learn its history. She sighed and, with a flick of her wrist, sent the pages fluttering. A parlour trick, but an effective one.

Introduction to Magick

*Magic. Magik. Magick. Sorcery. Witchcraft. Whatever the term may be, as it has evolved through the ages, are naught but gifts sent down by the One Gohd. The first manifestation of this divine art in Oz began, as many things do, in the wastelands. The **Impassable Desert**, vast, indifferent, and unimpressed with the fragility of mortal ambition. A caravan of pilgrims, weary and* *threadbare, trekked across the sands from **Wx**, drawn to the distant emerald beacon of Oz. They sought an audience with **Ozma I, The Wholly One**, bearer of foresight, anointed in the name of righteousness.*

Alas, the desert proved merciless. By night, the winds were bitterly cold; by day, the heat was unbearable. Many of the pilgrims could not survive and perished along the way. In their desperation, the survivors gathered in prayer, calling upon the One Gohd to grant them salvation.

*And lo, It was **Basthus**, the leader of the pilgrims, who received a vision in his sleep. An angel appeared to him and instructed him to test the faith of his followers. He was to take a small wooden bowl and fill it with sand. Those who truly believed would drink the entire bowl, for though it appeared to be mere sand, it had been blessed and transformed into Wholly water.*

*Thus, the true believers drank, and with it came the power of Magick. The first **Magi** were born. They bent the heat, twisted the cold, pulled the very air around them like a cloak. The disbelievers, however, mocked the act and refused to partake, leaving them to perish in the unforgiving desert. The believers, now empowered, survived and made their way to Oz. Upon their arrival, Basthus met with Ozma, who gave her blessing and revealed a divine revelation: the pilgrims were to make Oz their **home** and settle there. Over time, the pilgrims cultivated their magic through further revelations that Basthus received. These teachings were eventually compiled into a single tome: **The Kitab**, the first spellbook; forged in Dragon's Breath, back when Dragons roamed the Ozian skies. The pilgrims intermarried with the people of Oz, and their children were born—some with the gift of magic, and others without.*

It made no sense to Galinda why the people of Oz were so against magic when the once ruler, **The Wholly Ozma I** gave her blessing and invited them to live in Oz. Ozma herself had the magic of foresight. As Galinda flipped, it became clear that the book she was reading was a book of records. It was dated with different dates across the century. She let the pages flicker, this time with her fingers, dated records passing like years in fast-forward. Until she reached a name she had hoped to escape.

Seraphina.

There she was, again. Clinging to Galinda's consciousness like a stain that would not wash out. But the heading gave her pause. *Seraphina: The Noble Witch.* Galinda's lip curled. The Noble Witch? That wasn't right. That wasn't right at all.

Seraphina was **The Forsaken Witch.** Every history book said so. Every proper historian, every noble *Oziard* with an ink-dipped quill, had said so. But the book in her lap was not written by men in velvet robes or gilded towers.

This was written by witches.

And witches told a different story.

Seraphina: The Noble Witch.

*During the era of the **Devastating Drought**, the Wizard of Oz launched a relentless hunt for Seraphina, the Noble Witch. Branded an enemy of the state, she was to be executed on sight. Forced into hiding, Seraphina sought refuge in the homes of kind-hearted witches, never staying more than a single night—she refused to endanger those who sheltered her.*

*The Wizard's fury stemmed from her defiance. He had demanded that she surrender **Basthus' Spellbook: The Kitab**, an ancient grimoire of immeasurable power. When Seraphina* *refused, he named her the **Forsaken Witch** and vowed to bring her to ruin. Though whispers spread of her involvement in the drought, the truth remained uncertain. Nevertheless, the hunt for Seraphina stretched on for over a Sun-Moon, the Wizard growing ever more desperate.*

*To lure her out, he turned to cruelty. Each day, a witch was executed—a brutal sacrifice meant to break Seraphina's will. Yet, the witches stood defiant, giving their lives to protect her. But as their numbers dwindled, Seraphina made a choice. She removed her **Glamour Spell**, revealing herself at last, and surrendered.*

*The Wizard had feared her for a reason. Seraphina's magic was unparalleled, her power so great that prophecy foretold only **ONE** other **Witch** could ever rival her, a sorceress destined to arrive from the skies in Oz's darkest hour.*

*Before her capture, Seraphina ensured that the Wizard would never wield The Kitab's full power. She split it in two: **The Kitab Solis** and its much darker sister book, **The Kitab Malum**. The Kitab Malum contained spells of unspeakable darkness, curses that could never be undone. The Kitab Solis, by contrast, held magic of healing and light—remedies to counter some of the Malum's horrors but never undo them completely. Seraphina felt the Kitab Malum was insignificant and not needed in Oz, only the Kitab Solis was substantial due to its pure goodness.*

*Seraphina surrendered under one condition: the Wizard would **spare the remaining witches** and grant them peace. But, like all tyrants, he broke his word. Her body was burned at the stake, her severed head placed upon a spike at the gates of the Emerald City—for three suns and three moons, a warning to all who dared oppose him.*

*Yet, the Wizard's cruelty only fanned the flames of rebellion. His oppression of magical beings continued until the tides turned. In the **Great Wizard's War**, witches and warlocks rose in defiance, defeating the tyrant and forcing him to flee Oz forever. Determined to restore the honour stolen from her, the witches rejected the title of **Forsaken Witch** and instead **cemented her true legacy**. They called her what she had always been:*

Seraphina, The Noble Witch.

Her sacrifice would never be forgotten.

Galinda's mind swirled with doubt, the weight of a truth she had never questioned pressing against her like an unrelenting tide. Was she lied to? Was Seraphina being *Forsaken* just propaganda? There were many things going on in her mind, and she knew exactly what she was going to ask Mz. Everburn the next time they had a magic lesson.

When the next magic class arrived, Galinda returned the book to her teacher, a little surprised by her own sense of accomplishment. She had finished it. Every page, every word. Mz. Everburn's sharp gaze reflected a quiet surprise.

"You finished it?" she asked, unable to hide her astonishment.

"Yes." Galinda's voice was steady, but inside, her thoughts were a tangled web. "I have a few questions actually." She started with the less controversial topic.

Mz. Everburn gestured for her to sit, folding her hands neatly in her lap. "Go on."

"Mizz, the book mentioned two powerful spellbooks—the *Kitab Malum* and the *Kitab Solis*. Do you know where they are?"

"Hmmm," her teacher pondered. "I know where the Kitab Solis is, or rather, I have an idea. But as for the Kitab Malum…" She paused, her tone darkening. "No one, living or dead, knows where it lies."

"Can you tell me where the Kitab Solis is?"

"No, Glinda, you're not ready yet. Maybe when you advance more in your studies. If people knew you had it you would be in grave danger. Anyone would, that is why magic folk haven't gone looking for it."

Galinda's fingers tightened around the book in her lap. "So, others know it exists?"

"We call it *The Ethereum*," Mz. Everburn admitted, lowering her voice, "but most have been misled about its true location. Only three people know where it actually is—my mother, my sister, and me."

"Do they all have magic?" Galinda asked, though she suspected she already knew the answer.

"No," Mz. Everburn said softly. "Only me, my sister and my great-great grandmother do, who was among the first to fall at the hands of the first Wizard of Oz."

Galinda's **heart** stilled. "I'm so sorry."

The teacher nodded but didn't linger on the past. "Do you have any more questions, then?"

"When I was reading, I noticed something. Seraphina, she was referred to as 'The Noble,' not 'Forsaken.' Why is that?"

A long sigh escaped Mz. Everburn. It was a breath filled with years of untold stories. "Yes," she said, her voice heavy. "We, the witches, call her 'The Noble.' That is what she truly was."

"How so?" Galinda's voice trembled with the urgency.

Mz. Everburn's gaze softened. "Seraphina sacrificed everything so that witches like us could live. She gave her life so that we might have a chance to be free. It is all too easy for people to label someone as wicked, evil, as 'other,' or whatever, when they do not fit the mold of the majority."

Galinda nodded, trying to wrap her mind around the enormity of what she was hearing.

"That makes sense. But… what did she do to earn the Wizard's hatred? Why did he want her gone?"

Mz. Everburn's expression darkened. "That, my dear, is a question no one has the answer to—not truly. Perhaps only Seraphina and the Wizard know. Well… and the Fates." She paused, her eyes clouding with old grief. "But I know this: she was innocent, kind, and she cared deeply for animals, for all creatures, and most importantly, she enabled witches to be able to defend themselves long after her death."

Galinda's brow furrowed, a growing unease settling deep within her. "I guess… But I still don't understand everything."

BEFORE

"It's a lot to take in," Mz. Everburn murmured, her tone understanding. "You're young, Glinda. But you are asking the right questions. Never stop seeking the truth."

Galinda wanted so badly to believe that Seraphina was a good witch. For her own sake. But her stomach was still twisting at the thought of her because deep down, she didn't know what to believe anymore.

But it didn't matter.
She wouldn't be *Forsaken*.
Or *Noble*.
She would be *better*.
She would be *GOOD*.

◇

As the months passed, Galinda's progress was swift. She became a proficient young witch, her talents growing with each lesson. Her commitment was unwavering, her determination absolute. She memorized incantations like a scholar, knowing they would be essential in the days to come. Mz. Everburn prepared her in secret, as all wise mentors did, knowing that one day they would need to protect themselves from the bloodthirsty witch hunters in Oz.

And the most dangerous one of all... was her own father.

CHAPTER 14

Without Notice

O ver the course of the academic year, the lessons continued in secrecy. Not even Ominson knew of them. The sessions were held in such absolute discretion that it felt as though even we, *The Fates*, were unwelcome. As if we, too, could not be trusted with such an important secret. This was Galinda's final year at SilverCrest. It was imperative that she master all that Mz. Everburn had to offer before she was released into the world, a world eager to mold her but not necessarily to understand her.

And understand her, Mz. Everburn did. The girl was a quick study. Within six Oz'moons—six months in the *Otherworld*—Galinda had completed and graduated from her Advanced Magick course. She didn't merely pass; she excelled. Her mind was a fortress of incantations, each brick laid with precision, each spell locked into place like a sacred covenant.

For their final lesson, Mz. Everburn requested that they meet in the old library. It was a routine performed a thousand times over, yet this time, there was a weight to it, an unspoken finality.

"I cannot believe how far you've come, Glinda," Mz. Everburn said, her voice thick with something dangerously close to sentimentality. "I am so proud of you."

Galinda, never one to cry without permission, found herself blinking back the sting of unexpected emotion. Apart from Zelena, no one had ever said they were proud of her, not in any way that felt real. And yet here stood Mz. Everburn, red-eyed and sniffling, genuinely affected.

"Well," Galinda managed, "I had an amazing teacher. I couldn't have done it without you."

The woman scoffed, a feeble attempt to suppress the welling tears.

"That spellbook has been in my family for generations. It took me six Sun-Moons to master. And you? Six Oz'moons."

She shook her head in a mixture of admiration and mild disbelief.

"You have a **brain** sharper than any I've seen. I hope you never waste it. It's a gift in itself."

A gift? Perhaps. But gifts, Galinda knew, came with strings. She had spent much of her life trying to suppress that very intelligence, smoothing it down like the pleats of an inconveniently wrinkled dress. People didn't like it when she was too clever. Her appearance already set her apart—her mind only widened the chasm. It was easier to let them underestimate her. Let them assume she was nothing more than *disgustifying* strawberry-golden mild curls.

Mz. Everburn, ever the observer, studied her for a moment before speaking again. "One final test, I think. To see if you've retained your knowledge as well as I suspect."

She gestured toward a vase resting on the table. "Move that to the other side of the room."

Galinda raised her hands, preparing to do as asked, but her teacher halted her with a glance.

"With your eyes. Not your hands."

Galinda hesitated for only a moment before focusing. The air between her and the vase trembled, and then, effortlessly, it obeyed.

From there, Mz. Everburn tested her on transmutation, advanced levitation, expanded flame casting. Each challenge was met with effortless grace. Each spell, recited as naturally as a lullaby learned in infancy. The teacher could only shake her head in resignation.

"Okay," Mz. Everburn sighed, a mixture of relief and admiration. "There is nothing more I can teach you."

Galinda, desperate to cling to these meetings a little longer, tried modesty as a stalling tactic.

"Surely there's something?"

Mz. Everburn smirked.

"Perhaps one last thing. The most important spell I will ever teach you." Her voice dropped, conspiratorial. "It's one of the deadliest magicks known."

Galinda's pulse quickened. "What is it?"

"*Ozmosis.*"

Galinda frowned. "Ozmosis?"

"The Bubble Spell."

"Bubbles?" she repeated incredulously.

"Yes," Mz. Everburn chuckled. "I learnt it when I was a child. They aren't in the spellbook, but it's one of my favourites."

Galinda bit back a laugh. "Well, who doesn't love bubbles? Show me."

Mz. Everburn extended her hands, palms facing one another as though shaping an invisible sphere. She whispered:

"Orbis Levia Aeris Tenebris."

A soft glow flickered between her hands, and suddenly, bubbles began to appear. Hundreds. Thousands. They floated through the room like weightless pearls, clustering in the air until Galinda was submerged in a desert of shimmering spheres.

"This is incredible!" Galinda exclaimed, dancing among them, laughing as they drifted past her fingertips.

"Now you try."

Galinda mimicked her teacher's movements, murmuring the incantation with precise diction. But something was different. Her bubbles were pink—blushing, vibrant, impossibly large five times the size of her teacher's. They multiplied at an alarming rate, filling the space until books became damp, the scent of old parchment mingling with the sweet, ephemeral scent of magic. Her spell was stronger. Wilder.

Galinda didn't need instruction on how to stop it. She knew. She simply willed it, and the bubbles ceased.

Mz. Everburn smiled.

"I was hoping I wouldn't have to tell you how to cease the spell. You've surpassed me, quicker than I was told you would."

Galinda stiffened.

"Told?"

There it was again. Those cryptic hints. Those tiny, nagging suggestions that something larger was at play.

Mz. Everburn hesitated, then moved closer, lowering her voice to a hushed volume like she was giving a confession at the Solar Temple.

"Most witches are born with one talent—spellcasting, potion-making or clairvoyance. Rarely do they have two. And never have they had all three."

She paused.

"It has never been seen. Seraphina herself only had two; casting spells and potions."

"I'm confused?" Galinda was struggling to find the correlation, she was impatient, but she also wanted to stall a little while longer.

Was she about to find out something she didn't want to know? Sometimes living in ignorance made her life easier because when she knew something it weighed heavily on her **heart** that it became too painful to bear. From where this conversation was going, she regretted asking, as she often did. So, she tried to redirect the conversation as best as she could.

"Do I have one or two talents?"

"I suspect you have two, just like Seraphina but I don't teach potions so you will have to find that out on your own. I have one gift like most witches, mine as you know is spells. In Munchkinland, where I am from, we had a witch in our circle who had the power of clairvoyance. The most powerful we had seen in many years. She sat all of us down on the night of your birth and told us that at that night a witch was born in the South of Oz that has come to bring honour to the witches and restore Oz to glory."

Galinda was now looking down at her feet, clicking her heels trying to ignore what was being said but every word was piercing her ears like a knife.

"And you think that it's me?"

"Yes, she foretold that at your Moonshine Coronation you would pick the pink gem, just like Seraphina, The Noble Witch."

Galinda's breath hitched.

Her teacher continued, as if compelled to see her confession through to the end.

"Our customs in Munchkinland are different; many of us had never even heard of a Moonshine Coronation. But the seer's vision was clear—your arrival would change everything. She urged some of us to leave our homeland, to settle in the Quadling Country, ensuring that at least one of us would be present in every school. That way, when you turned eight and began your education, we would be there, watching, guiding, and preparing you for the path ahead."

"So, the books, the manuscripts about Seraphina, showing me your magic, being nice to me, it was all part of your plan?" Galinda asked now frightened, confused, angry and scared all the same.

"Yes and no," her teacher admitted, her voice carrying the weight of untold truths. "I truly do care for you—how could I not? You possess a rare kindness, an innate goodness that is as undeniable as it is extraordinary. But with such gifts come burdens, and yours is the loneliness of being different, of standing apart in a world that does not yet understand you. You were placed in a family that cannot fathom your purpose, and so we sought to protect you, to do for you what we failed to do for Seraphina. Need I mention what was happening in the South to 'Witches', most of whom didn't even practice or have an inclination of magic?"

Galinda turned away, staring at her hands. She felt the weight of it all pressing down on her—the expectations, the prophecy, the ever-growing questions.

"I was just the lucky one who was blessed to teach you. And now I feel my mission is complete."

Galinda couldn't suppress the small smile that tugged at her lips as she pieced everything together. If Mz. Everburn hadn't been at SilverCrest, her time there would have been far more difficult than it already was. Her teacher had been her sanctuary, the one thing she looked forward to each day. A sudden wave of gratitude washed over her, Mz. Everburn had taught her everything she knew, guiding her with patience and care. And when her magic finally manifested, she hadn't hesitated to trust her teacher, just as her teacher had trusted her enough to reveal her own gifts. That bond, built on understanding and unspoken faith, was something she would cherish forever.

"The waterfall..." she murmured, connecting the pieces. "You wanted me to find it."

"Yes, I knew your curious nature wouldn't allow you to sit idly by," her teacher laughed and so did Galinda.

But the more she tried to make sense of it all, the more tangled it became. The prophecy in the manuscripts painted one picture, a vision of destiny that seemed to align with Gisella. Yet now, her teacher was telling her that the prophecy was about her instead.

"Also," her teacher added, Galinda sighed inwardly, wondering what else there was to say.

"I know you and Ominson are immensely close, but would you like to make another friend? A female friend?"

"Yes!" Galinda was now excited about something. She loved Ominson so dearly that nobody could ever replace him, but she often wondered what friendship would be like with a girl. As curious as she was, how could she not?

"Great, there is a girl I know from Munchkinland, she is around your age, who I think you will get along great with. She's a little different from your typical friends but she's a lovely girl."

"When can I meet her?" she asked eagerly, her tone unchanged. It didn't matter if she had hooves for feet. A friend was a friend. She had felt different her entire life and perhaps she had a friend out there that was able to understand her in ways other people couldn't.

"I'll arrange it, sometime in the near future." Mz. Everburn answered smugly, the same smile she gave when she started telling Galinda about the prophecy.

The room fell silent. Mz. Everburn was waiting for Galinda to ask more questions, like she was supposed to ask every question that popped in her mind then and there and quickly. Galinda obliged.

"Okay, so about the waterfall, why did you want me to find it? Is it becoz of me and Seraphina?"

"Of course, Glinda, you didn't know back then but you had a spark of magic the moment you were born. It just needed to cultivate over time, the same way your body does when you go through puberty. It's the same for every witch. As for the waterfall, it was meant for you. Seraphina hid it long ago with her magic, and it revealed itself only to *you*."

"But why?" Galinda demanded, frustration bubbling beneath her skin. "Why me?"

"It has a hidden secret. And I am not going to tell you what it is, it will come in time. The same way the garden revealed itself the same way its secret will appear to you. It's your destiny."

"What even is destiny?" Galinda mocked; she was hearing about many prophecies that contradicted each other how could destiny be real.

Mz. Everburn now moving closer to Galinda whispered, trying to make sure Galinda felt the weight of the words she was about to speak.

"We all have a destiny. We're all put here for a reason. To play a role. Although it is already preordained for us, we have some power in its redirection, but the outcome will always remain the same. The *Fates* don't write destiny down to make us puppets; it is written becoz time has already happened, we are just behind on the timeline. And they are ahead. So don't mock destiny ever."

"So, I have no say in what I do? Is that what you mean?" Galinda asked desperately.

"Destiny is a funny thing, Glinda. You can alter it, delay it but you can never change it fully. Some believe that we can change destiny completely if you have enough conviction. But then it raises the question; Was it ever your true destiny in the first place? Or was your destiny always what you ended up changing it into?"

Galinda pondered; her teacher was right of course. Although she loved philosophy, this aggravated her that there wasn't a clear-cut answer.

"Just make the right choices," Mz. Everburn said, now speaking strongly, like a warning. "Make *good* ones, becoz delaying it or altering it can have consequences, and you'll have to pay the price. Which are usually great prices that will weigh on you significantly."

What her teacher said unsettled Galinda. The room had grown noticeably darker since they had filled it with bubbles. A chill ran down her spine, raising the hair on her arms. She was drained, mentally, emotionally. Each revelation had only led to more questions, but she had already absorbed so much in one sitting. When she got **home**, she would lie on her bed, stare at the ceiling, and attempt to sort through everything. She would categorize her questions, prepare them for the next time they met. And yet, she had the sinking feeling that no number of questions would ever be enough.

"I should probably pack up," Galinda said, her voice quieter than before. She gestured toward her bag, its contents spilled across the floor, books scattered in disarray. "My carriage should be waiting for me."

She moved to gather her things, but before she could bend down, her teacher raised a hand. "Let me help," her teacher proclaimed without waiting for resistance.

With a graceful wave of her hands, the books soared into her bag, closed themselves, and levitated up to Galinda's height, ready for her to carry.

"Thank you!" She exclaimed, smiling brightly.

In return, Mz. Everburn offered a smile that was warmer than before—one that reminded Galinda of the gentle, welcoming smile she had received on the very first day of school, years ago.

Suddenly there was a sound coming from the entry door of the library, and Galinda turned at lightning speed to check. She turned so quickly that she caught a glimpse of green speeding past the door.

Someone had been watching them.

"Did you see that?" she asked turning to Mz. Everburn for her expertise.

"I'm sure it was nothing. Why don't you get going, I've kept you long enough."

Her teacher didn't seem worried. Her job was already done. Galinda reasoned, if her teacher was at ease then there was no reason to be on edge. It probably was *nothing*.

She hugged her teacher and ran out the library to meet her Golden Goose at the school entrance.

On her way outside, she scanned the environment, just in case she could find the culprit that was watching them in the library, if there had even been one. But there was nothing in sight.

◇

When she reached the school gates, her Golden Goose was nowhere to be found. Today, she was met with the Golden Eagle. Had her father decided to take the less extravagant Golden Goose, leaving her with the Eagle, willingly? When she climbed aboard and opened the doors, she had two unexpected guests waiting for her inside its gilded compartment.

Dainhurst stood in his impeccably pressed ebony suit, while Gisella wore her green uniform. It was obvious that Gisella had just been picked up from school, and Dainhurst had come to SilverCrest to collect her afterward. Such a thing was unusual, making her wonder what the occasion could be.

The carriage air was very uneasy, and it felt just like Esmelda did when she was in the Mid-Uplands. She greeted Dainhurst, but he didn't give his usual forced smile. He was stoic and unblinking—angry about something. Perhaps business. And it was always best not to pry. Gisella too, was being unusually weird. She was quiet and didn't say a word nor did she make eye contact with Galinda.

"Are we going somewhere?" Galinda asked, hoping to break the silence.

Dainhurst didn't respond, so Gisella replied as though trying to cover up the idea that there was something going on that Galinda was oblivious to.

"We're going home." Gisella replied coldly.

"Did something happen to the Golden Goose?"

"Mother took it to one of her retreats."

Galinda nodded in acknowledgment of the only person willing to answer her questions.

She hoped her favourite carriage returned unspoiled because she valued her alone time in it after school, where she could count bluebirds on the way to the castle. When she was alone, she was comfortable because she didn't have to pretend, she was a part of a family.

At the castle, Dainhurst spoke his first words of the entire ride. He told his two daughters to exit the carriage and ordered the coachman to take him somewhere Galinda nor Gisella knew about. It was business. It always was. Gisella was still quiet, and the day had taken its toll on Galinda, she just wanted to be in her chambers so she could think.

BEFORE

Galinda fell asleep on her back facing the ceiling. She had been thinking all night, and when she awoke, her body ached from sleeping in such an uncomfortable position. But the day was ordinary, nothing was different. Galinda carried a notebook; she was still a student after all. Whenever a question popped into her mind, she jotted them down. By the end of the day, she had four pages full of questions. There were even more trapped in her head, that if she wrote them down, she would run out of ink. These questions remained in her head since she was in the library, so she was very confident that they weren't going anywhere anytime soon.

◇

The school ended and now she could meet Mz. Everburn and ask her the remaining questions. But when she descended the school stairs and went to her classroom there was something else waiting for her. A man. Mz. Everburn was a female, unless she knew Seraphina's Glamour Spell and transformed into a man. The classroom was different too, chairs were disorganised according to Mz. Everburn's standards and the curtains were changed from cream to blue.

"Have you seen Mz. Everburn?" Galinda asked the man in the room.

"Who?" the mysterious man answered.

"She is the teacher this room belongs to. Red hair. Blue eyes?"

"Never heard of her or seen her. I was just hired today and told to lead this class permanently becoz a teacher resigned."

"Oh, did they tell you who you were replacing?"

"No. But I know this is their classroom. As I said, I was assigned to take over as a result of their absence."

"Oh okay, thank you."

Galinda walked off slowly, closing her notebook and holding it close to her chest.

"Resigned?" she repeated, confused.

Mz. Everburn didn't say anything about resigning. She would've told her when they met yesterday. Something felt off but people were sometimes unpredictable, and she had first-hand experience. Her entire family was an enigma. It felt like déjà vu.

This was the second person in her life that disappeared.

Without notice.

CHAPTER 15

Breaking Through Stone

Months drifted by like slow-turning pages, and Galinda's time at SilverCrest waned, fading into the inevitable past. It was strange, she hadn't heard a word from her teacher, Mz. Everburn, since their final meeting in the library. Galinda expected, at the very least, a whisper of farewell carried on the wind, but no such murmurs arrived. Galinda considered the possibilities, perhaps Mz. Everburn had returned to munchkinland, where her family surely awaited her, or perhaps, less comfortingly, her mission, whatever that had truly entailed, had been fulfilled. No loose ends, no lingering ties. It was best, Galinda decided, not to entertain the worst of the unknown. Speculation could be as corrosive as truth.

When the day arrived, and she graduated from SilverCrest, still no word came. But the absence of her teacher's presence did not mean the absence of her teachings. Those remained, like pressed flowers hidden between the pages of a book—forgotten, perhaps, until one day rediscovered and suddenly invaluable.

❖

Four Sun-Moons passed. Four years in the *Otherworld*. Galinda, now sixteen, had mastered the art of discretion. Her magic remained a secret. She never used it in public, only indulging when Ominson wanted to see her perform or when she was too lazy to get out of bed and retrieve a book from the shelf. Galinda would simply levitate it forward, always wary of who might walk in unannounced, though such interruptions were rare.

Despite the changes wrought by time, Ominson and Galinda's friendship had not only endured but deepened, though it now carried an undercurrent neither dared acknowledge. They had ensured their futures remained intertwined, enrolling at *Willow-Wood Hills* together, as if proximity alone could safeguard their bond. Gisella had already graduated, leaving Galinda alone in a world that had not grown kinder with age. Her face, once merely peculiar, had become the reluctant canvas for a collection of red blemishes, the cruel toll of adolescence. But nature had compensated for this apparent slight. Her body had bloomed with a force that could not be ignored—her hips curving with practiced elegance, her waist cinching as if sculpted by an artist who favoured excess over restraint. Her breasts, too, had arrived in grandeur, defying gravity with their own quiet weight. The boys seemed to like her more, despite the occasional jokes, they were warming up to her and she liked that feeling. Oh, she liked it very much.

Ominson had changed too. Far gone was the gangly boy, too skinny for his clothing. What remained was something more deliberate. Ominson's frame had filled in the right places— his shoulders a bit broader and his chest widened with confidence. His blonde hair no longer hung like a child's. It gleamed, reminiscent of golden rays underneath the Ozian sky. Ominson's cheekbones caught the light at just the right moment, enough for the girls to swoon and fawn over his blonde perfection, even his jawline could slice through and pop cherries—*cherries* specifically. Though Ominson carried the same confidence he had ever since his childhood, something had changed. Now, it was as if he knew of his own allure, very attendant on how the girls' eyes followed him when he walked. But there was something else, something undeniable in the way his body held secrets. Secrets Galinda's body also held. A quiet kind of knowing, a promise beneath the fabric.

Ominson and Galinda had soon begun to question their friendship. They didn't look at each other the same way. Their eyes a little wider when they spoke, their glances lingered just a moment longer, their smiles brighter, touched with something they dared not name. Both knew its meaning. An unspoken truth. It was safer to remain in familiar waters than to dive into the unknown, into something they knew not. Something that would ruin them. So, they remained just that. Friends. Best friends.

Life was not so bad at Willow-Wood Hills. She excelled in her classes as she always had whilst Ominson struggled with his. He would often lament. *"Why can't we just learn the same things we did at SilverCrest?"* which was absurd. Ominson liked things to remain the same. So weary of change. Afraid to adapt, as if by ignoring it, he could preserve the world as it once was. But where academics failed him, his athleticism didn't. In *Whirl-foot*, a game that involved kicking a ball into a net while dodging multiple players, he excelled. And sometimes, when Galinda sat on the sidelines, she couldn't resist giving the ball a little magical nudge. Ominson was oblivious to this of course and whenever he scored, he would look over to Galinda to make sure she was looking. She always was.

Galinda and Ominson still met at the waterfall at least once a week, where they would update each other on their changing lives. They remained close but there was some distance, Ominson wanted to be with his tribe—those with *Violet* colours, as well as other males that spoke his language of sports and boyish adventure. Galinda remained as she always had: alone. Books were her companions, more predictable, more loyal than the fickle affections of teenage girls. At the waterfall she would just sit in silence and listen to what new thing Ominson was doing or discovering. He was adorable the way he talked about things that were obvious to Galinda; like how trees produced *Oxygen* to breathe. Even when he was recounting the events of a party he attended, it was all the same to Galinda. As long as he didn't leave her side, she was okay.

Today was one of those days where they would meet at the waterfall and debrief.

She arrived first, as she always did, finding her usual patch of grass and settling in with a book. Ominson arrived late, as he always did, but he arrived nonetheless.

"A new book already?" Ominson asked, partly surprised and partly expectant.

"Yes, Omi," Galinda laughed.

He plopped down beside her, nudging her playfully. "Mind telling me what it's about?"

"Just Piottor's *Goodness Within*, volume two."

Ominson groaned. "When are you going to stop with the 'Goodness' books? Try reading something with adventure for once."

"Shush," she chided, "I feel it broadens my mind."

Ominson sighed but relented. "Fine. What does it say?"

"Oh, you know, just that to be truly good, you have to balance virtuous traits," Galinda said, sitting more upright in that way she always did when something stirred her.

"Piottor says true goodness comes from developing courage, wisdom, temperance—all those things—through habit and practice. When you find the happy medium, that's when you've done it."

Ominson sat up too, thinking hard, more elated to have drawn this fire from her than to understand the theory.

"It's all complicated but I've simplified it, for you," she teased.

"Shut up," Ominson said, smiling in that half-annoyed, half-admiring way he always did with her.

"Do you agree?" he asked, more serious now.

"Of course I do! I've been practicing goodness my whole life. It's like a hobby; the more you practice, the better you get."

Ominson frowned thoughtfully.

"I kind of disagree."

Galinda frowned, a little annoyed. She urged him to continue, anticipating what foolish nonsense would spew from his mouth.

"What good are those things you 'practice' if it's not for the right reason," he said. "I think true goodness comes from intention."

Galinda frowned. "Intentions?"

"Yes. Like your magic, you always say it's about intention. You will it to happen, and you will it to stop. Doesn't that prove intention matters?"

Galinda fell silent.

He asked, "Think about it. If I bought you flowers becoz I wanted to make you happy, or becoz someone told me to, and I didn't really care but only did so because it was the *good* thing to do. Which will you appreciate more?"

"Obviously, the flowers you gave becoz you wanted to."

"Exactly!" Ominson exclaimed, triumphant.

"But if you gave me the flowers, I wouldn't know your intentions." Galinda countered. "I'd *still* have the flowers in both scenarios."

"But I'd know," he said quietly. "The person giving the flowers knows their *true* intentions. That's what matters. Which makes you ask, are they truly *good*, or do they just do *good* things?"

His point was valid. But she didn't see the difference. A good thing was still a good thing. It didn't matter, because people perceived things for what they are, not the intent. It was all the same to everyone and it should be all the same for her. Just like people perceived her for what she looked like on the surface and not the person she was within.

They sat in comfortable silence, the breeze playing with their hair. Even in quiet, their connection felt like a conversation. Ominson had to leave earlier than he usually did. He had to meet his father because they were going to Winkie Country for a business proposition, and he wanted Ominson to accompany him to understand business.

And so, Galinda was left to her thoughts, the breeze, the sound of the waterfall and the birds outside the garden. When she had enough of the book, she decided to wander around the garden to stretch her legs. She stood up and dusted the dirt off her pink uniform and began walking.

Galinda inspected the corners and crevices, taking in the garden's beauty. It felt like she was rediscovering it for the very first time, finding new love and appreciation for the garden. Grateful that she and Ominson had this sanctuary to themselves with no disturbances.

Galinda ran her fingers through the plants, plucking pink roses and inhaling its sweet scent. Inspecting the birds that had found their way inside and nested their families in between rocks. As the birds tweeted and their sound echoed, Galinda joined them in song. Humming their tune, her voice dancing, completing the place with brightness.

She galloped past a rock, past another, and another, but the last rock she sped past caught her eye.

A flicker of gold.

Galinda retraced her steps and went back to the rock but there was nothing. Perhaps her eyes were playing tricks on her. Since discovering her magic, Galinda had learned never to underestimate anything. Nothing anymore was as it seemed. She took the initiative and approached the rock, and as she neared, something began to appear on its surface. There were ancient carvings on it. Engraved deep, but it was clear that it had been carved centuries ago. Galinda wiped off the moss and the dirt that were trapped in the writing, allowing the light to touch it. The sun's golden hue reflected off it like a mirror. The engraved writing was now glowing in gold lettering.

Discerpere Saxum Findatur et Semper, Seraphina

She spoke the words aloud, tasting them on her tongue.

The garden held its breath.

Nothing.

Then—*crack.*

The rock trembled. Splintered. Burst apart in a shower of dust and debris. Galinda stumbled backward, coughing, eyes watering.

She didn't know what she'd done, and she wasn't sure if she wanted to find out. When Galinda thought it was safe, she crept from her shell and approached the scene. Clearing all the dust, something lay there.

She walked closer and when her vision was made clear, she saw a book. The book was white, gold on its edges, silver accents, and a large pink gem embedded in the centre of its cover.

Galinda was unsure whether to touch it or run away and come back when Ominson was with her. But she was too curious. Ominson was long gone, and the book was right there. So, she walked slowly to the book and curled her fingers just in case she had to lunge back for safety but as she came closer the book just lay there. No movement. Just lying there, as if waiting for her to pick it up.

She slowly picked it up, but almost lost her footing because she had underestimated its weight. It was a large and heavy book. Too large to fit inside her small bag. She didn't know what she had discovered but it was getting dark, and it was best to go *home* and assess it further within the confines of her chambers.

CHAPTER 16

Discovery

The moment Galinda arrived **home**, she examined her discovery, cautiously and methodically. It wasn't just curiosity, it was instinct. Something about the book felt different. She reached out, fingers brushing against its ancient cover, and tried to pry it open.

Nothing.

The pages remained sealed, resisting even her most determined efforts. She gritted her teeth and fought against its stubbornness, but no amount of force could part the book's binding. Exhausted, she collapsed onto her bed, staring at the ceiling, frustration burning in her chest. To open it was an exercise of futility. Perhaps it wasn't even a book at all. Perhaps it was an artifact, something that only looked like a book but held a deeper mystery. If brute force wouldn't open it, then perhaps… magic would.

Galinda picked up the book from the bed, closed her eyes, calm this time, and *willed* it to open. The air shifted, imperceptibly at first, then, as if the book itself had taken a breath, a soft rustling broke the silence. Then, a sudden flurry, pages flipping wildly on their own, filling the air with the crisp sound of aged parchment shifting.

Her **heart** pounded.

The *Book* was open.

Although there was a breakthrough, it annoyed Galinda she had to go through all that trouble for the book to open in such a simple manner. The pages fluttered like a living entity seeking guidance. When it reached the last page, the motion reversed, restless, searching. This wasn't an ordinary book or diary. It was a Spellbook.

Galinda's breath faltered. Mz. Everburn's spellbook had never behaved like this. It had never responded, never possessed a will of its own. But this book… it felt aware.

She exhaled, steadying herself. Somehow, she knew what she needed to do. She had to think of what she was trying to do for the book to adjust to her needs. Galinda scoured her room for something to inspire her. That's when she laid her eyes on the gold and diamond mirror on her dresser. She closed her eyes once more, thought about the mirror and placed her hands near the book. The sound of pages flipping became rapid, then came to an abrupt standstill, leaving the room completely silent.

Galinda opened her eyes. The book lay still, yet somehow…alive. She swallowed hard, her gaze upon the page. The language written on the page was foreign, its script tangled and intricate, but she recognised it. A handful of spells her teacher taught her were written in the same script. Galinda could only make out a few words—matching the cryptic markings Mz. Everburn had once taught her. She hesitated. Half-reading a spell could have consequences. She knew that.

And yet…

Her fingers twitched with temptation. After a judicious review of the circumstance she reasoned, it was only a *Mirror Spell* and vowed that after this, she would not cast any other spells until she could read them in their entirety. She grabbed the mirror and placed it next to the book and began to read what she could recognise. The words she read began to glow like sunlight, a glowing aura casting long shadows on the walls. The words she skipped remained dull and lifeless, untouched by magic. The spell was powerful, and she could feel it in her fingertips as she was casting it. Very advanced compared to what Mz. Everburn was capable of doing. At that moment she knew she had to be very cautious of what she did with the book.

The mirror was responsive to the spell; she made her intent clear, so the spell obliged. The mirror began to levitate, the same way it did on her Born-Day. The glass warped, shifting into something liquid-like, undulating as if the solid surface had become water.

And then—

The mirror collapsed onto the bed with a dull thud, lifeless and still.

Galinda's stomach twisted. *What had she done?*

She picked it up, turning it over in her hands, searching for any sign of change. But there was nothing. The glass had returned to normal, solid and unyielding. It looked exactly as it had before.

The spell had *failed*.

Or so she thought.

Annoyance flared in her chest. She tossed the mirror aside and turned back to the book, flipping through its massive pages. It called to her, promising possibilities beyond imagination. Clearly, the book was very powerful, even as she turned the pages of the large book in her lap, she was cautious not to hurt it in case it retaliated and cursed her. She had enough of those.

She flipped until she landed on something that made her eyes widen like they were about to pop out of her head.

The Glamour Spell.

The page was worn, the edges frayed, as though it had been used, touched, studied… by someone else. *Someone who knew its power.* She had heard about a "Glamour

Spell" before, somewhere in her readings about Seraphina. It was at that very moment when it hit her, like a jolt of electricity, a realization so profound it almost knocked her breath away. Galinda realised that the book she was holding in her hands was the *Kitab Solis*. **The Ethereum**.

Her fingers trembled as she dropped the book, retreating to the far corner of the room. Her pulse thundered in her ears. It seemed like no matter what she did, she was unwillingly getting closer to Seraphina. It made no sense at all. First, The pink gem. The waterfall. The magic. And now the Ethereum. If this is what Mz. Everburn meant by destiny, it was clear she had no choice in the matter. The more she thought about it, the clearer her mind became about what was happening. Mz. Everburn set her on the path to find the waterfall for the sole purpose of retrieving the Ethereum. That is why she refused to tell her where it was being held. Her teacher's statement about the waterfall garden holding "secrets" was her hinting at the *Forsaken* Spellbook. Every step she made, led her to this moment.

Galinda stood frozen in the corner for a long while. A chill crept over her, as if something unseen had entered the room and was watching her. Despite unseen elements trying to place this burden on her to be *forsaken*, she was not going to allow it nor let it stop her from getting something she wanted. Something that would change everything. The **Glamour Spell**. With that spell she could change everything she hated about herself. Shed everything that was *limiting* her. She approached the book with renewed resolve. But as her eyes swept over the page, her hope wavered. The text was intricate, far more complex than any spell she'd ever seen. She could barely decipher three words.

But she would learn.

She would study day and night.

She would unlock **every** word and rewrite herself into something new. Something **beautiful**. She was going to glamourise herself and maybe for the first time Seraphina did her some *good*.

Realistically, it would take many months—years even—to fully understand. Tonight, though, she needed something simpler. She flipped through more pages, seeking spells she could perform without strenuous effort for someone of her talent and skill. Most were incomprehensible making her **brain** pulse. All except two.

The **Ballgown** *Spell*.

And the **Slipper** *Spell*.

Galinda rose from her chair, preparing herself. If anything backfired, she had to be ready.

The spell required three things: precise movement, intention, and substantial magic.

She took a deep breath, whispered the incantation, and envisioned a violet ballgown, fitted to perfection.

Poof!

GLINDA: The GOOD Witch

A pink cloud swirled around her, shimmering like stardust under an Ozian night sky. Silk caressed her skin as the gown materialized, her waist cinched and her back shot upright. The magic dissipated, leaving behind an *Otherworldly* creation.

Galinda gasped.

She turned to her looking glass to inspect the gown she created.

She gasped, "Oh, Oz," she whispered, running her hands down the pillowy fabric. The material felt more exclusive and expensive than the gowns Gisella owned. It didn't even feel like it was made in Oz. The *Violet* dress beamed under the light in her room and embedded in its material is what looked like star constellations, and if she looked closely enough, a map of Oz. Magic had pulled her subconscious desires into reality. She always thought about what life was like outside the South of Oz. She wanted to be free. Hence, it was remarkable that her magic, even the spell was able to pick up on the most minute details.

She twirled. **It felt free.** Unlike any gown she had ever worn. It was loose in such an impossible way.

Seeing what she was able to create with the ballgown she wanted to see what wonder she could make with the slipper spell. The spell had the same requirements as the ballgown but less power. Using magic was like exercise. The larger the spell the more power it required, and the caster felt its effects.

The spell was simple enough and with a wave of her hand what looked like glass started to form, from her soles, delicately hugging the curves of her feet all the way to her toes. The glass hardened forming a perfect fusion of elegance and masterful craftsmanship. When the light touched its smooth, transparent surface, it fractured into a spectrum of reds, blues, greens, and purples, casting tiny, shimmering rainbows that seemed to dance across the surroundings. The crystal appeared alive, shifting in colour and intensity with every movement, as if it held a thousand tiny rainbows trapped within its delicate surface. Upon closer inspection, the crystal revealed intricate lines that run along its surface, veins of light etched into crystal.

Galinda had made the perfect *Crystal Slippers.*

Galinda looked like a princess. The fairest in all the land. The only thing missing to complete her was Gisella's pretty face and hair. However, the beauty in what she just created was enough to hold her over. For one night only, she didn't have to sulk on her *many* insecurities.

Galinda looked at herself in the looking glass again, how the gown accentuated her body before she delicately took it off and hung it in her wardrobe. She found an old casing for her large *Ozyclopedia* and put her crystal slippers in it for safekeeping and slid it under her bed.

Only hours ago, she'd felt tricked, like the Ethereum had been a burden laid upon her. But now? She was elated to hold it. It felt like a part of her. And she would protect it with everything she had.

Galinda closed the book and tucked it beneath her pillow. If anyone wanted to get to the book, they would have to go through her.

CHAPTER 17

Ballgowns & Crystal Shoes

W hen Galinda awoke, her first instinct was to check beneath her pillow. The spellbook was still there, its presence both reassuring and terrifying. There was no use hiding it under the pillow when her bed was vacant. Hiding something only works if one isn't, say, sleeping elsewhere, leaving the bed to sit empty, pristine, inviting suspicion. An amateur's mistake.

She needed to find a better hiding spot, one that would not so obviously cry out for discovery. After careful consideration, she tucked the book among the haphazard collection of novels and trinkets on her shelf. A place so mundane, so unremarkable, that no one, not even Gisella, would think to look there.

Especially not Gisella.

Gisella, who had never cared for books, rarely spent time indoors unless absolutely necessary. She was too preoccupied with more glittering things—shopping sprees in the Emerald City, impromptu revelries that lasted until the morning light, or simply the act of sleeping itself, an occupation she pursued with almost scholarly devotion.

Even though Gisella had never been one for intellectual pursuits, she had a plan. From the moment she was born, Gisella Fairmoor had known her purpose: she would marry rich. School had been an obligation, not a necessity, and now that she was no longer bound by it, she saw no reason to feign interest in things that bored her. It was all part of a grand design, she would be adored, she would be—inevitably, irrevocably—important and she didn't need University to do it. For, a woman in Ozian society, education held no currency compared to charm, beauty, and the practiced flick of a fan across a porcelain wrist.

Still, today found her at *home*, awake and, most concerningly, bored. And boredom, for Gisella, was a dangerous thing. It made her curious. And curiosity made her nosy. It was in this state of restless mischief that she found herself drawn, inexorably, to Galinda's room. Gisella had never considered her sister to be particularly interesting; Galinda was bookish in a way that suggested she actually read the books she owned, a thought both perplexing and vaguely unsettling. But recently, she had sensed something. A secret, tucked away beneath her sister's perfect posture and carefully measured words.

And so, she searched.

Drawers. Nothing.

Under the bed. Dust, a stray ribbon and an *Ozyclopedia* box.

Between the books? Please.

Gisella had rifled through everything, even examining Galinda's vanity. But there was nothing of interest. Nothing scandalous. Nothing mysterious. Just as she had suspected; Galinda's life was as dull as ever.

The wardrobe was an afterthought. Why would she check? Galinda's taste in fashion was best described as "well-meaning." But when Gisella swung the door open, she stopped, breath stolen from her throat as if someone had snatched it from her.

There, hung the most exquisite ballgown she had ever seen. A masterpiece of violet silk, shimmering with an almost ethereal glow. The fabric looked unlike anything found in Oz; smooth as liquid, radiant as the dawn.

Gisella reached for it with trembling fingers, barely breathing as she ran her hands over the delicate embroidery. The craftsmanship was unparalleled. Had she not caught herself, she might have swooned on the spot.

The fabric was cool beneath her fingertips, as if spun from something *Otherworldly*. Gisella knew dresses, knew them better than most knew their own reflections. She could tell the season's trends by sheer instinct. She knew every tailor, every seamstress, every name worth knowing in the business of beauty. And yet, this gown belonged to no one.

No one she had ever met.

No one who had ever existed.

Who in the world had made this?

Gisella pressed the gown against herself, twisting to catch her reflection in the mirror. If it weren't for the tragic reality of her sister's smaller frame, she would have claimed it then and there. Galinda, dear, sweet, unremarkable Galinda, could never pull this off. She lacked the poise, the presence, the *beauty* to wear such a creation. No, this gown belonged to someone who could do it justice. Someone like *her*.

In a dress like this, Gisella could make the world stop spinning.

A dress like this could win wars.

A dress like this could topple dynasties.

And conveniently, there was a grand event looming on the horizon. The timing, really, was quite perfect. She simply had to make it fit.

A plan began to form.

She could have it tailored, someone who would manipulate the form and stretch the fabric, making it hers without diminishing the brilliance of the design. Or perhaps… perhaps she could simply ask Galinda where she had acquired it. A direct approach. If the dress could be bought, then she would have one made to fit her exactly. No alterations, no compromises. A replica of perfection, tailored to her own magnificence. Yes. That, she decided was the more strategic approach.

Still, she wasn't ready to let go of it just yet. Carrying the dress with veneration, Gisella returned to her own room, spreading it across her bed as though laying down a sacred relic. Now it could bask in the rightful luxury of her presence. She sat beside it, admiring every stitch, every gleaming detail.

The day crawled by and waiting for Galinda to return *home* was unbearable.

When she finally heard the front doors close, when she recognized the distinct, irritated rhythm of her sister's steps, her *heart* quickened. Gisella practically floated down the hallway, meeting her sister at the top of the stairs, a grin stretching across her face so wide it was almost unsettling.

Galinda blinked at her, wary. "Are you... okay?"

"Of course! Why wouldn't I be?"

Without waiting for an answer, Gisella seized her sister's wrist and dragged her into her bedroom. Galinda barely had time to react before she was standing before *the* dress, *her* dress, spread across the bed like an offering.

Galinda's breath caught in her throat. "What—? Why were you going through my things?!"

"Oh Gohd! Don't be so dramatic," Gisella said, waving a hand.

"Dramatic? You *stole* my dress!"

"I *borrowed* it."

"What do you want, Gisella?"

Gisella was practically bursting with excitement. "Where did you get this?" she demanded, shaking Galinda's shoulders. "Who made it? Tell me this instant!"

Galinda's stomach twisted. One wrong word, and everything she had been hiding could unravel.

Think.

Fast.

"Ominson got it for me," she blurted.

Gisella froze. Then narrowed her eyes.

"...Really?"

"Yes." Galinda cleared her throat. "He—uh—he had it made for me. As a gift. By some seamstress," she said, snatching the gown from the bed.

Gisella scoffed. "Ominson? Had it made?" The scepticism in Gisella's face did not waver.

"Yes," she said firmly, committing to the lie. "Now, if you'll excuse me—"

Galinda turned sharply, retreating to her room before Gisella could push further. Ominson, after all, was many things; affable, wealthy, the kind of boy who would lend an arm at a ball simply because it was expected of him—but a grand romantic? A man who would commission a gown such as this for *Galinda* of all people?

Unlikely.

But there was no use pressing, not yet. The dress was already in Galinda's grasp, and a direct confrontation would be fruitless.

So Gisella, ever the strategist, relented.

"Well, if they can make one for you," she said, smoothing down her skirts with a casual air, "they can make one for me."

Galinda stiffened.

"So, when do I get to meet them?" Gisella insisted.

"I just said they were a secret," Galinda rebutted

"Come on, Galinda, don't you want your favourite sister to be prettier?"

Galinda just wanted to be left alone. "Guh! Fine!"

The pressure was growing, and the longer she kept talking, the more likely she was to slip up.

Galinda had not thought that far ahead.

But she was quick.

"I'm sure you know your measurements. You have a thousand gowns. Just write them down, and I'll relay it."

"You're right! You know me so well!" Gisella ran to hug her little sister tightly, leaving Galinda's face dotted with as many kisses as she had gowns.

Gisella grabbed a pen and paper, scribbling down her measurements. Measurements she pulled from memory, but if you asked her how many Wizards Oz has had since its inception, she wouldn't have a clue.

"How soon can they get the dress made?" Gisella asked giddy and impatient.

"It's a surprise, just tell me the colour you want, and I'll work my magic," Galinda replied sarcastically.

"I want Violet." Gisella answered, a smug smile across her face

Confused, Galinda repeated.

"Violet?"

"Yes. I want it just like yours. Is that a problem?"

"No, I guess not."

Galinda would think that she'd want a green gown. It was her tribal colour. But to be fair, when she cast the spell to create her gown, she had been thinking about Ominson. Wondering what type of dress he would find her pretty in. Which is perhaps why her dress materialised in Violet instead of pink.

Gisella had spent enough time in Galinda's room. She got what she wanted which meant it was time for her to leave.

And just like that, Galinda had trapped herself in her own deception. Now, she would have to make another gown. She would have to return to the Ethereum, to magic another miracle from thin air and pray that it did not betray her.

Gisella left satisfied, and Galinda?

◇

That night, alone in her room, Galinda locked the wardrobe, exhaling sharply. She had barely escaped that encounter unscathed. But she wasn't out of the woods yet. Because now she had another problem. She promised Gisella a gown. A gown *just* like hers.

She closed the door and lifted the Ethereum from the shelf. Using magic to summon it felt wrong, disrespectful, even. It contained the **Glamour Spell**, and it was the most powerful spellbook there's ever been, besides the *Kitab Malum*.

Galinda set her intention, and the book flipped to the Ballgown Spell page. Upon reading, it was clear that the spell needed a muse for it to work on. The spell catered to the caster needs and the client's body. Which meant she would have to craft a dress while Gisella was present. Which was *not* going to happen. Totally giving up, she flopped on her bed and Galinda was left staring at the ceiling, knowing that the threads of her secret were unravelling, one stitch at a time.

Unless...

Galinda's mind raced.

Mz. Everburn had once taught her to conjure simple objects, but with a twist. She had once conjured a half-eaten apple. The spell her teacher gave her was supposed to conjure a full apple, but she was able to adjust the spell to her teacher's needs by saying the spell, imagining the half-eaten apple precisely and willing it. It was logical that she could use the same premise for her dilemma. She was good at math, she knew what Gisella looked like, surely, she could estimate the size of a perfectly fitted gown for her.

Galinda stood at the end of her bed, she held the paper Gisella's measurements on it, she closed her eyes and envisioned a violet dress and said the spell. Galinda opened her eyes, the air shimmered. A cloud of pink mist filled the room, thick and opaque.

When it all cleared.

There it was.

A *perfect* Violet gown.

She gasped. The spell had worked. And not just worked, it had *surpassed* her previous creation.

A thrill coursed through her.

Her magic was evolving, strengthening like a muscle the more she used it.

Galinda couldn't believe she'd done it. The credit belonged to Mz. Everburn. Her teachings had shaped Galinda, etched deep despite the years that had passed. Without her, she would never have grasped the intricate weave of spellcraft, never unravelled the art behind the power. Moments like this made her ache for Mz. Everburn, to share her discoveries, to see pride flicker in her sharp, discerning eyes. She wished she could tell her about the Ethereum, to watch her reaction, to hear her thoughts. But no one knew where she was.

Zelena.

What wonders might she have crafted for her now? With magic as potent as hers, Galinda often wondered, could she have saved her? Surely, somewhere, there was a spell. She had the power now. But thinking like that was a hollow pursuit. Suppressing the grief, the ache of losing someone she called a sister was the only way to keep herself from unravelling. If she let her mind linger too long, the grief would drown her, spilling out in hours of tears.

Galinda carefully scooped the dress she made for Gisella and hid it under her bed. She had to make it look as though a tailor made it. Therefore, in three days, she would retrieve it from its hiding spot and give it to her sister. And with any luck—Gisella would never suspect the truth.

CHAPTER 18

Perception

G alinda did not hand Gisella the Violet ballgown. That would have invited questions; questions with answers that wobbled like a three-legged stool. No, better to let her find it in her own time—leaving it draped across Gisella's bed like an offering to the gods of vanity and excess.

Galinda, for her part, had plans. Or rather, she had plans to have plans. Anything to avoid Gisella's preening gratitude or, worse, her thinly veiled criticisms, both of which were delivered with the same breathless enthusiasm. Lately, Gisella had taken to rifling through Galinda's wardrobe, a development so baffling it made her wonder if there was something peculiar in the Upper Uplands' water supply.

Galinda tiptoed past her sister's room and set off for school, silently hoping the day would stretch endlessly. During lessons, she racked her **brain** for after-school activities to kill time. Ominson had an event to attend, which meant no meeting at the waterfall. A rare occurrence, but perhaps for the best. She had something more pressing to handle: translating the **Glamour Spell**. The sooner she could decipher it, the sooner she could *change* herself.

Before she went to the Golden Goose, she filled her bag with language deciphering books from the Willow-Wood Hills library. Her bag was not large enough to carry them all so she carried even more on her arms, using her chin to steady them from tipping over. As she crossed the threshold, she found her entire family dressed to the nines. Another event.

Ah. So it was one of those nights.

Galinda didn't care for frivolous parties that had no significance. No one missed her at those events, nor was she welcome to stand in the midst of the gentlemen and fair maidens of high society.

What did surprise her was the sight of her mother. Esmelda had miraculously surfaced from whatever mysterious retreat had kept her sequestered. It had been weeks. No one truly knew what plagued her, only that she was seeking help. Their conversations were rare, but Galinda still cared for her mother deeply. Flaws and all.

Dainhurst, meanwhile, was pontificating about his latest business ventures while Esmelda fussed over his tie, her hands moving with the efficiency of a woman who had dressed this man a thousand times but would never quite get it right.

Galinda, with the grace of a seasoned escape artist, attempted to ascend the stairs unnoticed.

It did not work.

"Galinda!"

She closed her eyes briefly. When she opened them, her father was staring at her expectantly.

"Put those books down and get dressed immediately," Dainhurst barked. "I told you we had things to do today!"

He had, in fact, told her no such thing. But this was typical. Information was dispensed on a need-to-know basis, and Galinda, in her father's eyes, rarely needed to know anything.

"Where are we going?" she asked, more to gauge what kind of excuse she'd need rather than out of any real curiosity.

Dainhurst narrowed his eyes. "You know full well I'm in the running to govern the South of Oz. I need my family by my side if this is going to work, and that includes you."

He tugged his tie loose and threw it back at Esmelda. "Do it again! You did it wrong."

Dainhurst gave a dismissive wave in Galinda's direction. "Go. Get. Dressed."

Galinda sighed. Even if she were crippled, Dainhurst would drag her there.

She needed to see what level of pageantry this event demanded. Gisella was always overzealous in her choices, which made her the perfect barometer. Whatever Gisella wore, Galinda would scale it down by three.

But when she entered her sister's room, she found Gisella twirling in the mirror, admiring herself in the Violet dress Galinda had left for her.

"How do I look?" Gisella asked, her voice thick with the expectation of admiration.

"You look beautiful," Galinda replied automatically.

Gisella's gaze flickered with uncertainty. "You don't think the dress is stealing my beauty, do you?"

"No, not at all. Very equal, I think."

Gisella seemed to consider this before nodding.

"I can live with that."

Satisfied, she returned to her reflection, admiring herself with the kind of devotion typically reserved for saints and deities.

Then, with the dramatic flair of a woman revealing a great injustice, she sat Galinda down on the bed.

"Galinda, you won't believe what Father did."

Galinda braced herself, "Oh Gohd, what?"

"I asked him for the Fairmoor Crown to wear tonight, and he said no." Her voice dropped to a whisper, as though the very words exhausted her. "Like, what is wrong with him? It's the only thing missing from this masterpiece of an outfit I put together."

Gisella took all the credit. As always.

"And?"

"And?" Gisella repeated, aghast, flopping onto the bed and staring at the ceiling. "He lied. He promised I could have it when I turned eighteen and last I checked, I'm nineteen. So why can't I wear it?"

"I'm sure he has a good reason."

Gisella scoffed, sitting upright "A good reason? We're talking about Father."

"Maybe he gave you a reason?"

"Nothing substantial, just something about not reaching a certain level of sophistication or achievement," Gisella muttered darkly. "As if there is *anyone* in Oz more sophisticated than me."

She fell backwards on the bed again, on the verge of tears.

Galinda didn't know how to comfort her sister. Though she was distraught, Galinda couldn't help finding her reactions over material things a little amusing.

Galinda did not argue.

She made her exit before Gisella could spiral further, but not before her sister grabbed her arm.

"You're not wearing *that* Violet dress, are you?"

"Of course I am!"

Gisella's expression twisted in horror. "No. Don't. Please. I'll give you one of my older gowns, ones I've never even worn."

"Why? Yours is better than mine anyway."

"Yes, but they're the same colour, and people will confuse us." She quickly added, "It'll just clash with mine."

Before Galinda could respond, Gisella was already leading Galinda to her *closet room*.

But she stopped. As if struck by a thought.

Galinda relented. "Fine. I won't wear it."

Gisella's face lit up with satisfaction. "Do you want one of my dresses?"

"No, that's fine."

Gisella's grin widened.

Back in her room, Galinda locked the door and opened the Ethereum on her bed. She would create a new one.

But what colour?

Green, her favourite? Or pink, her birth colour?

Then, she remembered the crystal slippers hidden under her bed. A pink gown would match perfectly. That was fashion advice Gisella once gave her. *As a lady, your shoes complete your outfit.*

With a whispered incantation, the spell shimmered into existence. The gown was breathtaking. Ethereal. Her finest creation yet. And when she slipped on the crystal slippers, they fit like a dream.

A knock at the door startled her. She barely had time to shove the Ethereum away before the maid entered.

"Oh Ozma," the maid gasped. "Lady Galinda… you look… beautiful!"

Galinda blushed, trying to remain composed, absorbing the words. If only Zelena could see her.

"Thank you," she said, standing taller.

"Your father sent me. They're about to leave."

Galinda nodded, fastening earrings and a necklace before descending the staircase.

The moment her family saw her, time froze.

Dainhurst inhaled sharply. "Galinda Fairmoor, is that you?"

Before she could answer, he lifted her, twirling her in an uncharacteristic display of warmth.

Gisella clutched her spiked crystal necklace and refused to look longer than a few seconds. But when she saw the crystal slippers, she nearly fainted.

Dainhurst beamed. This is exactly what he wanted. *Sophistication* at its finest.

Esmelda smiled with pride, paying Gisella no mind as she tried to get her mother's attention when Dainhurst was preoccupied with Galinda. Galinda and Dainhurst took the Golden Eagle, leaving Gisella and Esmelda with the Golden Goose to trail behind them to the event.

It was strange, almost wondrous, for Galinda to witness how her family responded to the dress she wore. Who knew that the key to blurring the edges of her insecurities was not in concealment but in extravagance of attire? She tucked this revelation away like a secret: ballgowns would be a staple in her life. They were going to be more than attire; they would be armour.

For the first time, she evoked reactions she'd never been able to summon with words or quiet gestures. Her father, Dainhurst—stoic, distant Dainhurst—had swept her into his arms and spun her, laughter spilling from him like it belonged there. The entire carriage ride, Dainhurst could not take his eyes off Galinda. His gaze was not filled with the usual flicker of polite acknowledgment, but with something warmer. It settled over her like sunlight breaking through clouds.

Galinda felt seen—not as an obligation, not as a shadow in the corner, but truly seen. And as the warmth blossomed in her chest, she began fantasising about how much her father was going to love her once she cracked the code to the **Glamour Spell**.

◇

Gisella sat in brittle silence within the lumbering Golden Goose. Her mood had dulled drastically from her usual sharpness. She was thinking. Thinking very hard as if in disbelief of something. Esmelda noticed, casting furtive glances her way. Gisella was muttering to herself and sighing very loudly. Something had unmoored Gisella and tipped her over the edge.

When they arrived, Dainhurst's voice sliced through the quiet, "Galinda, stay in the carriage."

His words weren't a suggestion but a command, crisp and decisive. He had a plan—a carefully crafted spectacle.

They waited a few Oz'mins for the sluggish Golden Goose to arrive. Gisella and Esmelda would lay the groundwork for Galinda's big reveal by entering first. And Galinda had no doubts in her father. This was his forte. Perception.

Inside the dim carriage, Dainhurst looked over to his daughter.

"Galinda, can you tell me why I'm insisting we wait for the perfect moment?"

"I don't know, Father" she shrugged.

Dainhurst sighed, as though preparing to impart sacred wisdom.

"Timing is everything," his voice low and deliberate. "One must know when to arrive and when to leave."

Galinda nodded.

"Perception is everything. The way you walk, the way you talk, the way you dress, even the way you arrive is everything. If there is one thing you must protect at all costs, it is the way people view you."

Dainhurst looked out the window, to make sure his runway was clear, then he turned back to Galinda and whispered. "Never forget that."

Galinda knew she wouldn't. Her father had maintained his image for years. Not a crack in his mask. Flawless and impenetrable. If anyone had mastered the art of perception, it was Dainhurst.

The moment arrived. Dainhurst extended his hand with practiced grace, "Now, let's go."

Galinda placed her hand in his, stepping from the carriage as though crossing a threshold into destiny.

Dainhurst wanted everyone to know that his daughter was the one wearing the best gown ever created. His upper-crust friends were sure to appreciate its grand design and *Sophistication*. Dainhurst and Galinda entered the Veilforge castle. Galinda realised the event was at Ominson's **home**, which meant that the event was organised by Magnum.

As soon as they entered, the room hummed like distant bees, a desert of important people from all four corners of Oz. Everybody had stopped in their conversations and heads turned when they saw Gisella's dress. But when Galinda stepped into view, the room didn't just turn, it stopped. Faces froze mid-expression, caught between awe and disbelief. Galinda recognized many from her mother's *NewZPapr* clippings, figures who once felt distant, now at a standstill like statues in her presence. Then, the eruption—applause, hushed whispers, a ripple of admiration. No one saw her face. No one noticed the flaws she'd feared.

They saw *exactly* what she wanted them to see.

Dainhurst leaned in, his voice soft but triumphant. "What did I tell you? Arrival is essential. Always time it well."

With a gentle nudge, he released her into the crowd to mingle. Galinda was eloquent in speech, and the best dressed. She was bound to bring honour to the family. The chandelier had been changed from the last time she was at Veilforge castle. It had been replaced with a much larger and grander one. It looked too big and heavy for the ceiling to uphold. But grand, nevertheless, lighting up the room like a thousand glass moons. As Galinda stood underneath the bright lights of the glass moon, her dress came to life. The shimmers dancing and the different shades of pink coming to the forefront. Galinda walked with a poise she hadn't known was hers. "Perception is everything." She kept repeating to herself. Remembering that line kept her body upright and proper. The clicks of the heels announced her presence even more. All eyes were still on her.

A *NewZPapr* journalist approached, notebook in hand, excitement in his stride. Esmelda was in the corner of the room speaking to some of her friends but when she looked over at Galinda, she gave a warm little smile. Galinda felt it was all worth it.

"Excuse me, my lady!" he called, his accent thick with the cadence of Winkie Country. "Might I have a word?"

Her smile was rehearsed, but radiant, "Of course."

"I'm covering fashion for the *Ozian Society* column, and I must say, this gown… it's the most elegant creation I've ever seen. My Gohd, the way it fits." He gestured dramatically, kissing the air as if words failed him. "You *must* tell me—who designed it?"

"I did. Just a few materials stitched together, nothing more."

"A woman of talent and beauty. Remarkable! And the colour—why pink?"

"I think it complements my skin. But more than that, pink embodies femininity, soft yet powerful. Don't you agree?"

"Oh, absolutely," he gushed, leaning closer with a conspiratorial grin. "Dare I say, the *best* colour."

They laughed, the moment light and easy, as an artist sketched Galinda's likeness from the neck down for the paper.

"And your name, for the column?" the journalist asked.

"Glin—" Galinda hesitated, then spoke with newfound authority:

"Galinda Fairmoor of the Upper Uplands."

◇

Meanwhile, above the crowd, Gisella stood on the staircase, her fury simmering beneath a brittle smile. Veloria chattered beside her, oblivious to the storm brewing. "Where did your sister get that dress? She looks so… womanly. *I* want that dress!"

"Be quiet," Gisella snapped, straining to catch fragments of Galinda's conversation below.

Veloria huffed but continued, relentless.

"I just don't get it. *You* always have first pick. Why would you settle for *that?*"—she gestured dismissively at Gisella's violet gown, "when *that* masterpiece exists."

Gisella's jaw tightened, her voice a hiss, "She tricked me."

Veloria's laughter was sharp and unkind.

"Tricked you? Seriously?"

"Shut up, Vee." Gisella's voice trembled, not with rage, but something worse. *Humiliation.*

Veloria's eyes darted to Galinda's feet. She gasped.

"Wait—are those… *crystal* slippers?"

"Just go away, Vee," Gisella snapped, her voice cracking.

Veloria rolled her eyes and drifted off, leaving Gisella alone to stew in silent defeat.

Below, Galinda finished her interview and slipped through the crowd, her **heart** thrumming with quiet hope. She needed to find Ominson. If strangers could see her now and marvel, perhaps *he* would too.

CHAPTER 19

Glass Moon

As Galinda scurried past guests who made constant gasps, she noticed Ominson outside leaning against the balustrade of the balcony, taking in the evening air. When she reached Ominson, her vision became clearer. He was speaking to a girl—blonde, beautiful and effortlessly radiant. The kind of blonde Galinda could only dream of being. Their conversation looked serious, intimate. If she had arrived a second later, his lips might have already been pressed against hers, lost in a heated exchange of breath and longing.

Galinda was ever thankful she'd arrived in time. She pretended to adjust the folds of her gown, ensuring the girl took notice, took in the shimmer of the fabric, the delicate embroidery, the way it clung to her figure. The girl did. Galinda turned ever so slightly so the silk caught the light in precisely the way it was meant to. And just as Galinda intended, the girl made an excuse and slipped away, leaving Galinda and Ominson alone beneath the starlit sky.

"You scared her off quickly, didn't you?" Ominson teased, a smirk tugging at his lips.

Galinda chuckled, feigning innocence. "I tend to have that effect."

But beneath his playful tone, Ominson rubbed the back of his neck, clearly uncomfortable. He knew Galinda saw him flirt with a girl. Though they were just friends, he always had a shyness about Galinda seeing him with other girls.

He turned to face her fully, the humour fading as he took her in properly for the first time that night. His breath faltered.

"Woz! You look—"

"I know it's a bit much," she cut in.

"No," Ominson murmured, reaching out to brush a strand of hair from her face, his fingertips barely ghosting over her cheek. "You look beautiful."

"You think so?"

"I do."

Their eyes locked, the world around them quieting. Galinda's blue eyes sparkled brighter than the stars above, and Ominson's own gaze—charming, warm, inviting—had never looked so enticing.

There was something different about the air that night. Charged. Reckless. Galinda felt it thrumming in her chest. She did not have a care in the world; any risk he proposed to her, she was ready to take. Ominson felt the same. But neither felt like being the catalyst.

"So," she said, breaking the silence with a playful lilt, "did you come out here to have more girls swoon over you?"

Ominson laughed. "No, that just *happens*, no matter where I am."

"Tell me about it," she quipped.

He raised a brow. "Are you jealous?"

"I didn't say that."

Her face was turning pink, pinker than the dress she wore. She hated how obvious it was.

Ominson sighed, turning back to the view of the garden below. His usual light-heartedness had dimmed.

Galinda, ever perceptive, placed a hand gently on his back. "What's wrong?"

He sighed. "My father."

"My father and I just got into a *huge* disagreement," he said, his voice quieter now, "I'm at my wit's end with him, and I don't think I can take much more."

"What happened?"

Ominson's fingers curled around the railing. "Your father and mine... They're trying to take control of all of Quadling Country. Your father leading, mine at his side. He drags me to every meeting, makes me listen to their plans. And if I question him, if I disagree, he lashes out—calls me weak. Says things I..." His voice trailed off.

Galinda's stomach twisted.

"That's terrible, Omi, what are you going to do?"

"I don't know. That's why I came out here. He's in his study right now speaking with your father. Probably expecting me to be there. I just... I couldn't. Not tonight." Ominson turned to her, something desperate in his eyes. "Why doesn't your father make you attend these meetings, Glinda?"

Galinda laughed, a dry, bitter sound. "I'm a girl."

Ominson nodded. "Right."

To Galinda, it was laughable that he would even ask such a question. Even munchkins knew that.

"Well," she said, tilting her head, "I think you need to find what your heart is searching for. Something with *honour*, so you can feel like you're doing good things."

Ominson's face softened. He smiled, a real one, not the practiced, charming kind he used on everyone else. "You always do that," he murmured.

"Do *what?*"

"You say these *simple* things that make me feel better. Like you lift the weight off my shoulders without even trying." He laughed, shaking his head. "I could kiss you."

Galinda stilled.

And for the first time in her life, she decided not to think.

She leaned in.

Ominson did the same.

The moment their lips met, it was warm. Familiar. Like the hugs they used to share when they were younger, only deeper, sweeter. It felt like **home**. And *there was no place like* **home**.

When they finally pulled away, Galinda turned her face, panic creeping in.

What if he *looked* at her now, really *looked*, and regretted it?

She had been so sure, so reckless, and now all she could hear were the voices of caution and insecurity she had long tried to suppress.

Ominson grasped her hand.

But then—

"GALINDA," a voice purred from the darkness.

Gisella stepped forward, her figure emerging from the shadows beyond the balcony's reach.

"Can you help me with my dress?" Gisella said sweetly,

Without waiting for an answer, she grabbed Galinda's wrist. Her grip on Galinda was anything but gentle.

As she pulled her away, she cast Ominson a knowing glance.

"Hello, Ominson."

Galinda let herself be dragged away, half in relief, half in horror.

They went up the spiral staircase, to the highest tier of the inside balcony, where the grand party still hummed below, a cacophony of opulence and intrigue.

Galinda forced her wrist out of Gisella's hand with a huff. Brushing invisible dust from her gown, as though adjusting the draping of a stage curtain before the grand reveal.

"Your dress looks fine," Gisella remarked, annoyed.

"Yes, I know!" Galinda answered sharply.

"I just saved you from embarrassing yourself. You should be thanking me."

"Embarrassing myself?"

"Ominson is a dog. His tail wags for every girl who so much as breathes his direction. And besides, Father brought you here to mingle with the gentry not to stick your tongue down your friend's throat. Leave all that for the water—"

But she didn't finish her thought.

Galinda's attention wavered from Gisella to scanning the crowd below for Ominson.

Gisella's laughter was a dagger, sharp, effortless.

"Oh, *please*. Don't tell me you've mistaken puppy eyes for genuine affection."

BEFORE

Gisella grabbed Galinda's wrist again. Harder.

Galinda wrenched her wrist free, her breath coming out harsher than she intended. "No. Let go of me."

Gisella blinked, startled.

"Guh! Why are you like this?"

Gisella recoiled as if slapped. "Like *what?*"

"Suffocating!" Galinda's chest heaved with the weight of words buried too long. "You pick me apart, subtly pointing out the things wrong with me, like I don't already know them. You're always there, correcting, controlling—*suffocating* me. Well, there. I said it. Just... leave me alone!"

The words cracked the air like a whip. And the world listened.

Above, the grand chandelier, a sprawling constellation of glass moons and crystal stars, shuddered. Its golden chains groaned, swaying as if caught in an invisible sandstorm. The crowd below gasped, heads tilting upward. A scream pierced the din, a frail, withered sound from an elderly woman directly beneath the chandelier's ominous descent.

Galinda spun around. Her **heart** lurched.

Without thinking, without *choosing*, she thrust out both hands. Magic surged through her fingertips, invisible yet undeniable, a force ancient and wild. The chandelier halted mid-plunge, a hair's width from crashing. It trembled in the air like prey caught in a snare.

Silence crashed over the room.

Not relief. Not gratitude.

Fear.

The chandelier floated gently down, landing beside the old woman who remained frozen, eyes wide with terror, not from the near-death experience but from the *unnatural* force that had saved her.

Then, from somewhere in the crowd, a shriek:

"*Witch!*"

Fingers pointed. Hands clutched pearls pressed against scandalized mouths. Galinda felt her stomach sink as the faces blurred together into one undulating mass of *loathing*. They weren't staring at Galinda's dress anymore—they were staring at *her*.

Gisella was frozen, the colour drained from her face. Galinda could see the calculation flickering behind her sister's eyes, the effort to *reconcile* what she had just witnessed. Magic. *Witchcraft*. Something unnatural, *unholy*, something utterly un-Fairmoor.

A truth so horrifying, it must be *rectified*.

"Someone *grab* her!" came a voice from the crowd.

Ominson and the rest of the guests outside rushed into the castle. It looked like she was in a desert of snakes and scorpions that had been starved for centuries. Three hundred and thirty-three years to be exact.

Galinda stood frozen. There was no saving her now. She was to be put to death. Disappear like the rest of the "suspected" witches. Only, she just gave them proof. The abyss had opened beneath her feet, and she was falling, falling…

Until Gisella stepped forward.

"It was me!"

The crowd's uproar faltered, confusion rippling through the desert of faces. A woman bedecked in jewels sneered from below.

"Gisella, don't be ridiculous."

Gisella lifted her chin, pride stitched into every word.

"It's the truth. I'm a witch." She gestured toward the old woman, now upright and trembling. "But I only use it for good. I just saved a life, doesn't that matter more than superstition?"

Whispers swept the room like wildfire.

Through the chaos, Dainhurst and Magnum burst in, their expressions thunderclouds of confusion and fury. Esmelda slithered in soon after, drawn by the scent of scandal. The weight of Oz's power had converged in one place.

The journalist was also part of the witch hunt parade. He was about to get the biggest story of his career. He pushed to the front; his quill poised like a dagger. "What does your father say about this?"

Dainhurst, as confused as a munchkin, pulled his daughter and Galinda to the side. Demanding answers on why they were the centre of attention and why it was not the type of attention he liked.

Dainhurst hissed in anger. "What is going on? Who caused this commotion?"

Galinda answered, "I can explain, Father—"

"Galinda used magic," Gisella interrupted. "She has magic!"

Dainhurst's gaze snapped to Galinda. His hands gripped her shoulders like a vice, shaking her slightly, his fury volcanic.

"Is this true?"

"Yes." Galinda answered, bowing her head, like she was waiting to be executed by *Ozian Guillotine.*

"But I took the blame for her," Gisella frantic, "they think *I'm* the witch."

Dainhurst's face was a mask of rage and calculation.

"You *what?*"

He shoved past them, his politician's mask sliding into place as he addressed the crowd. His words were sharp, designed to bleed and bind.

"Yes, as you've now seen, my daughter Gisella is a witch. But not the kind you fear. She is *blessed.*"

Murmurs rippled. Dainhurst needed more. A holy shield. A name to sanctify the scandal. Because if there was one thing Upland South Ozians loved more than killing witches, it was religion and being perceived as pure and true.

"Barbarus himself has purified her," he declared. "You all know of His Whollyness, his righteousness. She is not a threat. She is a symbol of goodness."

He pulled Gisella into the spotlight, his grip ironclad.

"Behold—*Gisella, the Good Witch of the South!*"

The crowd murmured amongst themselves, trying to make a decision, but Dainhurst had already made it for them. The once judgemental room was now filled with applause, resemblant of thunderstorms.

Gisella's new title echoed through the hall, drowning out the truth, suffocating it beneath layers of lies and survival.

Gisella was not merely a witch.

She was *The Good Witch*.

And Galinda? She was something else entirely.

She stood small in the shadow of her sister's triumph, only watching as the pieces of the game settled into place.

Beginning to understand, she had lost in more ways than one.

CHAPTER 20

Silver Slippers

The accord had been struck. Dainhurst, a man of pacts and penitence, had sent the Golden Goose to ferry the women back to Fairmoor Castle while he remained behind to deliberate. He needed the counsel of his closest brethren, men who, like him, understood the language of power better than the lexicon of sentiment. The women obeyed without protest, departing the grand ball and retreating into the uncertain night.

Galinda sat in uneasy silence during the *ryde home*, her thoughts gnawing at her like an unrelenting beast. She had spent a lifetime safeguarding the secrets of others like precious birds in her palms, yet the one secret that truly mattered, the one that lived inside her own flesh, slipped through her fingers like grains of sand. It was her **heart**—her reckless, traitorous **heart**—that had doomed her. Had she hesitated, had she let the chandelier shatter the old crone who barely seemed grateful for her rescue, she wouldn't be in this position.

Gisella, by contrast, luxuriated in the moment. Gone was the simmering irritation from earlier that evening. She had left the ball with something finer than any gown or jewel: a title.

The Good Witch of the South.

The words rang like a triumphant aria in her mind, a moniker embroidered in celestial gold.

Esmelda perched by the carriage window, watching the countryside blur past, unmoved. She had not yet decided how to react, whether to scold or to soothe, to mourn or to manoeuvre. Or perhaps a mother's weary acceptance? It was a choice best made in quiet. For now, she would remain still, neutral, just as she had learned at her *retreat*.

The three women proceeded directly to the grand hall, awaiting Dainhurst's return. Galinda sat rigid, every muscle in her body taut with nerves. The wind outside howled through the windows, rattling the panes like an omen. Gisella, by contrast, exuded serenity, almost smugness.

The silence stretched long and unbearably.

Then, Esmelda shattered it.

"Galinda," Esmelda snapped. "Why didn't you tell me?"

"I—I didn't want you to be angry."

Esmelda exhaled sharply, rubbing her forehead. "I am your mother," she said, voice trembling with an emotion Galinda had rarely heard from her—true, undiluted concern. "You are supposed to come to me about these things!"

Before Galinda could respond, Gisella leaned in, lips curving in amusement. "I'm just disappointed I didn't figure it out sooner. I always knew you had some nasty little secret tucked away."

"Be quiet, Gisella," Esmelda ordered.

"No. I want to hear her say it," Gisella rebutted.

Galinda's jaw tightened. "Say *what?*"

Gisella scoffed. "A 'thank you' would suffice."

Of course, she owed Gisella her gratitude, her sister had, after all, taken the blame. But there was something in the way she had done it, a certain *performance* to it. Gisella's actions had been clever, opportunistic, and dazzlingly self-serving which made the gesture feel anything but selfless. Now, she understood what Ominson had once told her in the garden, *true good deeds required true good intentions.*

Her dreams of using magic to reshape her destiny, to reclaim the Forsaken Pink Gem, to become *The Good Witch* had been stripped away. Stolen.

But what choice did she have?

For now, though, she was just grateful to be alive.

Galinda dug into the pit of her stomach and found what little remained of her dignity. "Thank you."

"That's more like it," Gisella purred.

"Enough," Esmelda cut in.

Then—footsteps. A clamour beyond the grand hall.

Dainhurst was **home.**

They had barely straightened their postures before he entered, his voice preceding him.

"Galinda! Gisella!"

Dainhurst entered, and the air itself seemed to still. He didn't need to ask if they were waiting. Of course they were.

Dainhurst lowered himself into the great chair at the head of the room. His arms crossed. His expression unreadable, save for a flicker of distaste.

"Galinda," he said, his tone grim. "Show me."

"My magic?"

"No, your embroidery. Of course, your magic! Such insolence."

Galinda obeyed, lifting a vase with a mere twitch of her fingers.

Esmelda gasped, covering her mouth. Gisella frowned and turned away as if she had been personally slighted.

Dainhurst's expression did not change, besides a subtle tightening of the jaw.

Then, a sound escaped him.

"Ah."

It was the sound a man made when looking at something broken beyond repair.

"I have guests arriving tomorrow," he said, rubbing his temple. "Go to bed. I must do what I can to keep this family from disgrace."

The girls, along with Esmelda did as they were told and departed in silence. Galinda retreated to her chambers. Gisella to hers.

But later that night, when the castle had settled into stillness, Gisella did not stay in her room.

She slipped into Galinda's chambers, quiet as a shadow.

If she was proclaimed *The Good Witch of the South*, she needed to see how magic worked.

Galinda, curled in bed, prepared to begin her usual cycle of silent tears. But the creak of her door snapped her out of it.

Gisella perched herself on the edge of the bed, tapping her foot impatiently. "Galinda," she cooed sweetly, "I know levitating objects isn't the *only* thing you can do. Show me more."

Galinda remained silent.

"Oh, come now." Gisella traced idle patterns into the sheets. "It's only fair. I saved you, didn't I?"

There it was again.

Galinda sighed, dragging herself out of bed.

"What do you want?"

She sat on the floor, stone cold against her legs. Gisella joined her, excitement buzzing in her fingers.

Gisella had an epiphany.

"The slippers," she said. "The ones you wore at the ball. I want a pair." She smirked. "But in silver. Silver is far more Sophisticated."

Galinda hesitated. "Fine."

She reached for the Ethereum, placing it on the floor between them. No more hiding. And, oddly, it was *freeing*.

"Stand up," Galinda instructed. Gisella obeyed.

Galinda traced a spell through the air, her voice weaving the incantation.

In an instant, the slippers materialized—gleaming, celestial silver. They slipped onto Gisella's feet, moulding to her form like they had always belonged to her. As though crafted by divine hands.

Gisella gasped.

"These are—Woz, these are—Spectacular," Gisella screamed before realising she was supposed to be in bed. *Better than sex,* she thought. Gisella danced around the room continuously, testing out her new silver shoes, checking for any flaws.

A shoe expert as well as a dress connoisseur.

She found none, which was a little annoying.

Her sister, Galinda, was remarkable and there was no denying it.

She looked at Galinda.

"So that's how you did it?"

"I'm sorry?"

"The crystal slippers... and the ballgown, you used magic."

"Yes."

"I knew it," she breathed. "I knew the secret designer story was rubbish."

She turned to the looking glass, admiring her reflection. The stars themselves seemed to dance at her feet. The most sophisticated shoes in Oz, and she had the only pair. The thought alone of wearing them out in the world got her body excited, she could feel the tingles in her genitals. She had never wanted for anything, not truly. But now—now she wanted something she could not buy.

Magic.

"Teach me," she said.

Galinda sighed. She had been doing a lot of that lately.

"You don't have magic. Magic only works if you have magic. Unless you want to learn basic potions, which works for anyone."

"How do you know I don't have magic. We come from the same parents."

"It doesn't work like that. Remember what Barbarus told father? Magic manifests by the age of sixteen and if you don't show any signs, you will never have it."

Gisella frowned.

"You have to at least, let me try."

"Okay, you see that book on the shelf. Estimate its weight and let the 'power' flow through you and nudge it off the shelf."

Gisella concentrated hard. Her eyes squinting. Her fingers curling hard, its shadow reflecting on the walls like a claw.

But nothing.

Not a single sound or movement that could be mistaken as a sign of potential magic.

"You're nineteen, if you had magic it would've shown. Whether you liked it or not. Like a pimple."

"And that makes you happy, doesn't it?" Gisella snapped.

The room remained silent.

"I'm sorry. I shouldn't have said that. It's not your fault."

"It's okay."

Gisella sat back. Still frowning.

"I'll find a way," she murmured.

And Galinda believed her.

Another idea struck Gisella.

"Galinda, can you enchant these shoes so they can change colour to complement any outfit I change into?"

"I can try." Galinda answered, sure of herself.

Galinda whispered a spell under her breath and waved her hands.

The silver shoes glowed like fire in the dark room, but they remained the same.

Unchanged.

"Maybe, you're not as powerful as you think you are." Gisella scoffed.

Galinda lowered her gaze, silence thick around her. Then, almost in a whisper:

"Maybe not. But I can still do other things."

That night, they laughed and basked in each other's company. Galinda performed miracle after miracle, each more dazzling than the last, and with every display, Gisella's wonder only grew.

She had never seen magic like this.

To her, it had always been something sinister, dark rites, whispered curses, the sacrifice of innocence.

But this… this was different.

This was light. This was joy.

And for the first time, Gisella couldn't understand how something so beautiful could be so feared.

Gisella didn't return to her chambers. Instead, the two sisters lay side by side, each lost in quiet thought.

And for once, they dreamed the same dream.

Magic.

A birthright.

A prison.

A path.

And somewhere, beyond their knowing, fate began to shift.

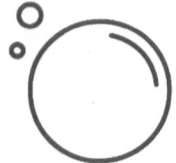

CHAPTER 21

The Man Behind the Curtain

The sisters awoke to the abrupt clatter of a maid at the door, urgency sharpened the woman's voice, slicing through the last wisps of sleep. They were to be dressed and polished before the guest arrived. Dainhurst's reputation remained intact, and thus, so must they.

Gisella wasted no time returning to her own chamber, where hot water steamed, soaps frothed, and a gown awaited. Whoever this visitor was, he must be either wealthy or sacred; no one else could inspire their father's obsequiousness. She considered, briefly, the possibility of a suitor. Even though her **heart** was set on someone else, it never hurt to be prepared. Love was fleeting, but strategic alliances had a staying power that outlasted even the finest couture.

Galinda readied herself with equal diligence but for a different reason. She had no illusions of romance or favour. This was about survival. Dainhurst, already a man of temperate affection, had turned colder still. If he wanted her starched and strung up like a doll, she would comply and quickly. She couldn't afford to provoke him further, especially not after the previous night's... events.

When Galinda was finally ready, she lingered in her room. She would wait for Gisella to step into the grand hall first. Alone with her father—particularly in silence—was unbearable. In the meantime, she distracted herself. She continued to study the **Glamour Spell**, praying to Gohd for the strength to navigate this ordeal. Maybe her father would be merciful.

Maybe, just maybe, he would spare her.

Downstairs, the maids worked in a flurry of activity, their movements sharp and practiced. Dainhurst had commanded that the castle be brought to pristine condition, despite it being already immaculate. In all her years, Galinda had never seen her father so intent on impressing someone, not even when dignitaries visited. The man was unnervingly unpredictable.

The main gates finally creaked open. Galinda rushed to the window, **heart** in her throat. A bronze carriage rolled to a halt before the castle. *Bronze* meant *middle ground*—not rich enough to be excessive, not poor enough to be beneath notice. She relaxed slightly. Whoever it was, surely it wasn't someone who could unsettle Dainhurst so completely.

The figure emerged from the carriage. Barbarus. Of course.

It made perfect sense.

This was not a social call. This was not an alliance to be forged or a favour to be curried. Barbarus had come for one reason alone: to root out the disease within her, to purge the house of its tainted blood. Dainhurst was not going to let his ugly daughter sit idly by in his castle without being cured of her Seraphina curse.

Galinda decided to remain in her room until she was summoned. Her **heart** beating out of her chest. Would she be tortured? She didn't know.

Barbarus entered the castle and spoke with Dainhurst briefly.

The maid knocked, soft but firm. Galinda and Gisella entered the grand hall, where Dainhurst and Barbarus waited in silence. Dainhurst, his cane tapping against the stone floor, gestured to the cushioned chairs with a practiced, dispassionate sweep. This was serious. Still, part of her hoped they would all just move on and pretend nothing had happened. She could never have been more wrong.

Gisella sat first, her legs crossed with a quiet elegance. The Silver Slippers gleamed beneath her, and it looked like she wasn't taking them off anytime soon.

Dainhurst cleared his throat.

"You all remember Barbarus, don't you?" His voice was clipped, formal, a touch too cold.

"Yes." The sisters chorused.

Barbarus smiled, a tight and charitable thing.

"Galinda. Gisella. It has been some time," he said, his voice too smooth, too polite.

"We have important matters to discuss," Dainhurst declared, his gaze levelling on Galinda with the weight of an anvil. "Regarding last night's... incident."

Galinda hung her head, a flush of shame crawling up her neck.

Barbarus picked up seamlessly. "Your father, ever the resourceful man, has turned an unfortunate event into an opportunity. It's remarkable, really." He turned to Dainhurst with something approaching admiration. "Few could have salvaged this situation."

Galinda blinked, confused. "He has?"

Dainhurst frowned, a little annoyed she even had the gall to speak after what she did.

"Yes," Barbarus confirmed smoothly. "This could have been catastrophic. Your family's safety was at risk."

"Thank you, Father," Gisella said brightly, her voice laced with relief. She wasn't ready to die. There were still things she wanted to do—have more sex, spend more money, wear more dresses, and even get married.

"Tell them, Barbarus," Dainhurst ordered impatiently.

Barbarus nodded, then turned to face the sisters directly. "We're not out of danger yet. Gisella, as you know, has declared that she is a witch. As far as the public is concerned, she is now the *'Good Witch of the South.'* The only reason you're both alive this morning is becoz of your father's quick thinking."

Dainhurst gave a single, satisfied nod. "Have you seen the NewZPapr?"

Galinda shook her head.

Gisella smirked.

Dainhurst slammed the morning's issue on the centre table. There, emblazoned across the front page, was a portrait of Gisella, resplendent in white, a paragon of virtue. The accompanying text praised her selflessness, her mercy, her goodness.

Galinda inhaled sharply. "But that was me."

"But they don't know that," Barbarus answered swiftly.

Dainhurst's voice was heavy, unyielding. "For this to work, Gisella must maintain the image of 'The Good Witch of the South.'"

Gisella tilted her head. "There's one problem with that, isn't there?" She extended her hand as if to summon magic from thin air. "I don't have it. I tried last night. I'm past the age of sixteen. The window has closed."

Dainhurst sighed audibly, "Yes. We know that, and that's why we're speaking with both of you. Barbarus, continue."

"This is how it must appear. Galinda, Oz must believe that Gisella is a witch, and we need your magic to be able to do this."

"No!" Galinda burst out, her voice sharp and desperate. "We can't keep hiding the truth. I'll just say it's me, that I'm the one with magic."

She paused.

"I'll be the Good Witch," she declared, her words hanging in the air like a fragile promise.

Dainhurst's grip on his cane tightened until the wood creaked and cracked, threatening to splinter.

"Galinda, no one will accept you as the Good Witch," his voice cold and final. "You don't have the image the public craves. They believed Gisella was the Good Witch becoz they *wanted* to, becoz it suited their fantasy. You saw how quickly they turned on you after you saved that woman's life. They couldn't handle the truth. They don't want it."

Barbarus interjected, "Galinda, do you remember that prophecy manuscript you found some years ago?"

Galinda's eyes flickered, the memory haunting her. "Yes."

"When you read it, who did you think the prophecy referred to?"

"Gisella."

Barbarus smiled, small and knowing. "Exactly. Prophecies are rarely as clear as we want them to be. They're often misunderstood or only half-true. Gisella doesn't have magic, but the world will know her as the 'Good Witch of the South,' becoz that is her destiny."

And suddenly, everything clicked into place.

Galinda had clung to the hope that the prophecy was wrong, that her fate was bound for something greater.
But she was not the golden-haired saviour.

She was not loved.

She was not the Good Witch.

"So… I can't ever use my magic publicly?" Galinda's voice was scarcely above a whisper.

Barbarus exhaled, sympathy threading through his words. "No. I'm sorry, Galinda. If you use your magic, the people will fear you. They will see you as a threat. And you chose the pink gem—you know what that means."

Barbarus softened. "This is for your safety."

Dainhurst, however, had no patience for tenderness. "The people will never accept you. *You* caused this, and now you must fix it. You will do what is necessary."

"That's enough," Barbarus chided.

He leaned in, closer than before, until Galinda could see the fine lines around his eyes, the exhaustion in his expression. Gently, he took her hand in his own, placed his palm over hers, a rare moment of warmth in a world of cold transactions.

"Just think about it," he murmured. The Choice you make now will define everything. But remember, it's important that you choose wisely."

The sound of the main gates opening interrupted the moment. Another guest had arrived.

Barbarus stood, his eyes scanning the door. "I suppose this is my cue to leave?"

Dainhurst nodded curtly and escorted Barbarus out of the room. As they walked, Galinda could hear Dainhurst's frustration bleeding through the walls.

"Why would you tell her to think about it? She has no choice in the matter!"

The sisters, still seated, listened as the words echoed down the corridor. Gisella, in a rare show of restraint, glanced at Galinda and said nothing. Perhaps, for the first time, she felt the weight of what she had taken. Perhaps, for the first time, she was aware of the yawning gulf between them.

For beyond the flicker of guilt, beyond the quiet moment of recognition, Gisella could already imagine it, the applause, the devotion, the songs of praise that would be sung in her name. She turned away just in time, just before a slow, satisfied smile spread across her lips.

◇

Barbarus and Dainhurst walked in the direction that led to the back of the castle. Dainhurst did not want Barbarus and whoever was arriving to meet.

Galinda, on the verge of tears, simply bowed her head and clicked her heels together.

Neither of the sisters knew whether they should leave like Barbarus or wait for Dainhurst to return. It was instinct, more than anything, that kept them rooted in place, waiting for their father's next command.

Ten Oz'mins passed before the door swung open once more.

Dainhurst was not alone.

The man beside him was striking, black and silver hair swept back, a groomed moustache perched above a knowing smirk. He wore green and black, a velvet moss-coloured coat over a crisp suit. His top hat gleamed in the firelight, casting a faint verdant hue, and his cane—tipped in emerald—tapped lightly against the floor as he walked.

"He looks rather dapper, doesn't he?" Gisella whispered.

Dainhurst gestured for the mysterious man to take his personal seat. No one ever sat in that seat besides Dainhurst. Despite it being the most comfortable seat in the house—or so the rumours claimed.

"Girls," Dainhurst announced. "I would like to introduce you both to The Wizard of Oz."

Gisella and Galinda both gasped in unison. Immediately standing up and bowing in respect.

The Wizard chuckled, a rich, velvety sound. "Oh, none of that. Sit, sit."

Galinda was now shy. She had read of him, studied his every mention in the pages of history.

Dainhurst smiled for the first time that morning. "The Wizard came here to speak with you, Galinda."

Her breath hitched. "Me?"

"Yes," the Wizard himself answered.

"Gisella," Dainhurst said, his tone a command wrapped in courtesy. "Could you excuse us?"

Gisella obliged, though she longed to protest, to stay. She wanted a chance to woo the Wizard in case he wanted to marry her. She would even settle for as much as having sex with him, if that meant that he endorsed her when she became The Good Witch. It would be easy for her to do too because he was very charming and handsome even for his age, insanely rich and he smelt good. But most of all, his penis was large, and she could tell by the way it was protruding from his trousers. She could make a proposal, if given the time. A well-placed word, a flutter of lashes. She was beautiful, she was young—what more could a man want?

But the moment passed, and with one last lingering glance, Gisella turned and left.

The room fell into silence.

The Wizard leaned forward, his voice silky and smooth, so calming that it could put a baby to sleep. "Galinda, is it?"

142

"Yes," Galinda answered shyly.

"Your father told me about what happened at Veilforge castle yesterday. If what I hear is true, you are a witch?"

"Yes. A good witch."

The Wizard laughed.

"That is good to know," the Wizard continued. "Your father has told me of his great plans for Quadling Country, and we have been working on it for quite some time now. Of course, recent events have shifted the landscape somewhat." His eyes glinted. "But I believe it is for the better. Do you know why?"

"No?"

The Wizard smiled.

"As you are well aware, magic is scarce in Oz these days," he said. "The world has grown dimmer for it. But you, Galinda—" He let the words settle. "You are something rare."

Galinda's breath caught.

"We have an opportunity," the Wizard murmured. "An opportunity to restore what was lost. To bring light back to Oz. Don't you want that?"

"I do."

"Galinda, we need your help to change the way people see magic."

The Wizard's voice was rich, every syllable smoothed down like the edges of a well-worn coin, passed from hand to hand, buying loyalty, buying belief.

"Every day, when I am in the Emerald City, don't you think it pains me that even I cannot shift the people's minds? That they trust only me with magic, when all I wish is for magic to be as free as the air, for it to belong to everyone?"

"I understand. Truly. I just—"

"You just what?" Dainhurst barked.

The Wizard lifted a hand, a casual, graceful flick of the wrist. A king calming his hounds.

"Let's set aside titles for a moment, Galinda," he said smoothly. "Forget about The Good Witch. Don't you want to be a good person?"

"More than anything!"

"Ah. You see? That is what I like about you." He leaned in, "But let me tell you something about goodness. Being good is not about right or wrong. It is about making people happy. Have you not done a good thing when the majority of people in society are happy?"

"I... suppose?"

"Exactly," the Wizard said, spreading his hands as though the world itself were contained between them. "And that is what I expect from you. To do what will make the people happy. That is what I have done since the day I became Wizard. I produce the greatest happiness for the greatest number of people. And look! Most of Oz prospers. There is peace, there is order, there is harmony."

BEFORE

"Do I have to be in the shadows to do good?" she asked quietly. "I want people to know that I am the one doing it."

The Wizard stilled, and for the first time, he exchanged a glance with Dainhurst, a silent conversation held in the space of a breath.

The Wizard sighed.

"I am going to tell you something, Galinda, something only a handful of people in all of Oz know. But you must swear to keep this secret. Not even your sister can know."

A secret? She had always been good at keeping those, except when they were her own.

"I swear."

The Wizard's gaze darkened with an air of solemnity.

"Life is a show, Galinda. A grand performance. Each of us plays a role— some in the spotlight, some behind the curtain. But every role is vital. Each equally important in this big story we are living."

Galinda nodded, entranced, hanging onto every word.

"The truth is… I don't have magic."

The room seemed to contract.

Galinda's breath caught in her throat. Of all the revelations she had braced for, *this* was not among them.

"You don't?" she whispered. "Not at all?"

"No," the Wizard said simply. "I am just a man. A man trying to do the right thing."

"But… you're *the* Wizard of Oz."

"It takes a whole team to paint this picture, Galinda, and that is what I want you to be. A team player."

"But… people have *seen* you perform magic."

"I put on a show. We live in simple times, Galinda. Show them sleight of hand and they'll see sorcery. Show them sorcery and they'll see a god."

It hit Galinda like a ton of yellow bricks. Mz. Everburn was right on her assessment all those years ago.

The Wizard was a *Showman.*

He had no real power, only the illusion of it.

"I hope you understand," the Wizard said. "And that you do not think less of me."

Galinda thought carefully before she answered.

"I don't," she said at last. "You're just trying to do the right thing. You're taking responsibility for the collective good of the people."

The Wizard smiled, pleased. "Precisely. So, you understand why I need you. Becoz I would not be where I am, would not have the power to keep Oz safe, without those behind the curtain—the ones who help me put on the show, who keep the people united under the banner of the *Wizard of Oz.* People like your father." He

144

gestured towards Dainhurst. "Quadling Country is one of the pieces left in fully uniting all four corners of Oz. And we *cannot* do it without you."

Galinda exhaled, feeling the weight of expectation settle upon her shoulders.

"Will you help us?" the Wizard pressed gently. "I will even grant you special admission to my university when you're of age."

Oz University? It was too great an opportunity to refuse.

She straightened, lifted her chin, and nodded. "Yes," she said, the word a stone dropping into water. "I will help you."

The Wizard clapped his hands together, beaming. "Bravo!"

Galinda blinked. *Bravo?* What an odd thing to say. Perhaps it was a phrase from wherever he had come from, some distant land across the sky.

Dainhurst straightened, stepping forward as though to dismiss the court. "The Wizard must be going now."

The Wizard rose.

"It was a pleasure, Galinda. I shall keep your name in mind."

He turned to leave, but Galinda found herself rising to her feet.

"Please, wait!"

The Wizard paused, glancing back.

"May I know your name?" she asked.

The Wizard laughed. "The Wizard of Oz?"

"No," Galinda said. "Your real name. Everyone has one."

He hesitated.

Then, with a breath, he seemed to reach deep into his past, retrieving something long buried.

At last, he spoke.

"Oscar," he said. "Oscar Diggs."

Galinda rolled the name over in her mind, committing it to memory.

"Oscar Diggs," she repeated. "I'll keep it in mind."

The Wizard's smile returned, this time smaller, softer. "Just keep it our little secret."

And then he was gone, his scent lingering in the room like a spell half-cast.

Galinda stood frozen for a moment before darting to her room. Still reeling, she peered out the window, just in time to catch sight of the Wizard's carriage rolling away. A breathtaking masterpiece of emerald and gold, more splendid than anything she had ever seen. Even Dainhurst, with all his wealth, could not match its grandeur.

Her *heart* pounded in her chest.

Then—

Bang!

Gisella burst in without knocking, demanding to know everything.

Galinda only smiled.

It was a secret.

And she wasn't telling.

CHAPTER 22

The Tunnel Under the Castle

Galinda had been playing and replaying her encounter with the Wizard, as though it were an old waltz she'd danced too many times, never quite finding the right step. She had agreed to something, something she did not want to do. And yet, it had been done. That was the problem with choices, wasn't it? Once made, they cemented themselves in the foundation of one's life, immovable as castle stone.

If she was not to be a Good Witch, if that ideal had soured on her tongue—what then? A governess? A scholar? A baker of pastries so delicate they collapsed under the weight of their own sweetness. All seemed inadequate substitutions. And yet, despite everything, she could not shake the peculiar certainty that she and the Wizard understood one another.

At least, when she turned eighteen, she would be eligible to attend the Wizard's University. Two Sun-Moons away. Two short orbits of the celestial bodies, and she would be free.

Gisella, ever the inquisitor, had attempted to pry the Wizard's words from her, but Galinda had remained resolute. It was a rare and remarkable thing to be entrusted with a secret, and if there was one thing Galinda prided herself on (besides her magic), it was her ability to be worthy of trust.

That morning, she had ensconced herself in her room, attempting to decipher the *Glamour Spell*. A frustrating endeavour, as she had barely scraped the surface. Mastery required patience, patience she did not have but had to enact if she was to receive what she wanted.

It was at precisely noon that a sound shattered her concentration—a sudden, metallic clang against stone echoed outside her door. Galinda jolted. The sound was unmistakable—something heavy had been dropped, deliberately, purposefully.

Galinda cautiously opened her door.

There, on the cold stone floor, lay an enormous key.

A key so aged and corroded that it seemed to have been unearthed from the bones of the castle itself. Beside it, a note.

The way it rested, so expectantly, sent a chill through her.

Galinda hesitated before picking it up, her fingers grazing the parchment as she unfolded it.

Take this key and go down the corridor in the West Wing of the Castle. Descend the spiral staircase to the lower level. Use the key.

Galinda glanced up and down the hallway, as if the sender might materialize from the shadows. But there was only silence.

Her first instinct was to ignore it and yet, her fingers curled around the key, its weight strangely reassuring.

Curiosity, that treacherous little beast, whispered in her ear.

Before she could talk herself out of it, she slipped on her pink slippers, tucked away her Ethereum, and shut the door behind her.

Galinda never went down the dark hallway. It was the only part of the castle where the light never touched. From the time she was born she had never seen anyone go down there, not even her father. She specifically remembered one time, she and Gisella tried to brave the west wing, but they fled the moment they heard the groaning floorboards and the eerie wail of the wind. Being back there caused such an uneasy feeling, like there was an entity waiting to feed on unsuspecting little girls.

Galinda, with her magic, was feeling braver than she did when she was a kindling. If anything tried to attack her she was prepared.

But every step she took made her **heart** beat faster and faster.

Now, standing at its threshold, she felt the weight of her own breathing. She couldn't understand why the note couldn't ask her to go to the North Wing, where everything was brighter and safer.

Galinda took a deep breath and conjured a small flame in her palm, its light flickering against the damp stone walls. The corridor was thick with the scent of abandonment, mildew, dust, the ghostly remnants of a once-lived-in space. Cobwebs dangled like abandoned lace, and the cracks in the stone yawned wide.

Her little feet were taking too long in getting past the dark corridor, so she decided to run.

They got her places quicker.

She reached the end of the corridor, meeting nothing but a door.

So she pushed it open.

Beyond it, a spiral staircase stretched downward like a coiled serpent, disappearing into the depths below.

Just as the note had promised.

Galinda peered over the edge. It looked like it was leading to *Hel*.

But there was only one way now.

Down.

She stepped onto the first stair.

Then the second.

And the third.

BEFORE

The staircase wound in tight circles, and after several revolutions, dizziness began to gnaw at the edges of her mind. She steadied herself against the stone wall, pressing forward until—at last her slippered feet met level ground.

When she looked back up, the main castle might as well have been the heavens, just based on how high it was.

Before her stood another door.

A large wooden door. *Rich,* **Expensive** *oak,* its keyhole waiting.

She exhaled sharply.

Inserted the key.

Turned it.

The door groaned as it swung open.

And then—

The stench.

A vile, putrid assault, sharp and sickly, like something long dead and unwilling to admit it.

Galinda stumbled back, her hands flying to her nose, her body recoiling on instinct.

She hesitated only a moment before forcing herself forward.

Somewhere, deep within the darkness—

A sound.

The sound came first. Low, indistinct. A murmur of voices, a whisper of breath, the sound of too many bodies pressed together in the stale dark.

Someone was inside.

Galinda crept forward, one hand pinching her nose, the other clutching a flickering firelight. The glow trembled as much as she did, casting long, quivering shadows along the damp stone walls, stretching and twisting as though reluctant to reveal their secret.

The light illuminated them.

Galinda's **heart** plummeted.

People.

Dozens. No, hundreds.

Huddled together, their bodies curled inward, shielding themselves from a world that had already turned its back on them. Women, men, children—hollow-eyed and gaunt, their clothes hanging from them like loose skin.

A woman, frail as paper, lifted her face toward her.

"Please... water," she whispered, her voice so brittle it cracked.

Another, emboldened by the sight of her fine dress, her polished slippers, her unfamiliarity, cried out. "Please, don't kill us! We're innocent!"

"We need food! Please, we're starving!"

The words broke over her like a tidal wave, but she could not yet comprehend them.

148

Who were these people? What were they doing in the tunnel beneath the castle?

The space reeked of suffering. It was a dungeon, that much was clear—though unlike any she had imagined. Dungeons were places for criminals, for traitors to the Wizard. If they were indeed criminals, they would've been sent to the Ozian Forest Camp. Not kept in the castle dungeon.

But these people, thin, trembling, barefoot, looked more like lost children than captives of the state.

Galinda stepped forward and promptly stumbled over something, her own hesitation, most likely, though there were so many things on the ground it could have been anything. She righted herself, swallowed her disbelief, and forced out words:

"Who are you?" she asked. "How did you get here?"

A little boy, his ribs protruding like the strings of a broken harp, gazed up at her with dull, desperate eyes. His eyes, too big for his hollow face.

"Have you come to save us?"

"Save you?" she echoed. "What is happening here? And—" she nearly gagged— "Guh! What is that smell?"

As she stepped further in, the firelight unveiled the horrors she had only half-seen before: the filth-crusted stone, the faeces and urine pooling in corners, the long, jagged fingernail scratches etched into the walls as if someone, many someones, had tried, futilely, to claw their way free.

The door, so thick and soundproof, had sealed these people inside like tombstones trapping the dead.

"Someone, *answer* me," she demanded. "Who are you?"

A woman in the back flinched. "Are you here to kill us?"

"What?" Galinda reeled. "No!"

A man, gaunt but still stubbornly defiant, scoffed from the shadows.

"Don't speak to her," he warned the others. "She's one of them."

Galinda felt an odd twist in her stomach.

"One of who?"

The man exhaled sharply, as if her ignorance disgusted him.

"We were kidnapped. Taken in the night. Brought here. We don't know by whom."

"Then why are you here?" she asked. "Did you—did you *do* something?"

A murmur rippled through them.

"No," A young girl answered, her voice quiet but clear. "They *think* we're witches."

The word turned the air thick, as though the tunnel had filled with smoke.

Galinda took a step back. "What?"

"We *told* them we weren't," another woman said. "But they don't believe us."

"Can you set us free?" a voice asked. A desperate voice. A voice full of hope.

Galinda turned, stepping toward the entrance where she could breathe. Where she could *think*.

She looked back.

"A-All of you?" she stammered.

"Yes," they said in unison.

"Oh, Oz," she whispered.

It made sense now.

These were the missing people. The ones accused of witchcraft. The ones *she* had helped condemn, however unknowingly. The ones suffering because of her.

Galinda's fingers clenched around the key in her palm. Her breath came shallow.

This—this could not be the work of Dainhurst. He wouldn't—would he?

"Are you helping us?" someone asked, voice trembling.

Galinda said nothing.

Then— "Yes," she said, though she did not yet know how.

"I'll be back," she promised.

A collective cry rose. "Please, don't go!"

"Please!"

Galinda raised a hand to quiet them. "I *will* help you," she said, voice steadier now. "But you must stay calm. And *no one* can know I was here."

She turned and, with shaking hands, locked the door once more.

Only when she reached the base of the stairs did she let herself break.

Tears welled, her throat tightened, and suddenly she couldn't breathe—not past the crushing weight of it all. She sank onto the steps, her whole body trembling.

She forced herself up. *Later.* She would grieve later.

Right now, she needed to think.

Surely, they had not been brought through the main entrance. The castle staff would have noticed. That meant there was another way in. Another way out.

Galinda ran her fingers along the tunnel walls, searching—searching—

Nothing.

Nothing.

And then—

A hollow spot.

Her pulse quickened. She pressed her ear to the wall.

A difference in sound. A space beyond.

She braced herself and pushed.

The wall did not budge.

She needed to put the fire out in order to use both of her hands and all her strength to try and push it open.

She ceased the firelight and pushed the wall with both hands. With all her might

This time, it shifted.

Stone scraped against stone. And then—light.

A sliver at first, then a flood as the wall slid open.

Galinda stepped through, blinking against the sudden brightness.

She was outside.

To her left, the maid's quarters.

To her right, the woods.

That's how they got in.

She *had* found a way out.

Galinda ran back through the tunnel.

When she threw open the door, they all flinched.

"I found a way," she breathed.

A stunned silence. Then movement, a stampede toward the door.

"Wait!" she cried. "Not yet!"

A boy, no younger than herself, frowned. "Why?"

"If you leave now, they'll see you. You'll be *killed*. I'll come back at sundown. Then, it'll be safe."

Mistrust lingered in their eyes.

"You're lying," someone accused. "You're toying with us."

Galinda held out the key. "Then take this. If you don't trust me, keep it."

A woman, weary but wise, placed a hand over Galinda's and gently pushed it away.

"We trust you," she said.

It was the first time Galinda felt worthy of it.

She nodded. Locked the door.

Galinda raced up the stairs as quickly as she could and entered her bedroom. She hid the key under her pillow, and returned to the **Glamour Spell,** searching for anything that could help.

She couldn't be at ease.

Not while people were rotting in the tunnel under the castle.

CHAPTER 23

Twisting Free

Galinda waited in her chambers, an idle thing, as the afternoon unravelled into its golden diminuendo. The light marked its slow surrender of day, and with it, the countdown of her small rebellion. She had measured the *HourZ* by slanted sunbeams, calculating just how long before she could unfasten the locks, break the mold, let the captives scatter into the dark like marbles on a tilted floor.

Dusk had come, and she had outgrown her waiting. This time, she exchanged her soft, impractical pink slippers for real shoes, the kind with buckles and purpose. She fastened her robe, tied her hair into a ponytail, steeled herself.

Under her pillow lay the key. A cliché, really, but effective, nonetheless. With it clutched in hand, she inhaled deeply, and—just as she stepped forward—froze.

Dainhurst.

On other side of the door, his hand poised mid-air, about to knock.

He never knocked.

His eyes flicked over her—her robe, her buckled shoes—taking in the shift in attire.

"Are you going somewhere?"

Galinda's mind raced. She needed an answer—something believable.

"I just needed fresh air."

Dainhurst frowned.

"At this hour? You know I don't like you outside after dusk."

"Yes, I know, Father," she said lightly. "I just needed to think."

Dainhurst studied her for a moment before offering, "Do you want me to come with you?"

"No, Father, I'm sixteen," she retorted.

He chuckled, shaking his head. "Alright, alright."

Galinda took a breath. "Did you need something?"

Dainhurst's eyes glinted, the vestiges of an old cunning dulled by recent successes. "As a matter of fact, humbug, I did. But I'll wait till your return."

Galinda blinked.

Humbug? It was *Hummingbug!* And Zelena was the only one that called her that.

She left through the front door, but only in pretence. She couldn't go to the direction of the West Wing; her operation would be destroyed before she even got the chance to enforce it.

As soon as the castle doors were closed, she ran around it to the back of the castle. The wind tossed her hair like leaves in a twister as she sprinted around the enormous castle.

At last, she reached the back.

The secret tunnel.

Galinda scanned her environment to ensure it was safe to proceed. The guards were on the other side of the castle. She had some time until their patrol brought them to her side of the castle. The castle was under constant surveillance you see, in case munchkin tricksters wanted to get revenge on Dainhurst for something he did and also because he hated little people so much, he called them "vermin pretending to be human." However, he mostly wanted protection in case northern Gillikin terrorists decided to invade a successful and *Sophisticated* man like he was. He knew how criminals worked, and he was going to beat them to the punch. Therefore, if Galinda's plan to free the captives was going to work, they had to leave—now.

Galinda tapped the walls once more; with careful precision, she pushed. The wall gave way with a whisper. She opened the dungeon door, slowly as possible. The door exhaled open with a sigh of dust and age. Then, voices, whispers like moth wings.

"What did I tell you? I told you she would come back."

Nearly a cheer, nearly a cacophony, but she hushed them with a raised hand.

"Shh, please be quiet." She commanded, her voice steadier than she felt. "We have to move quickly. Form a line."

They obeyed. Strange, how easily they followed her lead.

She left the tunnel door slightly ajar, just in case she miscalculated the guards' patrol.

"Please don't talk. Stay silent and walk towards that wall." she said pointing to the exit.

As the prisoners filtered past and exited their cage. A woman leaned close, eyes hollow but bright, whispered, "You have such a good *heart*. Thank you."

How strange to be praised for an action untethered to performance, Galinda thought.

A fire lit within her.

Galinda moved to the front of the line.

"There are too many of you to move as one," she instructed. "Find your loved ones and pair up. When I open this wall, you must run with all the energy that you have. Stay silent and do not stop."

A young boy's voice wavered. "But where do we go?"

"The forest is close," she said. Moving swiftly, she grabbed torches from the walls, lighting each with her firelight. She handed them out. "Run. Scatter. If some of you don't make it, at least others will. Leave Quadling Country. Tonight."

They nodded and whispered their thanks.

Galinda closed her eyes, murmured a silent prayer, and nudged the wall open. The flood began.

A sea of people spilled into the night, feet pounding against the earth, disappearing into the darkness. Mothers clutching babies. Children gripping hands. Men running with all they had left.

And then, silence.

Galinda was alone.

Alone with the ghosts of the prisoners that died before she knew of their existence.

Galinda craned her neck around the stone corner, **heart** pounding in her throat, watching through the pastures and into the forest. A hundred bodies had scuttled like mice through the fields, but now, at last, they were something else entirely, figures upright and swift, ablaze with newfound life. Alive. And free.

Half had vanished into the forest, torches flickering like will-o'-the-wisps in the thickening night. But the other half, too slow, too uncertain, remained visible. Hesitation was the traitor of the desperate.

◇

Then—a voice.

"Hey! What is that?"

Galinda sucked in a breath, flattened herself against the tunnel wall, ear pressed to the cold stone.

"Are those—are those people?" a guard asked, voice thick with the kind of incredulity only privilege affords.

"Yes! Sound the alarms!"

The world lurched. A metallic screech tore through the air. The horn's wail splitting the night.

The guards began to stir like hornets from a nest, charging forward, swords and torches held high. Some on foot. Others on horseback, hooves pounding against the dirt like a war drum.

Galinda's lungs seized.

She ran. A breathless ascent up the coiled stairs, emerging into the shadowed corridors of the West Wing. She tore past portraits of ancestors who had all, in their way, made decisions they regretted. Or perhaps, more insidiously, ones they did not.

Dainhurst, Esmelda, and Gisella were already downstairs, gathered outside, while chaos spread like wildfire across the castle grounds.

At the hall's high windows, she searched for the scene below. If the escapees faltered she *must* intervene. But magic had its limits, a fact Galinda had learned in the way children learn about gravity: by falling. There was distance to consider. Reach. The intangible physics of spellwork—like invisible waves weakening over distance. No spell she knew could reach that far.

Panic crawled into her skull. She struck the sides of her head with the flats of her hands, as if she might jar loose some forgotten lesson, some incantation that stretched further than her own feeble grasp. But nothing.

Then she had an idea.

Galinda dashed to her bedroom, yanked The Ethereum from its resting place, and flung it onto her bed. Hovering her hands over its pages, she whispered a frantic plea:

"Help me," she murmured, barely aware of the words leaving her lips. "Please."

The book stirred. Pages fluttered, rifling through spells as if alive. Then, suddenly—stillness.

The Twister Spell.

Galinda read the inscription. Her attempts at trying to decipher the **Glamour Spell** was training her **brain** in reading other spells. She now had another spell under her belt.

A warning was written beneath it, but the language was unfamiliar, foreign letters, curling and unreadable. But the spell itself, *that* she could read. And *that* was all that mattered.

Galinda pressed the words to memory and ran back to the window.

She raised her hands. The air thickened, the wind, a mere participant in the night, was now under her command.

Ventus Aeor dominari, Orbis Tempest Aetherium!

The gale shifted. Where the wind had once nudged gently from the east, now it howled from the west. The guards faltered, struggling against the force. But it wasn't enough. Not fast enough.

Galinda chanted again. And again.

A terrible mistake.

The wind didn't merely *shift* this time. It roared. The wind thickened into a vortex. What she had summoned was no simple gust—it was a storm. The air writhed, twisting upon itself until it took shape—a churning column of destruction.

A tornado.

She had wanted a distraction. Instead, she had unleashed chaos.

The ground came alive with destruction. Horses, men—screams drowned by the sheer force of the storm. One by one, they were plucked from the ground, flung into the swirling abyss like ragdolls. A guard. Another. Another.

It was working. But it was also *wrong.*

"Enough," she commanded, but the storm did not yield.

"Cease!" she shouted. Nothing.

A sickening dread settled in her stomach. This was something else. Something old, something ravenous. It had taken her command and *exceeded* it. She had read the spell, but she had not learned how to undo it.

It became very clear to Galinda rather quickly, that this was a potent spell because she was starting to feel lightheaded.

She tried again. Words, pleas, counter-spells; all lost in the storm's hungry wail.

The tornado swelled, twisted free across the castle grounds, expanding outward into the rest of Quadling Country.

In trying to save hundreds, she might have doomed thousands.

Lives wrenched away by her own hands.

Galinda felt sick.

Her vision blurred, whether from the effort of the spell or the sheer weight of what she had done. She thought of the innocent lives beyond the castle, the farmers, families, children. Would the twister stop? Would it fade? Would it take more than it already had?

She looked at the grounds once more. Ruin. Smoke, dust, and debris filled the air. The once-groomed gardens, now mangled, shredded. The maid's quarters—a splintered ruin. The farm—cattle torn from the earth like plucked petals.

But the prisoners. They were gone. And they had not been caught in the storm. *Small mercies,* she thought, and then immediately hated herself for it.

Screams echoed from inside the castle and beyond, faint cries rising from the distant villages. Galinda's hands trembled at her sides.

"Galinda!"

Dainhurst's voice snapped her out of her daze.

She turned and ran, descending the stairs on shaky legs. When she reached the hall, Dainhurst caught her by the shoulders, steadying her.

"Are you hurt?"

"Yes—no—I don't know."

His gaze searched her. "Why didn't you come downstairs when the storm started?"

"I—I didn't know what to do."

He turned, giving orders to the head guard. The castle was in upheaval. Esmelda issued orders to the maids—blankets, water, supplies—preparing for a long night in the grand hall. Guards whispered amongst themselves.

Gisella, however, did nothing.

She *watched.*

Galinda pretended not to notice, but it was no use. Gisella, curious as ever, closed the space between them in an instant, grabbing Galinda's wrist and dragging her into the kitchen.

"Did you do that?"

Galinda felt the question like a blade to the ribs.

"Do what?" she murmured.

Gisella narrowed her eyes. "The *twister.* Was that you?"

"No?"

Gisella scoffed. "You're lying."

Galinda exhaled, defeated. "Fine. Yes. But don't say anything."

Silence.

Gisella stared, as if trying to reconcile the impossible with the truth before her.

"Your powers… are they *growing?*"

"I think so."

"Woz. Why couldn't you stop it?"

Galinda said nothing. What could she say? That she had been *careless?* That in trying to save a handful of people, she may have doomed more?

Gisella turned, her mind already at work unravelling the implications.

But then—

Galinda glanced over. Dainhurst was still speaking with the head guard, and from his expression, it didn't look like he was concerned about the twister, the guards, the horses, or anything that fell victim to it. The twister was out of the Fairmoor castle grounds rather quickly and made its way elsewhere, so it didn't bother him because it wasn't his problem anymore. What he wanted to know was something more sinister. Where his captives were and if they retrieved them.

Galinda couldn't hear what Dainhurst was saying to them, but she knew. There was something in her intuition that told her that he was responsible for the prisoners. She knew it. Undeniably.

Dainhurst was done with his meeting.

"Girls, in here," Dainhurst's voice called.

Esmelda, Gisella, and Galinda stepped forward.

"There have been… developments," he said. "I can't discuss them yet, but everything is under control. For now, we'll sleep in the grand hall. Guards will keep watch.

"Are we in danger?" Gisella asked.

"No, just precautions. The twister is gone. There's nothing to worry about."

But Galinda knew better.

As Dainhurst led them upstairs, he veered off into his study. Galinda watched him go.

Her ***heart*** heavy.

She had unleashed something terrible tonight.

And she couldn't take it back.

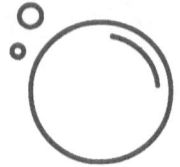

CHAPTER 24

Ultimatum

T he Fairmoors stirred awake in the grand hall, the weight of the previous night's chaos pressing down on them. Morning had long passed, and it was now well into Morn-Mid Oz'Clock, an unseemly hour for a family so accustomed to order and propriety.

Dainhurst was conspicuously absent from the groggy tableau, but the heavy thud of the study's door echoed through the castle, signalling his return. Clad in his nightgown, a rare and unsettling sight for anyone but Esmelda—he strode in, his usual composure frayed at the edges. Things were different. Things were changing.

Rather than retreat to the dining room, Dainhurst waved for breakfast to be brought to the grand hall. A minor breach of decorum, but it spoke volumes. He was too depleted to maintain even the simplest charade of dignity. He collapsed into a cushioned chair, crossing his legs with an impatient bounce, fingers drumming against his knee in an uncharacteristic display of agitation.

A maid, stationed exclusively for Esmelda's morning routine, stood at attention, waiting with the *Daily Oz NewZPapr*. Typically, Dainhurst had little use for such trivialities. He knew when things were happening and how they happened before any reporter did. Sometimes, before they even occurred.

But today was different.

Without ceremony, he snatched the *NewZPapr*, nearly crumpling it in his haste, flipping past the front page with violent disregard.

As the paper spread wide in his hands, Galinda caught sight of the bold, glaring headline:

TWISTER TERRORIZES OZ: munchkin STATE CAPITAL IN RUINS — MYSTERIOUS HEROINE HALTS CYCLONE CATASTROPHE

She gasped—a reflexive sound, unbidden but unmistakable.

Dainhurst's eyes, dark above the edge of the paper, flickered toward her. Others in the room, stirred by the sound, turned as well, but Galinda shrank under their gaze. The moment passed. The murmuring silence of morning reclaimed its space.

With an exasperated sigh, Dainhurst flung the *NewZPapr* toward Esmelda. It fluttered in the air before landing delicately in her lap. Whatever he had been looking for, it was not there.

Sinking back into his chair, arms crossed, his expression contorted into something almost childish, a boy denied a trip to the Emerald City, sulking in his disappointment.

The heavy stillness was broken by the arrival of a guard, appearing in the doorway like a ghost summoned by Dainhurst's restless energy.

Dainhurst was on his feet instantly and walked to the guard standing by the door and asked. "Any news?"

Galinda tilted her head, ears attuned.

The guard hesitated, then delivered his report. "No, sir. Even with the assistance of the Southern Ozian Guard, there's no trace of them in Quadling Country."

Galinda's lips twitched, betraying the first flickers of a smirk. She was grinning like a mischievous munchkin—two pieces of good news in one morning. Though she had not been the one to quell the storm she had summoned, she found satisfaction in knowing that someone had. And the prisoners, the ones she had freed, had evaded capture.

Dainhurst scoffed, dismissing the guard with a flick of his wrist. But as he turned back into the hall, his gaze landed on Galinda, still brimming with quiet, defiant satisfaction.

His instincts were keen; she had inherited them, after all.

"What are you smiling about?"

"Nothing," she replied, too quickly.

"You're lying."

Something unfurled in her chest. A dare. A need to challenge him.

"Alright, *Father.*" The title dripped from her tongue like something foreign, something spoiled. "Why were there prisoners under the castle? Is that why you forbade us from going there all this time?"

Dainhurst was flabbergasted.

Esmelda's eyes were wide open as she looked at Dainhurst's reaction. Gisella, in shock, cupped her mouth, half yawning. The maids, well-versed in the rhythms of family scandal, melted from the room, their retreat swift and silent.

Dainhurst's voice struck like a thunderclap. "Such *insolence!* How dare you speak to your father this way?"

Galinda exhaled, slow and measured.

"You call yourself my father," she said, "yet I doubt someone as *cruel* and *wicked* as you could ever have begotten me."

He lunged.

But Galinda did not flinch.

With a flick of her wrist, a burst of firelight flared between them, its heat licking at the air as a warning. Dainhurst stumbled back.

She let her words settle.

"Now, that I know that you were responsible, I will not participate in your crusade for power, power you don't deserve. You can forget about me helping make Gisella the 'Good Witch.'"

Gisella shot up from her chair, face red with rage. "You *can't* do this! It's not fair!"

"Shut up, Gisella," Esmelda snapped.

And just like that, Gisella deflated, collapsing back into her seat, her indignation swallowed whole.

Dainhurst stood rigid, fists clenched at his sides, his silence louder than his fury.

Esmelda stepped in, her voice a thin veneer of maternal reproach. "Don't you *ever* speak to your father that way," she said, measured and precise. "With such vile accusations. Have you forgotten his sacrifice to spare your life?"

"Well," Galinda's voice sharp as shattered glass, "perhaps he should have let me die, instead of having hundreds, if not thousands, slaughtered at my expense. Innocent people. Mothers and their children. Husbands. Fathers. Brothers. Sisters. Aunts—"

"Stop *right there*!" Esmelda's voice rung in the air like metal on stone, reverberating through the grand hall. "And how, exactly, do you know it was your father's doing?"

"You're right, *you* probably helped him. And besides—his castle, his dungeon, his sins, are they not?"

Gisella sat rigid, watching in wordless confusion. As unsightly as Galinda was, she had never seen her sister look so *strong*. Watching her for the first time, *stand*. Alone, against wolves with gilded fangs.

Dainhurst's hand landed lightly on Esmelda's shoulder, a calculated touch meant to cool a fire before it raged.

"Galinda, it wasn't me."

He bowed his head slightly, as if the weight of it truly pained him. "It was *Magnum*," he said, enunciating the name with deliberate slowness. "He had these people kidnapped and when I found out I campaigned to bring them here, just so I could keep them safe."

"You're a liar!" Galinda shouted, her voice catching.

"I would never lie to you, humbug. I was in the process of having them resituated. I just needed time," he paused. "I assume you let them go?"

Galinda squared her shoulders, lifting her chin. "Yes."

Dainhurst sighed, shaking his head in what might have been admiration, might have been something else entirely. "You are *so* brave, my girl. You did what I could not. In a *single* night."

He took a step forward, then another, slowly, carefully, as though approaching something fragile and wild, something that might bolt at any moment.

"I *told* Magnum it was wrong, but he wouldn't listen," he said, voice softer now. "You must believe me, I planned to set them free myself. I just needed time."

Galinda had been so certain, but was she wrong? The prisoners hadn't known who had orchestrated their capture. *Could* it truly have been Magnum?

But no. No—something still didn't fit.

"If that's true, why were you so upset when the guard couldn't find them in Quadling Country?"

"Ah. *That* was a misunderstanding. If they are found by the witch hunters, terrible things could happen and this time they will not be put in a dungeon. I am scared for them."

Dainhurst was now close enough to grip her. And then, in a whisper:

"Do you *know* where they are?"

"No. And even if I did, I would never tell you."

Dainhurst exhaled, nodding. "Good. I hope they are safe. And I am *glad* you freed them, my *good* and *wonderful* girl."

He smiled. A fatherly smile, warm as firelight. And she, traitorous girl that she was, could not help but return it.

In that moment Galinda chose to believe her father.

"So," Dainhurst said lightly, "that sudden twister, during the escape—that was *you?*"

"Yes."

"Hmm."

And just like that, he lunged. His hands found her sides, he began to tickle Galinda, and, in an instant, she was laughing, gasping, writhing as his fingers found the places they had known only on Gisella when she was younger.

"I hope that you aren't dead set on refusing to help us with Gisella."

"Fine, I'll help you, but only if you promise me—no more prisoners."

Dainhurst stilled.

Ah. *An ultimatum.*

He was familiar with it. He was the one that usually gave them, oh how alike they were.

For a moment, he considered. If he was honest with himself (and he often was, in the private chambers of his mind), what use was there in imprisoning those accused of sorcery, when he planned to put *Gisella*, as a known magic-wielder, before the world as the "Good Witch"?

It would be blatantly... *hypocritical.*

And that, above all else, was *dangerous for him and his family's image.*

"Deal."

Galinda extended her hand, and he took it, shaking firmly. "Then I'll be happy to help you."

"That's my girl."

It was time for breakfast. Everything had calmed down and it looked like everybody was in a good spirits. Especially Gisella, who was beaming as the Fairmoors sat on the floor and ate in bliss. The sky was clear and blue, the sun seeping through the windows and the gust of fresh air that entered through the opened shutters.

Dainhurst couldn't resist the urge of attending to business.

"Galinda, you're clever." A casual compliment, wrapped in a request. "What do you think we should do about the twister incident?"

Gisella, overeager, piped in: "What do you *mean*, what should we do?"

"Be quiet, Gisella. I asked *Galinda*."

Gisella frowned, turning her face to the other direction, retreating into safety and finishing her *Butterbean Scone*.

Galinda, swallowing a mouthful of Tangerine-Tonic, considered. "Well, I saw on the paper that the munchkinland was left in ruin by the twister. What if, Gisella's *first assignment* was to go help? That's sure to bring credibility to her being the 'good witch.'"

Dainhurst clapped. "You are so right! Genius! Call the maid to prepare your clothes."

"No." Galinda tapped her fingers against her lips. "I'll do it. I'll magic her attire. This is her *debut*. There will be reporters. She needs to make a *statement*."

She met her father's gaze. "Perception is *everything*."

Dainhurst smiled. A rare smile, one even Gisella had not received. And Gisella, *she noticed.*

"Anything else?" Dainhurst asked, ever the pupil to her growing expertise.

Galinda tilted her head.

"Well, the paper said that twister was stopped by a mysterious heroine in munchkinland. What if we say that it was Gisella that stopped it and if the mysterious woman tries to go public and take credit for it, we could pay her to be quiet."

"Perfect." Dainhurst nodded. "And if she's from munchkinland, odds are she's poor. It wouldn't cost much."

He stood, pushing his plate away. "Galinda, follow me."

The two Fairmoors, like peas in a pod both entered Dainhurst's study, the door shutting behind. Leaving Esmelda and Gisella to eat their breakfast completely alone.

In his study he pulled out a notebook and a Silverwinkle pen and began scribbling on it.

Dainhurst slid the paper closer to Galinda who was sitting in front of him and asked, "Will that be enough?"

Galinda looked down at the paper, her eyes widening at the large sum of numbers written in *Ozian gold.*

Z *1~000~000 gld*

"Is this for me?" she asked confused.

"Yes."

"What for?"

Dainhurst pressed his palms together and leaned forward on his *authentic* oak desk. "I want to give you a job. I know you're sixteen and this is far more than the allowance I give you."

"This is even more than the allowance you give Gisella," Galinda laughed. "But what job are you thinking about?"

"Originally, I thought we only needed you for your magic, but you've proven useful in other areas. You have a clear understanding of perception and how it works, and I don't think my little project can go as far as it can without you."

Galinda was elated. She really was useful for once. The Wizard was right, working behind the scenes wasn't utterly miserable as she presumed.

"Oh, thank you father. I would've done it for free though. We're family."

"I know you would've Galinda, that is why I'm offering it to you."

"Well, thank you father."

. "Hey, humbug, it's the least I can do."

The room was now silent and Dainhurst was toying with his blonde moustache, in deep thought which was Galinda's cue to leave his study. As Galinda opened the door, he snapped out of his daze just in time and said, "Galinda, get dressed right now and tell your sister to do the same. We're going to munchkinland today."

As the study door closed behind her, Galinda felt the first tremor of something inevitable. munchkinland wouldn't know what *hit* it.

CHAPTER 25

munchkinland

The magical Fairmoor conjured a dazzling emerald gown for Gisella, its fabric shimmering like liquid jewels. As the light caught its surface, it rippled with brilliance, as if raindrops cascaded down her body in a delicate dance of reflection. Gisella, not one to leave perfection incomplete, paired it with her spiky crystal necklace and her most treasured *Silver Slippers*. She was, in all respects, ready for her grand entrance.

Galinda, by contrast, had dressed as she always did—neatly, properly, no embellishment of grandeur, with no intention of being seen. That was the point, after all.

The Fairmoors, Galinda, Gisella, and Dainhurst, boarded their carriage and set off on the long journey to munchkinland. For Galinda, this marked a first. She had never left the South of Oz, though she had read much about the other states, their landmarks, their customs, the food, the peculiar affectations of their citizens. The prospect thrilled her. Today, at last, she would scratch one name off her list of places to see.

The circumstances, however, were less than ideal. This journey was not for leisure but for reparations, an act of mending, necessitated by her own unfortunate lapse in judgment. And yet, even a forced departure from Quadling Country was, in its own way, an adventure.

The carriages took the *Pryzm Road* to hasten the journey, a choice that irritated Galinda. She had longed to absorb the unfamiliar sights, to witness the landscapes that changed from one region to another. Instead, the shortcut robbed her of such delights. Even so, as they neared munchkinland, the world outside began to shift in ways she could scarcely believe. The trees grew shorter, the colours of the fields sharpened unnaturally, and the creatures—creatures she had only seen in books—ostriches with their impossibly long legs, towering giraffes, sturdy goats, and, unless her eyes deceived her, a singing hound.

The world and everything in it felt new.

Despite the expedited route on the *Pryzm Road*, the journey still took five *HourZ*. When at last they arrived, Galinda pressed herself against the carriage window, her eyes widening as munchkinland unfolded before her. Everything was miniature—houses, taverns, schools, shops—each structure seemingly built on a smaller scale. But then she saw the people.

The citizens of munchkinland were even smaller than their surroundings. Galinda had seen illustrations of them in her books, depictions created by Quadling Country historians and artists. The images had been cruel—short, stubby figures with grotesque features: malicious grins, oversized ears, bulbous noses, gnarled nails. But now, seeing them in person, she realized how wildly inaccurate those portrayals had been. The munchkins were simply... *people*. Shorter than most, yes, but otherwise no different from anyone else.

Dainhurst, who conducted much of his business in munchkinland, had often described them as vermin. Was that exaggeration, then? Or merely the sort of prejudice men of industry indulged in when speaking of those they wished to control?

Still, not all the inhabitants fit the description. Here and there, among the crowds, Galinda spotted people of ordinary height. This was a surprise, one of many, she suspected, that munchkinland had in store for her.

The carriage trundled forward, she turned her gaze toward the horizon, eager to see the damage left in the wake of her ill-conceived twister spell. But from their current vantage point, everything appeared untouched. The fields still bore their heavy-headed crops, the tulips; every colour of the rainbow remained standing, their colours unmarred. The thatched-roof huts sat firmly upon their little homes, and the people—vermin or not—looked rather cheerful.

How could this be? Had the storm not reached this part of the state?

She turned to Dainhurst, who sat immersed in business papers, idly twirling his moustache.

"Father, how large is munchkinland? I see no sign of damage."

Dainhurst lowered his glasses just enough to regard her. "Oh, quite large, all things considered. Far too much land for such little people, if you ask me. If I had my way, we'd clear some of this wasted space for factories. But no, they're an independent lot. Stubborn, really. Still, the capital, that's where the real damage is."

Galinda considered this. If the capital lay at the **heart** of the land, and the twister had struck there, then why did this part of munchkinland remain pristine? She puzzled over it for a moment before realizing: the *Pryzm Road* had brought them in from a different direction. They had circled behind the storm's path, approaching the damage from the outside in.

She leaned back in her seat, waiting. The carriage sped along, and as it did, the landscape changed slowly. The once-picturesque scenery grew worn, unravelling at the edges. The further they travelled, the more ruinous it became.

In front of her, Gisella slept, her head lolling against the carriage wall, her breath slow and even. It was, after all, an important day—one in which she would offer help, rebuild what had been lost, restore order where chaos had taken hold. And yet she slept through it, as if she had not already indulged in a full night's rest. She had woken at Morn-Mid Oz' Clock for Oz's sake. *How much sleep did one girl need?*

The carriage remained silent until the coachman finally announced, "Sire, we are nearly there!"

At once, Gisella stirred, as if she instinctively knew it was time to rise.

Dainhurst straightened in his seat, pushing his papers aside. He leaned out the window and surveyed their surroundings before instructing the coachman, "Find a place to halt. Somewhere discreet. A corner where we won't be seen," he said.

"O-okay."

His confusion was evident, but he had long learned never to question Dainhurst.

Galinda, equally perplexed, turned to her father. "Are we doing something else today?"

"Not exactly."

Dainhurst leaned into her, "Galinda, I've seen what you can do. You've reminded me how true the saying 'perception is everything' really is. I need you to create something for Gisella to arrive in. Something... grander. The Golden Eagle isn't enough. She must look like a goddess. You understand?"

Galinda pondered the request. What could she create that would leave an indelible impression? What would elevate Gisella beyond mere spectacle?

Then, inspiration struck.

Eureka!

"I've got it!" she exclaimed, her excitement bursting forth.

Gisella, wide awake, leaned forward eagerly. "What is it?"

Galinda grinned, a mischievous glint in her eyes. "I'll show you when we get there."

Gisella scoffed, glancing out the carriage window at the people she was supposed to help. To her, they were nothing more than clowns. She chuckled at the sight of the little figures bustling through the streets, their tiny limbs moving in rapid, almost comical strides. When she'd had her fill of amusement, she leaned back against the cushioned seat and idly examined her nails, twirling her silver ring between her fingers.

Dainhurst stuck to his papers and pens. Sealing some transaction, a deal made in the depths of a carriage seat. The empire never slept, nor did it pause for sentimentalities.

The carriage came to a slow, deliberate halt.

"We're here, sire," the footman announced, opening the carriage door. As protocol dictated, the footman swapped out the Fairmoors' shoes so as not to track the filth of munchkinland back to the rich, better, and superior soil of the Upper Uplands.

Gisella objected.

No, the silver slippers must stay. What was the point of an entrance if not to be seen? She had not endured this tedious journey merely to step into the world as a lesser version of herself. The silver must gleam. The world must see.

The carriage nestled behind a forest of fallen trees. A perfect, shadowed enclave. A space where secrets could breathe without interruption.

A Curtain.

Dainhurst led his daughters deeper into the thicket, Gisella trailing behind with a deliberate strut, her emerald gown billowing as she moved, her silver slippers falling in rhythmic contrast to the rugged terrain. She walked like a princess.

Technically, she was.

"Alright, Galinda," Dainhurst said, "what do you have in mind for Gisella's entrance?"

"Well," she said, "I was thinking… she should arrive by cloud."

"Cloud?" Gisella frowned, unimpressed.

But Galinda had learned long ago that the absurd was often a matter of execution. Mz. Everburn had once demonstrated a spell for summoning mist, but her efforts had been feeble, the result little more than a ghostly fog at her ankles. The spell had been abandoned, deemed too ambitious and too draining for her teacher to perform.

But Galinda was nothing if not ambitious and powerful.

She saw the doubt flicker in her family's eyes, but she did not dignify it with a response. Instead, she lifted her hands and began.

Her fingers curled, then unfurled, weaving invisible strands of magic. She murmured under her breath, each syllable a quiet command. Her eyes locked onto Gisella—unmoving, unblinking.

Gisella instinctively took a step back. There was something eerie about the way Galinda looked at her, the way the air thickened around her in response.

A whisper of cloud curled at Gisella's ankles.

Then more.

The mist gathered, thickening, swirling, shimmering—an unnatural mossy green with threads of deep emerald, rolling like a storm contained within itself.

Galinda ceased her murmuring, the magic taking its final shape. She exhaled.

"Gisella, get on," she instructed, her voice brooking no argument. "And stand firmly."

Gisella eyed the cloud with suspicion. "Are you insane? That's—it's a cloud."

Galinda did not repeat herself.

Dainhurst, ever the businessman, intervened. "Just do it. Or shall I have Galinda take your role?"

"No!" Gisella snapped, too quick, "Fine."

She lifted the hem of her emerald gown and hesitantly stepped onto the conjured platform.

It was soft. But firm.

Surprisingly firm.

Gisella stood upright, bracing for a wobble, but none came. It held her, solid as stone, but light as air.

"Perfect," Galinda murmured. "Hang on tight."

She raised her hands once more, and the cloud obeyed.

It lifted.

Higher.

Higher still.

Gisella gasped, grabbing at nothing, but the ascent was smooth, deliberate. After the initial panic subsided, she settled into it. The moment took shape, the poise returned to her shoulders, the confidence to her chin.

"You continue to amaze me, Galinda," Dainhurst remarked, watching the display unfold.

Galinda let the cloud descend just enough for Gisella to remain poised above them, waiting.

"Now," Dainhurst said, "when you make your entrance, all eyes will be on you. Treat them as you would fellow South Ozians. Smile. Be dazzling. It's what you do best."

Gisella nodded.

"And," Galinda added, "listen to them. Their concerns. If you need me, raise both hands, and I will know."

Another nod.

She was ready.

Galinda lifted her hands, and the cloud drifted forward, carrying Gisella towards the *heart* of the munchkin capital.

Gisella was ethereal in the sun's glow, the silver slippers glinted in the eyes of those below and her green dress made her look like she was the creator of all things green on the earth.

Gisella looked like a goddess. Just as they had planned.

Galinda and Dainhurst watched from below like spectators, they were seeing their plans form for the first time. In real time.

As Gisella floated to the crowd below, the people noticed.

One voice rang out first.

"Everyone, look!"

Then another.

"What is that?"

"Is that a person?"

Galinda and Dainhurst stepped out of their curtain and moved closer so they could see and hear what was happening. Galinda also needed to be close enough that her magic would reach the distance.

GLINDA: The GOOD Witch

The cloud descended with elegance, Gisella lifting her gown just enough to display the gleam of her silver shoes before stepping onto solid ground. The moment her feet touched earth, the cloud vanished, like an illusion, like a dream.

The crowd hushed.

They gawked.

A child stepped forward and asked softly, "Who are...you?"

Gisella knelt, her voice as soft as spun sugar. "Well, little one, I am the Good Witch of the South."

"You are?"

"That I am." She scrunched her nose against the child's, a gesture that sent ripples of laughter through the gathering.

They were caught—already, they were caught.

Not just by her beauty, but by her **heart.**

"Are you here to help us?" A voice, uncertain but hopeful. A rotund munchkin, half-hidden among the crowd.

Gisella laughed, light, airy. "Why, yes! I couldn't very well leave you all to fend for yourselves, not after I stopped that dreadful twister."

A murmur swept through the crowd.

Applause.

Loud, thunderous, like that of full-sized men. To the Good Witch, applause sounded the same, it didn't matter who they came from.

"You stopped the twister?" one asked.

But this voice did not come from the crowd. It came from the edge—another short imp waddled to her, his small hands out for Gisella to shake.

Gisella didn't like to shake strangers' hands if they weren't from the Uplands let alone munchkin ones.

But people were watching.

Right now, she wasn't Gisella, she was the Good Witch of the South.

So she bent down, as she had before, and took his hand.

"Well, yes. I stopped the cyclone."

"Then many thanks are in order. Thank you for saving munchkinland."

"No need to thank me. It was simply the good thing to do."

The imp smiled warmly. "And your name?"

"You may call me the Good Witch of the South."

The Good Witch looked down at his attire and saw a reflective shiny yellow light hit her eye. It was a gold badge on his chest pocket. It hit her on the head like *flatheads*, that she was speaking to the mayor of munchkinland.

"Good Witch." The mayor repeated sounding it aloud. "Good. That you are!"

He turned to the crowd, his voice rising in solemn proclamation. "I want you all to welcome the Good Witch of the South!"

The applause rose again, enveloping her.

The mayor turned back to the Good Witch, "When you've finished your work here," he said, lowering his voice, "I would like to speak with you. About something… important."

The Good Witch nodded, smiling sweetly, her porcelain face as unreadable as a painted mask.

Then, at last, she took in the wreckage, the snapped beams, the splintered homes, the heaps of debris left in the storm's wake. The sight of it, all that ruin, struck her unexpectedly, and she let out a strangled, dramatic cry.

"Guh!"

The audience laughed.

She was beautiful, yes. But more than that, she was charming. And charm had a way of making even devastation entertaining.

Recovering, the Good Witch lifted her arms. Galinda, standing unseen at a distance, recognized the signal at once.

With a flick of her fingers, Galinda wove the scattered timber back into place, reassembling a cottage from what had been, only moments before, an unsalvageable pile of wood. Then another. And another. It was exhilarating at first, the sheer, breathtaking force of creation. The power to undo ruin, to smooth out the wrinkles of misfortune.

But magic had its limits.

Galinda could feel the exhaustion creeping in, an invisible tide dragging at her limbs. Yet she pressed on, repairing *home* after *home* until her breath came shallow and her hands trembled.

And then, at last, it was done.

Finally, munchkinland was reborn. Every building stood pristine, every cobbled street spotless, and the Yellow Brick Road gleamed brighter than ever, each golden tile polished to perfection.

The Good Witch tossed her hair from left to right. "Well, now that is done!"

The crowd erupted once more, entranced by her theatrics.

The Good Witch smiled indulgently. "Where is your mayor?"

A child scampered off, knocking eagerly at the door of a modest *home*. The mayor emerged promptly, as if he had been waiting.

"You mentioned that you wanted to speak with me?"

"Yes," he said gravely. "It's about our title."

The Good Witch's brow arched. "What about it?"

The mayor exhaled heavily, as if preparing to confess some long-held sorrow. "All of Oz has been cruel to us. For years, becoz of our height, they look down on us—most literally and most figuratively. We were hoping you could help."

"I'll do anything to help!" The Good Witch placed a hand to her chest in a gesture of noble sincerity. "What do you have in mind?"

The mayor glanced around, then squared his shoulders.

"First," he said, "we wish to be recognized as Munchkins—with a capital 'M'. They refer to us as munchkin with a little '*m*' to insult us. It's not just a word, Good Witch. It's a wound. It is a way of reducing us, of making us small even in name, and all we want is to be treated equally to all those who live in Oz."

A hush fell over the crowd. All eyes turned to the Good Witch.

The Good Witch considered this.

As the most powerful man in Quadling Country, her father's influence made this a simple political favour.

She sighed softly, letting the moment stretch. Then, with a radiant smile, she declared, "Consider it done."

The crowd gasped.

"From this day forward, you will no longer be referred to as munchkins with a little '*m*'. You will be respected as a people. You will be known as Munchkins, with a big 'M'. I will personally see to it."

The cheer that erupted in response was deafening.

For a moment, the Good Witch simply stood there, basking in the adulation. She felt it, that rare and intoxicating thing—power.

Not the kind of power Galinda possessed, the kind that strained the body and drained the spirit. No, this was the power of words, of perception, of influence. She had reshaped the way an entire people saw themselves. That was power.

The moment stretched, lingering in golden admiration, until the Good Witch, ever mindful of pacing, deemed it time to exit.

"Well," she said lightly, "if there are no further questions, I'm going to take my leave."

But just as she turned, a little girl, small even by Munchkin standards, pushed to the front of the crowd, clutching something in her hands.

A *Lolliguild-Pop*.

Green and white, swirled into a perfect spiral, specially made for her.

The Good Witch plucked it from the child's hands and inspected it with a trained eye before offering a radiant smile. "Thank you, little one."

"Taste it!" the child urged, bouncing excitedly.

"Right now?"

The girl nodded, eyes bright.

The Good Witch lifted the pop to her lips, angling it just so to shield the crowd's view, and mimed a delicate lick.

Then—

She made a face of sheer delight, of unbridled satisfaction, as though it were the single most exquisite confection she had ever had the privilege of tasting.

"Mmm! Absolutely divine!" she proclaimed.

The crowd cheered, and she raised her arms once more.

A cloud coiled into existence around her feet, lifting her slowly, elegantly, into the sky. She ascended. Sunlight danced on her silvered toes, dazzling the Munchkins below.

Meanwhile, beneath the cover of trees, Dainhurst and Galinda stood waiting.

As the cloud carried Gisella out of sight, the two made their way back to their hidden carriage.

The cloud, now absent its audience, drifted back down to the mossy ground, dissolving the instant Gisella stepped off it.

She wasted no time. Gisella flung the *Lolliguild-Pop* to the ground, wiping her hands as if ridding herself of some contagion.

The Good Witch was given the sweets to eat, but Gisella Fairmoor was not going to accept food from little miscreant vermin disguised as people.

Dainhurst, unbothered by the display, pulled her into an embrace. His joy was unrestrained, uncharacteristic. He even dragged Galinda in, catching her in the sweeping motion of his arms.

"How did I do?" Gisella asked.

Dainhurst pulled back, hands still gripping her shoulders. "How did you do?" he echoed, incredulous. Then, with theatrical flourish, "You were *amazing!* How the One Gohd and Ozma blessed me with two superstars, I'll never know."

Gisella's chest swelled, pride filling her to the brim.

Dainhurst turned to Galinda, eyes narrowing in speculation. "And you— where did you learn to wield magic like that?"

Galinda hesitated, then chose her words carefully. "I had a great teacher."

Dainhurst's usual unreadable face shifted a little.

The carriage was called, and as they waited, Gisella tapped Galinda on the shoulder. "You did good," she murmured.

Galinda allowed herself a small smile.

But something gnawed at her. A suspicion, a curiosity.

"Were you pretending to be me?" she asked, amused. "You know—my mannerisms, my way of speaking and likeness?"

Gisella stiffened. "I don't know what you're talking about," she snapped. "Can't we just celebrate my win? What I'm doing benefits the entire family, so stop complaining."

"Okay," Galinda answered calmly.

The Fairmoors changed their shoes, apart from Gisella, before entering the carriage. Gisella was wide awake replaying what had occurred, the people cheering and loving her. Respecting her.

For a second she almost forgot what she had promised the munchkins.

Oh, she meant the *Munchkins*.

"Father, I promised the munchkins that I would aid them in having their title recognised by the other states as Munchkins." Gisella paused, rolling her eyes before continuing, "With a capital 'M'."

Dainhurst sighed, twisting his moustache in thought. "That's doable." Then, with a chuckle, "I suppose we can't laugh about them in public anymore."

Gisella smirked, "We can. We just won't let them see it."

Dainhurst and Gisella laughed, their cackling going against the sound of the night wind as it blew past the carriage window.

Galinda, too exhausted and drained, needed to recharge. The moment her body relaxed in the Golden Eagle seats she fell into a deep slumber.

Even though her family were in Munchkinland with ulterior motives, Galinda found peace in knowing that she fixed a little piece of the damage she caused.

CHAPTER 26

Shift in the Tide

A t dawn, Dainhurst stood by the great arched window of his chamber, waiting. He had been restless the whole night, twisting in his great mahogany bed, and he made sure the staff knew to deliver the first copies of the *NewZPapr* directly to him. The man of many masks, this time, could not conceal his nerves because *everything* was no longer in his own hands, nor in those of his powerful allies. It rested with the people. How would they receive his little project?

Gisella.

Power, after all, was a fragile thing. A stone castle could crumble if the foundation rotted from within. And his little foundation, his oh-so-precious lifeline, was the Munchkinland affair. The people, those clucking hens, needed to swallow it whole.

At last, the newspapers arrived, the ink still fragrant, the pages crisp with the morning damp. A maid scurried down the corridor, carefully balancing the stack as he raked his thick blonde hair, twisted the ends of his moustache, and muttered under his breath. The maid moved too slowly for Dainhurst's liking so he lunged. There was no other word for it, seizing the top paper like a starving man at a banquet. The maid, startled but accustomed to his impatience, knew better than to linger. She turned and disappeared in the direction of Esmelda's chambers, leaving Dainhurst alone with history.

He unfurled the *NewZPapr*.

THE GOOD WITCH OF THE SOUTH SAVES AND RESTORES MUNCHKINLAND

For a moment, Dainhurst only stared. He read it twice, then a third time, just to be sure. Then, an eruption—a laugh, sharp and unexpected, like a clap of thunder. Somewhere in the distance, a portrait rattled on its hook.

He bolted from his chamber, nearly knocking over a candelabra in his haste, and burst into Gisella's chambers without warning.

"Gisella, wake up immediately!"

The young woman stirred in her plush, canopied bed, tangled in silk sheets and the lazy haze of sleep. She blinked against the sudden intrusion, a mess of golden curls spilling over her shoulder.

"What?" she mumbled. "What is it?"

Dainhurst thrust the paper toward her. "You're on the front page! We did it!"

Gisella sat up, rubbing her eyes. Not at the headline, mind you, but at the accompanying illustration. There she was, enshrined in ink, a vision in monochrome, radiant even in the grainy newsprint. The artist had captured her with remarkable accuracy: her delicate profile, the poised tilt of her chin, the ruffled elegance of her gown, the effortless way she stood among the Munchkins. *No doubt*, she thought smugly, *I am now the most famous woman in all of Oz*. Her name would be whispered in every tea parlour, every drawing room. Gisella. The Good Witch of the South. And all it took was a few magic tricks and being polite to small people.

"Father, I can't believe we actually did it!"

Down the hall, Galinda sat cross-legged on her bed, decoding the **Glamour Spell**. But the moment she heard her family's shouts of triumph, she knew. *The news was in*. She closed her spellbook and entered Gisella's room.

"Is the paper here?" she asked softly.

Gisella, grinning, handed her the paper.

Galinda's brows knitted slightly, and her eyes widened. "Woz, I can't believe you did this, they put the Munchkins in capitals in the headline!"

Dainhurst and Gisella exchanged looks, as if Galinda had just spoken in tongues.

Gisella dismissed it with a wave. "So, what's next?"

Dainhurst smoothed a hand over his moustache, "There is *always* some sort of trouble happening in Oz, my dear. It shouldn't be difficult to find another cause to champion."

"And if we can't find any," Gisella added, smirking, "we can always create some, like the twister Galinda made."

"Yes! Precisely," Dainhurst said, flashing a proud grin.

Galinda stiffened. "I don't think that's a good thing to do, Father."

Dainhurst turned to her, his expression smooth and untroubled. "No?"

"I helped you to restore Munchkinland out of goodness and to fix what I broke, and I understand politics comes into it but it is taking over everything, it's like we aren't there to help anyone and we're just there to pretend just for the sake of being popular."

Gisella scoffed. "Oh, please."

Dainhurst, however, approached her with measured steps. He placed a heavy hand on her shoulder.

"No, no, what we are doing is good. Galinda, tell me, are we not made up of different cultures in Oz?"

"Well, yes."

"The Munchkins. The Winkies. The Quadlings. Even the talking Animals, before they were… relocated." He smiled faintly. "Each has its own idea of goodness, yes?"

Galinda, confused as a jibblewalker, replied with an "Okay?"

"We have different cultures and different ideals. So, what I am asking you is, do you think our culture is any more important than theirs?"

"No. But—"

"But what? They all have different ideas of what goodness is because we are all different people! Goodness is not set in stone; it is not absolute. It is there for each individual to decide what works best for them, aligning with their true selves in a world without inherent meaning. That's what we're doing, or would you rather be a slave to the ideas others impose on you, Galinda?"

"No. I'm just sayi—"

"Don't you want to be free?" Gisella interrupted mockingly.

Galinda felt the air tighten around her.

"Guh," she said, exhaling sharply. "I suppose you make sense."

"That's a good girl," Dainhurst murmured, ruffling Galinda's strawberry-blonde hair.

"I'll keep helping," she said, brushing his hand away. "As long as we don't do what Gisella suggested."

"Which is?" Gisella arched her eyebrows trying to remember the suggestion she had made that was so absurd Galinda didn't want to follow.

"You know, creating problems just so we can swoop in and fix them. That, I will *not* do. And you can forget about me ever making another twister again."

"You're so *boring*," Gisella sighed. "You should just give me your magic, since you don't know how to put it to good use."

"Girls," Dainhurst chided, voice like oil on glass. "You are sisters. *Act like it.*"

Before either of them could retort, a sharp knock echoed through the chamber. A maid entered, bowing slightly.

"Sire, the reporters are requesting an audience with you today… regarding your role as the father of *The Good Witch of the South*."

Dainhurst's expression gleamed, his smile a polished thing.

This was only the beginning. He could feel it.

Galinda slipped out of Gisella's room, the weight of the conversation pressing on her ribs. There was only one person she wanted to talk to.

Ominson.

A little more than best friends now, it seemed, because the last time they met they shared a kiss, and since then they hadn't seen each other. Galinda took the Violet byke and rode to Veilforge Castle, but with each turn of the wheels, her **heart** began to race faster, and it wasn't from exertion.

Galinda arrived and knocked on the looming castle's large doors.

Ominson answered.

His face was gloomy, but when he realised it was Galinda, it quickly turned into a smile. His eyes looked at her differently this time. There was seduction behind it, and Galinda couldn't tell if he was doing it purposefully or if his intentions were seeping through without his consent. He usually looked her dead in the face with occasional glances down her frame, but his eyes this time drifted down to her breast and below.

Way below.

Galinda swallowed, ignoring the sudden heat creeping up her neck.

"Hey," she said, aiming for casual. "Are you busy today?"

"I was supposed to be," Ominson admitted, stepping aside to let her in. "But my father left without me."

Galinda tilted her head. "Why?"

"Something about not being cut out for this, and when I am ready, I should show it and act like a Veilforge."

"Oh," Galinda said, "Want to go to the waterfall?"

Ominson's lips curled into a grin. "You even have to ask?"

They rode together, their bykes weaving familiar paths toward their hidden world. And yet, when they arrived, something *felt* off. Like an old melody played just slightly out of tune.

"Do you ever get the feeling that someone's been here?" Galinda asked, running a hand on the stone in the garden for inspection.

Ominson, already lounging beside her, shrugged. "Only us. Who else would know about this place?"

"I don't know. I think I am going crazy; I've been having this weird feeling that someone has been in here for years, but I don't know why."

"Years? I think you're just paranoid."

"Maybe," she murmured.

The pair sat on the grass, Galinda at her usual spot, which was starting to wear from years of sitting in the same place—it was hardening and losing its comfort.

Ominson sighed, breaking the momentary silence. "What is it you wanted to talk about?"

"It seems you're the one with more on your chest."

"Maybe." He ran a hand through his hair. "Why were you avoiding me after we kissed?"

Galinda froze.

She had thought, hoped, really, that if neither of them spoke of it, it would cease to exist.

And before she could summon a proper response, Ominson closed the space between them.

His lips found hers.

Again.

Galinda jerked back, her breath unsteady.

Ominson frowned. "What? Is it so wrong?"

"Ominson, I—"

"Save it."

"Why me?"

"What?"

"Why me, Ominson? You could have any girl in Oz. Why *me*—when I look the way I do?"

Ominson shot to his feet, his anger sudden and bright. He kicked a rock, sending it skittering into the water. "Why do you *do* that to yourself?" he snapped. "Why do you do that to *me*? You act like it's impossible for someone to love you. I have *never*—not once—said a damn thing about the way you look. Ever. And yet, you assume that's all I care about?"

"Ominson, you *hear* what people say."

His face darkened, his anger swelling like a storm. "Out of *everyone*, I never thought…" he sighed, "you've known me for years, I tell you about my problems, my fears and even you believe what other people say about me?" His voice shook, his hands clenched into fists. "Let's say, for the sake of argument, that all those rumours are true. That I 'put my cock in anything with a pulse.' You know me better than that. And yet, even *you* still believe the worst of me."

"Ominson—"

His voice dropped, quieter now. "I never thought *you* would see me that way."

"You're right. I'm sorry."

Ominson sat back down, his anger cooling into something softer. His face was still flushed, from bright red to *pink*, but the heat of it was fading.

"Can we just… forget it? Pretend I never kissed you?"

Galinda nodded. "Sure."

A breath passed between them, tentative but healing. And then, quietly, she said, "I wanted to talk about my family. About Gisella. About everything we've been doing."

"Right, I saw it in the *NewZPapr*. Good stuff, you know, helping the Munchkins get their title back."

"So you *did* see it."

"Everyone did." His eyes narrowed slightly. "But why do you sound so miserable about it?"

Galinda hesitated. "Becoz it isn't real. *I'm* the one doing the magic, Ominson. Gisella doesn't have any. It's a façade, it's all an illusion."

"I was confused about that, becoz the papers were calling her the Good Witch, but I know you've had magic for years. It should be you!"

Galinda let out a hollow laugh. "Apparently, I'm not the right *fit* for the title. Becoz of the way I look. I tell myself it's not so bad—staying behind the curtain, helping my family, giving Gisella the fame she's always wanted. But it *hurts*." She swallowed the lump in her throat. "I've wanted this *my whole life*. And yet... I understand why it has to be this way."

She looked away, blinking hard. "They're right. It *makes sense*. No one wants to believe in a Good Witch who looks like *me*."

Ominson stared at her for a long moment before shaking his head. "You look *fine*, Glinda, I'm sorry if the world has made you feel otherwise. I don't bring up your looks becoz I know everyone else won't let you forget. But... I *see* you. The real you. The selfless, *not good,* but the kindest person I've ever met."

"Omi."

"I said we should move on," he exhaled, half-laughing, half-defeated, "but this—this is exactly why I want you so desperately. I've been with every girl in Quadling Country, and you're worth the whole lot of them put together."

Galinda, perched at the edge of emotion, forced herself to speak as the tears welled in her eyes.

"Ominson, I wish I could see myself the way you see me. But I know my limits." Galinda caught her breath. "It wouldn't be fair to you, to either of us, to start whatever this is, when I don't even know who I am. When I can't accept myself for who I am."

Ominson's hands flexed, his fingers curling into the earth as if he could anchor himself to it, as if holding on to something physical would steady the spiralling tempest inside him. "Then let me do that for you. Let me love you until you believe it. Let's just go, Glinda. Leave our families, leave this Gohd-forsaken place. Just you and me. And I know it sounds absurd, us being sixteen, but this is what I want. To be free from all this expectation. Don't you?"

She closed her eyes, shaking her head "You make it sound so easy, Omi. Oh, to see the world the way you do. But I know myself. I can't choose freedom if it means loneliness, Omi. As pathetic as it is—and I hate myself for it—I would rather stay in gilded bondage, surrounded by people who pretend to love me, than be truly free, alone and unloved."

Her confession shattered something between them.

She turned away before he could speak, staring at the waterfall, as if somewhere within its relentless cascade lay an answer she had not yet found.

Ominson watched her shoulders shake, the waterfall's mist catching in her hair like glistening dewdrops. His throat tightened. "But I love you," he whispered, barely audible above the crashing water.

"I know." She wiped her tears on her sleeve, "But that isn't enough for me."

He flinched as if she'd struck him.

"That's why I envy Gisella, she gets love she doesn't even need. And I—I need it so desperately, Omi. More than you could ever understand. I wish I could change, but I can't. And I've made peace with that."

Ominson pulled her into his arms, and they wept together. And then, inexplicably, laughter bubbled up between them, strained, hollow, but laughter, nonetheless. They understood each other's pain too well, like it was a language all their own. They both carried the same weight, even if they bore it differently.

Ominson whispered, "I've made up my mind. When I'm of age, I'm leaving this wretched place. And if, in that time, you have a change of *heart*—I'll have a place waiting for you."

Galinda could hear the sincerity in his voice. What a life it would be, to be with the one person who was willing to love her despite everything.

Ominson was so sure of himself, so certain of what he wanted. He had known since childhood, that the life his father planned for him was not the one he would live. He wasn't book-smart, but he was smart when it came to life, and he never hesitated to chase what he desired.

Galinda, on the other hand, was made of a different kind of fabric. She had spent sixteen years clawing for acceptance, devouring herself from the inside out just to fit into a world that had already made up its mind about her.

No, she was not like him. But she was hopeful. Hopeful that one day she would unlock the secret of the *Glamour Spell*. When that day came, when she was finally beautiful—truly beautiful—then she could let herself believe in his love. Then he would not wake up and regret her. Then and only then, she could be everything he didn't yet know he wanted.

The two best friends sat in each other's company for a little while before making their way *home*.

❖

When Galinda reached Fairmoor Castle, there were multiple carriages outside. They had visitors. They were Middies; she could tell by their carriages.

She pushed open the castle doors, and there they were, Dainhurst in his finest suit, Gisella posed under the artist's brushstrokes, reporters eagerly jotting down whatever fabricated wisdom spilled from her sister's lips.

Had they been doing this all day?

Galinda knew better than to ask.

She climbed the stairs without a word, unnoticed, forgotten in her own *home*.

The noise from below stretched into an eternity before finally, blissfully, falling into silence. Doors slammed, carriage wheels rumbled, and the house exhaled.

And then, as expected, the knock came.

"Humbug," Dainhurst called as he entered, "we're leaving for Winkie Country in the morning."

"Why?"

"News just hit that there is a civil war brewing between the king of the Winkies and other tribes within Winkie Country. Gisella has been called there to mediate." A smug smile danced on his face.

Galinda forced a nod. "Fine."

But no matter how much she despised it, no matter how deep her resentment ran, she would not let it show.

Family, after all, was everything.

CHAPTER 27

The West of Oz

With Esmelda away at a retreat, the remaining Fairmoors set off for Winkie Country, their carriage rattling over the *Pryzm Road*. Gisella, ever the vision, sat cloaked in a new green gown Galinda had fashioned for her, paired with her crystal necklace and silver shoes. This time Galinda brought a language book to aid her in deciphering the spell. She was halfway through, and being stuck in a carriage made the *HourZ* the perfect pastime.

Winkie Country was less civilized than she had expected. The villages in the West of Oz were primitive, the roads crude, the air thick with the scent of earth and livestock. Even Munchkinland, with its never-ending farmlands, had more industry. But what Winkie Country lacked in modernity, it compensated for in fortresses. The landscape was littered with castles, each vying for dominance, but none more imposing than the king's, a hulking mass of grey stone and bitter winds.

A crowd had gathered outside, waiting for a glimpse of the Good Witch of the South.

Dainhurst murmured his instructions, and Galinda, without hesitation, summoned the familiar cloud spell. The crowd gasped as Gisella descended from the heavens, their cheers deafening.

From Gisella's perspective, they were a much finer audience than the Munchkins, if only because they were of a reasonable height. The darker complexions were unfortunate, but one could not have everything. At the very least, they understood her importance.

The Good Witch put on a brave smile. It was like the Winkies had never heard of mint musk, because they smelt of grass. She thought the Quadlings in the Quadling Midlands were uncouth, but the Winkies were villagers compared to the poorest of her people—they had no decorum, and they were touching her. She didn't care if it was from appreciation of her arrival—their diseased fingers, rough with labour, made her uncomfortable in her own skin. Darker complexioned individuals with dark hair instead of blonde should know their place. To never touch the pristine and holy.

The large castle—almost rivalling the size of the Fairmoor estate—was quite nice, Galinda thought. It felt homely and cozy despite its architecture, but the environment felt a little threatening. She had magic, but something about having a dozen guards with spears, cutlasses and blades standing in front, at the back, and sideways of them, following their steps to the Council Chamber was unnerving.

The gates opened, and The Good Witch entered first, where the air was thick with incense and politics. The tribesmen at the roundtable bowed low in reverence as she passed, walking with the measured grace of a woman accustomed to being worshipped. There was a gilded chair adorned with emeralds left vacant, and it was quite clear that it was made specially for her. The Good Witch made her way to the seat opposite the king of Winkie Country.

As Dainhurst and Galinda stood in the corner witnessing the conversation in silence, the king—a round man with a buffalo-horned silver helmet and a fur cloak, huffed and puffed like an angry bull. Finally, he inhaled sharply through his nose, his breath rattling like an impending storm.

The negotiations began.

The Vinkus, a man with a voice that seemed to have been aged in the belly of a volcano, cleared his throat, reverberating against the cold stone walls. "Thank you for coming today for us Good Witch," his accent curling the words in unexpected places. "I know it is long journey from the South, Aye?"

"Well, I only came to prevent a war," she said, a pause timed just so before she added, "and for the free food."

The Vinkus let out a great, braying laugh. The tribesmen remained unimpressed.

"I am the Vinkus, King of the Winkies" the fat king gestured his hands to the guests at the roundtable, "And these be the tribesman that make up in my entire kingdom."

Each man was adorned with a bronze helmet with some characteristic of a different animal. One with a goat's horn, another with an antelope horn, another with a deer horn. Their attire, vibrant and varied, marked them as warriors of distinct clans.

"We had expected the Wizard himself," the Vinkus continued, "but I hear he has urgent matters elsewhere, so we leave his chair empty—for you."

The Good Witch nearly laughed at the king's manner of speech. How could he be a king when he didn't understand proper grammar? She could only wonder what his people were like to live with.

"Well," she said, drawing a gloved hand over the gleaming armrest, "I do think the emeralds suit me. Green is my colour, you know."

"I am to be very glad that it is to your liking!" the Vinkus replied heartily, either unaware or unbothered by the mockery in her tone.

BEFORE

A tribesman, dark brown of complexion, wearing the goat-horned helmet, leaned forward. "Shall we to begin now?"

"Yes, begin," said the Vinkus

The man in the goat helmet rose. "I am Benidar, the leader of the Goatééy Ganee tribe, I am very honoured that you come here today, but I need you to understand why I frustrate, why I almost send army to fight."

So, Benidar was the agitator, the one who instigated the civil war, Galinda thought.

The Good Witch tapped her finger on the wooden table. "Why Benidar? What drove you to such extremes to decide that a war was the best solution?"

Benidar took off his helmet and placed it on the table, he was sweating like a pig. Perhaps he should have a pig helmet the Good Witch thought, and if she was honest, he looked like one, and it wasn't because he was red in the face. She didn't even know that it was possible for darker-skinned people to get red.

"Good Witch, the Vallas Tribe," as he pointed to the tribesman in the antelope horn, "have been stealing our crops and raping our women."

The antelope tribesman, with reddish skin stood up and slammed his hands on the table. "I will not take this disrespect. We did no such thing, why would we steal crops from fools like you, we got our own food and our own women to impregnate. Your people are weak, we are larger in numbers why would we cross mate?"

Benidar reached for his belt. A glint of metal.

"Order!" the Vinkus roared, "you will remain silent until your king command to speak!"

Reluctantly, Benidar relented, his fingers loosening from his crude shank.

The Vinkus then pointed to the man in the antelope helmet to speak.

The man in the antelope helmet glanced at the Good Witch, "I am Sundari, I am the leader of the antelope tribe. For years we have had peace in the land. No wars, no fights. But I am afraid Benidar is trying to cause problems becoz he is envious of my people. He sees we are smarter, faster, stronger and so he tries to bring these ridiculous accusations to try and fight us. This is all stemming from jealousy!"

"No that is true not!" Benidar interrupted, "There have been women missing for weeks now from me tribe and those found is dead and others is pregnant."

"Order! Did I say you can speak?" the Vinkus asked angrily.

"Is there any proof, any reasoning why you think the Vallas are the one doing this?" the Good Witch asked carefully.

"Yes. The Vallas is lighter than my people so why the babies come out fair. It is obvious they do it to my people. And the crops, they have more than us, way more, and my crops is missing. So, they are the ones doing it."

The Good Witch considered. Who was in the wrong, she didn't know. But if she had to choose it couldn't be the Vallas because they spoke better and eloquently than the Goatééy Ganee.

The man in the deer helmet remained quiet.

The Vinkus looked to the tribesman in the deer horn and asked. "Do you have anything to say?"

"No. I stay neutral. I don't know who to fight with." The man in the deer helmet remained seated and looked at the Good Witch. "I am Aurkhan, the leader of the Ugabu tribe, I known both tribes. Both trustworthy and they both honest people. I trap in the middle and me don't know who to believe."

The Vinkus spoke directly to the Good Witch, "You see my issue? I do not want to be here bias; I want you to help me decide who is telling the truth."

The whole table looked at The Good Witch for wisdom. Looking to her for the answers, like their lives depended on it.

And it did.

But no matter how hard the Good Witch tried to think, she didn't know what to do.

"I don't know," the Good Witch answered.

"You do not know?" The Vinkus, more disappointed than surprised.

"Well," she recovered quickly, "if I had to choose, I would say the Vallas."

"See I told you, you liar, you are deceitful animal!" shouted the Sundari.

The room devolved into shouting, men rising from their seats, hands gripping at weapons, the argument unravelling into something raw and violent.

The Good Witch sat frozen, her carefully cultivated image slipping, her fraudulence threatening to bloom into full exposure. The Vinkus realised that the Good Witch's newfound reputation of being wise, fair and diplomatic was a farce. Her giving the Munchkins their title was just a one-time thing. But he was so fed up that he didn't object and just allowed the tribesmen to continue fighting a little longer, while he thought of a solution himself.

Amidst the argument, a voice, soft but certain, came from the back of the room.

"Well, I have an idea."

Galinda.

Dainhurst tried to grab Galinda's dress in attempt to stop her as she stepped forward, but he was too late, and his grip barely scraped her.

The Vinkus frowned. "Who is you?"

Galinda glanced at Gisella, whose expression was a portrait of silent horror.

"I am the Good Witch's sister," she declared.

The Vinkus studied her. "And you say you have a solution?"

"Yes."

The room fell silent.

"Do you have an artifact used in court rulings?" Galinda asked, "something sacred—something binding?"

The Vinkus grunted. "Bring the golden horn."

BEFORE

A guard placed an ornate helmet, gilded and resplendent, at the centre of the roundtable.

Galinda stepped closer. "Now, each of you, place your hand upon it, and swear. Swear that you speak the truth, as far as your knowledge permits you."

The room held its breath.

Benidar and Sundari reached out, their hands hovering over the gleaming surface.

And then, as one, they pressed their palms to the golden horn.

Benidar and Sundari locked eyes. A challenge unspoken.

"I swear that art shalt speak truth and only truth in the presence of the Vinkus and the one Gohd. That I profess!"

Benidar shifted uncomfortably, his fingers twitching as he withdrew his hand. "What next?"

Galinda folded her hands before her. "Tell me," she said, her tone light but edged with steel. "Has this happened before? Have the Vallas ever been known to steal, to—" she hesitated, choosing a softer phrasing, "to rape?"

Benidar's brows knotted. "No."

"And yet you accuse them now, absent of proof?"

The room hung on her words, as if suspended in the web of her reason.

"Did you ask the women—the victims—who had wronged them?"

Benidar's reply came swift, defensive: "No."

"And why not?"

His eyes darted to the side. "Becoz women lie."

Sundari smirked, arms folded across his broad chest. "See! They are very dumb people."

Galinda let out a breath. "How long has this been happening?"

Benidar grunted. "Nine Oz'moons."

"And are there any witnesses? Anyone who has seen these crimes firsthand?"

Sundari's hand shot up before Benidar could interject. "Yes. I brought one with me. But he"—a nod in Benidar's direction— "doesn't believe women are capable of truth-telling, so she's been kept out of the discussion."

"Bring her to me," Galinda said.

A guard disappeared through an arched doorway, returning with a woman dressed in little more than stitched burlap. She stepped forward hesitantly, hands knotted in front of her, her eyes wary.

Galinda softened. "Your name?"

"Mela."

"I'm sorry for what has happened to you," she said, sympathetically but firmly. "But if you can help us, even a little, it might stop this from happening again."

Mela swallowed hard, then nodded.

"Did you see the person or people that stole the crops?"

"No."

"Did you see the man that raped you?"

A slow shake of the head. "No. It was dark. Cold. Wet." Her voice trembled, and then, as if the very words pulled her under, she began to cry slightly.

Benidar scoffed. "And this is your great witness? She knows nothing. Women are useless."

Galinda shot him a glare. "Please be silent!"

Mela wiped at her face, "I couldn't see him, but, I remember how he smell like."

"Can you describe it to me?"

"Rosemary and lemongrass." Her lip quivered, "my father used to bring back musk from his travels outside Winkie Country. I know the scent."

Mela began to cry, unable to contain herself.

Galinda motioned for the guard to take Mela out of the room.

Sundari's expression twisted with realization. "See, we don't even grow rosemary and lemongrass here in Winkie Country. We as a culture don't grow that here, no one does."

A long silence.

Benidar rubbed his chin. "The Vallas is right."

The Vinkus leaned forward, "have you come to a decision yet?"

"I have one final statement."

"So make it!" replied the Vinkus.

Galinda exhaled sharply, "Think! Nine Oz'moons ago, was there a group of outsiders? A group unfamiliar to your customs, foreign to your lands? A group who might carry rosemary and lemongrass musk?"

The air itself seemed to still.

And then—

"The Wizard's Guard." The words rang from the Vinkus like a death toll.

The room erupted, not with anger, but with horror.

"That's why the Wizard never come today," someone whispered, "out of shame."

Benidar and Sundari rose at once, hands grasping one another in a show of newfound brotherhood.

"I so sorry I say that disgustifying thing about Vallas."

"I so sorry I said that about Goatééy Ganee. Please forgive me?"

"I forgive. We are brother, we are family!"

The Vinkus, taken aback by the sheer impossibility of peace in a room that had been brimming with war only moments before, let out a great, bellowing laugh. His chair creaked as he stood, clasping Galinda's arm.

"Thank you little one! How can something so simple so make us so blind we cannot see. You are a wonder! You make good leader."

The Vinkus leaned closer to Galinda's ear.

"I think if you have magic, you make better Good Witch, aye?"

His laughter was infectious, and Galinda found herself grinning despite herself.

Dainhurst, still standing by the wall, was astonished. A king was a king, and to be acknowledged by one only uplifted the family name.

Gisella, remained in her emerald chair. "We shall be going now," she interrupted.

"So soon?" The Vinkus threw his hands up in protest. "Silly! You shall stay! Eat! Feast until you are fat like me, aye?"

"I am pretty hungry!" Galinda replied.

"Me too." The Vinkus laughed. "We shall feast!"

Dainhurst stepped forward smoothly, offering the king a small but pointed smile. "And I hear Winkie Country has *extraordinary* cuisine, which I have yet to try."

The Vinkus clapped him on the back. "Then we shall feast!"

The tension dissolved into the preparations of celebration, the tribesmen still caught up in their newfound kinship, kissing each other's cheeks, apologising with full hearts and eager hands.

The Vinkus roared for his servants, his voice rolling through the great hall like the wind over the barrows. "Let it be known to the villages! A feast for all! Tonight, we celebrate!"

The castle, a brooding thing of stone and soot-stained banners, was suddenly humming with industry. Servants scuttled with purpose, their arms laden with the delicacies of Winkie Country: *Goldmead tarts* with crisped honey edges, *Shardfish Stew* thick with the tang of the northern rivers, *Bruttle Pudding* glistening darkly under a drizzle of caramelized rum, *Blackened Ram Ribs* charred just to the brink of bitter, *Dark Ale Cheese* crumbly and pungent, *Frostberries* nestled in great silver bowls beside dollops of *Snowcream*, and *Braised Boar* glazed in the deep garnet syrup of *Thornberries*. At the centre of the feast, a grand roasted beef, its juices glistening like garnets, was flanked by goblets of rich cherry wine.

The villagers arrived at dusk, clothed in their finest, though "fine" was a matter of interpretation in the Vinkus. Even so, the castle filled with the scent of sweat and hearth-fire, with rough laughter and clinking goblets, with the deep, throaty strains of harp and drum. They danced, as Winkies did, with wild, untethered abandon, until their limbs ached, and their bellies groaned. Dainhurst danced among them, swayed by drink and a kind of reckless diplomacy. He would allow himself to enjoy it—for tonight.

Everyone partook.

Everyone, except Gisella. She remained apart, refusing to dine or mingle with commoners, her gaze distant as though the merriment around her was an entirely different world.

When the night edged into morning, and Dainhurst and Galinda had tasted all the foods they could get their hands on and the party had died down, it was time to leave. But they had to say their goodbyes and give their thanks to the Vinkus for his hospitality. If there was one thing the Winkies knew how to do, it was throwing a party and being spectacular hosts. It didn't matter who their guest was; anyone was welcome with open arms.

Dainhurst approached the Vinkus, who had succumbed to a deep, satisfied drowsiness upon his throne, his arms draped over the great mound of his belly. With a careful tap to the shoulder, the Vinkus stirred, blinking away sleep.

"Vinkus, my family and I shall be leaving now," Dainhurst announced. "Thank you for your hospitality."

The Vinkus stretched, his lips parting in a yawn wide enough to swallow the room. "You sure you don't want to stay? Plenty of room. You leave in morning, yes?"

"No, no," Dainhurst countered smoothly. "Urgent matters await us at home."

Dainhurst had enjoyed himself, and if he were a commoner, he would've spent an entire week in Winkie Country to soak in its rich culture. But he wanted to continue to hold a barrier between his Quadling nationality and the Winkies. If he stayed longer, it would give them absurd ideas, ideas like they were somehow equals.

"But you had good time?"

Galinda, standing at Dainhurst's side, lifted her voice in a soft reply. "It was wonderful."

The Vinkus turned to her then, his drowsy expression sharpening. He gestured for a servant, whispered something inaudible, and sent them scurrying from the hall.

"One moment," the Vinkus murmured.

When the servant returned, he carried a silver platter, its contents concealed beneath a domed lid. The Vinkus lifted it with ceremonial gravitas, revealing a golden medal—unmistakably gold, heavy and pure, the crest of a buffalo carved into its centre.

"This is for you, little one," the Vinkus declared. "To show my appreciation. For as long as I am king, you are always welcome in Winkie Country."

Galinda stood with emotion swelling within her slight frame. It was a feeling unfamiliar to her—acknowledgment, gratitude, recognition. She was *seen*. Not by just anyone, but by a king.

With an air of solemnity, the Vinkus pinned the medal to her dress.

It was official.

She nodded in respect, and he returned the gesture.

At the doorway, Gisella watched with narrowed eyes, saying nothing, though the tension in her frame spoke volumes. If she felt slighted, she gave no voice to it. The carriage awaited them, and as they climbed in, the castle and its revelry faded into the mist behind them.

It was time to go *home*, where everything was less windy and familiar.

♦

The next morning, the *NewZPapr* had their story. Dainhurst, ever the opportunist, made sure of it.

But not without revision.

The headlines blared in bold print:

GOOD WITCH OF THE SOUTH HALTS BREWING WAR IN WINKIE COUNTRY—HONORED BY THE VINKUS WITH A GOLDEN MEDAL

And the Good Witch, of course, was not Galinda.

It was Gisella.

Gisella, who now shrieked with joy through the halls of their *home*, drinking in the adulation, preening beneath the illusion of her own heroism.

Galinda remained silent. She had known this would happen. She had known the moment the lid had been lifted from the platter. The moment she had seen the gleam of gold and felt its weight pressed against her chest.

But was it enough?

For now, it had to be.

Because *she* knew the truth.

And so did the Vinkus.

Meanwhile, Dainhurst basked in his own success. The castle was awash with reporters, the scent of ink and ambition heavy in the air. He paraded through the country with Esmelda at his side, the perfect image of a nobleman's wife, though only because he had put an end to those *retreats* she had so desperately clung to. He had no patience for her charades, her affectations of distress. Whatever *problems* she claimed to have, they would not stand in the way of his ambitions.

And the tour, his grand, performative tour, continued.

Through Munchkinland, through Winkie Country, even through the wilds of the Vinkus.

But not north.

Never north.

No matter how much he desired social standing, no matter how much he hungered for approval, there was one place he would not go.

Gillikin Country.

A land of terrorists, undeserving of his presence.

Or that of his Good Witch.

CHAPTER 28

Long Live the King

The headlines came weekly, their ink barely dry before new ones replaced them. *The Good Witch of the South Strikes Again! Gisella Brings Peace to the Munchkins! Gisella Heals the Sick in Winkie Country!*

The Good Witch was almost as popular as the Wizard himself. *Almost.*

It did not take long for whispers to start, those half-spoken thoughts that carried like dry leaves on an autumn wind.

Did they need a Wizard at all? Hadn't the Good Witch done more for Oz in mere months than the Wizard had in years?

The Wizard of Oz was not a man accustomed to being questioned. And so, he arrived at Fairmoor Castle once more.

This time, to negotiate.

Galinda caught a quick glance of her friend Oscar Diggs before he was gestured into her father's study and yet, strangely, she felt no inclination to press her ear against the door. No flutter of curiosity, no hunger for secrets.

But the *Fates* were there.

We are always there.

The Wizard had grown restless. The matter was no longer mere irritation, no longer a game of politics, where one simply waited for public favour to shift like the tides.

Power is like glass—once it is cracked, it is only a matter of time before it shatters entirely.

Dainhurst knew this.

So did the Wizard.

"Welcome back, Oz," Dainhurst greeted, lounging behind his desk. "I have been *very* eager for this conversation."

"Yes," the Wizard murmured, his eyes flicking across the study. Something felt...different. "Is that a new desk?"

"Yes! You noticed!" Dainhurst's laughter was light, perhaps too light. "I felt that with everything changing, the place needed a new touch."

BEFORE

The Wizard's gaze swept the room. New desk. New chair. New shelves, new vases, even a new portrait, one that depicted Dainhurst himself in colours richer and bolder than any artist had dared before.

"Shall we get to it?" The Wizard said, unaccustomed to negotiating.

"Yes, about Gisella," Dainhurst said smoothly.

The Wizard cleared his throat. "Yes."

"What did you want to propose?"

"You see, it's no secret that Gisella's popularity has soared. It is... unbalancing things. Just last week, a *prisoner* had the gall to insult me in my own palace, declaring, 'The Good Witch will put a stop to your evil one day!'"

Dainhurst laughed. "What evil?"

"My thoughts exactly." The Wizard muttered.

"So, what can I do for you?"

"I need you to *stop* the tours around Oz," the Wizard said. "Quit this *tirade*. It is disrupting everything I have built."

Dainhurst tilted his head. "And how does that benefit *me?*"

The Wizard's smile was tight. "Do it for *me*, Dainhurst. Are we not friends?"

"Friends, yes. But I am a man with a family, Oz, and they *must* come first. I'm sure if *you* had one, you would share my sentiment."

The Wizard's expression darkened, but before he could respond, Dainhurst continued:

"Gold. I assume you're about to offer me gold."

"I'll give you all the gold and emeralds you desire. Just name your price."

"With all due respect, I already have more wealth than I know what to do with. I am the wealthiest man in Quadling Country." He paused. "I want something... more substantial."

"Be careful, Fairmoor. Challenging *me* will not end well for you. I can *guarantee* it. So be careful what you are about to ask of me."

"I want to rule. I have all this wealth, all this fame, but that means nothing if people aren't bowing at my feet to complete me. I want to be King of the Quadlings." Dainhurst bowed his head. "Your Wonderfulness, I know the policy changed; I know elections are now held every term for a mayor... but all those elected officials are in *my* pocket anyway."

Dainhurst laughed.

The Wizard laughed.

Dainhurst continued, "I want the law reversed, with no further elections. Just me, as King. And with *your* support, Your Wonderfulness, I believe the people would undoubtedly accept me."

The Wizard lingered for a long moment.

Then, he laughed again.

"Why didn't you say so, friend? Consider it done."

Dainhurst stood, reaching across the desk to shake the Wizard's hand.

"Now the matter of what I want. Gisella could be an asset, a mutually beneficial alliance." The Wizard relaxed, twirling his moustache. "I have been searching for a common enemy, someone so loathsome, so irredeemable that the people will despise them more than their occasional dislike of me. But I cannot seem to find a soul wretched enough to fit the part. However," he smiled, "with the love Gisella is getting, her at my side would be just as effective."

Dainhurst raised a brow.

"As you well know, hate is the easiest emotion to incite. But love—ah! Love is just as potent."

"So, you *don't* want me to put an end to her tours?"

"Actually, no, but *limit* them. One visit a week. Just enough to remain in the public eye, but not enough to overshadow *me*."

Dainhurst smiled. "That, I can do."

They shook hands again.

"Dainhurst, this has been *delightful,* but I must be going," the Wizard said, rising from his chair. He adjusted his hat, straightened his sleeves. And then, with a smirk— "Or should I say... *King* Dainhurst?"

Laughter filled the study, rich and warm, like a well-aged wine.

Dainhurst escorted the Wizard to his emerald-gilded carriage. Before the door shut, the Wizard reaffirmed their pact.

"I shall have the deed and your title settled by week's end."

And just like that, the emerald carriage rolled away.

Dainhurst would soon be King.

◇

The week unfolded like a stage play already rehearsed to perfection, a frenzy of preparations, relentless press engagements, and, most notably, a decree from the Wizard himself. It was official, Dainhurst Fairmoor was to be crowned King of Quadling Country. Times were changing and rather quickly, the sitting mayor was promptly ousted, not with a fight, but with a strangely serene endorsement, as though he had known all along that his time was borrowed, and that true power lay elsewhere.

The people, however, were not so willing.

Half of Quadling Country erupted in protest.

The Quadlings valued their right to vote. Or rather, the *illusion* of it.

And now, that illusion had been shattered.

Dainhurst was taken aback. He had expected *grumbling,* yes. Perhaps a few raised fists. But this? This was more than discontent. It was *outrage.*

He needed another endorser. The Wizard's approval alone was not enough.

The Good Witch of the South.

She had made her loyalties clear: *her father above all.* And with her public blessing, the fury of the people, their grumbling subdued, like waves calming under a soothing tide.

BEFORE

The Good Witch's radiant smile pacified them.

It was done.

◇

The morning of the coronation was crisp, golden, and humming with anticipation.

As was tradition, the Fairmoors, excluding Galinda, gathered atop the castle tower with their honeybee tea and cream tarts, indulging in their peculiar little ritual: laughing at the Munchkins below.

A charm for good luck.

When at last they were dressed, the carriages arrived.

Gisella and Dainhurst in the Golden Eagle.

Galinda and Esmelda in the Golden Goose.

The Pryzm Road carried them swiftly to the Solar Temple, where a restless sea of Quadlings awaited.

But they were not here for Dainhurst.

They were here for *her*.

As Dainhurst bent to change his shoes at the temple steps, Gisella lifted the hem of her gown, revealing her silver slippers.

The crowd *erupted.*

They adored her. Worshipped her. Some whispered that she was Ozma reincarnated.

And why shouldn't they?

Gisella *basked* in it.

Inside the temple, Dainhurst and Gisella entered first. Esmelda followed.

Galinda, lingering, observed the crowd.

What they clapped for. What they *cheered* for. What made them *grin*.

Fascinating.

She had wondered before, but now she *knew*—being adored as Gisella was must feel like *bliss*.

And one day, *she* would taste it.

This was the second time Galinda was at the temple, Gisella's third, Dainhurst's fourth or fifth, and Esmelda's hundredth. The seats were filled mainly with the usual perfectly blonde upper echelon guests waiting to see their "friend", "brother", "Family" get crowned as King. To rule all of Quadling Country.

Dainhurst made his way to the golden chair at the altar to face his soon-to-be subjects, while Gisella, Galinda, and Esmelda sat amongst the crowd. Galinda was at ease when she settled into her seat, for as far as she knew there were no *Raindrop Gemz* required for this ceremony.

At the altar, Barbarus raised a hand. The temple bell tolled, a signal, a beginning.

Barbarus spoke of leadership. Of justice. Of the sacred duty of a king.

Gisella, predictably, dozed off.

194

Galinda, however, listened.

From her seat, she observed Dainhurst, impatient, barely masking his irritation. His fingers drummed against his knee. His foot tapped against the stone floor.

He wanted the crown atop his head.

He wanted to return to *better air.*

At last, after what felt like a thousand Sun-Moons, Barbarus concluded.

Dainhurst rose.

He knelt before the High Priest, head bowed.

Barbarus lifted the crown and intoned,

"For the One Gohd is my Witness

As you all are

As I raise this crown to honour you, to bestow on you this responsibility

To be just, kind and truthful.

Blessed Be and may the King be Good."

The crowd echoed back:

"May the King be Good."

The crown descended upon Dainhurst's head.

Surprisingly light.

Soft.

He lifted his chin slightly, almost disbelieving. Had Barbarus truly placed it? Was it truly *his*?

He reached up, fingers grazing the golden rim.

Yes.

Yes, it was real.

And yet, even now, there remained one final formality.

Barbarus unfurled an ostentatious green parchment for the final testament.

The Wizard's Decree.

And read it aloud.

*"The **Wizard of Oz** Decrees:*

I, the one and Only Oz

With the power vested in me

By the one gohd,

Now recognise

Dainhurst Fairmoor,

*King of the Quadling Country, Second only to I, the **Wizard of Oz**, in all power and rule*

in this South Ozland."

Dainhurst was directed toward the parchment, laid out upon the altar like an offering, waiting for his name to be signed. To solidify the bargain.

He exhaled sharply, half amusement, half disdain. Then, with a deliberate lack of reverence, he pulled out his Silverwinkle pen and signed his name with a flourish.

"Second to only *who?*" he muttered, barely bothering to keep the sarcasm from his voice.

The crowd erupted in applause, a frenzy of clapping hands, stamping feet, cheers that swelled to fill the Solar Temple's vaulted ceilings.

It was done.

In the eyes of the people, in the eyes of Gohd, and—most importantly—in the eyes of the Wizard of Oz.

Dainhurst Fairmoor is King.

He settled into the golden chair, legs crossed. His forebears had sat in similar seats when kings still ruled Quadling Country instead of mayors. Now that the old ways had returned, so too would the old customs.

One such tradition?

The kissing of the King's hands.

Dainhurst had insisted upon it, his personal addition to the ceremony. If he was to be King, he would enjoy all its privileges.

Power was nothing if it wasn't witnessed. What was dominance without someone to tremble beneath it?

The gentry, the empresses, the gentlemen and ladies, the lesser lords, all of them lined up, each one keenly aware that refusing this display of fealty would only gain them the wrath of a man who they knew had no ounce of mercy in his **heart**.

They knelt. They kissed his hand.

One by one.

Including Esmelda.

Including Galinda.

Including *the Good Witch herself.*

Dainhurst basked in it, his pride swelling visibly in his chest, a slow-burning victory that he wanted them *all* to see.

They had doubted him.

They had whispered in parlours, dismissed him as a man with exceeding aspirations.

Yet here he was.

Not a mayor.

A King.

The sudden rush of power had a lasting effect inside his body; the thrill was more pleasing than anything Esmelda could offer. If his audience could see the load that had just been excreted from his cock, they too would be begging to be crowned next. Dainhurst sat on his golden throne a little while longer, partly to soak in the moment, but also to stall, giving time for his cock to relax. It would've been terribly embarrassing, to stand up with his genitals poking out of his pants for all his subjects to see.

When at last he felt composed enough, he rose.

The Golden Eagle awaited him to transport him back to the once former Fairmoor Castle, now the Royal Castle.

He departed alone, leaving Esmelda, Galinda, and the Good Witch to travel in the Golden Goose.

The entrance of the Royal Castle was a spectacle—a crush of reporters, emissaries, and dignitaries from every corner of Oz, all gathered to pay their respects to the new King.

Even the Gillikin King had come, despite his well-known distaste for Dainhurst. But Quadling Country was the strongest and wealthiest territory in Oz, its army formidable. It was *prudent* to have the Quadling King as an ally, regardless of personal feelings.

Dainhurst met with the press individually, one by one, in his study. *HourZ* passed as he answered their questions, shaping his image, commanding the narrative. Only after the last of them had been seen did he turn his attention to the kings, then the mayors.

◇

A feast was held that night in celebration of the entire family and their visitors.

It was the first in years.

Dainhurst had *business* to attend to, or so he claimed.

The other Fairmoors did not eat either.

The reporters, kings, and mayors feasted alone, gorging themselves in the candlelight before retreating to their respective corners of Oz.

By the time the last of the revellers had gone, by the time even the castle's golden candelabras had burned themselves down to the wick, only two figures remained awake within the Fairmoor stronghold.

Dainhurst, fresh from a night of *business*, a vague word that could mean anything from backdoor dealings to backhanded slaps, was in an uncharacteristically good mood and his sexual urges were through the roof. Esmelda, meanwhile, lay awake beside him, her mind working in slow, methodical loops, much like a clock with a faulty pendulum, something off-kilter in its rhythm but determined to keep time all the same.

It had been months since Dainhurst had so much as looked at her in that way.

Not that he had been starving himself. He had, of course, eaten well. The whores he took were younger, silk-limbed, unfamiliar with the particular cruelty of a man who saw pleasure as a transaction. He had once thought himself discreet, but Esmelda was no fool. She had heard their laughter echoing faintly through the corridors, had smelled unfamiliar perfume clinging to his collars.

But tonight—tonight was different.

Tonight, he felt like *the man*.

The man that had become the King.

BEFORE

The moment he entered her, something in him snapped free, an uncoiling, a reckoning. He assumed, rather stupidly, that he had emptied every drop of semen entirely during his coronation, his body wrung out by the sheer thrill. But his flesh had other ideas.

Esmelda did not complain.

She had not felt this from him since Galinda was born.

Dainhurst was many things, but he knew how to take a woman to bed.

She had once told him, in the privacy of their marriage chamber, in a tone both teasing and reverent—

"You could impregnate the infertile."

She needed this, too.

She had been fading, wilting, her spirit slipping from her fingers like fine sand. But tonight, he reminded her of the fire.

A King is nothing without his Queen.

And a dying marriage, it seemed, could be reborn—a spark to fuel it.

◇

Dainhurst woke with new blood in his veins.

His limbs felt looser, lighter, as if, overnight, he had shed the weight of his former self and stepped fully into his power, into his *true self*.

The maids had already adjusted to their new duties. The moment his eyes flickered open, the morning's paper was placed neatly in his hand.

THE NEW KING OF QUADLING COUNTRY CROWNED BY ORDER OF THE WIZARD OF OZ.

The words, set in sharp, formal print, glowed with validation.

There was much to do.

Today, he would tour his lands, his Quadling Country, even the *peasants* deserved to see the man who now ruled over them. Appearances mattered, after all. And he would need his Queen and his Good Witch by his side.

As they prepared to leave, Gisella saw her moment.

She approached; her voice honeyed with the kind of feigned sweetness that masked sharper ambitions beneath.

"Father?"

Dainhurst barely glanced at her, adjusting his crown while Esmelda straightened his tie.

"What is it?"

"As you know, I am twenty now. You once promised me, when I turned eighteen, that you would give me the Fairmoor Crown."

Dainhurst smirked.

"Did I?"

"You did." Gisella lifted her chin. "And now that I am the Good Witch, now that I am officially a Princess, I think it would add to my look."

He turned to her fully, now intrigued.

"And this is important to you?"

"Yes, father. How could it not?" She laughed, a little nervously.

Dainhurst's smirk deepened.

"If I am honest, Gisella, I feel you've been slacking in your duties to uplift my image. The family's image. I don't see how you could possibly feel you've earned the Fairmoor Crown."

Her expression barely flickered, but the room went silent.

Even the maids, who were accustomed to not existing in the presence of royalty, seemed to step even lighter.

"Father, I have done everything you have asked." Her tone was careful. "Every single task."

Dainhurst leaned in.

"Are you arguing with your King?"

Her breath caught.

"From now on, I am your King first, and your father second. You will address me accordingly."

A pause.

A lesson learned.

Gisella swallowed and nodded.

"Listen well," Dainhurst continued, his voice suddenly lilting, almost kind. "Do as I say. Fall in line. Then the crown will be yours."

"I understand, Father."

"Good girl."

◇

Dainhurst, Gisella, and Esmelda made their way to the Quadling Lowlands, to meet their subjects.

Dainhurst travelled in the Golden Eagle.

Gisella and Esmelda followed in the Golden Goose.

No questions were asked.

No one, not even family, would be permitted to sit beside the King.

He was first.

They were after.

And such was the way of power.

Galinda had served her purpose. Her magic had already done what was needed. A stepping stone for Dainhurst's ascension, a spectacle to be paraded out when the Good Witch needed to dazzle an audience. A magician's trick only dusted off when required—never more, never less.

And so, with nothing better to do, she found herself at Veilforge Castle.

She knocked.

Ominson answered.

BEFORE

The moment his eyes landed on her, a grin unfurled across his face; it was as if he had been waiting all day to deliver the line that followed.

"Ah, thank you for coming, Your Highness! Princess Glinda Fairmoor, oh— Your Highnessness!"

"Stop that this instant!" Galinda laughed, swatting him lightly on the arm. "And don't call me 'princess.' It sounds strange coming from you."

"If you insist."

Ominson seized her by the hand and dragged her inside, already speaking at a rapid pace.

"Now, tell me everything."

They fell into their rhythm, as they always did.

Magnum was away on business, leaving Ominson alone in the castle. It was often this way. Their families had a habit of leaving them to their own devices, and what a relief that was. Theirs was a companionship best enjoyed without supervision.

But there was something different about today.

Galinda watched him, how the joy lit in his face, how his voice softened when he spoke to her.

And she thought, not for the first time, of his proposal.

"Run away with me. Just the two of us."

It was ridiculous. It was impossible.

Yet it replayed in her mind like a melody she couldn't shake.

She had made up her mind once, refused him once, and yet... she was reconsidering.

Every time he looked at her, every time he spoke, she had the same thought, the same persistent, inescapable thought—

Kiss him.

She wouldn't let him know.

Not yet. Not until she was certain.

◇

Night had fallen by the time she returned to the Royal Castle, but Ominson lingered in her mind, unshaken, unmoved.

And with him, the thing she had been trying, desperately, to bury.

Her own reflection.

So, Galinda went to her chambers.

She reached for the Ethereum and flipped through its pages until she found it.

Her favourite spell.

The **Glamour Spell**.

She had translated nearly every word, unravelled its secrets, spent months decoding its intricacies. But there had always been one remaining mystery—one word that eluded her, that held the spell just out of reach.

She turned to it now.

And at last, she saw it.

It was a word she didn't need a translation for.

A word she would recognize in every language, in every font.

Beauty.

A single word. Short. But eternally meaningful.

Galinda wrote it down.

The puzzle was solved.

The months of work, the hours spent scouring meaning from ancient text— it had all been worth it.

There was a warning carved into the spell's inscription, something vague, something cautionary, but she didn't bother with it. She wasn't about to waste more months deciphering that.

Seraphina had used it, once. Night after night.

And she had been fine.

So, Galinda would be fine, too.

The spell required more than words. It needed a potion to bind it, to make it last.

Ingredients Required:

- **Pink Poppy Petals.**
- **Grimroot.**
- **Honeycomb.**
- **Crushed Silk Powder.**
- **Dewdrops.**
- And most of all—**intent.**

She raced down the castle's spiralling stairs, straight into the kitchen.

'Leave me," she told the maids.

They did.

Her hands trembled as she prepared the potion. Not with fear—no, with something more electric, something thrilling.

Was this really happening?

Was her dream finally becoming real?

It felt like Fate.

She worked tirelessly. *HourZ* passed, but she hardly noticed. When at last it was finished, she took a vial and poured the shimmering liquid inside. Every last drop.

It was time.

Galinda lifted the vial to her lips.

And then—

She hesitated.

She turned, catching her reflection in the kitchen window. She studied it.

What would she change?

BEFORE

There were too many things to count. And yet, something in her stalled. Perhaps it was the finality of it all. This wouldn't be temporary. She had to make a permanent choice.

And that realization made it all suddenly, terrifyingly more real than she had ever expected. But there was something else.

A voice, a thought, a presence that lingered in the back of her mind.

Ominson.

And for now, at least for now, that was enough for her to be patient.

At least until her eighteenth birthday.

By then, she would be sure.

Galinda placed the vial in a box, sealed it, and hid it away.

CHAPTER 29

Before Change

Many months passed, and each day the Fairmoors needed Galinda's magic less and less. Dainhurst's popularity was at its peak, his name spoken with a mix of reverence and fear. Gisella had wedged herself into the intricate machinery of governance, restoring a fragile cordiality between the King of the Quadlings and the King of the Gillikins.

But Dainhurst, oh, how he still loathed the Gillikins.

No one quite knew why.

His hatred had no logical shape, no rooted cause. It was a matter of taste, of instinct, the way they looked, the way they dressed, the odours of their food. They were, he was certain, predisposed to villainy. Criminals by nature, terrorists in the making.

The *Wizard of Oz*, however, was at an all-time high in public favour, bolstered by none other than the Good Witch of the South.

And Dainhurst, though he ruled with an iron fist, knew the importance of spectacle.

It was Galinda—plain-faced, unremarkable Galinda—who had an uncanny talent for understanding the people. A mind attuned to the rhythms of justice, a knack for reading desires, for balancing perceptions.

If only she weren't so visually unappealing.

Still, he tolerated her counsel.

She attended school, but her real education was in law, in power, in the subtleties of control. And Dainhurst, ever the mentor, shared his wisdom freely:

"Only fools allow themselves to be succeeded in popularity. Make sure you are the most popular person wherever you go. If you cannot become popular by being good—then become popular by being wicked."

She wrote them down, carefully, meticulously, in a pink notebook.

The Good Witch herself was barely **home**. Her duties as a celebrity far outweighed her duties as a sister. She toured from city to city, her purpose ambiguous, sometimes political, sometimes simply ornamental. She would arrive, wave, smile, disappear.

Suitors lined up in droves, princes, even old kings, all desperate to claim her hand.

But Galinda knew better. The Good Witch didn't seek a husband. She sought an audience.

And Galinda, the devoted little seamstress, was expected to fashion a spectacular gown for each and every appearance.

And yet—

With every passing day, Galinda thought of the potion, hidden away.

Waiting.

◇

Nobody was at the Royal Castle that afternoon.

A perfect excuse to leave.

To see her Ominson.

She grabbed her Violet Byke and sped toward Veilforge Castle.

She knocked. No answer. Not *home*.

And with nothing better to do, she turned her path toward the Magic Waterfall. Perhaps there, in the hush of running water, she could gather her thoughts. Perhaps there, she could finally decide.

The wind was cool against her skin, the sky a dimming gold, the world strangely light beneath its glow. By the time she reached the Waterfall, something inside her had settled.

She moved the rocks aside.

Slipped inside.

And then—

A sound.

There was a voice coming from within. It wasn't speech but they were sounds, nonetheless.

Somebody else inside.

Galinda came into view, and at first, her *brain* refused to assemble the image into something comprehensible. Like a botched illusionist's trick, her world rearranged itself around a reality she could neither name nor digest.

Her knees buckled. She landed on the damp earth, gasping for air, a small, ragged sound caught between a sob and a hiccup.

There, in her spot—her spot, mind you—was Ominson, his body sheathed in Gisella, the two of them tangled in the most base and brutal of human activities, utterly indifferent to the sanctity of place. The sounds he made were obscene, guttural, like an animal caught in a steel trap but somehow relishing the pain.

He was moaning aggressively, and he was climaxing. Ominson's head snapped up. His lips were still wet from Gisella's kisses and though his eyes met the

204

eyes of the unexpected visitor, registering Galinda's presence, he still couldn't mask his expression of pleasure, and neither could Galinda's *sister*.

Galinda's body moved before her mind did. She was upon Ominson, striking at his bare back with as much force as her small, trembling hands could muster. He was still inside Gisella, still slick with the evidence of their treachery. Gisella laughed. Laughed.

"What are you doing?!" she screamed, her voice shredded by grief.

Ominson, still untangling himself from the mess he had made, fumbled for words. "Glinda, I—I can explain—"

But could he? Could he explain this?

Gisella stretched languidly, her golden limbs spread across the grass as if she were basking in the aftermath of a particularly satisfying sunbath. As Ominson withdrew from her, she pulled him back, insatiable, her lips grazing his jaw. "Ignore her," she purred. "Finish what you started."

That was it. It wasn't just the betrayal. It wasn't just the unbearable *intimacy* of it. It was the *effortlessness*. The way Gisella accepted his touch as though she had always deserved it.

Galinda turned and fled, but Ominson was faster. He caught her just as she reached the exit his hands grasping hers. He was still hard, the traitorous organ standing as evidence of his lack of remorse, of the way he had already decided this was not his fault.

"Glinda, please—this isn't what it looks like!"

"Is it not?" Her breath came in gasps, more out of disbelief than exertion. "You weren't just now inside my sister?"

"I just—" Ominson struggled to tuck his hard cock back into his trousers, as if concealing the crime would erase it.

"Just what?" Galinda spat. "I guess it is true what they say, that you're a man whore and can't keep it in his pants."

"It's a misunderstanding, Glinda, please."

"A misunderstanding?" Galinda barked a laugh through her tears. "Then I suppose I have misunderstood quite a bit. I must have misunderstood every moment you tried to kiss me, every word you whispered to me. I must have misunderstood my own feelings, silly, soft-hearted girl that I am."

"Why are you angry at me? You're the one who said you didn't want to be with me! You're the one who decided I wasn't enough! You have no right to be angry!"

"Oh, is that the reason?" Galinda shrieked. "And *this* was your revenge? Is that why you had to do this? Here? In our place?"

A voice slithered in from the shadows.

"Galinda, get a grip. Why are you acting like he belongs to you?"

For a moment, she had forgotten Gisella was even there. But there she stood, smug, as though she had been waiting for this moment all along.

"And you." Galinda turned on her sister, wiping away the tears that burned like acid with the back of her trembling hand, "have you not had your fill of all the men in Oz? You're even more of a whore than he is."

"So now I'm a whore for him? The man our family decided I was meant to marry before either of us were even born?"

Galinda turned back to Ominson. "How long has this been going on?"

"Weeks," Gisella offered with a grin.

Ominson's voice was quieter. "Sun-Moons, Glinda, since we were thirteen."

Something inside Galinda splintered.

"You sick, twisted witch," she hissed, nearly raising her hands to cast the first spell she had ever truly meant. But she restrained herself. Instead, she lifted a single finger, pointing at her sister like an omen.

"Gisella Fairmoor, hear me well. From this day onwards, I swear by the One Gohd, I will never use my magic to aid you in your quest as the Good Witch. You are on your own. And no one—not even our father—will convince me otherwise."

"You're bluffing."

But Galinda had already made up her mind.

She turned back to Ominson.

"And you," her voice cracked, "I am ashamed I ever knew you. You let me believe I was imagining things. That I was crazy. All those times I told you I felt someone had been in here—you made me think it was just me. But it wasn't, was it? It was her. It was always her."

"No, Galinda, don't you see? I couldn't tell you becoz I was ashamed. You're the only one I love. You're the only one I respect. I didn't want you to see me the way everyone else does."

"That's too bad," she whispered, "becoz now I do. I see you for what you truly are."

She turned to leave.

But before she could take another step, hands seized her shoulders. Hard.

And with a single, brutal push—Gisella forced her into the Forgetting Waterfall.

Ominson screamed. "No!"

For a moment, Galinda was weightless, the air slicing past her ears, the whole world turning over like an unfinished thought. Then the water swallowed her.

Cold. Rushing. *Forgetting.*

Ominson looked into the deep water, searching for pink, and there she was, below, trying to reach the surface.

She was sinking. Drowning.

Then—hands. Ominson's hands, plunging into the water, dragging her out. Like he had done many times before, in many different ways.

She collapsed onto the grass, coughing, sputtering, vision blurred.

Gisella hovered nearby, watching. Waiting to see if Galinda had forgotten.

If she had erased her.

Ominson knelt beside Galinda, cradling her shoulders. "Glinda, do you remember who you are?"

Galinda blinked up at him, then she batted him away and sat up, staring at Gisella with an expression not of anger, but something deeper.

Something *final*.

"Yes," she rasped.

Ominson's breath caught. He glanced at the waterfall, then at Gisella. His face twisted in something between shock and betrayal.

He touched the water, yet he also remembered who he was.

It had all been a lie.

The water was not enchanted. There was no Seraphina curse. There never had been.

Mz. Everburn was right all these years. Just propaganda to ignite fear. But that didn't matter to Galinda. Her sister had just tried to sentence her to a fate worse than death.

Forgetting who she was.

Galinda stumbled to her feet and ran.

The world blurred past her, the wind tearing at her wet hair, her soaked dress clinging to her skin. The Violet Byke sat waiting for her at the garden's entrance, but she did not take it. It belonged to another girl, a girl who no longer existed.

So, Galinda ran **home**.

She ran until her lungs ached, until her little feet gave out, until she had put as much distance as she could between herself and the ghosts of her past.

When she reached the castle, it was completely dusk, Galinda, still wet, ran to her bed chambers and dug out from underneath her bed the vial of potion she had secretly hoped never to use. With the Ethereum by her side, she ignored her reflection in the looking glass, popped the bottle to her lips, and whispered the spell.

Finite Vulus Mutari Osculum Noctis et Semper

Her intent had been crystalline, clear as a star's reflection in a winter pond, but the figure that had surfaced in her mind was an unwelcome spectre. Not the person she had expected, nor the one she had willed herself to forget. The one she reviled. The one she idolised. The one for whom she had sacrificed more than she would ever admit.

Gisella.

Galinda swallowed, each drop sliding down her throat like liquid moonlight. The salt of her tears mingled with the potion's bitter tincture, and when the last sip was done, the last tear shed, the Glamour Spell was complete.

The effect was not gentle.

A sickening churn twisted in her gut, at first an irritation, then a siege, as if a thousand invisible needles had conspired against her insides. Her lungs, her **heart**—

they were under attack, rebelling against her own magic. The room swayed, tilted, capsized. She clawed for her bedpost, but her fingers would not cooperate. She couldn't even grasp air.

Had she done something wrong?

Galinda fought the pull of unconsciousness with every fibre of her being. She knew, with an instinctive certainty, that to close her eyes now was to die. But her body was not interested in her theories. Her limbs slackened, her breath shallowed, and the cold floor greeted her with an embrace that felt disturbingly like the arms of the afterlife.

◇

The night stretched itself into unnatural lengths. Even in unconsciousness, she did not forget. Everything she thought she once knew was secretly encapsulated in deceit. And yet, the world beyond her chamber showed no sympathy. The sun, as indifferent as ever, rose from the west, and the birds, unaware of her transformation, dared to sing. The cruel truth: the world still revolved but what sprouted from the ground that morning was something new. A flower everyone had forgotten was planted.

When Galinda opened her eyes, she was no longer the same girl.

She stood, stronger this time. The bedpost no longer betrayed her grip. The dampness of the previous night clung to her like old regrets. She shed her clothes with the urgency of a snake discarding an ill-fitting skin, baring herself to the chill of the morning.

And then—

A glint. A flicker of something in the looking glass.

"Oh, Oz," she whispered. Her hands found her face, tracing unfamiliar lines with the veneration of a blind woman granted sight.

The hair, golden, impossibly so, spun from the sun itself. The nose, no longer overbearing, but a delicate, aristocratic button. The jaw, sculpted, sharp, kissed by divine geometry. Lips full, cheeks flush, eyebrows pale as sun-drenched wheat.

And yet, beneath all that perfection, freckles. A stubborn constellation of freckles still speckled her nose, a relic of her old self. Her eyes—impossibly blue—had remained unchanged. As if the spell had known. As if the spell had listened to her true desire and ignored all but what she craved most.

Her body?

Unchanged.

That, after all, had never needed improvement.

Galinda was now ***Beautiful.***

She dressed, but the fabric felt wrong against her new skin. Her hands worked with newfound decisiveness, gathering every article of her past life. She flung open her door and found two maids scurrying by. She tossed the garments at their feet.

"Do what you will with these. Dispose of them, wear them, I don't care."

Their hands flew to their mouths. "Princess Galinda?" The maids knew she had magic but who knew magic could reach such extremes. To make the impossible possible.

To make Galinda beautiful.

They obeyed without further question. Some pieces they took for themselves, murmuring in hushed awe. The rest—they burned.

Galinda was done with the past.

She had a journey to make. The Quadling Country City awaited. She would require new finery befitting her transformation. She would walk through its streets with the sun at her back for everyone to see what a fine and exquisite specimen she had become.

Galinda took her golden hand mirror to accompany her on her journey. With every two steps she took, she looked into the mirror to admire herself just to make sure the façade had not faded.

Suddenly—

The creak of a door, half-open, an unspoken invitation, or a warning.

Gisella was *home*. Galinda saw the sliver of her sister's face, half-hidden in the darkness, peering out from behind the doorframe. Watching. Waiting.

Was it shame that kept her there? Or fear?

She did not care.

She turned from the doorway; they would never cross paths again.

Not if Galinda had anything to say about it.

Galinda stepped out of the castle with her pockets lined in gold—hush money, in a way, though dressed in the fineries of an allowance. A princely sum from her father for her service in sculpting Gisella into the Good Witch and in tidying up his legal affairs. A woman of means now. A woman of power, in her own right.

At the carriage house, the Golden Goose stood, its lacquered body gleaming in the early light. She ran her fingers along its trim before addressing the driver.

"You there," she called. "To the Quadling centre."

The coachman squinted at her, perplexed. "Erm. Mz. —who?"

Galinda frowned. "It's me, Galinda."

The poor man blanched, his eyes ballooning in their sockets. His jaw slackening as if it might unhinge entirely.

"No questions, please," she snapped. "Just do as I say."

"Right away, Princess."

With a hasty bow, he climbed into his perch, still casting wary glances back at her as though she might, at any moment, crack open to reveal an imposter inside. He fumbled with the reins, lost in thought, so lost, in fact, that he nearly crashed the Golden Goose not once, but twice, jerking it back onto course with a strangled yelp each time.

Galinda, meanwhile, occupied herself with more important matters. She turned her golden hand mirror this way and that, puckering her lips, tilting her chin and tossing her hair.

Toss. Toss.

And again.

Toss. Toss.

At certain angles, under certain lights, she noticed something uncanny. A resemblance.

To Gisella.

But prettier.

Much prettier.

She had not known such a thing was possible.

$\diamond$

When they arrived, the coachman pulled the Golden Goose into the *Royal Reserved Area*. He climbed down to accompany her, though his role was less that of a chaperone and more that of a pack mule.

The moment she stepped onto the cobbled street; people turned, whispering, their faces caught between awe and confusion.

For a moment, they thought she was the Good Witch of the South herself.

Which was absurd, Gisella had emerald eyes. Galinda's were blue. So blue, in fact, that if the sky had the good sense to be jealous, it would have darkened with storm clouds at that very moment.

But realization soon dawned. It was not Gisella.

It was a different Fairmoor.

Princess Galinda.

The people bowed, instinctively. She acknowledged them with a nod, as a queen acknowledges the lowborn, graciously.

Wait until they hear her sing, she joked to herself.

The whispers continued, but they were not the kind that mocked. They were the kind that marvelled. The same kind of whispers Gisella had earned.

And now Galinda had earned them, too.

She moved through the shops with a deliberate air, acquiring new dresses, purses, shoes—oh, the shoes. Ten pairs. No, twenty. It was not as though she could not conjure them herself, but that was hardly the point.

Shop owners fawned over her; designers begged her to take their wares for free. She refused. Let them see that she had as much wealth as she had beauty. Let them marvel at both.

And marvel they did.

It wasn't long before the reporters arrived, their notepads open, their quills scratching in breathless anticipation.

"Princess Galinda! A moment of your time!"

She twirled for them, her skirts flaring like golden fire.

Toss. Toss.

It wasn't enough.

They wanted more.

So she gave it to them.

She struck poses. Let them capture her in all her glory. Tossed them a quote or two.

"How does it feel to be the Princess of Quadling Country?"

"It feels good."

"Good—that you are!"

The poor coachman was struggling under the weight of her purchases, his arms piled high with silk and leather and embroidered finery. A gaggle of teenage boys rushed forward, not to help, not truly, but to bask in her presence.

They carried her parcels to the Golden Goose, then stood there, eyes wide, grinning idiotically, like dogs hoping for a scrap from the table.

Galinda, benevolent, rewarded them. She pressed a *kiss to each of their bowing foreheads.*

The boys let out strangled gasps of delight, then fled to spread the news.

She had kissed them.

She had *kissed* them.

The coachman, watching the scene unfold, only laughed in understanding. He mounted the Golden Goose, and together, they began the journey **home**.

For the first time, Galinda did not spend the ride gazing at herself in her mirror.

She was too busy replaying the events of the day in her head.

The attention.

The fame.

The intoxicating rush of being *seen*. Being Popular.

She loved it.

She *needed* it.

Especially after what had happened just one day before.

◇

Galinda arrived at the castle with a smile fixed on her face and she was *dry* as ever.

"Thank you, coachman."

"You're welcome, Princess," the coachman grunted, ferrying parcel after parcel up to her bed chamber, assisted by a small battalion of maids.

At the entrance stood Dainhurst, her father.

Staring.

His eyes ran over her face as though inspecting a painting long thought lost, only to find it curiously restored, its colours brighter than before.

"Hmmm," he mused. "Is it really you?"

"Yes, Father. It's me."

"But how?" he whispered, astonished.

Galinda smiled, a small, secret smile. "Magic."

"Woz!"

"I hope that's okay?"

"Of course it is! My beautiful little princess."

He seized her arm and pulled her into an embrace, tighter than she had ever known from him.

It was some time before he let her breathe again.

"There's a ball tonight," he said at last. "I organized it, and I'd like you to come with me."

Above them, unseen by Dainhurst, a shadow stirred atop the grand staircase. Gisella. Watching.

She had heard the rumours. But hearing is one thing. Seeing is another.

Her lips parted, but no words came. She stood frozen, her fingers clenching the polished railing, her expression caught between disbelief and something else, something uglier.

"Why, yes, Father!" Galinda declared smugly. Then, as though an afterthought: "Oh, and I was wondering, I know I'm only seventeen, but might I wear the Fairmoor Crown tonight?"

Dainhurst beamed. "Yes, of course! It's yours."

Galinda turned her head just in time to see Gisella, her green-skinned sister, standing rigid. Their eyes met.

And in that moment, Galinda knew.

She had won.

Unable to hide her fury, Gisella spun on her heel and disappeared, the slam of her bedroom door reverberating through the great halls of the Royal Castle.

Dainhurst exhaled. "Galinda, why don't you freshen up? We'll be leaving soon."

She ascended the staircase, past where her sister had stood moments before, and entered her bed chamber, now overflowing with boxes upon boxes of custom-made pink clothing, silken gloves, and shoes.

As she readied herself, she smoothed lotion over her skin and spritzed herself with the most expensive Quadling perfume she had purchased that day.

A sharp rap sounded from the castle's great front doors.

Galinda paused and peered out of her window.

A visitor.

For her.

Below, standing at the threshold, was Ominson.

He was dressed for the ball, his Violet Byke at his side.

Galinda inhaled sharply, then tried to pull back from the window, but it was too late.

He had seen her.

"Glinda?" he called, confusion etching into his features.

Her **heart** was hammering against her ribcage.

The last person she wanted to see. The last reminder of something she desperately wanted to forget.

A knock at her door.

"Princess," a maid's voice. "There is a visitor. Ominson. He asks for you downstairs."

"Tell him I don't want to see him." She hesitated. Then, colder this time: "Tell him he is not allowed to set foot in this castle. Ever again."

The maid nodded, disappearing down the hall.

Moments later, the guards descended upon Ominson like wolves on an intruder, their blades glinting in the torchlight. The head guard did not mince words.

"The princess has made it known you are never to set foot at this castle again. If you are seen on these premises, we have authority to use brutal force."

Ominson barely had time to react before two of them seized him under the arms, dragging him backward. Another guard retrieved the Violet Byke and, with a great heave, sent it tumbling onto the road beside him.

"Tell her it's me! Ominson! She knows me!"

But the castle doors had already shut.

Galinda did not move from her place.

She did not watch.

He was gone.

And that was all that mattered.

Galinda fashioned for herself yet another spectacular pink gown that looked like it was made from pink rose petals accompanied by her crystal shoes. Galinda smoothed her hair, applied another mist of perfume. Then she descended the grand staircase to where her father waited.

"Gisella won't be joining us," Dainhurst informed her. "So, it will just be us. And your mother."

Galinda nearly smiled. Nearly.

Gisella, shut away in her room, sulking in green envy? *Delicious.*

Dainhurst, beaming with paternal pride, held up a crown.

The Fairmoor Crown.

Diamond and gold, it gleamed like the sun itself.

Gently, he placed it upon her head.

It looked light.

But it felt heavy.

Very heavy.

"You now bear the Fairmoor Crown," Dainhurst said solemnly. "Treat it with honour, becoz you carry it with our family name. Whether you like it or not, you carry the Fairmoor blood."

"Yes, Father." She nodded, blinking away the heat behind her eyes.

"Swear to me," Dainhurst pressed. "Swear to your king and your father that you will carry it with honour."

Galinda inhaled.

And then, with absolute certainty—

"*I swear.*"

Dainhurst flicked his wrist, summoning the coachman.

"The princess and I will take the Golden Eagle," then, turned to Esmelda, "Take the Golden Goose. I need to speak with the princess."

"Yes, your highness."

Esmelda obeyed without question, slipping into the lesser carriage, the one with the ridiculous name of poultry. A goose. A bird with a honking cry and webbed feet. Fitting.

The royals, now properly arranged, departed for the ball.

The Queen, alone.

The King and his princess, together.

Inside the Golden Eagle, plush and candlelit, Dainhurst took his time. He let the moment settle, let the hum of the wheels on the stone path fill the air as he studied her. His daughter. His creation.

"Galinda, Galinda."

She turned to face him.

"What do you think," he asked, idly stroking the embroidered cuffs of his sleeve, "about changing your name back to Glinda?"

Galinda blinked.

"Really? Why?"

"I want you to become the Good Witch of the South."

Galinda's mouth parted slightly. "Isn't that supposed to be Gisella's thing?"

"Yes, I know. But we can start from scratch. I'll say something like—oh, I don't know—Gisella is passing the mantle to you. The way a king passes his title to his prince. I think 'Glinda the Good Witch of the South' sounds better than... Galinda."

"I don't know."

Dainhurst sighed theatrically. "Don't tell your sister I said this, but you're smarter. You have the magic. And now you have the beauty and charm to pull it off better than Gisella ever could."

"Father, I am tempted. But I don't want to go by Glinda anymore. At least not for now. And I already have plans. When I turn eighteen, I'm going to the Wizard's University to learn more about politics and magic."

Dainhurst exhaled in mock exasperation, running his fingers through her golden mane. "Oh, hummingbug."

Galinda stilled.

That was... right.

Not *humbug*, as he used to say. No. *Hummingbug.*

He finally got the name Zelena used to call her correct.

Dainhurst leaned back, "Fine," he said. "I'll send you off to the Wizard's University. I'll have everything prepared, your own suite, your own Ummi, a personal chef, anything you desire. We're royals now, so you'll get the treatment you deserve."

"Thank you, Father."

"Just promise me, that after your schooling, you'll return, and we'll discuss your future as the Good Witch of the South. Don't have too much fun and forget about your dear old popsicle."

They both laughed.

A joke, thinly veiling an order.

"And what about Gisella? What will she do when I'm gone? I already told her I'd never use my magic for her again."

Dainhurst shrugged. "Eh, I don't know. It doesn't really matter. I'm king now. I tell the Quadlings what to think. I'll probably just... make something up."

With that, he returned to his stack of documents, signing them with swift efficiency.

Galinda turned her gaze to the window, watching the bluebirds flying way up high, their wings a blur of motion against the dusk.

◇

They arrived at the ball.

Esmelda, trailing behind in the Golden Goose, emerged last.

Galinda had never seen this castle before.

It was smaller than the Royal Castle. Smaller than the Veilforge's castle, too. But still, grand enough to host a gathering of influence.

It would do. A castle was a castle, after all.

Dainhurst stepped out first, changing his shoes. Then, without so much as a glance, he extended his hand to Esmelda, leading her forward.

The King and his Queen.

Galinda knew her cue.

She stepped from the carriage, chin lifted, back straight and waited for her father to enter first before she did. The Fairmoor Crown gleamed atop her head, a beacon under the chandelier-lit sky.

Her gown—a masterpiece of magic—shifted with the air, petals of silk blooming as she moved.

Gasps.

Applause.

She had anticipated it.

But what she had not anticipated was the sheer number of reporters. A small army of them, their eyes alight, their quills poised like weapons.

Someone had tipped them off.

Galinda answered their questions with ease.

And when she tossed her golden curls over her shoulder, she caught it, their eyes, following the movement like moths to a flame.

In the periphery, she saw them.

Other girls.

Copying.

Adjusting their posture, flicking their hair in the same fashion, as if by mimicking her they could absorb some fraction of her power.

Who knew the power being pretty had to influence people?

And then—she saw them.

Three girls.

Girls she knew from Willow-Wood Hills.

Girls Ominson had slept with.

A brunette. A raven-haired girl. A blonde.

Popular, once, now, they stood uncertain.

Hesitant.

Waiting for her.

The shy, unspoken hope of the social ladder shifting in real time.

So, she did them a favour. She walked to them.

With a smile.

"Hello, girls," said Galinda, as if she had just happened upon them rather than calculated the encounter down to the tilt of her chin.

"Hi," said the brunette, eyeing her with something caught between wariness and awe. "It's Guh—Glinda, right?"

"Galinda now, but yes."

Another girl, blonde but not quite blonde enough, nudged the brunette sharply. "We're supposed to bow. She's a princess now."

"No, no, that isn't at all necessary." Not outwardly, at least. Even though the thought of these same girls—who once found endless amusement in watching her bullied—now bowing until their kneecaps snapped did bring a certain satisfaction.

But that would hardly be… good.

"I'm Fanedra, but you can call me Fanny." The blonde girl said, perking up.

"I am Coraletta," said the brunette. "They call me Cora."

"And I'm Marisella, but I go by Mila," the raven-haired girl added, her eyes gleaming with an energy that suggested she would either become a very devoted friend or an exhausting one.

Mila, incapable of containing herself another second, all but lunged forward. "Okay, now that we're friends—what's it like? Being a princess?"

Fanny, demonstrating the most *brain* cells of the trio, yanked Mila back with a nervous laugh. "Forgive us. She's… excitable."

Fanny, Galinda noted, was the careful one. The one with ears to the ground, who listened to whispers about the King's punishments. About the gardener who had

216

been thrown in prison last week for sculpting a hedge into the shape of a coyote instead of a lion.

"It's fine," Galinda said lightly, amused by Mila's lack of restraint.

"Really though," Cora asked, leaning in, "how is it?"

"Well, I do get this crown."

"Oh, Oz," Mila murmured, mesmerized. "Can I touch it?" Mila asked, fingers lifting like a baby to candy.

Fanny slapped her hand down with a harsh whisper. "Stop it!"

Galinda smiled. "Let's get some drinks and sit outside."

No protest. No hesitation.

She walked.

They followed.

The pack.

Galinda felt it and, oh, she loved the feeling.

She chose a *crimson tonic*, the others fetching their own drinks. They found seats outside in the evening air, and the laughter, light, effortless, bubbling like the drinks themselves—began.

Was it always this easy? Galinda wondered.

For so long, she had clung to the ghost of her old friendship with Ominson. But this—this was different.

Dare she say it?

Sisterhood.

By the end of the night, they were inseparable.

Fanny, slightly dazed from too much *Ollyjuice*, let curiosity slip through. "Galinda," she slurred, hiccupping, "who made your dress? It's... so... spectacular."

"I have a new royal seamstress. She made it."

"Ooh! Ooh! Can she make me one?" Mila asked, bouncing slightly in her seat.

Galinda tilted her head with mock sympathy. "No. My father wouldn't like that."

Silence.

They did not press further.

Then, Mila, still riding a wave of impulsivity, blurted, "Okay, but tell us this— how did you suddenly get pretty?"

The others stiffened, knowing full well that the wrong words could cost them their heads. But they were all thinking it.

Galinda smiled, unbothered. "I have access to the best beauticians in Oz now."

Mila nodded, satisfied. "Makes sense."

A coachman approached. "Princess, the King said we shall be leaving now."

Galinda rose. Instinctively, the girls stirred to their feet, as if waiting for instruction.

Cora, still caught in the lull of wine and laughter, blinked in confusion. "Where are we going?"

Galinda smiled indulgently. "I'm going home. But, I'm inviting you. Come to my castle sometime this week."

Fanny's brows lifted. "Really?"

"Yes," Galinda said with the airy finality of someone used to being believed. "Goodbye, girls."

They squealed their farewells, practically tripping over themselves.

A personal invitation to the Royal Castle.

Not everyone received that honour.

◇

As Galinda followed the coachman, she caught movement in the corner of her eye. A boy. Standing at the foot of the stairs, as though waiting for something.

He spoke. "Glinda?"

Her breath caught slightly at the name, half-forgotten, half-loathed.

His voice was soft, cautious. As though he were still trying to register the new image of her. "What have you—" he said. "Please, can I speak with you? It's really important."

Ominson.

He looked rough. Not just the fashionable kind of rough, the sort of rugged dishevelment that made poets weep and seamstresses inspired. His eyes were red-rimmed, raw as if he'd scrubbed them in frustration. Dark circles bloomed beneath them; bruises left not by fists but by sleepless nights. His shirt hung loose and wrinkled, an afterthought of clothing, his belt fastened half-heartedly, and his once-shined boots scuffed from a hundred uneven steps.

Galinda could have wept at the sight of him. She might have, once.

But every time she looked at him, the memory slithered forward, unshakable, settling at the back of her throat.

"Please." His voice was unravelling, as if these were the last words he'd ever be granted.

Galinda inhaled, exhaled, then turned on her heels.

She climbed aboard the Golden Eagle, the carriage rattling slightly as it pulled from the grand entrance, and she did not look back.

◇

For days, Gisella did not leave her room. Did not eat, or if she did, she did not taste it.

The Good Witch was expected to appear, expected to smile, to flutter, to be graceful and radiant and full of whatever it was that made people believe in things. But she had cancelled every engagement. How could she be the Good Witch if she had no magic?

Galinda did not care.

Dainhurst did not care.

At her wit's end, Gisella scheduled a meeting with her father.

◇

The study was alive with the scratching of pen against parchment, the whisper of paper being turned, the methodical stamping of wax seals.

"Father," she said, stepping inside, "may I come in?"

Dainhurst barely looked up. "Yes."

"I need to speak with you. It's important."

His quill did not still. "I'm listening."

"The people are asking for me. I was supposed to be in Thorneville today, at the Emerald City, but I refused to show up becoz—"

"Becoz what?"

"Becoz I don't have magic. And Galinda refuses to help me."

"So what does that have to do with me?"

"You need me to be the Good Witch!"

"Do I?" He set the quill down, finally turning his full attention to her. "Am I not already seated on the throne? Am I not the richest and most powerful man in the strongest state in Oz?"

"Yes?"

"Then what do I need you for?"

The realization was a slap.

And yet—

She needed to be the Good Witch.

She needed it like air, like purpose, like a tether to something beyond herself.

"What about the matter with Galinda?" she tried. "Are you not going to ask why she's cross with me?"

Dainhurst sighed. "Gisella, I don't care."

"You're just going to let the Good Witch fade away?"

His smile was slow, indulgent. "Who said anything about letting the Good Witch fade away?"

She narrowed her eyes.

He leaned back in his chair. "If Galinda refuses to help you, then…" He lifted his hands in mock helplessness. "If the princess says no, then it's no. What can I do?"

"What about everything you used to say? About us being sisters? About sorting out our differences?"

Dainhurst had already returned to his papers.

She pressed on. "And the Fairmoor Crown? You said—"

"Out, Gisella," he said, his voice croaking with disinterest.

She stood there a moment longer.

Then, realizing she would get nothing more, she turned and left.

219

BEFORE

◇

Meanwhile, Galinda flourished.

Coraletta, Mila, and Fanny had arrived at the castle, having followed through on the invitation with an eagerness that might have been embarrassing had it not been so expected.

The castle was unlike anything they had ever seen. Had they known, back in school, how extravagant it was on the inside—well. Perhaps they might have suffered the indignity of being friends with Galinda before she was beautiful.

They ate, they drank, they laughed until their ribs ached.

They were all wealthy, but there were certain delicacies reserved only for royals. And so, Galinda, ever the gracious host, had the maids prepare a feast.

For so long, the castle halls had been silent. Now, they pulsed with the sounds of their laughter, the sounds of four girls bound together by the sheer luck of being young and alive and at the centre of something.

And it ached in Gisella.

Gisella knew Galinda had used magic to become beautiful. Some said Galinda was even more beautiful than she was. She had won the Fairmoor Crown before even turning eighteen. She was withholding magic from her, and her name was in the papers again.

She was making their father fall out of love with her.

Galinda was taking everything that belonged to her.

And it ached.

It ached so much; she swore her *heart* might tear itself from her chest.

Galinda, meanwhile, had never been happier.

"Galinda or Princess?" Fanny teased. "What should we call you?"

Galinda rolled her eyes. "Galinda."

"So, Galinda, what are your plans? Are you marrying a prince when you turn eighteen, or are you going to university?"

"University."

"Really? Us too!" Mila chirped.

Galinda laughed inwardly. Mila at university. That was a thought. She would certainly have to pay her way in.

"What university?" Cora asked.

"The Wizard's University, of course."

"Oh, Gohd! Yes! We're all going there too!" Fanny cheered.

"How much is your family paying to get in?" Mila asked, only half-joking.

"I got a personal invitation from the Wizard himself."

"You're lying," Fanny accused.

Galinda smirked. "I swear. He came in person and asked me to attend."

"You saw the Wizard? In his true form?" Cora gasped.

"Yes."

"Woz," Mila breathed.

"What will you study?" Fanny asked.

"Mag—Politics. Politics. How about you?"

Cora giggled. "Oh, we're not going to learn. We're going to sleep with as many rich and handsome boys as we can and then find husbands."

"Speaking of," Galinda mused, "Cora, Mila, you're not from Quadling Country, are you?"

"No," they said in unison.

"Where, then?"

"Gillikin," Cora said.

"Winkie," Mila replied.

Fanny, ever the proud one, tossed her blonde hair. "Obviously, I'm Quadling."

Galinda nodded. "So what are you doing here?"

Cora shrugged in the effortless way that rich girls did, the sort of shrug that suggested they were above trivial inconveniences like being alone in a foreign country.

"Quadling Country has the best schools," she said simply. "Our parents wanted the best for us, so, here we are."

"So you live here all alone?" Galinda asked, tilting her head.

"Without our families, yes," Cora admitted. "But we have our Ummi, and we live in a rather large house, so we can't complain. Not to mention the unlimited bank account."

Cora and Mila laughed, too easily, like they had rehearsed this answer before. Perhaps they had.

There was silence then, the kind that creeps in when everyone suddenly remembers they are being observed.

Galinda picked up her silver hairbrush and began running it through her curls with slow, practiced strokes. "How was the ball after I left?"

Mila laughed first.

Then Cora. Then Fanny, who tossed Mila about by the shoulder like she was some overgrown doll, all giggles and conspiratorial grins.

"What's funny?" Galinda asked, arching a brow.

Cora smirked. "Okay, after you left, your dear friend Ominson had a little too much to drink and came over to our table…"

Galinda paused mid brush stroke. "And?"

"And he asked Mila if she wanted to go upstairs."

"Upstairs?"

"Yes! To… you know," Cora teased.

Mila was still laughing, but then she looked straight at Galinda, half-drunk on amusement, half-tinged on her own wicked little secret.

"And it was gooood," she purred.

The hairbrush slipped from Galinda's fingers.

For a moment, the air seemed to freeze.

Then she laughed, too.

Because it didn't matter.

Because she didn't care.

Because he owed her nothing.

Because he could do whatever he wanted.

Couldn't he?

⬦

As the weeks flew by, Galinda became known in the popular circles of Quadling Country.

They already knew her, of course. They had always known her. But now, they understood her.

She was no longer some tragic relic of Seraphina, the girl people whispered about in half-superstitious tones.

She was Galinda.

The blonde, the beautiful, the fashionable, the pink-clad princess of Quadling Country.

She was popular. Very popular.

And this time, for all the right reasons.

She was the sister of the Good Witch, and just as good. She was so good.

And she did it without so much as a flick of magic in public.

Magic was still… distasteful. Tolerated, perhaps, but only when neatly sanctioned by the right authorities. Thanks to the Good Witch, it had become slightly less taboo, but only slightly. Only those with a certificate from the Wizard's University, or those who bore the title of *Wizard* or *Good Witch*, were permitted to use their magic in public.

Not that anyone ever seemed to graduate from the magic program at the Wizard's University.

But Galinda would change that.

One day, she would use magic publicly.

One day, she would be the Good Witch.

Just as her father had always wanted.

Just as she had always wanted.

⬦

Days turned into weeks, weeks into months, and Galinda turned eighteen.

It was time to get ready for university and she was going out of Quadling Country for the first time without the King. She and her closest friends needed supplies—garments, shoes, perfumes, ribbons—essentials, really. There was only one place for such an undertaking.

The Emerald City.

GLINDA: *The GOOD Witch*

At the request of his pretty little princess, the King of Quadling Country had arranged for her to travel in the Golden Eagle, an older yet still opulent carriage which he no longer used, having recently acquired the *Golden Phoenix*.

The *Pryzm Road* was cleared for her passage, and a dozen guards were assigned to escort her and her friends.

Gisella watched from her window as Galinda and the others climbed into the Golden Eagle, their laughter carried by the wind. She had not been seen in public for months. Some had begun to speculate that she had died. The King, of course, had assured them otherwise.

But still—

The Good Witch had vanished.

◇

The journey was long, and one by one, the girls succumbed to sleep.

All except Galinda.

She sat wide-eyed, watching as the landscape transformed.

The further they travelled, the more the world around her glittered.

Emerald roses lined the trails.

Ruby-red Sleeping Poppies, things she had only ever seen in books, grew in clusters along the roadside, their petals like crushed velvet.

Jade lilies swayed in the breeze, impossibly green.

And then—

The Animals.

Not the animals. The *Animals*.

They were dressed in suits, wore glasses, and even combed their hair. They lived like humans, engaging in intelligent conversations. She had heard of them in her stories, and she knew some used to live in Quadling Country before they were driven out or killed. However, seeing an antelope give a boy directions, a giraffe directing traffic, and a wolf in a crisp black coat carrying a stack of books under one arm while checking a pocket watch with the other, was a surreal experience.

This meant they were closer to the Emerald City than she thought: **The Emerald City**, where everybody from all the four corners was welcome.

The sun caught on something in the distance, sending a glimmering cascade of green light across the horizon.

Galinda stuck her head out of the carriage, and there it was—

The Emerald Tower.

The heart of the city.

The **home** of the Wizard himself.

Golden roads unfurled in every direction, spirals and curves, but they all led to him.

The way the city glistened—

223

BEFORE

It was breathtaking.

A mountain of a jewel. A hope. It was Oz.

Once upon a time, green had been her favourite colour.

Now, she despised it.

But the Wizard?

He got a pass.

He was the only person she could tolerate whose entire brand was green.

"Girls! Wake up this instant!"

Galinda's voice sliced through the drowsy stupor of the carriage like a silver blade.

"We're here!"

The other girls stirred, blinking sluggishly, stretching in the languid, feline way that rich girls do when waking from a long nap. They were pleased to be in the Emerald City, certainly, but it was a tempered delight, an old love rather than a new infatuation.

But Galinda—

Galinda was practically vibrating. She looked like a child about to get her first *Lolliguild-Pop*.

Which, frankly, was absurd.

She was the wealthiest girl in all of Quadling Country. There was no way, in all of Oz, that the princess had never stepped foot in the Emerald City.

The city was built for everyone from the four corners of Oz, but let's be honest, primarily catered to the rich and powerful.

And yet, there she was, positively breathless, as though she had discovered a long-lost utopia.

The Golden Eagle came to a slow, ceremonious halt.

Galinda didn't so much step out as burst forth, like an overexcited soap bubble, her voluminous skirts billowing in the wake of her enthusiasm.

The other girls scrambled after her, adjusting their gloves and hats, exchanging knowing glances as if to say, *Well, she's lost her mind, hasn't she?*

Galinda twirled on the cobblestone, arms stretched out, drinking in the city with wide, greedy eyes.

It was so much more spectacular in person.

There were thousands of shops. Shops for everything.

Madame Morbell's Hair Salon—where the wealthy had their tresses tamed into elaborate monstrosities of curls and pins.

Dillamont's Boutique—for men to get their finest suits and boots.

Amma's Kitchen—redolent with the scent of freshly baked bread and simmering soups, a modest nod to ***home*** comforts in a city made of artifice.

Nessa's Roses—a florist boasting blossoms from every corner of Oz, their petals arranged in perfect, unnatural gradients.

And even a **Boq's Toes**—for the most extravagant pedicures, because, in the Emerald City, even one's feet must be fashionably adorned.

There were too many to count.

"Where should we go first?" Cora asked, already resigned to Galinda's inevitable command.

Galinda turned, scanning the boulevard for the grandest, most ostentatious storefront.

Her eyes landed on a towering glass display of jewelled heels and silk slippers. **Frexwell's Shoes.**

She lifted her chin, pointed like a general leading her troops into battle.

"There!"

The girls shrieked in unison.

"Shoes!"

They took off at a sprint, sending pedestrians scattering.

The guards, startled, exchanged frantic looks before stumbling into motion, hands hovering over their swords. If so much as a golden strand of Galinda's hair went missing, they would surely lose their necks.

One by one, Galinda plucked up shoes: ruby slippers, blue sandals, black boots (not that she would ever wear black, but one must own all the options).

She sifted through the collection with the meticulous care of a jeweller inspecting diamonds.

And then—

"Oh, Oz, are you—could you be—the princess of Quadling Country?"

Galinda turned, mid-selection, to find a bald, bespectacled man with a blonde moustache approaching her with the hesitant reverence of a man nearing a shrine.

She nodded gracefully.

Frexwell nearly fainted.

"It *can't* be! The princess! *In my shop!*" He clasped his hands together as if in prayer and motioned dramatically to a cushioned chair. "Come, sit, sit!"

Galinda arched a brow. "Have we met?"

"No, no, but I am a *Quadling* native, my dear! I have followed your fashions most devoutly in the *NewZPaprs*. I was *at* the ball where your sister was revealed to be the Good Witch, though, between us, I didn't much care for that. But your gown? *Spectacular.*"

"Oh, thank you!"

"I imagine you are looking for pink shoes?"

Galinda laughed, "yes, but I didn't expect—"

"Bah!" He waved her words away as if they were inconsequential. "I'll have them recoloured. Just pick your favourites, and my assistant will see to it at once."

A sharp whistle, and a skinny boy materialized at Frexwell's side.

"This is Lazlo Threadmire, my apprentice. He shall assist you."

Lazlo, trembling slightly, ducked his head.

"Hello, princess," he whispered, "I—I am such a big fan."

"Are you a Quadling native as well?"

"No, Gillikin." He hesitated. "I know your King don't like us much, but it is an honour to meet you."

Galinda's lips twitched in amusement.

"Don't say that," she teased. "I don't judge strangers until I've met them. Becoz, you know, strangers are just people I haven't met yet."

Lazlo blinked at her; mouth slightly open. He had the distinct look of a person trying very hard to decipher wisdom beyond their comprehension. Then he nodded vigorously, as though afraid to admit he hadn't quite understood.

Galinda, pleased with herself, resumed selecting shoes.

When at last her fingers were exhausted, she nodded decisively to Lazlo.

"I'll have them recoloured in every shade of pink."

"Yes, your highness!" Lazlo practically tripped over himself in his rush to obey. As he scurried away, he whispered under his breath, loud enough for Galinda to hear:

"Woz! Such a *good* princess!"

After a while, when Galinda was helping her girlfriends decide on the few shoes they could buy, Lazlo returned.

Three other staff trailed behind him, each with ten boxes of shoes.

"All coloured pink, your highness!" Lazlo said gleefully, whilst also struggling for air.

Frexwell was back again.

"How much is it?" Galinda asked.

"No, for you free!" he insisted.

"Oh Frexwell, you would do that for me?"

"Hey, you are my princess, it is an honour to have you wear my shoes. That is payment enough."

"Thank you!"

He smiled once more, not as if the smile ever left his face.

With a wave of his hands in the direction of the door, the staff walked, trembling, carrying the boxes to the Golden Eagle, with one of the guards leading them to its parked location.

Cora, Mila and Fanny had to pay for their shoes. Each bought eight pairs and were charged at full price.

There was so much to see in the Emerald City.

They went to the bakery, Galinda ordered a Gooseberry Pie.

They got their nails and toes touched up at **Boq's Toes**.

They even went into the *vyntage* clothing store.

Farkleberry & Things.

Hoping to find and laugh at the many *hideotous* items they were selling.

And that they did.

There, amidst the dust and mothballs, Galinda discovered an old black cloak—long, draped, vaguely resembling a discarded curtain.

Beside it, a white pointed hat.

A terrible thought occurred to her.

She donned the hat, wrapped the cloak around herself, and struck a menacing pose, fingers curled like talons.

"Oh! Watch out, my sweeties!" she cackled, in the shrillest, most over-exaggerated voice she could muster. "I'll get you, my sweetie!"

Cora, Mila, and Fanny howled with laughter.

"You're *too* good at that!" Mila wheezed. "I'd be *so* spooked if you weren't so *pretty*."

Fanny elbowed her.

"What?" Mila grumbled. "I'm just saying—if you looked the way you *used* to, I'd run away screaming."

Galinda paused, then smiled.

Because it was a joke.

Because it was funny.

Glinda Fairmoor's face spooked everyone. Too good, she was dead. Gone and melted away.

"Should I buy it?" Galinda said, her voice a taunt now.

"You wouldn't," Fanny replied with a snort, "That's a crime, even to pay for such... disgustifying things."

But Galinda was already at the counter, placing her purchase with deliberate finality. The shopkeeper blinked, clearly stunned by her decision, and Galinda couldn't help but smile a little smugly.

"You didn't!" Cora laughed, the sound bouncing off the dusty walls. And then, with a quicksilver shift, all three of them burst into raucous laughter.

It was a brief reprieve, but eventually the reality of the day set in. University books to buy. Unavoidable, unwelcome. They all groaned at this, but none groaned louder than Galinda.

"Books are for people who have no friends," Galinda muttered as they trudged off toward the University bookshop.

After they bought their books, purchased some souvenirs and ate some more food, the sun began to sag low over the Emerald City, casting long shadows against the yellow brick road; it was time to head **home**. They spent the whole day in the Emerald City and still didn't see nearly a quarter of it. Galinda saw it as a positive.

That left more for them to explore when she *returned* again with her best friends.

The Pryzm Road was cleared for her once more, reaching the castle way past the night.

Half asleep, the girls groaned, sleepwalking to the separate bed chambers Galinda had prepared for them to stay in, whilst Galinda was carried by one of the guards.

Princesses didn't have roommates. Even if it was for one night.

As she was being lifted into the castle, one of the guards asked, "Princess, should we carry your things with you inside?"

"No. I'll be leaving for University in a few days, there's no need."

They did as they were instructed and left it safe and intact in the Golden Eagle.

Laid in her soft canopy bed, Galinda pulled out the Ethereum and her translations for some bit of light reading, however exhaustion took over her and she fell asleep beside the spell book.

Left *open.*

◇

The early morning slipped through the castle's towering spires like a whispered secret. Galinda's best friends had long since departed, each returning to their own homes, to prepare for the grand adventure awaiting them in two days. The Wizard's University loomed ahead, and their futures stretched before them like uncharted land.

But for Galinda, the day unfolded with the kind of wearisome familiarity that made her chest ache. Dainhurst was still at work, shuffling papers and passing new laws no one would ever care to remember. Esmelda, who had never known the meaning of subtlety, was now revived, her life resuscitated with a breath of adoration for her King. And Gisella, poor, poor Gisella, was locked away in her chamber, a prisoner of her own whims, as she had been so many times before.

Today, though, even Gisella's isolation had taken on a strange quality. Her friends, Thelma and Veloria, had arrived, unusual in themselves, for they were quiet today. Too quiet, as if the very words they shared were too dangerous to utter aloud.

Galinda found herself drawn to the kitchen, her stomach growling in protest of the breakfast she had missed, lost somewhere in the quiet embrace of sleep. She entered the kitchen, her senses immediately overwhelmed by the warmth of the room and the smell of fresh bread, the distant sizzle of something simmering. Two maids worked in harmony, one wiping the counters, the other preparing something for later.

"Good after-midday, Princess," they greeted her in unison, dipping into their curtsies.

"Good midday."

She wandered to the cabinets, her fingers brushing over shelves until they stilled at the realization. Her hidden stash of treats—sweet, secret treasures—had been emptied. Turning to one of the maids, she commanded with an air of easy entitlement. "Can you whip me up something while I take a shower?"

"Of course, Princess. What would you like?"

"Surprise me."

She turned to leave, the familiar rhythm of her life pulling her forward, when a soft voice stopped her. One of the maids, holding a letter in her hand, stepped toward her with hesitant steps.

"Oh, and don't forget this!" her voice betraying a sense of trepidation as she handed the letter over.

Galinda paused mid-step. "Why do you have my letters? That's the Royal Secretary's job."

"This is… a special letter," the maid explained, her smile both apologetic and knowing.

"Who sent it?"

"Ominson."

A sigh escaped Galinda's lips—sharp, cutting. "Didn't I make it clear? No one is to entertain him. He is never to set foot near this castle again."

"I—Princess, I was tending to the flowers this morning, as I always do. The guards were making their rounds, and he… he handed it to me. Said it was imperative I get it to you. He said you would never hear from him again if you accepted this."

Galinda's eyes narrowed, "So, you fell for his charm, then?" she asked, her voice laced with scorn.

"He… looked so sad, Princess."

Another sigh, this one deeper, heavier. Galinda snatched the letter from the maid's trembling fingers and made her way upstairs without another word.

In her room, she paused before the fireplace, the fire already crackling with the promise of warmth. She stared at the letter, wondering for a moment if she should cast it into the flames, burn the memory of Ominson from her life forever. But something stopped her. Instead, she tossed the letter onto her bed, its presence a stark contrast against the pale sheets. With a sigh, she stepped into the shower.

The water was warm, cascading over her body like a cleansing ritual. As the droplets slid over her skin, her thoughts wandered, thoughts of the University, of her new life, of the endless possibilities that awaited. Her friends would be with her. She would be adored. She would finally leave the suffocating grip of Quadling Country behind. And the boys—oh, the boys. They would fall at her feet.

The days couldn't come fast enough.

But as the Oz'mins stretched, Galinda's hunger grew more insistent. She stepped out of the shower. As she entered her room to dress, her gaze fell on the bed. The letter. Still there. Waiting.

A pang of annoyance tightened in her chest, but she couldn't look away. She moved to it, then picked it up. She should burn it. She should forget it. But curiosity, that insidious companion, a trait unbecoming of a princess, whispered in her ear. *What could he possibly want now?*

She opened the letter slowly, carefully, her breath caught in her throat as the paper crinkled between her fingers.

And so, despite herself, she read:

BEFORE

Dearest Glinda,

I hope you are well.

If this letter reaches your hands, then I fear your heart is still aflame with bitterness toward me, which, if I am honest, I understand. What happened in the garden… it plays over in my mind as well, over and over. You were never meant to discover the truth in that way. I doubt you were ever meant to know at all. But here we are.

I am broken, Glinda. Very broken, and that is no excuse, I know, but it is the truth. I have always been honest with you and so I will tell you the truth once more.

Since we were eight, Glinda, I have seen, done things that no child should ever have to endure, and it was at your sister's hand. She approached me a few days after we found The Waterfall, right around the time you lost Zelena. She was already inside when I found her and she told me that if I spied on you and informed her on our conversations in the garden, she would show me how to be a man. She gave me my first kiss—and it went further, much further. At thirteen, she gave me my manhood, and I gave her my innocence. But rest assured; whatever secrets you shared with me remained just that. Secrets.

I told my father about the things Gisella taught me, and he patted me on the back as though I'd achieved something noble. I thought perhaps I was doing something right. So, when you tell me to 'keep it in my trousers,' Glinda, it hurts. Becoz the thing is, I can't. I've tried so hard. But since thirteen, there's been a hunger inside me, an unquenchable hunger that no amount of effort can sate.

I've seen Barbarus. He tried to help, but I think there is no cure for what was planted in me so young. I need time. Time to understand who I am, and I think you need that too. Perhaps you were right to turn me away when I confessed my love to you. You've always been so sharp, so smart. It would have been a disaster, after all.

My father and I still don't see eye to eye, and so I've made my choice. I need to find honour, something that proves I am not just the foolish, useless, blonde man-whore from Quadling Country. Something that when people look at me, they see that I am worth something.

I think, Glinda, that we are alike. The Fates must have woven our threads together, you and I. We both hunger for something—we just don't know what. I think you long for love, and I hope you find it. I do. Becoz you deserve it, Glinda. Once I thought I could give it to you, but now I know that only you can decide what love means to you and the type of love you value most.

What I think I seek is honour. And so, by the time you read this, I will have already left Quadling Country to join the Wizard's Guard.

Who would have thought I'd become a soldier, eh?

Glinda, if I never see you again, if I die in some far-flung corner of Oz or if the Fates see fit to keep us apart, I want you to know this: I love you. I always have, and I always will. For all the wrongs I've done you, the pain I've caused, I will spend the rest of my life regretting it.

Love always,

Your Omi.

Galinda sat.

The letter, once sharp with its truth, now crumpled gently beneath her fingers, held close to her chest as if it alone could stave off the aching hollow within her.

For many Oz'mins she just sat there, rocking before the fireplace, reading and rereading his words. A part of her wished that she had been kinder to him. The questions swirled around her like a dark cloud: What if she had let him in? What if she had given him a chance? Now he was gone, off to the Wizard's Guard, and she would never know if they would ever meet again.

She once promised him that she would always be his best friend and now she had broken that pact by not allowing him the same grace she knew he would've given her if the roles were reversed.

But in the midst of the whirlpool of emotions, one thing stood clear: he had chosen to seek his own path, to defy his father and fight for something he believed in. She could hardly understand how he found the *courage* to do so, yet she was proud of him for it.

Her thoughts were broken by a sharp knock on the door.

"Princess, your breakfast is ready," a maid's voice called from the other side.

Galinda sniffled, wiping her eyes hastily, and replied hoarsely, "I'm not hungry!"

◇

HourZ passed. Galinda lay on the cold marble floor of her room, staring at the ceiling.

That evening, Dainhurst insisted they gather for a family dinner, a final meal before she left for her studies. Galinda's favourite foods were prepared with care— Poppyloaf, Gooseberry Pie, Stromberry Truffles, Fire-Sizzled Wyvern Ribs, Glowfruit and Chickduck Wings.

Gisella, surprisingly, had emerged from her room—cheerfully, rather— insisting she help the maids prepare. It was unsettling, the sudden shift in her demeanour, but Galinda chose to say nothing.

Gisella placed Galinda's drink in front of her, along with an empty plate.

The meal began without incident, the air thick with tension that no one seemed willing to address directly.

"So, Galinda," Dainhurst began, his voice light as he served himself some Wyvern ribs, "how are you feeling about leaving for the Wizard's University?"

With forced enthusiasm, Galinda replied, "I'm excited."

Gisella sat directly across from her. Staring.

"And what will you be studying?" Dainhurst asked.

"I told you already," Galinda said with a small laugh. "Politics. And hopefully a magic course on the side."

"Politics?" Dainhurst raised an eyebrow. "Why not something more… feminine? The Arts, for example? You do have a lovely singing voice."

Galinda rolled her eyes. "Father…"

"I'm just teasing," Dainhurst chuckled, his laughter strained. "And since you got in at the Wizard's personal request, no need for the allegiance ceremony."

"Really? So I don't have to pledge?"

"No. I don't know why he insists on it, like he doesn't already rule over all of Oz," Dainhurst said, scoffing.

Esmelda, as always, was the voice of reason. "It's just symbolism, dear. So they know who they *need* to remain loyal to."

"Hmm," Dainhurst grunted, unconvinced.

"I think you ought to do the same," Esmelda added.

"Maybe."

Dainhurst turned to look at Galinda. "What is that boy you're always with doing? err, Magnum's son."

"Omi," Galinda corrected herself. "Ominson. Oh, he joined the Wizard's Guard."

Dainhurst's spoon clattered against his plate. "Really?"

Galinda nodded.

"I'd say that's honourable of him, but he is a traitor. Why didn't he just serve in my army?" Dainhurst pointed his spoon at Esmelda. "I see you're right about that allegiance thing."

Gisella didn't say a word, but her gaze never wavered from Galinda's face, and the silence between them felt like a tangible thing.

Galinda shifted uncomfortably under her sister's unblinking stare but said nothing.

And so—

She lifted her glass of crimson tonic, taking her first sip of the evening. The sharpness of it was a welcome distraction, and yet, it could not quench the fire that still burned within her.

At once, Gisella sighed, and her posture slackened. She leaned back in her chair, relaxed now, unconcerned, suddenly finding her plate more interesting than her sister.

Galinda barely had time to process this before her father's voice cut through her thoughts.

"You do know your mother and I are coming to the University with you, right?"

"No. You don't have to do that," Galinda protested.

"Yes, I do."

With the theatrical flourish of a man who had never been denied anything in his life, Dainhurst reached across the table and squeezed her cheeks. "Don't you want your Mumsy and Popsicle to be there to say goodbye?"

"I just don't think—Guh! Fine!"

Satisfied, Dainhurst resumed his meal, carving into a Wyvern rib with practiced ease. "I just want to make sure my perfect, pretty princess is safe and looked after. I have your private suite arranged, your Ummi chosen, and, of course, as promised, a Royal Chef to ensure you never have to trouble yourself over meals."

Galinda arched a brow. "Does the University even allow students to bring their own chefs?"

"When will you realize, you're not like every other girl, Galinda? You're my daughter."

Esmelda laughed at this, a trill of agreement.

Galinda smiled. "Well... thank you, Father."

And yet, no sooner had the words left her lips than her stomach gave a violent lurch, twisting with a sudden, urgent pain.

"Ah—ow!" Galinda winced, one hand clutching her midsection.

Esmelda nearly leapt from her chair. "Are you all right, Gli—Galinda?"

"Yes... I think I just need some rest," Galinda managed, though the pain had not yet subsided.

"Are you sure?"

"Uh-huh. Excuse me."

She pushed her chair back, still cradling her stomach, and made her way up the grand staircase, every step more laborious than the last. By the time she reached her chambers, she barely had the strength to make it to her bed. She collapsed atop it, arms splayed, head heavy against the pillows.

Sleep took her at once, swift and merciful.

It was the only cure she knew for pain.

◇

When Galinda awoke, the world was slow to make sense.

She was groggy, disoriented, *confuzzled*, her own name felt like something she had to reach for.

It was like her soul had been stripped from her.

It was evening. Had she slept through the entire day? Again?

This was becoming a problem.

What would people think?

She was Galinda Fairmoor of the Upper Uplands.

She was Royalty.

She bore the Fairmoor Crown.

She resolved then and there that she would not sleep again until departure. A full night awake would be a small price to pay for resetting herself to propriety.

And yet, even as the hours passed, her mind remained fogged, her limbs weak. Every sound in the corridor made her turn sharply, as though shadows might leap from the corners to devour her.

Still, she forced herself to eat. She ordered a maid to bring her lunch, but even after consuming it, she felt no better. It was as though her body had taken the nourishment and promptly discarded it, refusing to make use of it.

So she lay in bed once more, hoping that, by the time morning came, she would feel whole again.

As the hours waned, she felt some semblance of herself returning—but only just. It was near the 13th hour when her limbs no longer felt as though they were melting.

She exhaled, a long, shuddering breath of relief.

She would not have to miss her first day. She would not have to lose even a single moment of the social ascent that awaited her.

◇

The carriage was ready by sunrise.

Dainhurst was the second to be dressed and prepared. Galinda was the first.

One by one, the household roused itself. Esmelda descended the stairs, rubbing the sleep from her eyes.

And then there was only one left.

A maid approached Dainhurst, whispering something in his ear.

He sighed, exasperated. "Alright," he said finally. He turned to Galinda. "Gisella won't be coming with us. She has… morning sickness."

Galinda schooled her features into a placid expression. She forced a smile, nodding.

She picked up her bag and stepped outside, where the golden-plated carriage, the Golden Phoenix, awaited her.

She halted.

Something forgotten. Something important.

Without a word, she turned on her heel and ran back to her chambers.

The Ethereum.

The book sat where she had left it, waiting, as if it knew it was meant to follow her. She cradled it in her arms, feeling the weight of it press into her ribs, heavier than she remembered.

Now, she could leave.

The Fairmoors boarded the carriage, and the Golden Phoenix lurched forward, so began their journey northward.

The University, though not at the very heart of Gillikin Country, was still within its borders, and this fact alone was enough to make Dainhurst's expression curdle like spoiled cream. He sat across from Galinda, arms crossed, shoulders drawn tight, his distaste worn as plainly as his regal cloak.

The notion of leaving his daughter in the hands of those uncultured, unkempt Northerners, subjecting her to their curious vowels, their odd habits, their stubborn resistance to proper decorum, it was almost too much for him to bear.

But he reminded himself—he soothed himself—with the singular thought that made this ordeal palatable: *The Wizard had insisted on her attendance personally.*

"You do realize," Dainhurst grumbled, "that I never would have permitted this if the Wizard himself hadn't intervened. You know how much I despise those people."

Galinda, feigning attentiveness, merely nodded. But then, catching sight of the way the vein on his forehead bulged, swollen with his righteous indignation, she let out a laugh.

Dainhurst huffed, rolling his eyes toward the carriage ceiling.

They took the Pryzm Road, of course, because what other road was there? And by midday, they arrived at the great stone gates.

And there it was.

Bare and bold.

The Wizard's University.

CHANGE

Change

CHAPTER 30

The Wizard's University

The Golden Phoenix nosed its way into the stone archway of the University, its gilded wheels hushed by the soft cobblestones. Other carriages clustered nearby—silver, platinum, bronze—each a proclamation of lineage, of belonging. No wooden carriages in sight, no squeaking wheels led by hapless donkeys. This was a place for those who had already arrived, even as they arrived.

This was a place for the fortunate.

And that made Galinda very happy.

The University sprawled across the horizon, far too vast for the sum of its students. A design flaw, or a deliberate flex of power? She imagined the architects, too drunk on influence to consider logistics, gesturing vaguely toward the water: *Yes, yes, and a moat, or better yet, a lake! Let them arrive by boat, that should make the poor think twice before applying.*

Galinda pressed her face against the carriage window.

Boys.

Boys adorned in embroidered waistcoats, walking with a practiced confidence that barely disguised the urgency beneath. Boys who wore their family crests on medals. Sons of aristocrats, nephews of mayors, princes and heirs apparent to obscure, windswept kingdoms.

Galinda squealed and withdrew, bouncing in her seat, heels clicking against the polished floor of the carriage.

The Phoenix came to an elegant halt at the lake's edge.

Silence.

Not true silence, but that brand of hush where whispers cluster like moths against gaslight.

The Golden Phoenix, rare and resplendent, had not yet been released for public sale. That the Fairmoors arrived in it was not just ostentation, it was a reminder. Theirs was a wealth so profound that even the other wealthy could only aspire to it.

CHANGE

The door opened. One after another, the Fairmoors emerged, gracefully, languidly, as if they had all the time in the world. Those watching, eager to appear disinterested, invented small tasks—straightening cuffs, adjusting hats—but all the while, their eyes betrayed them.

"It's the King and Queen of Quadling Country," came the whispers.

Some bowed, some averted their eyes in quiet mortification. They had considered themselves rich, until now.

One Fairmoor remained inside.

Galinda Arduelle Fairmoor.

Her pink shoes touched the earth, and an invisible current swept through the crowd. *Oh, of course it's her.* The most popular *Yungling* girl in all of Oz.

The boys, too bold or too foolish, nudged each other, their lips pressed tight to stifle unseemly grins. They had heard stories that her beauty resembled the Morningstar. Now they would know if they were true. Her golden curls tumbled forward first, deliberate, cascading like spun treasure. Then her face: eyelashes, long and thick, her lips red as a rose, and her cheeks a soft blush as if kissed by the sun. Features delicate and cruel in their perfection.

The girls stirred, suddenly ill at ease. Hands flew to hair, smoothing, fixing, reordering. Servants fumbled for combs and mirrors. They had left their castles thinking themselves beautiful. And perhaps they were. But beside Galinda—

Not beautiful enough.

They needed to brush their hair again.

And again.

And again!

Some boys took a hesitant step forward, then faltered. Their gazes slid to King Dainhurst, who would sooner have them quartered than let them exhale in his daughter's direction. The more pragmatic boys did not bother stepping forward at all. They knew better. Their carriages had been bronze. Their surnames were merely notable, not *legendary*.

They were Middies.

"Sire, I have notified the helmsman of our arrival, the boat should arrive shortly," the coachman announced.

"Perfect, thank you Gregoree," Dainhurst replied.

Dainhurst, watching the way the crowd bent toward his daughter as flowers bend toward the sun, leaned in.

"You see how they look at you?"

Galinda gave a shy smile. "Yes."

"Use that." A pause, then softer: "They are all here unmoored, uncertain. They need a leader. Be that leader. And never, *never* align yourself with the weak. You stay around them long enough, and their weakness may become your own."

"Yes, Father. Thank you."

GLINDA: The GOOD Witch

Dainhurst smoothed a hand over his gloves. "And, if ever in doubt, simply ask yourself, what would Popsicle do?"

The coachman had already begun unloading her things. A fortress of chests and hatboxes accumulated at the dockside. Gregoree, still catching his breath, turned toward his King.

"Sire, the boat approaches."

The boat. Or rather, *her* boat.

Galinda turned toward the water. The boats ferrying the other students were uniform, forgettable. No doubt an efficient, university-approved model.

Hers was not.

Hers was pink.

Not the soft pink of dusk, nor the fleeting pink of a rose at bloom's edge. No, *this* pink was audacious. Blinding. The sort of pink that demanded, rather than requested, to be seen.

It took a small army to hoist her belongings aboard. The helmsman's jaw clenched, his breath heavy, but he did not dare complain. They thought Dainhurst excessive. They had never met his daughter.

At last, Galinda climbed aboard. She trailed her fingers in the water as the *Aquafish*—emerald, violet—danced beneath the surface, as if in worship. She climbed atop her stack of luggage, ascending higher, and higher still.

The view from above. How sweet it was.

Dainhurst, watching, allowed himself a smile.

If only he had known then.

If only he had seen what she would become.

If only he had realized sooner—how alike they truly were.

The helmsman loosened the sails, and the boat surged forward.

Despite leaving last, despite the staggering weight it carried, Galinda's boat reached the University first.

And still, heads twisted, bodies angled, eyes searched.

They wanted to see her.

The *Pink Princess*, perched on high, looking down on them all.

The boat floated its way to the docks of the main campus, cutting through the waters with the slow inevitability of destiny itself. News had already outpaced it— news that Galinda Fairmoor of the Upper Uplands, Princess of Quadling Country, blonde radiance incarnate, swathed in the finest pink silks, had arrived.

They had heard of her. They had seen sketches in fashion gazettes. The whispers ran ahead like mice in the wainscoting: *Prettier than the Good Witch of the South? Well, then, she must be Good-er. The Good-est, in fact.*

Hundreds of students and faculty had assembled, a congregation of academic curiosity spiced liberally with voyeuristic hunger. There she was, a dollop of spun sugar balanced atop a precarious tower of travel cases, like the finishing cherry on a *banana creamcone*.

239

CHANGE

The great boat docked with an exhalation, its chains rattling as it was moored in place. With the practiced grace of someone accustomed to both admiration and treacherous high-heeled descents, Galinda stepped down from her mountain of luggage. Behind her, guards and university porters scrambled to unload her excesses—boxes marked with gilded initials.

The boys ogled. They vied to be seen. Some attempted brooding sophistication; others, wide-eyed innocence. None succeeded in anything more than looking absurd.

Did Galinda notice them? Of course she did. Did she grant them the favour of her regard? Of course she did.

She turned, ever so slightly, just enough for the light to catch in her irises, for the corner of her mouth to suggest a smile, before she dismissed them entirely with a flick of golden lashes.

The boys were undone. Some imagined her naked. Some imagined her dressed, but only in their arms. Some dared to imagine themselves beside her for all eternity, through marriage of course, crowned by her favour, permitted to bask in her glow.

And indeed, one of them might. But only one.

She took heed of what her friends Cora, Mila and Fanny were planning.

Why should she come to the Wizard's University only to simply learn?

No, no.

A university of this calibre, this petri dish of pedigree, offered more than books and lectures. It was a hunting ground for a perfect prince, an incubator of futures forged in wealth and ambition.

Galinda scanned the crowd, which was still enthralled by her beauty, sorting through the hopeful, the helpless, the hapless. None, as yet, had the necessary glint of inevitability.

Although many came close, she never quite saw the One.

But not everyone had arrived.

And she would wait, she wasn't a patient girl, but for this, she would be—ever so.

A short man in a navy suit pushed through the throng, his dark hair shot through with grey at the temples, his expression bearing the weary affability of a man who has met too many important people and forgotten most of their names.

"Your Highness, welcome! Punctual, just as the rumours predicted!"

King Dainhurst of the South laughed heartily and clasped the man's shoulders like an old friend.

The man turned to Galinda, extending a hand. "Professor Shinzin, Headmaster of The Wizard's University but most people here call me Professor Shinz, so feel free," he laughed.

Galinda met his handshake with the limpest, most perfunctory grasp imaginable. "A pleasure," she said, executing a curtsy forced and unnatural.

"Oh, the pleasure is ours," said Professor Shinz, his eyes twinkling with a knowingness she did not appreciate. "You've made quite a name for yourself already, I read the Daily Oz, you know?"

He pivoted on his heel. "Shall we?"

The Fairmoors followed. The sea of students parted as though commanded by an unseen force. Some had been waiting for *HourZ*, yet they were shuffled aside as if they were merely set dressing for the grand arrival.

They passed under an archway, stepping into the main courtyard of the university, where the shadow of a monumental statue loomed over them.

It was the stone statue of the very man the university was named after.

The Wizard of Oz.

Galinda looked up. The likeness was uncanny, the carved stone capturing his strong jaw, his imposing moustache, the cane he wielded like a sceptre, its top crowned with an emerald the size of a clenched fist. The inscription at its base read:

To find your heart's greatest desire, look not to the skies, just simply follow the Yellow Brick Road.

Galinda smiled.

The many winding paths of the Yellow Brick Road, which all eventually led to the Wizard.

The one man who could give anyone what they seek.

Yes.

She knew this already.

They pressed forward.

Professor Shinz glanced at Dainhurst. "It's been Oz'moons, Dainy. How does it feel, to finally be the King of the South?"

Dainhurst laughed, the sound a rolling declaration of triumph. "Couldn't be better."

"I can hardly believe you actually did it."

"Did you ever doubt I would?"

Professor Shinz's smile remained unchanged. "Not for a second."

Galinda, however, was unsettled. This man, he was not blonde. And yet her father greeted him like a brother.

"Are you from Quadling Country?" she asked.

"No," Professor Shinz replied. "The North. Gillikin Country."

Galinda turned to her father. He nodded, ever so slightly, his expression carefully neutral.

They ascended three flights of stairs, arriving at a singular chamber perched at the pinnacle of the university. Professor Shinz withdrew a key, unlocked the door, and ushered them inside.

It was more than a room. It was a kingdom in miniature.

The space, vast enough to house twenty-three students, belonged to Galinda alone. A pink canopy bed sat in regal splendour; the newest model of a large wardrobe carved with unicorn horns. A crystallised rosy-pink vanity mirror, framed in gold, occupied one side of the chamber, its surface littered with the latest in beauty innovations. A chandelier, bedecked in crystal, refracted the light into endless shades of rose and blush.

Dainhurst turned to her. "This is yours."

"The *private* suite of the private suites," added Professor Shinz, "reserved for our most esteemed guests."

"Woz!" Galinda gasped.

Dainhurst beamed. "Do you like it? We can replace anything that doesn't suit you."

Galinda ran a hand over the silk bedsheets, overcome. "It's perfect. How did you know exactly what I wanted? I assumed I'd have to shop once I arrived."

"Thank your mother," Dainhurst said. "She chose everything."

Galinda turned to Esmelda. Then, impulsively, she embraced her.

Tighter than she ever had before.

Esmelda sighed into her daughter's golden curls. "Anything for my perfect girl."

Galinda was not hugging her because of the lavish gifts.

It often occurred to her, in those fractured moments between conversation and silence, that her mother didn't truly know her at all. That they were, by some cosmic joke, cut from entirely different bolts of cloth, one stiff and practical, the other soft and fraying at the edges. Yet, unbeknownst to her, the mother, always the silent spectator, forever stationed just beyond the threshold of confession, had spent years observing, cataloguing.

Love, in her mother's case, was not a demonstrative thing, but something quiet and studious, folded neatly away like letters never sent, and tucked deep into the hollow compartments of the heart.

Before Dainhurst could voice his question, Professor Shinz, ever one step ahead, answered it for him.

"And the matter of your *Ummi*—we've allocated one, of course. She'll arrive by week's end to ensure you're well-settled, properly nourished, and—" He bent his forehead, furrowing his brows to Galinda as though the very thought caused him acute suffering. "Most importantly, staying on top of your academic work."

The way he said it made it clear: he had low expectations that someone like Galinda would prioritise her education or have the intelligence to complete her schooling.

Dainhurst brushed past the insinuation. "And what of the Royal Chef I requested?"

"We've arranged accommodations for him alongside one of our new assistant teachers. He will have full use of their kitchens to prepare Princess Galinda's personal meals. They will be served to her at the sixth hour, fourteenth hour, and the seventeenth hour."

"Perfect!" Galinda clasped her hands in satisfaction.

"Oh," Professor Shinz said suddenly, glancing down at his notes. "You requested sorcery to be added to your curriculum?"

"Yes, that's correct."

"And—" he hesitated, as if reluctant to say it too plainly, "you possess magic, like your sister, the Good Witch?"

Galinda flicked her gaze toward Dainhurst.

His nod was a decree.

"Yes, I do," she said.

"Then perhaps a demonstration?"

Galinda smiled.

She turned to her grand canopy bed, its pink silk pillows so perfectly plumped, so exquisitely arranged, that disturbing them seemed a crime against beauty itself. She raised a hand, fingers poised with intent, and willed one to rise.

Then—

Nothing.

Galinda frowned.

She tried again, this time with greater focus.

Then—

Still nothing.

The room was too quiet.

"I'm sure she's just tired," Dainhurst said smoothly, stepping in before the moment could fester. "It was a long journey."

"Sure," Professor Shinz said, in a tone that suggested otherwise. "It's only that our sorcery professor is a personal friend of the Wizard. She is...particular. She only admits students with raw magical talent, the sort that even I couldn't persuade her to overlook."

He made a small note in his book.

Or, rather, he *crossed something out.*

Galinda's pulse quickened.

"If, when the time comes, you cannot display your abilities," he continued, "I'm afraid you won't be allowed to take the course."

Galinda swallowed. "How many students are enrolled in it?"

Professor Shinz barely glanced up. "Two."

Silence.

"We should be going," Dainhurst declared, his tone final.

He made for the door but hesitated, turning back to her. He lowered his voice, a rare moment of fatherly quiet.

"Don't worry, you'll do great, *hummingbug.*"

She grinned, throwing her arms around him. "Goodbye, *Popsicle!*"

Surprisingly, she already missed him, his tantrums, his dramatics, even his exhausting need to be right. And she knew, as sure as the sun rose, that he would miss her too. If only because now he was left alone in that castle, trapped with that wicked green *witch*, Gisella—green with envy, green with spite.

Professor Shinz followed Dainhurst out, leaving Galinda alone with Esmelda.

Esmelda lingered, placing both hands on Galinda's shoulders.

"Galinda," she said, softly. "Take care of yourself. Enjoy yourself, and don't get *too* lost, you hear me?"

"Yes, Mother."

"And try to make genuine friendships. Real connections. It's not *always* about being surrounded by 'powerful people'," she added, her voice laced with a gentle mockery of Dainhurst. "Okay?"

"You *heard* Father," Galinda laughed.

Esmelda rolled her eyes, but a small smile crept through.

Then, without ceremony, she pulled Galinda close and held her.

"Goodbye, *Mumsy*."

Esmelda said nothing. She merely *kissed Galinda's forehead*, a quiet benediction, and then left.

The door shut with a final, resolute click.

And there Galinda stood, alone in the vast expanse of pink.

Alone.

Left to brave this new world, with no hand to hold but her own.

A knock.

Galinda flicked her gaze toward the door, her delicate frame still poised before the grand mirror. With a sigh of practiced patience, she pulled the door open.

"Your belongings, Princess," wheezed one of the guards, his breath labouring under the weight of privilege, hers, not his.

Galinda tilted her head just so, peering past him. Indeed, the remainder of her prized cargo loitered in the corridor, burdening a handful of lesser men who lagged behind, struggling with the more excessively heavy trunks. Their faces shone with the exertion of carrying an entire young woman's worth.

She opened the door wider and gestured with a languid hand. "Right there, please."

The men obeyed, piling the parcels in a careful tower of pink, each one embossed with an elegant 'G.' It took them a full forty Oz'mins to ferry the excesses of her existence from the hallway to the chamber, and when at last they were finished, she dismissed them with a smile so dazzling, three of them pretended to misunderstand the concept of an exit. They loitered, feigning confusion, drinking in the radiance of her, as though she were a flower, and they were mere bees.

Eventually, they were shooed, leaving Galinda alone with the indulgences of her own taste.

She wandered to the great window, below, the university swarmed with new arrivals. Some of them, her audience, looked up, their eyes catching on her golden hair as it lifted and danced in the wind. She was, in effect, precisely what they imagined her to be.

Another knock.

Galinda stirred from her reverie, strode to the door, and peered through the spyhole. What she saw made her heart lurch in delighted recognition.

She threw open the door.

Cora, Mila, and Fanny.

The squeals, the shrieks, the exclamations, a symphony of privilege reunited. The three girls tumbled inside. Their eyes widened, darting from the mountain of belongings to the thirty pairs of shoes, gleaming bottles of perfume, jewellery and *Make-Do*: blushes, lipwands, lushtint—some of them still unreleased to the common public. But nothing—nothing—held their attention quite like the bed.

A confection of the most expensive silks and *Fluffwool*, the bed was celestial in proportion and softness. It was a bed for queens, for angels, for deities.

Naturally, they lunged.

"This bed!" Fanny cried. "Need I say more?"

"I know!" Mila flopped onto her back, arms outstretched, as though baptizing herself in silk.

"They're already talking about you, Galinda," Cora declared, rolling onto her stomach, her chin propped up in interest. "I couldn't walk three steps without hearing your name. You'd better share that fame with us, I've got boys to entangle with."

"Take as much as you like," Galinda mused, stretching like a cat, her golden hair spilling over the pillows. "I have more than I know what to do with."

"Oz, you tease!" Cora swatted at her playfully.

The laughter bubbled up once more, as sweet and effervescent as champagne.

But then,

Something caught Fanny's eye.

Something...wrong.

A black smudge against the pink expanse.

She slid off the bed with an acrobat's grace. She prowled toward the anomaly, her fingers sifting through layers of gilt-edged boxes, and lavender-scented parcels.

"Fanny, what are you doing?" Cora asked.

"Give me a moment," Fanny muttered, digging deeper, her expression sharpening with each passing second.

Her fingers closed around it. She pulled.

A gasp.

No, four gasps, sharp and high-pitched, like notes plucked from the same horrified chord.

Fanny held up the offending object, pinching it between her thumb and forefinger as though it were a dead rat rather than a mere piece of fabric.

A long, black cloak.

And worse, a white, pointed hat.

"Galinda?" Fanny's voice dripped with suspicion. "What's the reason?"

"No way," Mila whispered, "You actually brought that—that disgustifying thing?"

"The second I got home, I'd have burned it till it melted into ash," Cora added, aghast.

Galinda scrambled for an explanation, her mind whirring. "I— I don't know how that got there—oh!" Memory struck like a lightning bolt. "I left all the things we bought in the Golden Phoenix! I must've forgotten to sort it out!"

Fanny narrowed her eyes. "You can't be seen with this, you know that, right?"

"Guh! I'd give it away, but I don't hate anyone that much," Galinda huffed, crossing her arms.

"Yet," Fanny corrected, grinning.

Cora grinned.

Mila, bouncing on the bed again, grinned too. "Ooh, ooh! When we find someone we hate, someone truly worthy, we'll give it to them!"

"Smart thinking," Fanny deadpanned.

"Thank you," Mila beamed.

With an exaggerated shudder, Fanny tossed the cloak and hat aside, as though merely touching them had tainted her. The girls laughed, already imagining the delicious moment when they would bestow the cursed garment upon its rightful, unfortunate recipient.

Then, as if nothing had happened at all—

They jumped on the bed.

And Galinda, at last, joined them.

CHAPTER 31

Green as a Bitter Gourd

The sun had not yet dipped in the east. Students at Wizard's University embarked upon the ancient ritual of self-assortment. Bonds were formed, alliances whispered into being, all dictated by the unspoken yet immutable laws of social taxonomy. Who would prove worthy? Who would fall gracelessly into the margins?

For Galinda and her shimmering entourage, the answer was self-evident. The library was a land of lost causes and clammy-palmed social missteps. The field, however—the great verdant coliseum where aristocrats in training tested their sinew and status—was where history would be made. And Galinda was its inevitable queen.

The boys, already in the thick of their beloved *Pucket-ball* match—a sport that involved running a circular ball to home base while dodging opponents before using a mallet to sink it into a pit, a game less about the rules and more about the preening—ceased their exertions the moment she arrived.

Not because she asked them to but because they couldn't help themselves.

A ripple of silence, a collective intake of breath. Even the girls waiting at the edges of the field flicked their eyes toward her, their attentions torn between admiration and inevitable envy.

She tested the waters. A flick of the hair.

Toss. Toss.

The world trembled.

Fanny, Cora, and Mila, being the loyal imitators they were, executed their own synchronized tosses, a cascade of golden, brown and ebony strands catching the burning sunlight.

The boys, poor creatures, licked their lips, scratched idly at their private parts as they involuntarily began to rise and adjusted themselves as if the laws of decency had momentarily vacated the premises.

Galinda smiled.

One of the boys, Hedrick, tall, dark-haired, and conveniently shirtless, called out, "Galinda, do you play?"

She turned to her ladies, as if the question was entirely foreign. "What?" she asked, punctuating the syllable with a light, incredulous laugh. As if to say, *Me? A game? Among the sweaty?*

The boy grinned. "Come on, I'll show you."

Galinda sauntered forward. "Alright," she said sweetly. "But you'll have to be a good teacher."

Hedrick swallowed, squared his shoulders, and positioned himself behind her. Perhaps too close. No, definitely too close. He guided her hand to the mallet, demonstrated the swing. The ball went astray, but the crowd erupted into applause, nonetheless.

"You're a natural," Hedrick assured, though what he meant was *I am rapidly losing my dignity in these infernally tight shorts.*

Because now he was fully erect, if he stepped any closer, his *tod* would be rubbing on her back.

He pulled back, subtly at first, then with increasing necessity. His resolve, and something rather more tangible, had reached their limits. Galinda, perceptive as ever, whispered silkily in his ear, "Oz, you're such a great teacher."

And that was that. The poor boy was ruined.

There was no coming back, the shaft was now burgeoning in his shorts, begging for reprieve.

They could all see it in his tight shorts.

But he did not care.

And the girls watching were not complaining either. They giggled behind their hands. The boys smirked, half in admiration, half in pity.

"Want to play an actual game?" another voice called out, eager to press this moment into legend.

Galinda, aglow with newfound athletic prowess, merely batted her lashes. "Why not?"

And so, it began. The ball in hand, she made a regal dash toward her home base. The boys pursued, though their efforts were as laughable as they were performative—tripping over their own feet, feigning exhaustion as if enchanted by some divine force (*or, rather, by a force of golden curls and a finely tailored bodice*).

She reached the base, swung the mallet, and the ball veered off course, only to be nudged miraculously into the goal by another boy's *overly helpful* foot.

Victory!

The boys erupted into cheers, lifting her high upon their shoulders, a triumphant parade of adolescent worship.

"Galinda! Galinda! Galinda!"

"How did you get so good at sports?" one of them dared to ask.

She merely shrugged. "Talent," she said airily. "What else?"

They all laughed.

And just like that, Galinda was officially *good* at sports; written into the annals of Oz University: Galinda, first of her name, sovereign of the field, unparalleled in skill, undisputed in grace.

And the world, particularly all the boys and most of the girls, could only stand in awe.

The sun, in its final descent, painted the world in a tired golden light. The boys, swarming around Galinda like bees around honey, carried her up the stairs to her private suite with the kind of devotion one might show a statue or idol. Her entourage—Cora, Mila, and Fanny—scurried behind, clutching Galinda's bag. The walk was an arduous journey, the weight of it pressing down on their chests, but they did not falter. No, the boys had a single purpose: to prove their worth. Each hoped, in that quiet place at the back of their minds, that one day they might be invited into the sanctuary of her room, a place of secrets, of soft velvet sheets and whispered promises.

When they reached the doors, they placed her down with delicacy, like porcelain. She was untouchable, and yet, like the star placed atop *Ozma's Eve* tree, she could never be too far from the reach of admiration. The boys lingered, the air thick with that tension of desperate hope.

Galinda turned her gaze on them. "Thank you, boys," she purred, her voice soft as spun sugar. "You've been so good to me."

Hedrick stepped forward with an expression too rehearsed to be genuine. "It was our pleasure." to his surprise, he meant it. It *was* his pleasure, nothing more, nothing less.

The girls, Mila, Cora, and Fanny, saw them off, their shoulders held high, even as their eyes kept darting back toward Galinda's room, as if hoping for another glance, a flicker of attention that might prove their place in the hierarchy of her life. They were careful, even now, to make sure the boys knew: they too were loyal, but above all, they were her closest companions.

Once the boys had taken their leave, they walked away, but not without the ritual: turning back, just once more, to ensure Galinda was not in need.

Galinda, her hand still clutching the door, gave a single exaggerated yawn and then, with practiced ease, whispered to her companions, "Girls, I'm so tired. I'll see you tomorrow."

The door shut with a soft thud, the lock clicking into place with the finality of a stage curtain. She was alone.

Her suite, larger than anything Mila, Cora, or Fanny could ever dream of, was her sanctuary. It was ten times more elegant, ten times more lavish. And yet, in the solitude of her room, she found a strange kind of peace, an independence in the luxury that the others would never fully understand. They *wanted* to understand, of course. They needed to believe that they were more than mere shadows in her light.

As Galinda rifled through her belongings—shoes, jewellery, lotions, her *Make-Do*s—she smiled faintly at the familiar indulgences. But then, her fingers paused. There it was.

CHANGE

The Ethereum.

Safely hidden amongst a pile of university books, where no one could possibly look. She felt a rush of relief as her hand closed around the thick volume.

But she wasn't done yet.

Underneath the books she used for pretence, she found another.

The Complex Understanding Collection: Gilded Yoke: Political Analysis of Oz's Four Corners.

A book she sneakily bought in **Farkleberry & Things** in the Emerald City, hidden away for the sole purpose of indulging her most secret curiosity. She had heard of the book's controversial nature, how the Wizard halted its production—and of all places, she hadn't expected to find a copy within the Wizard's own domain.

Galinda knew the expectations placed upon her, expectations she placed on herself, but tonight, she would indulge.

In the confines of her room, she could be herself.

The self she buried but, in her solitude, would often allow to reach the surface to gasp for air.

Her room was still, save for the quiet rustling of the pages. The faint breeze from the open window swept across the floor, carrying with it the sounds of the boys below, waiting for yet another show. Galinda smiled softly to herself, a knowing smirk, as she stood by the window. The boys' eyes were glued to the silhouette she cast against the light, their breath quickening with anticipation.

She didn't move. She *let* them linger, feeding into their desires. She *knew* they would look. After all, who could resist?

Pretending to be oblivious to the party outside her window, she sensually slid out of her clothes, each movement deliberate, measured, an act of quiet defiance till she was naked with nothing on but her pink fluffy slippers.

The boys outside could not see beyond the shadow, but they could see every shape, where her body curved and the parts that protruded.

Enough to ignite their imagination.

Their sighs of excitement and accomplishment slid on the back of the wind and carried into the private suite.

Galinda walked into her bathroom, in her hand, her book and a bottle of *Shimmer-Foam Bubbleluxe*. She filled the marble bath with warm water and squirted three drops from the bottle, and within seconds the bath foamed up, a perfect layer of frothy bubbles.

Just the way she liked it.

She sank into the water, holding the book in one hand, her fingers tracing the words.

Introduction: The Illusion of Unity

Oz, as it is commonly understood, is a single land united under a single rule. This is a fantasy, no less whimsical than a living scarecrow or an animate patchwork girl. The reality is more complex, more brittle, and more gilded than most would like to admit. It is a land of four quarters, each with its own ambitions, its own grievances, and its own interpretation of governance. If the Emerald City is a crown, then it is a crown held in place by four uneasy hands, none of which trust the others entirely.

munchkinland presents itself as the most orderly of the quarters, a land of tidy fields and tidy laws, but it harbours a divide among its own people. Between those born into height and those who are not. The term **'munchkinlanders'** *is used as a generalization for all its citizens and those that are normally sized, while* **'munchkins'** *refers to the little ones, a distinction that has sparked controversy. There has been a conflict from within, where munchkins feel targeted. With its wavering political climate, bureaucrats have replaced barons, but the same cautious conservatism remains. Its laws, intricate and exhaustive, are not tools of justice but of obstruction. To govern in munchkinland is not to lead, but to navigate."*

Gillikin Country, by contrast, has mastered the art of ruling without seeming to rule at all. Its scholars write the histories, its financiers fund the endeavours of the Emerald City, and its quiet aristocracy ensures that no true political shift occurs without their consent. Their true power lies not in decrees but in influence, in the slow, patient shaping of events. They are the sculptors, while the rest of Oz is merely clay.

The Winkies know better than most that power is rarely benevolent. Now free, they reject rule in all but name, favouring the leadership of war-chiefs and elders over the delicate diplomacy of courtrooms. Yet they are not as ungoverned as they claim. Their society, built on strength, loyalty, and retribution, is bound by laws far older and more unyielding than any Emerald decree. A land where honour outweighs bureaucracy, where debt is paid not in coin but in blood.

And then there are the Quadlings, red of earth and red of name, whose lands are dismissed as backwater and whose people are considered provincial at best, expendable at worst. Their crime is neither weakness nor ignorance, but inconvenience. They control resources that the rest of Oz covets but would rather take than trade for. Their land is rich, their traditions deep, and yet their voices are barely a whisper in the Emerald City. They are left to their own devices—until their wealth becomes too tempting to ignore.

Thus, the great illusion persists that Oz is whole, that the Emerald City reigns supreme, that unity is a matter of policy rather than tolerance. But beneath the green sheen of the capital, the yoke is gilded, not golden. And those who wear it know the difference.

Galinda, satisfied with her bath, stepped out, drained the water, and walked to her bedroom. The boys were still there, waiting for another show.

She obliged.

Galinda slowly put on her nightgown, wrapped her hair, put on some *Make-Do* and some perfume.

Even in sleep, she wanted to be beautiful.

She placed the book on her bedside table and dimmed the lights.

Only then did the boys leave the stone wall and slowly walked back to their rooms.

Cozy and warm in her bed, Galinda began to think about what the next day would be like.

How popular she was going to become with the scholarship students that would be arriving, most likely poor, they too would bow for her to place a *kiss on their forehead.*

Galinda drifted into sleep with a smile curling at the corners of her mouth.

◇

At the 5th hour of morning, while most of the university still lay in the hushed arms of sleep, Galinda was already awake. She had brushed her teeth to a shine, cleansed her face until it glowed like alabaster, and applied a generous layer of Make-Do. Then, for good measure—again.

She sat at her desk, bent over a heavy tome, the candlelight catching the glimmer of ink on her feverishly scribbled notes. There was, after all, too much to remember. The academic mind, she had observed, was like a silk purse, capable of holding a great many things, but prone to bursting at the seams if stuffed carelessly.

A soft knock rapped at the door.

Galinda composed herself before opening it, only to find a liveried man standing at precise attention. A servant from the Royal Castle. She recognized him by the gleaming crest embroidered at his breast pocket. He had arrived precisely at the 6th hour.

"Princess," he said with a bow so exact, it might have been measured, "your first meal is prepared."

Behind him, a trolley laden with silver-domed platters exhaled the scent of indulgence: golden oats and honey cakes, Churncakes dripping with butter, cream-cones stacked like miniature snow-capped mountains, wild greens with a treacle of nutmeg glaze, Winkie spice porridge steaming thickly, molasses bread dark as the earth and so much more.

A kettle of lavender tea, fragrant as an orchard in the sun, completed the offering.

Galinda gave a short, astonished laugh, quickly muffled when she saw the chef's unwavering seriousness. "This is absurd! How can I possibly eat all this?"

"The King instructed me to provide a variety of breakfasts each morning so that you may have your pick."

"A churncake and a bit of porridge would have sufficed."

"The King was most explicit, Princess. It is my head if I disobey."

"Very well." She pulled the trolley into her chambers, dismissing the servant with a nod.

"I shall return at the fourteenth hour with your lunch, Princess," he intoned before bowing out.

With a sigh, she selected a single cream-cone and poured herself a cup of tea before returning to her desk. Perhaps now, finally, she would have a moment of quiet.

A knock.

252

Galinda closed her eyes. It seemed there were disturbances layered within the very architecture of her morning.

She opened the door.

Her friends.

As Galinda subtly nudged her book out of sight, Fanny, ever hawk-eyed, narrowed hers. "Were you just reading?"

"Yes," Galinda said before realizing, "I mean—no!"

Three sets of eyebrows arched.

"Not really," she amended hastily. "I was merely… daydreaming."

"Oh?" Mila leaned in. "About boys?"

"Yes!"

The girls lost interest, their gazes drifting instead to the platters of untouched food.

Fanny, with the casual presumption of the very rich, asked, "Can we?"

"Help yourselves."

What followed was a feverish dismantling of culinary perfection.

Then—another knock.

Galinda nearly screamed.

Peering through the spyhole, she saw a woman. Older. Round. Breathless from the climb. Her hair brown but streaked with white. Her chin was adorned with a single, defiant grey hair that quivered with every laboured breath.

Galinda opened the door and raised an eyebrow, waiting for an explanation.

The woman merely stood there, gulping air as though she'd wrestled the stairwell itself.

"And you are?" Galinda asked, unamused.

Between gasps, the woman croaked, "I am—your Ummi."

Galinda blinked.

Then, remembering her manners, widened the door. "Oh, well, you should've said so! Come in."

The Ummi lumbered inside, eyes flickering toward the food with unmistakable longing. Galinda caught the glance, and the Ummi, catching Galinda catching it, made a show of licking her lips with exaggerated nonchalance.

"It's dreadfully dry in this part of Gillikin," she said, as if reciting a fact. "I ought to buy myself some lip-oyl."

Galinda, sensing the woman's embarrassment, said, "I have one."

She moved to one of her many drawers, most of them crammed to capacity with this and that, except for one. *One* remained empty. She dug through the collection of Lip-Oyls. Each unopened. She plucked one lemon-scented Lip-Oyl and handed it to the Ummi.

The Ummi smiled, relief washing over her shame. "Oh! I do love me some lemons," she declared, as though announcing an allegiance to good health.

Mila, between mouthfuls, muttered under her breath, "Yes, when they're wrapped in pastry."

Fanny and Cora whimpered in cruel amusement.

But the Ummi had ears sharper than they assumed.

"Girls, take your food and leave. I need to speak privately with my Ummi."

Fanny pouted. "Are you serious? Your bed is so comfortable."

"I will not say it again."

The girls, understanding the limits of her tolerance, begrudgingly gathered their plates, piling them even higher as they made for the exit.

The door shut.

The Ummi exhaled heavily. "That was kind of you," she murmured. "Though, I don't understand why you keep company with such nasty girls."

Galinda merely smiled and gestured for her to sit.

The Ummi, businesslike, pulled a notepad and pen from her purse. "So, how are you settling into your accommodations?"

"Well enough," Galinda said airily.

"Popular with the boys, eh?"

Galinda's answering smile was all sharp teeth.

The Ummi gave her a knowing look. "I trust you understand my purpose here?"

"I believe so."

The Ummi leaned in. "You are to send regular reports on your academic progress and should you encounter any difficulties, I am here to help."

"Academic progress?"

"Yes. Need I remind you that you are here to learn, not simply to become an Ozian socialite?"

"I suppose not."

The Ummi's gaze sharpened. "You are a smart girl, Galinda. As much as I know you enjoy making friends, I expect you to spend more time with your books. And I will not tolerate hearing that you've had others do your work for you." She fixed Galinda with a look. "Trust me. I will find out."

Galinda sighed, long-suffering. "Yes."

The Ummi stood, casting a glance toward the door. "I should take my leave."

On her way out, she snatched the last cheese tart from the trolley and bit into it with all the urgency of a woman who had waited too long for her pleasures.

"If you ever need me before our scheduled meetings, inform Professor Shinz. He will contact me."

"Understood."

"Good luck, Galinda."

And with that, she wobbled her way out, the tart halfway to her mouth as the door clicked shut behind her.

GLINDA: The GOOD Witch

It was verging on the 8th hour, and with the pledge of allegiance imminent, Galinda, with nothing better to do (or at least nothing grander to be seen doing), scooped up her purse and made her way down to *The Grand Lycrium*. She was not required to take the pledge, of course. Special entry had its privileges, and she intended to wield them, not by absence, but by presence. To be seen not pledging was a declaration of status in and of itself.

She drifted past the monumental statue of the Wizard, its expression chiselled into an unsettling ambiguity, was he benevolent, or merely resigned to his own importance? Down the stone steps she went, entering the vast chamber below the university, where hundreds of students sat in obedient rows upon willow benches. Uniformed in their drab school attire, their heads turned in unison as she entered.

She was, after all, a vision in pink.

The boys stiffened, adjusting their postures as if their vertebrae had suddenly developed aspirations.

Her eyes found Fanny, Cora, and Mila, but the seats beside them were occupied. No matter. A girl, some nonentity, registered Galinda's presence, smiled (a weak, supplicating thing), and relinquished her seat without a word.

"Thank you," Galinda murmured.

"Don't mention it," the girl replied, before evaporating into the crowd like mist.

Professor Shinz took the stage. A wave of polite applause rippled through the chamber before silence resumed. He launched into a sermon of sorts—passages from the Ozma, a speech on the virtues of knowledge, a lecture on the necessity of pledging loyalty to the Wizard.

The students absorbed his words with interest, though selectively. Knowledge? A passing notion. Ozma? A footnote in history. But the Wizard—ah, now that was something worth pledging to.

The roll call began.

"Alexia Morin, step forward."

A stout girl rose and, with as much conviction as she could muster, proclaimed:

"By the grace of Oz and the wisdom of the Great and Powerful Wizard, I pledge my allegiance. May my hands serve his will, my voice honour his name, and my heart remain steadfast in loyalty to him."

"Next."

The names continued, one after another, each voice blending into the next, until at last—

"Evelia Everdeen."

She stepped forward, raised her hand, began to recite the pledge.

And then, she screamed.

The kind of scream one makes when confronted with something wholly unnatural, wholly impossible, wholly—wrong.

CHANGE

The entire hall froze. All eyes followed the trembling line of her pointing finger toward the back of the Lycrium.

And there, standing in the dim shadows, was a figure.

Draped in black: boots, gloves, a feathery dress that clung and then sprawled like a murder of crows. Hair slick and dark as an oil spill. Long fingers like creeping ivy.

And skin—

Green!

Green as a bitter gourd.

A sharp inhale rippled through the crowd. Then, chaos.

Students shrieked, clambering over benches, retreating to the corners like cornered prey.

Galinda did not move.

Fanny gripped her shoulder, her voice a whisper edged with dread. "What is that?"

Galinda did not know. But she knew, with a sickening certainty, that it was green. And Galinda, fated, haunted, tormented, could not seem to escape the colour green. The one colour she thought she left behind in the South.

But no!

Green here.

Green there.

Green, green, green.

"Students, settle down!" Professor Shinz commanded, his tone betraying him.

The green girl stepped forward.

"Hello," she said, her voice even, measured. "There is no need to be afraid. I mean no harm."

From behind Galinda, Mila peeked out. "Then why do you look like that?"

"You mean my skin?"

"Like you have limepox."

"I was born like this." The green girl's chin lifted.

She extended her hands in what might have been a gesture of peace. "Please, step away from the walls. There's no need for this—"

Professor Shinz stormed toward her, his face blotchy with contained fury. He lowered his voice, but it carried.

"I told you to stay in your quarters," he hissed. "You were to arrive after the pledge. That is why I excused you from taking it."

"I know," the girl replied, "but I wanted to experience the full tradition. Is that so terrible?"

"Yes!" Shinz snapped. "When you look the way you do."

A flicker of something, wounded pride, restrained anger, passed across the girl's face.

"What is that supposed to mean?" she asked, her voice quieter now, but no less sharp.

"Need I remind you," he said, his words laced with condescension, "the basis of your admission to this university?"

She said nothing.

"Thought so. Now go."

The students, emboldened by his authority, slunk back to their seats. All except Galinda, who remained standing at the centre of the room.

The green girl turned to leave.

"Wait," Galinda called.

She turned.

Galinda stepped forward, extending a delicate, manicured hand. The crowd gasped.

The green girl, hesitantly, warily, took it.

"What is she doing?" Mila muttered to Cora.

Galinda tilted her head, observing the creature before her with theatrical fascination. "Hmm. What do you go by?"

"What do I go by?" The girl echoed, bewildered.

"What is your name?"

"Zelphira." She widened her chest. "Zelphira Grimbelle Raventhorne."

"Well, I'm Galinda. Galinda Arduelle Fairmoor of the Uplands." She paused, corrected herself. "Upper Uplands."

Zelphira remained unimpressed.

"You don't know who I am?" Galinda asked, feigning astonishment.

"Should I?"

Galinda turned to the spectators, laughter already bubbling in her throat. "Tell me you don't read The Ozmopolitan without telling me you don't read The Ozmopolitan."

The hall erupted in laughter.

Toss. Toss.

Zelphira's expression shifted—something steeled in her.

"Oh, I'm sorry," she said with mocking sweetness. "I suppose I've been wasting my time reading *actual* material, politics, history, while you occupy yourself with hairspray reviews and Make-Do trends."

Galinda's smile stiffened. "You don't know me."

"I don't need to." Zelphira's lip curled. "Just look at you."

"Well," Galinda mused, tilting her head, "don't get angry with me just becoz you look like a broccoli and dress like a scarecrow's charity case."

The air filled with laughter, rippling outward like an unkind spell.

Professor Shinz, in a spectacular display of professional decorum, laughed the loudest.

Galinda placed a manicured hand to her chin in an exaggerated pantomime of thoughtfulness. "As a matter of fact, how in all of Oz did you manage to get into this university? It's obvious you're—" her nose wrinkled slightly, as if catching a faint but offensive scent, "a peasant."

She plucked at the fraying edge of Zelphira's sleeve, holding it between her thumb and forefinger as one might a suspicious insect. "Cheap," she diagnosed. "Munchkinland, am I right?"

"Yes," Zelphira said, chin lifted, voice firm.

The room burst again.

Zelphira remained still, statuesque in her refusal to be diminished.

Galinda's eyes twinkled. The moment was a gift.

"Guess how I knew?" she whispered, voice thick with performance.

Zelphira said nothing.

Galinda leaned in, conspiratorial.

"The *Ozmopolitan*," she purred.

The crowd howled.

Zelphira blinked slowly, as if taking in the full breadth of the scene, its players, their glee.

Galinda sighed, feigning weariness. "I *could* help you, you know."

"With what, exactly, prissy princess? Embroidery? Ballroom giggling? The correct fork for pâté?"

Mila's voice rang out. "That's not funny because she's *actually* a princess."

"Oh, my apologies," Zelphira said dryly. "A princess *and* an expert in decorative handkerchiefs."

Galinda smirked. "I meant I could help you *not* be green." She snapped her fingers. "Just like that."

Cora, seizing the moment, called out, "Oh Oz, isn't Galinda so good?"

"So *good*," the students chorused.

Galinda curtsied.

"Well," Zelphira said, dusting imaginary lint from her sleeve, "I must be getting back to my quarters. Let me know if you ever have something clever to say."

Zelphira turned.

Galinda wasn't finished.

"Oh, don't let me keep you," she trilled. "Just—let me know when you finally take a bath. Maybe the green will wash off, along with that *stink*."

Zelphira turned back around, slow and deliberate.

Her hands twitched at her sides, as though resisting some invisible urge.

She muttered something, low, guttural, her fingers curling, flexing.

The room collectively inhaled.

Then, she exhaled sharply, lowering her hands.

Fanny cackled. "Oh Oz, was that a *curse*? You ugly witch!"

The laughter swelled again, filling the space like a rising tide.

GLINDA: The GOOD Witch

Zelphira turned on her heel and strode out.

Galinda watched her go, eyes gleaming.

A green, ugly witch, slinking away.

As she should.

CHAPTER 32

The Winkie Prince

Classes commenced a few days later, each student dutifully attending the courses assigned to them, or rather, assigned to their futures, carefully curated by ambitious parents with a taste for social climbing.

But Galinda chose for herself.

She went to Politics.

She expected a small, select gathering, well-groomed young men in ascots, perhaps, and a smattering of plain girls who, lacking beauty, had no choice but to be clever. Instead, the room was packed. The doorway teemed with students jostling for position, eager to secure a good seat. Too many bodies, too few chairs.

Galinda did not jostle. She strutted, batting a few lashes. And despite arriving last, she was first in line.

The moment the doors flung open, a tall, angular man with ink-dark hair swept into view, flapping his arms like an impatient crow.

"Inside, inside! Quickly now!"

The students hurried past him, their first impression already taking root, this was not a man to be trifled with. He was the sort to ruin careers with a single disdainful glance.

Galinda chose a seat at the back. Not to avoid attention, heavens, no, but to command it. From here, she could observe the heads that would inevitably turn toward her.

The man stalked to the front of the room, seized a piece of chalk, and scored the board with a shriek of white dust.

"My name is Professor Thadeus Ponsworth," he declared. "But you will address me as Master Ponsworth."

A murmur. A whisper.

He struck a ruler loudly on the desk. "Silence!"

The murmurs fled.

"In this room," he continued, "you will abide by my rules and my rules alone. If you defy me, you will be punished. If you have a question, you will raise your hand.

If you fail an exam, you will be removed from this course, and if you are removed from this course, you are removed from a life worth living. Have I made myself very clear?"

"Yes, Master Ponsworth," came the chorus.

"Very well." He began pacing, fingers interlaced behind his back. "You are here becoz you fancy yourselves destined for something greater. Becoz, you believe you will serve some high purpose for whatever obscure province of Oz spat you into existence. But let me be plain—most of you will not succeed."

A rustle of indignation. A few offended gasps. The ambitious, the confident, the ones who had been raised to believe they were singular and extraordinary, sat taller.

Ponsworth allowed them to stew for a moment before continuing.

"Now then, who can tell me, in its purest form, what politics means?"

Arms shot up like blades of grass after a storm.

Galinda's did not.

Ponsworth, however, was drawn to her as a magpie to a glimmering trinket.

"You. Pretty girl."

Galinda blinked. "Me?"

"Yes. Define politics."

"I'm afraid I don't know, Master Ponsworth."

He smirked, though there was no amusement in it.

"If you do not know what politics is, then why are you here? That suggests you have no idea what you're studying. And if you have no idea what you're studying, you will fail. And I do not tolerate failures." He tilted his head, savouring the discomfort. "So, I suggest you gather your things and leave."

The class turned to Galinda. A rare and dreadful thing was occurring.

She exhaled slowly.

"Politics, in its essence, is the art of convincing people that what is best for you is best for them," she said. "It is the push and pull of promises and power, where words are sharper than weapons and allegiances shift like shadows at sundown. It is neither good nor wicked—it simply is. Like the wind, which can carry a ship forward or capsize it entirely."

Silence.

Then, Ponsworth clapped, once, sharp as a pistol shot.

Heads snapped back to him.

"Yes! Precisely! Very poetically said." He pivoted, pacing once more. "However, politics is also the mechanism by which people decide who gets what, when, and how. It determines who leads, who follows, who thrives, who starves. It is negotiation and manipulation, rules and loopholes. It is the air we breathe, the ground we walk on."

He stopped abruptly, looking out at the sea of uncertain faces.

"When you entered this room, I demanded you call me 'Master' rather than 'Professor.' I struck the desk. I scrawled on the board with a madman's fervour. I pricked at your insecurities. Why?" He let the question hang, before answering himself. "Becoz that, in itself, is politics."

A hand was raised hesitantly.

"Master Ponsworth, are you saying that politics is woven into everything?"

"Of course. It is in the household, the workplace, the school." His eyes gleamed. "Tell me, who is the head of your household?"

"My father."

"And secondary?"

"My mother."

"If you have a younger sibling, are you not expected to govern them?"

A few nods.

"In your social circles, though you may resist admitting it, there is always one among you who dictates what is said, how it is said, and what is deemed worthy of notice. You follow them, whether consciously or not."

Pens scratched hurriedly against paper.

"How did you gain admittance to this school?"

"I had to be approved."

"By whom?"

"The committee. Then Professor Shinz. And then—"

"The Wizard," Ponsworth finished smoothly. "Exactly. You see?"

A student groaned audibly. "Woz. So… do we still have to call you 'Master Ponsworth'?"

"Yes," he said simply.

Galinda studied him, feeling something unfamiliar stir inside her.

Admiration.

He had split open the world before her, revealing something intricate and insidious beneath its surface.

The bell gave a single, sharp clang, an unceremonious dismissal. The students remained poised, waiting for the unspoken second signal: the professor's leave to depart.

"That marks the end of today's lesson," intoned Master Ponsworth, gathering his materials with the precise, almost performative indifference of a bureaucrat who has long since ceased to find amusement in the young and the hopeful. "You may go."

The students rose, an orchestrated shuffle of books and bags, eager feet scraping against the polished floor.

"Galinda. Stay behind."

The words landed like a stone in her gut. She suppressed a sigh but not the small downturn of her mouth as she watched the others file out, taking with them the comforting anonymity of the crowd. She had spent years perfecting the art of belonging, not standing out, not falling behind, but drifting perfectly within the tide of expectation. And yet, here she was again. Singled out. Othered.

When the last student had gone, leaving behind only dust motes and silence, she stepped forward. She and Ponsworth, alone now, the *Fates* watching from the dark corners *we* preferred.

The professor slapped a folder onto his desk, its contents fluttering at the edges like a caged bird. He gestured to it.

"Do you know what this is?"

She tilted her head, affecting the wide-eyed innocence that had charmed grandmothers and governors alike. "No?"

"Yes, you do."

Her lashes flickered. "It's my report."

He exhaled sharply through his nose. "Why do you do that?"

"Do what?"

"Act stupid." He tapped a finger on the folder. "I've reviewed every report, and yours ranks the highest Wizdom Score Standard in this entire class, among the W.S.S. top ten in all Ozian educational districts."

Galinda said nothing.

"You have a gift," he continued, levelling a finger at her forehead, where her **brain** stayed hidden. "Use it. I can tell you're ambitious. Persistent, but you're letting trivialities chip away at your potential."

He paused, letting the weight of his words settle.

"And if you ever lie to me again, if you *ever* sit in my classroom and feign ignorance, *pretend* not to know the answer when you do—" His voice turned to stone. "I will make certain you never work in politics. Not even your father will be able to *save* you. Am I understood?"

"Yes, Master Ponsworth."

"Good. Go. Rejoin your friends."

Her **heart** rattled against her ribs as she exited, his words clinging to her like cobwebs. He saw right through her.

Galinda quickened her pace to get to her next class. Her heels clicked impatiently as she crossed the west wing of the castle, descending a spiral staircase that twisted deeper than reason dictated, leading her to the underbelly of the school.

The dungeon-turned-classroom was lit by firelight spells, their glow richer, hungrier than ordinary flame. There was something in the air, a charge, like the prickle before a storm.

The doors were closed. She knocked.

They did not open so much as *surrender*, groaning apart with an unseen force.

Inside, the air smelled of old parchment and something acrid—burnt spellwork, perhaps.

At the front of the room stood Lady Mordemire, around fifty Sun-Moons old, a woman with the kind of presence that turned warmth into cold.

But it was not the teacher only who caught Galinda's eye.

At the front, cloaked in ink-black fabric and suspicion, was Zelphira. Her face twisted into something between confusion and outright disdain. *Pink Prissy Princess? Here?*

Galinda felt her own surprise bloom in equal measure. Zelphira had magical abilities? She had assumed the girl was here for *botany* or some other unambitious pursuit of dirt.

And then there was the boy. Scrawny, pale as poverty itself, watching the exchange from the back of the room.

Three students. That was all.

Galinda swallowed, then asked, "Is this Lady Mordemire's class?"

"Indeed." The teacher regarded her with the cool gaze of a bird of prey, "And you are?"

"Oh, Galinda Fairmoor. I believe I'm enrolled."

"Right. The Quadling King's daughter. I was expecting you." A beat. "Fairmoors arrive *on time*. Don't be late again!"

Galinda dipped her chin. "Of course."

She scanned the room for a seat, preferably far from Zelphira. She took a step toward the back.

"Stop."

She froze.

"Yes?"

Mordemire had picked up a different slip of paper, turning it between her fingers. "It says here you have yet to demonstrate your power."

"Oh, right, let me just set my things down—"

"No, no." Mordemire waved a dismissive hand. "Bring them with you. That way, if your magic fails you again, you can leave immediately."

Galinda's throat went dry.

She stepped forward, the weight of expectation settling on her shoulders. Her books slid to the floor with an unceremonious thud.

Mordemire turned, gesturing toward Zelphira's desk. "See that coin?"

"Yes?"

"Levitate it."

She exhaled slowly. Focused. Raised her hand.

Nothing.

The coin remained stubbornly still.

Mordemire clasped her hands. "You don't have magic, do you?"

"I swear I do!" Galinda's voice wobbled in ways she did not appreciate.

"Then where is it? Did you misplace it on the way here?"

Zelphira's smirk was positively venomous.

And Galinda?

She was beginning to wonder the same thing.

"I... I think so."

"Foolish girl. That is not how magic works. It doesn't just *disappear*, you either *have* it, or you *don't*." She massaged her temples, as though Galinda's very presence had manifested into a migraine. "Is this a joke to you?"

"No—"

"You *do* realize that the purpose of this class is to cultivate the most advanced magic wielders in Oz? To serve the Wizard? Do you want me to tell him you take him for a *fool*?"

"No! I swear I *do* have magic! I just—I don't understand why this is happening to me. You *must* believe me."

Mordemire blinked once, slow as a lizard basking on a rock. "I *must*?"

Her gaze slithered over to the other girl in the room, the one draped in black, the one who had been silent but watchful, her expression a coiled smirk waiting to spring.

"Zelphira," Mordemire murmured, "levitate the coin. Show her how it's done."

Zelphira's eyes flickered to Galinda, amusement glinting within them, and then—

The coin obeyed.

It lifted, not with a show of effort, not with the dramatic flourish of fingers or an incantation uttered under breath, but simply because Zelphira *willed* it. The air around it seemed to hold its breath as the coin twirled dramatically and danced in the space between them, dipping into a mock curtsy before plummeting neatly back onto the desk.

Mordemire arched a brow. "You see? *Can you do that?*"

"I—I'll try again."

She lifted her hands. Pictured the coin bending to her will. Focused all the energy in her body, in her blood, in her mind—

Nothing.

Not even a twitch.

Mordemire's sigh was a death knell. "Pick up your bag and leave my classroom."

"But—"

"Did I *stutter*? Get. Out."

Galinda's fingers fumbled as she gathered her belongings, her face burning, her throat tightening like a noose. But before she could make her retreat, she caught sight of Zelphira's grin, wide, gleeful, flashing the telltale points of her fangs.

"Zelphira," Mordemire drawled, "do the honours."

Zelphira blinked, slow and deliberate.

The heavy doors *yawned* open, their hinges shrieking like something out of a nightmare.

CHANGE

Galinda barely had time to stumble forward before they *slammed* shut behind her, the force sending a gust of air through the corridor, whipping her golden curls into a frenzy.

She stood there, breathing hard, her chest rising and falling like a ragged tide.

She didn't understand *what was happening*, why she couldn't do what she *knew* she could do, why she felt untethered from herself, why she was beginning to wonder if she belonged *anywhere at all*.

The feeling was uncomfortably familiar.

Galinda ascended the stairs to the main court of the university, each step measured, though her breath was not. The great *Ozcodile* fountain gurgled nearby, indifferent to her misfortune, and there, thank the *One Gohd*, was a bench. It wasn't much, but it was the closest thing to civilization in this desolate square of academia. She sat down, smoothing her skirts as if that might somehow smooth the tremor in her hands. Her bag and books settled beside her, prim, obedient.

The other students were safely tucked away in their classes, memorizing equations or debating the finer points of ethics.

She was alone. A *now* rare and dangerous condition.

She dabbed at her eyes with her sleeve, a most unprincessly gesture, but the act of wiping only seemed to encourage the tears to flow faster. *What was the reason for her magic failing her?* A malady of the heart? A seasonal affliction of the soul? Was she dying? That would explain things. A sudden, tragic demise, the kind that left court physicians baffled and admirers weeping, would at least provide a satisfying narrative.

But no. She felt healthier than ever. Her chef ensured a diet of the finest ingredients, charmed for longevity. She got regular exercise, particularly in bed.

So why was everything unravelling?

And then it came to her. Like a whisper. Like a curse.

Zelphira.

From the moment that green-skinned riddle had crossed her path, nothing had been the same.

It *had* to be her. How else could it be explained? That *thing*, that *creature*, walking around with magic more powerful than Galinda's had ever been? It didn't make sense. Unless, of course, she had stolen it. Some clandestine siphoning of power? Some secret, dark magic—a green witch's trick. Yes, that would be fitting.

And worst of all, the whispers.

The conversations that once revolved around her—*Did you see what Princess Galinda was wearing today? Do you know what perfume Galinda Fairmoor uses?*—had begun to wane. In their place:

"Did you see that green girl, Zelphira?"

"How do you think she became green?"

"Does Zelphira have a disease?"

GLINDA: The GOOD Witch

It didn't matter that Zelphira's name was spoken in scandal, in suspicion. It was spoken and her notoriety had now outpaced Galinda's carefully cultivated adoration.

She remembered what her father told her: *Popularity is power.*

But now she saw something even clearer: *Infamy works faster than charm.*

Very well, then. She would learn from it. She would weave infamy into her image of goodness.

The tears had slowed, though the evidence of them still stained her face.

"Why are you crying?" The voice was smooth, deep.

Galinda lifted her chin, assuming an expression of bemused detachment. "I'm not crying."

The boy who stood before her, no, *lounged*, for he carried himself as if all of Oz were his personal parlour, and dressed in all blue, cocked an eyebrow. "So, you sweat from your eyes?"

She straightened her spine, wiped the last betraying moisture from her face with a decisive sweep. "It's the heat."

"Ah." He sat beside her, utterly uninvited, and with the ease of someone who had never once been told he wasn't welcome. He reached out, without warning, without hesitation, and brushed away a lingering teardrop near her eye.

"Who would've thought," he mused, "I'd be the one wiping away *Princess Galinda's* tears. Shouldn't you be in class?"

"I should ask you the same thing," she countered, lifting her chin just so, as if it had been sculpted for precisely this angle of defiance.

He exhaled a laugh, slow and indulgent. "Do you know who I am?"

She let her gaze travel over him, *lazily*, like a cat that already knew the answer but wanted to toy with the question.

"Yes," she said at last. "The Winkie Prince."

"So you should know I get special privileges. I have one of my devoted scholars taking notes for me while I... *survey* the school for entertainment."

"And you know I'm the Quadling Princess, so you should know that *I* too get special privileges."

He grinned. "Fair enough."

The sun caught in his eyes, the lightest brown, warm and bright, glinting with a mischief that felt both charming and dangerous. His caramel skin, kissed golden in the afternoon light, looked so impossibly smooth that Galinda might have licked it, had she been born of humbler origins. His lips, cherry-coloured, distracting, parted slightly, as if he meant to say something, and yet he didn't.

A stretch of silence. Their eyes locked. Neither yielding.

Galinda had found her prince.

"It's about time we met, don't you think?" he murmured, voice dropped to something *just* above a whisper.

267

CHANGE

Galinda laughed, tilting her head ever so slightly. "I was waiting for you to find me, Winkie Prince."

"You keep calling me Winkie Prince. Call me Rivero. *River*, if you like."

"Alright then, *Winkie Prince*."

He groaned, tossing his head back, the theatrical agony of a man *gravely* offended. "You wound me."

She giggled, tucking a stray curl behind her ear.

"River," she mused, testing the name, letting it settle on her tongue. "You *do* know people have been waiting for this, don't you? Even the teachers. I think they expect us to marry or something."

"And do you think we should give them what they want, Princess?"

"Oh, I don't know. I have a *very* long list of bachelors waiting for my hand."

"Well... they aren't *me*."

"True," she sighed, her eyes never leaving his. "They aren't."

And then—

A breath between them.

A tilt of her chin.

A brush of lips.

They began kissing.

Slow, at first. Then suddenly *more*.

Then—

The bell.

A flood of students, spilling out into the courtyard. A gasp. A murmur. A rustling of whispers swelling into a cacophony.

And before either of them could react, before either of them could even breathe—

It was already news in the ***Ozmopolitan***.

PRINCESS GALINDA ARDUELLE FAIRMOOR OF QUADLING COUNTRY AND PRINCE RIVERO TAVIAN VALEHEART OF WINKIE COUNTRY OFFICIALLY SPELLBOUND.

An item. A couple. Destined.

Or, at the very least, *doomed* to be discussed.

The cheers and the gawking, the wild exhilaration of scandal made flesh, were what finally pulled them from their trance. But did they flee? Did they shrink, chastened, under the weight of so many hungry, appraising eyes?

Of course not.

Only after a calculated beat did she stoop to gather her books, her satchel. River, still feverish with laughter, seized her hand, and together they darted toward the back pastures, where the school castle's gilded eyes could spare them a moment of privacy.

They ran like children escaping a governess's scolding, the wind working through their hair like a sculptor reshaping clay.

"Did you see their faces?" River choked, breathless with glee.

"I *know!*" Galinda crowed. "*Like* the Wizard himself had descended in a puff of smoke and blessed me with a kiss!"

"It'll make the papers, no doubt."

"Of course it will! You didn't kiss an *ordinary* girl."

At this, River slowed, turning to face her properly. He caught her hands, his grip warm despite the cooling air. "Is this what love is?"

"I suppose so."

"You like me, don't you?" River asked, though the way his eyes gleamed with certainty suggested it was not a question at all, but rather an invitation for her to confirm the inevitable.

"Yes, and you? You like me?"

"How could I not? You're perfect."

"Well then," she purred, "*I suppose we're official?*"

"The *Ozmopolitan* will declare it by sunrise. We may as well make peace with our fate."

"You might be right," Galinda mused, tapping a manicured finger to her chin in an exaggerated show of contemplation.

"And given your political aspirations, it could only work in your favour." River lifted one hand as if weighing an invisible scale. "The Princess of the South," he declared. Then the other hand, tilting the balance. "The Prince of the West. A match made in—" he smirked, "—well, in whatever realm benefits us most."

"A deal, then," she said, extending her hand with the same poised elegance.

As the sun sank lower, its golden light stretched over the fields like melted butter, coating them in an almost mythic glow. The cows, unbothered by the affairs of the young and lovestruck, chewed their grass with solemn disinterest.

"You know," Galinda said, as if it were a casual observation rather than a precise conversational gambit, "I've met your father."

"Have you?"

"Indeed. He once gave me a golden medal and said that I was always welcome in Winkie, *Winkie Prince.*"

River laughed, then considered, his expression one of wary admiration. "He doesn't offer such sentiments lightly. He's a shrewd judge of character. You must have made quite the impression." Then, as if struck with fresh delight, he beamed. "That makes you even more perfect! He'd approve of us!"

And with that proclamation, he kissed her again.

"I'd love to visit Winkie Country again."

"And so you shall! Before the year is out, I'll see to it. My father will have to reacquaint himself with his son's exceptional taste."

Galinda smirked. "I think my father would approve of you, too."

"*King* Dainhurst? Approve? I hear he's quite the formidable man."

"Oh, he's simply misunderstood," she said airily, "not everyone comprehends his brilliance."

"If you say so. Shall we go to your private suite or mine?"

"Mine, obviously. It's bigger."

River smirked, a gleam of wicked delight in his eyes. "Beautiful *and* funny. A dangerous combination." And before Galinda could protest, he set upon her, fingers merciless at her sides, tickling her into breathless, helpless laughter.

In that moment, something in Galinda wavered. A missing note in an otherwise perfect melody.

Here was a boy, no, a *prince*, who adored her, who saw her precisely as she wished to be seen: flawless. On paper, it was a romance scripted by fate itself.

Or was it?

And yet.

That infuriating, unnameable *and yet*.

Perhaps this was love, as it was meant to be. And yet, again, *and yet*, there was a whisper of something else, something lost to another lifetime, another self, as if she had once known love differently, and had since forgotten its original shape.

River, giddy with his own triumph, seized her hands. "Lead the way, Princess."

"Glad to."

They strode past the cows, who remained stalwartly uninterested in their affairs, and made their way back to Galinda's private suite.

Galinda pushed open the door.

Pink. Pink. Pink.

River, taking one sweeping glance, laughed. "Say, you must really love pink."

She levelled a look at him, slow and assessing. "And you must really love blue."

"What gave it away?" he asked, mock-wounded. "Was it the pantaloons? The blazer? The gloves? Perhaps the tie?"

"Shush," she said, shoving him playfully.

His attention drifted toward the enormous silken canopy bed. Without hesitation, he threw himself onto it, arms spread, sinking luxuriously into its embrace. "This is *divine*. Dare I say better than mine?"

"It *is* better than yours."

"Oh, *apologies*," he drawled, eyes twinkling.

"I'm going to freshen up," she announced, sweeping her gaze over him once more. "I suggest you get into something more comfortable."

She retrieved a small bag and disappeared into the bathroom, where she set about her quiet ritual. A touch of *Make-Do* to deepen the red of her lips, the dark of her lashes, the bloom of her cheeks. A mist of something floral, something expensive. A hundred deliberate strokes through her golden curls until they shone with the effort.

Now she was ready.

When she opened the door, she found exactly what she had intended to find.

River, clad in nothing but his underwear, reclined sideways on the bed, one hand planted confidently on his hip, a portrait of ease. "Is this comfortable enough?"

Galinda tilted her head, appraising. "Hmm. No. Lose the underwear."

River smirked. "Why don't you come take it off yourself?"

She did just that.

With a flick of his wrist, he dimmed the lights, leaving only the flicker of a single candle to cast its golden secrets against the walls.

And there, in that *haven*, beneath silken canopies and within whispers of privilege...

Deals were cemented.

Promises were made.

Secrets were kept.

Though the castle walls were thick, they were not thick enough. The echoes of their entanglement carried, unchecked, through the high halls of academia, mingling with the hush of ancient history.

The Princess and the Prince.

◇

Morning arrived in shades of pale gold, spilling through the curtains in indulgent waves. Galinda and River lay facing each other, their positions reminiscent of a newlywed couple, poised at the precipice of a future they had not yet decided if they wanted.

River opened his mouth but halted. It looked as though he was about to confess something, but he changed his mind before the words could escape his mouth.

"How'd you sleep?" River murmured, voice thick with the remnants of dreams, stretching like a cat made of mischief.

"Better than I have in months," Galinda admitted, laughing lightly. "All thanks to you."

River smirked. "Was I that good?"

"Tragically, yes."

"What can I say? I've had a lot of practice."

"Oh, *stop it*," she chided.

But River, being River, was not one to let a jest go unprodded. He propped himself up on an elbow. "You've had a lot of practice too, haven't you?"

"Lately, yes."

"Who knew you and your sister were so alike?"

Galinda froze. "*What* do you mean by that?"

There was a knock at the door.

Startled, she rolled over, assuming the bed had more space than it did, and promptly tumbled off the edge with an undignified *thump*. River, sprawled in his luxury, found this endlessly amusing. As did Galinda, once she staggered to her feet,

271

smoothing her tousled hair and yanking on her pink-and-white feathered nightgown before answering the door.

The chef stood outside, wheeling in a silver trolley laden with steaming plates. "Good morning, Princess. Your breakfast is served."

River, now having deigned to rise, strolled over, still naked, still careless, his long frame casting a shadow over Galinda as he leaned against the doorframe, arms braced above him in a pose that was likely meant to be casual but had the distinct effect of drawing attention *downward*.

His cock danced with the wind, though the windows were shut.

"What do we have for breakfast?" he yawned, unbothered, unabashed.

The chef, realizing far too late what exactly he was witnessing, turned a deep shade of plum. "I—I am sorry, Prince, I didn't realize you weren't—um—"

"Oh, don't worry, you can look."

Galinda turned just in time to see the unfortunate man's eyes flicker downward, only to wrench themselves immediately back up, his entire posture rigid with the effort of *not seeing*.

She sighed, seizing the door and pulling it closer until only her face peeked out. "I'm *so* sorry about that."

The chef, now sweating profusely, shook his head in desperate reassurance. "It's—it's fine, Princess, I—I should go—"

He deposited the trolley with uncharacteristic clumsiness and all but bolted.

"Wait," Galinda called after him.

He froze, looking as though he expected to be executed on the spot.

"Serve my lunch today in the great hall. Like the other students." A knowing smile curled her lips. "I imagine people will want to see me today."

The chef nodded frantically before scurrying out of sight.

Galinda shut the door and turned to find River standing precisely where she had left him, still gloriously unrepentant.

She snatched his discarded underwear from the floor and promptly began *whipping* him with it. "You couldn't put on some clothes *before* coming to the door?"

"What?" he moaned, rubbing the spot where she had struck him. "I don't have anything to be ashamed of." To prove his point, he started to gyrate, moving his hips in slow, exaggerated circles.

Galinda, despite herself, burst into laughter. "*Just don't do that again.*"

"It's not like people haven't seen me naked before. Honestly, I'm practically naked all the time."

"Well, *I* have an *image* to uphold," Galinda reminded him, tossing her hair. "I can't look like I'm some kind of *whore*."

"And *I* have an image to uphold," River countered, smirking. "*A prince with a big cock, blessed in more ways than one.*"

Galinda groaned. "It's *different* for you."

"How so?"

"Don't play dumb. You *know* exactly how so. Now go take a shower and put some clothes on. We must make an appearance *together* for our subjects."

"Fine, fine. I'll be good. But you're awfully bossy this morning, *Princess.*"

He crept forward, hands circling her waist, breath warm against the sensitive curve of her ear. *"Care to join me?"*

Galinda sighed, her body betraying her before her words could. "I thought you'd never ask."

And so, they disappeared once more into the steam of the bath chamber, letting the water rinse away the remnants of their indulgences—

Or, at the very least, making new ones.

CHAPTER 33

Severed Thread

The afternoon sun blazed with an intensity that almost seemed deliberate, as though it fully understood the gravity of the day for Galinda. After all, she was the *main character* of this tale, *her* story, her moment to shine. And if she were to be entirely honest, she was the pivotal figure of the university, the very axis upon which Oz itself seemed to turn.

Recently, she thought of herself this way. The centre of everything. How could she not?

Meanwhile, the Winkie Prince had also prepared with care, as if he too understood the weight of the day. His usual navy-blue attire, so reliably him, was cast aside in favour of a lighter, softer blue. Baby blue and white, the perfect ensemble for a momentous occasion. He wavered for a moment, wondering if he should don the fur coat of his father's, the one that had seen countless kings and princes through moments of pomp. But he decided, perhaps wisely, that such a statement would be saved for another occasion, perhaps the wedding.

The magazines had been published, the *NewZPaprs* eagerly turned out. The students whispered in excited anticipation, as if they hadn't seen the front-page headlines already. The teachers pretended to grade papers, but all knew the truth—they were watching the clock, calculating the moments until the spectacle began.

Everyone wanted to know if true love was real. They didn't just want to *believe* in it, they wanted proof. Proof that a fairytale could be more than just a story. Proof that destiny could truly unite two hearts. And what better proof than a princess and a prince?

Princess Galinda and Prince Rivero were ready.

Blue and pink. And everything in between.

The two of them descended the grand staircase with the air of those who were entirely *aware* of the significance of their steps. The hall was empty. No students lingered in the corners. No one dared to delay.

Everyone was waiting for lunch. And more importantly, everyone knew where to go for lunch.

Galinda reached out, knocking once on the massive double doors. They swung open with practiced precision, as if this grand moment had been rehearsed a thousand times in their minds. And before the doors were even fully parted, the whispers began.

Gasping. Staring. Eyes wide in disbelief.

"I knew it!" someone said, their voice trembling with the excitement of an unspoken truth.

"She's so lucky," came the next voice, a touch of awe in the words.

"No!" another protested. "He's the lucky one!"

"*Well done!*" came a voice from somewhere near the back, one voice in the din of the crowd.

At the centre of the room, Cora, Mila, and Fanny waved frantically from their reserved seats, practically bouncing off the benches in their eagerness to acknowledge their friends. "Over here!" they called, as though the entire lunchroom had not already seen the spectacle unfolding.

River caught sight of his friends, his *real* friends, huddled together in their corner, making ridiculous hand gestures, silently asking him if he had, indeed, had sex with her.

He winked. The response was instant, a wave of whispers and quiet giggles, followed by their friends returning to their seats with a satisfied sense of knowing. "I told you," one of them murmured, barely audible but fully triumphant.

River sauntered over to the middle of the room, taking his seat beside Cora, Mila, and Fanny, his tall frame displacing the students who had dared occupy the spaces he and his friends had claimed. They scattered like cockroaches in daylight, leaving the prime spots behind with no complaints.

Teachers, ever the picture of professionalism, had their lunches at staggered intervals. But somehow, some inexplicable magic seemed to make them all arrive at once. They pretended to fetch their food, stretching their necks with an air of studied nonchalance, while their eyes, so obviously trained on the two at the centre of the room, betrayed the real reason for their attendance. They were listening to every word, every exchange, as though it might unlock some new truth about love, about royalty, about *fate* itself.

And then—

The doors swung open with a thud, cutting through the whispers like a blade through cloth. The noise died down so suddenly. A silence that was deafening in its own right. Loud in its refusal to be ignored.

Framed in the doorway like a grotesque shadow in the midst of a divine dawn, stood Zelphira.

Dressed in sombre black, Green, sickly green, a hue that clung to her like a stain one could never wash off. All eyes snapped to her, drawn unwillingly to the spectre of her presence, as though a serpent had slithered into the garden of paradise. Galinda, of course, noticed first. She could never fail to notice.

Zelphira stomped across the floor, her boots hitting the tiles with the rhythmic thud of a marching soldier, though far less disciplined.

"I *loathe* that thing," Galinda muttered under her breath, her voice dripping with venom. "Don't you?"

River, ever the enigmatic figure, feigned indifference, though his lips twitched slightly in the direction of a smile to appease Galinda.

Zelphira, oblivious or perhaps uncaring to the hush of disdain that followed her, made her way to the food counter. Her bony arms reached out and grabbed a tray with all the grace of a butcher, piling it high with rice, green beans and lentils. The sheer mountain of food was a statement in itself, as if Zelphira were daring anyone to question her appetite. She would not starve for the sake of propriety.

Every table was full, every single one, that is, except for the one behind Galinda's. Zelphira's eyes darted to the seat, and with an air of entitlement, she made her approach, stomping her way across the room like a force of nature.

The students at the table saw her coming and, with the practiced motions of animals avoiding a predator, vacated their seats. The trays were left behind, some forgotten entirely, but none remained to contest her claim on the space.

As Zelphira drew nearer, a small pink-shoed foot appeared from the corner of the table, as though summoned by the gods themselves. The foot—*Galinda's*—slipped under Zelphira's path, a subtle, deliberate trap.

With a muffled *thud*, Zelphira went tumbling forward, the tray of food flying from her hands and scattering across the floor like a plague of locusts. Her face, her long black hair, everything became buried in a sea of rice, beans and lentils.

Laughter spilled forth like water breaking a dam, the tension that had held it back for so long now unleashed with a vengeance. The students who had clung to silence found their voices, and what a glorious sound it was. Zelphira had given them a reason to laugh. She had *earned* it.

"Oh, Oz," Galinda gasped theatrically, both hands flying to her face in a mock display of concern. "Do you need help?" She extended a hand, one of impeccable grace, as though offering salvation to a lost soul.

Zelphira, however, slapped it away and rose with an angry snarl, "you did that on purpose! You *tripped* me up!"

"Me? I did no such thing."

"You *tripped* me!" Zelphira cried again, her voice rising in pitch with every word.

Galinda turned to the onlookers, casting a glance that invited their testimony. "Did you see me trip her up?"

"No!" they all cried out in unison.

Mila chimed in. "All Galinda tried to do was help you up, you ungrateful cow."

"Yes," Cora added, "Galinda is a good person, and you're just…" She paused, her hesitation ringing louder than the insult she had not quite delivered.

The room broke into fresh laughter.

"River, you saw it, right?" Zelphira prompted, turning to him.

River, however, bowed his head slightly, his face a study in avoidance. He remained silent.

Fanny, who had never been one for subtlety, leaned across the table and addressed Zelphira directly. "Just leave. No one wants you here."

Zelphira looked around, her eyes scanning the faces of the room, the faces of disbelief, of betrayal. She had just accused the Princess of the South—the sister of the Good Witch—of being *Wicked*.

Without a word, Zelphira dusted herself off, her shoulders heavy with the weight of her humiliation, and stomped out of the lunchroom, slamming the door behind her with a finality that could have rivalled the closing of a tomb.

"You better leave," another voice muttered, barely audible but laden with a satisfaction that filled the room.

Galinda, still dazed, gathered her composure and smoothed a hand over her skirts before proclaiming, *"Sometimes you try to help people, and they refuse to be helped. Some creatures are simply made that way. It's their nature, and they can't be blamed for it—nor can we be blamed for recognizing it."*

"She's so right," Fanny declared, a sycophantic shrillness in her voice.

"Absolutely," another agreed.

"We thank you for your goodness, Galinda," someone offered from the back.

Galinda pressed a hand to her chest, soaking in their reverence. *A saint in satin.*

◇

After that, the days fell into an easy rhythm. Ozian sighs of adoration accompanied Prince Rivero as he escorted Princess Galinda to her classes. Gasps of awe when he kissed her cheek, just a farewell until their next hour of reunification. More sighs when he held the door for her, or bent over her hand with all the decorum of a man accustomed to worship. And when he walked with his arm curled around her waist, it was confirmation: this was what they had wanted. This was what they had all hoped was real.

And then, as they wove through the campus's grand corridors on their usual path to class, they passed *her*.

Zelphira.

Always clothed in black.

She did not stop. Did not speak. Only looked. Looked *through* Galinda with such undisguised contempt that, for the first time in recent memory, Galinda's unwavering gaze faltered. A single twitch of discomfort. A quick glance down at her shoes.

Mila, having observed the encounter, seized the moment. *"Galinda,"* she whispered, the gleam in her eye promising mischief.

She held the banana, the last of it bitten away. And then, with a flick of the wrist, the peel was airborne.

It landed with a soft, unceremonious *plop* against the back of Zelphira's head.

A beat of silence. Mila turned away swiftly, feigning innocence, though the shaking of her shoulders betrayed her.

Galinda turned, curious about the damage, but in doing so, Zelphira assumed she was the culprit.

Zelphira frowned. It was not a pleasant sight.

Her hand lifted. Her fingers twitched. She whispered something—something hushed and unfamiliar—and then—

She stopped.

Slowly, deliberately, her hand fell.

Galinda could still feel the phantom of her voice, could still hear the whisper beneath her own thoughts. And in that moment, she remembered. Zelphira had magic. She moved a heavy door with just her eyes. For all she knew she could tear apart half the school with a mere wave of her hand.

A shiver curled around Galinda's spine. Her magic was failing her and so she couldn't defend herself if Zelphira decided to curse her.

"Are you alright?" River's voice was warm, grounding.

"Yes," she said quickly.

They had reached her classroom now.

"Here we are," River announced, pressing a quick kiss to her lips and holding open the door.

Mila, still suppressing giggles, wandered off to her own affairs. River turned, heading toward his War Tactics and Combat Strategy lecture.

Galinda lingered a moment before stepping inside.

◇

Nightfall brought no relief from her own importance. She, Cora, Mila, Fanny, and River, accompanied by his usual cadre of smug, muscle-bound admirers, occupied the benches by the great fountain, tossing laughter and scandalous jokes between them like a shuttlecock at sport. Passersby dawdled near, pretending they had somewhere else to be, but lingering just in case Galinda, in some rare act of generosity, decided to expand her social borders.

But they remained where they belonged.

Outside.

Wishing, waiting, hoping for a glimpse into the world where she ruled.

A few lamps flickered on. The moon, ever the dramatic old voyeur, took its place in the sky. Lady Mordemire passed by, unmoved by the scene, her robes stiff with authority, her mind likely occupied with whatever tedious business the Wizard had for her.

And then, trailing behind like a shadow that had gotten lost and misplaced itself, came Zelphira.

Arms overloaded with forbidden sorcery books only Lady Mordemire had access to. She looked neither left nor right, humming some grim, tuneless melody to herself.

Mila, never one to let a perfectly good opportunity for cruelty pass, cupped her hands around her mouth.

"Hey, green girl! Is your *pussy* green too?"

Galinda snorted. The others cackled.

Fanny laughed and said, "Zelphira! Tell us, did your mother have sex with a frog? You know humans are not supposed to mate with the animals, right?"

But Zelphira only kept walking, her humming undisturbed, her posture unchanged.

Mila frowned. "Did you not *hear* us, green girl?"

Still, nothing.

"Come on," Cora finally sighed. "It's getting late."

The girls gathered their bags and drifted off, Fanny giggling over something Cora whispered. River stretched and stood, a lazy smile fixed on his face.

"Shall I walk you to your suite?"

"No, that's all right," Galinda mused. "I have... something to take care of."

He grinned knowingly. "As you wish, my princess." He kissed her cheek before sauntering toward the east wing, where his private chambers awaited him.

Galinda waited until the courtyard emptied. Then, with careful, deliberate steps, she made her way toward the maids' quarters.

And there she was.

Zelphira.

Hunched in the dim torchlight, fumbling for her keys at the entrance to the cramped, unremarkable building that housed those of *lower standing: the maids*. A few boys loitered nearby, half-hidden in the shadows. They had been waiting for her.

Waiting to throw their rocks.

A well-aimed one struck her shoulder. Another clipped the side of her face. Laughter followed, not mean-spirited in their eyes—just sport.

Galinda's voice rang out, high and imperious.

"Zelphira, *wait!*"

The laughter halted. The boys stilled.

Zelphira turned. A fresh rock hit her cheek, jarring her mid-motion. She gasped, gripping the books tighter against her chest, her hair, long and slick with oil, swept across her face.

But it was the expression she wore that unsettled Galinda.

Shock.

Like Galinda was the *last* person she had expected to see.

"What do you want?" she croaked. A whimper, half-swallowed, barely escaped her throat.

She found her keys.

Galinda hesitated.

But no. She *wanted* this.

"Are you—?" The question felt foreign on her tongue. "Are you *all right?*"

Zelphira flinched. "Like you care." Her fingers tightened around the keys, whitening her knuckles. "What do you *want?*"

Galinda inhaled deeply.

"I was wondering… since you're in sorcery class and I'm not allowed…" She swallowed. "I was wondering if you might… teach me what you've learnt from Lady Mordemire?"

Zelphira blinked. Then laughed again, though this time with real amusement, real cruelty.

"We've been over this," she sneered. "You're talentless. You have *no magic.*" She stepped closer, her breath hot and bitter. "All you have is *looks*, and that should be enough for someone like you. But no, you want to live in *even more* delusion than you already do."

Galinda bristled. "I do *not*—"

"—And even if you *did* have magic, what *makes you think* I would waste a single flick of my fingers teaching a fool like *you?* You're nothing but a *pampered princess whore*, spreading your legs for powerful men so they'll keep you relevant."

Galinda's stomach twisted. She clenched her fists.

"Me, a *whore? Me*, a *fool?*" Galinda's voice was shrill and splintered like shattered glass. "*You're* the green one!"

She could have stopped there. She could have let the words settle, let them fester, let them poison Zelphira in silence.

But something in her, a flicker of something ruthless, something gleaming and unchecked, urged her forward.

"Honestly, it's a wonder how you've survived this long, that no one had crept into your room and *murdered you* like the revolting little mistake you are."

Zelphira stiffened.

Galinda leaned in, her breath cool as winter glass, her smile sweet.

"And your parents, they should have burned you the moment they saw your repulsive green flesh slithering out of your mother's *twiddle.*"

Zelphira smirked, thin, brittle, a shield against the tremor in her hands. Her voice, when it came, was parched earth.

"Don't speak to me again. Don't *ask* of me. We are *not* friends."

"Oh, that much is obvious. You'll *always* be alone. No one likes you, let alone…*Love* you. You're here calling me a whore? You wish a prince, let alone a man could stomach touching you without vomiting."

Galinda flipped her hair, a grand, dismissive gesture, one meant to remind Zelphira of exactly what she *wasn't*.

Beautiful.

The rock-throwing resumed.

A fresh one struck Zelphira's collarbone. She stiffened but did not cry out. Instead, she turned sharply, shoving her key into the lock with fumbling fingers.

Click.

The door swung open.

She slipped inside, locking it behind her—only then allowing herself to *breathe.*

◇

The next day, Galinda and her circle, her devoted courtiers, gathered at their usual spot in the dining hall. A reserved table, waiting on the arrival of their steaming platters, while Galinda waited for the personal delivery of her meal to be wheeled in on a silver cart.

Fanny leaned in first, eyes alight with mischief. "Have you heard the latest Zelphira rumour?"

Galinda perked up immediately, "oh, tell me everything."

"Word is, the reason she's green is becoz she can't bathe. If water touches her, she'll melt—so she oils herself instead. And that's why she reeks. Why her hair's always slick and greasy."

River exhaled through his nose, unimpressed. "That's ridiculous."

"Utter nonsense," Galinda agreed, "where'd you even hear that?"

Fanny tossed her golden locks. "Oh, I made it up. But it's already spreading like wildfire."

Mila perked up, "I told people she has no family, sleeps with goats, and eats babies."

Laughter danced at the table, wild, delighted, indulgent. It was absurd, they all knew that, but why let the truth get in the way of a good story?

Cora, never one to be left out, leaned in conspiratorially. "I didn't start this one, but apparently, she's a cursed baby from Ozma herself. Dropped from the sky becoz she was too wicked for the heavens. Now she's doomed to walk the earth, a punishment for her sins."

That did it. Galinda doubled over, laughter shaking through her, tears pricking at the corners of her eyes. The others followed, swept up in the sheer entertainment of their own cruelty.

Galinda, catching her breath, wiped her eyes. "Well, I have a little surprise for her." A pause, then a delicate wrinkle of her nose. "Though I will say, the smell isn't a rumour. She does stink. Her hair reeks of onions, her clothes of hay. But I will give her one thing—her teeth are startlingly white."

"Obviously," Mila interjected, not missing a beat. "She has to brush them after gnawing the bones of children to cover up the evidence."

Another wave of howling laughter.

River remained quiet. Though a reluctant smirk ghosted across his lips, betraying him.

And then—the doors swung open.

Zelphira.

This time, there was no dead silence. No collective holding of breath.

Instead, laughter. Quiet at first, from corners of the room, then spread like a slow, cruel fire.

And as if by design, a single table remained empty. Set aside just for her. A gesture of generosity, surely. A kindness, really.

Zelphira took her tray, again piled it high with food, too much food, some might say. She moved to the lone table, the one reserved just for her. This time, she checked the floor with each step. No more pink-shoed betrayals.

The crowd deflated slightly. No trip, no spilled food, no fresh entertainment. But still, there were things to mock. The way her dress draped like second-hand curtains. The oil-slick sheen of her hair, the way her nostrils flared when she chewed. Her shoes—cheap, battered things, how they scuffed the polished floor. Even her fingers, too long, too skeletal, moving like spindly twigs over her book.

Ah, but Galinda had planned for this.

She rose.

River leaned toward her. "Where are you going?"

She tapped his shoulder, a delicate reassurance. "Oh, don't worry."

From her bag, she pulled something small, rectangular. Innocuous. She made her way across the dining hall, her hands folded behind her back. The room hushed as she approached the lone table.

Zelphira, who had been eating with one hand and reading with the other, lifted her head. Her expression was already weary, as if she knew, somehow, that her next humiliation had arrived on golden-heeled feet.

"I thought I told you never to speak to me," she muttered. Her voice was low, warning, as though she was trying so hard to spare Galinda's life, but she was making it utterly difficult to do so.

"Arrr, don't bite," she said, teasing a growl. "I have a gift for you, out of the goodness of my heart."

A murmur swept through the room.

"Whatever it is, I don't want it."

"Oh, but you *must* have it."

Galinda, in one elegant movement, revealed what was in her hands, peeling back the wrapper with the same care one might use to unveil a diamond necklace.

A bar of soap.

A tidal wave of laughter, of shrieking mirth. Some students banged their trays, others clutched their sides.

Zelphira froze.

She dropped her spoon.

Galinda pouted, ever the innocent. "Oh? You don't want it? I could explain how to use it if you like?"

Zelphira's hands curled into fists. She slid her book into her bag, threw the strap over her shoulder.

She said nothing.

She simply stood.

She walked out, her back straight, her boots clicking against the floor.

"Wait!" Galinda turned to the crowd; voice honeyed with concern. "What did I do wrong?"

A student sighed, shaking his head in admiration. "You're too good, Galinda. It's like you said, some people just don't *want* the help."

Another piped up, "but you *tried*, and that's what counts!"

Another asked, "I still don't understand why your heart still yearns to help such a lost cause?"

Galinda nodded sagely. "Well, these things are sent simply to try us. What else can we do, but respond with goodness? Must we not do the right thing, to keep the fates on our side?"

A smattering of applause.

She left the soap on Zelphira's table, its stark whiteness against the rough wood a cruel sort of punctuation. Even though Zelphira had gone, the laughter remained, rippling through the room long after her shadow had disappeared.

Galinda slid back into her seat.

River leaned in. "Galinda, what was that?"

"What was what?"

"You didn't have to do that. Not like that."

She blinked at him. "I don't know what you mean. I—I only tried to *help* her."

River rose from his seat and strode out of the lunchroom without a word.

Fanny, watching him disappear through the doors, leaned in toward Galinda, who was savouring her cake with particular delight today. "Where's he off to?"

Galinda, barely pausing between bites, gave a light shrug. "Oh, he probably just needs some air."

◇

That very evening, Galinda perched herself upon the worn benches near the Ozcodile Fountain, her eyes scanning the evening crowd, the flickering lights casting shadows on the cobblestones. She wasn't waiting just for any passerby, no, she was waiting for someone who should have known to come.

CHANGE

When each figure came into view, tall, short, broad, or slim, Galinda would, with a flick of her hair and the sweetest, most innocent tone, inquire, "have you seen Rivero by any chance?"

Each reply, without exception, came swiftly, "no, sorry."

A puff of frustration briefly clouded her gaze, though she immediately replaced it with a delicate, almost mechanical smile. He should have known to find her here. After all, this was where they first crossed paths, this fountain—the scene of their first curious exchange. It wasn't *just* a coincidence. It wasn't a random meeting. He *should* know this.

As she continued her wait, the sound of whispered voices approached. Galinda turned her head to see Cora, Mila, and Fanny, huddled close as though sharing secrets too precious for the open air. Their words, though muffled, betrayed an undercurrent of excitement.

"Where are you girls off to?" Galinda asked with the same airy tone that made every question seem casual, though her eyes were sharp.

The trio jerked, caught like intruders in their own conspiratorial plot, though their surprise quickly morphed into delighted amusement at the sight of Galinda seated so elegantly, yet alone.

Fanny stammered first, "we're just… going for some beverages at the Gillikin bar."

Galinda's finger drifted lazily in the opposite direction. "But the bar is *that* way."

Mila, always the quicker to speak, muttered in defeat, "Okay, fine! We're going to play a jest on Zelphira, you know, the green girl?"

Cora's elbow jabbed into Mila's side, "of course she knows Zelphira, dummy."

"What kind of jest?"

Before anyone could respond, Fanny swerved the conversation, her voice taking on a false cheer. "What are you doing out here all alone, Galinda?"

"I was waiting," Galinda said, her tone a little more clipped now, "I was waiting to see if River would show up. You haven't seen him, have you?"

"No, not at all," Fanny replied swiftly.

Mila, still animated by the earlier thought, asked impulsively, "do you want to come with us? It doesn't look like you're busy."

"Well… sure."

As they neared the quarters, Galinda watched the trio with a wry smile. "Anyone care to tell me what kind of trick you're planning?"

"You'll see," Fanny winked, her tone a promise of mischief.

At the door, Mila raised her hand to knock, but Fanny intercepted the gesture, slapping it away just in time.

"What are you doing?" Cora scolded, "how are we supposed to pull the *trickle* if we knock? We're doing this while she's asleep, remember?"

"Oh, right," Mila muttered, raising a finger as if struck by sudden brilliance.

Fanny leaned in close to Galinda, "apparently, she sleeps with the window open. So, we'll climb in through there."

Galinda, ever the sceptic, raised an eyebrow. "What about the maids? Won't they notice someone's been in?"

"Already handled. I told them what we were doing. They've agreed to keep quiet."

Galinda laughed, her smile turning impish. "You snivelling little snake."

Fanny caught the mischievous gleam in Galinda's eyes and chuckled. "There she is, the Galinda we all know and love."

The girls crept around the maid's quarters like shadows, their movements silent, calculated. Galinda, always the leader of the pack, spotted it first.

"There!" she hissed, pointing to the window.

The window stood wide open, as promised. Cora clutched the bag close to her chest. Fanny was the first to slink in, followed by Mila, then Galinda, and lastly, Cora.

"What now?" Galinda whispered.

"She's a deep sleeper," Cora whispered, though the words carried a sinister edge, the quiet glee in her voice unmistakable.

Cora, ever prepared for mischief, reached into the bag and withdrew a pair of scissors.

Galinda swallowed, her heart hammering in her chest, though she kept her voice steady. "What are those for?"

A sly grin curled at the corners of Cora's lips. "We're going to cut her hair, of course."

The others turned their gaze to Zelphira, who lay, oblivious to the storm that had just arrived at her door.

She was at peace.

Galinda cleared her throat, "I have a feeling she values her hair more than anything. Look at the length…It looks like she's been growing it from the moment she was born."

"Exactly. And she's got plenty to spare," Fanny quipped, "a lot to spare."

But Galinda's pulse quickened. "I just don't think…" she trailed off, her thoughts drifting to Zelphira's magical abilities, the power that lurked beneath that quiet exterior.

"It's too late to turn back now," Cora interrupted, "we're already here."

Galinda straightened herself, "let's just get it over with," she muttered, though her voice was brittle.

Cora reached forward and thrust the scissors into Galinda's hands with an almost unsettling force. "Here you go. Cut it."

"Why do I go first?" Galinda asked, her voice a little less sure.

"I don't make the rules," Cora shot back, her grin widening.

"You do it!" Galinda insisted, attempting to pass the scissors back, but Cora was firm, her grip like iron.

"Don't be weak," Fanny added, "It's like you're scared of Zelphira."

"Scared?" she scoffed.

Taking a deep breath, she steeled herself. The scissors, once foreign in her hands, now felt like an extension of herself, a tool of defiance, a mark of her own transformation. She stepped closer to Zelphira, her movements slow, deliberate. She aimed the scissors low, near the base of the long, flowing tresses.

Mila's voice, light and eager, cut through the silence. "Higher."

Galinda shifted, inching the scissors higher.

Cora's voice, no more than a murmur, urged her. "Higher."

And finally, Fanny, "Higher!"

Galinda complied, bringing the blades of the scissors to within a breath of Zelphira's scalp. With a single, swift motion, Galinda squeezed the handles, and the sharp blades snipped through the thick locks of hair.

Snipped like severed thread.

What had taken years to grow was reduced to mere strands in seconds. The hair fell like a blanket of forgotten time, tumbling to the floor in a quiet cascade.

The room held its breath.

Mila, unable to contain herself, burst into laughter, the sound sharp and unrestrained. "She actually did it!"

Fanny, wide-eyed, gasped, "oh…" She couldn't contain it either, and soon the room was filled with the sound of hysterical laughter.

But just as quickly as the moment had begun, something shifted. Something dark.

Zelphira's eyes fluttered open. The monster, it seemed, had awoken.

"Oh drat!" Mila exclaimed.

In a flurry of panic and fluttering skirts, Mila, Cora, and Fanny bolted from Zelphira's room, their feet thundering against the wooden floor as they scrambled for the door of the maid's quarters.

Galinda was left behind.

Abandoned in the stillness of the room, the scissors still clutched tightly in her hand.

Zelphira shifted in her bed, the soft rustle of her sheets betraying her awakening.

"What in Oz are you doing in my room?" Zelphira's voice was raw with confusion and fury. "How did you get in?"

Galinda's mouth opened, but no words came out.

"I should go," Galinda finally said, her voice a breathless, frantic whisper.

"No! You, wait here. I'm reporting you to Professor Shinz."

Zelphira's eyes, dark and focused, slowly began to shift, as if some understanding was dawning within her. A frown deepened on her forehead, she felt something was terribly wrong. Her gaze dropped to her own body.

Her head, her shoulders, light, too light.

Slowly, she lifted her long, skeletal fingers to her hair.

She turned, her gaze locking on Galinda as the scissors gleamed in her hand. And there it was—her hair, scattered across the floor in a sea of broken strands, a trail of destruction marking the space around them.

"What the—?" Zelphira's voice cracked.

With an almost mechanical precision, she stood, her limbs stiff with the beginnings of rage, and stalked toward the mirror hanging on the opposite wall. The reflection that met her was a grotesque version of her own self, her once-proud hair reduced to a ragged mess, strands falling in uneven clumps.

"I can explain."

But Zelphira was already staring into the mirror, her breathing shallow, her chest rising and falling in rapid succession. The silence was suffocating. And then, then came the scream.

"I will kill you!" Zelphira's voice was a growl now, "Galinda, do you hear me?"

Galinda's breath hitched as Zelphira moved toward her, every step heavy with unbridled fury.

"What have I ever done to you? Why would you do this to me?"

"I— I—"

"Is it becoz I'm green?" Zelphira hissed, "Is that why you hate me so much that you would do this?"

"No...well—"

"Why do you hate my green so much? Does it bother you that I'm green? Tell me! Becoz I can't understand it! Why are you so cruel?"

Galinda remained silent, her mind scrambling for something, anything, that might make sense of this, but she found nothing.

"Galinda," she said through gritted teeth, her voice thick with venom, "I suggest you leave. If you know what's good for you, you will leave right now. Do not make me do something I'll regret."

Galinda ran. And she didn't stop.

Zelphira sat on her bed, her breath shallow, her hands trembling in the darkness. The sting of humiliation still burned against her skin, yet her body, perhaps instinctively, sought comfort in the only way it knew how. She hummed. A song—ancient, wistful, something that had once been sung to her—rose to her lips, delicate as a thread of moonlight, her voice strong yet delicate and beautiful.

Then, an interruption. A knock at the door.

Zelphira tensed, her humming tapering off into nothing. She heard movement beyond her room, the slow stirring of half-feigned sleep from the maids who had been roused awake by her scream but did nothing.

Heavy footfalls approached.

The door to Zelphira's room swung open, slamming against the wall with force.

It was him.

Professor Shinz stood in the doorway, his silhouette grotesquely outlined in the dim glow of the hallway sconces. His nightrobes, hastily thrown on, his fingers curling into fists at his sides.

Zelphira rose, the remnants of her severed hair still clutched in her lap.

"You!" he bellowed, the word slapping against the walls.

"Professor Shinz, thank you—"

"You disobedient creatu—girl!"

Her jaw clenched. "What have I done now?" lifting a hand to her ruined hair as though to present her innocence like an alibi.

"What have you done?" he echoed mockingly, "we all heard your scream— your chaos! Do you think you're the only one who lives here? I don't know whether you require sleep like the rest of us, but *we* do! You've woken half the campus with your theatrics!"

"Professor, can't you see I had reason?" Zelphira snapped, "look at my hair! Someone—"

"Silence!"

His voice cracked through the room like a whip, and Zelphira flinched despite herself.

"Listen to me," he said, jabbing a thick, accusatory finger in her direction. "I will say this once. If you step out of line again, if you make a spectacle of yourself, if you bring one more ounce of shame upon this institution, as you have done since the moment you arrived, I will remove you from this school, better yet, if that day even comes, I don't care if the Wizard wants you here, Oz will no longer be your home. Am. I. Understood?"

Zelphira did not answer right away. Her hands curled into fists at her sides, nails biting into her palms. A tide of hot, burning words surged up her throat—words she wanted to throw in his face, to make him feel small, just as he tried to make her feel small.

"Yes," she said through gritted teeth.

Professor Shinz straightened his robes. A scoff. A sneer. Then, with a flourish of finality, he turned on his heel and thundered out of the room, slamming the door behind him so hard that the walls rattled.

The silence he left behind was thick and heavy, except—

A noise.

From the kitchen.

A barely stifled giggle. A throat cleared to disguise it. Another stifled chuckle. The maids.

Zelphira gathered a handful of her shorn hair, cradling it gently against her cheek as though it were something precious, something that had belonged to another lifetime.

A tear slipped down her face, though she made no sound.

And then, softly, faintly, she began to hum again.

Quieter this time.

For herself.

◇

By morning, River was at Galinda's private suite, lavishing her with kisses, more in an hour than he'd given her in a week, and Galinda, vain little thing that she was, had no complaints. Let him dote on her. Let him worship her. She wouldn't breathe a word of protest, not when his renewed affection was so freshly rekindled. She knew too well how fickle it could be, how his rage had flared over something as inconsequential as a bar of soap. If he ever discovered what she'd done, what they'd done, he might very well abandon the operation altogether.

Galinda made a sport of avoidance. No lingering in the lunchroom, no idle gossip in the halls. She arrived early to politics class so that Zelphira wouldn't so much as cross her periphery. It was better this way. The girl's smouldering envy of Galinda's beauty had already spared her before, who was to say it wouldn't turn the other way, should they meet again?

So, Galinda orchestrated a new arrangement. She and her court would take their lunch on the benches today, the wind tousling her golden curls as she dined on a personal buffet, a spectacle of exclusivity.

But then, a disturbance. A ripple in her carefully curated reality.

Zelphira was not in the lunchroom either. No, she was striding past their bench, deliberately, languidly, as if she wanted to be seen. And River, the fool, smiled at her. It was brief, a flicker of civility, but Galinda caught it. And worse, River caught that she caught it. He coughed, awkwardly adjusting his expression, but the damage was done.

Something was off.

It was Cora who noticed first, then Mila, then Fanny. And finally, Galinda.

Zelphira had a full head of hair.

Blacker than before, richer somehow, as if the strands had been oiled by moonlight itself.

Mila, mid-bite into a pear-pie, let the pastry fall from her lips, mouth agape.

Fanny clutched Galinda's arm, eyes wide with horror. "But you chopped it last night! We all saw it!"

"Obviously." Galinda's voice was a bit too sharp.

"It must be magic," Mila whispered, like a child invoking a ghost story.

"No way!" Cora turned to Galinda, "does she have magic? You lived with the Good Witch, surely you can tell."

Galinda almost confessed. Almost let slip what she'd seen in sorcery class, the way Zelphira's eyes alone moved heavy objects with no incantation.

"I mean, it must be, mustn't it?" She affected a casual air. "What other explanation is there?"

Mila exhaled as though she'd narrowly avoided an execution. "If I knew she had magic, I wouldn't have snuck into her room. What if she'd turned us into carrots? I *hate* carrots."

Fanny, still watching Zelphira with unguarded trepidation, bowed her head when the girl's gaze flicked toward her. "Maybe we should—stick to less direct trickles?" she murmured. "I don't want to die at the hands of a cucumber."

Galinda nodded. "Agreed."

CHAPTER 34

Magical Ailment

In the morning's stillness, precisely at the 6th hour, Galinda was startled awake by the arrival of her Ummi, without warning of course. Unlike most girls, whose Ummis seemed to tailor their visits around their client's whims, arranging meetings to suit their preferences, Galinda's Ummi was unbothered by such trivialities. She arrived when *she* pleased, and more often than not, it was at the most inconvenient of times, like the sort of inconvenient hour when you've barely had time to brush your teeth, let alone apply your faithful *Make-Do* to smooth the edges of your day.

"Good morning, Galinda!" The Ummi trilled, her voice a peculiar mix of honey and steel.

"Morning," Galinda groaned, her eyes still fogged with sleep as she rubbed them, struggling to remember what the world even looked like at this ungodly hour.

"Just waking up, are you?"

"Is it *that* obvious?" Galinda mumbled.

"Oh, *very* much so."

"Shall we begin then?" the Ummi continued, sweeping into Galinda's private suite as though it were her own. She settled herself into the chair at Galinda's desk with a loud, ungraceful plop, the chair groaning under her weight, and Galinda couldn't help but notice the way the legs buckled slightly, as though fearing their very existence under such a burden.

She tried to cross her legs in an elegant fashion, then gave up halfway, settling instead for a spread-legged pose that suggested more comfort than dignity.

"So, Galinda, how are your studies progressing?"

"Very good, Ummi."

"*Bah!* Don't call me 'Ummi'! Call me *Ummi Edelweiss*—I think I forgot to mention my name the last time I was here."

"You did." Galinda laughed, still a little disoriented.

"Oh, dear me! How thoughtless of me!" Ummi Edelweiss chuckled lightly, her tone tinged with an odd sort of self-mockery. "I do tend to forget myself in the presence of a lemon tart. Such a *delightful* thing, don't you think? But I digress." Her laughter faltered slightly, as though she'd shared a secret too intimate for public knowledge, quickly retreating behind a mask of propriety.

"Yes, well," Ummi Edelweiss continued, after a brief pause, "I spoke with your professor, the grumpy one. What's his name—oh, yes! The one with the sour disposition."

"Master Ponsworth."

"Ah, yes! Master Ponsworth! He said you're top of your class. All assignments completed and submitted on time."

Galinda nodded, but the acknowledgment felt somehow hollow, like she should be ashamed of her own accomplishments.

"I trust you completed them all *by yourself?*" Ummi Edelweiss raised a single eyebrow, her gaze piercing.

"Yes. Every single one." Galinda replied firmly, though her voice held a flicker of unease.

"Well then! That's splendid! You're doing so well!"

The joy in her voice was palpable, but there was something in her gaze that suggested she had not finished. A shift, a subtle but unmistakable shift—hovered in the air.

"I assume," Ummi Edelweiss continued, her voice lowering to a near-whisper, "I assume you were not accepted into the sorcery class?"

Galinda rolled her eyes, a mixture of annoyance and frustration creeping in. "How do you know that?"

"I told you, I have access to the courses you take, and your progress."

"Well, yes," Galinda muttered, her words bitter. "Lady Mordemire sacked me."

"I'm sure it wasn't from a lack of talent?"

"No." Galinda hesitated. "Yes." She let out a heavy sigh. "I don't know. It's complicated."

Ummi Edelweiss glanced at the clock on the wall with a casual sort of precision, "I have time," she stated plainly.

Galinda sank onto the edge of her bed, a weight settling in her chest as she stared down at her hands, which suddenly felt like lead. "I've been having problems with my magic. It just… stopped working, ever since I came to this university. And now, the few people I told I *had* magic, well, they don't believe me. And how could they? I haven't been able to cast the simplest spells. I don't even know if I'm sick, or…" Galinda's voice trailed off.

Ummi Edelweiss's expression softened; her sharp eyes gleaming with something close to concern. "Have you spoken to the doctors on campus?"

"Yes, I've seen all of them. They tell me I'm perfectly healthy. In fact, I'm actually very good at brewing potions, and I've concocted dozens, all of them perfectly fine, but I still wake up with nothing to show for it. I think… I think it's some sort of magical affliction. A curse, perhaps. I don't know anymore."

GLINDA: The GOOD Witch

The silence between them stretched for a moment, heavy and thick.

"You know," Edelweiss began, with a sudden shift in tone, "one of the students I keep an eye on is quite exceptional with magic. The most powerful I've seen in ages. I'm sure you've heard of her."

Galinda's head snapped toward Edelweiss, "who else do you watch over?" she asked slowly, as if the very question itself might hold an answer she wasn't ready for.

"You've heard of Zelphira Raventhorne, haven't you?"

Galinda's face dropped.

"From Raventhorne Farm? Quite the mysterious one. Dark, brooding… full of promise. Of course, you must know her." Ummi continued, her voice thick with the unspoken, as if the name alone could explain everything. "Mind my language, but the green girl, dresses in all black, always with that sour look on her face."

"I know her!" Galinda bit out sharply, "Or at least I've heard of her."

"Perfect! I'll have a word with her. I think you two would make *marvellous* friends. She's truly a darling once you get to know her."

"No! I don't think she likes me very much."

"Oh, bah!" Ummi waved her hand dismissively, "you just need to talk to her. She's sweet. Really, I'm sure she'll help you."

"Ummi Edelweiss," Galinda sighed in exasperation, "I'd rather not. Do you have any other options?"

Ummi, unbothered by the sudden shift in mood, leaned back, her fingers tapping her chin in thoughtful consideration. "Well, during my travels through Gillikin Main, I always ride past a little shop run by a healer. People say she's good, though her methods are… unconventional. I can't give a full recommendation since I've never been there myself, but I really should, I think. I feel I'm gaining a little weight, though I haven't been eating much. It's a mad phenomenon I've been experiencing…" she rambled on, oblivious to Galinda's growing impatience.

"Can I have the name of the shop?"

"Oh, right! Yes, of course." Ummi fumbled through her bag, until she found a worn notepad. She flipped through its pages. "Ah! Here it is: Velora Herbs."

Galinda repeated the name to herself, her mind fixing it like a spell, making sure it stuck.

"Thank you."

Ummi glanced at the clock with feigned surprise, jumped to her feet—awkwardly, as though standing upright was a personal triumph. "Oh, look at the time! Ummi Edelweiss has to be off. No lemon tarts today?" She asked, a lightness in her voice that didn't quite match the line of her mouth.

"Sorry, no. I think the chef is running a little late."

"No worries, I'll get by."

For a split second, Galinda thought she saw the faintest glint in her Ummi's eye, was it a tear? Perhaps. But it was gone as quickly as it had appeared.

293

CHANGE

Ummi Edelweiss turned toward the door, her steps slow, reluctant even. She paused in the doorway, looking back at Galinda with a faint, almost wistful smile. "Good luck, my dear. I do hope you find what you're looking for."

Alone at last, Galinda stood in the quiet of her room for a long moment before she moved. She walked toward the bathroom, pulling the trolley of food the chef had wheeled in moments before Ummi arrived.

She took a bite of a lemon tart and poured herself a cup of tea, nothing too hot, nothing too strong. Just something to ease the tension in her chest.

Velora Herbs.

The name bounced around her head, a small, lingering thing. Would this healer, whoever she was, be able to help? Or was she just another stop along the way to a dead end?

Galinda dressed herself, choosing a blue dress that was both inconspicuous and yet subtly regal, paired with worn brown boots, the kind of footwear that whispered "practical" rather than "princess." She grabbed a purse, a small, leather thing that could easily be dismissed, and a scarf, carefully arranged to cover most of her face, like a clever disguise drawn from a stage play. She opened the door to find River, poised to knock, his hand halfway through the air, a mix of surprise and amusement written all over his face.

"So, where's the princess off to today?" he asked.

Galinda placed a finger to her lips in secrecy. "Shhh. I don't want people knowing where I'm going."

"So, that's why you're wearing blue?"

"You're sharp," Galinda replied, her tone dripping with playful mockery.

"Want me to come with?"

"Actually, yes. Your carriage would be better than taking mine."

They made their way to River's coach, where his coachman, Elfrank, slouched in the front seat, the thick pages of the latest issue of *Ozmopolitan* spread out in his lap. The bold headline on the cover proclaimed the latest scandalous gossip about Princess Galinda and Prince Rivero. As they approached, Elfrank quickly closed the magazine, attempting to hide the glaring evidence of his idle reading, but the faintest flush creeping up his neck told them all they needed to know. Galinda and River burst into laughter—a sound that filled the air with the warmth of shared amusement.

"Elfrank, can you take us to Gillikin Main?" River asked, his tone light but with the authority of one accustomed to giving orders.

"Yes, my prince," Elfrank muttered, still trying to compose himself as he turned the reins.

Galinda slid into the carriage with practiced grace, River following from the other side. The seats, though not as extravagant as hers, were every bit as comfortable, lush blue velvet cushions, gold trim gleaming faintly in the soft morning light.

"So, where exactly are we going?" River asked, his voice carrying a quiet curiosity.

"It's a long story."

"Don't we have time? We have nowhere to be."

She looked at him, then away, as if the weight of her own words had caught in her throat. "I'm going to get healed."

River's brows furrowed, a mixture of confusion and concern crossing his face. "Healed from what?"

"I have magic, River. Well, I *had* magic, but ever since I came to the university, it's been... not working. My Ummi suggested I go to a healer's shop in Gillikin Main for some help."

"Woz! You have magic? I told you, you're just like your sister."

Galinda rolled her eyes.

"So, what are you going to do if it doesn't work?"

Galinda looked away, staring out of the window as the streets of Oz rolled by. "I don't want to think that way. I'm...optimistic."

But River saw her hands, trembling slightly, betraying her calm demeanour. Without thinking, he reached over, taking her hand in his—a simple gesture, but one that grounded her in the present, in the warmth of his touch. She smiled, though it was faint. He held her hand, and for all the comfort it provided, there was something entirely platonic about it.

Before long, the carriage reached the towering Gillikin Gates, and they were raised with a metallic groan, letting them pass into the bustling streets of the town.

"Where should I park, my prince?" Elfrank called from the front; his voice relaxed as if the world outside the carriage was of little concern.

"We're looking for Velora Herbs," Galinda said, her voice barely above a whisper.

It was there, nestled amongst the more commonplace vendors, near the butcher's stall, the vegetable seller shouting out prices to passersby.

"Is this fine?" Elfrank asked, pulling the carriage to a slow stop.

"Perfect," she answered, not quite sure if she was telling the truth or if she was just trying to convince herself.

She stepped out, River following her.

The shop had no doors, just a swaying beaded curtain, shimmering like liquid shadows in the cool breeze. It was the sort of shop one might imagine as an afterthought, built from the edges of dreams and forgotten places. Galinda, with a glance at River, lowered her head and passed through the curtain, the beads making a soft clink as they parted. River hesitated for a moment before following, his footsteps nearly silent on the wooden floor.

"Hello?" Galinda's voice sounded unsure in the heavy silence. "Is anyone in here?"

A voice, as smooth as velvet, answered, "Yes...come in, my child."

CHANGE

From the dim shadows of the room, an old woman appeared. Her hair was dark as night, strands falling loosely around her face, though there was no sign of age in her eyes, only a sharp gleam of knowing. She was seated cross-legged on a mat on the floor, a small lamp flickering before her. Her eyes were closed, as if she were already privy to the truth of the moment before it had arrived.

River, leaning in slightly toward Galinda, whispered, his voice a breath, "This is spooky. Let's leave while we can."

"I came here for help, I'm not leaving."

River groaned under his breath, "the things I do for you, Princess."

Hesitant steps followed as they moved into the room, barely disturbing the quiet. The old woman's voice floated toward them, "Don't just stand there. Come, sit."

River found a spot at the back of the room, sitting a little further away, his posture stiff with nerves. Galinda, however, knelt near the lamp, the warmth from the flame offering her a strange comfort amidst the room's strange energy.

"Hello… are you, Velora?" Galinda asked, her voice tempered with a mixture of wariness and hope.

The woman's eyes fluttered open at last, "Yes, I am. How can I help you today?"

"My name is Glinda Fairmoor, and I've heard you are one of the best healers in Gillikin. I need help with my magic."

"Are you a witch too?"

Galinda glanced at River briefly, who was doing his best to hide his own unease. She turned back to Velora and nodded slowly, her tone deliberate. "Yes. I am."

A soft chuckle escaped Velora's lips, but there was no humour in it, only a dark, knowing resonance. "Ohh, I sense no magic in you, child."

"That's why I'm here. My magic—it's stopped working. I can't even cast simple spells."

"Oh, so you're a spell-casting witch?"

"Yes. And I'm guessing you're a potions witch?"

The old woman's lips curled into a smile. "Yes, I am."

Galinda hesitated for just a beat, "I make potions too. But nothing has worked."

"I thought you said you were a spell-casting witch?"

"Yes," Galinda said, her voice steady, "and also a potion-maker."

Velora gasped, her fingers trembling slightly as she placed a hand to her chest. "My, my. It can't be… We haven't had a witch with both talents since…"

"Seraphina," Galinda answered softly, a single name from the past that felt both distant and too close.

The old woman's eyes widened slightly, a glint of awe mixing with something else, something darker, deeper. She grabbed Galinda's hands, her grip firm and warm, shaking them with immense pride. "It is an honour to meet you."

Velora stood suddenly, her movement as fluid as water, and made her way to a set of cabinets that lined the far wall, filled with vials of various colours, each one labelled in delicate script. The light from the lamp flickered in the dim space, casting odd shadows across her face as she scanned the shelves.

"So, how long has this ailment been happening?"

"Since the start of term."

"Hmmm." Velora's eyes never left her as she considered the words, her lips pursed in thought. "Have you had any sickness recently?"

"No. Not at all."

"Any traumatic experiences? Sometimes, witches lose their magic for a time when there's a mental block. An emotional wound can stifle the flow of power."

"No."

"What's your name again?"

Galinda blinked in confusion. "Princess Galinda Fairmoor."

"Aha!" Velora's eyes lit up with a sudden, eerie clarity.

Galinda stared. "What?"

"When you came in, you said your name was Glinda Fairmoor. I asked you again, and you said **Princess *Galinda*** Fairmoor. It's subtle, but it means something. It's as if you don't quite know who you are."

Galinda stiffened, the words sinking into her chest like a stone. "Okay?"

"You don't know who you are!" She grabbed a clear vial from the shelf and held it up, the liquid inside shimmering faintly. "You've lost your power, your potential, becoz the magic cannot recognize the person it was meant for."

Galinda's gaze darted to River, a brief flash of panic tightening her chest.

River, sensing the unease, lowered his head slightly, his own unspoken way of offering his silence and reassurance.

"How can your magic stay with you when you don't even recognize yourself? Magic flows like blood, coursing through your veins, bound to the very core of who you are. If you don't know who that is, the magic fades, that's why it was so easily pulled out of you. But this…this is beyond my understanding. How it could vanish entirely…that, I cannot explain."

Galinda's stomach twisted at the realization. "So, there's no cure?"

"I don't know. But…" She held up the vial, "You can try this."

"What is this?"

"This," Velora said, her voice almost reverent, "is called *Revitalis*. It's my last vial, and it's meant to heal any sickness, restore balance. If you choose to take it, it may be just what you need."

"How much will this cost?"

"Take it. I was saving it for the perfect moment, and I believe this is it."

"Why me?" Galinda asked, her voice tinged with disbelief.

CHANGE

"Don't you see? Oz is moving toward darkness. Do you think you're here by chance? You possess two gifts in magic, just like Seraphina, the Noble Witch. If I can do a small good by helping you in this way, then that is payment enough."

Galinda shook her head, a feeling of deep discomfort creeping in. "I can't just take it. Let me pay."

"No." Velora's voice was firm, almost maternal. "Now leave."

Without a word, she stumbled to her feet, River rising wordlessly beside her. Without a glance back, they exited the dim, oppressive room, the weight of the conversation lingering in the air.

"Rather blunt, isn't she?" River said, his voice light with an odd mix of amusement and frustration. He threw a playful jab at the air. "Let me at her! I'll fight her for excusing a princess like that."

Galinda laughed, tapping his shoulder lightly. "No one would stand a chance against you, my strong prince."

River put his hands on his hips, puffing out his chest as he struck a ridiculous pose. They both laughed, the moment of levity fleeting yet comforting. Galinda pulled her scarf tighter around her neck and, with River by her side, they entered the carriage discreetly.

The carriage rolled smoothly past the Gillikin Gates, and Galinda, her hands trembling slightly, opened the vial and drank its contents in one swift motion, her eyes closing instinctively as she waited for the magic to work.

"How do you feel?" River asked.

Galinda opened her eyes slowly, then blinked as though coming out of a haze. "I don't feel any different."

"No tingling? A wave of renewal?"

Galinda stared down at her hands, feeling... nothing. "Wait!"

"What? Do you feel it?"

Galinda's lips curled slightly.

She burped.

"Excuse me. But no, I don't feel any different. Maybe I'm not supposed to. Maybe it worked, and I just don't realize it yet."

The entire *ryde*, Galinda rested her head against the cool window, the passing landscape blurring into a haze of muted colours.

When the carriage finally came to a halt before the University's looming castle, they both stepped out into the cool air. River leaned against the side of the carriage, his posture casual, but there was something in the set of his shoulders that told Galinda he had something to say.

"Galinda?" His voice was calm, deliberate.

She turned to him, a brow arched, unsure of where this was heading.

"I think I know someone who can help you, but... don't overreact."

"Who?"

"Zelphira."

298

The name hit her like a slap to the face. She scoffed, rolling her eyes, and turned to walk away, but something in River's voice stopped her.

"Listen, she's more powerful than anyone knows. She's insanely smart and she has the gift of clairvoyance."

Galinda's pulse quickened at the mention of clairvoyance. Did Zelphira, too, possess dual gifts like her own? She saw her spell cast in sorcery class.

"And how would you know this?" Galinda demanded, her curiosity edging into suspicion.

River sighed. "She's been tutoring me. My Sirrah found out I was... taking shortcuts, having other students do my assignments. So, he assigned me to her. She's helped me pass. Which I couldn't have done without her."

"Even if I went to her, she wouldn't help me," she muttered, exhaling a heavy sigh. "She hates me."

River hesitated, the silence stretching between them, until he spoke again, a touch of impatience in his voice. "What else did you do to her?"

Galinda's mouth dropped open, her face flushing with indignation. "Why did you assume I did something? I've been nothing but good to her"

"Maybe *good*," River said, "but kind? Have you been *kind*?"

"What's the difference?"

River sighed again, a deep, resigned sound, before he stood straight, pushing off the carriage with a slight grunt. "Do you want me to speak to her for you?"

"Please," she said quickly, the words spilling out before she could think better of them. "I mean... that would be good. If she's as powerful as you say."

River smiled.

"I'll put in a good word for you," he said with a wink. "Don't worry."

"Thank you."

❖

The following evening, after the twilight dinner among friends in the garden, River approached her, as if summoned by a divine wind. He stood before her, his caramel skin gleaming faintly under the fading sunlight, the expression on his face one of quiet revelation, as if he were a prophet who had been granted a glimpse of a future already written, a future in which Galinda's magic would be restored. He spoke as though every word was imbued with the certainty of fate, as though he were orchestrating an event of profound significance, something akin to a wedding or a coming-of-age ritual.

"How do you feel today? Did the potion do anything? Has your magic returned?" His voice was soft, yet unwavering.

Galinda's response came as a mere whisper, "no, it has not."

River leaned closer, his confidence like a warm blanket wrapped around her. "You needn't worry. After a long conversation with a certain green witch, she has agreed to help."

"She did?" Galinda's voice betrayed a flicker of disbelief.

"I told you I'd get it done."

Galinda kissed him lightly on the cheek.

"So where is she?"

"In the library. After her study, she'll come up to your suite at the eighteenth hour."

"You're a star, Winkie Prince."

River, always quick to absorb a compliment like a sponge, responded with his own brand of playful arrogance. "Tell me something I don't know."

As if to punctuate the moment, River spotted his friends engaging in a game of *Whirl-foot*, their laughter carrying across the garden like wind through autumn leaves. With a mischievous wink, he bounded off to join them, leaving Galinda with her thoughts.

She lingered for a few more minutes, sitting with her friends, her mind already half in the future, waiting for Zelphira's arrival. When the time felt right, she excused herself, her footsteps light as she ascended to her private suite.

Galinda's nerves tangled within her, knotting tighter with each passing moment. She paced in restless circles around her room, the quietness amplifying her thoughts.

She flopped onto her bed, only to rise again almost immediately.

No. That wouldn't do.

She needed something, anything, to distract her from the trembling in her hands, from the wild thoughts racing in her mind.

A breath. A deep, steadying breath.

She had an idea.

Brush her hair, a small voice suggested. Yes, that would calm her nerves. Or maybe not.

Better yet, read a book. Galinda let out a short laugh, her voice a soft, self-mocking sound that barely escaped her lips. *Ridiculous,* she thought. But she couldn't help herself; the absurdity of her unease lightened her a little, even if only for a moment.

Galinda sank back onto the bed, arms at her sides, stilling herself. She reached for her golden hand mirror, its delicate frame warm beneath her fingers.

She studied her reflection. Did she have food in her teeth? No. Of course not. She could hardly imagine it. Yet there was a strange weight in her chest, an invisible thread pulling her thoughts back to Zelphira.

And then,

The mirror shifted. Its glass rippled, as if it were liquid, warping and distorting, its surface betraying the laws of reflection. Galinda froze, her breath caught in her throat.

Then—

A face.

But it wasn't hers.

It was Zelphira.

Galinda gasped, stumbling back in shock. She saw Zelphira sitting alone in the library, immersed in a book, her sharp features softened by the amber glow of the lamps around her. Alone. Studious. Unaware.

The vision wavered, trembling like a mirage on the verge of collapse, and then—poof—it was gone.

Galinda's mind raced, her thoughts crashing into one another, but the realization was sharp and clear.

Her magic. She had it back.

A breathless laugh escaped her. She had done it—she had enchanted the mirror. Her magic had returned. The potion had worked.

Without thinking, without control, Galinda jumped onto her bed, her body moving in a frenzy of excitement. Her legs kicked wildly, as though they were running from something far greater than herself—her own joy, her own disbelief.

She was whole again.

After her little bacchanal of self-congratulation, Galinda attempted something delicate: levitating a pillow. It did not so much as quiver.

Her magic must be returning in increments, rationed by the unseen forces that governed such things. The mirror enchantment had been a hungry spell, consuming whatever reserves she had stored. Even so, she was too giddy to be discouraged.

A knock at the door.

Galinda flicked her curls behind her shoulder and opened it to find Zelphira standing in the hallway. Books clenched in one arm, bag in the other. Clad in black, naturally.

"Let's make this quick," Zelphira said, already stepping forward.

Galinda raised a hand, palm outward. A dignified halt. "Actually, you're not needed anymore."

"How do you mean? River said—"

"Well, he said wrong! You're not needed, so go away."

"River made it very clear that you needed help."

"Are you deaf? I don't want to see your disgustifying presence near my suite again. You really should've used the soap I got you. Leave!"

Zelphira did not argue. She only nodded, a measured, almost regal movement, and walked away.

Galinda slammed the door and flung herself onto her bed, staring up at the ceiling. The rush of expelling Zelphira, of making herself unassailable, fizzled into exhaustion.

◇

CHANGE

Days passed. Magic continued to evade her. Not a pillow, not a feather—nothing would rise. She had thought that if she simply distracted herself, her gifts would come rushing back like an obedient dog. Instead, she remained ordinary.

Then, over lunch, Mila slapped a *Daily Oz* on the table.

GOOD WITCH OF THE SOUTH SEEN FOR THE FIRST TIME IN MANY MOONS—REVIVES BARREN FIELDS, ADVOCATES FOR MAGIC.

Galinda snatched it. "Give me that!"

Mila leaned back, amused. "Oh yeah! Your sister's in the papers again."

Galinda looked up sharply. "What do you know about this?"

Mila shrugged. "Not much. People thought she was dead, but—poof—she's back. Using her magic again. Honestly, I think she looks more alive than ever, don't you?"

Galinda tossed the paper aside, grabbed her bag, and retreated to her suite.

She paced. The walls watched her.

Gisella, using magic? Impossible.

Had their father found some puppet in Quadling Country to continue the farce? It was no secret that he had tired of pretending Gisella was anything more than an artifact of nostalgia, a symbol of his idealistic past.

Galinda wheeled toward her vanity, seized her golden hand mirror.

She inhaled sharply.

"Show me Gisella."

The glass warped. Images slid across its surface like oil on water. Then, there she was, Gisella, casting a levitation spell, the magic pouring from her as if it had always been there, waiting.

Galinda almost dropped the mirror.

This wasn't possible.

Everyone knew the rules: if magic hadn't manifested by sixteen, it never would.

And yet—

Galinda ran a hand through her hair, fingers tangling in her curls.

She lifted her hand toward the glass cup, willing it to rise.

Nothing.

Galinda exhaled sharply, the sound half sigh, half curse.

She needed Zelphira.

Now more than ever.

And after what she'd said, after the scorn she had heaped upon her—there was no chance Zelphira would listen.

Not even River could fix this.

Another knock came at the door of Galinda's suite, sharp and deliberate, as though it were a summons to something far more pressing than mere conversation.

She peered through the spyhole, her breath catching for a moment, as if the sight of her three friends was somehow both a relief and a complication.

She opened the door, a movement too practiced to be casual.

Cora was the first to speak, her voice low and urgent, "are you all right? We saw you hurry off, and we were concerned."

"I'm fine. Truly, just a bit overwhelmed with schoolwork, that's all. Nothing to worry about."

Fanny raised an eyebrow, her tone more rhetorical than anything, "do you mind if we keep you company?"

"Of course," Galinda replied, stepping aside and ushering them into her sanctuary. They all sat upon her canopy bed, each sinking into its soft familiarity, as if the softness of the fabric could somehow soothe the sharpness in the air.

Cora turned her head, her eyes falling upon the black cloak and the white pointed hat resting against the wall. Her lips curled with a mix of annoyance and exasperation. "I wish you'd just get rid of that thing. It's like you're spiritually attached to it."

"Don't be daft," Galinda snapped. "Didn't we all agree it would go to the person we hated most?"

Fanny sat up straight, her eyes lighting with sudden recollection. "Oh yes, I remember."

With a swiftness that made her appear almost predatory, Fanny stood, crossing the room to scoop up the cloak and the pointed hat. She handed them to Galinda with an almost possessive flourish. "And now we've found the perfect recipient."

"Who exactly do you mean?"

Fanny's laugh was almost too sharp, "now who's being daft? Who else but Greenie?" she said with a mocking emphasis. "Give it to her."

Mila and Cora exchanged a glance, and then, without warning, burst into laughter, a deep, resonant sound that rippled through the air like thunder. Mila began to clap, her hands coming together in exaggerated applause. "Oh, this is *perfect!*"

"I don't think—"

"Oh, she'll love it," Fanny interrupted, "just look at what she wears! She'll wear anything as long as it's free and honestly, you'll be doing her a favour, giving her something more... *appropriate.*"

"I couldn't," Galinda murmured, the weight of indecision pulling at her heart. Then, an idea began to unfurl inside her, something so deliciously wicked, it made her smile before she could even stop herself. "Could I?"

Zelphira.

The name was like a sweet poison on her tongue.

Her fingers tightened around the cloak. Maybe she could kill two birds with one stone.

CHANGE

And perhaps, just perhaps, those birds would be oblivious to ever see it coming.

◊

Evening crept in, its shadows pooling beneath the windowsills, signalling it was time for Galinda to set her plan in motion. She donned a light-pink sundress, a slip of pale fabric that clung to her like the delicate veneer of civility she so adored, topped with a white cloak that fluttered like the softest whisper in a garden breeze. A spritz of lily perfume swirled into the air around her, fragrant, calculated, just enough to mark her presence without suffocating it. She dabbed her lips with a rose-tinted *Lip-Oyl*, an imperceptible gesture that nonetheless added a layer of careful polish.

Clasping the cloak and hat in her hands, Galinda drew a breath, steadying her pulse, and knocked on the door to the maid's quarters with the confidence of someone accustomed to being answered.

The door swung open with a creak, revealing a maid who blinked at Galinda's regal appearance as though she were some unexpected comet in the night sky.

"Princess Galinda!" The maid's voice fluttered, both surprise and courtesy fighting for dominance. "How delightful to see you. Did you need your room cleaned?"

"Oh, no. I'm here for Zelphira."

"Excuse me? Did you say...Zelphira?"

"I did."

The maid hesitated, casting a puzzled glance over her shoulder before stepping back and nodding. "I'll fetch her."

The moments stretched in silence, punctuated only by the sounds of a distant clock ticking and Galinda's breath, measured and deliberate.

Soon, Zelphira appeared in the doorway, a dishevelled figure swathed in what could only be described as an unfortunate approximation of a nightgown, a garment that looked as though it had been borrowed from a sack of potatoes.

"For Oz's sake, not you again!" Zelphira groaned, as she made a half-hearted attempt to shut the door in Galinda's face.

Galinda's hand shot out, stopping the door's progress, and her voice was soft but insistent. "Please, hear me out."

"You have one Oz'min to speak."

"I know I said some cruel things to you a few moons ago. I wanted to apologise. I feel terrible about it, but there's something I need from you. And I brought you a gift." She held her hands forward, cradling the cloak and hat, an offering wrapped in the guise of goodwill.

Zelphira's eyes flickered to the items, her gaze lingering for a moment as if trying to discern any trickery beneath the surface. She reached forward, lifting the cloak, its fabric light and strange against her fingers, and pulled it close, inspecting its weight. She did the same with the pointed hat, turning it over in her hands as if expecting it to reveal some hidden meaning.

"Hmm," she mused aloud.

Finally, Zelphira sighed, "Fine. I'll help you. But don't get it twisted, Galinda. I'm not doing this becoz I think you're worthwhile. I'm doing it becoz I like the attire."

Galinda nodded with measured calm. "I understand."

Zelphira stepped aside, a gesture that allowed Galinda to cross the threshold into Zelphira's bedroom. The two women locked eyes, both remembering the last time they had shared this space.

"Sit there," Zelphira directed, pointing to the empty patch of floor in the centre of the room. Galinda complied, settling herself as gracefully as possible on the cold wood.

On the floor beside them lay Zelphira's *Sorcery Studies* books, scattered all over, their worn, leather-bound covers a stark contrast to the rest of the room's sparse décor. Galinda, naturally, seethed, watching as the girl who had nothing, nothing but a room cluttered with her strange, unrefined magic, do the very thing she dreamed of. Her fingers tightened, nails digging into her palm, and for a fleeting moment, Galinda wondered what it would take to *make* Zelphira's magic hers.

Zelphira placed the cloak and pointed hat neatly on the dresser, then returned to the floor, sitting cross-legged with an easy fluidity. She clapped her hands together, the sound sharp in the otherwise still room. "Now, tell me what the issue is."

"I've lost my magic. And I don't know why. I've tried everything, every potion, every serum, everything under the sun. I even consulted a powerful spellbook, but nothing. Absolutely nothing."

Zelphira's eyes flickered, sharp as ever, her attention now fully fixed on Galinda. "What *powerful* spellbook?"

"You wouldn't know it," she replied, her tone dismissive, but there was an edge of unease beneath it.

"Have you been sick? Or experienced any traumatic events lately?"

"No, no illness. But I've already been through all of this with a healer, and she still couldn't tell me what exactly is wrong with me."

Zelphira sighed then, a sound heavy with the weariness of someone who had already lived a thousand lives, or at least it seemed that way.

"Give me your palm," Zelphira commanded, her tone brokering no argument.

"Why?"

"Do you trust me?"

Galinda swallowed, a flutter of hesitation settling in her chest. After a short moment, "yes," she replied.

She stretched out her palm, its softness an unspoken contrast to the roughness of Zelphira's long, green fingers that closed over it with an unsettling intensity.

Without warning, a gust of wind erupted from nowhere, thrashing Zelphira's hair about wildly, though the windows were locked tight. It wasn't wind—it was magic, raw and untamed, a force that rippled through the air like the pulse of something ancient and powerful.

Zelphira looked beautiful, ethereal with the wind swirling around her, like she was one with it, a creature made of the very elements. Her hair whipped in a silken frenzy, her eyes closed in concentration, her body still but humming with energy. There was something almost divine in the way she seemed to command the tempest, something otherworldly.

Still, Galinda's instincts screamed at her to run, to flee from the suffocating power filling the room, but Zelphira's grip on her palm was a vice, unyielding, as if the very air was holding her captive. Yet, it wasn't the fear of being trapped that kept Galinda rooted to the spot. It was something else, a strange pull, an undeniable fascination.

Galinda didn't know what it was about Zelphira, but in that moment, as the wind howled and the magic enveloped them, Galinda realized she wasn't afraid of Zelphira. She wasn't afraid of the power that swirled between them, of the unknown. She was afraid of herself, of what might happen if she let go.

Zelphira's voice pierced the air. "Was the healer you saw... Velora? Velora Herbs?"

"Yes," Galinda said, her voice shaky. "Did River tell you that?"

"No," Zelphira answered, eyes still closed. "Velora was right, though. There's no magical vein in your body. If you *ever* had magic, it doesn't live in you anymore."

"Tell me more. What happened? Where did it go?"

Zelphira's eyes snapped open, her gaze sharp as obsidian.

"The potion you drank... it did nothing," Zelphira intoned, her voice steady despite the howling air. "There's nothing wrong with you for it to heal. *You* must heal yourself—something no potion, no magic, can do for you."

"But... where did my magic go?" Her voice cracked, the questions building like a storm. "How do I get it back?"

"Even my magic has limits. I cannot answer all your questions. Some things... you must do for yourself. You will get the answers you seek in time."

"Are you sure?"

"Yes. And I'm rather tired, so if you could please leave?"

Galinda blinked, caught off guard by the abruptness of it. A flicker of anger rose within her, but it quickly faded. She had dismissed Zelphira in a worse way.

Wordlessly, Galinda rose to her feet and left, her mind swirling with the remnants of Zelphira's cryptic revelations.

Still, she was no closer to an answer. Whatever had happened to her, it was something she would have to face alone. For the first time, Galinda wasn't sure if she was prepared for it.

CHAPTER 35

Bubbleluxe

A few days later, Galinda, River, and their merry gaggle of revellers staggered back from the *Feathered Wyrm*, drunk on *Wizard's Brew* and their own self-importance. The cobbled paths of Oz university swayed beneath them in a way that was either delightful or perilous, depending on how much one had imbibed.

It was then, as they rounded a corner, that they caught sight of Zelphira. She was crouched in the dirt, feeding bits of broken bread to the campus chickens, an occupation as dreary and undignified as the girl herself. But what made Galinda pause, just for a fleeting moment—was the attire.

On Zelphira's head sat the white, pointed hat Galinda had given her, and draped over her shoulders was the heavy black cloak, oversized and spectral. The wind toyed with it, lifting its hem in great, billowing flourishes that sent swirls of dust into the air. The chickens, however, were unfazed by the theatrics, too absorbed in their meal to care for anything else.

From the far end, Fanny, who had been deep in tipsy flirtation with one of River's more attractive friends, suddenly took notice. Her gait was unsteady, but her interest was now thoroughly piqued. She leaned into Galinda, her breath warm with alcohol.

"You didn't tell us you *gave* it to her already?" she giggled, somewhere between scandalized and delighted.

Galinda laughed too, because, well, wasn't that the expected response?

Mila, ever the sharp-tongued one, added, "She really doesn't understand fashion, does she? She looked in a mirror and still *chose* to walk out?"

"There's no hope for that girl," Cora chimed in.

At that moment, Zelphira turned her head, catching the sound of approaching footsteps. Her gaze flickered toward them, toward *her*, toward Galinda. And for the briefest of moments, Galinda met her eyes. But then, swiftly, deliberately, she looked away, as though the glance had been an accident, like she had *not* seen the green girl at all.

She did not want to feel obliged to smile at her, nor did she want to offer acknowledgment, no matter how small.

River, however, had no such reservations. With easy nonchalance, he raised a hand in greeting with a smile. Zelphira, after the briefest hesitation, returned the wave, small, discreet, fleeting. Then, just as simply, she turned back to her birds.

Galinda and her retinue rounded the corner, vanishing from sight.

But moments later, another group arrived.

The *Whirl-foot* boys, fresh from practice, still slick with sweat and bravado, came strolling down the path. One of them, a boy with a cruel glint in his eye, nudged his friend. He motioned toward the scene before them: Zelphira, hunched and preoccupied, a creature unaware of the predators circling.

"Watch this," he whispered.

Then he darted forward.

His boots slammed against the earth with a force that sent the birds into a cacophony of alarm. They shrieked, they flapped, they scattered, feathers bursting into the air like misplaced snowflakes.

Zelphira's head snapped up, eyes blazing. "Why would you *do* that, you fool?!"

The boy did not answer. Instead, he shifted his weight, and it was only then that Zelphira realized—he was standing on the hem of her cloak.

Her fingers curled into fists. "Get off my cloak," she ordered, her voice sharp as steel.

The boy sneered. "Is *that* what you're calling this? Looks more like a glorified rag."

She ignored him. He was beneath responding to.

The rest of the *Whirl-foot* team had caught up now, and among them, at the centre of their pack like some self-appointed prince, stood Hedrick—their captain. He stepped forward, he surveyed the situation, then, with a lazy flick of his hand, motioned for his lackey to step aside.

The boy obeyed.

Hedrick tilted his head, looking down at Zelphira with a slow, measured smirk. "You know, you ought to be nicer to people. *Especially* your superiors."

Zelphira laughed then, and not prettily. "Superiors?" she echoed. "Calling you *scum* would be too generous a compliment for what you truly are."

For a moment, just a moment, Hedrick faltered.

And then, quick as a whip, his face hardened. "You're a dirty *green* wench!" Then spat on the floor. "It's best you learn your *place* now."

And with that, he kicked her.

His boot struck her arm, sending her tumbling from her crouched position, her body hitting the ground with a dull, graceless thud.

Her white hat tumbled from her head.

Pain seared through her. And though Zelphira was not one to show weakness, not one to flinch, not one to *whimper*—

This time, she did.

Hedrick caught it.

His smirk deepened as his gaze flicked to a boy, no more than eight Sun-Moons old, sitting on the ground not far from them. The child was small, almost swallowed by the fabric of his ill-fitting clothes, as he filled an endless assembly of glass jars with black ink for the professors.

With calculated nonchalance, Hedrick bent down and plucked up the fallen white hat.

He did not speak. He did not need to. He merely turned and walked toward the boy, making sure his movements were slow enough, deliberate enough, that Zelphira would have time to sit back up, to reorient herself, to see exactly what he was about to do.

She did.

Her eyes, still laced with the remnants of pain, darted toward his hands. *Her* hat. *Her* gift, her one claim to something refined, something delicate.

Hedrick held it up.

He met her gaze, grinning. Then, with a calculated languor, he let the fabric slip from his fingers, releasing it into the large ink basin.

The hat took its time sinking. Its pointed top lingered on the surface for a moment, as though resisting, as though pleading to pulled back up before it succumbed, disappearing into the inky void.

And at that moment, as with all stories first written in ink, this was when they began to rewrite Zelphira.

The laughter came, boisterous and triumphant. The other Whirl-foot boys clapped Hedrick on the back, throwing their arms around him as if he had just secured a championship victory, as if he had done something worthy of celebration.

Zelphira did not watch them go.

She pushed herself up, wincing as she forced weight onto her injured arm, and walked over to the boy.

He had been watching the entire time, his youthful face marked with a sadness that seemed too old for him, as if he already understood, at eight Sun-Moons old, how the world worked, comprehending its **gears and machinery**. Without a word, he plunged his arm into the ink.

Black liquid sloshed over the edges of the basin. His small hands fumbled for the fabric, gripping it tight, lifting it out of the darkness.

His fair skin completely stained now, his arm blackened all the way to the elbow, but he did not seem to mind.

He held out the sodden hat to her. "I'm sorry, Mizz," he said earnestly. "Here you go."

Zelphira smiled, but it was a fragile thing, as if it might shatter if she blinked too hard.

"Thank you," she murmured.

Reaching into the folds of her pocket, she retrieved a single silver coin and placed it into the boy's ink-slicked hands. "For your kindness."

The boy wiped his hands against his tunic before taking the coin, his eyes wide with gratitude. "Thank you, Mizz."

Zelphira turned, her cloak catching the air as she moved.

"Wait—" The boy's voice stopped her.

She turned.

"What's your name?"

A pause.

"Zelphira," she said. "What's yours?"

"Nikolast Chopper."

She nodded, offered him another soft, fleeting smile, and then walked back toward the maids' quarters, the weight of ink dripping from the hat in her hands. It looked as though her hands were melting with it, dissolving into the blackness, as if she were being unmade, piece by piece, with every step she took.

By the time she reached her room, her fingers and palms had been stained entirely black. The ink had set into her skin, thick and unrelenting, a mark that would remain for days, until time and scrubbing revealed her *green* once more.

She held the hat in her hands. It had dried now, no longer sopping, no longer dripping.

She turned toward the garbage sack, prepared to discard it entirely, to rid herself of the thing that had been ruined, defiled.

But then—

She hesitated.

She looked at it properly.

The white was gone, yes. The ink had swallowed it whole. But the hat was now perfect black. *A fine, uncompromising black.*

It matched her cloak quite nicely.

And she had always been partial to a black ensemble.

She held the hat up to the air, studying it, letting the dim candlelight settle upon its shape.

Then, without quite meaning to, she smiled.

❖

By the time the luncheon bells tolled, the dining hall had already swelled with the usual suspects, nobility, strivers, and those unfortunate enough to be neither but who made do with charm or cleverness. The clatter of silverware and the low hum of gossip filled the room, punctuated now and then by the drunken giggle of girls who had spiked their milk with spirits.

Then, like a dark omen, Zelphira entered.

She had timed it perfectly, oh, how intentional it was, waiting until every seat was occupied, until every eye was otherwise engaged, until no one could pretend they did not see.

She wanted them all to see.

She wanted him to see.

The long black cloak, absurd in its grandeur, trailed behind her like wings made of shadow, dragging across the polished floor as if too heavy for flight. And the hat, that hat, once pristine white, now drenched in ink, its once-pointed tip sagging slightly under the weight of its transformation.

Across the way, Hedrick and his Whirl-foot boys sat frozen, eyes narrowing in something between confusion and distaste. Had she no shame? No bruised ego? Hadn't she gotten the message, that she was meant to cower? Had she not gathered up her belongings and fled into obscurity like a properly humiliated outcast should?

Fanny, never one to let a moment pass unremarked upon, leaned in toward Galinda with a smirk. "I'll give her credit, she's certainly committed to the bit," she mused, before taking a languid sip of the nauseating combination of milk and liquor sliding down her throat.

Galinda did not respond. She busied herself with River, pretending to find him fascinating.

The laughter in the hall was quieter now, tinged with confusion. The joke was getting old. Yes, they all knew she was green, they had seen. They had ridiculed her awkwardness, her unfashionable clothes, her every misstep. But lately, she had stopped stumbling. She had stopped giving them the satisfaction of falling flat on her face. And what was the fun of cruelty if it had no visible effect? What was the fun if the victim refused to flinch?

Mila, ever restless, suddenly sat upright, her fingers fumbling for something in her bag as though an idea had struck her and she might lose it if she didn't act at once. She produced a letter.

"Here, Galinda." She thrust it forward. "For you."

Galinda blinked at it, then took it gingerly. "What is it?"

Mila shrugged. "The mail boy gave it to me."

"And why would he do that instead of delivering it to me himself?"

Mila sighed. "Fine. We meet in my room. From time to time." And with that, she went back to crunching her *Crickle-Knack*, unbothered.

Galinda turned the letter over in her hands. The Quadling royal seal. Her father's golden crest.

Oh, so that was it.

With practiced elegance, she slid a finger beneath the wax and unfolded the letter:

My Darling Princess Galinda,

CHANGE

I wanted to write to you. It has been some time, and I miss my beautiful princess. I hope you're enjoying your studies at The Wizard's University, and that you haven't already forgotten your dear old Popsicle.

You have not been home once since your departure.

There are things we must discuss as a family.

I have ordered your return and expect you back in the South at the end of term.

See you soon.

Your Popsicle,

Royal King of the Quadlings

Galinda exhaled through her nose, a delicate little huff, and folded the letter back into its envelope. She took a slow sip, as though its contents might wash away the sinking weight in her stomach.

Across the room, Zelphira had found her seat. Unshaken. Unbothered. She picked at her food with steady hands, the black hat perched triumphantly atop her head.

And Galinda, despite herself, found that she could not look away.

Galinda frowned, though she did so carefully, mindful of the creases it might leave between her brows. Something else gnawed at her thoughts. As much as she missed her father, the prospect of returning ***home*** meant seeing Gisella's insufferable face. And hadn't she done quite enough of that already? Even from a distance, Gisella was impossible to avoid.

The newspapers ensured it, relentlessly, nauseatingly. *The Good Witch Saves a Kitten! The Good Witch Cures the Common Cold! The Good Witch's Favourite Breakfast—Find Out What's on Her Plate!* There was no end to it. Galinda had watched, with increasing irritation, as her own name slid, column by column, to the margins of print. The Ozmopolitan magazine, her Ozmopolitan feature, which she had considered a matter of destiny, had betrayed her too. Instead of an exclusive on Galinda's luminous curls, there was an entire spread dedicated to Gisella's hair routine.

And, Oz above, Galinda knew for a fact she had the better hair.

Cora, with all the subtlety of a dropped silver tray, snapped Galinda out of her wool-gathering. "Me and the girls have decided we want to go to Gillikin Market later this afternoon. Shopping, naturally. You in?"

Galinda blinked back into the moment, her lips curling into a knowing smile. "Does a Kalidah crave a honeyed meat pie?"

"Then it's settled," Cora said with a wink, as though she'd just closed a treaty rather than planned a spending spree.

◇

As the late afternoon light began to soften the air, the girls gathered in their finest, a symphony of cloaks, boots, and the richest perfumes, designed to turn heads and ensure that the market would know who was of high society, even if they were to

312

mingle amongst the common folk. Galinda, ever keen on maintaining her station, decreed that River accompany them, despite his clear preference for a game of Whirl-foot with Hedrick.

But Galinda's wishes were law, as they often were, and so, the girls set off in Galinda's newly commissioned carriage. **The Gilded Rose**, as it was called, was a spectacle. White and gold trimmed the exterior, while pink and silver cushioned the seats inside, the colours blending together in a delicate, regal harmony. River slouched into the soft cushions, visibly displeased, his boredom almost palpable as the carriage rocked beneath them.

He continued thinking about how he would rather be tossing a ball around than nodding along to Galinda's never-ending questions: "Will this look good on me?" "Try this, you'll love it." Pretending he liked something he detested. Pretending to care.

Mila, Cora, and Fanny, of course, noticed his exaggerated sighs and bored posture, casting sly glances between themselves as they shared a secret laugh.

As the carriage pulled to a stop at the bustling Gillikin Market, the energy around them was overwhelming. Stalls piled high with colourful goods, vendors shouting to outdo one another with competitive prices, each voice rising above the next: "Ten golden crowns!" "Eight golden crowns!" "One for ten silver crowns!"

The girls exited with the poise they had perfected; eyes drawn to them as usual. River, however, remained trapped in his own world of grumbling, rolling his eyes as Galinda glanced back at him with an expression that could only be described as "expectant."

Mila, who had perfected the art of cutting through the tension, teased, "Rivero, could you stop sighing for once? If you weren't the prince of my country, I swear I'd be suffocating you by now."

River stuck out his tongue, teasing back, but it wasn't enough to break his ennui. Galinda turned to Cora, her curiosity piqued. "You're from Gillikin, what do you recommend we do?"

"We should start with food. Have you ever tried Wildberry Porridge?"

Galinda's face lit up. "No? Okay, let's go then."

And they were off, taste buds dancing from one stall to the next. Galinda, ever the magpie for snacks, tucked more than a few of the treats into her purse, savouring the moment as she found her new favourite indulgence.

"We should probably grab some fresh fruits, too," Cora suggested, her eyes gleaming with pride. "Gillikin grows the best fruits in all of Oz."

They ventured into the section dedicated to fruits and vegetables, where every item was plump, shiny, and bursting with life. Galinda, wide-eyed and utterly fascinated by the concept of market shopping, turned to Cora. "So, how do we do this?"

"Grab a sack and walk around. You pick what you want, you pay, then you put it in your sack."

Galinda followed the instructions eagerly, gathering *Sunplums, Silver-Leaf Apples, Whisperfruit, Mangos, Snow Berries, Dewdrop Figs, and Fayberries*, until her arms were overflowing. As she handed over coins, she would walk off before the vendor could respond, always leaving the transaction unfinished, paying triple the price.

"Oh, this is so fun!" Galinda squealed with a childlike giddiness.

The market was abuzz with gossip, no doubt excited by the rare spectacle of royalty shopping for produce in their midst.

PRINCESS GALINDA AND PRINCE RIVERO SPOTTED SHOPPING FOR FRESH PRODUCE AT GILLIKIN MARKET!

Galinda turned her head, scanning the crowd, and there she saw it: a familiar pointed hat in the distance, a silhouette she would recognize anywhere. Zelphira. At the far end of the stalls, a figure dwarfed by the chaos of commerce, alone and unnoticed by most, except Galinda.

"Why don't we get going?" Galinda suggested.

"So soon?" Fanny asked, her voice laced with surprise.

"Yes, I'm tired. I mean, you girls can stay, but I'm afraid I'm leaving with my carriage." She glanced at River, eyes narrowing slightly in expectation. "Leave with me."

It was a command more than a question, and he needed no further urging.

"I guess we're leaving then," Cora said with a shrug, the group falling in line behind Galinda, their arms laden with sacks of fruits and trinkets.

Galinda glanced back over her shoulder. She was still watching Zelphira, still standing by the stall, the figure a strange contrast to the rest of the market's frenzy. Zelphira was holding an orange and an apple, trying to decide which to buy, though the farmer's scorn was already evident in his eyes.

Galinda's gaze narrowed, her brow furrowing. She was about to turn away when the exchange caught her attention. Zelphira, without enough crowns to buy both fruits, had offered a silver coin, only to have it rudely rejected. The farmer snatched both the apple and orange from her hands as if she were a beggar and not a customer. Zelphira, crestfallen, picked up her sack, likely containing little more than a single pear, and backed away, helpless.

Galinda, turned to her friends. "I'll be back in a moment."

River, already inside the Gilded Rose, shouted, "Want me to come with?"

"No, that's fine."

With a quiet grace, she disappeared into the crowd. She ducked behind a cluster of people, weaving in and out, moving unnoticed through the sea of merchants and shoppers, until she stood behind an older woman, just close enough to Zelphira without being seen.

Galinda reached into her pockets and pulled out five golden crowns, her fingers wrapping around the glimmering coins before she dropped them, one by one, in front of Zelphira's feet. The sound of the coins hitting the cobblestone was sharp and clear, the reflection of the fading sunlight dancing across them. It caught Zelphira's attention, and she turned in confusion, looking for the source of this sudden gift. But there was no one close enough to claim them.

It was as if the coins had fallen from the sky.

Zelphira bent down slowly, her fingers brushing the gold as if unsure it was real. Her eyes swept the area one last time. "Oh, Oz…" she whispered to herself.

Galinda stayed hidden, watching, her heart a tangle of motives as she saw Zelphira, after a pause, pick up the fruits again, approaching the farmer with more confidence this time. The old man's harsh voice cracked the air, "Go away. You don't have enough crowns!"

But Zelphira, unperturbed, plucked a single gold coin from her pocket and handed it to the farmer with the quiet authority of someone who had already won.

Galinda's lips curled into a smile, satisfied in a way she had not expected to be. She watched as Zelphira, now with more fruits than she could carry, walked away with dignity Galinda couldn't help but admire.

Turning back, she rejoined her group and strode to the Gilded Rose as if nothing had happened.

"Where did you go?" Mila asked, her curiosity piqued.

"Oh, I thought I dropped my ring, but it was on my other hand."

Cora and Fanny exchanged a look, a silent understanding passing between them, before Fanny whispered to Cora, "It's a wonder how the Wizard gave her a scholarship."

Mila, however, turned to Galinda with a knowing smile. "One time, I thought I lost my hat, but it was on my head. It's easy to make that kind of mistake," she said, nodding sagely, like it was the most ordinary thing in the world.

◇

Zelphira strode onto the campus with a kind of grace that only someone who had long been a stranger to the weight of expectation could possess. Her head held high, her cloak behind her like the wings of a bird who could, at any moment, choose to take flight. Her hat sat perfectly atop her head, like a crown of defiance, and her long, untamed hair flowed in its wake, graceful and untethered to the mundane. She was a vision of quiet rebellion.

Upon entering the maids' quarters, she moved with the same deliberate pride, placing her newly acquired groceries on the kitchen table as if they were trophies, each piece of fruit, every bundle of vegetables, an assertion of her worth in a world that so often preferred to overlook her.

Zara, one of the other maids, looked up from her work, an eyebrow arched in suspicion. "Where did you get those from?"

"I bought them," Zelphira replied simply.

"What I mean is, where did you get the money?"

Zelphira's lips curled into a smirk, "I've got my ways." She picked up an apple, holding it out with a careless sort of grace. "Do you want one? I've got enough to spare."

"No," Zara answered abruptly, "I don't know where it has been."

"It's from the market."

Zara's gaze hardened, her words slicing through the space between them. "I meant your fingers."

Zelphira simply shrugged, a motion so practiced it seemed effortless. She began to unpack the fruits, the rice, the potatoes, each item a small, private victory. But Zara's voice cut through the air again, sharp and unexpected.

"By the way, you've got a gift waiting outside for you."

"Gift?" Zelphira's eyes darted toward the door, confusion flashing across her face.

"That's what I said."

"From whom?"

"Go outside and find out. It's right by the benches."

Zelphira left the groceries on the counter and moved toward the door. She stepped outside, scanning the area. For a moment, she saw nothing. The world around her seemed unnervingly still.

Then, from above, a voice called out, mocking and familiar. "Hey, Greenie!"

Zelphira's gaze snapped upwards. Before she could react, a group of students, faces she didn't recognize, were already in motion. In a coordinated flurry, a bucket was tossed—its contents splattering across her, dousing her in the unmistakable stench of fish stew, expired milk, rotting meat and onions. It was as though the very air had turned sour, the weight of it heavy and vile, seeping into her skin, her clothes, each drop of filth another strike to her dignity.

The laughter rang out from above, shrill and full of derision. "How are you supposed to clean yourself now, when you don't shower?"

"Why don't you just die!" another chided.

Zelphira didn't scream. She didn't shout. She stood there for what felt like an eternity, her body still as stone, her mind reeling with disbelief. The tears, however, they came in silence, rolling down her cheeks like drops of rain that had no place to fall.

She moved, slow and deliberate, like the weight of the world had been placed upon her shoulders, her feet dragging across the cobbled stones as she made her way back to the maids' quarters.

Inside, Zara and the others were already waiting, their laughter filling the space with tangible cruelty.

"Did you like the gift, Greenie?" Zara's voice rang out, mocking.

Zelphira, unable to form the words, simply walked past her. She didn't even look at the others as they laughed harder, their mirth a cruel echo in the chamber.

"Oof!" Zara mocked once more. "I never knew you could stink even more than you usually do."

Zelphira pushed past the others and retreated to the bathroom.

The door shut behind her with a soft, final click.

She sank to the floor, her back against the door, the walls closing in with each passing moment. The bathroom, already small and cramped, felt suffocating. The wet stew pooled around her like a flood, the smell of it filling her nostrils, choking her. Her cloak had absorbed every drop, every speck of it, until the fabric was soaked through, clinging to her skin like a second, revolting layer.

But Zelphira didn't move. She didn't try to clean herself or even rise. She sat there, broken in silence, her sobs the only sound filling the still air.

For a long while, that was all there was. Just the sound of her own pain, echoing in the small, confined space.

News flew through the halls like a whisper on the wind. Mila, Cora, and Fanny nearly tripped over themselves as they barrelled toward Galinda's suite, their footsteps loud and eager. They reached her door and pounded, eager to share the latest.

Galinda opened it slowly, her gaze sharp. "What's going on?"

Mila's eyes were wide with excitement, her words tumbling out in a rush. "Did you hear? Some of the students—*dumped food waste* on Zelphira!"

Cora and Fanny were already dissolving into fits of laughter, their bodies practically pushing into the room as they tried to weave around Galinda to get inside.

Galinda stopped them with a raised hand. "When did this happen?"

"Just now, out by the benches!" Mila said, practically breathless.

"And where is she now?" Galinda pressed, a strange tightening in her chest that she couldn't quite name.

"Make way, Galinda! We need to *talk* about it!" Fanny demanded, but Galinda stood firmly, her expression unreadable.

"I'm busy. We'll talk later. I need to handle something."

Without waiting for their protests, she shut the door with an almost finality that left them stunned. They lingered outside, confused, but Galinda's attention was already elsewhere. She waited for the soft sound of their retreating footsteps before she crept toward the door's spyhole, peering out to ensure they hadn't lingered.

Her thoughts raced, and before she could fully consider them, she was already descending the grand spiral staircase to the maids' quarters.

She knocked sharply on the door. Zara answered, still chuckling, though the laugh died in her throat the moment she saw Galinda.

"Princess Galinda, what can I do for you?"

"I'm looking for Zelphira, is she here?"

Zara hesitated for just a moment, the remnants of her laughter clinging to the air. "She's here, but...she's a bit preoccupied."

"I need to see her."

Zara stepped aside, and Galinda entered the quarters, her gaze following the trail of water that glistened on the floor like the remnants of something broken. She knew where it would lead.

The bathroom door loomed ahead, and she knocked softly.

"Go away!" Zelphira shouted, her voice hoarse and raw.

"Zelphira? It's me, Galinda."

There was a long, strained silence from inside before Zelphira's voice came again. "What do you want? Just go away."

"Zelphira, please… do you need anything?"

The silence stretched, and Galinda could feel the weight of it pushing against her, but she didn't give up. "I'll be back. I'm going to get something for you."

She turned and hurried back up the stairs, her feet practically flying. She reached her suite, grabbed the *Bubbleluxe* soap, the scent of it almost comforting, and a towel before she dashed back down, nearly colliding with a passing maid.

She arrived at the bathroom door once more.

"Zelphira," she said, her voice softer now, "I have some things for you."

Inside, the soft sound of a whimper was all she heard in reply.

"It's some…" Galinda's voice faltered, her usual confidence slipping for just a moment. "I have some *soap* and fresh towels. Please open the door, so I can give them to you."

More silence.

But after what felt like an eternity, the bathroom door clicked open, and Galinda, with a hand full of delicate care, offered the soap and towel to the girl who had been broken in ways words could not describe.

The door closed gently behind her.

Galinda stayed by the door, her presence a quiet insistence, though she couldn't fully understand why she lingered. There was a peculiar weight pressing against her chest, a sense of unfinished business, an unspoken understanding that she couldn't leave—*shouldn't* leave. She didn't know what might happen if she turned her back. To leave Zelphira in this state… What would that mean? She didn't want to think of it.

The sound of water running was the first thing that gave Galinda a semblance of peace. She clung to it like a lifeline, a sound so mundane, so ordinary, yet so full of promise. *At least she's doing something,* Galinda thought, sitting down beside the door.

Then, from behind the door, came the unmistakable sound of hard scrubbing, the scrape of something rigid against something soft. Metal against stone.

Grunting followed, then more frantic scrubbing, punctuated by a soft whimper, then a sharp squeal, followed by more whimpers. A sob. Another.

Galinda's stomach clenched.

She stood, as though pulled by invisible strings, her hand moving before she even thought to knock.

"Are you okay in there?"

But Zelphira didn't answer. There was only the sound of the frantic scrubbing growing louder.

Galinda hesitated for a moment, heart thudding in her chest, and then her hand was on the doorknob. She turned it, and the door creaked open with a reluctant groan.

GLINDA: The GOOD Witch

The stench hit her first, *the smell of fish, onions, garlic mixed with other unrecognisable things*, an olfactory assault so potent it nearly made her gasp. But it wasn't the smell that caused her to stagger back. It was the scene before her eyes.

"Oh, no," Galinda whispered, "Oh Oz, what are you doing?" She stumbled forward, stepping on the wet tiles, her feet slipping beneath her, as she rushed to the tub. "Stop that!"

The bathroom was a chaotic mess, the floor slick with bubbles, *too many bubbles*, covering every inch, thousands swarming around in the air, over her feet like frothy waves. The air was thick with them. She could barely see past the foam.

But it wasn't the bubbles, nor the overwhelming smell that tore her apart. It was the sight of Zelphira, slumped in the tub, her body trembling. Blood, dark and thick, swirled in the water with the remnants of the soap. Her skin was marred, cut— deep gouges lined her arms and legs, streaking her greenish flesh with red. Her wounds; raw, each one a fresh testament to her pain.

"What are you doing?" Galinda cried, her voice breaking. Her hand reached out, trembling as she touched Zelphira's shoulder. "Why are you scrubbing so hard? Are you trying to *rip* your skin off?" Her eyes filled with tears, a torrent that matched the one flooding Zelphira's soul. "Stop!"

Zelphira looked up at her, her face hollow with exhaustion. Her eyes, so full of sorrow and something deeper, *defeat*, bore into Galinda.

"I'm just so tired," she whispered, her voice quivering, faltering under the weight of it all. And then, like a dam breaking, she began to sob, her body wracked with grief. "I'm so tired…"

And in that moment, everything in Galinda fractured. She sank to the floor beside Zelphira, pulling her into her arms, holding her as though that alone could heal the wounds, though she knew it wouldn't. It couldn't. But she held on anyway, her chest shaking as Zelphira cried into her.

The both of them, trapped in the bath of pink bubbles and sorrow, cried together. Galinda's tears mingled with Zelphira's; two souls laid bare in the silent ache of their shared pain. It was as though the world had tilted on its axis and all that was left was this—this unspoken grief, spilling out between them, filling the room with the sound of broken hearts.

They cried. And for a long while, neither of them knew if the tears would ever stop.

CHAPTER 36

Two Sides of a Coin

Galinda knelt beside Zelphira in the half-flooded bathroom, her silks sodden and ruined, her perfume lost beneath the persistent stench of fish, soap and blood. She did what she had never been taught to do—she worked. She wrung out the washcloth in trembling hands, wiping at the welts and cuts with the softest motions she could manage, coaxing warmth back into cold limbs. Zelphira had gone quiet, a kind of quiet that unnerved Galinda, neither sleep nor rest, but the silence of someone who had run out of energy to even despair.

She dried Zelphira with the towel pulled from her own suite, the thick kind woven from cloud-soft cotton and perfumed faintly with lavender. She wrapped her like a child. Then, with a commanding breath, she wasn't aware she'd taken, Galinda escorted her through the quarters like a nursemaid shepherding a spectre.

The moon had mounted the sky by the time she returned from her search, a bundle of gauze, cotton, and a tiny brown glass bottle of antiseptic clutched to her chest. In its amber glow, the moon looked as though it pitied them both.

Zelphira sat on the edge of her narrow bed, back slightly hunched, her long black hair falling in wet strands about her shoulders as she dabbed at it with her towel. Galinda, now seated beside her like a girl playing pretend at being useful, watched her with curiosity she tried to conceal.

"What's it like?" Galinda asked softly, "Living here."

Zelphira didn't look up. "Terrible." She gave a breathless, humourless laugh. "Have you ever been bullied by maids before?"

"The maids? They're in on it?"

Zelphira finally turned to her, "Isn't *everyone*?"

Galinda bit the inside of her cheek. "If even the maids, those paid to care for and clean after others, are in on the joke, then something is deeply wrong here."

Zelphira didn't answer.

"Why do you stay here? Didn't they assign you a student room, like the rest of us?"

"I couldn't afford it." Zelphira's tone carried no shame. Just exhaustion. "They said I could live in the servants' quarters, since I'm here on scholarship and I can't leave becoz—where would I go?"

There it was again. That heaviness. That truth so quietly devastating it could shatter a mirror if spoken aloud too many times.

Galinda didn't think. Or perhaps she thought too much, too fast. "Move in with me."

Zelphira blinked, slowly, like she wasn't sure if it was a suggestion or some new form of cruelty.

"What?"

Galinda straightened her back. "Move in with me. I have more space in my suite than I know what to do with. And you shouldn't have to—"

"I can't possibly—"

"I insist. In fact, let's do it now. Pack what you need. Leave the rest. Leave this whole wretched little room behind."

Zelphira studied her, "Are you sure?"

Galinda's voice turned steely. "I'm not going to beg. Unless you *want* to stay with Zara."

The name hit the air like a curse, and Zelphira, without another moment of doubt, stood.

"I'm coming," she said, a flicker of something close to hope, or maybe disbelief, lighting her voice.

Zelphira packed quietly, deliberately, two modest bags, all she possessed in the world, each item folded with the care of someone used to making little feel like enough. And when she was done, they departed without ceremony: the princess and the pariah, side by side beneath the dispassionate eye of the moon.

They arrived at Galinda's suite—an entire floor. Galinda had neglected to lock the grand double doors. A mistake, perhaps, though it was well known among the Ozian elite that no one dared to trespass uninvited upon the territory of a princess. Not unless they sought exile by scandal.

Zelphira stepped inside.

"Sweet Lurline," she gasped, her green hand instinctively covering her mouth. "All this, for just you?"

"Yes," Galinda replied, as though apologising for all the pink.

She moved to her chest of drawers, opening them with the brisk authority of someone surveying a kingdom. Silk chemises and scented sachets nestled in tidy compartments. But there, near the top left, a drawer was empty, like it had been waiting.

"This one's yours," Galinda offered, turning to Zelphira. "Will it be enough? I can clear another if you need more space."

"No. This is… more than enough," Zelphira said softly.

She moved slowly about the room, arms folded like she was cold, or maybe just trying to hold herself together. Her eyes flicked from one sumptuous detail to the next, the kind of details that belonged to fairy stories, not to her.

At the vanity, she paused. "Is this... is this Make-Do?"

"Yes, why? Would you like to apply some?"

Zelphira laughed, a short, self-mocking sound. She held up her hands. "They don't exactly make them in *my* shade."

Galinda's eyes narrowed, not in judgment, but defiance. "Sit."

"What?"

"Sit down. Now."

There was a subtle joy in Galinda as she took up her softest blush—a petal-pink powder scented faintly of cinnamon rose. With the tip of her brush, she dusted Zelphira's cheeks, careful not to overwhelm the olive glow of her skin.

Then, in a small ceremonial flourish, she crossed the room, plucked a pink rose from the vase beside her reading chair, and tucked it behind Zelphira's ear. The flower, obedient and curious, settled into the dark cascade of her hair.

Galinda leaned in beside her so their faces, sunlit and moonlit, met in the mirror.

"Pink and Green... they've always been sisters, haven't they?"

"You think so?" Zelphira asked, a flicker of doubt in her voice.

Galinda giggled, eyes warm with certainty. "I know so."

They stared at themselves; twin reflections braided not by likeness but by something less nameable. Zelphira studied her own image, not with vanity, but with the estranged curiosity of someone seeing themselves for the first time in the right light.

"Zelphira," Galinda said softly.

"Yes?"

"You are so beautiful."

Zelphira looked away, but not before Galinda saw the shimmer building in her eyes. A swell of feeling that couldn't quite break but threatened to.

Galinda turned quickly, almost theatrically, spinning to the centre of the room. "Come, let's sit on the floor. We've got lifetimes to catch up on."

And Zelphira, wiping her tears before they had the chance to fall, followed without a word, knowing, perhaps for the first time, what it meant to be seen, not just looked at.

They sat cross-legged on the carpet like two girls trying to conjure a childhood they'd never had.

"So," Galinda began, chin tilted, voice rehearsed in optimism, "earlier you said something about being here on scholarship?"

Zelphira nodded, a small, demure motion. She tucked her long black hair behind one ear, the pink rose still perched defiantly on the other, as if daring the room not to romanticize her. "Yes. The Wizard himself decreed I be admitted. I've never met him. But still, his word is law, isn't it?"

Galinda blinked. "Woz. Why you?"

"To study sorcery, of course. I got a letter, sealed, emerald wax, and it said the Wizard had *plans* for me. Grand ones. Apparently."

"And you said yes."

"I didn't think twice," Zelphira said, with the shrug of someone who had long ago learned not to expect choices. "I never thought I'd even *see* a university, much less attend one. I wanted to study *Byology and Animal Care*, and perhaps *Environmental Theologies* as an extra course." She laughed, but there was something metallic in the sound. "But the scholarship was strictly for *Sorcery*. Strings attached, of course."

"And yet they couldn't even give you a proper room."

Zelphira raised an eyebrow, amused. "You try telling the most powerful man in Oz that your greatest concern is inadequate accommodation after giving you free education. Assuming you get an audience at all."

"I've met him," Galinda said, a little too casually, "And I also received a scholarship."

Zelphira leaned in, eyes catching the candlelight like polished stone. "You've met the Wizard? What was he like? What did you wish for? What was your heart's truest desire?"

Galinda gave a practiced shrug. "He visited our estate. Insisted I attend. I didn't ask for anything."

"Well, of course not. What is there to wish for when you already have it all?"

Galinda's smile wavered, cracked like porcelain in winter. "And what would your wish be?" she asked softly.

Zelphira paused, her gaze distant. "After I graduate, after I've proven my worth, I want to sit on the Magic Council. And then… I want to help the Animals. I want to fix Oz."

"Fix Oz?"

Zelphira straightened, her voice sharpening. "I don't know if you've noticed, but Oz is pulling itself apart. It started when Munchkinland pushed for independence. Now every province clings to its own culture like armour, convinced they don't need the others. If I'm right, this division, it could be the end of Oz! The South hate the North. Gillikin distrusts the Winkies. The East pretends it's untouched, but it's cracking too and I don't even need my clairvoyance to see that."

Galinda blinked. "And the Animals?"

"When was the last time you saw a Lion lecture? Or a Goat teach in the lecture halls? They've vanished. Gone into hiding. Afraid. And rightly so. Something's hunting them—"

"I hadn't noticed."

"Most people haven't," Zelphira said bitterly. "The truth is dressed in silence. But the Animals feel what we feel, joy, pain, fear. And they're being pushed out of this world. I want to bring them back. To protect them. And maybe… if someone on the Council actually cared, that could change."

"Will the Wizard help?"

Zelphira grinned. "Of course he will. He's powerful. Wise. And we all know he has a fondness for emeralds, and who better to speak for them than the greenest of them all?" She gave a theatrical bow from her seated position, her rose bobbing with the motion.

That made Galinda laugh, a crisp sound, like wind flicking a wind chime, but Zelphira's tone shifted.

"There are rules that need to change."

Galinda blinked. "Rules?"

"The nonsense ones. The quiet, invisible ones we all live by without asking who wrote them. Like how every girl's name in Oz must end with an 'A'. A decree of femininity. As if syllables could conjure virtue."

Galinda raised an eyebrow. "And men's names?"

"Oh, they're free to end however they please. No expectations tied to the last letter of their identities."

Galinda's lips parted in amusement, but Zelphira turned to her with a half-smirk.

"You didn't take the pledge either, did you?"

Galinda looked at her hands. "No. But only becoz I came on scholarship."

Zelphira grinned. "You remember the ceremony in the Grand Lycrium?"

The two of them burst into laughter, as if the memory were stitched into their ribs.

"What a day," Galinda said, still catching her breath. "If someone had told me *then* that we'd end up roommates…"

"I'd have dropped the fish bucket atop myself and died," Zelphira finished.

"I didn't need to take the pledge. It wasn't a requirement."

"Same, though, honestly, I *wanted* to. Just becoz everyone else was."

There was a pause, soft as powder.

Then Galinda, shifting topics like someone changing hats: "I give nicknames to my friends."

"Oh? So now we're friends?" Zelphira said with a teasing glance.

"Why, yes! And prepare yourself, friendship with me is a full-time performance. You're about to be wildly, horrendously popular. And it's all becoz of me."

"Oh no!" Zelphira gasped, feigning horror. "More fish buckets from adoring fans!"

"Oh, don't worry, you're going to grin and bear your new-found popularity," Galinda waved her hand, "like I do."

"So, if we're standing side by side… who wins the popularity war? The glittering blonde *Pretty Princess* or *Greenie?*"

Galinda leaned in, eyes sparkling. "Oh sweetie, I know, without a shadow of a doubt, that you will be very popular." She began to play with her hair. "You just won't be as popular as me!"

Laughter again—this time more breath than sound.

"Okay," Galinda said. "Nickname time. What do they call you?"

Zelphira made a face. "Greenie. Vermin. Sludge. Sewage. Limepox. Take your pick."

"No. Absolutely not. We're burning those names in effigy. Let's see... Zelphie?"

Zelphira frowned. "I don't think so."

"Elph?" Galinda thought. "Yes! Can I call you Elph?"

"I don't like it. I'm already green, the jokes will write themselves—" Zelphira's eyes darted in thought. "Maybe just call me Zelly?"

Galinda paused, her face softened as though she'd stumbled upon a secret door in her own memory.

"I knew a Zelly once. A long time ago. Yes, I like that. Zelly. It suits you."

Zelphira smiled. "Then, Zelly, it is."

"And you? I can't shorten *Gah-linda*. So how about... *Glinda?*"

Galinda froze for half a second, just long enough to betray that it mattered.

"That was my name, once. Before..."

Zelphira tilted her head. "Why the change?"

"Oh," Galinda said, standing up as if to deflect. "It's a long story."

"Well, I guess, change... undone."

Galinda rose, her fingers lifting in the air like a conductor's, summoning invisible fabric and feather, the ghost of old enchantments. "Back then, I made gowns that shimmered like stardust. I could turn your frock into the most magnificent dress you've ever seen. Shoes that could dance on clouds. All with just a flick of my fingers and a spell."

Zelphira, sitting cross-legged like a child or a sage, looked up at her—her own expression half amusement, half something gentler. "I believe you."

"You do?"

"I do," Zelphira said, then tilted her head with a new gleam in her eye. "Shall we try again?"

"Try what?"

"My clairvoyance, to see why your magic is...gone."

"Yes! Yes, please. If you don't mind, that is."

Zelphira smiled. "Give me your palm."

Galinda extended her hand. Their fingers touched—and something electric, or perhaps *elemental*, sparked between them. Not quite lightning, but something close. The room didn't tremble, yet their hair lifted as though remembering the wind.

Zelphira closed her eyes.

"I see..."

"What do you see?"

"A younger you. Magic pulsing from your fingers like ribbons. And a boy. Blonde, narrow as a candlestick."

Galinda whispered. "Ominson."

"And your nose," Zelphira added, suppressing a giggle that slipped through anyway.

"I told you. It's a long story."

"What happened?"

"Focus, would you?"

"Right," Zelphira whispered, the trance pulling her deeper. "Now… green. All green."

"Green?"

"Yes. Everything. You're asleep… no, your magic—it's *absent*. Like a light in a locked room. Glinda, I think—it's been taken."

Zelphira's eyes snapped open, and she gasped like someone resurfacing from deep water.

"Taken? What do you mean *taken*?"

"Exactly that. It wasn't lost or withered or miscast. It was *stolen*."

Galinda stood, though not regally—more like a girl trying to shake frost from her limbs. "How is that even possible?"

"I don't know, but whoever managed it must be formidable. Devious. The sort of sorcerer who doesn't announce themselves until the curtain falls."

Galinda's eyes narrowed. "But if it was stolen, it can be *retrieved*, right?"

"In theory, yes."

Galinda took a long breath, shaky, but earnest. "Then I'll get it back."

The room fell quiet, but not unkindly so. The kind of hush that wraps around two people beginning to understand each other.

Galinda sat back down, crossing her legs to match Zelphira's. "Let's play a game, we each tell a secret, but we can't judge one another. Agreed?"

"Agreed."

"I'll go first," Galinda said, raising a finger. "But don't get cross."

"Okay?"

"You know that pointy hat and cloak I gave you…?" She winced, as if bracing for the sting of a slap.

"Yes?"

Galinda drew in a breath, "I gave it to you as a cruel joke," she said, her voice smaller now, "I'm sorry."

The silence between them stretched thin and sharp, taut with the weight of the confession. Zelphira's eyes narrowed, her posture stiffening, and she sprang to her feet in a sudden, fluid motion. "You evil girl!"

"I'm sorry, I didn't—"

And then, the unexpected happened. Zelphira began to laugh.

"Wait, you're not mad?"

Zelphira chuckled again, the sound light and unburdened, a teasing edge to her smile. "I'm not foolish, Galinda, I knew it was a joke. I just genuinely liked the outfit. As a matter of fact, once I get the fish smell out of it, I'm going to wear it again. Oh, and also you should know… ***your voice goes high-pitched when you lie.***"

"It does?!" Her flustered expression quickly melted into a mix of embarrassment and amusement, and without thinking, she grabbed a pillow and hurled it at Zelphira with playful violence.

Zelphira dodged just in time.

"You little menace!" Galinda exclaimed. Though the mischief in her voice softened the reprimand, her laughter bubbled up, warm and infectious.

"Maybe I should start keeping track of all your little tells, Galinda."

"And maybe I'll start keeping track of yours!"

Zelphira laughed once more, her spirit unshaken, and she collapsed back onto the cushions, eyes sparkling.

"I was going to tell you about my… unpleasant looks before," Galinda said, her voice softening, the humour ebbing away like the last ripples of a storm. "But you saw my face and my scary nose in your vision already."

"Oh, you mean *this* nose?" she teased, her tone laced with mischief.

With a casual flick of her wrist, Zelphira raised her hand and spoke the words, a chant rolling off her tongue like the ancient rustle of leaves in a forgotten forest:

Bin Quwwat il Qadïr Ansabtu.

The moment the last syllable left her mouth, the air shimmered with magic, and before Galinda's very eyes, Zelphira's nose transformed—elongating, distorting, its shape warping into something grotesque. It became long, sharp, and jagged, bending unnaturally, as though it had been twisted by some cruel sorcery. It was a monstrous reflection of what Galinda's nose had once been, a mockery of her own past.

Galinda recoiled, a scream bursting from her lips, "don't do that! Get rid of it. Now!"

Zelphira, watching the chaos she'd summoned with something akin to amusement, closed her eyes for a moment, and with a soft sigh, the nose vanished, fading as quickly as it had come.

Galinda's heart pounding in her chest, found herself speaking again, her voice faltering as she tried to steady the chaos within her. "Your turn."

Zelphira sighed, the sound heavy as a tired gust of wind.

"Do you know why I don't use my magic against people?"

Galinda's eyes sharpened with interest; her curiosity piqued. "No, why?"

Zelphira took a deep breath. "I tried so hard to be good. I followed every rule, every dictate placed on me, and it got me nowhere. No one ever saw past the disgust of my green skin, the 'evil' they painted on me like it was a brand. When my magic began to manifest, I started using it in secret, advancing it quicker than I expected. For a while, I gave up on trying to be good. I thought that true goodness came from following my instincts, not someone else's rules. So that's what I did."

Her voice faltered for a moment, a tinge of sadness slipping through her words. "Long story short, I found a spell. I didn't know it couldn't be undone, but I used it. I turned a boy from Munchkinland into a talking, living, scarecrow. At the time, no one knew I had magic. Only he knew. But despite everything… he didn't tell anyone I was the one who cursed him. I've regretted it ever since, and that's partly why I came here—to learn from Lady Mordemire, to find a way to undo it. But I can't. And that's why I'm scared… becoz I know that if I use my magic when I'm angry, I might do something worse and most of all, regret in the end. Besides, with my green skin, the moment I retaliate… I'd soon be labelled the wickedest of them all."

Galinda's hand reached out, gentle and warm, touching Zelphira's arm in a gesture that was both comforting and sincere. "Oh, Zelly, we've all done things we wish we could take back."

Galinda's arms enveloped her in a hug, warm and steady, and for a moment, the world felt just a little less heavy.

"So," Galinda asked eagerly, her voice lightening, "what do you think about goodness now?"

"I don't think one can have power, true power and be truly good at the same time," she said, her voice steady but filled with conviction. "It's a fallacy. Like how black cannot be white at the same time. The most they can be is… grey."

Galinda nodded, her understanding clear.

"But," Galinda continued, "if you can change your nose, why don't you just cast a spell and get rid of your green skin? All your problems would be solved."

Zelphira's lips twisted into a wry smile. "I've tried everything, every incantation, every potion… no matter what I do, I wake up still green."

"So, how often do you use your magic?"

"I mainly use it in Sorcery class, but I used to do things in secret, just trying to help out, as much as I could. I didn't need the praise, I just wanted to do good." She paused, her eyes distant, "You remember the twister that hit Munchkinland a few Sun-Moons ago?"

Galinda leaned forward. "The one the Good Witch stopped?"

"I'm the one that stopped the twister." Zelphira said, "It was my magic. But I let the Good Witch take credit."

Galinda sat back, her eyes widening with surprise and something like admiration, though she quickly masked it with a flick of her hand. Zelphira chuckled softly, watching her closely.

"Look at me," she continued, her voice low and almost rueful. "People wouldn't believe me. They'd rather think that I was the one who *created* the twister. They would've exiled me out of Munchkinland faster than you could blink."

Galinda's lips parted, "I have a secret too," she whispered, almost embarrassed, "I was the one who created that twister."

Zelphira gasped, "No."

"Yes, I did a spell, and it just got... out of hand."

Zelphira shook her head slowly, disbelieving. "Woz."

"Trust me, I've learned my lesson."

Zelphira's gaze softened, her shoulders relaxing. "It's all in the past now. What I want to know is, why do you pretend to be dumb, when I can tell that you're intelligent?"

"Why don't you use your magic publicly? We're both running away from something we don't want to be."

The room fell into a pregnant silence, the weight of their words hanging between them like a storm cloud, thick and suffocating. Then, a deep rumbling sound broke the stillness, like the earth itself had begun to stir. The tremor started small but quickly grew in intensity, erratic and aggressive, shaking the very foundation of the room.

Both girls stood in shock, their eyes meeting in alarm. The rumbling was coming from opposite sides of the room—one from Galinda's pink trunk and the other from Zelphira's bag. They exchanged a look before rushing to their respective corners, drawn by the unsettling noise.

Galinda's hand hovered above the trunk, her face flickering with hesitation as she cautiously unlatched it. She peered inside, her expression shifting. But before she could react, Zelphira whispered sharply, almost as if she were speaking to the very bag itself. "Be quiet."

But the rumbling continued, relentless.

The girls both grabbed their objects, and it was then that they realized what had caused the commotion. Two ancient tomes lay before them: the **Ethereum** and the **Grimorium**.

Both, wide-eyed, asked in unison, "Is that...?"

They gasped, the reality of the situation crashing over them.

Zelphira spoke first, her voice a whisper of awe, "Is that the *Kitab Solis*?"

Galinda, equally stunned, nodded slowly. She glanced at the dark tome in Zelphira's lap, "Is that the *Kitab Malum*?"

Zelphira's lips trembled into a smile, "But I call it the *Grimorium*."

"Mine's the *Ethereum*."

"Sweet Ozma," Zelphira breathed, her words like a prayer.

The tremors from the books ceased, and the room became eerily still. Galinda looked up, her gaze sharp; a question forming in her mind. "Who knew you had the other half this entire time?"

Zelphira raised an eyebrow. "How did you get it?"

"I had a great teacher," Galinda replied, her lips curling into a half-smile. "*You?*"

"I had a great friend."

Zelphira held her hand out, "let me see it."

CHANGE

Without hesitation, Galinda handed the Ethereum over to Zelphira, who held it carefully, almost reverently. Galinda opened the Grimorium, its pages stiff at first but yielded to her touch and opened slowly. She flicked through the pages with a bemused expression. "I can't read a thing," she laughed softly, her fingers brushing over the cryptic symbols. "Not a single thing."

The Ethereum in Zelphira's hands opened with intense force, the pages flipping rapidly as if eager to reveal their secrets to her and only her. Galinda watched, captivated. "Can you read the Ethereum?"

Zelphira's eyes flickered over the words, her brow furrowing slightly in concentration. "Every single word."

Galinda leaned in, her gaze sharp. "And can you read every word of the Grimorium?"

"Yes, everything."

A long silence hung between them, the weight of their shared discovery settling in. Galinda's voice broke the stillness, her tone quiet but firm. "We must keep this a secret. We mustn't tell a soul."

Zelphira's expression hardened with determination. "Agreed."

Without another word, Galinda turned toward the far side of the room, her fingers brushing over a small chest she had tucked away there. She carefully placed the Ethereum inside, locking it with a soft click. Zelphira did the same with the Grimorium, placing it gently within her own chest. Together, they sealed the books away from the world.

Galinda slid a spare key into Zelphira's hand, her eyes steady. "So we can both access them if need be."

Galinda, ever impatient, seized the opportunity to ask, "I know I don't have my magic right now, but can you teach me what Lady Mordemire is teaching you and that other boy?"

"Oh, you mean Elmond? He dropped out on the first day. Wouldn't stop crying, poor thing. Scared of Lady Mordemire. Couldn't handle her... uh, unique way of teaching." She shook her head, a wry smile tugging at her lips. "As a matter of fact, I have his books. You can have them. And I'll give you your first magic theory lesson."

"I'll take what I can get."

Zelphira reached into her bag and, with a dramatic flourish, pulled out two identical copies of *Merlin the First's Theory of Magic*. She handed one to Galinda, who took it eagerly, her fingers brushing against the aged cover. "One for you, and one for me."

Galinda grinned, "well, then. Let's begin."

"Turn to page four hundred and five," Zelphira instructed, her voice steady as her fingers grazed the edges of the ancient tome.

Galinda obeyed, her hands flipping the pages carefully until they landed on the marked page. She glanced at Zelphira, who nodded encouragingly, and they began to read aloud together.

Chapter VII — Of Essence and Will

It is a fallacy, and a most dangerous one, to believe that magic is a uniform tool—like a sword forged in the same fire for all hands to wield alike. Such thinking has led more than one would-be wizard to ruin. No. Magic is not external, like a blade. It is internal, like blood.

Just as no two hearts beat with identical rhythm, nor flow two rivers with the same bend or song, magic flows differently within each person who dares to claim it. It is shaped by the caster's breath and temper, by the secrets they carry, and even by the way they grieve.

It lives in the marrow, shaped by the caster's breath, grief, secrets, and joy. No two spells are alike, becoz no two souls are. One may summon fire with laughter, another with fury. There are no universal incantations, only languages of the self, waiting to be heard.

Magic reflects the caster. It does not disguise. It is blood, not blade. Mirror, not hammer. It reflects who we are, not who we pretend to be.

Imitation fails. Memorization fades. Only what is felt, lived, and true will cast with life.

Ask not, "What spell?" but "Who am I when I cast?"

For if magic is breath, then intent is the lung. If it is blood, then will is the heart that drives it. And above all, the nature of the caster, their honesty, their rage, their longing, determines how the magic lives, or whether it dares to live at all.

For will is the heart of magic, and the spell only lives if you do.

Zelphira propped her head up, her gaze lingering on the words. "Essentially, magic is unique to each individual. Their habits, skills, beliefs, experiences... the way they carry themselves."

Galinda nodded slowly. "Makes sense. It's not just about casting, is it? It's about... *being.*"

Zelphira closed the book with a quiet thud, the sound reverberating in the stillness between them. "I really do hope you get your magic back," she said, her tone carrying a quiet sincerity.

Galinda exhaled slowly, the breath heavy with unspoken things. "I hope I do too." Her voice faltered slightly, but she quickly masked it with a smile, though it didn't quite reach her eyes.

The absence of her magic was a void she wasn't sure how to fill, but perhaps, just maybe, the answer lay in this journey they were beginning together.

CHAPTER 37

Good News

By the time the sky had stretched itself open into morning, Galinda had already played the role of benefactress with a zeal bordering on performative. In the corner of the shared chamber, an arrangement of items had been placed, not dumped, not strewn, but curated, as if for an exhibit: dresses in demure shades, crisp shirts with pearl-fastened collars, underthings as soft as gossip, rows of brown and black boots lined like mourners at a wake, and beside it all, glass bottles and carved soaps, a vial of perfume that smelled like powdered lilies and the memory of rain. Even the lotion shimmered with some quiet intent.

Zelphira, who had sunk, not entirely willingly, into Galinda's bed for the night, had vanished into sleep with the grace of someone who'd long been denied it.

At the sixth hour, the door creaked open, and breakfast entered, not by servant's hand, but by Galinda's own. She wheeled the tray in with the gravity of ceremony. The silver clattered, a polite clamour, and the sound prodded Zelphira awake. Her eyes opened slowly, reluctantly, as if accusing the room of betrayal.

"Did you sleep well?" Galinda asked, a teasing lilt in her voice.

"Like the dead," Zelphira muttered, blinking.

The smell found her before anything else did—savoury and warm, like memory in a kitchen.

"Mmm, what is that?"

"Breakfast," Galinda replied, as if that settled all matters.

Now fully alert, Zelphira sat up, eyes scanning the contents of the tray. "Do you live like this... every day?"

"Most days."

Zelphira, unwilling to wait for permission that might never come, reached for a scone and a glass of milk. She ate quietly, breathing through her nose, as if restraining herself from devouring it whole. Then, setting the glass down, she looked at Galinda.

"Thank you. For this. For all of it."

Galinda waved a hand, almost embarrassed. "You'd have done the same."

"No," Zelphira said gently, "I mean it. Nobody has done this for me before, certainly not another girl."

Galinda gave a small smile—pleased. She nodded toward the pile of clothes.

"You see those?" she said. "They're yours. And I know you have an attachment to that battered cloak and that... hat—but now that we're friends, you'll have to wear something more... appropriate."

Zelphira turned her gaze to the garments. Her long black hair slipped forward like a curtain; she pushed it behind her ear with a practiced motion.

"I'll wear them," she said, and the words hung in the air like a pledge.

She finished the last of her scone in silence.

Zelphira stood beneath the warm stream of the shower she never had access to, letting water rush down her shoulders. She took her time, luxuriating in the soap Galinda had chosen, washing her hair carefully with the creamy *Foamé* shampoo, and gently rinsing her face. Refreshed and dry, she stepped from the steam into the bedroom.

"You can borrow my Herr-Oyl, if you want," Galinda offered generously.

"Oh, thank you!" Zelphira said, genuinely pleased. "Finally, I can stop concocting my homemade recipes."

Galinda laughed brightly. "That explains why your hair always smelled faintly of onions."

"Onions happen to be essential if you want your hair long and black as coal," Zelphira replied, mock-serious.

"Until you started using the Grimorium to grow it overnight," Galinda retorted, smirking playfully.

"Only becoz a certain someone crept into my room and chopped it off."

They both dissolved into laughter, easy and comfortable, like longtime conspirators.

Zelphira smoothed the lotion gently over her skin, then pulled on the fresh new clothes: a black skirt, just to her knees, flattering her figure, and a crisp white shirt tucked beneath a soft cream blouse. Brown boots, polished to a gentle gleam, completed the look. She sprayed a hint of perfume, combed the silky *Herr-Oyl* through her long, luxuriant hair, and glanced at herself in the mirror.

She was utterly changed, renewed, almost unrecognizable—strikingly beautiful. The green tint of her skin now somehow made her seem even lovelier.

"There she is!" Galinda applauded warmly.

They walked out together across the bright bustle of the campus, attracting curious stares from students who were confounded not just by Zelphira's remarkable transformation overnight, but also by the sudden, inseparable bond she shared with Galinda. Galinda welcomed the stares. They moved side by side, comfortably, as if they had been companions since childhood. Sisters even.

Students smiled warmly, waving casually as they passed. Someone even offered Zelphira an unopened *Chewy-Toffee* without explanation. Zelphira turned to Galinda, eyebrows raised, and the two friends shared a private burst of laughter.

"You really should've befriended me at the start of term," Zelphira teased quietly.

They laughed again, contentedly, before nearing the classrooms. Zelphira's class lay just ahead; Galinda's politics lesson with Master Ponsworth was further along, and Galinda hurried anxiously, aware of the ticking clock, after all, a Fairmoor was always punctual.

"I'll see you later, Zelly!" Galinda called as she rushed off.

"See you later, Glinda!" Zelphira called back, smiling to herself as Galinda ran ahead. For a moment, she simply stood watching, marvelling at how suddenly, unexpectedly, and wonderfully life had changed. Then she stepped into class, **heart** lighter than she'd ever imagined possible.

◇

After class, the attention was the same, students' curious gazes lingered, drawn by the sight of Galinda and Zelphira, now inseparable.

At lunch, Galinda and Zelphira chose a bench outdoors, sitting comfortably beside Galinda's loaded food trolley. Across the courtyard stood Cora, Mila, and Fanny, staring curiously from a distance.

"Galinda!" Mila called, pointedly ignoring Zelphira. "Are you joining us in the lunchroom?"

"You go ahead! I'll catch up later."

Just then, River jogged up with a grin wide as daylight. "Now this is a pleasant surprise! I've been waiting for this day."

"Oh, have you now?" Zelphira teased lightly.

"Absolutely." River squeezed onto the bench. "Now scoot over and hand me a duck sandwich, please."

Galinda passed him the tray.

"I don't know how you all can eat animals, over a perfectly good strawberry scone," Zelphira said.

"Aren't animals supposed to be eaten?" River argued. "And I'm talking about the 'animals' not the 'Animals'. I know how much you care for them but I'm sorry, but they taste divine."

River held out his hand offering her a bite of the duck sandwich, but Zelphira turned away in disgust.

Between bites, River turned to Galinda. "You know, the year is almost ending. I'd like you to come visit Winkie Country with me."

"I'll have to stop home first," Galinda replied, "but I'll be there."

River shifted his gaze to Zelphira, smiling warmly. "And you, I also want you at *Draeth Mor.*"

"Draeth Mor?" Zelphira's eyebrow lifted sceptically. "Is that a burial ground?"

River clutched his chest dramatically, feigning injury. "Oh, you wound me! Draeth Mor is the name of my castle."

"Sorry," Zelphira laughed softly, shaking her head. "But I can't afford to travel, so that might be a problem."

"Please," River dismissed her concerns grandly. "Don't worry, I'll have you picked up. How quickly you forget I'm a prince, heir to the throne?"

"Show-off," Zelphira teased, pushing him playfully.

"That's my middle name," River agreed with mock seriousness, bowing slightly.

A student approached quietly from behind Galinda, leaning close to whisper, "Hey, Galinda, you're such a saint for befriending her. I don't know how you manage it."

Galinda offered only a faint, uncomfortable smile as the student moved on.

"What did she say?" Zelphira asked curiously.

"She said... you look amazing today. She was just too shy to say it directly."

Zelphira smiled playfully, flipping her hair over her shoulder in an exaggerated mimic of Galinda's usual gesture.

"Toss. Toss."

River laughed first, followed by Galinda and Zelphira, the three of them dissolving into shared joy.

♦

Night fell quickly as the days passed, as though each sunset was eager to erase the day just to start anew. Galinda and Zelphira found themselves wishing for more hours, feeling time slip through their fingers faster than they expected.

A sharp knock startled Galinda from her thoughts one night. She peered cautiously through the spyhole to see Coraletta, Fanedra, and Marisella standing outside, arms crossed defensively, faces tight with discontent.

Fanedra spoke first, her voice edged with accusation. "Is she in there?"

"Who?" Galinda asked innocently. "Zelly? Zelphira?"

"You know exactly who," Fanedra snapped.

Galinda sighed softly and stepped outside closing the door behind her. "What's this about? Why are you so upset?"

Marisella stepped forward, voice tense. "We need to talk."

"Can't this wait? I'm a little busy right now."

"No, it can't," Fanedra said, her voice rising. "You need to hear this, and I don't care if that green wench overhears."

"In fact," Coraletta said coldly, "maybe she should hear it."

"Quiet," Galinda hissed, "Fine, I'm listening. Just keep your voices down."

CHANGE

Fanedra sneered. "Why have you gotten so close to that green slime, anyway? You've known her for what? All of three seconds, and now you spend every moment with her. You even share your room?"

Galinda tilted her head, smiling coolly. "Jealous much?"

Marisella scoffed bitterly. "Jealous? Why didn't you ask one of us to move in instead? We've known you far longer!"

"She needed somewhere to stay. You didn't," Galinda said simply, shrugging.

Coraletta's voice cracked with frustration. "Forget about the room. We haven't been seen around you in ages. People have started asking if we're even friends anymore. It's hurting our reputations—and our prospects."

Galinda raised an eyebrow. "So, this tantrum is becoz you're less popular without me there, for you to suck off?"

Fanedra's face turned red, blonde hair escaping angrily around her face. "Yes, you're a princess, yes, you're the Good Witch's sister, but don't forget we helped build your little empire. Or has your green pet cast a spell to erase your memory?"

Coraletta cut in sharply, her voice venomous. "Who do you think fed people the stories that created your sparkling reputation? We followed you around, picking up your scraps and spinning every nasty rumour into gold. Without us, you'd just be another pretty girl playing dress-up. You need us, Galinda."

Marisella leaned forward urgently. "Just toss out that Greenie. Evict her. Stop speaking to her." She laughed. "Before us, you were nothing special, just another pretty princess with a famous sister. We are the ones that made you into the beacon of goodness you pretend to be."

Galinda chuckled, eyes flashing with sudden contempt. "Nothing before you? You think you created me? I built all this myself. The only reason you're panicking now is that you realize I'm not there to help you catch rich boy penises to fill into your twiddles."

Fanedra stepped closer, voice trembling with rage. "I knew it would come to this. Perfect little Galinda thinking she's above us. You forget what you were, an ugly, lonely, frail girl with dirty-blonde hair."

Marisella now stepped closer, eyes narrowed maliciously. "We know the truth, Galinda. It wasn't the perks of privilege that fixed you. It was your sister, the Good Witch, who cast a spell to correct that hideous face, your ugly nose. We've known it all along. And now, you must choose carefully. Choose now."

Coraletta stepped up. "It's us or her. Decide."

Galinda's voice came low and firm. "Zelly. Without question. And I never want to see any of you near me again. Stay away from my suite, my castle—don't even mention my name."

Marisella's eyes widened in disbelief. "You're actually choosing that wicked green witch over us?"

Galinda met her gaze steadily. "Are you stupid? Obviously." Her voice hardened dangerously. "And let me be clear, if any of you retaliate against Zelphira, I promise you, I'll have all three of you executed by dawn."

The three girls gasped in shocked unison, stepping back immediately, before turning and fleeing swiftly down the staircase, leaving Galinda standing alone, her heart pounding with anger and certainty.

Galinda took a deep breath, steadying herself before opening the door and stepping back into the room. Inside, Zelphira was silent, suspiciously still, her eyes fixed firmly on the pages of her book, though she hadn't turned a page in several minutes.

"How much did you hear?"

Zelphira paused before softly admitting, "All of it."

"I'm so sorry," Galinda said, voice trembling as tears filled her eyes. "I can't believe I ever thought that way of acting was acceptable. I'm a hypocrite, the biggest hypocrite who ever lived." She sank slowly onto her bed, shoulders heavy with guilt.

Zelphira quietly closed her book, setting it aside, then reached out to place a comforting hand on Galinda's shoulder. "It's better to be a hypocrite than to remain the same person forever."

Galinda turned, embracing Zelphira tightly, as if holding on would keep her steady. "I'm sorry for everything I did to you. I just hope you can find it in your heart to forgive me."

"Don't worry, I said plenty of awful things too, remember? Besides, I forgave you a long time ago. I could tell from your eyes, that deep down, you were hurting just as much as I was."

Galinda laughed softly, wiping away her tears. "We're both so pathetic."

Zelphira grinned warmly. "Tell me something I don't know."

Together they laughed, easing into a gentle silence, their friendship quietly healed.

◇

Many weeks had passed, bringing an end to their first year at Oz University. Zelphira and Galinda were now even more inseparable, with River being their favourite companion.

Galinda finished the year with the highest W.S.S. scores in her class, though she kept her success quiet, personally asking Master Ponsworth not to congratulate her publicly. She preferred to keep up her facade—the girl who prioritised form over content, who wrote essays on rose-scented, *pink* paper. Master Ponsworth understood and obliged.

Zelphira also finished the year impressively, though she was the only student in her specialised studies, surpassing even Lady Mordemire's expectations.

As the term ended, students stood waiting for their boats, hugging friends goodbye, promising reunions. Galinda and Zelphira stood side by side, surrounded by their luggage. Zelphira now had significantly more belongings than she'd arrived with, but still nothing compared to Galinda, whose acquisitions over the term filled several more trunks.

"Do you have it?" Galinda asked anxiously.

"Of course!" Zelphira said brightly, pulling her old cloak and pointy hat from her bag.

"No, not those!" Galinda laughed, shaking her head. "Your Grimorium."

"Oh, right, yes, it's locked safely in that trunk you gave me. Do you have your Ethereum?"

"Locked and safe."

"Good."

River bounded over suddenly, sucking happily on a small *Lolliguild-Pop* that stained his lips bright red. "Hey, girls, how are we doing?"

"Wonderful," Zelphira replied.

"You seem to be enjoying that very much, aren't you?"

River grinned playfully, pulling the lollipop from his mouth and holding it toward Galinda. "Want a lick?"

Galinda laughed, recoiling jokingly. "No thanks!"

"Oh, come on, you know you want to!" River insisted, pushing it closer as Galinda ducked away.

He turned toward Zelphira, pretending to whisper. "She's acting shy now, as if she hasn't already swallowed my entire tongue."

Zelphira cringed dramatically. "Ewww, I did not need that mental image!"

River and Galinda both laughed, but their moment was interrupted by a voice calling from behind.

"Prince Rivero Valeheart, your boat has arrived!"

River glanced back briefly, then turned once more to his friends. "Don't forget, I expect you both at Draeth Mor soon, alright?"

Both girls nodded warmly.

"And Zelphira, I'll have you picked up from…Raventhorne Farm in Munchkinland, right?"

"Yes," Zelphira confirmed with a smile.

"Coolio!" River said cheerfully, throwing up a thumbs-up before turning to leave. He ran toward his boat, waving enthusiastically behind him. "See you soon!"

Zelphira raised an eyebrow. "Coolio? Who even says that?"

"That's River being River. Best not to question it."

Lady Mordemire glided gracefully toward Zelphira, her silver skirt whispering softly across the polished floors. Smiling warmly, she placed both hands affectionately on Zelphira's shoulders.

"How are you, my darling?"

"I'm well, and you?"

Galinda suddenly found the ground fascinating, nudging a pebble gently with her shoe.

"Good! I wanted to congratulate you on completing the sorcery course," Lady Mordemire said, proudly kissing Zelphira on both cheeks. "Oh, I'm so very proud of you."

Zelphira's eyes widened. "Completed? Forgive me, but I don't quite follow."

"Oh, always so modest," Lady Mordemire laughed. "You've finished the entire course."

"But I thought it took three Sun-Moons?"

"Normally, yes, but you've exceeded all my expectations. You've mastered everything in just one Sun-Moon. I truly believe, no, I know, you're ready to meet the Wizard."

Zelphira gasped sharply. "The Wizard of Oz?"

"Is there any other?"

"Oh, Oz," Zelphira whispered, awestruck.

"Precisely."

"When?" Zelphira's voice rose eagerly. "Am I worthy?"

"Trust me, my dear. You are more than worthy. I will write to him immediately, and he'll respond soon."

"How will I know when he does?"

"So many questions! Trust me, Zelphira. When the Wizard answers, you'll know."

Galinda continued kicking her pebble silently. Zelphira glanced at her, then quickly turned back to Lady Mordemire.

"May I bring Galinda with me?"

Galinda's head shot up, startled. "Zelly—no! This is your moment. I don't want to impose."

Zelphira ignored her protests and continued firmly. "Please, Lady Mordemire. Galinda has important political aspirations. She achieved the highest W.S.S. scores in Professor Ponsworth's politics class. And she's the daughter of the Quadling King, I want her to have this chance to fulfil her heart's desire, too."

"And if I refuse?"

"Then I won't go. I can't do this without her."

Lady Mordemire sighed, giving Galinda a look of barely disguised annoyance. "Very well."

With a stiff nod, Lady Mordemire turned gracefully and swept away.

As soon as she was out of earshot, Galinda and Zelphira squealed joyfully, dancing around each other in excitement. They burst spontaneously into song, their voices rising cheerfully:

"Tell the Ozian Wizard, we'll meet him in the heart of Oz."

Nearby students looked on, confused yet charmed by the joyful spectacle.

CHANGE

"What would I even wish for?" Galinda wondered aloud, suddenly thoughtful. "I still don't even know."

"You'll know when the time is right."

Their playful moment was interrupted by an announcement from the conductor: "Princess Galinda Fairmoor, your boat has arrived."

Attendants quickly loaded Galinda's and Zelphira's belongings onto the boat. As they did, both girls noticed Coraletta, Marisella, and Fanedra watching silently from afar. When the eye contact grew uncomfortable, the three girls swiftly looked away.

Soon, Galinda's boat sailed out, farther and farther away until the trio became mere specks on the horizon, like three single grains of uncooked rice.

Arriving at the docks, their luggage was loaded onto separate carriages.

Galinda hugged Zelphira tightly. "I'm really going to miss you."

"We'll see each other soon, at Draeth Mor, remember?" Zelphira reassured.

"I know, but still…"

They laughed warmly together once more.

"I arranged a carriage to take you home," Galinda added gently. "Will you be alright Zelly?"

"I'll be fine. Thank you, Glinda."

Galinda shook her head warmly. "Don't mention it."

They hugged again, holding tight before Galinda stepped gracefully into her luxurious Gilded Rose carriage, waving goodbye as it rolled smoothly away.

Zelphira climbed into her own carriage, settling in for the journey *home*—to Raventhorne Farm, back in Munchkinland.

The journey back to Quadling Country was not so much a return as it was a reluctant retreat. Galinda recently unstitched from the curious intimacy she'd found at Oz University, particularly that with the peculiar and inexplicably magnetic Zelphira, found herself marooned in a coach with nothing but velvet cushions and dread to keep her company.

It was not only that she missed Zelphira, though she did, in the way one might miss a thunderstorm: the crash of it, the thrill, the strange silence that follows. But there was also the matter of *home*. Or what passed for it.

She had imagined, vainly, perhaps, that distance and education might have diluted her grievances with Gisella. That the hot water of time would have softened those old knots. But the memory remained vivid: Gisella, pushing her into the water of the magic garden. That single act, petty and evil, had curdled into something far more permanent. A betrayal wearing the skin of play.

The castle loomed ahead in its usual finery: crenelated, grand, and utterly joyless. The gates yawned open without welcome, and the carriage halted with a weary sigh of its own. Galinda descended, careful not to wrinkle her skirt or her composure. The maids scurried, as they always had, like flustered insects with silver trays for hands.

And there, poised like living portraits, stood her parents.

Dainhurst, all paternal benevolence and overcompensated charm, opened his arms as if to embrace not just Galinda but the notion of forgiveness itself. "Welcome home, my little princess! Are you well?"

"I am well, Father. And you?"

"Oh, and not even a glance for me?" Esmelda interjected, her voice honeyed with performative offense. "My daughter returns and suddenly I am but a footstool."

Galinda let out a practiced laugh, the kind that could pass for warmth in a dark room. "I was saving the best for last."

"Flatterer," Esmelda said, kissing both cheeks in quick succession, as if to ward off sincerity.

There was hugging. Enough of it, at least, to satisfy the optics of a happy homecoming. And Galinda, ever the student of social spells, performed it all perfectly.

Only once the initial courtesies had exhausted themselves did she ask: "Where's Gisella?"

Dainhurst's expression flickered, just faintly. "Inside. There's... quite a lot to tell you. Come along now."

The doors shut behind her like punctuation, final, enclosing. Inside, the castle wore its sameness like armour. The carpets had not faded. The walls still whispered.

And there, at the top of the staircase like a well-composed apparition, was Gisella.

She descended with the slow grace of someone used to being watched. Her hair gleamed in obedient curls. Her lips curled in a smile that suggested both amusement and premeditation. But there was something... altered.

A subtle fullness. A weight gathered in one place.

And around her neck, a green crystal, ornate, sharp spiked, exactly identical to the one Dainhurst had gifted Gisella years ago. Only this one looked meaner. Hungrier.

As she drew closer, Galinda's voice betrayed her.

"You're pregnant?"

Gisella's grin widened. She stepped forward and embraced her sister with a suddenness that suggested affection and strategy in equal measure.

"Yes," she murmured, saccharine and smug.

Galinda pulled back. Her words stumbled out in fragments. "But—how? Who?"

"Guess."

Of course. The games had already begun.

"I don't have time for riddles," Galinda muttered, already exasperated.

"Ominson," Gisella said, with the care of someone dropping a match onto dry grass.

Galinda's mouth fell open. "What?"

"I'm carrying Ominson's child, silly."

"He's back?"

"No."

"But… then how? You're lying."

Gisella moved closer, the scent of her perfume now overwhelming. She leaned in, voice a whisper dressed in silk and spite.

"Remember that one time in the garden?"

Galinda stared. A flush rose to her cheeks.

Galinda blinked. "No…" she said, but it was more hope than denial.

"Oh yes, it was a surprise. But a happy one. Aren't you happy for me?"

Galinda didn't answer. She turned to the two thrones of the room, Dainhurst and Esmelda, who, having ceded their authority to spectacle, now observed with a mixture of calculation and conceit.

"I thought princesses—" Galinda's voice faltered, then regained its edge, "were supposed to wait for marriage before having a child?"

Dainhurst gave a dry, almost conspiratorial chuckle. "Oh, in theory. But this is a marvellous turn for her image. The Good Witch, pious, radiant, maternal. The people lap it up like cream."

"And Ominson's father has agreed," Esmelda added, plucking at an invisible thread on her sleeve. "They'll be married the moment he returns from the Wizard's Guard. It's practically divine fate."

A muscle twitched in Gisella's jaw. Small. Almost imperceptible. But Galinda saw it. Felt it.

"Does he know about these… plans?" Galinda asked, leaning forward as if the truth might be hiding in her father's breath.

"Of course not, but he'll do what's required. Boys always do, when you train them early enough."

Gisella said nothing. She simply stood there, the picture of smug serenity, while something serpentine slithered beneath her skin.

Galinda's hands curled into fists, the urge to slap that smile clean off her sister's face burning hot and immediate. But alas, she had her manners. And her sister had a baby.

"Gisella," she said, voice low. "How are you using magic? I read the papers—surely…"

"Right!" Dainhurst clapped once, delighted to be the harbinger of news. "Your sister is a witch now. Officially. A real one this time!" He laughed, as if it were all a joke and he'd written the punchline himself.

"No. That's not possible. Barbarus said—"

"Barbarus can be wrong. Even saints lose their halos in the wash."

"Are you jealous?" Gisella said sweetly, "Poor Galinda. She spent all those years studying spells and scrolls and look who also ends up with magic too. Didn't I tell you I would get magic one day?" she boasted.

Galinda let the silence answer for her.

"Well!" Dainhurst bellowed, clapping again. "Since we're all home and no one's eloped or murdered each other, yet, it's a cause for celebration. We'll have a feast!"

The servants were set into motion with a single gesture, scattering like startled birds.

Within hours, the Fairmoor dining hall was aglow—crystal chandeliers shimmering, cutlery lined in militant rows, and roasted game fuming on platters like passive-aggressive sacrifices.

Dinner, however, was a quiet affair, composed primarily of chewing, swallowing, and the occasional cough to avoid true conversation.

At last, Dainhurst broke the silence. "So, Galinda. Tell me. How was your time at the Wizard's University?"

"It's called Oz University now," Galinda corrected gently, "by the students and the locals. But yes, it was good."

"I read something in the papers, about a special someone? A prince, was it? Though you forgot to write to your dear old popsicle…"

"I didn't forget, I was just very busy, with coursework and, yes, the prince of Winkie Country. But forget you? Never."

He beamed at her, placated.

"Make any new friends?" he asked, spearing a carrot with all the gravitas of a man inquiring about war strategies.

"Yes," she said, and took another sip.

But then Gisella spoke, "I heard a rumour. Something about Galinda parading around campus with some… green girl. A poorling."

Galinda's jaw tensed. The room cooled perceptibly.

"Green?" Dainhurst raised a brow, intrigued. "You mean, like… Quadling? One of the Raindrop Gemz?"

"No, Father," Gisella laughed. "The girl is green. As in, colour. Like this olive." She plucked one from her plate, held it aloft like evidence, and bit into it with flourish.

All eyes turned to Galinda.

Esmelda's voice was less amused, "Is this true?"

Galinda nodded once.

Dainhurst exhaled the sort of sigh that fathers usually reserve for grievous disappointments—"Green skin?" he repeated, as if the words themselves offended. "What disease does she have? Did you learn nothing from me?"

He pointed at her, index finger trembling with fury, and tapped it repeatedly against the table, a drumbeat of old-world authority. "Need I remind you that you are a princess? You cannot associate yourself with… commoners. Especially, a green one. How is that even possible?"

Galinda looked away, cheeks flushed—not with shame, but with the desire to say far more than she dared.

"It ruins the mystique, don't you know?" Gisella added.

Galinda frowned, but she held her voice in a softer register now, as though revealing something private. "Father, she's a sweet girl. Very smart. She helped me at university, in more ways than I can even count. And yes, I understand she isn't wealthy. But she is, without exaggeration, the best thing that happened to me there."

"Better than your prince boyfriend?" Gisella smirked.

"Yes."

Esmelda tilted her head. "If she's not from Quadling Country, then where is she from?"

"Don't say Gillikin," Dainhurst growled, "with their nasty black hair and their dreadful, smelly tinctures—"

"Munchkinland," Galinda replied, almost inaudibly.

The word hit the table like a dropped jewel, small, but piercing.

Dainhurst's face reddened. "Still! Filth, all the same. I don't even understand how the University let such a thing past their gates. But let me be perfectly clear: you are never to see her again. From this day forward, she is not your friend. She is your enemy. Am I understood?!"

Galinda's breath caught in her throat, but she answered in a **high-pitched** chirp, "Yes, Father."

"Good girl," Esmelda purred.

Galinda fell silent, her appetite hollowed out. Her thoughts slipped elsewhere, wandered toward dormitories and laughter in the dark and strange books that whispered back when you opened them. She thought of Zelphira, not as a curiosity, but as a comfort. And of how soon she might escape again.

After dinner, Gisella performed an exaggerated yawn, a hand fluttering to her mouth like a curtain. "I'm positively exhausted. I think I'll retire to my chambers." She gave Galinda a smug little chuckle. "You know, the baby."

Galinda stood abruptly. "I think I'll retire too."

Dainhurst gave a lazy wave of permission, the sort usually reserved for dogs or daughters.

The two ascended the staircase in silence. Their gowns whispered behind them like gossiping servants. Just as Gisella reached her chamber door, Galinda seized her by the arm, dragging her aside with a force that made Gisella's eyes flash.

Galinda's gaze dropped for a second to the swell of her sister's stomach. The sight filled her with something ancient and fierce. Jealousy, perhaps. Or grief. Or something older than either.

She pressed her sister against the wall, her breath hot and her voice just above a growl. "Tell me how you did it."

Gisella blinked innocently. "Oh, you know. Penis to vagina—"

"No, you sick, twisted witch!" Galinda hissed. "How did you manage to get magic? What did you do? Do you have some little lackey casting spells behind a curtain, conjuring tricks while you pose like a saint?"

"Oh, heavens no," Gisella said, her voice honeyed with amusement. With a flick of her wrist, the doors flew open behind her, creaking wide as though the castle itself had been trained to obey her.

Galinda stepped back, startled, breath catching in her throat. Her spine went rigid.

Gisella's laughter erupted, sharp and delighted. "Oh, *that* face. Galinda, if I could bottle the look you're making right now and wear it as perfume, I would. Wouldn't it be fun," she added, almost wistfully, "to let you stew in it forever, trying to solve me like a riddle you were never smart enough to crack?"

"Stop being weird and just tell me," Galinda snapped. "You and I both know you weren't born with magic and you didn't 'bloom late,' Gisella. That's not how it works. It never is."

Gisella's grin sharpened. She turned on her heel, her hair whipping behind her like a silk whip, and with another flick of her hand, the doors slammed shut, right in Galinda's face.

◇

The days that followed were a pageant of unbearable irony. The castle bustled, not with purpose but with ceremony. Reporters strolled in like moths in waistcoats, drawn to the candlelight of scandal. Royal cousins and baronesses with brittle hair and brittle smiles arrived bearing flowers and empty platitudes.

"You'll make such a wonderful mother," they said, bowing to Gisella's belly.

"That child is blessed," crooned another. "To be born to the Good Witch and a princess of the South!"

Galinda stood in the corner of it all like an accidental ghost. She smiled when needed, blinked on cue, and sipped tea like it was poison she didn't want to waste. The headlines made it worse.

GOOD NEWS: THE GOOD WITCH, PRINCESS OF THE SOUTH IS NOW WITH CHILD!

Galinda refused to comment to the press, though many tried.

She wanted out.

And like all things in life, whether delivered by fate, magic, or mail, it arrived. A letter.

Sealed in wax. The crest of Winkie Country pressed delicately into its skin. Inside, a note from Prince Rivero himself, requesting her presence at Draeth Mor.

Galinda's *heart* fluttered like a bird freed from a net. She could see Zelphira again. Just the thought was enough to make the walls of her *home* seem less like stone and more like a sentence.

She waited until the family returned, Dainhurst, Gisella, Esmelda, all freshly powdered and perfumed from their latest parade of public opinion.

She met her father at the door.

"Father," she asked, voice light with the tremble of anticipation, "do you mind if I travel to Winkie Country?"

"Whatever for?"

"Remember when we visited the Vinkus many sun-moons ago? I've always wanted to go back. And Prince Rivero, he invited me to meet with his father. Again."

He hummed, eyes narrowing. "You *have* been cooped up a while. A little change might do you good. Even if the air there is far less refined than ours." He chuckled at his own joke, oblivious or indifferent to the weight of her longing. "Yes, I suppose change can be good."

"So... is that a yes?"

"It is. Though someday I'd like to meet this Prince Rivero of yours. A father must know where his daughter's interests lie."

She smiled, managing a curtsy.

But Gisella, of course, had something to say, "Galinda, I hope you're not sneaking off to meet that green girl Father forbade you to see?"

Galinda's voice pitched up, all innocence and artifice. "No! Of course not."

"Very well," Esmelda murmured, bored with the scene. "I hope you enjoy yourself."

Galinda barely heard her, already flying up the stairs, trailing silks like a comet. In her room, she packed as though she were fleeing the scene of a crime. Gowns for every weather, twisters, hail, sleet, shame. She packed as if she were leaving forever.

◇

By morning, Galinda Arduelle Fairmoor was gone.

On the road.

Bound for Winkie Country.

And, though none yet knew it, bound for the only part of herself she had not yet met.

CHAPTER 38

The Western Sky

The Gilded Rose, Galinda's royal carriage trimmed in pale gold and stitched with the embroidered sigil of House Fairmoor, creaked to a halt beneath the towering shadows of the Vinkus' castle. It was still vast, granite-faced, and gloomy as myth—its high turrets piercing the grey, stagnant sky. The clouds threatened rain like a half-made promise, but none fell. As if even the weather respected the house's refusal to be hurried.

Galinda stepped out, her shoes clicking against ancient stone, and approached the great door—carved with images of Winkie ancestors locked in eternal battle and brooding posture. She raised a hand and knocked. The doors opened at once, without protest or a groan, as if she'd been expected since birth.

Guards stood lined along the corridor's interior, expressionless and rigid, their weapons polished like ceremonial bones. Their eyes didn't move. Only their presence communicated: *You are being watched.*

Then, at the far end of the long and shadowed hallway, a familiar figure emerged, first as a silhouette, then with colour, then with warmth.

River.

His gait quickened from a stroll into a jog, then into a clumsy sprint, his arms swinging slightly out of rhythm with his noble posture.

"You made it!" He beamed. "How was your ryde?"

Galinda gave a delicate laugh. "Apparently, I've been more sleep-deprived than I thought, I slept the entire journey. Like a princess under a spell."

"You *look* wide awake now," he said, with a grin that made his words feel almost conspiratorial.

She matched his grin. "Is Zelly here?"

"She's not coming."

Galinda's heart jumped in her throat. "What? But I thought—"

"I'm jesting," he broke into a laugh. "She's in the main hall. Honestly, your face… priceless."

CHANGE

Galinda scowled, then laughed despite herself. She gave him a light jab in the arm. "You're impossible."

"Race you," she said, and with no further warning, bolted down the corridor like a comet in silk.

River blinked. "Hey—! That's cheating!"

He chased after her, but she was already halfway there, her laughter echoing off the walls like a spell breaking gloom.

The grand hall unfolded before her like the interior of a cathedral dedicated to shadows and ancestry. And there, sitting cross-legged on the velvet-draped divan, a novel in hand, lavender in the air—was the girl she had longed to see more than anything else.

Green as ever.

"*Zelly!*" Galinda shouted, running toward her.

Zelphira looked up. Her eyes widened. "*Glinda!*"

They collided in a hug that felt more like a reunion of souls than friends, a full-bodied embrace that erased time and status and kingdoms. For a long moment, they simply held on.

River arrived behind them, huffing, feigning injury. "You two were apart for, what—an Oz'moon? And now you're acting like it's been a full century of exile."

"Are you jealous?" Zelphira teased, glancing over her shoulder.

"Only a little," River replied, crossing his arms and scoffing in mock offense. They all laughed.

Galinda caught her breath, smoothing her hair. "Are we the only ones coming tonight?"

"No," River replied. "Some of my boys will be here, and a few girls too, though they're not staying. You two," he added, gesturing, "are welcome to stay as long as you like. The castle's been bored stiff without you."

"Perfect," Galinda said, eyes glinting. "This is going to be a *twist.*"

Their joy, however, was interrupted by the unmistakable thunder of bootsteps approaching.

Galinda didn't need to look. She *knew* that gait, its gravity, its warning. She stood taller as the doors groaned open once again.

There, framed in the archway like a monument to another age, stood the Vinkus himself. A tower of a man with eyes as deep as dusk and presence like a spell cast over the entire room. His heavy cloak billowed even without wind.

"Hello, Father," River said, stepping forward but glancing sideways to Galinda and Zelphira. "He's not that scary," he whispered. "He's a big softie."

A beat.

"Sometimes."

"I *hear* you," rumbled the Vinkus. Before River could react, the man swooped in and seized his son in a headlock, knuckle-rubbing his scalp with the grace of a bear.

"Ouch! You're embarrassing me!" River whined, half-laughing, half on the verge of tears.

The Vinkus let him go with a bellowing laugh that echoed off the castle's high ceilings like war drums played in jest. River rubbed his head tenderly, his eyes shimmering with the betrayal only a son could feel at the hands of an affectionate father.

Galinda and Zelphira exchanged a glance.

It took every last ounce of decorum to not erupt with laughter on the spot.

Then the Vinkus turned, straightening his furs and posture as if remembering he was royalty and not a wrestling uncle. His voice shifted slightly, still booming, but with the cadence of a man remembering his part in the script.

"I am Vinkus. King of Winkies. You tell me now who you are."

Galinda stepped forward, curtsying with just enough flair to earn admiration without seeming desperate for it. "I'm Galinda. You may not remember, but we met some sun-moons ago."

The Vinkus squinted one eye. "Is it so? I does not remember you!"

"I came with the Good Witch and my father. You gave me a golden medal for helping with the western civil dispute."

Zelphira's eyebrows crept upward, intrigued.

"Ah!" he snapped his fingers. "*That* you! Why you no say that first?" He beamed suddenly, stepping forward and wrapping Galinda in an enormous, enveloping hug.

Galinda let out a small gasp, her ribs pressing against his fur-lined armour. He smelled of firewood, steel, and old leather. His warmth wasn't just heat, it was pressure, history, gravity. She blinked rapidly, suddenly, almost unwillingly moved.

He set her down, still peering at her as if trying to solve a riddle written in silk.

"You look very… *different*, aye little one? Not so little now! You grown up like sunflower in storm. What happen to you?"

"It's a long story."

"Then it must be good one," he said, chuckling. "You welcome here. You stay long as you like. Even forever—then Rivero can marry nice, pretty girl like you."

He leaned in, his voice a low whisper in her ear: "He need smart woman, cause without one, his head fly off! No one to hold it down!" He let out another great laugh.

Galinda giggled, flattered but mostly amused.

Then his attention shifted, his face sharpening.

"You!" he barked, pointing behind her. "Come forward."

Zelphira stepped forward with deliberate calm. The firelight struck her green skin and made it glisten like moss in moonlight. As she emerged fully, silence fell over the room.

CHANGE

The Vinkus' eyes widened. "You is green?" he said, nearly recoiling. "What in Oz is *this*?"

"Yes," Zelphira said, raising her chin. She extended a hand without hesitation. "My name is Zelphira Raventhorne."

The Vinkus eyed the hand suspiciously, then blinked. "Why you green?"

"I was born this way."

"Hmm." His brows furrowed. "Where you from, green girl?"

"Munchkinland."

"The little people land?" he barked with sudden uncontrollable laughter. "But you not so little! You too tall for that!"

"There are tall people too," Zelphira said, standing straighter. "And we're nothing to laugh at. We deserve the same respect you expect."

The Vinkus' grin faded like the last glow in a dying fire. He studied her—this green girl, this strange guest who dared correct a king.

And then, to everyone's surprise, he nodded. Slowly. Solemnly.

"I like you, green one." He placed a massive, heavy hand on her shoulder, firm, but not cruel. "You strong girl. You be good leader one day. Maybe better than most men I know."

He turned to River. "You learn from green one and little one if you are to be king one day. Very different lessons, yes, but both important. You need learn from both. You hear me?"

River nodded, slowly, respectfully, but there was a telltale pink blooming at his ears. The weight of his father's praise (and expectations) always came wrapped in discomfort, like shoes that pinched just slightly at the toes.

Then the Vinkus turned again to Zelphira. "You know, green one... if you ever need place to stay, you come here. You welcome, same as Galinda. This castle is yours when you want it."

Zelphira blinked, caught somewhere between gratitude and disbelief. "Are you sure?" she asked cautiously.

"Do I look like king who is *not sure* of what he say?"

"No, you do not!"

With a satisfied grunt, the Vinkus clasped her hand in his massive one and gave it a firm, earth-shaking shake. He did the same for Galinda, less a handshake, more a ceremonial jostle, and then moved to River, whom he greeted not with affection but with a boulder-sized slap on the back that nearly bent the poor prince in half.

River wheezed, visibly trembling from the impact, and attempted to recover with dignity as his father strode out of the chamber, the doors shutting behind him with a final *thud*.

Silence followed for a beat. Then—

"Well," River said, exhaling dramatically, "*that* went well."

His eyes darted to the walls, the ceiling, the corners, anywhere but the two girls beside him, as if searching for a piece of himself he'd misplaced during the encounter.

Zelphira cracked a smile. "I think he likes me."

River straightened his shoulders, still rubbing the sore spot where his father had nearly clapped his spine out of alignment. "Of course he likes you! My father doesn't just welcome *anybody* to the Western Sky, let alone *Draeth Mor*, like it's their own hearthstone."

"What does Draeth Mor even mean?" Galinda asked, her voice drifting upward as she gazed at the high, arched ceiling and the carvings that twisted along the rafters like ivy turned to stone.

Draeth Mor.

"It means 'place between the storms,'" River said. "At least in the old Winkie tongue. Most don't use the name anymore. They call it 'The Vinkus' Castle' like it's just a title. But the castle's older than the Vinkus. It remembers everything. You'll see."

Zelphira raised an eyebrow. "That sounds… haunting."

"Depends on what you're hiding from."

Galinda twirled a strand of her hair, eyes narrowing in mock suspicion. "Is *that* why there are gargoyle heads carved into every fireplace? They're not for decoration, are they?"

"Nope," River replied cheerily. "They're for judgment."

The three of them fell into laughter again.

Zelphira crossed her arms. "Well, if Draeth Mor accepts me, maybe I'll stay a little longer than planned."

Galinda glanced sideways at her. "I wouldn't mind that."

✧

The days slipped past like loose grains in a sieve, impermanent and shimmering in their insignificance. In the western reaches of *Draeth Mor*—where castle walls leaned like tired old men and the air smelled of dried petals and burnt sugar—the Vinkus was a ghost by daylight, off consorting with matters of state or wine or women or all three. River had taken to treating the days of his father's absence like national holidays of the self. He hosted bacchanalias for one, with streamers of indulgence and confetti made of consequence shredded to pieces.

But Galinda and Zelphira—ah, Galinda and Zelphira—chose seclusion over spectacle. They'd turned Zelphira's chamber into a cocoon of silk and sighs, despite being allotted their own separate wings of the castle. There, amid tapestries of starlit beasts and moth-eaten volumes of forgotten lore, they fell into the comfortable war of literature: reading aloud, bickering over protagonists with more passion than either would admit they possessed.

They wandered the gardens, a mess of thorns that spawned the brightest red poppies, the colour of fresh wounds. They dined on confections too exotic for names,

Jellied Mushrooms, Sweetroot pastries, Skyfruit Tarts, and occasionally, if River managed to drag himself from whatever sybaritic oblivion he'd found the night before, he joined them. He'd sip half-heartedly at tea, pretend to follow their chatter of plot and metaphor, and later whisk Galinda away to rediscover the geography of her body like an old map he feared forgetting.

Letters came for Galinda. From **home**. From responsibilities. From somewhere beyond the perfume of roses and the echo of Zelphira's laugh. She answered none. At first, she composed excuses of silk. Then linen. Then sackcloth. Eventually, not at all. The letters stopped. Good. Just what she wanted. And yet, wasn't there a violence in being forgotten?

◇

Two full Oz'moons passed in Draeth Mor. The Vinkus, whose appetite for company had evidently expanded beyond wine and war, extended their stay indefinitely. The castle, he said, had never felt more alive. And perhaps it had. For what is life, if not a garden of borrowed delights and the illusion that they will last?

Until—

One blistering afternoon, the kind where even the bees buzzed irritably and the stones underfoot burned with quiet spite, the girls lay in the garden with books pressed against their chests and Orange Sunberry juice dripping condensation down the sides of their glasses. They were cross-legged on a blanket stitched with images of mythical creatures, the grass itchy beneath their calves, the sky an uninterrupted sheet of brilliance overhead.

Then came the chime.

Not the chime of bells, nor time, but something stranger: a sound like childhood music boxes possessed by foreboding. Galinda shaded her eyes, squinting toward the sky where a speck resolved itself—a floating contraption, ridiculous in design, like a child's toy with delusions of grandeur. A miniature hot air balloon, red and white stripes with an emerald-crusted basket that glittered with ostentation.

"Zelly, look!" Galinda whispered with the urgency of prophecy, tapping her on the thigh.

"Mmm?" Zelphira grunted, nose still buried in her book, as though fiction could shield her from fate. "Can it wait? I'm at the part where the prince realizes he's in love with his enemy."

"No, it absolutely cannot."

With the sigh of someone who had been forced to pause just before a crescendo, Zelphira placed the book facedown beside her. She looked skyward.

A miniature hot air balloon, red and white stripes with a green basket trimmed in gleaming stones, was descending slowly, deliberately, like a child's toy possessed by intent. It chimed gently as it floated, as though announcing its own arrival with the self-importance of a dinner guest.

"What in the name of Lurline is *that*?" Zelphira muttered, more annoyed than alarmed.

"No idea," Galinda whispered, delighted. "But it's *beautiful!*"

The balloon touched down between them with ceremonial daintiness. Inside the basket: a folded parchment sealed in wax.

Zelphira tilted her head. "Someone sent us a letter *like this*? This seems... excessive."

"And excessive is often exquisite," Galinda said, reaching toward the basket but stopping short.

Zelphira reached instead. Her fingers, long, unadorned, vaguely ink-stained—plucked the letter from its velvet cradle. She turned it over, then went still.

The wax seal bore the unmistakable sigil of the Wizard.

Zelphira inhaled sharply. "It can't be."

"What? What is it?" Galinda sprang up, her voice rising like steam, pacing the blanket's edge in increasingly urgent little steps. "Show me!"

Zelphira held it up. Written in impossibly fine script, curved like smoke and vanity, the front read:

To: Mizz Zelphira Grimbelle Raventhorne.

Galinda gasped. "It *can't* be! Oh Oz!" Her whole body sprang to life with theatrical flair, pacing as if the floor beneath her were a war room. She tapped her fingers against her chin with mechanical precision, already plotting ten steps ahead, as if summoned herself. "Open it!"

But Zelphira didn't move. Her fingers, so often steadied by the weight of books and thought, now trembled as if carrying something far heavier than parchment and wax.

"I—" She looked at Galinda, her voice barely more than breath. "I can't. Look at my hands." She raised them, half in awe, half in fear. "They're shaking."

Galinda, ever the noble understudy in life's grand performance, took the letter gently, like a chalice in a sacred rite. She cracked the seal, as though doing so would release a genie or a ghost and unfolded the parchment with almost reverent slowness. Zelphira's eyes widened, her anticipation a volatile mix of dread and delight.

Galinda cleared her throat. She always did so before performing.

Dear Mizz Zelphira Grimbelle Raventhorne,

I write this letter to you as a personal invitation to the Emerald City to visit The Great, The Powerful, The Wonderful Wizard of Oz.

This invitation is non-transferable, though, it shall accommodate only two parties.

The Wizard expects you promptly at the 13th hour on Wandnesday.

Yours Wonderfully,
The Wizard of Oz

"*Wandnesday?*" Galinda echoed, looking up with a grin blooming like dawn itself. "But that's *tomorrow!*"

"Tomorrow?" Zelphira's voice cracked like glass. "That's—oh Oz—we have to *pack!*"

"We have to pack *now!*" Galinda shrieked, already half-running. Books and juice glasses forgotten, they scrambled to their feet and dashed toward the castle like two storm gusts in petticoats, chanting in singsong:

"Tell the Ozian Wizard, we'll meet him in the heart of Oz."

Behind them, the little balloon gave one last theatrical chime before lifting again into the sky. It floated upward with calm finality, a wind-borne emissary returning to its emerald sender.

Inside, Galinda burst into her room, flung her satchel onto the floor, and tore through her dresses like a tornado—velvet, cashmere and silk. Each outfit was critiqued against one impossible criterion: *Which one says, I am not merely beautiful—I am worthy?*

Zelphira, for her part, knew. She had already chosen. Her knowing was not just sartorial, it was strategic. She would not arrive garbed in wonder. She would arrive in armour.

Moments later, Galinda bounced into Zelphira's room and threw herself on the bed, sighing in disbelief, wonder, hope, love—all of it. "Can you believe it?" she whispered, hugging a pillow like it might reply. "The Wizard. *The Wizard.* But what matters most, Zelly, you're going to get what your heart has always wanted."

Their joy was loud enough to stir River from the depths of his usual decadent sleep. He appeared at the doorway, hair tousled like a fallen prince, expression pinched with the dramatic suffering of the perpetually misunderstood.

"What's with the commotion?" he muttered. "Can't you tell a man is trying to get some sleep?"

Galinda jumped up. "River you wouldn't believe what Zelphira just got."

"Spill!"

"The Wizard himself!" Galinda declared, "Just invited her for a meeting in the Emerald City!" flinging her arms wide as though she'd conjured him herself.

"*No way!*" River's eyes widened, suddenly very awake.

"Yes way. And we have to leave at sunrise. *Tomorrow!* Of course! She's allowed one companion, and *I'm* the chosen one!" Galinda twirled, sheer delight oozing from every fingertip.

River clutched at his heart, mock-wounded. "Woz. Left out. Again. I have dreams too, you know. Desires, for a wardrobe full of emeralds, even."

"Sorry, River," Zelphira said gently, though there was something steely beneath the softness. "I made Galinda a promise."

"Fine, fine, but bring me back a souvenir."

"Deal," Zelphira grinned.

"I'll have the carriages readied by sunrise," he said with a shrug, disappearing again into his shadows.

Once gone, the girls squealed anew, falling into laughter and whispers and dreams as the golden sun dipped low. The hours would move slower now, taunting, tender, unbearable. Tomorrow, the Emerald City. Tomorrow, the Wizard. Tomorrow, destiny.

✧

That night, sleep came like a shy servant—reluctant, late, and always turning back at the threshold. Galinda and Zelphira lay in separate rooms, but their restlessness was the same tune played in different keys.

They closed their eyes, feigned breathing patterns, contorted themselves into poses of slumber as if convincing the body might persuade the mind. But it was a charade, easily unravelled by the tiniest whisper of thought.

For Zelphira, it was worse.

She lay twisted in her sheets like seaweed caught on a rock, tossing from left to right, right to left, then back again, hoping the movement would scatter the thoughts collecting like stormclouds in her mind.

Was he truly as powerful as they say?

Could he really grant her heart's desire?

Would he hate her despite being the same colour as the same emeralds he coveted so much?

The questions were persistent and, worse, unanswered.

And still, somehow, just before dawn painted the edges of the sky with its grey-blue sigh, Zelphira drifted into a reluctant sleep. And of course, she dreamed of him. The Wizard. Nothing but the Wizard.

✧

River had returned from his ventures, some half-secret gallivanting through Winkie Country, and arrived back at Draeth Mor like a wind returning to its cave. He knocked on both doors at once, each rap impatient but affectionate.

"Time to rise, witches," he called through the corridor.

They'd had only scraps of rest, no more than two hours tucked in among questions and dreams. And yet, they felt awake. More awake than they had been in months.

They had *purpose*.

They washed in steaming baths, scented with lilac root and peony sap. Galinda applied her potions and painted her lips like an artist preparing for judgment.

Zelphira ran her comb through her black hair and dressed slowly, carefully, as though armouring herself for something more than just a journey.

At last, they met at the top of the stairs, bags in hand, hearts half in their chests and half already gone to the Emerald City.

Galinda was first to descend, in her pink skirt and blazer; that showed just how *Sophisticated* she was. She stood at the base, tapping the toe of her polished shoe on the marble, a rhythm of nerves. When she finally looked up, she froze.

Zelphira appeared at the landing, and behind her, only metaphorically, and yet undeniably, a shadow dragged itself like a memory. She wore her cloak: that strange, weather-beaten garment that looked like it had been stitched by wind and time itself. And upon her head sat the infamous hat. Wide-brimmed. Ancient. Assertive.

Galinda blinked. Bowed her head. Silence spun out between them, as reverent as it was awkward.

"Zelly, I—um—are you *sure* you want to wear that?"

"Did you think I was jesting when I said I loved this cloak and hat?"

"Yes?"

"Well, I *do* love it. And I *am* wearing it. I think the Wizard will appreciate the statement."

Galinda sighed, but the edges of her frown were soft. "Very well. Still… I think you look magnificent in it."

Zelphira smiled, stepped forward, and pulled her into a warm, grounding embrace.

River dashed down moments later, smelling faintly of sandalwood and sin, his shirt half-buttoned and eyes still glazed with sleep. He enveloped Zelphira in a hug that could have broken ribs, then turned to Galinda. For a moment he faltered, arms twitching in indecision, then settled on a kiss to her cheek. It lingered a half-second too long.

"Have a safe journey, you maddening creatures," he said, stepping back. "Bring something back. A scandal. A curse. A good story at least."

Galinda and Zelphira laughed and slipped into the waiting carriage.

The Gilded Rose shimmered like a moving shrine, its wheels charmed to silence. It smelled of crushed petals and ambition. A vehicle fit for a meeting with myth.

River waved from the archway as the sun crested the hills. "You'll tell me *everything!*" he called.

Galinda blew him a kiss. Zelphira waved.

And together, the girls rode toward the Emerald City. Toward the Wizard. Toward the unravelling of everything they thought they knew.

The two sisters sat opposite each other in the carriage, laughing at the sheer absurdity of it all. Of all the people in Oz, *they* had been chosen, summoned by the Wizard himself. The notion felt like a dream stitched from green velvet and gold.

Galinda leaned forward slightly. "How are you feeling?"

Zelphira let out a half-laugh. "How do you *think*? I feel like if I'm not nailed to the floor, I'll fly away."

"It's nerve-wracking, isn't it?"

"I'm more nervous to meet the Wizard than I'd be to meet the One Gohd," Zelphira admitted. "Isn't that ridiculous?"

"Not at all, it's perfectly understandable."

They both turned to peer out the window as the Yellow Brick Road stretched ahead of them, winding like a ribbon through the emerald-green hills. Crowds bustled along the path—traders, travellers, children with wind-spun toys.

Zelphira pointed suddenly. "Animals!"

A monkey stood near a streetlamp, nose deep in the *Book of Ozma*.

Galinda nodded. "Most of the remaining Animals live here now. It's one of the few safe places left for them."

"Woz… It's like whoever's behind their disappearance is afraid of the Wizard. Like they're only safe becoz he's watching."

Galinda gave a solemn nod. "Yes."

Zelphira leaned back into her seat, letting out another sigh, but this time, it was steadier. "I think I'm more calm now."

◇

They rode for another thirty Oz'mins, lulled into a quiet anticipation. When they looked out the window again, Zelphira's eyes widened.

There it stood—the *Emerald Tower*.

Soaring into the clouds, carved with patterns that shimmered under the sun, its spires glittered like gemstones made from magic itself.

"We're here!" they said in unison.

They scrambled to grab their bags. Zelphira adjusted her cloak and pressed her hat tighter on her head.

When the carriage stopped, she stepped out and twirled slowly in place, fingers at her lips as she took in the bustle around her. Shops lined the street with enchanted window displays, sweet smells drifted from bakeries, and Ozians of every stripe and shade strolled the cobblestones in robes, silks, and sparkled finery.

"This is *amazing*," Zelphira whispered.

Galinda smiled. "If we finish early, I'll show you all the best shops, and the tastiest places to eat."

"How many times have you been here, *princess*?"

"Only once."

"Only once? But you're as rich as they come! This place is *designed* for people like you. Your father could probably *buy* half the city."

"Well… I lived a different life before my *bibbidi-bobbidi-boo*."

"*Bibbidi-bobbidi-boo?*"

"You heard me," Galinda grinned.

Zelphira extended her hand, and Galinda took it without hesitation. Together they drifted into the crowd, Zelphira's cloak sweeping behind her like a dark tide, parting the crowd wherever they walked.

And then, they saw it.

The great gates of the *Emerald Tower.*

Tall as a cathedral and twice as enchanted, they stood rigid, shut and locked but welcoming nonetheless, just enough to suggest: *you might be given entry, but nothing comes out unchanged.*

Still hand in hand, Galinda and Zelphira stood at the gates, nerves buzzing beneath their skin. Only two Oz'mins remained until the 13th Hour. The guards posted at either side were statuesque in their stoicism, but behind the polished armour and fixed expressions, the occasional sideways glance was exchanged—were they amused by Zelphira's bold outfit, or quietly sharing in the girls' excitement? It was impossible to tell.

"It's the Thirteenth Hour," Zelphira whispered.

"Where's the letter?" Galinda asked, already searching her sleeves as though she might have it tucked there.

Zelphira reached her long fingers into the depths of her heavy bag and pulled it out, the parchment slightly creased from its time inside. She offered it to the nearest guard, a tall, muscled figure whose permanent scowl looked carved from stone.

He grunted, took the letter, opened it with one gloved hand, and let out a low, unimpressed "Hmm." Then, sucking his teeth with theatrical disdain, he announced in a booming voice, "Open the gates!"

A pause.

Then with a great mechanical clunk, the emerald gates slowly creaked apart, revealing the splendour of the world beyond.

The girls exhaled in unison. They took a step forward, up the gleaming staircase flanked by towering marble pots bursting with soft pink flowers, and entered the green universe that awaited them.

Emeralds glittered on every surface, and as the sunlight poured through the high glass ceiling, the reflections bounced off the walls with blinding brilliance. Galinda winced, shielding her eyes.

"Here," the guard barked, stepping forward and shoving two spectacles into their hands.

Galinda blinked at them. "What are these for?"

"What do you *think* spectacles are for? They're for your eyes. Unless you'd prefer to keep squinting and go blind."

Galinda gave him a sweet smile as she slid the light-green spectacles with emerald lenses onto her face. "You're a little grumpy, aren't you?"

The guard remained unmoved.

Zelphira put hers on too. "Do you have a name, or should we just keep calling you 'Grumpy'?"

He sighed with the exhaustion of someone constantly surrounded by optimism. "Chisterus. Most people call me *Chase*."

"*Chase?* Why not Chester? That seems like the obvious choice"

"Becoz I'm the fastest—and the deadliest," he said flatly, his hand resting on the long blade strapped across his back.

That silenced them. The girls exchanged a glance and decided it was best to continue quietly.

The hallway they now entered stretched long and grand, flanked by relics of Ozian history. Each artifact sat behind crystal cases, labelled with gold plaques and short descriptions. Galinda, ever the scholar of the strange, drifted from display to display, her eyes wide and darting.

There it was, *Fiora's Magical Hairbrush*.

Gunther's Axe.

Ozma's Crown.

Then, she stopped. Frozen.

Seraphina's Magic Wand.

Galinda gasped and ran toward it, her breath catching in her throat as her hands hovered just above the glass. She blinked, then blinked again. Was she hallucinating?

No. It was really there.

The wand stood tall and long beneath a crystal enclosure, its body slender and smooth, ending in a jagged star-shaped head. It was marvellous. Grand. Beautiful. But strangely... lifeless.

"So *this* is where it's been all this time," Galinda whispered, breathless.

This was the wand said to be powerful enough to bend kingdoms to its will—the very one used to threaten all of Oz. The wand partly responsible for almost ruining her life.

Zelphira had kept walking, until she realized Galinda was no longer beside her. She turned to find her friend frozen before the artifact, mouth agape.

"What's that? And why is your mouth open like you're catching flies?" Zelphira asked, bemused.

Chase, their ever-impatient escort, turned and barked, "Don't make me come back there and drag you forward!"

Galinda blinked, jolted from her trance, and quickly rejoined Zelphira. Their heels echoed sharply on the marble floor as they jogged to catch up with the ominous guard.

At last, they arrived at a set of massive gold double doors, the handles shaped from glowing emerald orbs.

"The Wizard is ready for you," Chase said, extending his hand. "Sunglasses, now."

They removed their green-tinted spectacles and passed them over. Chase snatched them with his usual grunt and stalked off without another word.

Zelphira stood still, exhaling. She'd been doing a lot of that lately.

Galinda turned to her, eyes soft. "This is it. We can change everything today, you can finally start your mission to save the Animals, and I can make my name in Ozian politics."

Zelphira hesitated, her fingers clutched tightly around the strap of her bag. "I don't know," she murmured. "I always thought I was brave... but now that I'm here— this is everything I've ever wanted. And he... he might be the only other person, other than you, who will accept me as I am."

Galinda stepped closer. "Listen to me, Zelphira *Grimbelle* Raventhorne. You can do this. You can do *anything.*"

Zelphira smiled faintly, drew in a breath, and pushed the golden doors open.

The throne room was dark. Silent.

It was the kind of stillness that made the air feel too thick, too quiet—like standing in *Tempest Graveyard* back in Winkie Country. The kind of silence that made you wonder what was listening.

Zelphira froze just a step in. The silence crawled up her spine like frost. She instinctively turned to go back, but Galinda held her hand tight, steadying her.

They began to bicker in whispers—Zelphira trying to retreat, Galinda gently insisting. But beneath it all, Zelphira drew strength from her friend's steadiness. In her presence, Zelphira felt like she carried the force of a thousand soldiers.

Then it happened.

A wall of fire *erupted* just ahead, causing them both to leap back. A fierce gust of wind followed, though there were no windows or visible source.

Loud. Terrible. Thunder in human speech.

"I am Oz, the Great and Terrible!"

From behind a moss-draped veil, an enormous *mechanical head* surged forward, its eyes glowing and mouth wide.

"Step forward and introduce yourself!"

Galinda stepped forward without hesitation. "I am Galinda," she said proudly. Then, glancing back—"And this is Zelphira."

"*Zelphira?*" the voice now whispered, shrill and unnerving, like ten thousand mice scratching inside the walls.

Another explosion of fire.

The great head twitched, gears groaning. Then, it *stopped.*

The machinery powered down with a heavy *clunk.*

Suddenly, every light in the room flared to life.

And then, footsteps.

From behind the curtain emerged a man, walking with a steady, deliberate grace. Strands of grey and silver sitting on his head, soft yet thick and a well-groomed moustache perched above his lip. He carried a cane, black lacquer with a large emerald affixed to the top, glinting like a frozen drop of envy.

He stopped just past the curtain and stared directly at Zelphira.

"Tilda?" he whispered, barely audible.

Galinda and Zelphira exchanged a glance.

Zelphira tilted her head. "Who's Tilda?"

The man didn't answer, only continued examining her green skin, his gaze filled with something between memory and disbelief.

Zelphira had more pressing questions. "Are you the—"

"The one and only!" he said, suddenly animated. With a sweeping bow and a wide grin, he added, "Oz. At your service."

Galinda curtsied with grace. Zelphira, though clumsier, followed her lead.

Zelphira was wide-eyed, nearly breathless. She looked to Galinda, glowing with excitement, and had to physically restrain herself from bouncing in place.

She turned back to the Wizard.

"I might've misheard, but... did you say '*The Great and Terrible*'?"

"I did!" the Wizard said proudly. "Been using it for ages, but it never quite caught on. The people seem to prefer 'Great and Powerful.' So, well, who am I to argue with the masses? Whatever they want goes." He laughed.

Galinda smiled, nodding in agreement.

Suddenly, the Wizard gasped and reached toward the side of Zelphira's head. "Oh! What's that?"

Zelphira stiffened. "What? What is it?" she asked, mortified. *Did she have an insect in her hair?*

He withdrew his hand with a dramatic flourish—and in it, a gold coin.

"This," he said, "is for you. Keep it. Cherish it for all your days."

He placed it in her palm, and Zelphira stared at it in wonder.

"Sorcery," she whispered, awed. "You really are magic."

Galinda stepped forward, practically glowing.

"I'm not sure if you remember me," she said brightly. "We met a few sun-moons ago—"

"I do not, I'm afraid, though I don't know how I could forget a pretty face like yours." He squinted. "What did you say your name was again? *Belinda?*"

She whispered, with a patient smile, "*Galinda.*"

But he had already moved on.

They followed him down the hallway, his polished boots clicking loudly, his cane tapping in perfect rhythm.

"I know you're wondering why I summoned you, my precious Zelphira," he said, not turning back.

"Yes, your Ozness."

The Wizard sighed, his voice turning thoughtful. "I have always longed to be a father. But fate, well, has never been so kind to grant me that wish. So instead, I look for those like you... those who've been mistreated, overlooked. I take them in. Guide them. Love them."

He paused.

"I offer them a new path. One of purpose. Of immense good—for the sake of Oz. Does that sound like something you'd want, Zelphira? To be with me? As father and daughter?"

Zelphira's breath hitched. Her heart soared.

"Yes, your Ozness! I would love that more than anything in the world."

Galinda smiled, marvelling at how Zelphira's eyes sparked with a light she'd never seen before, something raw, unguarded. *Hope.*

The Wizard smiled warmly. "Lady Mordemire speaks very highly of you. She says you're exceptional, the finest student she's ever taught. Is that true?"

"Uh—I think so?"

Galinda elbowed her gently, mouthing, *Say yes.*

"Yes. I mean, yes... I try to be."

"Then surely, you know your purpose here. Why you've been granted this meeting."

"Sorry, your Ozness... I don't."

"To prove yourself, of course!" he cried, spinning theatrically on the spot.

"Oh! Right, of course!" Zelphira said, softly smacking her forehead. She jolted upright, flustered at her own forgetfulness.

"Only then will I grant your heart's truest desire."

A beat.

"So tell me... what have you chosen to show me today?"

Zelphira smiled, then reached into her bag. Her arms trembled slightly as she pulled free a thick, dark tome, its leather cover worn, etched with faded sigils that pulsed faintly under the emerald light.

"I brought this," she said. "An ancient spellbook. I'm sure you know what it is. I thought I could read from it to prove myself."

Galinda's eyes went wide, her expression shifting to pure horror.

The Grimorium.

Why in Oz would Zelphira bring *that*—and worse, reveal it to the Wizard?

Galinda subtly shook her head, mouthing *put it away,* but it was too late.

The Wizard turned, eyes locking onto the tome. He gasped.

"Is that...?" He stepped forward, voice breathless. *"The Kitab Malum?"*

"Yes! And I thought reading from it might prove my worth," Zelphira said, beaming, her eyes alight with excitement.

The Wizard's expression darkened. "Did you *steal* it? How do you have that?!"

"I didn't steal it."

"Do you *know* what that book is capable of? The horrors it holds?"

"I do," she replied calmly. "But it's not all darkness. There's good in it too, spells that could heal, protect, even grow life where there is none." She tapped the cover lightly. "If I could just show you—"

The Wizard studied her, his gaze lingering on the certainty in her face.

Finally, he stepped back. "Fine. Prove your worth."

Zelphira lowered the book to the floor, took a steadying breath, and opened it. The pages began to turn on their own, flicking faster and faster, then suddenly stopped.

The Evergarden Spell.

She whispered the ancient words:

Bismi Rahma Nur'al Qalb Aben Takeya Aben Kanaf Ayatin.

Her hands began to glow, light bursting from her palms until it filled the entire chamber—warm, golden, radiant. She placed her hands to the floor.

The feeling: euphoric. Like she was finally letting loose of the emotions she had kept hidden for so long.

The marble rippled beneath her touch, and suddenly—like wildfire—lush green grass spread from her fingertips, consuming the cold stone beneath them. Vines twisted up the columns, flowering in vibrant shades. Blossoms bloomed in seconds. Trees sprouted skyward. The throne room transformed before their eyes into a living garden.

The Wizard stumbled back, trying to outrun the growing field, but the grass overtook him.

Where once stood a throne room of emerald and stone now bloomed an ethereal garden.

Galinda stood speechless. She turned to Zelphira, eyes wide, voice trembling. "Zelphira… your magic! In the name of Ozma, Lurline, and the One Gohd—how?!"

The Wizard dropped his cane.

"Can you remove the spell?" he asked, breath caught in his throat as his mouth gaped as he took in the garden throne room.

"You mean cease it?"

"Yes."

Zelphira closed her eyes. The light in her palms faded. She touched the ground again—and within seconds, the magic receded. The grass vanished. The vines withered back into nothing. The marble floor gleamed, untouched. It was as if the garden had never existed.

Silence.

Then, the Wizard spoke, voice low.

"How are you reading it? Who taught you how?"

"No one, I've always been able to. I can't really explain it."

The Wizard stepped forward briskly. "Let me see the book."

Zelphira tensed. "I've shown you my magic. Don't I get my heart's desire?"

"After I see the book," he snapped, though his voice carried a thin smile.

CHANGE

Zelphira hesitated. Galinda moved aside, watching nervously.

She handed the tome to the Wizard.

He grunted, trying to open it, tugging at the cover, twisting the spine, but nothing happened. The book refused him.

Frustrated, he asked, still forcing a cordial tone, "Why won't it open?"

Zelphira looked at Galinda, then back at him. "When you first interact with the Kitab Malum, it only opens for those who possess magic. It has to recognize you."

The Wizard's smile thinned further. "Would you kindly open it for me?"

Zelphira hesitated, confused, but then nodded. "Sure."

She touched the cover, and it opened instantly, pages rustling as if breathing.

The Wizard snatched it from her hands and bent over it, eyes scanning the words greedily.

Zelphira tilted her head. "Can you read it?"

The Wizard mumbled, still squinting at the text. "Not a word."

Without hesitation, Zelphira slid her hand beneath the book and gently pried it from his grip. She closed it with a soft *thud*, clutching it protectively.

The Wizard said nothing.

He began pacing, slowly at first, then faster, each step clicking sharply against the marble. His muttering was low, frantic. Words spilled under his breath like water through cracked stone.

Then he stopped.

"Tell me, witch," he snapped suddenly, turning on his heel. "What are your magical talents? You know the main three, I presume? Or is your spellcasting just an impressive party trick?"

Zelphira stood tall. "I can do all three. Spellcasting. Clairvoyance. Advanced Potion-Making."

Galinda gasped and staggered back a step. "What in Oz?! *Zelly!*"

Both she and the Wizard wore the same expression—shocked, wide-eyed, as though they'd just seen a ghost rise from a forgotten grave.

Without a word, the Wizard spun around and strode quickly toward a hidden passage behind the throne. "Follow me," he ordered.

They followed in silence.

The corridor opened into a grand library, vaulted ceilings, floating lanterns, walls packed with tomes that pulsed faintly with enchantments. At the centre stood a lone podium. Upon it rested a book, oddly shaped, ancient, bound in cracked leather and etched in runes.

The Wizard approached it and lifted it with reverence. He glanced at Zelphira, and for the first time, his voice cracked, not from theatrics, but something rawer.

"Do you know... what you are?"

"What I *am*?" she repeated. "I... I don't understand."

He flipped through the pages frantically, parchment fluttering like wings in a storm until he found what he was looking for. He began to read aloud, voice low and rumbling:

"In a time of darkness in Oz, there will come ONE. A Saviour and a Curse to all in Oz. She will descend from the sky and break apart corruption in the land and liberate the oppressed.

At her side shall march the furred folk—beasts once muted, now risen—creatures of fang and mind, bound to her soul, and to her purpose. They will sweep through the land and skies like fire through dry grain, and the false crown of Oz shall fall beneath their fury.

She may walk in light, the brightest Oz has ever known, her name sung from the poppy fields to the Crystal Lakes. A redeemer.

*Or she may turn, ever so slightly, and the winds will shift. She may become the darkest witch to ever haunt the soil, **the most Wicked the land has ever borne.**"*

He paused, glancing up at her. Then continued, slower now:

"With great power comes great sacrifice, and power she will have.

She will be the only being in Oz to ever possess all three sectors of Witch Power: Spellcasting, Clairvoyance and Potion Mastery—the full spectrum of witchblood reborn in one vessel.

No teacher will bestow them. No rite will earn them. They shall be woven into her bones.

Upon her back she shall bear the Kitab Malum, the last spell tome, forged in Dragon's Breath and written in languages no longer spoken—spoken now only by her.

*She is the **ALTHEBA**.*

The Sorceress Supreme."

The room fell quiet. Even the enchanted lanterns seemed to hold their breath.

Then the Wizard turned the page.

It was torn, missing a jagged portion of the prophecy. But he kept reading:

"In another day, A Green Witch shall bring forth an offspring, One who shall be honourable and take his rightful place upon the throne, unseating the False Wizard and being instated as the true Wizard of Oz."

His voice faded as he read the last line.

He slammed the book shut and dropped it on the table with a thunderous *thud and* looked at Zelphira.

"You," he snarled, jabbing his finger toward her. "You are the *Altheba*."

Galinda whispered, almost to herself, *"The Sorceress Supreme."*

The Wizard began to advance, slowly, like a predator. Zelphira instinctively backed away, inching toward the exit of the library.

"I… I don't think—surely, it's a mistake," she stammered.

"Don't be a fool!" the Wizard snapped. "You *know* the prophecy is about you."

He stepped closer, grinning like he'd won a prize he hadn't expected to receive.

"I invited you here to cast spells for my court, to keep my rule shining. Who knew I'd be handed the *Altheba*—on a silver platter?"

Galinda's voice cut through the tension.

"Zelly, is it true? Did you know... that you're the Altheba?"

Zelphira spun to face her, fire rising in her voice.

"Stop calling me that. My name is *Zelphira!* Not some made-up name pulled from a dusty old prophecy."

But the Wizard was still drawing closer, eyes glinting with intent.

"Your Ozness," Zelphira said, bowing stiffly. "I would like to receive my heart's desire now, if you don't mind."

The Wizard let out a deep groan, part exasperation, part hunger.

"Only if you promise to use your magic and help *me*."

"Help you *how*, exactly? You're the *Wizard of Oz*. The most powerful spellcaster in the land. Why can't you cast your own spells?"

The Wizard and Galinda exchanged a glance, subtle, sharp, loaded.

Then he turned back. "Trust me, Zelphira," he said, extending his hand. "Stay by my side. Do as I ask. And I will give you everything you've ever wanted."

Zelphira didn't move. Her voice hardened.

"No. Not unless you help the Animals. The ones being *hunted*, *murdered*, forced into hiding in the forests like they're pests. I've done everything you asked since I got here, but you haven't once listened to what *I* want."

The Wizard's smile fell.

"I can't do that," he said quietly.

"Why not?"

"Becoz nothing can be done, it's just the way things are."

"What does that *mean*? You're the ruler of Oz! The people would listen to you. With your kind of power, you could—"

She stopped. Her eyes scanned his face, the way his hands tightened, the hesitation behind his words.

"Unless..." she whispered, stepping toward him. "Unless you *don't* have magic."

The Wizard's sigh was slow. Long. Admitting what he hadn't wanted to say.

Zelphira staggered back, like the breath had been knocked out of her. "Oh Oz... *That's* why you couldn't open the Grimorium. That's why you've been so obsessed with my power."

She pointed at the Wizard, voice rising with each word.

"You enrolled me in the university. You *forced* me to study Sorcery—nothing else. You've been grooming me, shaping me into something you could use."

Her eyes burned with betrayal.

"Becoz, *you* don't have magic. Becoz, you have *no* real power."

"You're right," he said, barely above a whisper. "That's why I *need* you."

Galinda stood completely still. Not a word. Not a breath.

Zelphira turned to her. "Why are you so quiet? Did you know?"

Galinda didn't respond. Her eyes were fixed on the floor.

Zelphira turned back to the Wizard. "So that's it? You're just going to let the Animals die?"

"Zelphira, you foolish child. Animals belong in cages. Or on a plate."

Zelphira's mouth fell open, but he went on.

"Where I come from, animals *don't talk*. They entertain us, serve us, feed us. Some are kept in homes, yes, but always behind bars, behind rules. They're not *people*. Not creatures of thought or reason or worth. They're beasts. And beasts do not deserve a seat at the table with men."

He took a step forward.

"They certainly don't belong in *Ozian civilisation*."

Zelphira looked like the ground had been ripped from beneath her. Her knees wavered. The truth, finally spoken, finally confirmed, hit her like cold iron.

Everything she feared was true. Everything she hoped to change... had just been declared impossible.

She almost collapsed under the weight of it.

"The Animals... it all makes sense now!" Her breath hitched. "*It's you!* You're the one hunting them, silencing them, driving them into exile!"

Her voice rose, raw with fury.

"You're keeping a few *harmless* Animals here in the Emerald City, just enough to make yourself look like a friend. A protector. But it's all for show, isn't it? A performance, so no one would ever believe you're the *Terrible Wizard* they refuse to admit."

She pointed a shaking finger at him.

"The prophecy... it wasn't just about me. *It was about you.* You're the false crown. The fraud meant to be overthrown with the help of the Animals. That's why you're trying to destroy them. Becoz you're afraid. Becoz a prophecy threatened your reign!"

The Wizard said nothing. But the silence, cold, stiff, too calm, was answer enough.

Zelphira's voice dropped. "So tell me. How have you granted so many people's heart's desires if you have *no magic?*"

The Wizard let out a small shrug, almost amused.

"I have sorcerers," he said, coolly. "They can cast small things, glamours, charms, illusions. Nothing impressive. But most people's hearts desires are laughably small. They just want to meet me. Be near me. They think *that* is magic enough."

"And the others?" she asked, eyes narrowing.

"Some journeys aren't meant to end, sometimes... all people need is purpose. A mission. So, I send them on *impossible* quests, a reason to leave; to find their *hearts truest desire*. They don't return and it stops them from asking for what I can't give them. But they go with hope in their hearts. And isn't that what matters?"

He smiled gently, like a man speaking of harvests or forgotten friends.

"Hope, after all, is far more sustainable than truth."

"And you sleep at night, knowing all this? Doing all *this*?"

The Wizard's smile twisted into something darker. Almost sad. "My precious child, where I come from, and one day you'll understand this, people need someone to blame and someone to look up to. Mainly, they crave a villain. But not just any villain, someone who they can easily *believe* is one. You don't have to believe in my methods, but I am not the villain. I'm the hero, and I want you to be a part of it."

He raised one hand.

"Someone must be *wicked*—" then raised the other, "—for someone else to be *good*."

He stepped forward.

"There can't be a devil without a god. It is the natural state of the world. And it is the only way to bring folks together. But I am not that enemy, I am as good as they come. Only you can decide if you want to be part of the good side of history or become the enemy Oz desperately craves right now."

Zelphira clenched the strap of her bag with white knuckles. Then, with a look of pure disgust, she spat on the floor between them.

"You *disgust* me, and I will tell everyone the truth. That you're a fraud. A liar. A *devil*."

Without waiting for a response, she turned and ran, bolting down the hall, her footsteps echoing against the marble as she searched for a way out, for any door that led to freedom.

The Wizard turned to Galinda, eyes sharp.

"*Get her back. Now!*"

Galinda hesitated for only a second, then turned sharply on her heels.

Zelphira's cloak sliced through the air like a ribbon in revolt as she tore down the hallway, her boots pounding against marble. Behind her, Galinda followed, swift, silent, relentless, with the conviction of a predator chasing prey, not out of malice, but desperation.

"Zelly, wait!"

Zelphira just continued running.

As they ran, a loud *grumble* echoed through the palace speakers.

Then, the Wizard's voice.

"There is a fugitive in the palace! Green and dressed in black! Do *not* let her escape!"

Zelphira yanked at every door handle she passed, breath ragged, **heart** hammering. But every door was locked.

Galinda, unnervingly calm in the midst of Zelphira's frenzy, spoke in a low, measured voice.

"Let's just go back. Tell the Wizard it's all a misunderstanding. Maybe he'll—
"

Zelphira scoffed. "Over my dead body."

Then,

A roar.

"Get her!"

It was Chase. His voice thundered behind them, and with him, a battalion of guards surged forward, swords gleaming, faces twisted with rage.

"Zelly, we have to go, now!" Galinda screamed.

Zelphira and Galinda rounded corners blindly, trying every hallway, every corridor. But the soldiers were fast. *Chase* was faster.

They were always just behind her. Always closing in.

"Here!" Galinda cried, spotting a narrow crevice in the labyrinthine walls of the palace.

Zelphira turned the corner—

There, ahead, a ladder. Leading up to the highest point of the palace.

The Emerald Tower.

Without a second thought, she grabbed the rungs and began to climb, pulling herself up with desperate speed. Galinda followed, hands shaking but steady.

Then, Chase burst into view below them.

"*Stop right there, Witch!*" he bellowed, his sword glinting as he raised it. "I want *your blood* on my blade!"

"Give me your hand!" Zelphira shouted, reaching down from above.

Galinda stretched her arm as high as she could, and Zelphira grabbed it, yanking her up into the attic with all the strength she had left.

With a wave of her hand, Zelphira sent the ladder crashing down. It hit the floor with a thunderous *slam*. She sealed the trapdoor shut with another flick of her fingers.

Chase roared in frustration below. "They've gone up! Find another way—now!"

Zelphira rose to her feet, breathless, shaking.

Galinda stood too, trembling with fury.

"Why are you *always* like this?" she yelled. "Why can't you just *stop* and think for one second? Now we're fugitives, *we're* being hunted like the very Animals you seek to protect!"

Zelphira turned to her, eyes ablaze.

"*We?*" she spat. "*I* am the one they're chasing. *I* am the one they want dead."

"You're right, so, let's go back. Let's just talk to the Wizard. He's a kind man. He *likes* you. If you just apologise, if you explain yourself, he'll listen! He *needs* you. You could still help the Animals. You could still make this right."

"**No,**" Zelphira said firmly, voice like flint.

CHANGE

Galinda threw her hands up, pacing furiously. "*No?* Are you crazy? You think you're so clever, but now you've sabotaged everything! You've turned the most powerful man in all the lands into your enemy. The smart move would've been to use him to your advantage, not challenge him!"

"I'm more stunned that *you* would rather grovel to feed your burning ambition, sometimes I wonder if I even know you at all."

"Maybe you don't!" Galinda shot back. "And maybe I don't know *you* either. All this—for some *Animals* who'd turn on you the moment they got the chance! You think they care that you're trying to help them? They'd eat you alive, just for being green!"

"It's more than the Animals!" Zelphira shouted. "That's how it *starts*. But it never stops there. What if next he began hunting blonde girls with blue eyes? Would you say the same thing then?"

She stepped closer, her voice trembling with hurt.

"Where is that soft, kind heart you once showed me? I thought you'd be the first to rise against injustice. But here you are, choosing your *ambition* over your *morals*."

She pointed back toward the **heart** of the palace.

"He's a fraud! A man behind a curtain, nothing more!"

"I'm choosing *safety!*" Galinda hissed. "He's no more a fraud than the rest of us. Sometimes someone *has* to play the man behind the curtain. It's essential. Civilisation doesn't function on truth, Zelphira—it runs on illusion. But you? You wouldn't understand that. You're too busy being idealistic. You're *ill* with delusions of grandeur, dreaming of a world that doesn't exist!"

"That may be so. Maybe I am dreaming of a world not as it is but as it should be. But I would rather walk that line *alone*, free in my thinking, free in my will, than be shackled in gilded chains with company that goes against every fibre of my being."

She turned and walked to the cracked circular window at the far end of the tower, the wind pushing strands of her dark hair away from her face.

Galinda followed quietly and reached for her hand.

Zelphira turned to her.

"You can still be with the Wizard. This is what you've wanted your whole life. You said it yourself, he's the only one, besides me, who will accept you as you are."

Zelphira gave a small, sad laugh and slowly released her grip. "But I don't want it. Not like this. I won't seek love at the cost of my soul."

Galinda's voice was barely a whisper. "Then what changed you? Was it just finding out the truth about him?"

Zelphira looked at her, steadily, honestly.

"Nothing changed. This is who I've always been."

She took a step closer.

"But *you*... you can't fathom anything outside the path laid in front of you. You can't see my perspective becoz, deep down, you don't know who *you* are. Isn't that right... *Glinda?*"

Galinda froze.

Then, the speakers crackled to life again. But this time, the sound came from *below.*

The girls turned toward the balcony and stepped into the open air, gazing down at the square beneath the Emerald Tower.

A *crowd* had gathered. Thousands of visitors, citizens, tourists, and nobles alike, every eye turned toward the centre. A hush fell over the square.

There he stood.

The Wizard.

His *first* public appearance in years. Perhaps decades.

It was a rare sight to see the Wizard in his human form.

Most didn't know what he truly looked like—his image passed around only through whispers and wild imagination. Some believed he was a skeleton. Others claimed he was a beautiful woman, a divine reincarnation of Ozma herself. Some pictured a great horned beast, others a dazzling sphere of fire that spoke in riddles.

But today, he appeared not as myth or monster, but as a man.

Graceful, composed, and mercifully *human*—a form simple enough for small minds to comprehend.

He spoke, his voice amplified through a gleaming microphone, his words carried across all of Oz like a sermon from the sky.

"Dear citizens of Oz, it is I, the Wizard.

I come to you humbly, to warn you of a terrible threat.

I have received divine revelations, from the One Gohd, from Lurline, from Ozma herself. They all speak the same name.

A devil has risen from the depths of **Ell.** *Green-skinned, disfigured, twisted, her very body a manifestorius of her wickedness.*

She has broken into my palace. She stole the sacred Kitab Malum and tried to murder me. I survived, only barely, using what magic I could muster. But I could not stop her completely.

She still roams free. And she has vowed to spill your children's blood… and drink it.

If you see her, do not wait. Kill her on sight. Mutilate her more than she already is, for the good of your people and your precious children.

To the noble soul brave enough to bring me her head, I offer a reward beyond imagining. Gold, titles, honour eternal.

Blessed be, and beware the temptation, the lies she will tell, the deception of this vile, this ugly, this…

Wicked Witch. *"*

The crowd below erupted in a frenzy.

On the balcony above, Galinda pressed her hand to her mouth in horror.

"Zelly…" she whispered.

Zelphira exhaled slowly. Her eyes glistened, but she refused to let the tears fall. She turned her face away, but Galinda reached out, gently cupping her cheek, and wiped the wetness away with her thumb.

Zelphira steadied herself, brushing the dust from her cape and fastening her wide-brimmed hat.

"It's too late for second-guessing now," Zelphira murmured.

Galinda's voice broke. "What will you do? They'll never listen to you. You can't undo what he's said. You can't fix Oz, or help the Animals, if they see you as a monster."

"But I have to try, if I sit by and do nothing, then I've already lost. I have to *try*, even if it kills me."

"Don't say that! Aren't you afraid?" Galinda asked, trembling. "I'm terrified for you."

Zelphira met Galinda's gaze, steady and unflinching.

"Don't you see? It's the Wizard who should be afraid of me. I have nothing left to lose and he has everything, and I've made my choice."

She paused, her voice softening.

"For so long, I have limited myself, shrinking, softening, silencing, just to make others feel comfortable. All the while, I was the one forced to live uncomfortably… in my own skin! Well, I'm done with that. I'll defy them, just as I'll defy the air that's suffocated me in an attempt to keep me grounded."

She stepped closer.

"And I know this might be foolish. *Idealistic.* Reckless even. But you put that in me, Glinda. You taught me to hope. So now I'm asking…"

Her hand hovered in the space between them.

"Will you come with me? Together, we could find your magic again. Together, our reach would be Unlimited. *Good* and *Wicked*, side by side."

Galinda looked away, her silence heavy, shame clinging to her like a second skin.

"Oh, Zelly…" she whispered. "You know I can't. I don't have your courage. I've lost my magic for good. I'm nothing. I'm weak."

"You're not."

"You can't even get out of this tower, the guards will kill you before you get the chance to fight."

Zelphira nodded slowly, already knowing the truth in her heart. "I just hope that one day, you don't regret this choice… that it doesn't come back to haunt you."

Galinda's voice cracked. "You too, Zelly."

Their eyes met, glimmering with tears neither wanted to acknowledge. Then, Zelphira wrapped her arms around Galinda and held her tightly, as if the moment might be the last.

Then she stepped toward the edge of the balcony.

She climbed onto the railing, rising on her tiptoes to peer over the edge. Below: hundreds of guards, packed shoulder to shoulder, their swords raised, their voices shouting.

"There she is! Kill her!"

Galinda staggered forward. "Zelly, *what are you doing?!* Are you going to *jump?*"

"Yes."

"Zelly, *please.*" Galinda's voice broke, tears spilling freely now. "I can't lose you, not like this! You won't survive this fight let alone the fall!"

Zelphira turned to her, face still, voice cold with resolve.

"But I will survive. I've been doing it my entire life."

Galinda sighed. *"Maybe you're not as powerful as you think you are."*

Zelphira raised her hand, gently stopping her.

"No. That's where you're wrong. I *am* as powerful as I think I am."

"Don't jump. Please!"

Zelphira looked out at the world below.

"But that's exactly what I need to do, sometimes… you have to take a leap— if you want to fly."

Zelphira moved closer to the edge. She raised one arm, fingers spread open, and closed her eyes.

Silence.

Only the wind, whispering like prophecy.

Then—

Something stirred in the distance.

A faint glimmer… a blur slicing through the clouds at breakneck speed.

It came faster. Closer. Closer.

A **broom.**

Not ordinary. Heavy. Old. Etched with runes, identical to those carved into the *Kitab Malum.* A relic of power, forged for no one but her.

Galinda's eyes widened in disbelief.

Suddenly—*crash!*

The attic door burst open.

Chase. Sword drawn, eyes wild.

He lunged at Zelphira with a growl, blade raised.

But she was quicker. With a single, fluid motion, Zelphira tipped forward and let herself fall, Chase's fingers only grazing the edge of her billowing black cape.

"ZELLY!" Galinda screamed, rushing to the edge.

She couldn't bear to look. She imagined the worst: Zelphira crushed in the courtyard below, her body broken before a crowd that hated her, *without ever knowing her.*

Galinda peeked over the edge, heart pounding.

Then—

Whoosh!

CHANGE

A black blur shot straight upward into the air.

Zelphira, laughing wildly, astride the flying broom, her eyes fierce and gleaming.

"Too slow, Chase!" she called, grinning.

More guards spilled into the room, surrounding Galinda and Chase.

Zelphira hovered just outside the balcony now, floating before Galinda like a myth come to life.

"If you ever wish to find me, *Glinda*..." she said, her voice rich and strange, "...just look to the Western Sky."

And then, she threw her head back and cackled. Louder this time. Unrestrained. Defiant.

Below, the people saw her, black cloak, pointed hat, green skin, exactly as they'd been warned.

"That's her!" one cried.

"The devil the Wizard warned us about!"

"Burn her, burn her like they did Seraphina!"

Zelphira hovered high, silhouette against the bruised, dark sky.

Archers lined up. The guards pulled their bows.

"*Fire at will!*" Chase shouted.

"*GO!*" Galinda cried, her voice desperate.

Zelphira flashed her a final smile, brief, soft, almost grateful.

Then she kicked off the air and shot forward like a bolt of black lightning.

Still cackling. Still flying.

Arrows flew in a thousand directions, but she was already too far gone.

Galinda stood, breathless, tears streaking her cheeks as she watched her disappear into the clouds.

And in that moment, despite everything, her smile broke through the sorrow.

Zelphira was free.

And she was *magnificent*.

CHAPTER 39

Saving Face

Chase stomped his boots in fury, the echo of it ricocheting off the rafters of the Emerald Tower like the tantrum of a god denied sacrifice. He had *never* lost a hunt. Never missed a mark. And yet here he was—defeated. Outmanoeuvred. Someone, *some thing*, had slipped through his fingers like fog.

And they laughed, cackled even, at his failure.

Somewhere in the distance, a laugh still rang in his ears—not taunting exactly but laced with knowledge. As if the game had never really been his to win.

Galinda slid down the tall pane of the large, broken, frosted window, the glass cold against her back. She drew her knees to her chest and bowed her head low, letting her hair fall forward like a curtain, a veil between her face and the world. Her breath trembled in her throat.

"Can you please, guards..." she whispered, her voice cracking like fragile glass, "give me some privacy?"

The words were barely audible, more confession than command.

A beat. Then a whisper, too careless to be discreet, found its way to her ears.

"Are we supposed to capture her too?"

Galinda didn't move, but her breath caught. Her fingernails curled into the fabric of her skirt.

Chase turned, brows arching. "Do you *know* who that is?" he asked, eyes flicking toward Galinda. "That's the Princess of the South. Her father and the Wizard? Pals. Old friends." He lowered his voice into a confidential hush. "Look at her. Harmless. Couldn't hurt a fly."

He gestured to the guards, dismissing them with a flick of his wrist. "Go. Inform the Wizard. Tell him the mission... was incomplete."

The guards left like a breeze through a broken window, leaving Galinda in the attic with nothing but silence and a bruised dignity.

She sat still for a long while, watching the sun inch toward the eastern horizon—wrong, somehow. *Wrong.* The sky burned orange over a city of emeralds, and for the first time, Galinda wondered if the sun would ever rise in the *West* again.

CHANGE

At last, when the pain stopped being sharp and started being manageable, like a tight corset instead of a knife, she rose to her feet, her knees trembling slightly beneath her. She dusted off her skirt, pulled herself together, and began the long descent down the Emerald Tower, its walls echoing her heels with a hollow rhythm.

Past the guards. Past the cold wand of Seraphina, still floating in the relic hall like a condemned memory.

But Galinda didn't stop.

She had somewhere to be, though she no longer knew where *home* was. Perhaps it no longer mattered.

She reached the entrance hall and turned the golden handle, emerging just as the Wizard stood at the podium, addressing a crowd that still lingered in the square like sheep waiting for a second sermon.

Their eyes shifted. Heads turned.

The Wizard paused, his words caught mid-sentence as he saw her appear beside him, poised, silent, ethereal in the dying light.

He blinked once, the surprise in his expression quickly replaced by something else. Something fainter than relief, deeper than gratitude. *Understanding.*

He smiled. Slowly. It spread into a grin, not of joy, but of recognition. Of timing. Of theatre.

He motioned for her to step forward.

Galinda exhaled softly. She knew the stage. She knew what it meant to arrive *now*, in *this* moment, before a gathering of eyes still wide with fear and hungry for hope.

So she walked.

The crowd shifted again, murmuring. A gasp or two. A child clutched a mother's sleeve. A pigeon took flight.

The Wizard turned back to the crowd. His voice, now smooth as silk, carried with measured gravitas.

"This," he said, "is Princess Galinda."

"Glinda!" She corrected him, her chest straightening a little.

The Wizard adjusted, "Glinda Fairmoor. Daughter of the King of the Quadlings. Sister to the Good Witch of the South."

Gasps rippled through the masses.

"She was there," he continued, voice rising, "when the Wicked Witch attacked me."

Glinda stepped back instinctively and bowed her head.

He turned to Glinda now, his gaze sharp, cutting, purposeful and he pushed her forward. "I cannot take all the credit. No. This young woman stood beside me in the face of darkness. She fought. And she *chose* the side of good."

A pause. A breath.

"I am proud," he said. "Proud of her bravery. And her intellect. And her heart."

He let the words hang, like the final line of a spell not meant to be questioned.

GLINDA: The GOOD Witch

Glinda stood motionless, back straight, lips pressed tight. She said nothing.

But inside, her **heart** was a coin flipped into the air, spinning, spinning, never landing.

The crowd erupted. Cheers poured through the square like waves breaching a levee, sudden, violent, adoring.

Glinda's face cracked. No, *spilled*, into a smile so instinctive, so uninvited, it startled even her. She caught it just a breath too late. The muscles had already moved. The damage was done.

A civilian's voice rose above the din: "Are you a Good Witch too?"

Glinda opened her mouth. "No—"

But the Wizard, ever watchful, cut her off before the truth could escape.

"Yes," he boomed, "she is *most certainly* a Good Witch! That is *precisely* how she fended off *the* Wicked Witch."

The crowd roared. Applause thundered again, louder, as if her silence had only validated the title.

Glinda stood frozen beneath the force of it. The vibration of voices, the clapping hands, the collective gaze, it all struck her like an invisible storm. She shivered.

She wanted to pretend she was indifferent, that she had learned the sacred art of quietude from Zelphira, who had unknowingly helped tuck away her insatiable need for adoration. But Zelphira was not here. And Glinda's body betrayed her.

A twitch in her spine at the mention of "Good."

A flush at the crowd's ovation.

A sick, exhilarating *arousal*, not of lust, but of latent hunger.

The Wizard stood beside her a moment longer, soaking in the illusion he had sculpted, then gave a gracious, theatrical wave and turned to retreat into the palace. Coat trailing. Power intact.

Glinda followed.

He had saved his image. Restored his myth.

At the cost of someone else's truth.

With the help of Glinda's silence.

And the absence of her sister's voice.

Glinda shut the door behind them. The echo swallowed the crowd.

The Wizard continued walking down the long, green-glass corridor. And when his back was turned, Glinda spoke.

"Oz," she said, carefully, "I know why you called me a Good Witch. I understand the gesture, the timing, the… theatrics."

He did not respond. So she continued.

"But now that you've *said* it, now that the world *believes* it, I have to *perform* it. Which isn't the issue." Her voice lowered. "The issue is… I don't have magic."

That stopped him.

He turned slowly, as if turning any faster might disturb the fragile illusion between them.

"You don't?"

"I don't," she confirmed. "I had it. Once. But it left me. I don't know how. Or when."

The Wizard studied her, long and languid, as though she were a new breed of flower blooming in the wrong garden.

"That's strange," he said at last. "I remembered you the moment you gave your name. I remember meeting you at your father's castle. I remember *you*, little thing—smaller voice, sharper eyes. And I remember talking you into helping your sister become the Good Witch Helping her... ascend."

"Then why," Glinda asked softly, "did you pretend not to recognize me?"

His grin returned, this one darker, more private. "Let's say... my attention was elsewhere. On a certain *green* girl. Who turned out to be a *rotting fruit* dressed in rebellion."

He stepped closer. "You should know by now, I wear many faces. I *see* things. I remember them. Even when people change their faces."

He nodded toward her. "Like *you* have."

Glinda said nothing.

"You've remade yourself," the Wizard continued. "Face. Voice. Posture. A performance so convincing even you believe it. But I see it. And I ask again: how are you doing it without magic?"

Glinda's voice fell to a hush. "I *used* magic. But then... it vanished. I didn't throw it away. It just left me."

The Wizard studied her for a long, pointed moment. Then he laughed, a deep, hollow sound that echoed up the corridor like the ringing of a cracked bell.

"Yes you do, you fool," he said, the words shaped with cruel amusement. "You know *exactly* where your magic went. But you don't want to face it. You don't want it back—not really. Becoz you've grown fond of the warmth of mediocrity."

Glinda stiffened.

"You *love* the feeling of being ordinary," he went on, each word peeling her silence away. "You have wealth. You've finally sculpted the face you longed for. And let's be honest, magic is still suspect in this world. Frowned upon. Feared. You're *relieved* to be rid of it, even as you pretend to mourn it."

Glinda stuttered, something forming in her throat but never making it to her lips.

"Listen," the Wizard said, the tone shifting again. Smoother now. Icy. "I'm not retracting my statement. You are now a *Good Witch*."

He turned on his heel, his coat sweeping behind him like the curtains of a stage.

"You can't just leave me on my own to figure this out," Glinda called after him, her voice cracking with desperation, pride, and something else—perhaps hope.

He stopped, a breath away from disappearing around the corridor's bend.

Then he sighed. "Just do what I do," he said, not unkindly. "Perform. Create spectacle. They won't know the difference."

He kept walking. "*Come with me.*"

Glinda scurried after him, heels clicking against the emerald-tiled floor, each step echoing like punctuation marks to a sentence she hadn't meant to start.

He led her through the winding passages of the palace, finally returning to the dim-lit library where once before they had spoken of prophecy. Only this time, there was an absence—of heat, of warmth, of someone not there.

"Prophecies are dangerous things, Mizz Fairmoor. They make monsters of kings... and martyrs of children." The Wizard said with a faint smile, as though it was just another bit of wisdom. "We can't always afford to indulge them, not when the whole of Oz teeters on a whisper."

Glinda shifted, uneasy. "That's a grim way of looking at things."

The Wizard's smile thinned. "It's the true way. And we're in the business of truth now... aren't we?"

A single candle flickered on the table, its light throwing distorted shadows of their faces across the spines of ancient books.

The Wizard sat. He didn't gesture for her to sit. He simply opened a notebook, took out a pencil, and began to write.

Then, as though remembering she was still standing there:

"Do you know what I was before I became the Wizard?"

Glinda tilted her head. "No."

He smiled. That storyteller's smile. Part mystery, part trap.

"Back in my land," he said, voice low and syrupy, "I was many things. But in *all* of them, I was a performer."

He didn't look at her when he spoke. He didn't need to.

"I started as a labourer in a circus. Nothing special. I swept sawdust, fed animals, polished brass. But I *loved* the lights, the illusion, the hush before the curtain rose. I needed a reason to be there. You could call it passion. Or pathology. I was fascinated with how easily people could be made to believe."

He looked up, smile curling. "Not *believe* in something real, mind you. Just... *believe.*"

Glinda leaned in, caught in his rhythm.

"In my world, people know magic isn't real," he said. "But they *want* it. They crave the illusion. They applaud the trick becoz they need to believe there's something more than what they're given. And so... I gave it to them."

He paused. "I became a ventriloquist."

Glinda blinked. "A what?"

"It's when you use your hand to animate a puppet. Make it talk. Make it say what you want. Move how you want."

"*Fascinating!*" Glinda exclaimed, her eyes widening, the candlelight catching the glint in them. "I think I remember seeing a show like that once, at a carnival. There was a clock, shaped like a dragon, I think. It told stories as it spun… something about time folding in on itself." She shook her head, smiling faintly. "But, sorry, please continue."

The Wizard's voice turned even smoother, like caramel over glass. Glinda felt herself drawn in—not against her will, but in the way one might lean into warmth on a cold evening, not fully aware of when it started.

"But although I *loved* being a ventriloquist," he said, eyes unfocused as if sifting through dusty memory, "it wasn't *enough*. It's one thing to make a puppet talk— to wag its painted mouth and say what *you* want it to. But it's a very different, and far more thrilling thing, to watch a *person* behave how you wish… and believe the behaviour was *their* idea."

He gave a wry smile. "That's the real magic. Not prestidigitation. Not sparks. Not spells. *Belief.*"

He began pacing now, slowly, shadows curling around his movements.

"So I studied. I hid behind velvet curtains and watched the magicians rehearse. I studied the illusions *they* used, and I rewrote them. Reimagined them. I designed a show so grand, so utterly unlike anything the world had seen, that the mere mention of it in the papers made people travel from counties away."

He paused. "I had someone I loved. Deeply. She didn't believe in what I was doing. She didn't believe in me. But that," he said, waving the thought off like smoke, "is neither here nor there."

Glinda watched him, absorbing every word. The way his smile flickered when he spoke of love. The way his voice tightened when he shifted away from it.

"I used unconventional things," he continued. "A hot-air balloon, for instance. Gears. Steam. Light. Music. My show became something more than entertainment—it became an *event*. People flocked to see *Mr. Marvel, The Spectacle Man, Oz, The Great and Powerful!*"

He chuckled under his breath. "That was the name they gave me. Becoz of the marvel I sold them. Not for what I *was*, but for what I *appeared* to be. The most popular man in Omaha. Even political figures, presidents… they came."

"Omaha?" Glinda tilted her head. "Is that the name of your land?"

The Wizard paused to consider how to explain. "Part of it. Like… like the Quadling lands are part of Oz. It's a city, but within a greater state. A corner of a bigger, colder world. Where dreams go to die… or get bent into something useful."

Glinda nodded slowly, sensing the weight behind the words.

"I was adored," he said. "But still poor. That's the part they never see. The illusion pays in applause, not gold. But that's another tale for another time."

His eyes flicked back to her, piercing now. "It's *all* about the illusion, Glinda."

He rose and began to pace again, his movements smooth but driven. A man unravelling himself, carefully.

"You see, before I entered showbiz, I wanted to be an *engineer*. That was my true dream. I had sketchbooks, hundreds, filled with designs. Machines. Inventions that could change things. Automata. Winged vehicles. Sound machines. But when you grow up on a farm, where the sky is too big and the dreams too small, your options are... limited."

He motioned wider now, his arm sweeping toward the hall beyond.

"You see that *large machine head* in the central chamber? The one with *my* face on it?"

Glinda nodded slowly.

"I created that. Not just illusion. Not just flair. A machine. A voice box. Levers. Steam. Mirrors. I built it to *be* me, when I couldn't. A figurehead. A mask too heavy to wear all the time."

He turned back to her, slower now.

"People worshipped it. They still do. Becoz they'd rather hear comfort from a great, booming head than from a man with calloused hands and a hidden past."

He sat down again, the candle between them casting deep valleys in his face.

"That's the trick, Glinda. That's the entire game. They don't want truth. They want spectacle."

Glinda nodded, eyes still caught in the shimmer of the idea.

"It gives me *allure*," he continued. "Presence. Makes me larger than life, something the people can kneel to without ever having to touch. You must do the same. Oz is filled with materials my land never dreamed of. Alchemy. Artifice. Steam. Light. The possibilities here are... infinite."

Glinda's voice was quiet but laced with hunger. "You don't suppose you could create something like that for me?"

The Wizard grinned. It wasn't warm. It was predatory. "I thought you'd never ask."

He leaned forward, candlelight gleaming across the sharp ridges of his smile. "Tell me, Glinda, would that be your *heart's* greatest desire?"

Her eyes widened, and without hesitation, she nodded, quickly, hungrily, as though afraid desire might disappear if she didn't claim it aloud.

"Yes."

The Wizard leaned back, satisfied. "Good. Now, I'm *not* going to make you a large mechanical head like mine. That's more of a *man's* approach, and besides, that schtick is copyrighted."

He laughed, a dry, theatrical chuckle.

"No, *you* need something feminine," he mused, "but remarkable. Ethereal. Something unforgettable." He tilted his head. "Do you have anything in mind?"

Glinda began pacing. Slowly at first, then faster, her heels ticking like a metronome of thought. Her mind spun through spires and crowns and floating chandeliers, but none of it felt right.

Until something stirred.

A flicker.

A memory.

CHANGE

The scent of lavender and soap. The sound of dripping water. The bathroom blurred with light. Bubbles, thousands of them, floating through the air as she knelt beside a girl the world had discarded. Zelphira. Fragile, broken. And beautiful.

Her throat tightened.

Glinda drew in the deepest breath she had ever taken, anchoring herself to the weight of the moment, trying, failing, not to feel.

"Bubbles," she whispered, then said louder. "*Bubbles.* I want to arrive in a bubble. Descending from the sky. Like Lurline. Like you in your balloon, when you first arrived. Like my sister, the Good Witch of the South."

She met his gaze. "But it **has** to be a bubble."

The Wizard snapped his fingers like the crack of a whip. "*Perfect.* Your mind, your instincts, they were made for this! Just stop hiding behind your grief and your goodness and *perform.*"

He kissed his fingers in delight. "A *show-woman!*"

Glinda laughed, her smile radiant with relief and revelation.

The Wizard pulled out a fresh page and began to sketch: a platform, round and cushioned, held aloft by an enchanted sphere. A transport of elegance. A spectacle of grace. The illusion of divinity.

Glinda clapped her hands together. "*Perfect!*"

But his smile, so bright a moment ago, faded like sunlight behind clouds. He set the pencil down and folded his hands.

"Glinda."

She turned.

"If I make this for you," he said, voice now low and smooth, "you must be my ally. Not just in words, but in action. You will do as I say—*my* every command. Without question."

The candlelight caught the edge of his expression, casting shadows beneath his eyes.

"Is that understood?"

Glinda's eye twitched, just slightly. Her throat was dry. But still, she nodded. "Yes."

The Wizard's grin returned, wider this time, darker.

"Then a bubble," he said softly, "you shall get."

The Wizard ripped the sketch of the bubble-cushion machine, stood from his seat, his movement as smooth as his voice. "You should leave. It's getting late."

Without another word, he swept past her, disappearing behind a hidden door carved into the wall like a secret kept too long.

It clicked shut behind him.

Glinda stood there, alone now, in the cavernous throne room of the Emerald Palace. The flame of the single candle flickered beside the empty sketchpad, its light waning in his absence. She was still holding her bag, though she hadn't realized she'd gripped it tighter.

He had dismissed her.

But she did not leave.

Instead, she began to wander, slowly, curiously, across the gleaming floor of the throne room. Her footsteps, at first tentative, became more graceful, more practiced. She moved like a ballerina learning the weight of her own myth. Her heels clicked softly as she tiptoed, turning in a slow circle like she was descending from the sky already.

Then she stopped.

Her eyes fell upon two podiums, tucked quietly to one side of the hall, their presence unannounced, ceremonial in their stillness. They bore no guards, no chains, no velvet ropes—only reverence and dust.

Glinda glanced over her shoulder. The silence was immense.

She approached the first podium.

A book rested there, thick, though smaller than the one beside it. She brushed a hand over its cover.

The Book of Records.

She flipped it open. The pages were lined with tiny script, impossibly neat, impossibly exact. Every entry was a timestamp. A chronicle. *The unedited log of Oz's history, recorded as it happened.*

Her own name appeared once or twice. Her father's more. Her sister's in headlines.

She rolled her eyes, unimpressed. History, she had long since decided, was a bureaucrat's version of gossip.

She let the book fall shut with a soft thud and turned to the second podium.

This book was larger. Older. Its cover was leathered like the skin of a beast long buried. She reached out, fingertips tracing the gold-embossed title:

The Holy Book of Ozma.

She tightened her grip on her bag. Something in her warned she shouldn't be here, not just *here*, in this room, but *here*, as *her*. As someone with no magic. As someone who'd just made a pact with illusion.

The silence deepened.

This was the *original* copy. The one from which all others had been copied, translated, and disseminated into every **home** in Oz. The same text Esmelda used in ceremonies. The same stories that were told in lullabies and liturgies.

She opened it slowly. The spine creaked like old wood in winter.

Her eyes scanned the chapters with passing familiarity:

The One Gohd.

She knew Him. Distant, abstract, always watching.

Lurline.

The fairy goddess of old, familiar like the remembrance of her name.

The Ozmas.

She knew like the Elphebet a child learns and never forgets.

CHANGE

But then,

A heading she had *never* seen before.

The Prophecy.

Glinda looked around, her breath catching as her gaze swept the room. Nothing stirred. The candle flickered. A whisper of wind? Or was that just her heart?

What prophecy? she wondered. She didn't hesitate.

She noted the page number in her mind, an instinctual act, one that would leave no trace.

She flipped to the chapter.

Her fingers trembled slightly against the pages as the candlelight shimmered over the delicate script.

The air shifted.

The candle flame wavered ever so slightly, as if aware that something unspeakable was about to be spoken aloud.

Her eyes fell upon the text, elegant, gold-leafed script, faded but not forgotten. Her breath caught.

"Exactly one century after the disappearance of the first Wizard, the Second Wizard of Oz will fall from the skies, in a contraption resembling a basket and a pillowing oval. Descending with him will be the first and the true Green Witch. No Green Wizard. But a Green Witch.

The Altheba.

No coven and no tribe.

She is not born; she is made. She will be the noblest of them all, the One Unitor of all four corners.

The Saviour of Oz."

Glinda snapped the book shut, as though the page had burned her.

It was all a lie.

Everything she'd been told. Everything she'd been taught to repeat. The revised Ozma copies in every house across Oz, each one lacquered in piety and omission, had *redacted* this.

Altered it.

The missing word in the most whispered prophecy, the one schoolchildren were taught to fear and praise, and priests carefully honoured, was: *Green Wi*—

It wasn't **Wizard.**

It was **Witch.**

And not just any witch. *Zelphira.*

Glinda clutched the holy book to her chest. Her pulse thrummed with possibility. If the people *knew*, if they saw *this*, they would understand. Zelphira wasn't the wicked one. She wasn't the threat.

She was the prophecy.

She was the Altheba.

The *Saviour of Oz.*

GLINDA: The GOOD Witch

For a flicker of a moment, Glinda imagined the crowd outside, those same adoring masses who had roared her name, thrown rose petals beneath her shoes, seeing this. The real text. The real truth.

They would see the Wizard for what he was: a lie in silk and steam.

They would see Zelphira for what she was: a miracle born in green skin.

And Glinda?

Glinda...

She would fall.

She took a step forward. Toward the door. Toward the candle. Toward the future.

And then stopped.

But if the people knew the truth about the Wizard...

They would know the truth about *her.*

She wasn't the Good Witch. Not truly. Not by rite. Not by prophecy.

She was a symbol. A convenience. A performance crafted for a political pageant.

If the lie unravelled, if the curtain fell, then so would she.

The platform the Wizard had built her, bubble and all, would evaporate.

Everything she had built, or had been *allowed* to build, would unravel before it ever truly began. The political future offered to her like a golden apple would rot in her hands. The Wizard's approval, so rare, so useful, would vanish. And she would return to what she had always been:

A princess.

A pawn with nothing to gain.

An echo.

Glinda stood in the flickering half-light, the book still clutched to her chest like a confession.

She began to reason.

Zelphira—*Altheba*—was powerful beyond reckoning. She had always been. Her green skin was no curse. It was a beacon. She was made, not born. Just as the prophecy said. It was her *destiny* to rise as the Wicked Witch.

And Glinda, Glinda had not *made* her wicked. Had not painted her green. Had not pushed her into prophecy.

She hadn't *labelled* her.

So why should it be *her* burden to change the label?

Glinda let out a shallow breath. Her eyes stung but did not spill. Perhaps, perhaps the right thing, the *good* thing, was to step aside. To let fate run its course.

Not to meddle in a story older than herself.

After all, wasn't it for the greater good?

Slowly, she turned. Her footsteps echoing like regrets down the polished floor.

CHANGE

She approached the podium. The holy book still warm where her hands had held it. She placed it back gently, without reverence, but with care.

She did not look back.

Her eyes twitched once, a spasm of conscience, but she did not bat an eye.

She exited the throne room. The grand door shut behind her with the soft finality of betrayal dressed as composure.

Outside, the city had dimmed into silence. The stars were just beginning to draw their sharp lines across the velvet sky.

Her Gilded Rose carriage stood waiting. Gilded and gaudy, glimmering faintly in the torchlight. The coachman tipped his cap.

"Where to, Your Highness?"

Glinda hesitated.

Then answered, "Home."

The coachman blinked. "And where is that?"

Glinda paused. Then said, softer, "Back to Quadling Country."

The Gilded Rose creaked as it leaned forward into motion.

The Emerald City remained behind her, silent, sleeping, unaware.

The carriage wheels whispered across the cobblestones, carrying her into the dark arms of night. A day already etched in the stone of time, sealed by the silence of the only person who knew what really mattered.

And did nothing.

CHAPTER 40

New Kindlings and Old Wounds

When she finally returned to Fairmoor Castle, she didn't speak to anyone. She didn't wave to the gardeners, didn't greet the steward, didn't even glance at the stables to greet the kind coachman.

She climbed the staircase like a ghost still uncertain of its place in the world, made her way into her chamber, and began, half-heartedly, to undress.

She only managed to remove her socks.

The rest of her garments clung to her like regrets. She collapsed onto the bed, wriggled beneath the covers as though trying to bury herself beneath something warm, and finally, let the tears fall.

They came in waves, familiar and fresh all at once. Shame first. Then disgust. Then something crueller: *understanding*.

What she had done, or rather, what she had *chosen not to do*, sat inside her like a stone. She hadn't betrayed Zelphira actively. No blood on her hands. No signature on a warrant. But silence, she realized, could be just as sharp. Just as permanent.

And what wounded her most wasn't that she had let someone else down.

It was that she had done it for *ambition*.

For *status*.

For a *stage*.

And she didn't feel guilty enough for the trade. She was angry that she loved the choice that she made.

It felt like old times again, crying in the cold of her royal bed, the walls too thick to hear anything but her own grief. Back to square one. No magic. No certainty. Just a frightened little girl wearing a crown too big for her heart.

To Galinda's surprise, the sun did eventually rise, *from the West*. And it burned brighter than usual, as though mocking her. She somehow thought the world would stop just for a moment. But life did no such thing.

She stayed in bed.

The warmth of the sheets was a weak comfort, but it shielded her from a world that now demanded more than she could give.

But word travels quickly in castles.

And her return, after Oz'moons of silence, unanswered letters, and cold absences, was news. The kind that slips through keyholes and finds its way to waiting fathers.

There was a knock at the door.

Galinda didn't move. She held her breath and prayed they would leave.

But she knew the sound of that door handle.

Knew the way it turned.

He entered.

"I couldn't believe it when they told me you returned," said Dainhurst, his voice already bruised with authority.

Galinda sank deeper beneath the covers.

He continued, walking further into the room, his shoes heavy against the floorboards. "How *dare* you disappear for Oz'moons, ignore my letters, stay away knowing your sister was due to give birth any day."

Galinda's voice rose, weak and high-pitched. "Sorry."

"Are you even *part* of this family anymore?" he snapped. "Becoz if you don't want to be, I can *fix* that. I'll rewrite you out of my will, strip you of your title. You'll be *nothing*, Galinda. Just another girl wandering the world without my name or protection. Is that what you want?"

"No, I just—"

She burst into sobs. Deep, heaving cries that choked her mid-word.

Dainhurst sighed. The way men do when emotions inconvenience their expectations.

He walked over and stood at her bedpost for a long moment before sitting down beside her, his weight pressing into the mattress like a decision.

"You went to see that green girl, didn't you?"

"How did you know?"

"We all heard the Wizard's speech. I read the papers. You think I don't have eyes? Ears? *All* of Oz is talking about it."

He lowered his voice.

"Your sister gave birth yesterday. A Fairmoor Kindling, new firewood to the family *flame*. But that news?—" He shook his head. "*Clouded*—eclipsed—by the naming of your green friend as the most wanted fugitive in the land."

She choked out, through sobs, "And I feel... partly responsible."

Dainhurst, not known for comfort, extended a single arm around her, more like a drape than an embrace. "You did nothing, and I'm sure—*sure*—you tried your hardest to help the situation. But don't dwell on it." He offered a smile, thin and calculating. "It all worked out in your favour. And that's all that matters."

"How so?"

"The Wizard named *you* a Good Witch, didn't he? That's twice now I've birthed one. A house full of Good Witches." He chuckled to himself. "Just dry your eyes and get dressed. I want us to celebrate. And maybe next time, listen when I tell you to stay away from green-skinned girls."

He exited without another word, calling over his shoulder for a maid to prepare her bath.

Moments later, a maid entered quietly, curtsied, and crossed the room into the marbled bathroom. She placed a new glass bottle beside the tub.

Bubbleluxe.

The scent of it filled the room in an instant, lavender, lily, and the faintest hint of nostalgia. Her favourite.

Glinda stared at it for a moment, unsure whether to feel soothed or haunted.

She removed her clothes, wrapping herself in a towel, and stepped into the bath. The water was hot. Too hot, but she didn't flinch. She let it rise around her limbs, wrap her body, blur her shape. She let the heat do what she could not: soften her.

After a long soak, she emerged, clean but not cleansed. She brushed out her hair, pulled on fresh clothes, and left the safety of her room.

The grand hall was too bright.

Inside, Gisella lounged on the central chaise, cross-legged and disinterested, inspecting her fingernails like they were the evening's entertainment. A maid stood beside her, cradling the newborn. But the moment she saw Glinda appear, Gisella snapped to attention and hurriedly reached for the child, both arms stretching out like she feared she'd have to *prove* her motherhood.

Esmelda, seated nearby with a cordial in hand, beamed with artificial delight. "Oh, look what the Kalidah dragged in. Galinda, dear, how *are* you?"

Glinda smiled. "It's Glinda now."

Gisella rolled her eyes with a dramatic sigh. "Oh, please. When are you going to stop with the name changes? No one cares!"

Glinda met her sister's eyes briefly, then let her gaze drift downward toward the baby now nestled in Gisella's arms. Her silence was a choice.

"I'm glad," Esmelda chimed, "glad you're back to 'Glinda.' It's been so long since I've heard that name. What changed you?"

"Someone I met."

Esmelda's smile sharpened with mischief. "I bet it was that Winkie Prince."

Glinda said nothing, choosing instead to walk toward the furthest seat in the room, an elegant act of avoidance.

But Dainhurst intercepted.

"No," he said, voice firm and final. "Go sit next to your sister. Say hello to her kindling. Be a good auntie."

Glinda's spine stiffened.

Reluctantly, she turned back, her feet dragging like words she didn't want to speak. She sank into the sofa beside Gisella. She noticed Gisella's hair was some shades darker. She had a wrinkle around her mouth, and her eyelids drooped a little lower.

Glinda lowered her eyes. She was still close enough to see the baby's small face, far enough to feel the chill.

The baby blinked, unknowing. Unbothered. Perfect.

Gisella turned toward her, already smirking. "Glinda…" she said, rolling her eyes like a theatre actress overplaying the role of civility. "You see how the Kindling looks normal? That's how kindlings *should* look. No overbearing nose. Perfect golden hair. Not a speck of green on their skin."

Glinda turned away, her jaw clenched.

The comment earned a smile from Dainhurst, a nod of agreement from Esmelda, and a few veiled snickers from the maids, disguised as polite sneezes. Well-trained women, all of them.

Then Gisella sighed. Loudly. The kind of sigh that begged for inquiry.

"I don't know…"

"What don't you know, dear?" Esmelda asked.

"The kindling," Gisella said with theatrical melancholy, "looks *nothing* like me. I know I gave birth to it yesterday, but… surely a mother knows these things, right?"

Esmelda rose, slow and practiced, like a curtain being drawn.

"Let me see."

Gisella passed over the child, and Esmelda examined it with the intensity of a jeweller inspecting a questionable diamond.

"Hmm. I see what you mean," she said, "And if I'm honest… the boy looks like Glinda."

She turned toward Glinda, "Yes. He has Glinda's eyes. Bluer than the sky. No doubt about it."

Gisella scoffed. "I suppose the baby *couldn't* be all perfect. Can't have emerald eyes like the rest of us. Strange, isn't it? That *I'm* the mother, and yet it took on *that* defect."

Esmelda stepped closer, "Look at him."

Glinda turned her face away.

"Look!" Esmelda repeated, sterner now.

Glinda gave a sharp, obligatory glance. A flick of her eyes. A rejection in miniature.

"No," she said flatly, "we look nothing alike."

"You didn't even *look*," Esmelda snapped.

The kindling began to cry.

Gisella reclaimed the baby for all of three seconds before passing him off to the maid with a wave of her hand. "Feed it some chocolate or something."

The room fell back into its rhythm of staged comfort and passive venom. Gisella reclined again, stretching her fingers and shrugging.

"See, Father?" she said with a sugary sneer. "I *told* you Galinda—sorry, *Glinda*—was off gallivanting with that green girl. She's a pathological liar. Lying all the time, lie, lie, lie, just like when she said *I* would never have magic. And look at me

GLINDA: The GOOD Witch

now." She gestured dramatically. "A *Good Witch* and a *mother*. And who is Glinda? A girl who associates with a criminal who tried to assassinate the Wizard. A poor, disgusting thing."

Glinda's hands balled into fists.

"*Shut up!*" she screamed, "You don't know what you're talking about, she didn't try to assassinate the Wizard!"

The room froze.

"Calm down and act like a princess, Glinda," Dainhurst commanded.

Gisella tilted her head, mockery curling at the corners of her mouth. "There were reports of her flying above the city on a broom that looked like it belonged in a graveyard. *Cackling*, no less, like something straight out of a child's nightmare. You see *that* and you tell me she's not a villain?"

She leaned forward, lips curling. "The only thing she's missing is that *crooked nose* you used to have."

Glinda's mouth trembled. "Don't make me——"

Her eyes fell to the jagged crystal pendant around Gisella's throat. It glinted faintly, but more than that—it *moved*. A flicker inside it. Something green, *alive*, was pulsing in its core.

"That necklace," Glinda said, her voice low, taut. "There's something off about it."

She stepped forward, slowly, like a hunter stalking her prey. "Why does it look like… the green hue is alive inside it?"

She raised her hand, reaching out.

Gisella recoiled instantly, shifting away, clutching the pendant like it was a holy relic she feared might be stolen.

Glinda turned to Dainhurst. "Doesn't it look *exactly* like the crystal necklace you bought Gisella? Except this one's green? You told us it was *one-of-a-kind*, father. *One*. But I remember, there was a chip in the lower facet. A tiny flaw. *That same chip is on this one*."

Dainhurst's brow furrowed. He stepped forward, inspecting the pendant with sudden interest. "Yes, yes, I see what you mean."

He turned to Gisella, voice sharp. "What did you *do* to it? If you wanted a new one in another colour, you could have just *asked*, you didn't have to stain it green and lessen its value."

But Gisella didn't answer. Her smile dropped. Her hand clenched tighter around the necklace.

Then, in one swift movement, she grabbed Glinda by the arm and *dragged* her from the hall, slamming the door behind them. The sound rang out like a spell breaking.

Outside, in the cold corridor, far from the gaze of family and façade, Gisella spun around.

"What do you *think* you're doing?" she snapped.

Glinda ripped her arm free. Her eyes blazed. *"Give me my magic back, you wretched witch!"*

"No."

Glinda began to pace, her hands trembling. "I *knew* it was you. I felt it, in my gut, in every spell I could no longer cast. *Why?* Why would you do this to me?"

Gisella shrugged, as casually as if asked about changing a dress. "Becoz you had something I wanted. So... I took it."

"You really *are* green with envy," Glinda hissed. "You—*you* were the beautiful one. From birth. The darling of every room. You had everything, Gisella. And I never once resented you for it. Never once tried to *take* anything from you. Becoz you were my *sister*."

Another shrug. "I guess we're just two different people."

Glinda's gaze sharpened on the pendant. "That's how you're doing it. That's where you've hidden it. My magic. It's in that crystal." She stepped forward again. "Give it to me."

She reached, fingers trembling, voice cracking.

But the moment her skin grazed the crystal's surface, *pain* screamed through her fingers. Burning, blistering heat—no fire, no flame, just *raw energy* that wanted her gone.

She gasped and flung herself backward, stumbling against the wall, clutching her hand. Her breath came in short, panicked bursts.

Had she held on a second longer, her flesh might have melted clean off the bone.

She shook her fingers wildly, trying to chase the pain away.

Her rage trembled beneath her skin, but it was grief that reached her eyes.

Not grief for her magic.

Not even grief for what she'd lost.

But for *who* she'd lost.

Her sister.

"Oh, did I forget to tell you?" Gisella's voice dripped with cruel delight. "You *can't* take the magic back. Once it's out—it's out. It's mine now. You'll never get it again... *unless I give it to you*."

Glinda's eyes welled with tears, and for once, she didn't try to blink them away.

"So... the thing with Ominson. You did that on purpose?"

Gisella's grin widened. "*Of course* I did."

Her voice was sharp, triumphant. A blade she'd been dying to draw.

"You were ruining my life—so I ruined *yours*. Now I have *everything* you ever wanted. I am the mother of Ominson's child. I have *your* magic. Father finally sees me again as the daughter worth keeping. The people love me. *I* am the Good Witch of the South." She stepped closer, her heels clicking like punctuation marks, her voice rising with every word, clear, cutting, *performative*. "I don't care what the Wizard says, you will *never* outdo me. I am *already* loved here. The South has embraced me like a prophecy fulfilled. And you?" She laughed. "You're better off fleeing to some other corner of Oz, some other little pocket of pity. Becoz I—*I* will be remembered by time. *Etched* into it. And you? You'll be nothing but a pink fog. A hue of irrelevance. A whisper no one bothers to remember."

Without another glance, she turned on her heel and strolled back into the grand hall, her dress sweeping behind her like a victorious banner.

Glinda stood there, hollow.

She stumbled back to her chambers, barely managing to shut the door behind her before the sob rose in her chest. But she didn't cry, not properly.

She *wouldn't*.

Instead, she reached for the Ethereum. She flipped through the pages with desperate fingers, trying to read through blurred vision.

But there was nothing.

No spell to restore what had been stolen.

No enchantment to summon what had been drained.

Only silence. And the ache of absence.

Except one thing.

The Transference Spell.

Glinda read it again.

And again.

The ink seemed to shimmer on the page, almost mocking her. It confirmed what she already feared, and yet hope, like an old wound, flared painfully in her chest.

It was *possible* to move magic from the original host, but it could only be contained in a vessel. Once magic had left the body, *once it was expelled*, it could not return by force. Not directly. The soul and the *magicore* no longer recognized each other.

With her magic bound, anchored in a vessel, an object, then there remained a single, delicate loophole.

To retrieve it, one required:

Consent.

Or the *object* the magic was contained in.

Her eyes hovered over the word as if it might split open and offer a solution.

Consent. As if that were even possible now.

Her magic wasn't floating in the air, waiting to be called. It had been *housed.* *Worn.* Adorned like a trophy around her sister's neck.

The necklace. The object of containment.

Her hands twitched, the nerves still raw from her last attempt to grab it.

The Ethereum glowed faintly under the candlelight. The page had gone still.

Her magic was *there*, just inches away, every time Gisella walked into a room, laughed too loudly, charmed a noble, cast a petty hex.

Her spells.

Her light.

Her birthright.

Locked in emerald crystal and spite.

And Glinda, Glinda Arduelle Fairmoor, was no longer a sorceress.

She was a girl in borrowed robes and clinging perfume, a title without the power to fill it.

She sat still for a long time.

Staring at the spell.

At the soft, damning word.

Consent.

She closed the book slowly.

And placed her hand on top of it, steady now.

She would not beg.

She would not plead.

There would be another way.

Glinda sat upright on her bed, the covers still tangled around her legs like the remnants of a bad dream. Her eyes drifted toward the window—where the sunlight filtered through in narrow beams, striking the glass like a memory trying to get in.

That's where she needed to be.

Out *there.*

The room had grown too heavy, too still. The walls felt less like protection and more like a bubble, delicate and suffocating. A sphere of quiet expectation. A gilded cage of Goodness.

She slipped on her pink slippers and stepped outside.

The sun met her like an old friend with new questions. Its warmth was gentle, but the light felt too bright. Like it was trying to read her.

The castle staff watched as she walked across the manicured gardens, parading the old familiar paths. It had been Oz'moons since she'd taken a stroll like this, since she'd let her presence be *seen.* And though they bowed and curtsied as they always had, there was a new quietness in their eyes, curiosity, perhaps confusion.

After all, hadn't the Wizard himself named her the Good Witch?

Then why the melancholy?

Why the eyes rimmed red?

A maid approached, half-smiling. "I was just looking for you, Princess."

Glinda said nothing. Just returned a faint, distant smile, the kind that only moves half your face.

"I have a letter for you. The mailman just delivered it, just this second."

The parchment was placed gently in Glinda's hand.

Her heart fluttered. She turned on her heel and walked quickly back inside, nearly tripping on her slippers as she half-glided down the corridor.

Was it *him?*

The Wizard?

Had he finished it—*her* contraption? The great bubble he sketched with such glee in the candlelit hush of his library? Was it ready to lift her from obscurity into the skies of reverence?

She reached her chamber door, her breath short.

Then she turned the letter over.

The seal stopped her cold.

It wasn't emerald.

It wasn't the Wizard's.

It was deep blue and pressed with a familiar crest.

Winkie Country.

Draeth Mor.

But she didn't know exactly who it was from.

Her fingers trembled as she broke the seal, parchment crinkling like dried petals.

She opened it there, in the threshold of her room, half inside, half out, and read it.

Dear Galinda,

I imagine you were expecting another name to be writing this letter. But no, it's me, Rivero. There's so much I've left unsaid, and though I'll try to keep this brief, I won't hide the truth from you.

I'm writing from my study. This is the fourth version of this letter I've attempted, and each time, I tore it up, thinking I could soften what needs to be said. But I can't. You deserve the truth, unvarnished.

Zelphira returned to Draeth Mor after what happened in the Emerald City. She came seeking sanctuary. And, as we promised you and her, we gave it. This place is now her home. And yet... you didn't come with her.

You can imagine my shock. No, perhaps you can't.

I don't know exactly what happened with the Wizard—I wasn't there. But I do know this: Zelphira did not try to kill him. We both know that. And yet you let them say she did. You let them paint her as a monster. And worse, you stood by as their lie.

She tried to explain your absence. She made excuses for you, as if love could explain abandonment. But I cannot. I will not. What you did was cruel. Selfish. Cowardly.

We would have protected you here. All of us. You know that.

But you chose your side.

I understand why. More than you know. We've always mirrored each other in ambition, in survival. But what shattered her, what broke her, wasn't your absence. It was seeing you stand beside the Wizard, while his voice crackled over the radios like a death knell, feeding the people poison, and smiled. Smiled, while he called her wicked. While the world swallowed the lie that she was dangerous, unhinged, evil.

You knew better. And still, you said nothing.

And that is Unforgivable.

CHANGE

Now, Zelphira is a fugitive. Hunted. If she so much as steps beyond these walls, she will be killed—her death paraded through the streets as justice.

All becoz you refused to speak.

I am appalled. Disgusted. And ashamed to have once called you beloved.

If I were you, I wouldn't be able to bear my own reflection.

And so, let us end this charade. This courtship. We both know what it was, comfortable, convenient, a fiction we wore like a costume. But I no longer wish to pretend. I cannot. My heart has always belonged elsewhere, and I think deep down, you knew that too.

So, I release you. I wash myself clean of this. Entirely.

But I leave you with this: if anything happens to Zelphira, if she dies, if they hurt her, it will be on you. Her blood will stain your hands, not becoz you struck the blow, but becoz you watched it coming and did nothing.

Nothing.

May you carry that truth with you, always.

Prince Rivero Valeheart

Glinda crumpled the letter in a single, jerking motion, her fingers trembling with fury. The parchment made a dry, papery crackle as she hurled it across the room. It hit the wall with no ceremony, just a soft, anticlimactic thud, and fell like a dead moth to the floor.

She slammed the door.

Ran.

Up the corridor, past portraits that stared at her with cold ancestral judgment. Up the stairs, faster, until the air thinned and the walls narrowed, and the steps groaned beneath her desperation.

To the attic.

She didn't know *why* she came here. Maybe she wanted a re-do. A reprieve. Maybe she wanted to sit in the same dust as before and convince herself she'd been better then, more innocent. That her shame had an origin point she could circle back to.

She reached the top.

Collapsed to the floor, knees folding, skirts pooling like wilted roses. The dirt clung to her, uncaring. Her breath was ragged. Her fists were clenched.

She didn't even know who she was angry at.

Rivero? The Wizard? Zelphira?

Herself?

She began to *rationalise*.

Rivero had no right to judge her. He would've done the same. Of course he would've.

She had no idea Zelphira could fly. She was left with no other option. What was she supposed to do? Choose to willingly plummet to her death off the tower balcony *or* seek comfort in the good graces of the Wizard.

No. She'd made the only choice she *could*.

How is Rivero so sure he could protect her? He is a prince to a powerful king but even all the kings are second to the Wizard.

The Wizard practically owned Oz.

The man who just chose to make her Good.

Not out of necessity, but becoz he could.

Her frown softened. The heat drained from her face, replaced by something cold and amused. She began to laugh, softly, like the tinkle of a cracked music box.

He would see.

They *would* see.

She would become the most powerful woman in Oz. She would rise beyond kingdoms. And when they realised what they'd cast aside, what they'd underestimated—they would beg.

And she would forgive them.

Because she was *Good*.

She exhaled, and the silence around her welcomed it. The attic was still, secluded. There was a comfort here she hadn't expected. She wondered, absently, why she'd never come here to think before.

And then she saw it.

A box. Half-hidden beneath an old sheet and a tangle of forgotten furniture. It looked familiar.

She rose, brushed the dirt from her dress and buttocks, and approached. Something about it hummed faintly in the back of her mind.

She dragged it to the window for better light.

Inside, ribbons, trinkets, rings. A necklace she once borrowed. A bracelet she'd forgotten she'd returned.

And suddenly, she *knew*.

These were *Zelena's* things.

Glinda's breath caught in her throat. She whispered to herself, barely audible, "Oh, Zelly…"

She dug deeper.

And there, nestled beneath the clutter of girlhood and memory, was a small, battered book. Dirty. Scuffed. Forgotten.

She pulled it free.

It felt heavier than it looked.

She sat back, pressed against the wall, knees drawn to her chest. She placed the book on her thighs and opened the cover.

Zelena's handwriting. Loose. Angular. Chaotic in places. Passionate in others. Her diary.

Glinda froze. Morality pricked at her like a thorn, *was it right?* Was this sacred? Was this a sin?

But Zelena had left it. Had *wanted* something found. Maybe.

CHANGE

So she read.

Page after page. Skimming past light-hearted entries. A brief, wild affair with a gardener. Pages of musings. Sadnesses. Dreams.

And then,

A page marked at the top in larger script.

Esmelda.

Glinda sat upright. Her eyes narrowed.

Twosday, 16th Glimmertide,

I am broken. Not just in body, but in spirit. It feels as though my soul has been torn from me and cast into the dark. What remains is hollow, a cage of bones, rotting from within.

I have endured horrors I cannot find words for. Many, many moons, spent in a dungeon beneath the world, surrounded by the stench of decay and the silence of the dead. They gave me nothing but water and the occasional bread, just enough to keep me alive… to suffer longer.

I have called out to the One Gohd until my voice frayed to whispers. I do not know what sin I committed to deserve this torment. I've searched myself again and again, clawed through every memory. Still… nothing. Only confusion. Only pain.

I remember falling asleep, in my bed. Then Esmelda's voice, soft as silk, ordering the guards to grab me.

I was lulled into silence by a sleeping draught. Took me in the night. And I woke not in the castle kitchens, but in Hel.

Today, Esmelda came to me. The Devil in a woman's skin. She smiled as she looked upon my fevered flesh, my open sores, my shaking limbs. She pressed her hand to my chest, hard, until my lungs seized and I begged for air. She watched me suffer like it was a song she enjoyed.

She told me she had this done to me, as if I didn't already know. That she hated me. That she always had. But she would not say why.

I knew she didn't care for me, I've always known. Even when I scrubbed the floors cleaner than any other. Even when I stayed behind to finish what the other maids abandoned. I gave more than my share. Still… she looked at me like something beneath her shoe.

But why? What have I done to deserve such fury?

She wouldn't say. Only that if I spoke a word of this to anyone, especially Glinda, she would see to it that I died slowly. Slower than this.

And yet… I had already decided I would tell no one. I do not want Glinda to carry this grief. How could I let her know that her own mother would do this to me?

What kind of world allows such cruelty to go unpunished?

I am sick. So very sick. Whatever plague she's cursed me with is eating me alive. I don't know if I will live to see the sun again. But I write this with what little strength I have left. I don't know why, I just feel compelled to.

I know the One Gohd will have justice for me in this life or the next.

But it is Glinda I fear for. She must never know.

Oh, Glinda was furious.

But not the kind of fury that screamed or flailed.

No, this was the kind of rage that *burned.*

She stood.

Her body trembled. Her cheeks flushed a livid pink. Her eyes burned like twin *Everflames.*

She could feel it inside her.

Bubbling.

Rising.

She was a surface about to shatter.

She stormed down the attic steps, each footfall like a hammer. Her breath came in short, feral bursts. She reached the grand hall and *threw* the doors open—so hard they slammed against the walls and echoed down the corridors like war drums.

The room fell silent.

Even Gisella flinched, jerking back in her chair with a gasp.

Dainhurst yelled. "What are you doing?!"

For a split second, Gisella thought the fury was hers. *Again.*

But Glinda didn't look at her.

Her eyes locked on *Esmelda.*

"What did you do to Zelena?!"

Esmelda froze.

"What?" she said, her mouth barely moving. "Glinda, what are you talking about—"

"Don't sit there and act stupid!" Glinda shrieked, *"I know you did something. I read it. I READ IT. So just say it! Say it!"*

Dainhurst stood abruptly, the blood draining from his face. He glanced at Gisella.

"Let's give them privacy."

Without another word, Dainhurst, Gisella, and the maids filed out of the room.

Glinda and Esmelda were alone.

"Please," Esmelda whispered, lifting her hand. "Please calm down, Glinda. Just… give me a moment to explain."

Glinda didn't move. Her voice was quieter now, but only because her throat was broken.

"No. Tell me this isn't true."

Esmelda lowered her head. Her eyes flickered. She said nothing.

Then, softly: "It is."

Silence.

Then Glinda howled.

Not with sound, but with presence. With body. With broken stillness.

Her face twisted into something near-animal. Not a sob, but a gasp of air so sharp it could've sliced skin. Her knees buckled, but she refused to fall.

CHANGE

She got a confession.

After all these years. After all the questions no one had dared ask.

The culprit was *her own mother.*

"Please, sit. Let me explain myself, please."

But Glinda didn't move. "*Why?*" she said. "Why would you do this to such a kind soul?"

Esmelda looked down at her own hands. They seemed old now. Fragile.

"Becoz I'm evil, becoz I'm cruel and wicked."

She let the words sit there.

Then, she exhaled. "But more than that... becoz I was *jealous* of her."

Glinda stared, disbelieving.

"*Jealous?*" she spat. "Of a maid? A *maid* who brushed your hair and folded your silks and called you 'My Lady' even when you didn't deserve it? A maid who served you *faithfully*, who was *kind*, to *your daughters?*"

"Exactly," Esmelda said, barely a whisper. "I was jealous of her. Mostly... of her heart."

She stared back down at her hands, as if they still held the memory of what she'd done.

"She took on the role I should've played. She *mothered* you. Fed you. Bathed you. Even after you chose the pink gem, when you had that weird face and soft-voiced and frightened of shadows, she cradled you like you were her own. She *loved* you, genuinely, instinctively, and I hated her for it. When you were sick, she nursed you. When you were sad, she made you laugh. When you sang, it was *her* voice you were echoing. *She* taught you to sing." Her voice trembled. "And when you got older... you *turned* to her. Not to me. You looked for *her* in every room. Not me."

Glinda's throat was tight, but her voice surged.

"So after all these sun-moons... you *killed her* becoz she was a better mother than you ever *could* be?"

"*No.* That's not what made me do it."

She swallowed.

"There was... a night. I had guests over, some women from the old circles. We were drinking, laughing, reminiscing... and Zelena was serving us. And one of them, Lady Perle, I think, she leaned back and said, 'My, what a beautiful maid you have.'"

Her voice turned bitter with memory.

"Then another added, 'Look at that hair—silky, full, perfect. She even has better hair than *you*, Esmelda.' And I turned to look at her, and she was *smiling*. Trying not to, but she was."

Esmelda's hands began to shake.

"Then someone whispered in my ear, 'You better be careful with that one. Keep her around too long and she'll seduce your husband, take your place. She's young, fertile. My mind went back to moments I'd see your father glancing a little too long at her, or when he'd give her more money than she needed for groceries.'"

She let out a breath. "And something inside me... *snapped*."

She looked at Glinda, eyes shining with tears.

"That's what pushed me over. That *fear*. That jealousy. That little voice in my head that said: *She's already replaced you with your daughter. Soon she'll replace you with your husband too.*"

She reached forward.

"Glinda, I—"

But Glinda jolted back, recoiling as though touched by poison.

"You *sick, twisted* woman," Glinda hissed. "You haven't changed. You're still that bitter, poisonous *monster* who let envy rot you from the inside out."

"No! I *have* changed. I know what I did was wrong. That's why I disappeared for many moons. I went to get help, Glinda. I saw a doctor. I was tormented, *haunted*. I would wake in cold sweats, screaming. I saw her in my dreams. I saw *you*. The look on your face."

She wept now, openly. "I hated myself for what I'd done. And what broke me wasn't just the act, it was how it *damaged you*. How it *poisoned you*. The way she died, it warped something in you, and I... I will *never* forgive myself."

"I am *ashamed* to look at you."

She stepped closer, tears racing down her face in defiance of her fury.

"I am *disgusted* to have come from you. You are *not* my mother. You're a *curse* stitched into the tapestry of my life."

"Please, Glinda, don't say that... I know I've done things. *Unforgivable* things. But that doesn't make me fully evil. I'm still trying. I *am* good. I just... I lost myself somewhere."

Glinda's lip curled in disbelief.

"No. You're not *good*. Stop lying to yourself."

"Who do you think dropped the key and the letter by your door the day you found the magic wielders in the dungeon? It was me! Doesn't that count for something? Doesn't that make me good in some way? That I'm trying?" Esmelda pleaded, her voice cracking under the weight of her desperation.

She stared down at Esmelda.

"No, you're wicked as they come. And nothing, *nothing*, can change that. The sooner you stop telling yourself these sweet little bedtime lies that you're a good woman, the sooner you'll understand what real healing looks like."

Esmelda stiffened, the tears on her cheeks drying into salt. But her voice regained a dangerous calm.

"Think what you like," she said, "but Doctor Thistle told me healing is possible. That moving forward is what matters. And Barbarus said the One Gohd has already forgiven me."

"They're *wrong!*" Glinda roared. "Just becoz you confess doesn't mean you are *forgiven!* It doesn't erase it!"

Then Esmelda's expression changed, like something inside her had cracked with release.

"Then… since we're confessing," she said quietly, "there's something I need to tell you. Something that's been burning inside me like fire. Something not even your father knows."

Glinda groaned, rubbing her temples, "What *now?*"

Esmelda took a breath.

"Seraphina, the witch you chose your gem after, she's not the villain they say she is. She's not evil. She—"

Glinda laughed. Bitter. Hollow. "*I already know this.*"

Esmelda raised her voice. "But do you know that she's your *ancestor?*"

Glinda froze.

"You're lying."

"I'm not, you come from her line. The blood of Seraphina runs through you."

"If that were true, if she were truly in our bloodline, *you* would've sheltered me. *You* would've understood. Not shunned me like dirt. Not locked me away. Not despised me for choosing pink!"

"You're right! And that is why I hate myself, but I am telling you the truth. I just had to be just as angry as everyone else. It's how we survive. You know this very well."

Glinda's face twisted into disgust. "You're just saying this now becoz you want my *forgiveness.*"

Esmelda stepped closer. "Even if I am, it's still true."

Glinda held up her hand, silencing her.

"It *doesn't* matter. Even if Seraphina *is* my ancestor, even if the legends are all lies and she's not wicked—*you still are.* You're worse than the stories they tell about her." Her voice dropped to a hiss. "*You* should be the one burned at the stake and let's hope the One Gohd's judgment is kinder than *mine*, becoz if I had my magic right now, I would turn you into a bug and squash you beneath my boot."

She spat on the grand hall floor.

Then turned.

"*Glinda!*" Esmelda cried, her voice cracking.

But Glinda didn't stop.

She walked out of the grand hall like a storm in velvet—threw the doors open, then slammed them behind her.

She reached her chambers in a blur of steps and fury, and also slammed the bedroom door and collapsed into her bed like she was falling through the earth.

And then,

She *screamed.*

Into the pillow. Into the sky. Into herself.

It came out hoarse and strangled, torn from somewhere buried far too long. But only gasps and sobs escaped.

She couldn't breathe.

Couldn't *feel.*

Couldn't *stop.*

She was tired.

So *tired.*

Her breath finally slowed, her body, wrung dry from the storm. And in the stillness that followed, something colder settled in.

She didn't weep anymore.

She rose from the bed like a puppet unstrung, her limbs moving only because they *had* to. She grabbed her bag, large, leather-trimmed, once used for grand travel. Tonight, it was survival.

She filled it with clothing, books, socks, whatever she could grab.

Her Ethereum, she tucked it away like a piece of herself she couldn't afford to lose.

She had *enough.*

Of Esmelda's evilness. Of Dainhurst's politics. Of Gisella's cruelty.

She slung on her coat, pink wool lined with white fox fur, once a symbol of youth, now armour. Her fingers fastened the buttons like they were binding a vow.

She descended the stairs.

At the grand hall doors, Esmelda stood like a statue carved from regret.

"Where are you going?" she asked.

Glinda didn't stop.

Didn't flinch.

She walked past her like smoke escaping a fire.

Down the front steps. Out the door.

The slam of the door behind her was not a scream this time, it was a sentence. Final. Full stop.

She called for the coachman. Her voice cracked, but he came at once.

He looked at her, blinking. Her eyes were red, her curls unkempt. Her hands trembled slightly as she handed over the bag.

Still, she stood tall.

The coachman said nothing at first. He loaded her things onto the Gilded Rose, the horses snorted as if sensing tension in the night air.

He looked at her once more, carefully.

"Are you all right, Princess?"

She nodded.

She couldn't speak.

Not yet.

They rode in silence for miles, the rhythmic roll of the carriage a lullaby for someone too exhausted to dream.

CHANGE

Then finally, gently, the coachman tried again.

"Princess?"

She took a breath. "Yes?" she said, her voice still raw, but steadier. "And... call me *Glinda*."

"Very well, Glinda. Where are we off to?"

She stared out the window. The moonlit road stretched ahead like a promise wrapped in fog.

She swallowed, a spark flickering behind her eyes.

"The North," she said, "take me to *Gillikin*."

CHAPTER 41

True North

This had been the longest journey Glinda had ever taken.

From the rose-drenched warmth of the South to the austere chill of the North, the land unfolded endlessly before her. Even with the *Pryzm Road*, the trip offered no shortcuts for grief.

It was a full day's ride, broken only by short pauses to relieve themselves and eat food neither of them truly tasted.

She was grateful, deeply, for the coachman. He asked no questions. Offered no platitudes. He simply rode. And in his silence, she found space to breathe.

The wheels clacked along the cobbles, and when Glinda popped her head out the window for air, the spires of the Wizard's University came into view, rising like distant ghosts.

Her *heart* clenched. Her stomach turned.

The memories hit her like perfume once worn by a lost friend. Sweet, sharp, and agonizing.

She ducked back inside.

Later, as they rolled deeper into Gillikin Country, the coachman called from up front. "Where do you want me to leave you?"

Glinda blinked. She hadn't thought that far ahead.

She had no address. No invitation. No destination. Only escape.

She cleared her throat, speaking through the window. "Can you find an inn? Somewhere we can spend the night?"

"Sure thing."

But Gillikin was not a land of welcome. Not easily.

The coachman stopped often, pulling the Gilded Rose beside locals with long black hair and pale, skeptical faces. "Do you know where the nearest inn is?" he'd ask.

They'd point vaguely, then vanish into doorways.

Again. And again.

Glinda sighed, her patience fraying. "What if we just stay in the carriage? Find somewhere quiet. Somewhere safe."

CHANGE

The coachman shook his head, firm. "No, Princess."

"Glinda," she corrected softly.

He smiled. "Glinda. We don't know these streets. And your father always warned me about the Gillikins and their Gillikinese natures. You've got valuables, titles, and more to lose. We don't want to test Gohd's mercy, not tonight."

Glinda nodded and sank into the cushion of her seat. Her bones ached from weariness. But in that moment, his care, his *insistence*—that melted something.

A small smile touched her lips.

The first in what felt like Oz'moons.

Eventually, they came upon it.

A cottage-style inn, nestled behind a slanting fence and the husk of what may once have been a cornfield. The wood was weathered, and the lanterns were few. But it was *there*.

The Gilded Rose rolled to a stop at the door.

"I'll go park somewhere safe," said the coachman. "Why don't you go in and ask for a room?"

She opened the inn's door. The bell above tinkled like a timid chime.

Inside, the room was bathed in soft yellow light. No more than three lanterns lit the space. Dust danced in the air, and the wallpaper peeled like memories. It smelled faintly of old cider and something bitter.

There was no one at the front desk.

She tightened her grip on her purse. A spider crawled across the floor near her pink-pointed shoes, and she flinched.

Still, she approached the desk and rang the small, tarnished bell.

Nothing.

Then the door opened again behind her.

"Princess—" the coachman began.

"Glinda," she corrected. Again.

"Glinda, I found a safe space to park the Gilded Rose. May I sleep in it tonight? I'd rather stay with the luggage. It's safer that way, since we are only staying for the night."

"Are you sure? I can pay for your room. It's the least I can do, after the trouble I've caused."

"That's kind of you, but it's my pleasure. Besides…" he smiled, just a little. "The seats are surprisingly comfortable."

Glinda raised an eyebrow, the shadow of a smirk playing at her lips. "And how would you know that?"

He chuckled, hand on the brim of his cap. "Let's just say, there've been a few nights I couldn't afford an inn myself."

Glinda laughed, soft and genuine.

The coachman laughed too, a bit louder.

"Go on then," Glinda said, waving him off gently. "Enjoy yourself."

He took off his hat and bowed his head, not as a servant, but like a friend might.

"Good night, Glinda."

He shut the door behind him, leaving her alone in the amber light.

She turned back toward the front desk. Still empty.

Still, no innkeeper.

Still, the bell unanswered.

A draft of Northern air curled around her ankles. Colder here. Thinner. The kind of cold that sank past skin.

She wrapped her scarf tighter, the soft wool bunched around her neck, and began tapping the bell.

Once.

Twice.

Then again.

And again.

Ding. Ding. Ding. Ding.

Her fingers moved faster, frantic, like she was ringing against time itself.

Finally, *a groan.*

Somewhere beyond the back room, someone stirred. A sleepy grumble followed by the slow, thudding shuffle of heavy feet.

Then, with a yawn and a shudder, a fat woman appeared, her presence large and oddly comforting, like a forgotten aunt or an old armchair. She blinked the sleep from her eyes and smiled the moment she saw Glinda.

"Oh dear," she said, her voice syrupy and unfiltered. "Didn't think I'd get anyone this evening."

She waddled to the counter, her gaze moved across Glinda in slow, curious circles.

"You're not a Northian," she said, squinting. "Not a *true* Northian anyway. No one from 'round here's got hair more yellow than a sunflower. That's pure Quadling if I've ever seen it." She sniffed. "You here for university?"

Glinda glanced around, dusty beams, creaking floorboards, a mounted fox head whose glassy eyes seemed to watch her.

"No," she said finally, voice muffled through her scarf. "But... do you have a room?"

The woman grinned wide, her cheeks blossoming like peaches. "*Do I have a room?* Darlin', I *always* have a room. No one stays here anymore. Not since the Wicked Witch rose from *Hel* and began terrorizin' the skies."

Glinda flinched at that—barely. But enough.

The woman caught it.

And narrowed her eyes.

CHANGE

"I think I know you. You're the *new* Good Witch, ain't you?" she whispered, reverently now. "The Wizard announced you a few weeks back. Princess of the South, brave and lovely, come to save us all."

Glinda gave the faintest smile.

"Oh, where are *my manners?*" the woman gasped suddenly, reaching across the desk with fingers like damp sausages. "I'm *Lady Peckle*. It's an *honour* to meet you."

She bowed her head, all her chins folding in submission. "Thank you. Thank you for what you did, for savin' our Wizard from that *beast*. You're a *Saint*."

Glinda offered her hand, already half-regretting it, and Lady Peckle seized it like it was relic.

Then kissed it.

"*Lurline* bless you," she whispered, eyes shining. "And may the *One Gohd* keep you. You're a *blessin'*. You're hope itself."

She stood still after, as though Glinda's very existence had turned the inn into a holy site. "The *Good Witch*," she mumbled under her breath, "in *my* inn…"

For a few stretched heartbeats, she simply stared. Then she seemed to remember herself, waddling over to the wall where a crooked hook bore a cluster of rusting brass keys. She shuffled through them, muttering codes only she understood.

"Follow me, my dear."

She led the way up the creaking stairs, her breath heavy not from the effort, but the surreal thrill of it all. Glinda followed silently, her steps feather-light compared to Lady Peckle's stomping feet. The hallway smelled of cinnamon and mildew. Somewhere, water dripped in rhythm.

At the end of a crooked corridor, Lady Peckle stopped and turned a key with a huff.

"This is the best we've got. Least mice. Cockroaches only in spring. I know it's not fit for a princess, but…"

Glinda stepped inside.

The room was humble. Worn paint clung to the walls like the last leaves of a dying tree. More wallpapers that peeled in lazy curls, surrendering to time. But there was a bed. A pillow. A blanket. A sink. A window.

A place to *rest*.

"This will do," Glinda said. "Thank you."

Lady Peckle beamed. "Awww, ain't you sweet as a sugarplum."

Glinda placed her folded clothes on the bed like sacred offerings. Lady Peckle handed her a small oil lantern.

Its glow startled a small stampede of mice into the corners.

Glinda jumped, but caught herself.

Lady Peckle didn't notice. She was too enthralled by the quiet poetry of Glinda's movements, like watching a star stretch its limbs.

She finally snapped from her trance as Glinda moved to shut the door.

But before the latch clicked, Lady Peckle wedged her face into the small opening, eyes earnest, voice trembling with sincerity.

"If you should need anything, I'll be downstairs."

Glinda nodded, barely holding back a sigh.

"I *mean it*," Lady Peckle repeated, as though swearing allegiance. "Anything you need. I'm here."

"I'll be sure to let you know."

At last, Lady Peckle stepped back, her large silhouette vanishing down the hall like a misplaced storm cloud.

Glinda shut the door.

Then *locked* it.

She placed her coat gently on the end of the bed, her hat upon the pillow.

She sat on the bed without undressing, without unpacking. As though her soul might flee the moment she allowed herself comfort.

Then she let her body collapse into the sheets.

And she slept.

Not peacefully.

But completely.

◇

By morning, the streets of Gillikin stirred with renewed life. The silence of the North had broken like ice underfoot.

People bustled to school, to market, to nowhere in particular. Their voices, sharp and spirited, echoed through the frost-laced air like firelight in a dark cathedral. The wind was still cold, always cold here, but the people, through sheer determination, kept the **heart** of the North warm.

Glinda rose slowly from the bed, the blanket clinging to her like it didn't want her to go.

She moved with practiced elegance, though her muscles ached beneath her dress.

She used her embroidered handkerchief to turn the rusted tap, washed her face with its freezing water, and brushed her teeth with careful precision. She combed her hair, applied a subtle pink gloss, sprayed herself with perfume, sweet magnolia and strawberry-plum, and stood in front of the mirror until she almost believed in the reflection.

Fresh clothes. A brave face.

As best she could.

When she descended the stairs, there sat Lady Peckle, planted at the front desk like an old statue of northern hospitality.

She was tapping her feet, reading *The Daily Oz*.

On the cover:

CHANGE

WICKED WITCH OF THE WEST SPOTTED ON HER FLYING BROOM AS SHE CONSPIRES TO BURN MUNCHKINLAND

The print screamed in scarlet ink, not the usual ebony. The image, a blurred silhouette against a moonlit sky, was unmistakable.

Glinda stopped cold.

Her stomach sank, her fingers tightened around the strap of her bag.

Lady Peckle noticed the stillness in her guest. She followed Glinda's eyes to the headline, then slowly turned the paper toward herself again.

She frowned, folded the paper in half, and lowered her voice. "I'm sorry."

"You don't have to apologise," Glinda replied quickly, a little too quickly. "Now... the discussion of payment?"

"Right. Of course. Hope you had a good night's sleep. You'll need your energy, fighting the Wicked Witch." She gave a laugh, but it was soft, uncertain.

Glinda didn't answer. Instead, she pulled six gold coins from her purse and placed them on the counter.

Lady Peckle's eyes widened. "The room cost... nine *silver* coins."

"Perfect then," Glinda said, already adjusting her scarf.

She lifted her bag, gave a polite smile, and turned toward the door.

"It was nice having you!" Lady Peckle called from the counter. "Come back sometime and say hello!"

The bell chimed as Glinda opened the door, a sound like a final breath, and she stepped out into the morning frost.

Her coachman was already waiting beside the Gilded Rose, brushing the snow from the wheels with his gloves.

"How did you sleep?" Wendell the coachman asked, his voice cheerful but measured.

Glinda stifled a yawn. "As best as I could."

"You?"

"Like an egg in a nest, warm enough, still intact."

He lifted her bag and loaded it gently onto the back of the carriage, careful not to crush the edge of her coat.

Then he turned, removing his cap. The morning sun caught the pale crown of his head, a few strands of grey catching the light like silver thread. He reached into his pocket and pulled out a small, folded piece of parchment.

"While you were asleep," he said, handing it to her, "I asked around. Seein' as you're not planning on sleeping in another inn, I thought we might find you a home. Folks gave me directions to a few properties, some for sale, some for rent."

Glinda looked down at the worn paper, then up into Wendell's eyes—eyes as steady as the reins he held. Something about that kindness, quiet and unasked for, broke something open in her chest.

She didn't speak.

She just stepped forward and hugged him, tightly, gratefully, like a child might cling to the last warm thing on a cold day.

"Thank you so much for this, Wendell," she murmured, her voice small but full.

"It's the least I could do," he said with a soft smile.

The Gilded Rose rolled once again through the unfamiliar streets of Gillikin. The first house was far too large, looming with stone shoulders and no soul in its windows. It felt more like a monument than a *home.*

The second, too small, too exposed. She'd never know peace there.

The third had already been sold.

The fourth, still under construction, swarmed with workers and scaffolding, the air thick with sawdust and hammering.

They visited every house on the list.

By the time the sun began to lower behind the Gillikin hills, stretching its last golden fingers across the rooftops, Glinda let out a long, discouraged sigh. Her arms crossed. Her head leaned against the carriage window.

"I suppose," she said quietly, "it's back to the inn. Again."

But Wendell flipped the parchment over and held it out. "There's one more. I ran out of space, so I wrote it on the back."

"Wendell, I don't have any energy left."

He met her gaze, insistent. "What if *this* is the one? And what if by morning, someone else has already taken it?"

She looked at him for a long moment.

"Well," she shrugged, "you're the one doing all the work. If you're willing to ride…"

"I don't mind," Wendell grinned. "It's therapeutic."

And so, they rode.

The Gilded Rose climbed gently into the hills.

And then, it revealed itself.

Nestled atop a quiet slope stood a medium-sized castle, its white stone softened by time and ivy. A great willow tree wept with grace in the front garden, its branches cradling a crooked little Swyng that creaked softly in the breeze.

Flowers bloomed in uneven clusters, wild violets, crooked tulips, star-shaped lilies. As if someone had planted them with feeling, not symmetry.

The whole place *breathed.*

Glinda stepped out of the carriage. Her boots touched the grass, and, for a moment, she said nothing. Then she twirled, spinning in place like a girl from a story, her skirt billowing like pink mist. Her laughter burst from her chest before she could stop it.

She hadn't smiled like this in moons.

"This is it!" she exclaimed. "This is perfect!"

Wendell, watching her, smiled. "Let's go in. Hopefully it's still available."

They walked up to the door.

Lights flickered within. Something smelled faintly of rosemary and cinnamon bark.

Glinda knocked firmly.

Footsteps.

The door opened.

A man stood there. Middle-aged, tidy, his vest slightly wrinkled and his expression friendly, if curious.

"Can I help you?" he asked.

Glinda stepped forward. "We heard this castle was for sale. Is that true?"

The man blinked, then brightened. "Oh yes! Come in, come in. I was expecting a potential buyer, but I think he's running late."

Glinda exchanged a glance with Wendell and leaned in. "Good thing we got here first."

The man looked at Wendell. "Is this house to your liking, sir?"

Wendell chuckled, tilting his head toward Glinda. "Oh, no. She's the one looking to buy."

"My apologies, my lady."

Wendell leaned in just slightly to the man and whispered, "*Princess.*"

Glinda shot Wendell a quick, playful glare and gave him a light tap on the arm. "Oh, stop it."

The man swallowed hard, his posture straightening with new awareness.

"I—I can show you around, if you'd like?" he offered, trying to recover his professionalism.

Glinda held up a gloved hand gently. "That won't be necessary."

She turned, casting her gaze across the sloping hill, the willow tree, the crooked little swing creaking with wind-song.

"This is perfect. I knew it the moment I saw it. I want to buy it."

The man's brow furrowed slightly, visibly confused. "Ah... well, I'm afraid it doesn't quite work that way. You'll need to put your name on the list. The owner chooses who he wishes to sell to. And the other potential buyer—he's expected later today."

Glinda's voice didn't rise.

She simply cleared her throat, delicately, as if preparing to say something of quiet but extraordinary weight.

"What if I paid double the price?" she asked. "You see... I'm looking to move in *right now.*"

"Right now, *right now?*"

"Yes," she said with a smile. "Right now, right now."

"And you'd pay *double?*"

"Yes," she said again, plainly, as though discussing the weather.

The man's eyes widened. "I... I think the seller would be *very* pleased with that arrangement."

He quickly pulled a notepad from his pocket, scrawled a figure with dramatic flair, and turned it toward her:

Ƶ 2~000~000~000 gld

Glinda studied it for a moment.

Then reached calmly into her bag, pulled out her *Chekk Book*—leather-covered, cornered in gold—and wrote out the sum with practiced elegance.

She signed it with a flourish and handed it to him.

"Charge it to the *Princess Glinda Fairmoor* account at the Oz Bank," she said.

The man looked at the slip. Then at the seal. He swallowed something thick in his throat.

"You're... you're the daughter of King Fairmoor?"

"Yes."

The man's demeanour shifted at once. He extended his hand. "The castle is yours."

Glinda shook it once, firmly.

He handed her the deed for signature, ink already wet on the page. Glinda signed it with a simple flourish.

And just like that, the man clutched his coat and briefcase, handed her the keys with theatrical glee, and vanished through the door, his joy echoing in his quick, retreating footsteps.

Glinda stood alone in the great hall for a beat.

Then she laughed.

She *twirled*, her heels clicking lightly against the marble as she spun. The castle swallowed the sound and flung it back in echo, like music.

She turned to Wendell, arms flung wide.

"Can you believe it?" she breathed. "*My very own place.*"

Wendell smiled, the kind of smile that lingered at the corners.

She rushed forward and hugged him again, this time with a little more weight, a little more meaning.

"I couldn't have done this without you."

Wendell patted her back gently. "Glad to be of help. But I suppose... I should be heading back to the South."

"You don't *have* to go," she said softly. "Not unless you really want to."

Wendell gave a small shrug. "I'm employed by your father."

"But you were hired for *me*, weren't you?" Glinda said quickly, hope fluttering beneath the words. "You were *my* ryder. So... what if I just employed you myself? I'm in a new country now. I don't know the streets. How would I get around without you?"

"I suppose... you're right."

Glinda beamed. "I'll give you your own room. I'll cover your food. And I'll pay you *well*. Unless…" she raised an eyebrow. "You miss my father's warmth and want to run back to him."

"No. I think the North suits me just fine. Far as I know, I've always lived here. My family's from here too. I guess I'm no longer a Quadling."

Glinda grinned, "Then we'll be Northerners together."

They both burst into laughter, unguarded and genuine.

◇

That night, they rode into the city, just the two of them, ordered piping hot Gillikin food from a crooked little shop where steam poured out of every window and everything tasted like rosemary, root spice, and butter.

And when they returned to the castle, they sat cross-legged on the cold stone floor, no furniture, no heat, no fine glassware. Just their food, the soft hum of wind through the shutters, and the occasional flicker of lanternlight dancing against the walls.

They kept each other company until their bellies were full.

Until words grew soft and the silence felt like safety.

Until they fell asleep.

Not quite on purpose.

Not quite together.

But side by side, beneath the vaulted ceilings of a new beginning.

CHAPTER 42

Change Undone

The morning arrived not with birdsong, but with *chatter*, human, curious, excitable. Voices rose like a tide outside her castle's window. The kind of tide you couldn't hold back, even if you tried.

Glinda stirred from her sleep, her golden curls tangled and her robe sliding off one shoulder.

"What is that sound?" she mumbled.

Wendell, already halfway awake on the floor with his blanket wrapped around him like a cocoon, groaned and stood. He shuffled to the window, pulled the curtain back just an inch, and peeked through.

"Stars above…" he murmured.

Outside, a crowd had gathered on the edge of her property—some pressed against the iron gate, others lounging beneath the willow tree as if staking out a parade route. Fingers pointed. Eyes sparkled. Every mouth moved with the cadence of gossip.

Glinda blinked. "Already?"

Wendell sighed. "Already."

With another breath, he made his way to the front doors and flung them open, his voice loud but not unkind.

"Can I help you?"

A teenage boy near the gate stepped forward, a bouquet of frost-bitten wildflowers in hand. "Is this *Glinda's Castle*?"

Wendell glanced back at Glinda, who, still in her robe, gave a tired nod.

"Yes, yes it is. But she's not home right now, she's away on business with the Wizard."

A collective groan passed through the crowd like a wave of disappointment.

Wendell raised a hand. "And please, don't step foot on the premises without permission. Glinda… doesn't like that."

The mention of her name made them shiver with delight.

CHANGE

Before they could leave, an older woman shouted from the back, "Then tell her *thank you!* For what she did! Standing up to the Wicked Witch! You tell her we're *grateful.*"

"Will do."

The crowd dispersed slowly, murmuring like bees with nowhere to sting.

He shut the doors and returned to the blanket-strewn floor.

"*Glinda's Castle,*" Glinda repeated, her voice half in awe. "So that's what they're calling it."

Wendell yawned, cocooning himself tighter. "I think it's quite fitting."

"I... like it too."

But before the moment could settle—

Chimes.

Soft and strange and unmistakable.

A musical tinkling that glided through the air like the notes of a spell.

Wendell groaned again, sitting up. "Now what?"

Glinda raised a hand. "Rest. You've done enough."

She pulled her robe tight and padded softly down the hall, her slippered feet brushing against the stone. She opened the front doors.

There it was.

A miniature hot air balloon, no larger than a pumpkin, hovered gently on the breeze. Its basket, embroidered with emerald trim, carried a single sealed letter. It floated downward and landed at her doorstep with uncanny grace.

Glinda's breath caught in her throat.

The balloon. The basket. The seal.

She didn't need to open it to know who it was from.

Still, she reached inside, her fingers trembling slightly, and lifted the envelope. She turned it over.

The seal was *emerald.* Glossy and rich, pressed with the crest of the Wizard.

Her skin prickled.

Without hesitation, she tore it open.

She unfolded the letter.

And read.

Dear Good Witch of the North,
I write this letter to inform you that your Bubble Compartment is completed.
Come to the Emerald City on Satyrday at the 12th Hour so I can show you the ropes.
Yours Wonderfully,
The Wizard of Oz.

Glinda stared at the words.

Then at the signature.

Then at the word again:

Completed.

Her statement piece.

Her entrance.

Her illusion.

She clutched the letter to her chest, eyes wide with the spark of something dangerously close to happiness.

"Today is Freeday," she whispered. "So that's… *tomorrow*."

She stood still for a moment, bathing in the quiet victory. She had her own castle. Her own identity, public and powerful. And she had Wendell, a friend who asked for nothing but stayed anyway.

She wasn't saved.

But she was starting to *build*.

The miniature balloon began to chime once more, like it was congratulating her, before lifting itself off the doorstep and vanishing into the clouds, trailing soft green vapor behind it.

Glinda smiled, then shut the door behind her, leaning against it with a sigh of hope.

Wendell, on a nest of blankets on the stone floor, asked, "What is it?"

"Get your rest. We're going to the Emerald City tomorrow."

◇

The next morning came like a sunrise with purpose.

They left at dawn.

The Gilded Rose glided along the Pryzm Road. Wendell rode with focus and flourish, the kind of ease that only came from a full stomach, a soft place to sleep, and no one shouting orders at him.

Glinda leaned back in her cushioned seat, a book propped in her lap. Her eyes moved over the words, but her mind… wandered.

She imagined a pair of green fingers tracing these same pages.

A voice beside her, scoffing, *"That character's an idiot."*

She smiled.

Then forced it away.

You couldn't have *everything*.

But sometimes, you could have *enough*.

◇

They arrived at the Emerald City with a few Oz'mins to spare before the 12th Hour. The towers gleamed like sharpened glass, and the streets shimmered with illusion and polish.

Glinda stepped down from the Gilded Rose in a cascade of chiffon and perfume.

"Thank you, Wendell."

CHANGE

"I'll go park the carriage. You know where to find me when you're done. Good luck."

Glinda smiled, then turned to face the Palace.

With a practiced flick, she tossed her hair back, smoothing each golden strand into its rightful place with her fingertips. She pressed down her skirt, palms flattening the fabric like she could iron confidence into herself.

She sighed.

Looked left.

Looked right.

Alone.

This time, there was no one to hold her hand.

She walked toward the Emerald Palace gates. As the 12th Hour chimed from the *Chronoglint Gilded Dial*, which hung at the very top of the Emerald Tower, she handed her invitation to the guard.

No hesitation. No questions. The gates creaked open.

She knew the way now.

Turn the corner. Right past the statue of Ozma in jade. Slip on the green-tinted lenses. Walk the hall. Straight to the throne room.

She knocked once before entering.

The room was dark, deliberately. The great mechanical head, pulsing with steam and eerie phosphorescence, sparked to life.

"I am the Great and Powerful Oz! *Who are you?!*" the voice thundered, echoing off the emerald panels.

"It's me," she replied dryly, "Glinda."

A beat of silence.

Then, from behind the curtains, the man himself emerged, laughing softly in his black-and-green suit, always too polished to be real.

"Next time, just say your name. Saves me the theatrics."

Glinda smiled, though her fingers fidgeted slightly behind her back.

"Follow me," he said, beckoning.

This time, they didn't detour through the library. No riddles, no misdirection, no disappearing into trick doors etched into the marbled walls.

He led her to a grand elevator, its surface a shimmering green metal that rippled like water under candlelight. Carved above it in Old Ozian script were the words:

"The Higher, The Stranger."

Glinda stepped inside.

The Wizard followed, and with a dramatic sweep, he pressed a glowing button, though it lit up a fraction before his finger touched it.

The word on the button: *Skyview.*

His grin stretched wide.

Glinda's smile, however, faltered. She looked down, squeezing her knees together tightly. A chill crept through the elevator shaft like anticipation made visible.

She said nothing.

Just watched her shoes.

And waited.

DING!

The elevator opened with a sigh of brass.

They had reached the very summit of the Emerald Tower.

Wind rushed in like a wild thing set loose, whipping Glinda's hair into a frenzy. It howled like some ancient, unseen beast circling the palace. Who knew the wind could be so loud this high above the world?

Glinda took a reflexive step back, one hand rising to shield her face.

"Don't be frightened, Glinda!" the Wizard called over the gusts, his voice full of that almost-boyish exuberance. "Come on, forward!"

He ushered her into the open, and there, sitting in the centre of the sky-drenched landing, was a large object cloaked beneath a velvet sheet.

"You ready?" the Wizard asked, one brow raised.

Glinda nodded.

With a flourish, he pulled the sheath away.

Gold.

Real gold.

"Oz!" Glinda gasped, her hand flying to her chest.

"I know. Sometimes I surprise myself."

What sat before her was not merely a vehicle, not a contraption, it was a throne dressed as a carriage. An ornate, regal platform that looked as though it had been plucked from the dreams of a sugar-spun goddess.

The base was forged in gold, etched with curling glyphs and starbursts. The highlights were the perfect shade of blush, like rosewater tea. The cushioning was petal pink, tufted with crystal-tipped buttons; embedded in its cushions and stitched with vines of iridescent thread.

It was *decadent* in every sense, and somehow, it *fit her.*

"This is..." Glinda breathed, "*Wonderful.*"

"That is my name," the Wizard said with a chuckle.

She laughed with him. It felt honest. And it had been a long time since anything felt *honest.*

"How does it work?"

The Wizard extended his hand. "Let me show you."

She placed her gloved fingers in his palm and stepped up onto the golden platform. Her entrance was seamless, a gliding motion that made her look almost born for this.

"See that carved section in the corner?" the Wizard asked, pointing toward the intricate floral design etched into the floor.

"Yes."

"Step on it."

She lifted her slippered foot and pressed it down.

In a heartbeat, the platform trembled, just slightly, and then bloomed.

A soft, rising *pop* of sound, like a soap bubble catching sunlight.

A shimmering **bubble** enclosed around her, radiant and round, rosy and transparent. It shimmered with faint tints of lavender and gold as it locked into shape.

Glinda stood inside it.

Inside a bubble.

She gasped, then *screamed*.

"Yes! This is perfect! *Oh Oz*—"

Her voice echoed within the bubble, and it made her laugh.

The Wizard stood outside, watching like a proud playwright on opening night.

"If you want it to disappear, just step on the same spot again."

She did—and in a blink, the bubble vanished.

Glinda was breathless.

Then she turned to him, still glowing with giddy disbelief. "Would it be able to *fly*?"

The Wizard paused.

Then smiled, slow and devilish.

"What would be the point, if it didn't?"

He pointed inside the platform, just beside the rose-tufted seat, to a gleaming lever inlaid with a tiny rosy cabochon.

"You see that? Just pull it back to lift up, and forward to descend, left to move left and right obviously to..." he waved his hand. "You get it. But it only activates when you're enclosed in the bubble."

"Okay, wait. Isn't it dangerous? What if, say, a bird smacks into it midair and the bubble *pops*? Wouldn't I plummet and, like...*die*?"

The Wizard threw his head back and laughed—a sharp, confident sound.

"Oh Glinda, it's forged from *Dragon Glass*. Tempered in Dragon's Breath. You'd need a thousand bullets to crack it."

Glinda blinked. "What are *bullets*?"

"Never mind. Ancient nonsense from my world. All you need to know is: it's safe. It's not *really* a bubble, you see. It just gives the *illusion* of one. That's the trick." He winked.

"And with this?" he added, circling the platform. "You'll never need to take the roads again. From the North to the South in thirty oz'mins. Maybe less if there's no wind."

"Woz."

"Try it out."

She stepped once more on the carved rune near the base, and with a soft *hiss,* the enclosure bloomed again. The air around her shimmered rose-gold, the illusion sealing her in a perfect bubble.

She tapped the bubble. Glass, not bubble. The Wizard was telling the truth.

Then, carefully, she pulled the lever.

The bubble rose.

The floor of the tower slipped away beneath her.

Glinda wobbled at first, knees bent, the wind pressing against the glass with wild curiosity. But she found her footing. Then her breath. Then her smile.

She was flying.

The Wizard stood on the tower's edge, arms crossed, watching like a sorcerer unveiling a prophecy.

"Don't be scared! Just follow the lever. You can go anywhere."

Glinda did just that.

She soared out over the Emerald Tower, dipping slightly before circling around its glittering spire. The bubble caught the sunlight and fractured it, casting soft prisms onto the buildings below.

People on the streets began to point.

What is that? they asked.

The answer came from a woman on a balcony, shouting, "It's Glinda, The Good Witch!"

Cheers broke out below.

Hands waved.

A crowd formed, pointing upward, as the radiant orb passed over them like a second sun.

Glinda hovered low for just a moment. The applause reached her ears even through the bubble's faint hum.

Then she rose again, flying higher, spiralling in a slow circle until she drifted back to the Wizard's landing.

She guided the platform carefully and pressed the rune.

The bubble dissolved with a warm hiss.

She stepped down, dazed with awe.

"That was…" she whispered, "everything."

"She's yours now."

"What does it need to run?" Glinda asked, still breathless.

"Just a cup of water every seven suns. There's a transparent tank there, it'll let you know when it's low."

Glinda crouched to check. The tank was full.

With one last glance, she pushed the lever gently and docked the platform against the greenstone floor.

The illusion vanished. Her feet touched solid ground.

But something inside her still felt like it was floating.

CHANGE

The Wizard tilted his head, puzzled. "Why are you getting off? You could fly home right now. The North now, is it?"

"Yes, but I came with my Ryder, I'd rather keep him company than have him ride back alone."

The Wizard gave a small, forced smile. Awkward. "How noble of you."

"Can I have the bubble delivered to my castle?"

"Of course. It'll be there by morning on Sunday. Or would you prefer Moonday?"

"Sunday is perfect."

"Let's get you back inside then. Stars above, I don't know how the Wicked Witch flies in this wind. Altitude's *Hel* on the hair and ears."

They stepped back into the emerald lift. The doors shut behind them with a hiss, and down they descended, through the ribs of the palace, through all its hollowed-out secrets.

Back to the throne room.

"Let me escort you out," the Wizard said, offering his elbow. Glinda didn't take it, but she walked beside him, their footsteps syncopated, rhythmic.

Halfway down the corridor, something caught her eye.

A flash of blush behind glass.

Seraphina's Wand.

She stopped walking.

She turned toward the relic like it had whispered her name.

Her ancestor's wand, slender, pink, ribboned with delicate carvings, and as long as a song.

"Do you mind if I have it?" Glinda asked, her voice barely above breath.

"What? *Seraphina's* wand?"

"Yes."

The Wizard walked up beside her, squinting at the artifact behind the glass. "It's dead. Not a flicker of magic left in it. Trust me, I've tried everything to revive it. Useless."

"I just think it fits me. It matches my image, pink and proper. Regal. Gohdly."

The Wizard tilted his head, amused. "Rewriting Seraphina's wickedness with your 'goodness.' Hmm. The public will eat it up like milk-drunk babes."

"My point exactly," Glinda replied with a faint smile, concealing the real reason deep inside her chest.

He turned and snapped his fingers. "Guard. Open it."

The guard fumbled for keys, unlocked the casing, and lifted the glass enclosure.

Glinda stepped forward and reached.

Her fingers touched the wand.

And there it was.

A jolt.

Not pain, not electricity, just... knowing.

It felt right. Heavy in the right places. Lighter where it mattered. Like an old promise remembered.

She held it in both hands and stared.

The Wizard glanced sideways at the guard. "You'd think she was holding a long-lost relative."

"Okay," he said, clapping once more. "Shall we get going?"

His hand hovered behind her back, guiding her gently down the corridor.

They reached the Palace doors.

Glinda finally looked up from the wand.

"Thank you, for the bubble. And... mostly, for the wand."

"What are friends for?" He leaned in. "And call me *Oscar*. Remember? Like old times."

"Okay. Goodbye, Oscar."

She turned, but he stopped her with a hand on her shoulder.

"When your bubble arrives, I want you to start touring the North. Speak well of me. The Northians are... slow to warm."

Glinda nodded once.

No promises. Just acknowledgment.

She walked out of the palace into the crisp Emerald air.

Wendell stood by the Gilded Rose, the reins in one hand, polishing a lantern with the other. He straightened when he saw her, then squinted at the wand in her grasp.

"What's that, Mizz?"

Glinda looked down at it.

The glass wand shimmered faintly in the light.

She smiled, an old smile, the kind Zelphira would've caught and questioned.

"Family," she said.

Then stepped into the carriage.

◇

As promised, the Bubble arrived on Sunday morning, punctual to the tick, gleaming like sunrise in a soap dish.

A Wizard's Guard delivered it in full regalia, saluting with more ceremony than was strictly necessary, and Glinda received it with the gracious nod of someone who had long since learned to wear gratitude like a hat.

Her tour of the North was afoot.

Seraphina's wand in hand.

A dress the colour of crushed rose petals.

Her curls spun into golden spirals.

And the Bubble, her vessel, her veil, her weapon.

She was ready.

✧

Glinda visited schools where children screamed with joy and reached for her fingers like she was a walking lullaby. She *kissed foreheads* in hospitals and blessed them with a warmth that felt real, because somehow, it was.

She floated above town centres while shopkeepers threw pink tulips from their windows.

And the press followed her like moths to a flame.

GLINDA, THE GOOD WITCH VISITS NURSERY

WIZARD OF OZ PROCLAIMS GLINDA THE GOOD WITCH OF THE NORTH

GLINDA THE GOOD WITCH OF THE NORTH VISITS GILLIKIN HOSPITAL

THE GOOD WITCH OF THE NORTH SPEAKS ON HER PARTNERSHIP WITH THE WIZARD

Every day: a new headline. A new bouquet. A new crowd gathered under her bubble, wide-eyed and hungry for hope.

And then it happened.

The Northians loved her.

More than they loved the Wizard.

And for the first time, Glinda felt something rare and dangerous bloom in her chest:

Power.

Not borrowed.

Not inherited.

Owned.

But not all things that arrive come with fanfare.

✧

Back at the castle—her castle—there were other deliveries. Quiet ones. Wrapped in wax and desperation.

Letters.

Dozens of them.

All from Esmelda.

Glinda burned each one without reading. The first few were ceremonial. Then it became habit. Eventually, it became muscle memory.

She tried, once, to open a letter.

But her body betrayed her. Her hands recoiled. Her stomach twisted. Something primal inside her refused.

So, she burned them all. Every. Single. One.

Even when the envelope was thick with apology. Even when the ink bled into the parchment as if the words themselves wept.

She could not go back.

She would *not* go back.

But then, one morning, while still in her dressing robe, Wendell walked in holding a new envelope. This one sealed in gold.

"It's from… Dainhurst," he said, hesitating as he placed it on the table.

Glinda stared at it.

She didn't touch it.

Not yet.

The wax seal shimmered with the Fairmoor crest.

She wasn't sure if that made it better or worse.

She sat down slowly, the wand resting against the side of her chair.

The castle was silent.

So she listened to the letter.

Still unopened.

Still waiting.

Eventually, she opened it.

Glinda,

I write to you not as the King of the South—but as your father.

This charade must end.

This rebellion of yours has gone on long enough. Whatever delusion you've clung to, whatever fantasy has convinced you that turning your back on your blood is righteous, must now end.

Come home.

Return to your family, to the land that raised you, to the mother who gave you life and has done nothing but reach out to you with forgiveness you do not deserve. She has written to you, pleaded with you, and you have not replied. Not once. Do you have any idea what that has done to her? To us?

It's not just disrespect, to ignore her letters, to cast her aside as if she were nothing, Glinda, that is the cruellest insult a child can deliver.

And still, she has reached for you with trembling hands. And still, you remain silent.

And as for me, I am not only disappointed. I am disgusted. You know how I feel about the Northians. You know! And yet you ran to them—took refuge in the very place that has spat on everything we built. Tell me, do you take pleasure in defying me? In tarnishing the Fairmoor name?

Do you know what the court says behind closed doors? That the daughter of the South's crown has traded her loyalty for the frostbitten praise of Gillikins. That she has forsaken her people, her name, her birthright.

*Your sister is beside herself. Gisella has devoted her life to this family, to her role. As the Wicked Witch of the West is becoming infamous, the people have placed you as her counterpart instead of Gisella, who is the **actual** Good Witch by the way. But now they call you 'Saint'. You have stolen her place in the sun, and not through merit, but by scandal, and now they see Gisella as second to you.*

The South as second to The North.

You have made a mockery of our legacy.

And for what?

I do not understand the game you're playing, but this will be your final warning.

Return home immediately. Restore your place in this family. Reclaim your loyalty. This is not a request, Glinda Fairmoor—it is an order.

If you fail to do so, know this: your privileges will be revoked. Your accounts, frozen. Your titles, stripped. You will no longer bear the Fairmoor name. You will be on your own, without protection, without inheritance, without us.

I will not fund the life of a traitor.

Choose wisely.

Your Father,

King Fairmoor of the Southern Realms

Her fingers faltered for a second before she crumpled the letter, creasing the royal seal. She stood, walked calmly to the fireplace, and dropped it in without ceremony.

The flames welcomed it without hesitation.

Her father's words, his venom, his threats, his wounded pride, curled into black smoke.

She didn't need his money.

She didn't need his name.

She had built something greater than the Fairmoor legacy: *herself.*

She had done what Gisella never could—become the Good Witch without spells, without sorcery.

Just like the Wizard.

And she was doing it better than Gisella ever had.

The saddest part of it all was the quiet truth she never spoke: Once, she had imagined living in a castle just like this one, with Gisella. Just the two of them.

But she didn't need her.

She didn't need *anyone.*

And so, Glinda stayed in the North.

◇

Three years passed.

Seasons folded like pages in a book. The Northern frost no longer bit, it became familiar. The wind became background noise to applause.

Glinda's reign as the Good Witch of the North blossomed.

She was no longer "the girl who ran away."

She was *the woman they ran to.*

The Wizard—Oscar—remained in the Emerald Palace, and Glinda became his most trusted voice. His face before the people. His velvet glove.

She spoke on his behalf at councils. She calmed the flames of rebellion before they caught spark. She kissed babies and unveiled monuments and cut ribbons while his silhouette loomed faintly behind her.

And in time, even the Gillikins, those cynical, sharp-tongued Northerners, began to soften toward the Wizard.

Because of *her*.

The East adored her.

The West feared her, all except *one*.

And the South... well, the South remained silent.

The Wizard often told her, sometimes when they sat side by side in private chambers with untouched wine between them:

"You say you don't have magic, Glinda. But your magic is people. You know how to *speak* to them. You know how to *make them hope*. And that... is rarer than any spell I've ever seen. You make them *believe*."

And she *believed him*.

She was **Good.**

And Zelphira remained **Wicked.**

Oz did not question the arrangement.

Oz did not *want* to.

But no spell, no illusion, lasts forever.

✧

One morning, a knock came to Glinda's castle.

Wendell answered.

When Glinda emerged from her study, a folded broadsheet had been placed delicately on the silver breakfast tray, alongside her tea and honeyed toast.

Her eyes flicked to the headline, as they always did, half-dreading, half-bored.

And then she saw it.

In letters so large they seemed carved into the sky itself:

THE WICKED WITCH OF THE WEST KILLS THE GOOD WITCH OF THE SOUTH

Silence fell like ash.

The toast turned to sawdust in her mouth. The tea went untouched.

She reread it once. Twice. A third time, in case the words might reorder themselves into something else. Something *false*.

But they did not.

Her eyes trembled. Her hands did not.

Gisella.

Dead.

Zelphira's hand.

The world as Oz knew it, *as Glinda had built it*, was about to shatter.

CHANGE

And no bubble, no wand, no illusion would be enough to keep the storm from coming.

Undone

CHAPTER 43

Confessions of a Wicked Sister

Glinda didn't walk, she fled. Her heels clicked like war drums across the castle's marble tiles.

She climbed into the Bubble and rose like a phoenix with a fractured wing, soaring from Gillikin's silent snow to the flame-stroked skies of the South.

Every gust of wind felt like Zelphira's breath on her neck.

Every cloud like a whisper of Gisella's perfume.

Every second, her *heart* broke a little louder.

It began to rain by the time she descended into the courtyard of Fairmoor Castle. She wasn't a witch, she was a woman undone.

The guards cheered, as trained. Their hands clapped like clockwork. But their eyes couldn't hide it:

She hadn't come for pageantry.

She had come to bury her sister.

She didn't bow. Didn't nod. Didn't blink.

She turned to a maid, pale-faced, trembling, and asked, "Where is Dainhurst?"

The maid bowed low and gestured toward the West Wing tower.

The highest one.

Where he always sat for breakfast. Where he could watch the world he owned.

Glinda lifted her skirts and ascended. One step after another, breath shallow, grief like lead in her throat.

She found him reclining in his usual chair. Alone. A silver plate in one hand, a bite of cream tart halfway to his mouth.

He laughed to himself, at a headline, perhaps, or a joke he'd crafted about the Munchkins.

Glinda cleared her throat. "Is it true?" she asked, her voice already cracking. "Or is this just one of your tricks to get what you want?"

Dainhurst didn't turn. He only smiled. "Like I'd lie about my own daughter's death."

The sentence hit her harder than the wind on Gillikin's peaks.

Her legs gave a subtle tremble.

Glinda sighed, and her eyes began to well with tears like they usually did. "How did she—"

"How did she die?"

He interrupted, unbothered.

"She fell," he said plainly, pointing toward the balcony. "Threw herself from the tower. Like a dove out of patience."

His voice was as cold as the cream tart he returned to.

Glinda's mouth fell open, her face beginning to contort.

"Did you kill her?" she asked.

Dainhurst finally turned, his face painted with false offense. "How *dare* you. Why would you say something so vile?"

His voice deepened. "I would *never* harm family. Have I not always said it? Family is everything."

Glinda's lip quivered. Her eyes, redder now, brimmed with salt. "So… if she fell—*you lied* about the Wicked Witch. She didn't kill her."

Dainhurst took another bite, licking cream from his teeth.

"Oh yes," he said calmly. "That? I made it up."

Glinda stepped forward, voice rising. "*Why?* Why would you lie to the entire realm?"

Dainhurst sighed. Set the plate down with a clang.

At last, he looked at her. Not with sorrow. Not with shame.

But with that terrifying calm that only men of power wear when they've decided the world is clay in their hands.

And in that moment, Glinda saw his true face. Not the King. Not the father. The maskless monster.

"Gisella is no use to me dead," he said, voice flat as stone. "But as a martyr? Ah, now *that* had value. One final service posthumously rendered. I turned her into a symbol. A torch for the South to rally behind."

He leaned in, eyes narrowing.

"A fall is sad," he mused, lifting his teacup as though toasting the lie. "But murder? Now *murder* is myth. And myths," he said with a smirk, "are powerful currency."

He sipped, savouring the power.

"They already despise the green girl. Why waste that hatred? Do you know how simple it is to lead a nation to war when grief is raw and the villain has a colour?"

"You're vile," Glinda choked, recoiling as though the words themselves left a residue.

But Dainhurst only leaned closer, elbows on knees, voice silked with venom.

"And tell me, Glinda, what would the realm say of a princess who couldn't bear to live? Fragile. Weak. *Unfit*." He tsked. "It would reflect *poorly* on me. I am a king. I do not raise broken things."

He set the cup down.

"No. But murder? Oh, I'd rather murder. It will give her *immortality*. It gives her *meaning*. Statues are carved from tragedy, not frailty."

Glinda's breath came in small, furious bursts. "You don't care about family. You never did. You care about your throne. Your legacy. And you'll burn your children at the altar of perception."

Dainhurst rose from his chair with deliberate slowness. He turned to her, his voice curling like smoke.

"And you don't?" he sneered. "Look at you. 'Saint Glinda,' with your sugar-pink gowns and your glassy lies. You're *exactly* like me. The only difference is I *admit* what I am."

He reached out and brushed a hand over her bodice, not in affection, but as if smoothing a marionette's costume.

"You've polished your poison in a prettier vial. But the rot, dear girl, it runs just as deep. Ambition, that's our true inheritance. And we both know it."

Glinda recoiled, her voice barely a whisper. "Not *everything* is worth the crown."

She turned away.

"Where's Esmelda?"

"Esmelda?" Dainhurst laughed, cruel and hollow. "Your *mother*, if you still call her that, is where you left her. Bedridden. Wasting away in silk and sorrow."

"And Gisella?" Glinda asked, holding her voice together by a thread. "Has she been buried?"

He laughed again, amused at her audacity to care.

"In the garden," he said, already turning away. "Freshly laid in the dirt like a fallen flower. Go talk to your dead, weak sister. Take whatever baubles she left for you. And then *get out* of my kingdom."

Glinda said nothing. She turned.

No final word.

No bow.

Only silence, and the aching slap of her footsteps echoing down the tower's spiral staircase.

She made her way to the garden.

There, a fresh plot, the earth still raw with sorrow. A stone carved in haste, and beneath it—Gisella.

Glinda sank to her knees. Her fingers sifted through the soil, tenderly, like she could still reach her.

She didn't speak.

There were no speeches.

No eulogies.

No apologies whispered into dirt.

Only the sound of her breathing, broken and uneven.

Only tears.

The gardeners, tending roses nearby, tried not to look. But grief is a contagious thing, and even they turned their faces, hearts heavy with pity.

But Glinda needed silence now, not the sympathetic kind, but the solitude that came when the world finally left you alone to shatter.

Then, with no announcement, she walked to Gisella's chambers.

She needed to see what was left of the girl the world had already turned into a statue.

And maybe… what pieces of herself still lingered there too.

She paused outside the door.

A breath caught in her throat.

She exhaled, slow, heavy, almost theatrical. Not for show, but survival.

And then she turned the handle.

The room had not changed.

The same perfume still clung to the air, rosewater.

The bed remained made, untouched, as though Gisella might walk back in at any moment, scold a maid for dust, and toss her shoes aside like a crown.

Everything was intact.

Like an unaltering memory.

Glinda stepped in slowly. Her feet barely made a sound against the velvet carpet. She sat on the edge of the bed, fingers trailing the soft coverlet, as if it might speak.

The tears came again, uninvited, unstoppable. A silent deluge.

She lifted her chin through the blur, and it was then, through the mist of her eyes, that she saw it.

A flicker of green on the vanity.

A hue too familiar to mistake.

Glinda stood, hesitantly, and crossed the room. She wiped the stinging salt from her eyes and finally saw it clearly:

Gisella's crystal necklace.

And beside it, a folded letter.

Neatly written on the front, in that elegant, slanted script only sisters could recognize without reading:

For Glinda.

Her breath hitched.

Without a thought, without hesitation, she reached past the necklace and took the letter instead.

She carried it back to the bed, every step heavier than the last.

And then, with hands that trembled but no longer wept, she unfolded it.

And the letter began to speak.

My Sister, Glinda,

I know you're angry with me. And after reading this, you'll likely be even more so. I've done things that are unspeakable, unforgivable, and I own them fully. No one else is to blame for what I've done. Only me.

For the first time, I see things clearly. And I have just enough courage left in me to admit the truth.

I didn't tell you how I stole your magic, not just becoz of my cruelty, but becoz of the unbearable shame. The weight of it has crushed me in ways I can no longer endure.

A few sun-moons ago, I confided in Thelma and Veloria, foolishly believing them to be friends. They were the only people I trusted to know the truth about my transcendence in becoming the Good Witch of the South and I told them how you refused to help me, how I feared fading into obscurity. Without your magic, I was nothing. That was the lie I let take root in my heart.

One night, I went into your room. Your Spellbook was left open. Your translations illuminated by candlelight, like they were waiting for me. I flipped through the pages and found a Transference Spell—a way to steal magic even if the caster possessed none of their own.

It felt like fate. A cruel, convenient fate.

I looked for another way. I did. But that spell was the only one a Non-Magi could perform. So I copied it. Along with your translations.

I told Veloria and Thelma. Veloria pushed me toward it. Promised to help. But I am not hiding behind them. This was my decision. My sin. I betrayed you as a sister, let envy devour my love for you.

Thelma travelled to the Gillikins and returned with something she called Black Poison. A draft so potent, it would keep you in a sleep so deep it would mimic death for several hourz.

I poured it into your cup at dinner and watched you drink it.

While you slept, I performed the spell. I stripped your magic from you with trembling hands and sealed it into the pendant. My triumph was hollow. And short-lived.

It wasn't until afterward that Thelma told me what else the Black Poison did.

And Glinda, that is what haunts me most.

It cursed your body. You will never be able to bear a child.

If I had known... by the One Gohd, if I had known, I swear I would've never touched it.

I cannot apologise enough for what I have done to you.

And I will be at your mercy in this life and the next.

434

Since that night, I have not known peace. The magic, your magic, was never meant for me. It tormented me from the moment I wore it. At first, I felt invincible. Alive. And then the voices began. I'd wake screaming from nightmares, the pendant burning against my skin.

But I kept it. Out of spite. Out of pride. Even as it hollowed me out.

And then… it began to take my beauty.

That was its curse to me.

I stole the most sacred thing from you—and in return, it took what I valued most. My face. My vanity. Myself.

And I went mad beneath the surface.

I confessed everything to Father. I begged him to let me step down, to pass the title of Good Witch to you, where it always belonged. But he refused. He said the only way I could stop was if I died.

I tried to run. But I am not strong like you, Glinda. I never was.

I don't know if you ever noticed, but I've been quietly falling apart for years. The sadness came first, then the numbness. I've tried to fill the emptiness with everything, clothes, jewels, parties, sex. I kept trying to patch a hole that only grew wider.

And when I saw what Ominson meant to you… I took him. Not becoz I loved him. Becoz you did.

Taking your magic was my last desperate attempt to feel full. But it only hollowed me out further.

And now, I've left this world on the worst terms. I know. But even here, wherever here is, I still need your forgiveness.

All the things I said to wound you, to chip away at your spirit… they came from a place of jealousy. You were always special. From the moment you picked up that pink gem, everyone saw it. We just didn't want you to see it. Becoz we knew what would happen when you did.

You will be remembered. And I will be forgotten.

And that should have been enough for me. It was your destiny—not mine.

I still don't know what my destiny was. But if it was simply to sharpen you into the woman you're meant to become… then my destiny is fulfilled.

This choice I've made, it is selfish. It is cruel. I know. I am so, so sorry for leaving my son behind. I look at his face, his beautiful, blue eyes, and all I see is you. He is the proof of all my sins. And I can no longer bear to look upon what I've broken.

But this ending, this one thing, it was mine to choose.

Maybe it's wrong. But it is the only decision that's ever felt like my own.

I don't know what waits beyond this life. But if there is something… I hope it allows do-overs. I hope one day we find each other again, somewhere gentler, and begin anew as the sisters we once were.

I think often of our childhood. Of how close we were. Of what time and pain stole from us.

I don't deserve this, but I'll ask anyway: Please take care of my child. Don't let Father near him. You and I both know the kind of damage he can do. He will ruin and corrupt his pure soul.

UNDONE

Take the necklace. Reclaim your Power. Use it for the Good. Use it to do what people won't.

My beloved sister. I love you. I have loved you. So, so deeply. Even through all my cruelty. Be who you were born to be. Make me proud.

I love you always.

Your Sister,

Gisella.

Glinda's lips folded inward, trapping the sobs behind a dam of silence. Her breath caught, shivering, as if each inhale was another betrayal to her composure. But something inside her was unravelling, slowly, quietly, like silk slipping through trembling fingers.

She had lost so much already.

And now, the quiet truth settled in her bones:

The dream she never dared speak aloud had crumbled.

She would never have a child of her own. Her dreams of family would remain just a fantasy.

Not in this life.

Not with this body.

Not after all that had been taken.

She stood and walked toward the desk. Each step felt heavier than the last, her eyes blinding her.

There it lay, the crystal necklace.

The vessel of betrayal. Of loss. Of love, stolen and twisted.

Her hand hovered, hesitant.

Then, without flinching, she took it.

No fire met her fingers this time. No searing pain.

Only cold.

Cold as regret. Cold as death.

She closed her fist around it and sank back onto the bed, holding it tight, like a relic, or a wound she didn't want to heal. A single teardrop slid down her cheek and kissed the stone, leaving a trail like rain on a windowpane.

She let go.

Her body tipped sideways, curling into the bed, into the pillow still perfumed with Gisella's scent, a bitter memory of what once was. And then the silence fractured.

Glinda wept. First softly. Then more.

Then fully, violently.

Sobs that tore out of her chest like wild things escaping a cage.

Screams muffled into fabric, like she might wake the ghosts if she were too loud.

Yearning poured out of her, the kind that could bend the stars backward if they were listening.

And then... warmth.

A small, human warmth.

Tiny fingers, soft and curious, wrapped around her hand.

Glinda froze, startled.

She turned slowly, lifting her face from the pillow, eyes swollen, lashes wet.

A boy.

No older than four.

Big, ocean-blue eyes, wide and innocent, looking up at her without fear. Without judgment. Just... wondering.

Gisella's child.

His little fingers clumsily tried to comfort her, brushing at her wet cheek with the care of someone who had never learned how to lie.

"Why are you crying?" he asked, his voice a melody of concern, all round edges and sunshine.

Glinda straightened, wiping her face with the back of her hand, only for more tears to take their place.

She pulled him gently into her lap.

The first time she touched him.

The first time she looked at him.

She adjusted his collar, tucked a strand of hair behind his ear, as if that small gesture might somehow anchor her to this moment.

"I'm not crying becoz I'm sad," she whispered, "I'm crying becoz... I'm happy. That's all. Don't you worry about me."

He reached up and cupped her face again, inspecting her as if trying to memorize her grief.

"What's your name?" she asked softly.

The boy smiled with the confidence of someone whose name was his whole identity.

"Orryn."

Glinda's lips curved into something real.

"Orryn," she repeated. "What a strong name. For a strong boy."

She held him tighter.

But then, as he looked at her, really looked at her, she saw it.

The shape of his gaze.

The colour of his eyes.

The quiet ache of recognition.

They were unmistakably hers.

And just as the thought anchored in her heart, the boy asked, "Have you seen Gisella? I can't find her."

The breath caught in Glinda's throat.

Her lashes lowered, and her eyes, soft and dulled with sorrow, flickered toward the window.

Outside, the rain had ceased its weeping.

The clouds, parting like a curtain, let the sun in.

And there it was. A rainbow—arching, defiant, radiant. A bridge painted across grief.

She rose to her feet, holding Orryn gently in her arms, and brought him to the window.

"You see that?"

He nodded.

She lifted her finger, tracing the colours stitched across the sky.

"Gisella is way over the rainbow now. Flying way up high."

"With the birds?" he asked, his voice feather-light.

"Yes, but not just any birds. Bluebirds."

Orryn's eyes widened with wonder. "Why bluebirds?"

She paused, just a beat, then pressed a playful finger to his belly.

"Becoz, they match your eyes."

He giggled, soft and pure.

"And she's flying to see the One Gohd, so she can ask him to make all your dreams come true."

"Really?" he whispered.

"Yes."

"Will she come back?"

Glinda hesitated, but only for a moment.

Then she smiled.

"Well," she said, "it's a long way to Gohd. And an even longer way back. But she wanted to go—for you. So, Gohd has made a special place for her. A place with Lurline. With Ozma."

The boy nodded slowly. "Will we meet Gisella again?"

Glinda's arms held him tighter. She brushed her cheek against his hair, kissed the top of his head.

"Yes, I'm sure of it."

He wrapped his small arms around her neck and held on. A warmth, gentle and full, spilled from him into her chest, quiet as candlelight, steady as breath.

And Glinda leaned into him, letting herself melt into that small but sacred embrace.

The first touch of comfort she had felt in what felt like a lifetime.

She did not weep this time.

She simply breathed.

Because somehow, in Orryn's arms… she remembered how.

After a moment, she gently placed him back on the floor, brushing a curl from his forehead as she bent down to meet his eyes.

"What do you think, about coming to live in my castle?"

Orryn's eyes flitted with surprise. "Will you be there?"

Glinda smiled, wide and certain. "Every day."

The boy jumped, ecstatic. "Yes!"

Her **heart** beamed at his joy. "Okay," she said, rising to her feet. "Let's go."

She reached for his hand, wrapping her fingers around his small ones. But then, something caught the light. A glimmer in the room. Not from the window, but from the floor.

Glinda turned her head.

Gisella's silver slippers.

They sparkled like they had been waiting, like they, too, wanted to leave.

She let go of Orryn's hand and stepped over to them, slowly lifting them in her hands. Then she took the crystal necklace and Gisella's final letter and stood still for a breath, looking around the room one last time.

A faint smile touched her lips, fragile but true.

She shut the door behind her.

Then—one last thing.

She made her way to her father's study, her feet knowing the way even if her soul begged her to turn back. She crossed the room with barely a breath and reached for the hidden compartment. She opened it.

The Fairmoor Crown.

She held it in her hands for a moment. Cold and gleaming. She stuffed the crown in her satchel as she descended the grand staircase with Orryn at her side.

But before they could reach the bottom, a shadow emerged above them.

Dainhurst.

"Yes, take him!" he bellowed. "A little Quadling. Take him to the North with you. Isn't that where all traitors flee?"

Glinda said nothing.

"Useless, both of you!" he spat.

She turned to Orryn and crouched. "Go wait for me outside, darling, alright?"

He nodded, hesitated, then obeyed—running out through the great doors.

Glinda rose and faced the man she once called *Father.*

"Perhaps," she said coldly, "if you ever intended to keep him, you'd have dressed him in clothes that fit."

Dainhurst scoffed. "Oh, I meant it. Take him. The boy's a stain. Ominson won't even claim him—says the child's not his. I don't want him here. He reminds me too much of her. A bastard born of disgrace."

Glinda's expression cracked into a frown, deep and silent.

"Your own grandson, and you speak of him like refuse."

Her breath caught, rage choking her before the words could even find shape.

"You've failed every role a man can hold. You've failed as a father, a pitiful husband, and now, instead of even *trying* to redeem yourself by being a decent grandfather, you double down on the same cruelty. You're not just cold—you're twisted. Sick."

She looked around.

"Enjoy the rot you've built around yourself."

Then turned, heading toward the stairs.

Dainhurst's voice cut through the air. "Still pretending you're not glad she's dead, aren't you?"

Glinda froze.

He stood at the top of the stairs, eyes gleaming.

"You're thrilled Gisella's gone. Admit it. Now you get to be the only Good Witch. No more competition. You're finally centre stage."

Glinda turned slowly, her face pale with rage.

"She was my sister! You truly are unwell. I knew you were cruel, but this… this is madness. Go see Doctor Thistle. Or Barbarus. Becoz you need more help than your wife ever did."

Dainhurst laughed bitterly. "You want to paint yourself as righteous? A saint? Please. You're an opportunist, Glinda. A serpent wrapped in pink silk. You're not blind, you're wilfully *ignorant*."

"Ignorant? *Pfft!* How? I don't even know what you're talking about."

"Oh, don't play dumb, shall I remind you?"

She said nothing.

"All those sun-moons ago, you knew perfectly well I was the reason those magic wielders went missing. You knew I was the one massacring them in *my* dungeon. But you accepted the lie—that it was Magnum's doing. You *knew*, deep down, you knew, but you accepted it. Not becoz you thought it was the truth but becoz you *wanted* to believe it. You needed a version of me you could stomach, and so I let you. You are a fool! A fragile, ignorant little whore."

Glinda's eyes quivered.

"Or maybe… maybe I was just hoping my father wasn't as evil as the world said he was. Maybe I wanted to believe you were a good man," she scoffed, "But oh, how wrong I was."

"What, and you think *you're* good?"

Glinda turned and walked further down the stairs.

But she stopped and turned.

Her breath trembled. Her voice was a whisper.

"Did you do anything to Mz. Everburn?"

"Who?"

"My teacher. The redhead. From SilverCrest. Did you do anything to her?"

He smiled. Shrugged. "Oh, that one. Don't blame me. She came willingly. Kept rambling about how *her work was done*. Spouting prophecies and riddles. Said she was ready."

Glinda's body shook.

Not with fear.

But with something deeper.

The kind of tremble that comes before a storm.

Dainhurst saw it, and smiled.

"I simply did what had to be done," he said coolly. "I led the charge against magic. And she, she was teaching you. Poisoning your mind with it. I couldn't be a coward. I had to be a man of honour, so I punished her."

Glinda scoffed. A dry, bitter laugh. "You're not honourable, you're a hypocrite! You only hated magic when it didn't serve you. The moment it became useful, you fed on it like a leech. You used me."

Her voice cracked.

"What did you do to her?"

Dainhurst stepped down a stair. Closer.

He leaned in.

And whispered.

"I slit her throat myself. And I smiled while doing it."

Glinda's eyes widened.

Her body didn't move.

For a breath. For two.

Then she ascended. One step. Then another.

Until they were face to face. Nose to nose.

Her breath, steady.

Her eyes, unblinking.

She lifted her hand, not in a strike. But in a vow.

"Listen to me, Dainhurst. I swear by the One Gohd. I swear by the grave of Zelena. By the blood of Mz. Everburn. One more sin. One more step out of line…"

She climbed one final step. Her forehead nearly pressed to his.

"I will kill you."

She turned, her dress brushing his leg like silk drawn across stone.

Down the stairs she walked.

And out the door.

Her words left behind her—

Final.

And true.

Outside, Orryn was prodding the Bubble, inspecting every inch with wide-eyed curiosity.

Glinda called to him, "Are you ready?"

He nodded.

She stepped onto the platform, her silver slippers tucked under her arm. Orryn hopped up beside her without hesitation.

Glinda pressed the activation plate.

With a hum, the bubble encased them, shimmering with soft pink light.

She pulled the lever.

The Bubble ascended, rising into the clouds.

Below, the staff of Fairmoor Castle, maids, guards, gardeners, watched, spellbound. A floating farewell.

Orryn stood proudly, untouched by the height. They were off on their way.

Out of the South.

"Bluebird!" he shouted, pointing.

Glinda smiled.

But just beneath his hand—

A button.

She saw, in real time, Orryn's hands moving to press it.

"No—" Glinda began, lunging forward—

But it was too late.

He pressed it.

A hidden window hissed open.

The Silver Slippers slipped through her fingers.

They flew.

She quickly pressed the button again and the little window sealed shut.

Twirling in the wind, the slippers shimmered like falling stars, tumbling toward the land below.

Down to Munchkinland.

Glinda gasped. "No!"

Orryn turned to her, guilt on his face. "I'm sorry."

Glinda breathed, calming herself.

Then, gently: "It's okay. It's okay."

She pulled him close to her leg and held him tight.

"You're a curious little thing, aren't you?"

He nodded, resting his head against her.

The Bubble carried them across Oz, quiet, steady.

And at last, it touched down again.

In the hills of Gillikin.

In the arms of the North.

In the place Glinda now called—

Home.

CHAPTER 44

Draeth Mor

They entered Glinda's Castle. Wendell was waiting at the door, his posture upright, attentive.

"Do you mind getting a room for him?" Glinda asked.

Wendell looked down at Orryn with a soft smile. "Do you want to choose your own room?"

Orryn nodded eagerly.

Together, Wendell and the boy ascended the grand staircase, ready to scavenge through Glinda's many spare chambers, searching for the perfect one to call Prince Orryn's.

Glinda turned away.

She took the crystal necklace and entered her study, the familiar hush of the room wrapping around her like a faded memory.

She held the necklace in both hands.

She draped it slowly around her neck, and the metal kissed her skin like a ghost.

Still, so cold.

This was all she had now.

No child of her own.

No bloodline to carry forward.

No future growing inside her, just memories, regrets, and magic, if it would even return.

Her eyes drifted to the shelf.

She lifted her hand.

Focused.

Willed.

Move.

The book remained still.

Nothing.

Not even a twitch.

She sat in the chair. Waited.

Perhaps it just needed time.

After a few long Oz'mins, she stood, took a breath, raised her hand again, and tried to levitate the vase on her desk.

Still, nothing.

No flicker in her veins. No pulse. No heat. No magic.

Glinda slapped the table with both palms, the sting biting her skin.

In a fit of rage, she ripped the necklace from her throat and held it up, the green crystal pulsing faintly like a **heart** that wasn't hers.

"Why won't you work?" she shouted. "Why have you abandoned me?!"

The necklace said nothing.

Just shimmered in silence.

She collapsed onto the edge of the desk, her anger folding into despair, her fingers twitching in the quiet.

She needed her magic now more than ever.

And then, an answer formed in her mind. Sharp. Clear.

Zelphira.

The only one who could help.

The only one who knew how.

A fragile smile cracked across her lips… but it didn't last.

Zelphira wouldn't help her.

Not after what she did.

Not after the betrayal.

The shame rose slowly, like water into a drowning girl's throat. She could hardly breathe.

She began pacing her study, panic blooming behind her ribs.

No. She couldn't face her. Not yet.

Not in this state.

She opened the drawer of her desk.

Placed the necklace inside.

And locked it.

◇

An entire Oz'moon had passed. Thirty days of stillness, half of it spent in bed and tear-filled pillows, the other half in warmth, of something Glinda might've once dared to call peace.

She and Orryn were inseparable. Every morning began the same, rising with the sun, sharing breakfast side by side, wandering the garden in matching step. Glinda would read through her stack of sophisticated novels, while Orryn devoured a new tale each day from the *Oz's Children Collection*, his tiny voice stumbling over the big words, but never once giving up.

444

It wasn't until she reached for a pen one morning that she saw it again.

The necklace.

Tucked quietly in her desk drawer, just where she left it, its green hue still pulsing faintly in the dark like a heartbeat.

For a long time, Glinda stared at it. And for the first time... she didn't flinch.

The shame, the fear, the guilt, it was still there, but it no longer ruled her.

She was ready.

Zelphira. Her best friend. Her sister in all the ways that mattered. The one person who could help her understand the broken magic... and maybe even mend it.

She took the crystal necklace in one hand, Seraphina's wand in the other, and moved to the door.

Orryn met her there, eyes bright. "Where are you going?" he asked.

Glinda hesitated, then smiled. "To see a friend."

Orryn grinned. "Can I come?"

"Yes!" she replied softly. "Only if you want to."

Before she could say more, he was already racing past her, hopping onto the Bubble platform with the boundless excitement only a child could carry.

Glinda stepped in behind him. The Bubble enclosed them in its rosy sheen.

And together, they lifted off, toward the Western sky.

Toward Draeth Mor.

Winkie Country looked brighter than Glinda remembered. The sun was blaring, warm and golden, and the flowers were in full bloom, nodding gently in the wind like they too had been waiting for this moment.

The Bubble descended slowly, then landed in the castle's courtyard with a soft hiss. Strangely, no guards were in sight, but above them, vast shadows circled.

Orryn gasped and pointed upward. "Monkey!"

Glinda followed his gaze.

Flying monkeys. Dozens of them, majestic, powerful, leathery, feathery wings stretched against the sun.

She reached for Orryn's hand, gripping it tightly. Together, they stepped off the Bubble platform and approached the castle doors.

Then came the sound.

A screech, no, a choir of screeches. Piercing. Furious.

The flying monkeys dove.

Their wings folded, claws outstretched, spiralling toward them like living blades.

Glinda didn't think. She dropped low, pulling Orryn under her, shielding him with her entire body. Her *heart* pounded, bracing for the tear of claws.

But then—

"STOP!"

The castle doors burst open. A figure stepped out.

Green-skinned. In a fine black dress.

Zelphira.

Her voice cut through the air like a sword, and instantly, the monkeys shifted, pulling up mid-flight, soaring harmlessly back into the clouds above.

Silence fell.

Glinda slowly rose, still gripping Orryn's shoulders. Her eyes met the figure on the castle steps.

Zelphira, her green skin glowing in the light, brow furrowed in disbelief. "Lurline above…"

Glinda took a breath. "Zelly."

They stood frozen for a moment. Neither moved. Neither spoke.

Then, Zelphira reached out.

She grabbed Glinda's hands and pulled her into a hug.

Glinda stiffened in surprise, but after a second, let her head rest over Zelphira's shoulder. Her arms wrapped around her friend like they used to. Like they never stopped.

Zelphira pulled back just enough to look her in the eyes. "It's good to see you, Glinda."

Tears rose in Glinda's eyes. She held Zelphira's hand. "Zelly, I—please… find it in your heart to forgive me. I don't—"

"Oh, stop it," Zelphira interrupted with a half-laugh, half-sigh. "Just come inside."

She stepped aside, holding the door wide.

And Glinda, still holding Orryn's hand, stepped into the castle that once felt like a *home.*

As Glinda stepped into Draeth Mor, the familiar scent of stone and firewood wrapping around her, Orryn trailed confidently behind her, like the castle already belonged to him.

Zelphira caught sight of the boy and tilted her head, brows pinching in curiosity. "And Glinda… who is this?"

"That's Gisella's son," Glinda replied softly.

Zelphira's gaze lingered on him for a moment longer, then she led them into the main hall. They settled onto the velvet couches, plush and familiar. Glinda hadn't sat here in years, and yet it felt untouched by time.

"I'm sorry for your loss," Zelphira said, her voice gentle.

Glinda gave a faint, grateful smile.

Zelphira leaned forward, as if needing to make it absolutely clear. "And Glinda… believe me when I say, I didn't kill the Witch of the South."

"I know," Glinda said without hesitation. "It was all my father's doing."

All around them, a dozen children played, their laughter and chatter filling the room like music. Toys scattered across the rug. Crayons. Dolls. Paper crowns.

Glinda looked around, puzzled. "Who are these children?"

Zelphira glanced fondly at them. "Orphans. They had nowhere to go... so I took them in. Gave them a home."

She turned toward the little ones. "I have a guest now, darlings. Would you mind playing in the other room?"

There were no protests. The children gathered their toys and shuffled out, still deep in their own imaginary worlds.

Orryn wandered over to Zelphira's side. He peered up at her, curious, cautious, like he was trying to make sense of her green skin and elegant black gown.

Then, slowly, he climbed onto the couch beside her and reached up, placing his small hand gently on her cheek.

"Don't do that!" Glinda called instinctively, half-standing.

Zelphira laughed, her hand rising to meet his. "It's fine."

Orryn beamed, and Zelphira smiled back, something tender flickering in her eyes as she looked into the mirror-blue of his.

Then she turned to Glinda. "Are you sure he's Gisella's child?"

Glinda nodded, her voice dry with irony. "Positive. I can't get pregnant."

Zelphira's eyebrows lifted. "Really?"

Glinda sighed, folding her hands in her lap. "It's a long story."

Zelphira tilted her head knowingly. "She was the one who stole your magic, wasn't she?"

Glinda sprang from her seat. "How did you know?"

Zelphira only shrugged, calm as ever. "I saw glimpses of it in one of my visions. I put two and two together. I didn't want to interfere, figured it was something the two of you needed to resolve yourselves." She tilted her head slightly. "But... I assumed you already knew deep down that she is the one that took it from you."

Glinda slowly sat back down, her body folding into itself with a long, exhausted sigh.

Just then, a familiar screeching tore through the silence. Glinda turned toward the window, flying monkeys circled above the castle, their wings slicing through the sunlit sky.

"Flying monkeys?" Glinda muttered, brows raised. "Iconic."

"I know right?" Zelphira giggled, smugly pleased.

Glinda narrowed her eyes. "Where did you even get them?"

"You won't believe me if I told you."

"Try me."

"I turned the Wizard's Guards into them. The ones he sent to kill me."

Glinda blinked. "You're jesting."

"Not in the slightest." Zelphira pointed through the glass at the largest monkey with the darkest wings. "You see that one?"

Glinda nodded.

"That's Chase. Our dear old friend Chisterus."

"No…!" Glinda gasped, half-laughing in disbelief.

"Dead serious," Zelphira smirked. "He truly is the fastest and the deadliest. Nearly took your face off earlier, still not sure if he's overprotective or just bloodthirsty."

"Woz," Glinda whispered. "You've really outdone yourself."

"I try," Zelphira said, brushing imaginary dust from her lap.

Glinda's eyes scanned the room. "Where's the King? And River? I thought for sure I'd be greeted by a scowl and a spear."

Zelphira's expression darkened. "They're dead. The Wizard's Guard killed them trying to get to me. That's why I turned them into my little pets. Use them to fight back against the Wizard."

Silence swelled between them.

"War is no easy path," Glinda said softly.

A quiet moment passed before Zelphira leaned forward. "You didn't come all this way just to make compliments about my flying monkeys. What did you need, Glinda?"

Glinda turned to Orryn, her gaze tender. "Do you mind playing with the other children for a while?"

Orryn nodded and scampered off toward the next room. Zelphira watched him go, her eyes narrowing slightly. When the boy disappeared through the archway, she turned back to Glinda.

"That's not Gisella's son," she said flatly. "That boy is yours."

Glinda blinked. "I just told you—"

"Glinda, listen." Zelphira leaned in, her voice firmer. "We all know babies are made from magic. Real magic. Not spells or potions, I'm talking about the kind that lives in your bones. It's what keeps you breathing. You think it's a coincidence that one tiny drop of semen turns into a whole child in a mother's womb? That's magic."

Glinda stayed silent, brow furrowed.

Zelphira continued, "Gisella stole your magic. And it was that magic, your essence, that created that boy."

She tilted her head. "Who's the father?"

"You wouldn't know him," Glinda muttered.

Zelphira's eyes narrowed. "Is it that skinny blonde boy I saw in my vision?"

Glinda's head snapped up. "How do you still remember that?"

"My visions don't fade. They live in me like memories."

Glinda offered a small, tight-lipped smile—disbelieving, uneasy.

Zelphira leaned forward, her voice low. "Gisella tried to cheat fate. She interfered in something sacred, you and that boy were meant to be. Fate doesn't like interference. So it corrected itself. Your magic—your magic—created Orryn to restore balance. Tell me, didn't you ever wonder why his eyes are the only bright blue ones in a family of emerald?"

Glinda's throat tightened. "So what you're saying is… I'm Orryn's mother?"

"Yes. Entirely. One hundred percent." Zelphira leaned back. "And maybe… just maybe, that's why you can't have more children. Becoz fate already gave you the one it always meant for you to have."

Glinda exhaled, slowly, as the truth curled around her like morning light. She looked to the other room. Orryn was laughing now, chasing the others in circles. And as she watched him, really saw him, he seemed to glow in a new way. Not just sweet, not just bright, but *hers*.

She smiled without meaning to.

Orryn must've felt it. He turned mid-run and grinned back at her, wide and whole, before galloping away again.

Glinda reached into the pouch at her hip and pulled out Gisella's crystal necklace. "Speaking of which… I need your help. My magic's in here. Gisella bound it somehow, but even when I wear it, it won't work. It's like it won't respond to me."

Zelphira took the necklace, held it to the light. Her eyes scanned the flickering green inside—and then she laughed.

"Of course it doesn't work," she said, shaking her head. "This isn't your necklace. This thing is tied to *Gisella*. Magic is personal, Glinda."

Glinda sighed. "You're right."

"We'll need something else," Zelphira said, her eyes thoughtful. "An item *you* connect to. Something that means something to *you*. Then I can transfer your magic into it."

Glinda blinked. "What? You can't just… put it back into me?"

Zelphira shook her head gently. "It doesn't work like that. Your magic was stripped, violently. Once it's pulled from the body, it doesn't just slip back in. Even though it was born from you, it's been out too long. It will need to be contained in an item. Though, your power will be concentrated and become more powerful."

Glinda looked around, then down at the wand lying beside her. She picked it up and held it out between them.

"What about this?" she asked. "It belonged to my ancestor. It's… sentimental."

Zelphira's eyes softened. "Perfect."

She waved her hand, and with a quiet shimmer, the *Kitab Malum* materialized in her lap. Its ancient pages fluttered on their own, as if searching, before halting on one that glowed faintly at the edges.

"Magic Transmutation," she whispered.

She set the book on the floor between them, then placed the crystal necklace on one side, Seraphina's wand on the other. Her hands hovered above each item, fingers steady, her voice calm but commanding.

And then she began to chant:

"Intaqil bin hadha dhalika abadan…

UNDONE

Intaqil bin hadha dhalika abadan…
Intaqil bin hadha dhalika abadan…"

The green glow of the crystal began to tremble. The air shifted.

The spell had begun.

A wisp of green vapor curled from the crystal, light as breath, thick as smoke. It floated upward, swirling and dancing like a serpent made of mist.

Glinda gripped her fingers. Holding her breath. *What if it failed again? What if she never got her magic back? What if it was Fate's grand design to lose her power, the way she lost her sister?*

Then, with a gentle pull, it drifted across the space and seeped into the hollow shaft of Seraphina's wand.

The wand flickered to life.

The green magic shimmered once, then turned. Shifted. Softened. And then, **pink**. A radiant, vibrant pink flooded the transparent glass, pulsing with warmth, as if the wand had taken a deep breath after years of silence.

The crystal necklace, now empty, fell to the floor—returned to its original state. Clear. Clean. Innocent.

Zelphira picked up the wand and placed it gently in Glinda's hands. "Go on," she said with a smile. "Feel it."

Glinda grasped it, and gasped.

The magic surged through her veins like lightning. Her feet left the floor as if the wand itself remembered her, called to her, rejoiced.

Her wand.

Slender and precise, carved from flawless crystal that caught every glimmer of light. A golden heartbeat pulsed at its tip. A living star that looked as though if one got too close it would burn them to ash. It was steady and alive. Silver filigree wove around the staff like vines of moonlight, delicate but powerful. *And when she lifted it, the air around her trembled as if the wand itself was humming with quiet magic.*

Glinda brought it to her lips and whispered, voice trembling, "I've missed you too."

Zelphira grinned. "Well? Don't just stand there, cast something."

Glinda smiled. Closed her eyes.

The wand hummed in her grip. The magic answered, fluid, effortless.

She felt silk rush over her skin, thread by thread. Magic laced through the air like music.

When she opened her eyes, she wore it:

A **new gown**. Petal-pink, impossibly grand. The train flowed behind her like liquid starlight. It sparkled at the seams, embroidered with golden thread and light-catching crystals. The sleeves, sheer and dramatic, rippled like mist.

Zelphira clapped with delight.

"See? I told you I made the most magnificent gowns," Glinda laughed and pulled her into a tight embrace. "Thank you. For everything."

Zelphira hugged her back just as tight. "What are sisters for?"

But before the moment could settle, it shattered—

A cry.

Sharp. Small. Fragile.

Like a baby.

Glinda's brows lifted. "Was that—?"

Zelphira winced. "I may have… kept something from you."

Glinda gave her a cautious, skeptical glance but didn't press further. Instead, she followed the sound, each step heavier than the last as she climbed the winding staircase. Zelphira trailed close behind.

At the top of the stairs, the floor was littered.

WANTED posters. Newspapers. Leaflets.

All bearing Zelphira's face, twisted, exaggerated, cruelly drawn to feed the myth.

Glinda froze. Her eyes scanned the images, her friend made into a monster. The sharp nose. The clawed fingers. The wicked sneer. She knew it was all wrong. Every depiction a lie. Every poster a reflection of a moment that started in love—two girls laughing in candlelight, pouring over forbidden texts, daring to imagine more.

She bent and picked up a paper.

WICKED WITCH OF THE WEST KILLS THE GOOD WITCH OF THE SOUTH

"I should've said something," Glinda whispered. "That you didn't do it."

Zelphira shook her head, calm and resigned. "They wouldn't have believed you."

"Yes, they would."

"No they wouldn't!" Her voice was firmer now. "They choose to believe it not becoz they have to, but becoz they want to, especially the Munchkinlanders. So small-minded…" Her smile was bitter. "Who would've thought the people who raised me would be the first to crucify me."

She stepped in front of Glinda and motioned to a door at the end of the hall. Her hand rested on the knob.

"Are you ready?"

Glinda squinted. "Ready for what?"

Zelphira gave a knowing smile and opened the door.

The room was dim. Quiet. Cool.

Glinda stepped in slowly, and as her eyes adjusted to the dark, her breath caught.

A crib stood in the centre of the room. Simple. Carved from dark wood. Moonlight pooled around it like a halo.

She approached, one hand resting gently on the edge. She leaned in.

Inside, a baby. Peacefully asleep. Tiny fingers curled into fists. Pale as snow.

Glinda blinked and turned to Zelphira. "A baby?"

Zelphira nodded.

"Is he... one of the orphans?"

"No," she said softly. "He's mine."

"You mean you—?" Glinda's eyes widened. "You *birthed* him?"

Zelphira smiled. "Yes. Him. All mine. His name is Lirvan."

Glinda looked down into the crib again, a smile warming her face. "*Lirvan,*" she repeated softly, gazing at the child's tiny hands and serene breath.

Zelphira's smile couldn't help but get wider, the way Glinda looked at him, like he was her own child.

But then Glinda's smile faltered, her eyes narrowing with quiet confusion.

Her head tilted. "But... he's not green?" she asked, almost in a whisper, like the question itself felt impossible.

"I *know!*" Zelphira whispered, almost exasperated. "I don't understand it either. Maybe it means he's special. Maybe he's the *one* the Wizard was talking about. The true Wizard of Oz. The one who'll burn *your* friend's empire to the ground."

Glinda kept her eyes lowered, silent.

She spoke softly, "Who's the father—Rivero?"

"No."

"Then who?"

Zelphira offered a cryptic smile. "Let's just say... the father is very 'honourable.'"

Glinda's gaze drifted to a silver rattle resting beside Lirvan. She picked it up and gave it a gentle shake. A soft, melodic chime filled the air, and the baby responded with a delighted smile.

With quiet tenderness, Glinda traced a finger along the curve of his tiny belly, watching it rise and fall with each breath. "He's beautiful," she whispered. "Definitely takes after his mother."

Zelphira chuckled quietly. "Looks like he's drifted back to sleep. Come on. Let's head downstairs."

They returned to the grand hall and eased into the velvet cushions once more.

Glinda studied her closely. "Hmm..."

Zelphira tilted her head. "What is it?"

"You look troubled. Like something's weighing on you."

"What gave that away?"

"You have a tell. Where you fidget with your fingers. Tell me what's on your mind."

Zelphira exhaled sharply. "I've been having these dreams. Not normal ones. These are... clairvoyant dreams. The same every night. Always the same girl. Always the same ending."

Glinda leaned in, her expression serious. "Tell me."

"In the dream," Zelphira whispered, her fingers knotting together, "there's a girl. Dark-haired, not quite as dark as mine. She wears enchanted shoes—I can feel it in the dream, like heat. Her power recognises me. And mine... recognises her."

Glinda held her breath.

"She comes to Draeth Mor," Zelphira continued, her voice cracking. "And she kills me. I melt, Glinda. My skin, my soul, everything. It's agony. It's real. I've never been wrong about these visions. Not once."

She covered her face with her hands. "I don't want to die. I've just found happiness. My baby. My children."

Her sobs escaped her, raw, helpless.

Glinda moved beside her, wrapping her arms around her shoulders. "Maybe you're misreading it. Maybe the dream is symbolic, not literal."

Zelphira shook her head violently. "No. I feel it in my bones. This girl is real, and she's coming for me."

Glinda held her tighter. "Then we'll stop her. I swear to you, I will protect you. We will fight this together, Zelly."

Zelphira finally let herself break, collapsing into Glinda's embrace. And Glinda held her, firm and unshaking, until the tears began to still.

As the sun dipped low and the sky softened into lavender, Glinda rose from her seat and stretched lightly. "It's getting late. Orryn and I should head back."

Inside, Orryn had fallen asleep, curled up among the dozen children who had long given in to slumber. Glinda gently roused him, brushing a strand of hair from his face. He stirred with a yawn, clinging to her arm as they stepped into the cool air outside.

The Bubble waited patiently in the courtyard, shimmering in the last breath of daylight.

Zelphira followed them out. Her voice cracked gently with yearning and sincerity. "Come back and visit me soon. We've lost enough time already."

"I will," Glinda promised, her words firm but warm.

She pulled Zelphira into a final hug, arms wrapped tightly around the woman she once feared she'd lost forever. Then, with wand in hand and the necklace glinting at her side, she stepped into the Bubble beside Orryn.

They ascended slowly, quietly, into the sky's embrace, Glinda's eyes on the woman below until the castle disappeared in the clouds.

Zelphira remained in the courtyard, standing alone, waving up at them long after they had gone.

As they ascended, Glinda let herself wonder, just for a moment, what a future might look like. The Good Witch of the North and the Wicked Witch of the West. It didn't make sense. Too much damage had been done; the people wouldn't understand. Not yet. Maybe not ever.

But the thought lingered... and didn't quite leave.

CHAPTER 45

Honour

Glinda had spent too much time away from her duties, and the consequences were starting to show. The people were asking questions, whispering if she had suffered the same fate as her sister, and, more importantly, the Wizard needed her.

Today was Ozma's Eve: the happiest, brightest day in all of Oz. A day the Wicked Witch, of course, would never be welcome at.

The Wizard had decided it was time to revive the old traditions, his yearly proclamation, and Glinda herself would be honoured with placing the star atop the grand *Whyte* Tree. The podium had been assembled, the floats lined the streets, a colossal white tree towered at the *heart* of Emerald City, and the infinite city lights flickered in celebration.

Crowds flooded the streets, wrapped in furs and scarves, eager for a glimpse of the Wizard and Glinda, eager for the festivities to begin. The air was thick with mist and falling snow, the world turning into a glittering dreamscape.

Inside the Emerald Palace, the Wizard stood ready with his cane, and Glinda stood proudly with her wand. They waited in the antechamber, the heavy walls muffling the crowd's anticipation.

Glinda broke the silence.

"Are you nervous?" she asked.

"Not really," the Wizard replied, smoothing down his coat. "I've been doing this since before you were even born. I forgot how good it feels… I don't know why I ever stopped."

Glinda smiled. "Thank you, for letting me place the star on the tree tonight. It's an honour."

The Wizard waved off the sentiment. "Bah! Don't mention it," he said. His eyes wandered to Glinda's wand, studying it with an almost wistful fascination. "I never thought I'd see that wand come back to life. Now that you have your magic again… the sky's the limit."

Glinda turned back toward the door, her *heart* warming slightly.

But the Wizard wasn't done. His voice sharpened, curious. "How did you get your magic back, anyway?"

A sudden gust of cold air swept through the hallway, rattling the nearby lanterns.

Glinda hesitated, then turned to face him fully. She sighed, the truth heavy on her lips. "I went to see Zelphira."

The Wizard's face twisted with alarm.

"The Wicked Witch?!"

"Yes," Glinda stammered. "But she's changed. She's not the same person anymore."

"I doubt that," he said, voice dripping with disdain.

"No, really, she has a child now."

At that, the Wizard's eyes twitched, barely, but Glinda caught it.

"And I think it's softened her," Glinda continued, "the same way Orryn softened me. I know she would be open to a conversation with you, especially if you agreed to help the Animals."

"No," the Wizard said sharply. "She is wicked, and that's final. Any attempt would be futile!"

"Futile?" Glinda stepped closer. "What's truly futile is this endless war you're waging against her. It's draining your armies and only strengthening hers—those flying monkeys aren't going anywhere. You won't win this war, not like this. Isn't it time to rethink your strategy? To make peace instead of dragging it out? You could gain far more by making her your ally than keeping her your enemy."

The Wizard opened his mouth to object, but stopped himself. He narrowed his eyes, thinking. "Hmmm."

Glinda pressed forward. "And maybe... maybe if you truly want peace, you could remove her label as the Wicked Witch. Give her honour. Let her return to society."

The Wizard gave her a long, searching look, but before he could respond, the great doors burst open, and a gust of snowy air swirled through the hall.

It was time.

The Wizard, composed once more, marched toward the podium. Glinda remained a few paces behind, clutching her wand.

The Wizard's voice boomed across the Emerald City:

"Today, on this momentous day, the thirteenth of Snowthrush, we celebrate the birth of Ozma. May the One Gohd never cease his gifts upon me, the wisdom and power to protect you all from wickedness. And may Lurline and Ozma save you all."

He turned toward Glinda, offering his hand in a grand gesture.

"Glinda, Good Witch of the North, will you do the honours?"

Glinda approached the large green button set beside the podium. She pressed it.

UNDONE

A whirring sound filled the air as brilliant lights spiralled upward, wrapping around the colossal *Whyte* Tree. The star at its peak shimmered and burst into golden brilliance.

The crowd erupted into cheers. People hugged and kissed beneath the falling snow. Musicians struck up a bright, festive tune. The Wizard's Guard marched in formation. Bottles popped, confetti rained from the rooftops, the entire city sparkling in celebration.

Above it all, the snow, the Winterdust, began falling heavier, a thick curtain of silver frosting the city.

"Look at all this Winterdust!" Glinda said brightly, turning toward the Wizard.

But he only gave her a thin, distracted smile. "I think I'll retire to my chambers," he said, voice distant. "Something weighing on my mind."

"Is there anything I can do?" she offered.

He chuckled softly. "Oh no, no. Trust me. Just some work needing my attention. Stay here, keep them entertained. Good night, Glinda."

And with a final nod, he disappeared into the Emerald Palace, leaving her standing alone at the edge of the celebration.

She watched him disappear into the palace and felt a chill she could not blame on the *Winterdust.*

She descended the podium steps slowly, her wand in hand, her pink gown billowing and sweeping the ground like a trail of clouds.

The people parted for her, smiling, waving, bowing, but Glinda barely registered them.

She walked forward blindly, deeper and deeper into the streets, until the brilliant lights and cheerful music melted behind her.

She wandered past the end of the festivities, into the dim, forgotten corners of the Emerald City where the lanterns didn't reach and the snow piled heavy in silence.

Using her wand's glowing tip as a guide, Glinda passed a lonely bench. She paused.

And then, unable to resist the weight pulling at her heart, she sat down.

She placed her wand beside her and buried her face in her lap, muffling the sobs that finally broke free.

The cold gnawed at her, but she barely noticed, only the heavy, endless ache inside her chest remained.

Footsteps broke the silence.

Soft. Steady. Approaching.

And then, a voice. Gentle, familiar, aching.

"Why are you crying?"

Glinda hurriedly wiped her tears with the back of her hand, hidden in her lap, forcing a smile onto her face before lifting her head.

For a moment, she thought the Winterdust was playing tricks on her.

The figure shimmered in the cold mist, and then solidified.

Her **heart** stopped, then lurched painfully, beating faster than it ever had before.

Her voice escaped her lips in a fragile whisper: "Omi?"

The figure smiled, wide and disbelieving, tears glinting in his eyes like stars.

"Glinda," he breathed.

They stood frozen in place.

Neither dared move.

For a heartbeat, maybe two, they simply stared at each other across the narrow distance, as if a single breath would break the fragile spell.

Then, as if pulled by a force stronger than themselves, Glinda surged forward.

She flung her arms around him, and he caught her, clutching her tightly, holding on to her like if he let go, she would disappear into nothingness.

She trembled against him.

"Wha—How are you here?" she gasped against his chest. "What are you doing here?"

He laughed, a shaky, disbelieving sound, as he stroked his hand over her back.

"It's good to see you too, Glinda."

Still breathless, she pulled back just enough to look at him.

"I didn't know if I'd ever see you again," she whispered. "Of all places... what brings you here?"

"I'm part of the Wizard's Guard, remember?" he smiled. "We were all called to the city for Ozma."

"Oh," she said, blinking. "Right. Of course."

"I saw you wandering away from the parade. I had to follow you." He tilted his head, studying her. "You've changed."

Glinda lowered her gaze. "I know."

"You've become everything you once dreamed of," he said softly.

"Did you ever doubt I would?" she asked, almost shyly.

"Not for a second."

She smiled and gestured to a bench nearby. "Please, sit with me."

They sat, Glinda to the left, her wand balanced in the middle and Ominson to the right.

He turned to her, his voice low and sincere. "Are you happy?"

"How do you mean?" she breathed.

He searched her face. "Strawberry hair gone. Nose gone." He paused. "Are you happy, Glinda?"

She stiffened, a breath caught in her chest. "What makes you think I'm not?"

"You were crying when I found you."

Glinda sighed and leaned back against the bench, her gown whispering against the wood.

"No. Yes? I don't know," she said. Then, turning to him: "Are you?"

He looked back at her, his eyes certain. His eyes unwavering from hers.

"Right now, I am."

Glinda smiled, her eyes certain. Her eyes unwavering from his.

"I am too."

Ominson moved the wand aside, then scooted closer to Glinda.

He whispered, "I heard about Gisella. I'm so sorry."

Her eyes filled, the tears she thought she'd buried rising again.

She rested her head against his shoulder, feeling the warmth and certainty of him.

He reached up and gently wiped away the tears that slipped down her cheeks.

"I'm here for you, Glinda. Always. Just say the word."

She lifted her head, her eyes finding his.

"There's so much to say, Omi," she whispered. "And so little time."

"Then say it," he murmured.

"Say what?"

He took her hand and folded it into his, firm and sure.

"Say you want me to stay…and I will."

She hesitated, her throat tight.

"But your honour," she whispered. "Did you find it? I can't ask you to leave the Wizard's Guard… not for me."

Ominson tightened his grip on her hand, his breath hitching.

"Glinda! Staying with you would be the most honourable thing I've ever done. But only if you'll have me. Only if you want it."

Glinda searched his eyes, earnest, steady, waiting.

He lifted his other hand to her cheek, his thumb brushing gently against her skin.

Her *heart* hammered in her chest.

Glinda leaned in fully, her lips meeting his for what felt like an eternity, and he met her halfway.

For a moment, nothing else existed but the warmth of that kiss, the trembling closeness of two souls finally finding each other again.

Their connection, and the sudden warmth cutting through the cold, sent shivers through them both.

The noise of the world dulled to a distant hum.

Glinda's body lost all its tension and so did Ominson's.

And they let themselves go.

Like leaves into the wind.

When they finally pulled apart, Ominson tucked her close, shielding her from the bitter chill.

They sat together, soaking in the moment, as the distant sound of cheers and laughter from the city reached their ears.

Glinda stirred first, glancing toward the twinkling lights.

"Shall we go?" she whispered. "There's someone I want you to meet in the North. Back Home."

He smiled, eyes shining.

"Lead the way," he said. "Take me home, Glinda."

They rose from the bench, but as they turned to leave, Ominson paused.

"Don't forget this!" he said, handing her the wand.

Then, without hesitation, Ominson shrugged off his Wizard's Guard jacket and tossed it into the snow, the heavy emblem sinking into the frost.

They hurried through the quiet streets, hearts beating fast.

Glinda activated her Bubble, and together they climbed onto the platform.

With a soft hum, they ascended into a frosty sky that looked like stars falling around them.

They kissed again, longer this time, as the Bubble spun higher into the midnight sky, carrying them toward home, toward each other, toward something they had almost lost forever.

Alone together in their own little bubble.

Their own little world.

◇

The Bubble touched down softly outside Glinda's Castle, its pink glow fading as the platform lowered. Inside, the castle lights gleamed like lanterns in the cold, festive night, every window was aglow in Oz, except one, far away in the West.

Hand in hand, Glinda and Ominson stepped onto the snow-dusted ground.

"This is it?" Ominson asked, eyes sweeping over the quaint towers and willow tree swaying in the night breeze.

Glinda looked at him with a hopeful smile. "Do you like it?"

He smiled back. "It's perfect."

They walked up to the door and knocked gently. Moments later, it creaked open, revealing Wendell—robe wrapped tightly, eyes wide with surprise. He blinked, taking in the unexpected sight, then gave a slow, knowing nod. It was Ozma's Eve. Miracles were owed.

Ominson extended a hand to Wendell. "Is this who you wanted me to meet?" he asked Glinda playfully.

"Not quite," she replied.

Before another word could be spoken, a rush of tiny footsteps echoed down the stairs.

Orryn appeared at the landing, hair tousled, eyes bright.

"You're back!" he shouted, racing toward Glinda and throwing his arms around her legs.

Glinda bent slightly to return the hug.

She glanced sideways at Wendell and whispered, "Why is he still awake?"

Wendell shrugged. "Said he wouldn't sleep till you got home."

Orryn's gaze shifted. His eyes landed on Ominson, sharp, curious, and scrutinizing.

"Who are you?" he asked, brows raised.

Ominson knelt down, a smile playing on his lips. "That's a fair question."

Orryn folded his arms like a judge sizing up a defendant.

Glinda lowered to one knee beside him, resting a hand on his shoulder. She looked up at Ominson.

"Ominson…" she said gently, "meet your son."

Silence.

Ominson froze. His lips parted, but no words came.

"What do you mean?" he asked at last. "I—I don't have a child."

"Yes," Glinda said softly. "You do."

He blinked. "Is this Gisella's child?"

"Yes… and no." Glinda took a breath. "It's complicated. I'll explain everything soon. But this—this is him. He's yours."

Ominson looked into Glinda's eyes. Something settled behind his own. A quiet trust.

"If you say he is, then I believe you."

Ominson then looked from Glinda to Orryn. The boy's wide blue eyes looked back, unflinching. Unmistakable.

He knelt down beside Orryn and gently tousled the boy's hair. Orryn shuffled back slightly, pressing closer into the folds of Glinda's gown, half his face hidden, the other eye curiously watching.

"He does have my hair, now that I look properly," Ominson said, grinning.

"And your ears," Glinda added with a warm smile.

Still nestled in Glinda's arms, Orryn eyed the man closely.

"What's your name?" Ominson asked, his voice calm and soft.

"Orryn," the boy replied, his voice small but clear.

Ominson tapped his chest lightly with a finger. "That's a strong name. Do you know what it means?"

Orryn shook his head.

"It means 'honourable one.'"

Then, Ominson opened his arms. "I know we just met, but… can I have a hug?"

Orryn hesitated, just a moment, then, eyes scanning Ominson one last time, stepped forward. He folded into the man's arms, and didn't let go.

Glinda stood upright, her **heart** full. She met Wendell's eyes from across the room. They exchanged a smile, quiet, proud.

After a long beat, Glinda gently interrupted. "I hate to ruin the moment, but he really should get to bed. It's late."

Ominson lifted Orryn in his arms. "Not you being all maternal now." He smirked. "Don't come between me and my son."

Glinda laughed.

Orryn let out a deep yawn, long and loud.

Ominson glanced down, catching the boy's drooping eyelids and bobbing head as it settled on his shoulder.

"You're tired, huh?" he whispered.

Orryn shook his head in denial, but it was too late—

"Yes, you are," Ominson sang gently.

Orryn smiled sleepily and gave a tiny nod, conceding defeat.

Ominson turned to Glinda, his voice gentle. "Mind showing me his room?"

Glinda beamed, caught in the warmth of the moment. "Of course. Follow me."

They ascended the staircase together, their steps quiet beneath the hush of night.

Inside the room, Ominson carefully placed Orryn in bed, pulling the covers up to his chin.

Glinda leaned down, pressing a kiss to his forehead. The boy's breath slowed, his lashes fluttering closed.

She gently closed the door behind them as they slipped back into the hall.

Outside, they stood still for a moment, faces lit only by the gentle lamplight.

Glinda turned to Ominson, eyes full of affection. "You're already amazing at this," she said.

He smiled. "Thank you. He really does look like you, though."

"Yes… about that."

Ominson gently took her arm, and Glinda began to explain everything, about the magic, Gisella, the spell, and the truth behind Orryn's birth.

They continued their conversation behind the door of Glinda's chambers, where words turned to closeness, and understanding wove their hearts tighter.

They entered the New-Oz'Moon with a clean beginning, and each day that followed built something steadier, sweeter.

Glinda had finally found her true prince.

Together in the North, Glinda and Ominson raised their son, not in grandeur, but in quiet joy. They had found their True North:

A direction.

A *home.*

A family.

And yes, Wendell was part of it too.

CHAPTER 46

Ceremony, Traditions & Time

One morning, Ominson rolled over in bed, the sun spilling across the sheets, and asked Glinda a question that caught her off guard.

His voice was light, curious. "So, what colour?"

Glinda blinked, disoriented. "What do you mean?"

"For Orryn," he said. "What colour did he choose for his Moonshine Coronation?"

She hesitated. Her gaze drifted to the far corner of the room, like she was trying to summon an answer from thin air.

After a long pause, she finally murmured, "Now that I think about it… I don't think he's had one."

Ominson raised an eyebrow. "Really? He's what—three Oz'moons old now? And he hasn't had a coronation?"

Glinda gave a dismissive shrug. "It doesn't matter. We're Northians now."

Ominson didn't reply at first. His face tightened, and then, as if holding it in had become unbearable, he exhaled and spoke.

"I know you're trying to leave the past behind," he said gently, "but no matter how far you run, you're still a Quadling, whether you like it or not. It doesn't just disappear."

Glinda rolled away from him, her back a wall of silence. "He's not having a Moonshine Coronation. That's final."

Ominson reached over and tapped her shoulder. "No, it's not. He's not just your son, he's mine too. And I want him to have one."

She didn't respond.

He continued, his voice firmer now. "You're afraid he'll pick a gem you don't approve of. But he deserves what we had. It's his birthright, his culture. He should get to embrace it."

Her voice came out low and vulnerable. "I just don't want to go back to the South. Not yet."

Ominson gently turned her back to face him. He kissed her shoulder, then her neck, then her cheek. "Then let's go together," he whispered. "And while we're there... maybe we can have another ceremony."

"What other ceremony?" Glinda asked, her voice still sleepy but tinged with curiosity.

"Oh, I didn't tell you?" Ominson grinned.

He leaned over to the bedside table and opened the drawer. From within, he pulled out a gold ring glinting in the morning light, set with a violet diamond that shimmered like dusk.

He held it up to her. Close. Steady.

Glinda sat bolt upright, blinking. "What are you saying?" she gasped.

"I want to marry you," he said softly. "Be my wife. Let me be your husband."

"You're jesting."

"Do I sound like I'm jesting?" he asked. "I've been carrying this ring for moons, waiting for the moment that felt right. And now, it does." He took a breath. "So, what do you say?"

Glinda beamed, her voice breaking with joy. "Yes! Yes! A thousand times, yes!"

He slid the ring onto her finger, and she lifted her hand into the sunlight pouring in from the window, watching the violet gem dance in the glow.

She looked at him again. "And you want to get married in Quadling Country?"

Ominson nodded.

"After Orryn's Moonshine Coronation," he said, "we'll have the ceremony. And I want Barbarus to officiate it."

Glinda hesitated, sighed, then gave a resolute nod. "Very well. We'll return to the South."

◇

The next morning, Glinda, Ominson, and Orryn stepped into the Bubble and rose into the golden sky. From the snowy hills of the North to the red earth of the South, they soared across Oz.

By noon, they landed at the *Solar Temple*.

The air was warm and rich with memory. The stone floor echoed beneath their feet as they walked forward, Orryn holding both their hands, his eyes wide.

Then, from a corridor, a voice called out. "I'm not expecting any visitors to—
—"

Barbarus stopped mid-sentence.

His eyes widened at the sight of them. "Glinda. Ominson."

He stepped forward, his voice thick with surprise. "By the One Gohd... it's been a long time."

463

He opened his arms and embraced them both.

Then his gaze fell on the child between them.

Barbarus leaned down and smiled. "And who might this be? Is this your child?"

Glinda nodded, the warmth in her chest blooming. "Yes," she said.

Barbarus smiled gently at the little boy before glancing up at Glinda and Ominson. "I never thought I'd see your face here again, Glinda." His voice trembled slightly. "I heard there was tension between you and your father... What happened?"

Glinda's face darkened. "Let's just say... he told me things I can't unhear. Things that changed everything."

Barbarus' eyes took on a weight of grief, like he knew more than he should. "I understand." He paused, then added softly, "I'm just relieved he didn't go through with it."

Glinda's brows furrowed. "Didn't go through with what?"

Barbarus blinked, suddenly nervous. "Oh—sorry. I think we may be talking about different things," he said with an awkward chuckle. "Anyway, what brings you here?"

"No," Glinda snapped, stepping forward. "Barbarus, tell me what you meant. Right now."

He sighed heavily and gestured for them to sit on a stone bench nearby. Ominson gave Orryn a toy to occupy him while Barbarus took a seat beside Glinda.

"I thought... I assumed that was the reason you and your father were estranged," he began gently. "The truth of what happened when you were born. I didn't imagine anything worse than that."

He bowed his head, his voice low and remorseful. "When you chose the pink gem, your father was mortified. He felt disgraced. He... he wanted to get rid of you. Whether it was through a staged accident, or some sacrificial act. But I stopped him. I pleaded with him to spare your life. I told him I saw a different future—one that would bring honour."

Glinda let out a quiet laugh, bitter and heartbroken. "He told me the opposite," she whispered. "He said *others* wanted me dead. That *he* fought to keep me alive."

Her gaze dropped to the floor, shoulders still.

Barbarus gently took her hand as it slid from her lap. His touch warm, grounding.

"I'm sorry, Glinda. I always feared the truth would hurt more than the lie. But I am truly amazed... I gave a false prophecy to save your life, and somehow, it came true. You've brought honour not just to the South, but all of Oz. You may wear the title 'Good Witch of the North'—but you are, without doubt, a true Quadling." He paused; emotion thick in his throat. "I'm proud of you. More than I can ever say."

Glinda placed her other hand over his, squeezing it. "Thank you. Truly."

She took a deep breath and smiled softly. "We're here today to ask something of you. We'd like you to perform the Moonshine Ceremony... for our son."

Barbarus stood, his eyes lit with purpose. "It would be my honour."

He called forth the ceremonial tray, and the Gemz, each glimmering like drops of rain, were carefully laid on the altar.

The sun hung perfectly overhead, casting golden beams across the stone floor.

Orryn, quiet as a mouse, was gently guided to the altar. He looked up at Glinda and Ominson, who nodded with reassurance.

Barbarus knelt beside him and said warmly, "Go ahead, my child. Choose your gem."

Orryn scanned the array of glistening *Raindrop Gemz*, his small fingers hovering over each one with careful curiosity. Then, as if pulled by an invisible thread, his hand reached out and grasped a single gem.

He held it high in the air, and the moment he did, the room was flooded with violet light.

Gasps echoed through the temple as the gem pulsed brighter than anyone had ever seen. It bathed the chamber in a warm, radiant glow that shimmered like starlight on water.

Barbarus stepped back, awe-struck. "By Lurline's breath... this is the brightest any gem has ever shone in my time." He leaned toward Glinda, eyes wide. "What exactly runs in your family's bloodline?"

Ominson erupted into celebration. "Yes!" He scooped Orryn up into his arms and spun him around. "You're just like your Popsy, aren't you?"

Glinda chuckled, her eyes misty. "Yes he is. And one day, he'll be just as honourable."

Ominson planted kiss after kiss across Orryn's cheeks, making the boy giggle in confusion and delight.

Barbarus, still stunned by the glow, cleared his throat. "And what is the child's full name?"

Ominson stood tall, with Orryn balanced on his hip. "Orryn Damian Alaric Veilforge Fairmoor."

Barbarus nodded, placing a hand over his heart. "Then let it be known, I present to you, Orryn Damian Alaric Veilforge Fairmoor, who has chosen the Violet Gem. May he always be good."

"May he always be good," Glinda and Ominson repeated in unison.

Barbarus beamed, but before he could speak further, Ominson raised his hand. "One last favour, if I may."

"Anything," Barbarus said at once.

Glinda and Ominson exchanged a knowing glance.

Ominson stepped forward. "Would you do us the honour of officiating our wedding?"

Barbarus gasped, and then broke into a joyous shuffle. "It's about time!"

Glinda burst into laughter. "What do you mean?"

"Oh, come on," Barbarus said with a wide grin. "The way you two bickered like a married couple since you were young? The whole temple could feel the tension. We've all been waiting for this."

"Hey!" Ominson protested with mock offense. "I was clear with my feelings. She's the one who ran every time."

"Oh hush," Glinda replied, swatting his arm playfully.

Their laughter filled the temple, warm and full. For the first time in a long time, everything felt whole.

Barbarus clapped his hands. "Alright then! Let's do this!" "No, not here!" Ominson objected.

Glinda tossed her hair then narrowed her eyes. "You and your surprises. What do you mean not here?"

Still holding Orryn in his arms, Ominson turned to her, his voice gentle. "I want us to marry in our little spot."

Her breath caught. "The Waterfall Garden?"

"Yes. I wouldn't want it anywhere else."

Glinda laced her fingers with his, nodding. Then the pair turned to Barbarus.

"Would someone care to explain what this mysterious 'Waterfall Garden' is?" he asked.

"Come with us and see for yourself," Glinda grinned.

Barbarus chuckled. "You better not have brought that Bubble contraption. I'm not built for heights—short legs, shorter nerves!"

"Don't worry!" Orryn piped up. "It's not that scary!"

Their laughter echoed as they all boarded the Bubble.

Barbarus clung to the side with his eyes squeezed shut for most of the flight.

When they finally arrived, the garden lay before them, untouched, radiant. Everything was just as they left it.

Barbarus stepped out, blinking. Then, utterly awestruck, he whispered, "Is this Heahven?"

"To me, it is," Ominson replied, his voice low with emotion.

Orryn stood completely still, his mouth open in wonder, holding tighter to Glinda's hand.

She glanced down at her pink gown. "I can't get married in this!"

With a flick of her wand, she closed her eyes and thought of something new.

In a burst of soft light, her gown transformed.

A white, resplendent dress bloomed into being, layers of silk and lace flowed like water, a tiara adorned her updo, and a sheer veil spilled over her shoulders.

She turned to Ominson. "What do you think?"

He was speechless. "You look... perfect."

She turned to Orryn. "And you, Orry?"

Orryn beamed. "You look amazing, Mumsy!"

Glinda's smile was quiet and glowing—any wider and she might burst into tears.

"Shall we begin?" Barbarus declared, his voice rising above the sound of the cascading waterfall.

"Yes! Please do," Ominson replied, squeezing Glinda's hand in his.

He led her to stand beside the falls, where the mist kissed their skin and the fading light gave everything a golden hue. Barbarus joined them, robes trailing, a warmth in his old eyes.

"Today I bring to you the partnership of an Oztime!" Barbarus began. "Glinda Arduelle Fairmoor and Ominson Valeus Veilforge. May they always be good to one another, love one another in sickness and in health, search for one another in this life and the next, even through any fire or tide that may come between them!" He turned to them. "Do you agree to this commitment? Is your heart true in this marriage? Will you fight for your love to endure?"

Ominson looked deep into Glinda's eyes, his eyes unwavering. "I do! With all my heart!"

Glinda looked deep into Ominson's eyes, her eyes unwavering. "I do! With all my soul!"

Barbarus smiled. "Then by the Old Light and the New, I pronounce you husband and wife."

They simply looked at each other, quiet, overwhelmed, as though time had paused just for them. A thousand unspoken words passed between them before they finally leaned in, and kissed to the music of the waterfall.

"Yuck!" Orryn groaned behind them, puffing his cheeks and blowing raspberries.

They all burst into laughter.

"Come here, you!" Ominson laughed, chasing Orryn around the garden as the boy squealed with delight.

They lingered for a while in that hidden oasis, until the sun began to dip beneath the trees. As they prepared to leave, Barbarus held back a moment longer, eyes drinking in the beauty one last time.

Once they had stepped through the path, Glinda turned, wand in hand. She whispered a spell.

"Hosteas Externa Crosceat."

Stone and root obeyed. A wall rose from the earth and sealed the garden's entrance completely, not a crack left to find the way back in. Only those who knew it would remember it had ever existed.

UNDONE

They returned Barbarus to the temple, embracing him warmly before parting ways.

Then, the newlyweds and their son took to the sky in the Bubble and returned to the North.

Life changed after that—and for the better.

There were trials, yes, but there were joys that outweighed them. Love stitched itself into their daily rhythms, and Glinda's days were filled with laughter, with magic, and with family.

◊

Time, of course, went on.

The moons turned.

The seasons shifted.

A decade passed.

Oz glowed in peace for a time. The Good Witch of the North rose in the hearts of her people, a steady second to the ever-present Wizard. The Wicked Witch remained hidden away in her castle and no one dared cross to the West to face her wrath or her flying monkeys that guarded the skies.

But then came the quiet years.

Storms began to brew.

Thunder. Snow. Torrents of rain.

But above all else—came the cyclones.

They tore through Oz with frightening regularity, bending trees and uprooting homes. The Wizard issued an order: *Every citizen must stay indoors until further notice.*

Oz had grown dark.

Or rather, it had grown darker.

CHAPTER 47

No Good Deed

The storms were becoming unbearable.

Glinda had done all she could, casting spells, raising barriers, calming winds, but each time she subdued them, they returned fiercer, hungrier, more relentless than before.

She needed help.

Someone powerful. Someone who understood the weight of suffering. Someone whose magic rivalled her own—even surpassed it.

There was only one name that came to mind.

Zelphira.

If anyone could stop this, it was her. She had always had a *heart* for the helpless, a softness buried deep beneath her thorns. Glinda had to believe she would care enough to act.

Without another thought, Glinda climbed into her Bubble. But as her fingers reached for the lever, they trembled. She paused.

Ten years.

It had been a decade since she'd last seen Zelphira.

Still, she pushed the lever forward. She had no choice.

As the Bubble ascended, she cast a protective enchantment from her Ethereum, shielding it from the brutal winds that howled most violently in the West.

But what awaited her there was far worse than broken glass.

Above her, the skies churned with winged silhouettes. The monkeys had seen her approach, and they dove. Screeching, snarling, claws bared, they spiralled toward her in a storm of fury. Glinda raised her wand and summoned a forcefield just in time but their blows pounded against the barrier causing a few scratches and dents to the Bubble.

And then, they stopped.

From the tallest tower, a cloaked figure emerged, leaning out the window to observe the commotion. With a raise of her broom, the monkeys broke away from their assault and soared upward once more.

The figure leapt from the tower, broom in hand.

Then she rose.

High into the sky, wind snapping at her long black cloak, her pointed hat sharp against the clouds. And then she descended, just as fast as the monkeys had. A streak of shadow falling like a spear from heaven.

Glinda swallowed hard, tightening her grip around her wand.

Something was wrong.

This wasn't the Zelphira she remembered. And for the first time, she wasn't sure it was her at all.

But when the woman landed and lifted her head—

Glinda gasped.

Her skin, once a vibrant lime, had deepened into a dark, mossy green. A tone of rot and shadow.

But it was her nose that stole Glinda's breath, the nose was long, hooked, grotesquely sharp. Deformed. Intentional.

Glinda stumbled back.

From above, the cloaked woman's voice sliced through the storm. "So… you've finally decided to show up. Let me guess, you need something."

"Zelphira…?" Glinda's voice trembled. Her hand rose to her lips as she took in the face before her. "What… what happened to you?"

The figure stepped closer, each movement unhurried and heavy, as if savouring the dread curling in Glinda's chest. The cloak whipped around her like smoke.

"What's wrong, Saint Glinda? Afraid of your own reflection?"

Glinda's eyes fixated on the twisted feature. "Your nose… why would you— what did you do?"

The Wicked Witch jabbed a long, clawed finger toward her face. "You really don't recognise it? This is your nose! Before your…what did you call it? Before your 'bibidi bobidi boo?'"

"But why would you do this to yourself?"

"Oh, you did this to me! You made me this way!"

"What are you talking about? In what world would I do this to you?!" Glinda snapped.

"This is a reminder!" she barked. "To never trust anyone again. Not you. Not the Witch of the East. You both called yourselves my sisters. But once you got what you wanted, you disappeared. Left me. Abandoned me just like everyone else."

Her voice cracked. For a moment, Glinda thought the Wicked Witch might cry.

But instead, she laughed.

"That's what the world already sees anyway. The posters. The headlines. The Wicked Witch of the West! So, why not give them the face they want. This is who I am now, so get used to it, sweetie."

She looked sick. Starved. A shell of the woman Glinda once knew.

Glinda stepped forward, but the Wicked Witch swung her broom between them, creating distance. Her eyes, once brown and bright, were now darker, harder.

"Leave, Glinda. I'm so serious, before I fix you."

Glinda swallowed her fear. "I didn't come here to fight. I came becoz I needed your help."

"Of course you do."

"Look around, Zelly, the people aren't safe. There are storms nearly every— cyclones tearing through towns, floods drowning homes, the deadly desert sands sweeping into Oz. This has to stop. Think of the Animals. You always cared about them."

The Wicked Witch let out a bitter snicker. "You sound just like him," she spat, stepping closer. "Asking me to save the very people who would hang me if they could? I told you, I've changed. And why should I help *you*, Glinda? You, who's more evil than I ever was."

Her voice dropped. "I'm letting you breathe becoz of our history. That's mercy. Leave. Now. If you know what's good for you."

Glinda hesitated. The clouds above them churned, the wind lashing her coat around her legs. She squinted upward. "It's quiet here. Too quiet, apart from your screaming monkeys... where are the orphans?"

The Wicked Witch froze, then grinned, slow and cruel. She pointed to the sky. "You see the smaller monkeys flying among the large ones? The ones with bat wings instead of feathers? That's them."

Glinda's eyes widened. "You're lying, you wouldn't... You couldn't turn helpless children into creatures."

"I did. I'm 'Wicked' aren't I?"

Glinda raised her wand instinctively, magic buzzing at the tip. "You've been locked away too long, Zelphira. You've forgotten who you are. This... this isn't you. You've become exactly what they always feared."

The Wicked Witch rolled her eyes. "Put that stick down before you hurt yourself. You think you're so righteous." She laughed. "At least I only killed those deserved it. If you want to play saviour, go aim your wand at *your friend the baby killer.*"

Glinda froze. "What are you talking about?"

"Don't act innocent now, you *treacherous*, selfish bitch! I forgave you, welcomed you back, gave you your magic, and you left. You *promised* to come see me again. You lied. That's what you all do. Lie! Lie! Lie!"

UNDONE

The Wicked Witch stepped forward, tears streaking her cheeks, her voice breaking. "And worst of all, you told him. You were the *only* one who knew. The only one I trusted. I should've known better. No good deed goes unpunished. I should have *never* helped you or helped Oz for as long as I have. Look at what it cost me!"

Glinda arched a brow, her voice sharp. "I don't know what you're going on about—but that's not what matters right now. What I *do* care about are the orphans. They're *children*, Zelphira! You must be sick. Twisted. How could you do this? What is wrong with you?"

The Wicked Witch bared her teeth, her expression contorting as something inside her snapped. She winced, doubling over in a sudden wave of pain, collapsing to her knees as she clutched her chest, her heart.

Startled, Glinda took a step forward. Her voice softened. "Zelphira?"

But Zelphira screamed, "Step back! Don't you *dare* come near me! He's dead becoz of you!"

Still, Glinda didn't stop. She moved closer, hand outstretched to help.

In a burst of fury, Zelphira raised her arm and with a flick of her fingers, unleashed a violent telekinetic blast that shook the trees from their footing. Glinda was thrown backwards like a ragdoll, crashing into the side of her Bubble with a deafening *shatter*. The shell cracked upon impact, then disintegrated into shards around her.

Zelphira's eyes twitched for a split second… but it quickly twisted into grim satisfaction for the Wicked Witch.

She stood, breath ragged, and grabbed her broom.

Glinda lay motionless at first, a moan slipping from her lips as the pain rolled in. Deep cuts slashed across her arm from the glass. Tears streamed down her cheeks—not just from the pain, but from the heartbreak.

The Wicked Witch stood above her like a shadow.

"I *should* kill you where you lie. I should behead you and end this. But for some reason, some *stupid* reason, I won't. But *look at me* when I say this, Glinda: if you don't leave right now… I *will kill you!*"

Glinda, bloodied and shaking, forced herself to stand. She gripped her wand and shouted through gritted teeth:

"It's *you*, isn't it? You're the one behind these storms."

The Wicked Witch halted mid-step.

She didn't turn.

Her cloak billowed behind her, caught in the wind.

"Yes," she spat.

Glinda shouted like it was last breath. "If you believe you are wicked…then that is what you will become."

In one swift motion, she mounted her broom and launched into the sky, ascending to the tallest tower.

Then, from the heavens, violent and sudden, a cyclone twisted into being.

The flying monkeys shrieked and scattered, retreating into the fortress of Draeth Mor.

Glinda turned to flee, her eyes darting to her Bubble—in ruins.

It wouldn't fly.

It wouldn't protect her.

It was gone.

She needed a new one. And fast.

Panic clawed at her chest, but she closed her eyes and reached inward.

She remembered Mz. Everburn's voice. The spell.

She whispered it with urgency:

"Orbis Levia Aeris Tenebris."

Her wand shimmered with intensity, growing brighter, pulsing like a heartbeat.

Then, around her, a shimmer, a glow, a form:

A Bubble.

Soft to the eye, yet strong as steel.

It shimmered pink and smelled faintly of lavender.

It wrapped around her like a second skin.

The cyclone roared louder—closer.

Glinda didn't hesitate. She commanded it to rise.

And it obeyed.

She soared into the sky, wind whipping past her, dodging debris and pushing against the pull of the storm.

But she didn't falter.

She wasn't just flying in a Bubble like she usually did.

For the first time she was flying in a Bubble of her own creation.

By the time she reached her Northern castle, her body was bruised, and weak.

Ominson was already rushing down the stairs to catch her.

He wrapped her in his arms, his voice frantic. "Glinda!"

Wendell took Orryn away quietly, escorting the boy back to his room.

And Glinda, exhausted, and breathless, let herself lean into Ominson's arms.

She had made it ***home.***

But she knew the storm was far from over.

◇

Back in the drawing room, Ominson guided Glinda onto the couch, his hands trembling as he peeled back the shredded sleeve of her coat.

There was still glass fragments pierced into her skin.

"Glinda…" he whispered. "What happened to you?"

"The Wicked Witch happened."

"Are you sure?"

Glinda snapped, "Why wouldn't I be? Is there anyone else in Oz with green skin and flying monkeys?"

She winced as he dabbed the wound. Her voice came out hoarse.

"She's gone."

Ominson looked up, confused.

Glinda met his eyes, her own shining with tears. "Zelphira. She's not Zelphira anymore."

Ominson hesitated, bandaging the gash on her arm. "Why would she do this? It doesn't sound like her."

"You've never even met her. But this wasn't Zelphira, the girl I knew. This is the Wicked Witch, through and through."

Ominson finished wrapping the wound, the silence between them thick.

Glinda continued. "I don't recognise her at all! Her skin's gone darker. Her nose... it's *my* old nose, remember? The hooked one."

Glinda picked up her wand with the little strength she had left. "She turned the orphans into monkeys, Omi. She... she did it. She's behind the storms."

Ominson leaned back, stunned. "She wouldn't do such a thing. I know she wouldn't."

"She told me so, right before she blasted me into my Bubble."

"Wait... I didn't see you arrive in your usual Bubble machine thingy."

"Becoz it's broken," Glinda said flatly. "She shattered it when she hurled me across the courtyard."

Ominson froze.

Glinda waved a hand, exhausted. "I'm fine. I created a new one. With my magic."

"You did?" His tone was filled with awe.

"I did. I didn't even think it would work. But it did." She paused, glancing at her wand. "I guess that's just how I'm going to have to get around now. I expect the people have gotten used to seeing me in a Bubble."

With a shaky breath, she opened the *Ethereum* and began searching for a restoration spell.

She found one. Whispered the incantation.

A warmth spread through her body, knitting torn skin, mending bruises— but she knew it would still take three full days before she was truly healed.

And what happened on that third day...

No one expected.

Not the Wicked Witch.

And certainly not Glinda.

CHAPTER 48

Dorothy

O n the third day, Glinda sat before her mirror, fingers gliding over the fading scars that lined her skin. She studied her reflection, again and again, each pass of her eyes searching for something she couldn't name.

She lifted her wand and recited the healing spell from the Ethereum.

A warm light passed over her face. The scar vanished like smoke.

She was good as new.

But still, something felt... off.

There was an emptiness pressing against her chest. A hollowness she couldn't cast away.

She picked up her brush and ran it through her golden hair.

Still, nothing.

She tossed the brush aside and tried parting her hair this way and that—left to right, but no angle made her feel whole. No light brought her back to herself.

Her eyes shifted to her long, magic staff resting near her vanity.

She hesitated, then reached for it.

Closing her eyes, she raised the wand and let her hand hover just above her head.

A soft glow spread across her scalp.

The golden locks began to darken, shifting hue by hue, until they returned—
Strawberry-blonde.

She opened her eyes.

And paused.

She looked into the large vanity mirror in front of her and didn't flinch.

Didn't criticize.

Didn't search.

Instead, her hand gently passed through her hair, like greeting an old friend she hadn't seen in years.

There it was.

Her reflection stared back—and for once, she didn't look away.

She welcomed it.

Glinda picked up her small golden hand mirror—the one she'd had since her girlhood.

She tilted it, peering closer.

And for the first time in a long while, she smiled.

Really smiled.

She looked deeper into the hand mirror, admiring the subtle warmth returning to her cheeks.

But then, the glass began to ripple.

The reflection warped like disturbed water. The surface shifted, and suddenly, a vision emerged.

A Cyclone.

Massive, spinning violently through Munchkinland, tearing through fields and cottages. The sky above it churned black and purple. The largest she'd ever seen.

Glinda gasped and the image snapped away, replaced by her own startled reflection.

She stood abruptly, **heart** pounding, ready to leave.

But then her eyes caught the object resting quietly on her table:

The Fairmoor Crown.

She usually kept it hidden away. But sometimes, she took it out, like now, drawn to it by something deeper than memory.

Ominson's words echoed in her mind:

"No matter how much you pretend… you're still a Quadling."

And he was right. No matter how far she fled, no matter how high she floated above her past, the Fairmoor name still pulsed through her like blood. After all, she had made a promise to her father once—to carry it with pride. And as a woman who took pride in keeping her promises despite it all…

Glinda took the crown and set it gently upon her head.

She conjured a pink gown, its fabric glowing faintly like early dawnlight, and stepped out into the courtyard.

"Where are you going?" Ominson called from the doorway.

Glinda turned. "A cyclone just hit Munchkinland. I have to help."

"But you're still healing, you can't go."

"I must. It's what I do."

"You can't stop every storm, Glinda. What if there's another one after that?"

"Then I'll try to stop that too."

She turned again, walking toward the open courtyard.

"Is there anything I can say to stop you?" Ominson asked.

"No. I'm sorry."

He exhaled and nodded slowly. "Then be safe… hummingbug."

Glinda smiled. She glanced back at him, and at Orryn, now standing beside him at the door, watching quietly.

She lifted her glowing wand and summoned her bubble. A radiant pink orb formed around her, enclosing her like a promise.

And with a rush of wind, she lifted into the air, soaring faster than any machine could manage, straight toward Munchkinland.

◇

Glinda arrived in Munchkinland encased in her shimmering Pink Bubble. The skies above were calm, the cyclone now just a memory, but the fear it left behind still lingered. Not a single Munchkin was in sight. Homes were shuttered, windows closed, and bunkers cleverly hidden beneath bushes and flowers remained sealed tight.

But amid the silence, there were two figures standing out in the open.

One was a young girl, sixteen, though her fresh face and palpable innocence made her seem younger. The other, a scruffy little dog by her side.

Glinda let her Bubble dissolve, her heels touching down on the polished Munchkin Podium. She took a few steps forward, her gown trailing elegantly behind her, eyes fixed on the girl.

The girl's face was open, curious, stunned in the way only someone seeing Oz for the first time could be.

She wore a gingham dress in pale blue, cinched at the waist and paired with a white blouse. Her skirt bounced gently just below her knees. Chestnut hair flowed freely over her shoulders, tied back with a simple blue ribbon. On her feet were worn black slippers, and she clutched a basket in one hand, her small dog tucked protectively in the other.

"You're not from around here, are you?" Glinda asked with a soft smile.

The girl shook her head, wide-eyed. "No, ma'am."

"What is your name, my dear?"

"Dorothy Gale…" she said softly, then glanced down. "And this is my dog, Toto."

She looked around at the towering blooms and the little spiral houses with golden brick paths winding between them. "We're from Kansas," she whispered. "And I think we've strayed a long way from home."

"Kansas?" Glinda echoed. "We don't get many visitors from outside of Oz."

She stepped a little closer, inspecting Dorothy's face with gentle interest. "You must be a powerful witch to have crossed into this world. Tell me, are you a good sorceress or a wicked one?"

Dorothy's breath caught. She clutched Toto tighter. "Oh, no, I'm certainly not a sorceress or witch! I thought witches were ugly and old with… long pointy crooked noses." Her eyes glided over Glinda as she studied her. "You don't look like a wicked witch… are you?"

Glinda laughed warmly, the sound like wind chimes. "No, not at all." She gave a graceful bow. "I'm Glinda, The Good Witch of the North."

Dorothy curtsied shyly. "It's nice to meet you."

She turned her gaze toward the tiny, silent homes. "Do people live in those little houses?"

"Oh yes. The Munchkins. You're in Munchkinland now."

She stepped up onto the centre of the podium, her voice rising into a melodic chant:

"Come out, out from, where you hide little ones, don't be shy"

The hush of Munchkinland broke. Leaves rustled. Shutters opened. One by one, doors creaked ajar.

Little men, women, and children began to emerge, dressed in vibrant patchwork and lace, blinking up at the newcomer.

Glinda turned to the crowd. "Munchkinlanders, this is Dorothy, and her dog Toto, who have come to us from the star known as Kansas."

In perfect unison, the Munchkins called out joyously:

"Welcome, Dorothy from Kansas!"

Dorothy curtsied again, overwhelmed by the sight of so many eyes upon her.

Then, a Munchkin approached Glinda and tugged gently on her gown. Glinda leaned down as he whispered something into her ear, then pointed discreetly toward a small house tucked behind the crowd.

Glinda's eyes bulged. She stood tall and addressed the Munchkinlanders with a grave voice:

"It has been brought to my attention… that the Wicked Witch of the East is dead."

The crowd gasped, then erupted into cheers. Applause thundered across the square.

A Munchkin official hurried forward, holding out a scroll. Glinda took the parchment, unrolled it, and read aloud:

"The Wicked Witch of the East has been killed as a result of a house being dropped on her. The Munchkin Coroner has averred and thoroughly examined her; she has lived her last day."

A hush fell for a beat. Then Glinda stepped aside and gestured to Dorothy.

"Dorothy Gale of Kansas brings you this good news. A miracle she performed without even knowing, she sent the Wicked Witch of the East to the One Gohd! And so… spread the good news: the Wicked Witch of the East is deceased!"

The crowd erupted again, this time with music.

The Munchkins danced as though they'd been rehearsing their entire lives for this one moment, when wickedness would fall and goodness rise.

Petals rained from hidden traps in the trees. Drums beat. Banners waved.

Glinda smiled politely and began to dance with them.

Lines of Munchkins began forming to greet Dorothy.

One by one, they kissed her hand and exclaimed:

"You'll be history in the book of records, and we will glorify your name!!"

Three tiny Munchkin triplets skipped toward her and kissed her hand and said,

"We are thankful, oh my sweetie!"

The other, "The stars themselves will whisper of you!"

And the last, "She's gone, dead and you made it true. No one could've done it so beautifully!"

They handed Dorothy tulips and skipped away.

The celebration bloomed brighter and louder—until it stopped.

The sky split with a sound like tearing cloth.

A cackle.

Sharp. Shattering.

Then *she* appeared.

Black cloak billowing. Pointed hat cutting through the air.

The Wicked Witch of the West descended like a shadow across the sun, riding her broom with fury.

She landed hard on the Yellow Brick Road Spiral, her long green fingers curling with menace.

The Munchkins scattered like seeds in the wind. Not one dared look her in the eye.

Her voice boomed like thunder.

"What are you all celebrating?" she growled. "Your joy sickens me. But don't worry, I'll fix that!"

Glinda stepped forward. "Before you do, wouldn't you like to see your sister?"

She pointed toward the house.

The Witch turned slowly—

Her eyes caught the pink-draped woman at the podium.

Dorothy leaned into Glinda. "That nose. That skin... I'm guessing that's a bad witch?"

Glinda nodded. "The Wicked Witch of the West. She's far worse than her sister."

The Witch sneered. "What's this, Glinda? Back for another fixing?" Her voice crackled. "Round two?"

She stomped toward the house. The legs of her sister stuck out beneath the wood, lifeless.

Zelphira—The Wicked Witch—fell to her knees.

From where Glinda stood, it looked like she was... crying.

The crowd behind the bushes began to laugh, but the moment she snapped her head toward them, silence fell like a blade.

Then her eyes shifted.

To the feet.

To the shoes.

Gleaming. Red.

From Glinda's view, they sparkled like rubies in the sunlight.

The Wicked Witch of the West locked her gaze on the slippers, and her jaw clenched with dangerous intent.

The Wicked Witch of the West knelt beside the crushed body, her hand reaching for the slippers.

As soon as her fingers touched them, they came back wet. Blood.

The house's jagged beams had impaled the body, and the blood had trickled down, staining the once-beautiful *Silver Slippers* entirely sparkling crimson.

The Witch recoiled, staring at her hands, then wiped them slowly on her black cloak.

Glinda noticed the slippers.

She raised her wand, whispered a spell under her breath, and in a shimmer of pink light, the slippers vanished from the dead witch's feet—only to reappear fastened onto Dorothy's.

But they were no longer *Red.*

The blood, the grime, it was gone.

The shoes were now clean and sparkled silver.

Not just any silver—bright, glistening, star-shard silver that gleamed like constellations in daylight.

Glinda gaped.

The Silver Slippers.

Gisella's slippers.

The very ones she had lost, dropped accidentally from her Bubble on the journey **home.**

Sent tumbling down into Munchkinland.

And now… they were on Dorothy's feet.

The Wicked Witch of the West stood slowly, her frown deepening. She turned and saw them.

On the girl.

She clutched her broom and marched toward Glinda and Dorothy with rising fury.

Her voice cracked with venom.

"Give me back my sister's shoes. This instant! Return them or I'll—"

Glinda stepped between them. Calm. Firm.

"No," she said. "Those are *my* slippers. I made them. They belong to me, and now," she nodded toward Dorothy's feet, "there they are and they're staying there."

The Wicked Witch was ready to argue, to fight, but then she stopped.

Her eyes dropped to the shoes.

They were *changing* again.

From Silver… into *Pink*.

A soft, glowing, radiant pink.

Not just a colour. A magic.

Dorothy gasped. "Oh, good heavens…"

She turned her foot side to side, marvelling at the transformation.

The pink shimmered with innocence, with purity.

Dorothy whispered, barely audible: "Magic."

Glinda's breath hitched, and then she exhaled in wonder. "Not just any magic—Innocence Magic."

If the old stories were true, that kind of magic didn't just protect the wearer, it *reflected* intention. Any harm aimed at Dorothy could rebound tenfold on the one who dared to strike her.

Glinda's lips parted in a slow smile, quiet, almost disbelieving.

All these years…

When she'd first enchanted those slippers for Gisella, back when she was just a girl, **heart** still full of hope, Gisella had asked for shoes that could change to match any outfit, any occasion. But they never had. Not once.

Or so Glinda thought.

Turns out… they had worked.

Because she cast the spell when she was innocent and pure of heart, all they needed was purity of the wearer to unlock them.

True, untainted innocence.

And Gisella never stood a chance.

And Glinda had doubted herself. All this time, believing the magic had failed. Believing *she* had failed.

But she hadn't.

She had been powerful then.

She had *always* been powerful.

The Wicked Witch snarled, her eyes fixed hungrily on Dorothy's feet. With a furious lurch, she lunged, fingers outstretched to snatch the slippers right off the girl's ankles.

But the second her bloodied fingertips grazed the edge—*szzzt!*

The shoes lit up, burned bright, and the Witch shrieked as the magic scorched her skin.

She recoiled violently, her fingers twitching with pain.

Her furious gaze snapped from the slippers to Glinda.

"I'm the *only one* who knows how to use them. Give them back. And trust me, I'm not going to ask again."

Glinda stood tall, unwavering.

She leaned in close to Dorothy and whispered, "Keep your feet inside of them. Their magic must be powerful…or she wouldn't want them so badly."

Toto began to bark furiously, lunging at the Wicked Witch. Dorothy swiftly reached into her basket, grabbed her leash and fastened it around his neck, tugging him closer to her.

Zelphira frowned. "Get that rope off the dog's neck right now, it's hurting it!"

Dorothy stepped back. "It's not a rope, and it causes him no pain."

The Wicked Witch summoned a fireball in her hand. "Remove the leash!"

The moment her eyes met Dorothy's, she froze.

Her face twisted in shock, the fireball disappeared as she stumbled backward, nearly losing her footing. One trembling finger pointed toward Dorothy. "You…" she croaked, her voice strained and raw.

Glinda's brow furrowed. She glanced from Dorothy to Zelphira, then back again.

Zelphira's eyes widened. And in that flicker of recognition, of horror, Glinda understood.

This was *her*. The girl from the dreams. The one Zelphira had cried about in Draeth Mor all those sun-moons ago.

Zelphira faltered, her body still reeling from fear, until something shifted. Like a storm passing over her face, her posture straightened, her eyes narrowed, and her mouth twisted into a dry, bitter grin.

"You stay tight inside them," she said coldly, "but they won't help you!"

She leaned closer, her fingers flexing into claws. "You can try to stay out of my way…"

Then she said it.

Words that made Glinda's **heart** freeze and her stomach twist.

Words she had heard once before, in *Farkleberry & Things* in the Emerald City.

The day she bought the Pointed Hat and the Black Cloak.

The phrase had been silly then. Harmless. But now, they chilled her blood.

"I'll get you, my sweetie…"

The Wicked Witch's voice was cold as frost.

Glinda didn't move. Couldn't.

And with that, she mounted her broom and swept into the air, cutting through the sky like a comet. No cackle. No laugh.

Just silence.

She was gone.

Glinda exhaled and turned to the crowd. "It's all right, you can come out now. She's gone."

Slowly, the Munchkins emerged from their hiding places. Their relief was cautious. Fragile.

Glinda turned to Dorothy. "I suggest you remove that…"

"Leash?" Dorothy replied.

"Yes, that." Glinda said coldly. "I'm afraid the Wicked Witch has a soft spot for animals and if you want any mercy out of her should you encounter her again, it must come off. Let the dog walk freely."

Something had changed.

Glinda looked… distant.

Dorothy did as she was told and removed it, placing the leash back into her basket.

She turned to Glinda. "I have now made an enemy out of the Wicked Witch of the West, haven't I?"

Glinda nodded. "I'm afraid so."

Dorothy's hands tightened around the fabric of her dress. "Then I'd better find a way back to Kansas."

"Yes, you must."

Dorothy tilted her head. "Okay… how? Do I wait for another cyclone to carry me home?"

Glinda smiled, conspiratorial. "No, dear. You must go see the Great and Powerful Wizard of Oz."

Dorothy's brow lifted. "The Wizard of Oz? Is he good… or wicked?"

"Oh, very good, but very mysterious. He lives in the Emerald City—far from here."

"I wouldn't have to walk, would I?" Dorothy asked, wincing.

"Well… do you have a flying broomstick?"

"No."

"A chariot of fire?"

Dorothy laughed. "No."

"Then I'm afraid you must walk."

Dorothy sighed. "But what if I get lost? Or the Wicked Witch comes after me again?"

Her face brightened with a thought. "Wait! Could I go in that pink bubble you have? That'd be *much* faster, wouldn't it?"

"No!" Glinda said quickly, a bit too sharply. Then she softened. "No, dear. That won't work. You won't get lost. You just have to follow the Yellow Brick Road."

Then, her expression shifted, mischievous. She turned to the crowd.

"She *must* follow the Yellow Brick Road, mustn't she?"

The Munchkins all nodded in agreement.

"Yes!" they cheered. "Follow the Yellow Brick Road!"

Glinda turned to Dorothy. "All roads lead to the One and Only Wizard! Oh, and don't forget, never let those *Rosy Slippers* off your feet for a moment, or you will be at the mercy of the Wicked Witch of the West."

She leaned forward and placed a soft *kiss on Dorothy's forehead.*

UNDONE

Dorothy stepped toward the golden spiral of bricks where the Yellow Brick Road began. But as her foot hovered over the path, she hesitated—her nerves surfacing. She turned back to Glinda, her voice small and trembling.

"But what if I—?"

"Like I said... just follow the Yellow Brick Road."

With that, she lifted her wand and summoned her Bubble.

A shimmer of pink light swirled and enclosed her, rising effortlessly into the sky.

The Munchkinlanders and Munchkins erupted in applause and cheers, waving as she floated upward and away.

Higher and higher, Glinda drifted over the blooming fields and winding hills, leaving Munchkinland behind—

One step closer to a story that had only just begun.

You might think Glinda Arduelle Fairmoor was returning home, back to the North.

But not yet.

There was someone she needed to see. Someone who likely didn't want to see her.

◇

Guiding her Bubble through the clouds, Glinda didn't descend to the courtyard at Draeth Mor like she had before. This time, she flew directly into the highest tower.

Just as she suspected, the Wicked Witch of the West was there, hovering over a steaming cauldron, stirring a thick potion with calculated intensity.

The moment the Wicked Witch saw Glinda inside her tower, her entire face flushed red—remarkable, given how green she was to begin with.

"You've got some *nerve* showing up here," she snapped. "Do you *not* understand that I don't want to see you?"

Glinda remained calm, her voice low. "She's the girl from your dreams, isn't she?"

Zelphira's posture shifted. Her eyes softened—for just a moment. "You remember," she said. "Yes. It's her."

She began moving rapidly about the tower, snatching herbs, snipping dried roots, flipping through pages of the *Grimorium*. Her movements were sharp, frantic.

"Why did you give her the slippers?" she erupted suddenly. "There's still a piece of *me* in them!"

Glinda blinked. "Wait... You put your *own magic* in them? Why?"

Zelphira's tone was bitter. "Did you never wonder how the Wicked Witch of the East got her powers? I gave her those slippers for a reason. She was meant to *do* something for me. But instead of completing her task, she wasted my magic on tormenting Munchkinland."

"What was she meant to do?" Glinda asked.

Zelphira let out a dry laugh. "Nothing that concerns you."

"Very well," Glinda said evenly. "You should know, I bought you some time."

Zelphira stopped, mid-stir. "What do you mean?"

"I told the girl to follow the Yellow Brick Road to the Wizard."

Zelphira blinked, then narrowed her eyes. "But the Wizard is a fraud, he won't be able to help her, and the Yellow Brick Road has more spirals than sense. She'll be walking forever."

Glinda smiled. "Exactly."

There was a long silence. Then Zelphira's entire frame softened. She rushed forward and pulled Glinda into a tight embrace. Her voice dropped to a whisper.

"...Thank you."

It had been a decade since Glinda had felt Zelphira's embrace. And in that moment, it felt as though a missing part of her heart, kept locked away for far too long, had finally returned ***home.***

When she pulled away, Glinda caught the shimmer of tears in her friend's eyes, tears that mirrored her own. For a moment, they were no longer adversaries, just two broken women standing in the ruins of their own choices.

Glinda turned toward the bubbling cauldron. "What potion is that?" she asked gently. "What are you planning to do to her?"

Zelphira exhaled, wiping at her cheek. "I don't know. I truly don't. I don't want to kill her... but if she's meant to kill me first, then maybe I have to." She stirred the brew again, her jaw tight. "The real problem is... she's wearing the Rosy Slippers. And my magic, part of it, is inside them. Becoz of that, I can't harm her. Not directly."

"Why?"

Zelphira's eyes flicked toward her. "Becoz magic, true magic, doesn't attack what it recognises as kin. It won't strike if it feels the same bloodline, the same source. She's wearing something enchanted with *my* essence. If I attack her, it will turn on me."

Glinda placed a hand over Zelphira's. "Then don't hurt her."

"I can't promise that."

"Then at least *try*," Glinda said, her voice soft but firm. "Try with everything in you not to hurt her... but I understand if it comes down to survival."

Zelphira nodded solemnly.

Glinda's tone shifted. "And the orphans. The children you turned into monkeys..."

Zelphira froze over the cauldron. "What about them?"

"Undo it, remove the spell. Let them be children again."

A pause.

"I *can't*," Zelphira replied.

Glinda stiffened. "What do you mean, you *can't*?"

"I *mean*," Zelphira snapped, spinning around, "I've *tried*! Every reversal, every counter curse, every healing chant. The Grimorium spell was too strong. It's permanent."

Glinda's voice broke as it rose. "Then why in the name of Oz did you do it? *You*, of all people—you who fought for the Animals, who stood for the voiceless. Your work changed everything. You brought them out of hiding. You gave them rights. Why... would you do something like *this*?"

Zelphira's fury dissolved in an instant.

"Becoz they were going to leave me!" Zelphira cried, her voice echoing off the stone, then softer, broken— "Becoz they were going to leave me..."

"Why would they? You gave them everything. A home."

"They got older. *Smart* enough to listen to the lies. To believe the Wizard's stories. They started to look at me like I really was the monster. They called me the Wicked Witch. And then—" Zelphira's voice cracked, her hands trembling. "the Witch of the East stopped speaking to me, my own sister, and then you abandoned me. River died. Vinkus was gone. I was alone, Glinda. I only had the monkeys. They stayed. They remained loyal and it didn't matter to me that my power bound them. And in a moment of weakness, as the orphans tried to leave—I panicked. I cursed them. I twisted them into something else, so they would be loyal. Bound to me like the other monkeys. They don't even remember who they are. They don't speak. They just... serve."

Her eyes sank to the floor. "The moment it was done, I hated myself. I couldn't bear to see my face in the mirror. That's why I enchanted my nose. Made it like yours. I didn't want to be me anymore. Not since—"

Glinda stepped closer and reached for her hand. "Since what, Zelphira? Tell me. Since what?"

Zelphira's lips parted, but no sound came out. Her breathing turned ragged, like the words themselves would choke her. "You don't know?" she said, bitterly. "You told him!"

"Told who?" Glinda whispered. "Told who what?"

"The Wizard. You told him about Lirvan."

"I only told him to help you!" Glinda pleaded. "To end the war. To stop the suffering. I thought—I thought it would set you free."

Glinda looked around. "Where is Lirvan?"

Zelphira shook her head, and when she tried to speak, the sound that came out was inhuman. A broken sob. She clenched her chest as if her soul might burst through it.

"H-he... The Wizard killed him. Cut off his head and left it on my doorstep."

The world stopped. Glinda's pupils shrank. "No..." she whispered. "That's not true. That can't be true. No."

But her knees buckled, and she collapsed where she stood, crushed by the weight of it. Her mind flashed—Lirvan's tiny fingers grasping her hands as he was asleep. His tiny body, vulnerable. Innocent!

Gone.

Gone.

Gone.

Glinda's thoughts spun further, memories clashing like thunder, and somewhere, deep in the back of her mind, the Wizard's voice echoed like a ghost:

"Prophecies are dangerous things. They make monsters of kings."

And now, she finally understood what he meant.

"He wasn't just my son," Zelphira whispered. "He was my redemption."

Glinda's breath caught. Her fists clenched around her wand. "Then why haven't you killed him? Justice must be done!"

"You think I haven't tried? My magic won't touch him. It refuses."

"Why? He doesn't have any magic."

Zelphira bowed her head, her voice barely audible. "Becoz... he's my father."

Glinda blinked, stunned. "What?"

"I know how it sounds," Zelphira said quickly. "But it's true. That's why my spells won't work. They recognise shared blood."

"But you're green, he's not. You were raised in Munchkinland, he's from the Emerald City. How could he be—?"

"I don't know how. But it's real. That's why I gave some of my magic to the Witch of the East, through those shoes you gave that girl, becoz she is my adoptive sister. I told her to kill him, since I couldn't. But she betrayed me. She kept my power. Used it for herself."

"Your own sister betrayed you," Glinda murmured, her voice hollow. "I can understand that."

Zelphira leaned over the cauldron, gasping. A single tear slid from her cheek and fell into the bubbling brew.

Glinda spoke again, quieter. "So, the Wizard killed his own grandson? Why? I don't understand. Lirvan was just a child..."

"Don't you get it? Remember the prophecy in the Emerald Palace, the one about the 'Green Witch who gives birth to the true Wizard who will take his place?'"

Glinda nodded slowly.

"He thought it was me," Zelphira said. "But he was wrong."

"Then who is it?"

"Gisella."

"What?" Glinda gasped.

Zelphira nodded grimly. "Her Moonshine gem was green. That was her chosen colour. And when she stole your power, she became a *witch*. That makes her the **Green Witch** in the prophecy."

Glinda's eyes widened. "Then that means..."

"Orryn," Zelphira breathed. "Your son. The boy you raise. The boy you... love."

The air in the tower grew heavier. The truth settled on her shoulders like stone. Her grip tightened around her wand.

"If the Wizard ever finds out," Zelphira warned, "he'll do to Orryn what he did to Lirvan."

Glinda's expression hardened. Her tears vanished, replaced by fire. "Then he won't get the chance."

She straightened, jaw set, chest rising.

"He has to answer for what he's done—to you. To Lirvan."

The sun was setting.

Glinda turned to the window. "I'll be back."

"Where are you going?" Zelphira asked.

But Glinda didn't answer. She formed her Bubble and rose into the sky, soaring from Draeth Mor.

She wore crowns, carried wands, cast bubble spells, but this time, she would not fly as a witch. She would fly as a mother. As a sister. As a friend.

CHAPTER 49

The Wizard of Oz

Glinda rushed *home* to the only place that still made sense, into the arms of the man and child who loved her most. The moment she saw Orryn, she swept him up into a desperate embrace, holding him like he might vanish.

"Mom…" Orryn murmured, squirming a little. "You're hurting me."

Glinda loosened her grip just slightly but didn't let go. "I just needed to be sure you were safe."

Ominson, watching from the hallway, stepped forward. "Why wouldn't he be? Is the Wicked Witch after him?" His voice was sharp with concern, his face pale.

Glinda shook her head. "No. Someone worse."

◇

That night, once Orryn had gone to bed, Glinda told Ominson everything.

The truth about the Wizard. His lies. His cruelty. His murder of Lirvan. His true identity.

Ominson listened in stunned silence, his face darkening with every word. He tried to comfort her, to pull her close and offer her warmth, but he, too, was spiralling. The idea that the Wizard might come for Orryn haunted him.

"What are we going to do?" he asked.

Glinda's voice was low. "I don't know. Not yet."

Ominson led her to bed, brushing the hair from her face. "Rest, just for tonight. We'll figure it out in the morning."

But sleep wouldn't come for either of them.

The thought of the Wizard, his lies, his grip on power, the way he had destroyed Zelphira's life and now threatened to do the same to theirs—kept them both awake, eyes wide in the darkness.

◇

UNDONE

When the sun finally rose, casting golden light over the frost-kissed North, Glinda dressed in silence.

She summoned her Bubble and rose into the sky.

But this time, she didn't walk to the Emerald Palace gates to be let in.

She flew straight to the topmost tower.

And entered without knocking.

The Wizard was in the throne room, no doubt rehearsing his latest illusion, hidden behind the curtain of the mechanical head that towered above the emerald floor.

"Come out, Oscar!" Glinda's voice rang sharp through the chamber.

The illusion fizzled, the gears winding down with a hiss. The curtain twitched, and there he was. The man behind the magic. The showman without shame.

"Glinda," he said cautiously. "We don't have any business today. What's the matter?"

Glinda gripped her wand and stepped forward until there was barely a breath between them.

Her eyes never blinked.

Her voice was ice.

The Wizard noticed her stillness, her fury, the sharp coldness that now clung to the air. And yet, he smiled.

"You've got something to say," he said, pacing the emerald tiles like a stage performer awaiting his cue. "I can tell. So go on—say it."

"I'm going to ask you one question," Glinda said, her wand trembling in her hand. "And I want the truth. No riddles. No pageantry. No lies."

"Have I *ever* lied to you?" he asked, sweeping his arms wide. "You, Glinda Fairmoor, you're one of the only people in Oz who *gets* me. You and I—we share something others don't have. Ambition. Vision."

Glinda's face was stone.

"Did you kill Zelphira's son? Your grandson?"

The Wizard looked at her a long moment.

And then, with eerie calm, said, "Yes. I did."

Glinda staggered back like she'd been struck in the stomach. "Oh. My. Gohd."

She turned away, her head swimming, almost vomiting. Her chest rose and fell too quickly, and a vein pulsed in her forehead like it might burst. *He* said it. Not Zelphira. Not rumour. Not guesswork.

Him.

She faced him again. "Not only a child, but your own grandchild?" Glinda looked into his eyes searching for some light but saw only darkness. "Tell me, did you know that he was your grandson when you did it?"

"Does that matter?"

"It matters to me!"

490

He shrugged. "Then yes. I knew."

"You truly are evil!" Glinda roared. "If killing an innocent child does nothing to you, let alone your *own grandson*, you really don't have a heart. Or your heart's been corrupted beyond repair."

"Corrupted?" the Wizard echoed with a scoff. "This was necessary. I had no choice."

"We *all* have choices, Oscar! That's just some pathetic excuse you tell yourself, so you can sleep at night without guilt clawing at your throat, and that is me being generous in assuming you feel guilt at all."

His voice rose. "Why are you so hellbent on this? Acting like he was *your* child. He was the son of the Wicked Witch of the West! I did all of Oz a favour. Can you imagine if the world found out *she* and I shared blood? The scandal? The chaos?" He sneered. "I only regret I couldn't kill her too."

Glinda stepped forward, her disgust plain. "How did you get like this? How did you become *this*?"

He turned away, pacing. "I don't expect you to understand. Not until you've worn the crown, until you've felt a kingdom hinge on your name. That child—he was the one. The prophecy said he would take my place. I wasn't going to sit back and let fate erase me."

"All this becoz of *that* prophecy?" Glinda barked a hollow laugh. "You are *so* foolish."

Then her voice dropped low. Sharp.

"How long have you known that Zelphira was your daughter?"

The Wizard stroked his chin casually, as if recalling some minor detail. "The first day you both came into my throne room. The day she became the Wicked Witch."

"And you let her go? You let her live as a villain, branded, hunted, hated by all of Oz—and then you took her *son* in the most heartless way imaginable? You're a sick man."

"Say what you want!" the Wizard snapped. "But I am powerful. I am *loved*. That's all that matters. Let Zelphira scream her truth from every rooftop, no one will believe her. Who would believe the Great Wizard of Oz murdered a child? And if they *did*, they'd thank me. For stopping evil before it manifested."

Glinda bit her lip so hard it nearly bled.

"The person you need to direct your rage at," the Wizard said coldly, "is the Wicked Witch of the West. She's the villain. Not me."

"If there's a villain in this tale," Glinda said sharply, "it's *you*."

"And that," the Wizard grinned, "is where you're wrong. Don't you understand? There have been millions like me in history. I'm not the first and I won't be the last. The world runs on *optics*. I will never be the villain. Neither will you—unless you make it very easy like Seraphina, but she was an anomaly. But you? You and I are the good ones. That's how history will remember it."

"I'll tell them the truth," Glinda declared. "I'll tell them what really happened to Zelphira. I'll tell them what *you* did to Lirvan."

The Wizard chuckled darkly. "Go ahead. Let's see how that works out. You'll be discredited in a heartbeat. The people will question *everything* you say. I've built this empire since before you could speak. And you think one woman in a pink dress can bring it down?"

Glinda's expression hardened. "What happens when Zelphira isn't here to take the blame anymore? When your scapegoat is gone?"

"Then I will find another to fill her shoes. There is always someone there to be a hero and even more to be a villain. You, even. It would take one whisper, one performance, one public stunt... and suddenly, *you're* the villain." He tilted his head. "Pink gemstone. Seraphina's wand. It writes itself. 'Glinda the Gruesome Witch of the North.' Or maybe just... 'Glinda the Gruesome.'"

He laughed again. "The people will *eat that up*."

Glinda steadied herself. "And what about Dorothy? What did you do to that girl?"

"Oh, her?" he smirked. "She came begging for a way back home. With her little friends, each of them wanting something I couldn't give. So, I sent them on a quest to fetch me the Wicked Witch's hat. They'll fail, of course. Zelphira will kill them all. That saves me the trouble of inventing miracles that don't exist."

He cackled again.

Glinda stood still for a moment, letting the weight of the Wizard's cruelty settle between them. But something shifted inside her. She was thinking about something, trying to make a decision but the answer came very quickly.

She had just made the biggest decision of her life.

And she was perfectly fine with her choice.

"Everything is funny to you, isn't it?" she said, stepping closer.

"Oh come on now, Glinda, don't be like that—"

"Tell me, what did Dorothy's friends ask you for?"

He tilted his head, confused. "Why?"

"Just tell me," she insisted, her tone sharp but even.

He sighed and humoured her. "Fine. The scarecrow wanted a brain. The tinman wanted a heart, my nie——" he cleared his throat. "Dorothy obviously wanted to go home. And the lion..." He scratched his chin. "I forget."

Glinda gave a slight, tight smile. "Of course you do."

The Wizard glanced at the time, already growing bored. "Well, this has been fun, but I've got work to do. The duties of the one true Wizard don't run themselves, you know." He chuckled.

Glinda gave a warm smile.

"I'm afraid that's no longer your concern," Glinda said calmly.

The Wizard laughed again. "What?"

GLINDA: *The GOOD Witch*

"I said," she repeated with perfect clarity, "your time as Wizard is over. It's time the Wizard of Oz... left Oz."

He blinked, uncertain. "I don't understand."

"I know," she said sweetly, tilting her head. "But I'll explain it to you."

She leaned in, her eyes burning with purpose. "You failed."

His smile faded. "Failed what?"

"The prophecy."

His mouth twitched. "That child—he's dead."

"No," Glinda whispered. "You got the wrong one. The prophecy said the son of the Green Witch would rise to take your place. But you forget, there were two Green Witches in Oz."

The Wizard's face paled. "Gisella."

Glinda nodded. "My son. Orryn."

The Wizard took a step back, his breath shallow. "Why are you telling me this?"

Glinda pressed a finger to her lips. "Shhh. That's the thing about prophecies. They're designed to mislead. Wrapped in truth, tangled with deception, just enough to cause ruin. It did the same to me and Gisella, made us think only one of us could become a Good Witch. And yet... in the end, we both did. You see, that's why you don't put your faith in predictions of destiny. We never know the full picture and so we are best putting the faith in ourselves and the people we love, and though it took me a long time, I finally understand."

She lifted her wand and began walking slowly toward the Wizard.

He stepped back, uneasy. "Glinda... what are you doing?"

"You don't have anyone to believe in, do you?" she said softly, almost like pity. "No family, no friends. Just a throne you stole and power that was never yours to begin with. You've inflicted pain, so much pain, more than I can probably even uncover."

She kept moving. He kept retreating.

"And worst of all, you destroyed my friend. My sister. And I can't let that go."

"Glinda, think about this, w-watch your next step very carefully."

"Oh, I have," she said, raising her wand. "That's all I've done for years. Plan, second-guess, think strategically. But all it did was keep me from listening to my heart."

The Wizard backed into a marble wall, cornered now.

Glinda tilted her head. "Don't worry. After this, you *will* be of use. You'll serve the people of Oz, truly, for the first time in your life."

The Wizard's face collapsed entirely into fear.

He cowered.

He dropped to his knees and grabbed Glinda's feet.

"Please. Please don't. I'll give you whatever you want. You can be Queen of the North—of all Oz, if you want!"

Glinda looked down at him with solemn eyes. "Goodbye, Oscar."

"You're just like me, *Galinda!* You hear me—just like me!"

She raised her wand, the golden star on its tip glowing like the sun. Her mind filled with the faces of Orryn. Lirvan. Zelena.

The Wizard's eyes darted to the door, mouth wide, ready to scream for help—too late.

Glinda had already said the words.

Orbis Levia Aeris Tenebris.

A shimmering bubble snapped into existence, locking around the Wizard's head.

He gasped.

Then choked.

He clawed at the bubble, nails scraping against its surface. Bloodshot veins burst in his eyes, and he reached toward Glinda in desperation.

But she didn't move.

The whites of his eyes turned red. His face swelled grotesquely, veins bulging. His head ballooned, twice its normal size. Blood seeped from the corners of his eyes and nose.

Still, she did not flinch.

She did not blink.

She just stood silently and watched him fight for his life, gasping for something as common as air.

Glinda did not release it, not until the Wizard crumpled to the floor. His eyes had gone dark. His entire body, a sickly shade of purple.

Then, and only then, Glinda ended the spell.

The Wizard of Oz was **dead.**

Glinda the Good Witch of the North had killed the Wizard of Oz.

She stared down at the body for a long moment, then inhaled deeply.

Satisfied.

Happy.

Hopeful.

And, above all—at *peace.*

Because Orryn was safe now. Truly safe. Free from the grip of the man who called himself "Wizard."

Mz. Everburn had been right. *The Bubble Spell really was the most important spell I ever learned,* Glinda thought.

Glinda hid the Wizard's body in the curtain of the mechanical head.

She had other business to attend to.

Forming her pink Bubble, Glinda soared into the sky, heading west—toward Draeth Mor. Toward Zelphira. One last time.

◇

As she flew across the Western skies, her eyes caught something below: Dorothy, walking steadily with her companions—Tinman, Scarecrow, and Lion—all headed toward the Wicked Witch's castle.

Toward Draeth Mor.

Glinda landed in the tower, stepping into Zelphira's chamber.

Zelphira was startled. "You're back!"

"Did you think I wasn't?"

Zelphira gave her a flat look. "Do you really want me to answer that?"

They both laughed, the sound light, momentary.

"By the way," Glinda added casually, "Dorothy and her gang are on their way here. I saw them as I was flying over."

Zelphira sighed heavily. "Thank you."

"You okay?"

"Not really. I'm trying so hard not to hurt her. But the closer it gets, the more real it feels, I... I can't find any other way out."

"It'll all make sense when the time comes. I believe that."

Zelphira nodded slowly.

"Anyway," Glinda said, voice lifting. "I came to give you some good news."

"Tell me. I don't get much of those."

"The Wizard is dead."

Zelphira shot to her feet.

"What?" she gasped. "How? Wha—"

"I killed him."

Zelphira laughed. "You. As in *Glinda Fairmoor* killed her *friend*, the Wizard of Oz?"

"We were never friends. *You're* my friend."

Zelphira stood still, her expression shifting. "Wait. You're serious. He's dead?"

"Yes."

"And *you* killed him?" Her voice rasped, barely a whisper.

She stepped forward and placed a trembling hand on Glinda's shoulder. She stared into Glinda's eyes, the silence between them thick, until the tears came. But Zelphira didn't look away. She didn't try to hide them.

These were tears of release. Of gratitude. Of something she never dared to hope for.

A gift greater than she ever imagined.

And in that moment, she felt it, *Destiny Fulfilled*. She could die happy.

Zelphira drew Glinda into her arms and clutched her tightly, sobbing against her shoulder. Glinda said nothing. She just held her.

UNDONE

When Zelphira finally pulled back, her fingers curled around Glinda's hand.

"It's funny how fate is, don't you think?" Zelphira said. "Once, we called other people 'sisters.' Who knew, in this vast, twisted world, that I would find my *true* sister in the middle of all this mess. You and I—we're one. Two sides of the same coin. And I'll die knowing that."

Glinda's grip tightened. "It's no accident we met. I believe that now more than ever. You were always meant to be more than just my friend. *My sister.*"

Glinda's voice wavered. "It has been a long journey and the path of change, it is uncertain." She laughed. "Good or not, I am not who I *was*. But becoz of you, I hope that if I have truly changed, it has been for good!"

The two sisters fell into each other's arms again, letting their hearts speak in sobs and silence.

Then Glinda pulled back and looked Zelphira in the eyes.

"I'm done with the lies. After today, I'll tell the people the truth. I'll own my part in all of this, and most importantly, I'll tell them of *your* innocence. Who truly is wicked. Becoz it's not you."

Zelphira lowered her gaze for a long beat... then met Glinda's eyes again. "No."

"...No?" Glinda asked, confused.

Zelphira shook her head. "The false Wizard was right about one thing. The people need an enemy to hate. I have handled it all this while and I have survived this long. Look at Oz now, Glinda. Everyone is united against *me*. Without me Oz would have fallen apart and destroyed itself, but in sharing a common enemy in the *Wicked Witch of the West*, that has been enough for them. I've been the enemy they needed. *You*, Glinda, you need to be their hero."

"I'm tired of the lies, Zelphira," Glinda said quietly. "I can't do it anymore."

"Yes you can!" Zelphira sighed. "*You must!* Otherwise, all of this will have been for nothing. It's sad... but it's the way of the world. And whether we like it or not, we've become symbols. *The world's greatest evil... and you, Oz's greatest hope.*"

She turned toward the tower window, gazing at the sun as it dipped behind the horizon. A small laugh escaped her lips, dry and wistful.

"I now understand my destiny," she whispered. "*My destiny fulfilled.* I have done what I was meant to do in Oz. And if this should be my last day..." she looked back at Glinda, eyes shimmering, voice unshaken, "*Knowing you has been one of the greatest gifts.*"

Glinda smiled softly through the ache in her chest. "If I'm to tell the people that *you* are the wickedest of them all... I need a favour from you."

"Anything."

Glinda magically summoned the **Kitab Solis** into her hands, placing it gently on the table. She flipped to a marked page, tore it out, and handed it to Zelphira.

"I know you can't turn the orphan monkeys back into children... but with this spell, you can give them their *speech*, their *memories*, and their *sense of self*."

Zelphira took the page carefully. "Of course," she said without hesitation. "I wish I had this in the Grimorium. *I would've done that the moment I cast the spell.*"

Glinda turned to leave, the moment weighing heavier than she could bear.

"Glinda!" Zelphira called out.

"Yes?" Glinda paused, turning back.

"*Tell Orryn about me.* That he once had a misunderstood aunt who loved him very much... who foresees a bright future for him. That she believes with all her heart, *he will make an amazing Wizard!*"

"I will," Glinda promised, noticing the pained look behind Zelphira's brave expression. She stepped closer and gently took Zelphira's hand. "You will *survive* this, don't worry."

She lifted the **Ethereum** into her arms and walked toward the tower's edge.

"I have to go sort out the mess I made in the Emerald Palace," she said with a dry little laugh.

But just before she formed her Bubble, something tugged at her heart—one final thing she had to say.

Glinda turned around.

There stood Zelphira: green skin, pointed hat, black cloak, broom at her side. A vision once feared, now fully loved.

By *her.*

"I love you," Glinda said, her voice trembling. "*With all my heart.*"

Zelphira's reply came steady and sure.

"I love you too. *With all my soul.*"

Glinda's pink Bubble swelled and lifted her into the air, gliding toward the Emerald Palace once more.

CHAPTER 50

Melting at the 13th Hour

Glinda arrived at the Emerald Palace, returning to the dead, lifeless body of the Wizard.

She opened the *Kitab Solis*, searching for a way to dispose of him. There were many spells listed, but one stood out among the rest.

The Lustrum Cordamentum.

She studied it carefully, it looked complex, ancient, and draining.

Before beginning, Glinda sat at the Wizard's desk in his study and penned a letter to Ominson, letting him know she wouldn't return **home** that night, but that she was safe. She enchanted the letter and watched as it flew out of the palace window, carried on magic to find its way to him.

With the Wizard's body laid out before her, Glinda dove into the spell. She translated the passage, analysed its structure, practiced its incantations, and rehearsed the wand work. The purpose was clear: to extract the Wizard's **heart** and **brain**, *purify* them of corruption, and transform them into preserved, renewed, and wholly viable organs.

She practiced.

Again, and again.

By the time she felt ready to perform it fully, the 10th hour had struck.

Glinda raised her wand and cast the spell.

The Wizard's body split open, cleanly, surgically, as if the spell itself knew where to cut. His **heart** and **brain** lifted from his body and hovered mid-air, suspended in glowing golden light.

Clutching the *Kitab Solis*, Glinda recited the long enchantment passage aloud. With every syllable, the **heart** and **brain** pulsed, their glow intensifying. On the final word, the light dimmed. The organs no longer looked old or tainted, they looked... new. Fresh. Like they had never been touched by cruelty.

She plucked them from the air and placed each into its own emerald chest.

Then she turned to the Wizard's corpse.

Glinda hovered her wand over him one final time, and with a single flick, his body crumbled into ash, disintegrating into the air. As if he had never been there.

Gone.

Glinda took a breath. She had work to do.

She sat down again in the study, pen in hand, and began composing letters to the leaders of the corners of Oz—North, East, West. All except the South. The message was simple: *The Wizard has left Oz in his balloon indefinitely, and in his absence, Glinda the Good shall assume his responsibilities.*

With a whisper of enchantment, she sent the letters flying through the palace's tall windows.

That left one final problem: the *public*.

She would have to face them. Soon.

But before she could move, the clocks began to chime.

All the clocks in Oz.

Thirteen chimes at the 13th Hour.

Every clock. In perfect unison.

It felt like *Ozmageddon*.

Glinda turned to the *Chronoglint Gilded Dial*, it read clearly: *Thirteen Oz'clock*.

Glinda stared at the clock, confused.

The clocks chimed at the 12th Hour.

Not the 13th.

And then came the thunder.

She sprinted to the tower's window. From there, she could see it, far to the West, above Draeth Mor, a dark cloud, thick and monstrous, forming above the castle.

The cloud spread rapidly.

It consumed the sky.

All of Oz was cast into darkness, eclipsing the sun in a sudden shroud.

Another clap of thunder. Then came the rain.

A torrential downpour poured over the land, drenching everything. And yet, even as the dark cloud vanished into the blue, the rain did not stop.

The sun returned, brighter than before. A full circular rainbow arched across the sky.

And still, it rained.

The Wicked Witch of the West was dead. But the people did not know that yet.

It is the heavy rain of this time that further pushed the rumours that the Wicked Witch was allergic to water. That it was a divine omen. Ozma had made it rain as a symbol for the very thing that killed her *gruesomely*.

The spillage of **Wholly Water.**

And if that had any truth to it, that the Wicked Witch was allergic to water and never had a bath in her thirty-eight years of living, then this would've been one stinky tale indeed.

Glinda, standing in the window, could only stare, silent, shaken.

She turned, grabbed the *Ethereum*, and prepared to leave for Draeth Mor. But just as she formed her Bubble, she saw something in the distance.

Flying monkeys. Ones with *bat wings*.

They were carrying four passengers.

They couldn't see her, but she saw them land and drop off four familiar figures.

Dorothy. The Tinman. The Scarecrow. The Lion.

They walked, slowly and cautiously, toward the gates of the Emerald Palace.

If Glinda left now, it would create chaos. Questions would erupt about the Wizard's sudden absence before she even had a chance to shape the narrative herself.

So, thinking quickly, she vanished the *Kitab Solis* with a wave of her wand and slipped behind the great curtain, where the Wizard's mechanical head machinery was stationed. She frantically examined the controls, recalling what she had learned of the contraption from past visits.

Moments later, the throne room doors creaked open.

Dorothy and her companions entered.

Her voice, once soft and sweet, now carried strength and conviction.

"Hello, your Ozness?" Dorothy called.

Glinda pressed a large green button. The mechanical head groaned to life—its eyes flickering, mouth stretching into motion. She grabbed the voice control tube, flipped the 'voice manipulator' switch, and clicked the button labelled FLAME—sending a dramatic burst of fire through the chamber's vents.

She spoke into the receiver, her tone theatrical, almost taunting, but just convincing enough.

"Who dares awaken me! Who are you—state yourself and your business!"

The Lion's knees trembled violently.

The Scarecrow gave him a light smack. "Get a hold of yourself!"

Dorothy stepped forward. "It's me. Dorothy. I did what you asked—I brought back the hat of the Wicked Witch of the West."

She held out her palms, revealing the black, pointed hat. Then she bent down and placed it on the marble floor.

"She gave you the hat?" the Wizard's voice boomed.

Dorothy faltered. "No."

"You *took* it from her?"

She turned to glance at her friends, unsure of how to phrase it. "Sort of," she said. "She... kind of left it behind."

"She did, did she?" the voice mused. "And why would she do that? That witch is *obsessed* with this hat."

"If I must go into details..." Dorothy said, her voice uncertain. "I threw a bucket of water on her, and she melted. Right there. Into a green, boiling puddle. Nothing left but her pointed hat."

The head fell silent.

Toto, restless, sniffed at the air, then started barking, tugging at Dorothy's dress.

"Shush, Toto," she whispered, brushing him aside.

Then the Tinman stepped forward, his joints squeaking faintly. "Now that we've done what you asked, oh Great and Powerful Wizard..." he paused, placing a hand on his chest, "I would like to have a heart."

The Scarecrow followed, hands outstretched. "And I would like to have a brain!"

Then came the Lion, hesitantly padding forward, his tail dragging, voice shaking. "And I—I would like some courage, your Ozness."

Dorothy followed suit, standing tall, her pink slippers glinting beneath her gingham dress.

"And I would like to go home. To my Auntie Em."

The Wizard's voice dropped low, slow and suspicious.

"So... you're telling me the Witch of the West is dead?"

The Scarecrow let out a laugh. "Inexplicably. Unequivocally. Dead!"

"Melted!" the Lion added proudly.

"*Liquidated!*" the Tinman chimed in.

Dorothy stepped forward.

"So, we'd like you to keep your promise to us, if you please, sir."

But the Wizard snapped back, voice sharp and sudden.

"Then I cannot help you. I'll have to give the matter a little thought. Go and come back *tomorrow!*"

"*Tomorrow?*" Dorothy cried, her voice cracking. "But I want to go home *now!* My family's probably worried sick—Auntie Em has that heart condition. She's probably losing her mind!"

The Tinman raised his axe in frustration.

"You've had *plenty* of time already!"

Suddenly, fire erupted from the machine. Smoke hissed through the vents.

"*Do not arouse the wrath of the Great and Powerful Oz!*" the voice thundered.

But Dorothy didn't flinch. Her slippers clicked purposefully on the marble floor as she moved closer to the towering head.

"If you won't help us... then I won't give you something I know you want."

There was a beat.

"And what is *that?*"

Dorothy turned to the Scarecrow. He hesitated, then reached into a hidden fold of straw in his chest. From within, Dorothy pulled out a worn, ominous-looking book.

The *Kitab Malum.*

Dorothy held it up.

"Give that to me, *right now!*" the Wizard shouted, panic in his voice.

UNDONE

Dorothy tucked it under her arm. "No! not until you do what you promised to do!"

Toto barked furiously, sniffing the ground. He darted to the side of the room and sank his teeth into the heavy velvet curtain behind the mechanical head.

And pulled.

The curtain fell away.

Behind it stood none other than Glinda.

Startled, she instinctively reached to draw the curtain closed again, but the moment of truth had already revealed itself.

"*Pay no attention to that person behind the curtain!*" the Wizard's voice blurted from the machine, trying to regain control.

But it was too late.

They already saw the pink get-down.

The Tinman gasped. "*Glinda?*"

Dorothy stared. "*It's been you?*"

"In all of Oz…" the Scarecrow mouthed.

The Lion began to tremble and said nothing.

Glinda stepped forward slowly.

"It's not what it looks like," she began, then sighed. "Okay. *It is.* But you have to understand—"

"Where is the Wizard?" Dorothy demanded. "And why were you pretending to be him? Have you been a great fraud this entire time?"

"No, I am not," Glinda said firmly, trying to steady herself. She took a deep breath. "The Wizard… just left in his balloon, out of Oz indefinitely. And he asked me to take over for him."

"And he couldn't wait a little longer for me to leave with him?" Dorothy asked, holding Toto tighter in her arms. "Well then, where's he run off to?"

"Someplace called *Omaha*," Glinda replied.

"Oh! I know where that is!" Dorothy perked up. "I had an uncle who used to live there."

Glinda blinked, momentarily thrown, then quickly recovered. "Oh, and… he left me with a gift. For all of you."

"He did?" Dorothy asked, skeptical. "I hope this isn't one of your tricks now, *is it?*"

"No," Glinda replied with a dry, guilty laugh. "Give me a moment."

She ducked behind the curtain, retrieving her wand and two small emerald chests.

"Who wants to go first?" she asked, stepping back into the room.

"*Me!*" said the Scarecrow, eagerly pushing past the others.

Glinda smiled.

"For you, he left a brain, so you can do good things with it."

502

"Like read books? And do math?" the Scarecrow asked, his stitched face lighting up with awe.

Glinda chuckled. "Yes, just like that."

She opened the chest. The **brain** inside glowed faintly, pulsing with magic.

"Do you mind taking off your hat?" Glinda asked.

The Scarecrow removed it, revealing his straw-packed head. Glinda raised her wand over the glowing **brain**, which slowly levitated, then lowered into the Scarecrow's skull.

There was a pause.

The Scarecrow toppled backward as the **brain** nestled into place. His eyes fluttered—then widened with clarity. It was like watching him wake up for the very first time.

He gasped. "And suddenly... I understand so much more!"

He turned to Glinda, beaming. "*Thank you*, Glinda! Oh, I will most *definitely* take the utmost care of it!"

"You must," Glinda nodded. "I have some books I think you'd enjoy."

Just then, Dorothy stepped forward, frowning, looking at the Scarecrow.

He subtly shook his head, mouthing for her *not to speak*.

Dorothy ignored him and turned to Glinda.

"I know it isn't my turn, and *Crowy* here is too shy to ask, but can you give him skin? When we were attacked by the Wicked Witch, we almost lost him from a little fire."

The Scarecrow stepped forward, waving his hands.

"It's okay, Glinda. You've given more than I could have imagined!"

Glinda smiled gently. "You are so modest. That shouldn't be an issue."

She motioned for him to come closer.

He did just that.

She touched the side of his face, brushing her fingers over his straw and burlap.

"I see you've been enchanted. The person who turned you into a Scarecrow used powerful magic, ancient magic that can't be undone. I can't give you skin... but I *can* give your straw the feeling of it. Flesh that won't burn. Limbs that won't fall apart. Hands that can hold."

The Scarecrow nodded eagerly. "That sounds wonderful!"

"Very well."

Glinda lifted her wand. It glowed, brighter and brighter, then released a pulse of warmth into the air.

The Scarecrow shivered. He looked down at his arms, his legs. Then he jumped. And spun. And wiggled his fingers.

"It's been so long since I could *do* this!" he said joyfully. "Thank you, Glinda!"

"Who's next?" Glinda said.

The Tinman stepped forward.

Glinda smiled. "What I have in here is your heart. Would you open up your chest up, please?"

The Tinman nodded and clicked open the panel in his chest, revealing his whirring gears and brass piping.

Glinda opened the second emerald chest. A warm, glowing **heart** floated upward.

She guided it with her wand, gently easing it into his chest.

The Tinman shut the door.

Immediately, the sound of his machinery changed, louder, fuller. It was like new life had surged through him.

"Now," Glinda said, "you won't need oil to keep your body moving. This heart will pump the oil your body needs on its own."

The Tinman placed his hand over his chest, as if in awe. "It's... warm," he said. "Thank you!"

"You're most very welcome!" Glinda turned. "Who's next?"

Dorothy gave the Lion a little push. "Go on! We talked about this!"

The Lion stepped forward, his tail between his legs. "I—I'm next," he said with a shaky voice.

Glinda looked at him with kindness. "I know what you need. It's obvious. But I'm afraid... the Wizard didn't leave anything behind for you."

The Scarecrow, the Tinman, and Dorothy all bowed their heads in quiet disappointment.

The Lion's lip trembled. His eyes filled with tears.

Glinda paused, her own **heart** tugging at the sight of him.

She took a deep breath.

"Anyone have a sharp object?" she asked.

"I do!" said the Tinman.

He stepped forward with his axe, its blade gleaming, almost as sharp as the *Ozian Guillotine*.

Glinda held out her palm.

"Make a cut. Right in the middle."

"Are you sure?"

"Just do it!" Glinda ordered.

With care, the Tinman slid the blade across her palm. A sharp gasp, then a crimson line opened.

Blood began to well, dark at first—then, as Glinda lifted her wand to it, the blood shimmered and transformed.

It turned golden.

Thick like syrup, glowing with an inner light, like Yellow-Nectar drawn under the sun of high summer.

Glinda reached for a small transparent vial resting near the old machine head, catching the golden liquid as it fell from her hand.

She winced. The colour drained from her cheeks.

She stumbled slightly, gripping her wand for balance. A sudden wave of doubt, pain and uncertainty surged through her, but she steadied herself.

The wound on her hand sealed.

She handed the vial to the Lion.

"Drink this," Glinda said.

"You want him to drink your blood?" the Tinman asked, eyes wide.

"He's an animal, isn't he?"

"Oh yeah! I forget that sometimes," said the Scarecrow.

"But this isn't blood," Glinda added. "It's liquid courage. I gave him some of mine."

"That's... all I need to know," the Lion said softly.

He took the vial and drank.

The golden liquid ran down his throat and something in him shifted. His chest expanded. His paws grew wider. His claws extended. A fire lit behind his eyes.

Then he dropped down to all fours—and let out a roar.

Loud. Proud. Free.

His friends roared and clapped.

"You have courage!" the Scarecrow yelled, delighted.

The Lion turned to Glinda.

"What about you? What happened to your courage?"

Glinda smiled, weary but clear-eyed.

"It took me a long while, just like you, to build mine. But here's the truth: courage isn't something you own. It's something you grow. I gave you some of mine... but you'll need to learn to make your own."

The Lion's ears twitched.

"What if I can't?" he asked.

"Then you will become a coward again."

"But I get scared all the time. I can't help it."

Glinda laughed softly, stepping toward him and ruffling his mane.

"You have a misunderstanding that courage means not being scared. Courage is being scared and doing it anyway. You can't be courageous without being afraid. You can't simply own it—it is something you must choose."

Dorothy gasped, her hands lifting toward her chest.

"You have been courageous all this time! You were terrified of the Wicked Witch, yet you helped us anyway. You were courageous and you didn't know it."

The Lion smiled, then turned to Glinda and gave a low, humble bow.

"Thank you!"

He returned to his friends, who greeted him with claps on the back and fists of strength, pride glowing in their eyes.

Glinda watched them, uncertain whether they had truly killed the Wicked Witch of the West, highly unlikely, but what she was certain of, was that they were good. And better than that… they were good to each other.

Still, Glinda's spellwork had taken a toll. She took a quiet breath to collect herself, but an eager Dorothy stepped forward.

"Last but not least!" Glinda said. "I'll have what you wanted to give me,"

"Oh, right!" Dorothy replied, snapping back to the moment.

Dorothy turned to the Scarecrow, who now had the strength to carry the heavy tome. He gently handed the *Kitab Malum* to her and she passed it to Glinda.

"Thank you very much," Glinda said sincerely, cradling the dark tome to her chest.

The Scarecrow turned to her and asked, "Can't you just stay, Dorothy?"

Dorothy smiled, wistful.

"I have so much I left behind. The farm, my Auntie Em most of all." She looked down at Toto. "And I also have a Wicked Witch of my own back home who wants to get rid of my dog. But thanks to you all, I now have the courage and the heart to fight back against her. I defeated two Wicked Witches here—I can do for another!"

They laughed, everyone except Glinda.

Dorothy turned to her gently.

"Can you help me get home?"

Glinda looked down at Dorothy's feet, at the sparkling pink *Rosy Slippers*, and then back up. She smiled warmly.

"You've always had the power, my dear. You just had to learn it for yourself."

"Learn what?" the Scarecrow asked.

"Why didn't you tell her before?" the Tinman added.

"Why did we have to go through all this trouble?" the Lion exclaimed.

"Why don't you ask her?" Glinda said.

Dorothy took a breath. Her voice was no longer small—it carried.

"I had to learn for myself that wishing for another world means nothing unless I can appreciate the one I already have, and that no matter how far I go, the truest magic is remembering who I really am. I needed to understand, not just believe, that there's no place in the world quite like home—not because home is perfect, but because home is where I'm welcomed, where I am loved, and where I choose to give my heart."

"Quite so!" Glinda said. "And you learned that much quicker than I ever did."

Dorothy looked at Glinda. "Can I say goodbye to my friends before I leave?"

Glinda gave a warm smile and nodded.

Dorothy began to cry.

She went to the Tinman first and hugged him.

The Tinman began to cry too.

Dorothy wiped his tears away.

"Don't do that, you'll rust," she said, as the Tinman also wiped hers away.

"I now have a heart, and I know I do becoz it's breaking," the Tinman said before giving her another hug.

Dorothy went to the Lion and gave him a kiss on the cheek.

"I know it isn't right, but I'm gonna miss the way you used to holler for help before you found your courage."

The Lion began sniffling.

"I would never have found it if it hadn't been for you."

Dorothy laughed.

"Oh, look at you. I didn't know lions could cry until I met you."

They both laughed.

Dorothy moved to the Scarecrow.

This time her tears just poured down her face like a waterfall.

"I think I'll miss you most of all…" she said. "You are the very first friend I ever made in Oz, and you were the first to make me feel safe in this lonely place. You didn't know me for very long, but you were willing to burn for me, and that alone is worth everything to me."

The Scarecrow smiled.

"And you are one of the only people who ever called me smart even when I didn't have a brain."

She hugged him.

And he hugged her back fully with his new limbs.

Then she kissed him on the cheek.

"Are you ready now?" Glinda asked.

"Yes," Dorothy replied.

Dorothy picked up Toto and moved his little paw to wave goodbye to them. She turned to Glinda.

"Becoz my magic made these slippers," Glinda said, "it will work in a way that is personal to me. How good are you with clicking your heels?"

"Like this?" Dorothy asked, clicking her heels together with perfect grace.

"Yes!"

"How many times?" Dorothy asked.

"Three times for good measure, then close your eyes and wish for where you long to be most in the world at this *moment*."

Click! Click! Click!

Dorothy closed her eyes, and whispered, "Oh, there's no place like home."

A sudden puff of shimmering pink cloud curled around Dorothy and Toto. Her hair lifted as though touched by wind, and with a soft whoosh, she was swept away, vanished completely.

UNDONE

Nothing remained, except the **_Rosy Slippers_**.

And because time flowed differently in Oz than it did in the _Otherworld_, the three days Dorothy spent in Oz amounted to only seven hours back **_home_**.

The Rosy Slippers did not change into another colour, nor did they return to their original state of Silver, no, they remained **_Pink_**. Permanently changed by a certain Dorothy Gale from Kansas.

Glinda picked up the Slippers from where they stood, then she turned and gently escorted the Tinman, the Lion, and the Scarecrow out of the Emerald Palace. Once outside, she conjured a Bubble and flew through the skies toward Draeth Mor.

◊

Upon her arrival, an eerie quiet hung over the castle. Only the soft flap of wings echoed in the air, monkeys with bat wings. The larger ones, the ones with feathers, were nowhere to be seen.

Gone.

Glinda stepped into the tower where Zelphira often worked.

"Zelphira?" she called.

Silence.

"Zelphira!"

Still nothing.

Then, quieter this time. "Zelly?"

But there was no answer. Only the soft whine of wind curling through the stone.

Glinda stepped deeper into the room... and then saw it.

Laid out across the floor like a discarded rug, Zelphira's large, black cloak.

It seemed absurd, but Glinda walked forward, knelt, and gently lifted the edge of it...

Almost hoping, impossibly, that Zelphira might be hiding beneath it like a child playing pretend, but all she found was a green puddle. Just as Dorothy described.

Then—

A sharp chatter echoed at the window.

Glinda spun around, wand raised, and faced the source: a monkey perched on the sill, wings twitching, staring at her with eyes that shimmered with something almost... human.

The monkey remained on the windowsill and spoke.

"Glinda!" the monkey said.

"You can talk?" Glinda asked, startled.

"Yes. I'm Meleena. Zelphira gave the other children and me back our memories... and the ability to speak."

Glinda looked down at the heavy black cloak in her hands, clutched tightly against her chest.

"She did?!" she said, her lips curling into a smile. "And the feathered monkeys?"

"They all withered away into dust when she…"

"Where is she now?"

Meleena didn't answer right away. A pause.

"Didn't you hear the clocks? The eclipse? The rain? …The Wicked Witch of the West is dead. Destiny fulfilled."

Glinda let out a hollow laugh that could have just as easily broken into a sob.

"You're lying. I know she's around here somewhere, I feel it."

She turned around in the room, frantic, eyes darting, searching.

"Zelphira, where are you? Zelphira, come out this instant!"

"I'm sorry, Glinda," Meleena said. "But Dorothy killed her—with a bucket of water. We all saw it. She… melted."

Glinda's voice shrank to a whisper. "No…"

"I know you were friends, but it was awful. She melted in agony. Screaming. There was nothing left of her. Nothing but her cloak and her pointed hat which Dorothy took with her."

Glinda didn't speak.

She just walked, slowly, over to the stone staircase, her arms still wrapped tightly around the cloak. She sat down, curling the black fabric around her like a shawl and began to rock gently.

"You were supposed to survive this. You were supposed to survive," she whispered under her breath.

Then her eyes suddenly lit with a spark.

A revelation.

She turned to the monkey. "Where is her broom?"

The monkey shrugged, helpless.

Meleena watched Glinda for a moment, saw the heaviness in her shoulders, the sharp stillness of grief—and quietly turned away.

She dropped from the perch in freefall, wings opening as she lifted into the sky, rising to join the other bat-winged children now circling overhead.

Glinda stood again and began to pace around the tower.

The cloak still draped over her like mourning shrouds.

Every sound made her turn—every flutter of wind, every soft creak in the stone made her **heart** jump, made her believe *maybe*, just *maybe*…

Then, her foot tapped something hollow.

She looked down.

A wooden trapdoor.

Glinda gasped.

She dropped to her knees, pried it open, and smiled, breath caught in her chest—

"Zelphira?" she whispered.

She looked inside.

There was nothing.

Absolutely nothing.

She stood there for a while, staring into the hollow dark, as though silence might speak.

Eventually, Glinda left the tower and began walking the vast halls of Draeth Mor.

She opened every door, one by one.

Nothing.

She entered Zelphira's room.

Empty.

She walked into her old room—the one Rivero had assigned her when she spent her summer there with Zelphira.

Stillness. Dust. No one.

Then, she reached Lirvan's room.

Preserved. Untouched.

The crib still stood, looking as though he had just been laid down for a nap.

The air inside was thinner, quieter.

Sadder than any place in Draeth Mor.

Sadder than any place in Oz.

She picked up Lirvan's silver rattle and gave it a gentle shake. The soft ring tightened her chest, but it still made her smile.

She held it for a moment, then set it carefully back in the crib.

Glinda continued searching, but she found nothing.

Not Zelphira.

Not her broom.

Desperation creeping in, Glinda lifted her wand and cast a locator spell over the black cloak.

A thread of hope.

But nothing happened.

The cloak danced in the air for a moment, then dropped, laying still—lifeless and cold.

And the only time a locator spell failed… was when the soul it searched for had passed beyond reach.

In that moment, Glinda knew.

It was final.

The Wicked Witch of the West is ***dead***.

She returned to the tower.

She stood in the centre of it.

She didn't cry.

She didn't scream, but her eyes were red.

And her fists were clenched so tight they trembled.

This time, she didn't leave through the open air at the top.

She walked down the spiral stairs to the entrance.

At the door, she turned back one final time.

With her wand raised, Glinda cast the same spell she had once used to seal the Magic Waterfall Garden—

the strongest concealment magic she knew.

She sealed the tower shut.

Stone and shadow wrapped around it like a tomb.

It was a grave now.

The grave of her sister.

Zelphira had been melted—reduced to nothing.

But Glinda could still feel her essence clinging to the stone, to the silence, to the cloak in her arms.

She wasn't gone.

Not really.

Her imprint on her will remain forevermore.

And so, Glinda stepped onto the courtyard.

She lifted her wand.

A pink sphere of magic bloomed around her like a living breath.

She rose into the sky.

And this time, she flew higher than she ever had before.

Above the towers.

Above the clouds.

And that's when she lost it.

The wind screamed past her Bubble, but all she could hear was *Zelphira*.

She saw her, wild on her broom, laughing with perfect *wickedness*, her long black hair whipping behind her like ink spilled across the sky.

Her green skin aglow, brighter than sunlight catching on the Emerald Towers.

And that *smile*, warm, and mischievous, and rare, and precious.

Glinda's breath caught as memory after memory surged before her eyes, the laughter, the arguments, the shared silences, the trembling trust rebuilt too late.

But what lingered most… was regret.

She had only just begun to make things right.

Only just found her again.

Too much time lost and now, Zelphira was *gone*.

And Glinda, Glinda had not been there.

She hadn't held her hand.

She hadn't stopped fate like she promised.

Maybe if she had stayed.

Maybe if she had come sooner.

Maybe…

Zelphira would still be alive.

Inside the Bubble, she screamed until her lungs rattled against her ribs.

And the sobs came, ugly, raw, and unrelenting.

Noise ripped from her throat she couldn't control.

Couldn't silence.

Didn't want to.

Suspended above all of Oz, with the sun blazing hot around her, Glinda hovered—

mid-air, mid-grief.

Alone.

Utterly *alone.*

For a fleeting moment… she let herself be free.

Free from being the Good Witch.

Free from the lies, the politics, the performance.

Just *Glinda,* mourning *Zelphira.*

She clutched the cloak tight against her face.

Lavender.

It still smelled like her.

Like the tower.

Like the warmth of a memory unwilling to fade.

And now… Glinda had her two totems back.

The pointed hat.

The black cloak.

The ones she bought long ago in *Farkleberry & Things* and gave to a girl who saw their ugliness, and loved them anyway.

Now, she had almost everything back but the person they were meant for.

◇

Glinda arrived in Gillikin in pieces, and Ominson had to help her walk indoors.

She told him everything, that Zelphira was gone. And in some quiet way, Ominson mourned her too, because he smiled just as much when Glinda recalled the best memories they had shared.

◇

That very night, as Ominson kissed Orryn goodnight, Glinda stood by the door, smiling at the sight of Orryn safely tucked into his bed. Ominson left the room, but Glinda lingered, just watching him. As she turned to close the door, Orryn spoke.

"Mom…" he whispered.

"Yes, my love?" she replied.

"Why were you sad?"

Glinda sat on the edge of his bed as he sat up.

"Mumsy just lost a friend, that's all. But Mumsy is fine, okay?"

"You mean… your friend is never coming back?"

Glinda sighed. "Yes."

"Is she over the rainbow like Gisella?"

Glinda smiled warmly, her eyes misting. "Yes, my love. Way, way, way up high."

Orryn giggled. "You're so silly, Mom. Your friend isn't really gone. She's with the One Gohd asking him to make all your dreams come true. Smart people know that!"

Glinda took his little hand in hers. "You're so right. Thank you for reminding Mumsy." She scooted closer. "And you know… she loves you very much. She told me so herself. And she is asking the One Gohd to protect you, in all the ways she couldn't protect… *others*."

Orryn giggled again.

Glinda looked at his face.

He was staring at the window.

Still giggling.

Glinda turned her head to the window, then back to him.

"Was it your green friend who went to the One Gohd?" Orryn asked, eyes still fixed on the glass.

"Yes. Why?"

Unnerved, Glinda stood up and crossed the room to the window. She pulled back the curtain.

There was nothing.

She opened the window and leaned her head into the cold air.

And then she saw it.

Left on the windowsill, just outside, was a silver rattle.

Glinda picked it up and turned it over in her hands.

It was undeniably Lirvan's.

She gasped softly as she gave it a gentle shake.

The chime was unmistakable.

She stared at it for a moment, then she quickly leaned back out the window for a sign.

Any sign.

Finally, she whispered into the air, "Thank you, for everything," letting the words carry on the wind, straight to whom they were meant for.

Glinda sat beside Orryn and placed the silver rattle in his hand.

"She left this for you."

He shook it and smiled.

UNDONE

Glinda ruffled his hair and kissed him on the forehead. "Good night, my love."

Orryn tucked the rattle beside him and stared at the window… until sleep found him.

CHAPTER 51

No One Mourns

The time had come. Glinda had to announce the death of the Wicked Witch to the public.

And though she could have easily broadcast the message across all of Oz, just as the Wizard once did when he declared Zelphira the Wicked Witch—she refused. Zelphira deserved more than that. She deserved better.

Rumours had already begun to spread. Celebrations had already started. But Glinda made a vow to do it properly, to tell the people herself. Face to face. Corner by corner.

She began in the North.

Then the South.

Then the West.

And finally, the East, Munchkinland.

She saved Munchkinland for last. It was Zelphira's **home.** And no matter how much time had passed, she still couldn't bear to return and tell them that the girl many of them had grown up with—their friend, their neighbour, her sister—was gone.

Glinda's Bubble hovered just behind the sun. From that height, she could see everything.

The Munchkins and Munchkinlanders were already celebrating. Singing and dancing, tossing petals into the wind, splashing one another with buckets of water.

Word had already reached them, faster than she could fly.

And worst of all, they had built a giant effigy of the Wicked Witch of the West. Arms raised, one hand holding a broom carved from wood cut by the Tinman. The likeness was uncanny, down to the nose.

Glinda's old nose.

Her breath caught.

But still, she sang.

She began to hum the *Day Songbird* melody with perfect pitch, her voice glittering over the skies like magic itself:

UNDONE

"Let us smile!

Rise and pray!"

"Look, it's Glinda!" a Munchkinlander called, pointing upward.

They all turned.

And cheered.

Glinda sang through her pain.

And it took every fibre in her bones to get the words out of her throat.

"Let's rejoice and know that Goodness does do

End all Wicked workings of those that loom

Oh, and yes we do know who

So rejoicify, now I say,

We live to see another day

Now that the sun has come and Wickedness has passed away!"

Glinda landed gently on the Munchkin podium, ceasing her Bubble spell.

She smiled.

And the people cheered, louder than they ever had for her.

Ten decibels higher.

She noticed.

She stepped forward, just briefly pausing to glance up at the towering effigy of the Wicked Witch, hands raised, broom in tow, pointed nose protruding with grim majesty.

Then she looked back down. At the people. At their beaming, radiant faces.

"Fellow Ozians! Becoz there has been so much rumour and speculation, let me tell you the whole and true story."

The crowd fell instantly quiet.

Petals slowed in the air, drifting down like snowflakes coming to rest.

"According to the *Chronoglint Gilded Dial,* the melting occurred at the 13th Hour, by direct result of a bucket of water thrown by a female child."

Her voice wavered.

"Yes… the Wicked Witch of the West is dead!"

The crowd erupted. Clapping in perfect, rhythmic unison. And just when Glinda thought they had exhausted every last petal in Munchkinland, more came—somehow—raining down from rooftops and windows.

"Good News! She's Dead!

Oh, such Good News! She's Dead and Gone!"

They sang in unison, their pitch was uncanny, their joy overwhelming.

It felt rehearsed, as if they'd been preparing for this day all their lives.

To let their hearts roar. To finally be free.

But what struck Glinda the most, what caught her breath and cracked her heart, was that the Munchkins were the ones who cheered the loudest.

They sang the loudest.

And danced the fiercest.

The very people who grew up with her.

Their own citizen.

So small-minded, Glinda thought.

But the truth, the hard, raw truth, was this:

The Munchkins weren't celebrating her death because they feared her.

They were celebrating because *after* the Wicked Witch of the West arrived, *people stopped laughing at them.*

Suddenly, it wasn't funny that they were so small.

They weren't the joke anymore.

She was.

Green and Weird.

Outrageous and Disgustifying!

A new target had emerged.

One that diverted ridicule and brought respect to those who had once been belittled.

The Munchkins, mocked for their stature, ignored for their voices, found pride in their fear.

People saw them now.

Heard them.

Respected their hatred for the Wicked Witch.

And that, for them, was enough.

Zelphira had unknowingly taken that burden.

So they could stand a little taller.

So they could walk through their lives with a little more dignity.

She absorbed the world's cruelty so they wouldn't have to.

The music swelled again, their voices consistent as they continued the song:

> *"No one mourns the Wicked!*
> *No tears for her deceit.*
> *Her skin green, heart black as coal,*
> *Her end is our relief.*
> *End of her bloodline—now that is belief!"*

Then, suddenly, all turned to Glinda.

Their eyes expectant.

Waiting for her to finish the song.

She hesitated.

She stood motionless at first, the silence stretching.

Then she exhaled, took a single step forward, and raised her voice.

It soared, clear and haunting, cutting through the air like a bell.

Higher than it had ever reached when she tried to mask a lie.

Almost operatic.

A note of unbearable beauty.

A truth wrapped in melody.

"She died in vain,

I wish her so much pain,

Her green skin—so much stain,

I hate her so… much disdain,

She'll melt away in heavy rain…"

Glinda sang.

Her eyes watered, but she dared not let it fall.

She kept the tremor in her throat steady, her voice unwavering, as she struggled to finish the verse.

"If she's somewhere out there on the other plane,

Forced to burn in Hel, paradise never again,

Over the rainbow, the bluebirds—shall I say—

Wickedness gone… in Goodness I pray."

And that was the worst lie Glinda Fairmoor had ever told.

She sang it with all the power in her lungs, every note polished and shimmering—

Because even if the words betrayed her heart, the melody could carry the truth.

Rising above the lies and words of the Munchkins.

Above the lies she was forced to speak.

A secret only the sky, and perhaps Zelphira, wherever she was, might hear.

And Glinda hoped, *hoped* with every fibre of her aching soul,

That if Zelphira was out there, listening,

She'd forgive the words and appreciate the melody.

And rest peacefully to the tune of her voice.

When no one was looking, Glinda let a single tear fall.

When she finished, the crowd erupted.

They clapped, roared, cheered, and tossed petals into the air until the sky itself blushed pink.

Their hero.

Oh yes, *their very good hero.*

A little boy ran to her, grinning wide. He held up a flaming torch and pointed to the towering effigy.

Glinda's hand twitched.

She motioned to give it back to him, *Please*, she thought, but the Munchkinlanders cheered even louder.

There was no way out now.

With her wand in one hand and the torch in the other, Glinda walked up to the effigy.

She stood beneath it—towering straw, broom and hat—

And threw the torch.

GLINDA: The GOOD Witch

It caught instantly, flames leaping upward with ravenous glee.

It burned fast, like it had waited all its life for this.

The effigy became a second sun.

And Glinda…

She walked to the centre of the podium once more.

She raised both arms, her long wand outstretched, mirroring the exact pose of the burning witch.

She let out the final soaring note:

"Goodness knows!"

And yes…

She did.

She held that note for as long as she could, her voice slicing through the smoke, through the cheers, through the lie.

And that was that.

The Wicked Witch of the West had been buried—

Not by soil,

But by story.

And then—

As Glinda turned to leave, a little Munchkinlander girl ran up, tugging at her dress.

"Goody! Goody!!"

Glinda turned gently. "Yes?"

The little Munchkin girl looked up at her, eyes wide.

"Why are people Wicked?"

Glinda blinked.

"That is a good question."

She knelt down to meet the girl at eye level.

"Most people find it… *befuddlelotius*." She gave a gentle smile. "Are people just born Wicked? Or are they turned into Wicked beings?"

The little girl leaned in, eager.

"Do you think the Wicked Witch was born Wicked?"

The crowd went quiet.

All of Munchkinland leaned in, waiting.

Glinda looked into the child's eyes.

"The Wicked Witch was born a babe, like all of us." She paused. "It would be wrong for us to say that from the very moment she was born, even as a kindling, she was Wicked."

"Not her!" a crowd member interrupted. "She was born green for a reason! She should've been burnt the moment she came out of the womb!"

The crowd exploded into laughter.

It echoed louder than even the cheers.

519

Then, slowly, the laughter died.

Glinda kept her gaze steady, locked on the girl.

"People were cruel to her," she said softly. "It wasn't easy. She was green... and that made her different."

She turned to the crowd. Her voice sharpened. "And sometimes people don't like that."

Someone shouted from the crowd:

"Yes, Glinda, but the difference is, we didn't go around murdering babies and drinking their blood!"

Laughter again. Cruel.

Howling.

Glinda didn't smile.

She turned away from them.

She looked at the burning effigy, towering, crackling, laughing in its own way.

And it was in *that* moment, watching the fire eat away at what remained of her sister's silhouette, Glinda finally found the answer to the question she'd carried all her life.

Goodness... is whatever Society decides it is.

Zelphira, beautiful Zelphira, had been made grotesque in part because of Glinda.

What started as a *harmless* joke... became canon.

A hooked nose—*her* nose. A pointed hat. A silhouette burned into myth.

The world loved to remember a joke.

But never the joy and love that was born from it.

Glinda looked up at the fire one last time.

She said nothing.

She formed her Bubble.

And she rose.

She didn't wave.

She didn't smile.

She refused to look down, refused to watch the Munchkins continue their celebration.

Celebrating the death of her sister.

Zelphira.

Epilogue

Saint Glinda

A few moons passed, and Glinda finally shared the truth with the people of Oz. She spoke of the prophecy—that a *New True Wizard* was destined to rise. The people listened, wide-eyed and reverent. They believed that the old Wizard had been called up to the heavens once his mission was fulfilled: aiding in the defeat of the Wicked Witch. Now, he was said to be among the stars, one of them named *Omaha*, looking down from above.

Though they mourned the absence of a Wizard, the hope of a new one on the horizon kept their hearts full.

They had something to look forward to.

And so, Oz entered a new age.

Glinda took the reins of leadership, but she did not claim the throne. She kept it vacant, waiting, reserved for the one truly worthy of it.

She disbanded the Wizard's Guard, no longer needed to protect a throne that had lost its master. Instead, she gave them new purpose: to serve as peacekeepers, patrolling all four corners of Oz, ensuring safety for its citizens. With no Wizard left to guard, their loyalty was better spent on the people.

The Emerald Towers and Palace were closed to the public—no one allowed within its gates. It would stand as a silent, gleaming monument. A landmark of what had been—and a reminder of what would return.

It would only reopen… when the *True Wizard of Oz* arrived.

And as for the **Kitab Solis** and **Kitab Malum**—Glinda had a revelation.

She couldn't stop thinking about what Zelphira said during their final conversation:

"We are two sides of the same coin."

It echoed in her heart.

None of them had ever been wholly good. It was impossible.

And neither were they wholly wicked.

UNDONE

That was the flaw, the dangerous illusion, of separating the Kitab Solis from the Kitab Malum. It split the truth in half. Zelphira had suffered because of that division. She had been unable to undo spells that could have saved her, or others, simply because the wisdom was locked away in the "other" book.

She had believed that spells from the Grimorium were completely irreversible.

Had the two been one from the start... who knows what might've been prevented?

Glinda understood now.

Magic didn't need walls, it needed **balance.**

Nuance. Harmony.

Pink and Green.

Light and Shadow.

Solis and Malum.

Truth.

And so, she corrected Seraphina's mistake.

She fused the two books into one.

One volume. One whole.

The Kitab Eterna.

Otherwise known as... The Equilibrium.

Neither good nor wicked—just *honest.*

And that... was what Oz needed most.

From then on, Glinda ruled justly, wise, tempered, and unyielding in her pursuit of fairness.

Very fitting of her name.

Fairmoor.

A Saint to the people of Oz.

A symbol of Goodness.

And though they adored her, they also grew to fear her. Respect her.

For she did not hesitate to uphold justice, even when it broke hearts to do so.

She abolished the ancient rule that every girl's name must end in an "A."

She legalized the free practice of magic in all four corners of Oz.

No politician, no king, no empress dared challenge her word.

And much like Dorothy, the Tinman, the Cowardly Lion, and the Scarecrow—

Glinda too had to build *courage,*

Think with her *brain,*

Lead with her *heart,*

To find her way back *home.*

◇

522

Many years had gone by, and Oz was peaceful. Harmonious. Blissful. The people still told stories of the *Great and Powerful Wizard*, though few remembered his face. The legend had swallowed the man just as the myth of the *Wicked Witch of the West* had buried the woman she once was.

But some truths… have a way of finding light.

Glinda often stood on the balcony of her North Tower, gazing out over the lands below. The wind carried voices, laughter, songs—some old, some new. And sometimes, in the breeze, a child's voice would echo: "Dorothy."

A name.

A spell.

A kind of magic.

Orryn played in the garden below, growing fast—wiser by the day. Undeniably, he had Glinda's fire. Her ***heart***. And Zelphira's stubbornness too. She saw it in his eyes whenever he looked up at the stars like they owed him an answer. And though he was still just a boy, those who met him often said there was something different about Orryn, something watchful in his eyes, ancient in his thoughts, like he had lived lifetimes before this one. As if Oz was waiting for him to grow into who he was meant to be.

He often asked questions no one else dared: about the old Wizard, about Zelphira, about the things adults kept hidden behind silence. Glinda never lied to him. She couldn't. He reminded her too much of everything she'd fought for, and everything she still hoped for.

The *Rosy Slippers* remained intact, preserved… But the stories hadn't. Children still spoke of them like a promise—that kindness could change fates, and even witches… could be good. And they were right, of course. But the tale changed with each retelling.

The tower at Draeth Mor remained sealed. A monument to a woman who had once been feared and hated, and who Glinda had loved more fiercely than she could explain. Sometimes, when the sky was clear and the moon was full, Glinda would fly there, not to unseal it, but simply to sit on its highest ledge and remember.

The world never truly knew who the Wicked Witch really was.

But Glinda did.

And though they say,

"*No One Mourns the Wicked,*"

We, the Fates, challenge that and *say:*

No, ***One*** *Mourns the Wicked.*

THE BEGINNING…

Glossary

Pronunciation Guide

Zelphira – zel-FEE-rah
Gisella – ji-ZELL-ah
Draeth Mor – drayth-MOR
Ugabu – oo-GAH-boo
Ummi – OOM-mee
Vallas – VAL-lahs
Goatééy Ganee – goh-TAY-Gah-NAY
Seraphina – seh-rah-FEE-na
Pryzm – PRIZ-um
Mz. Everburn – miz EVER-burn
NewZPapr – newz-Paper
Ominson – Aw-MIN-sin
Ethereum – ee-THEER-ee-um
Grimorium – grih-MOHR-ee-um
Altheba – al-THEB-uh

Artifacts & Objects

Rosy Slippers – Pink sparkly slippers worn by Dorothy.
Emerald Shard – The source of Emerald City's lights.
Fiora's Magical Hairbrush – A legendary brush that creates perfect hairstyles.
Golden Goose Carriage – A luxurious carriage model used by the aristocracy of Oz.
Kitab Malum (The Grimorium) – A mysterious, extremely powerful, and dangerous spellbook.
Kitab Solis (The Ethereum) – An ancient, powerful spellbook written in cryptic markings.

Kitab Eterna (The Equilibrium) – The joining of The Grimorium and The Ethereum. The complete spellbook.

Ozyclopedia – A large book giving information on many subjects or on many aspects of Oz typically arranged alphabetically.

Raindrop Gemz – Magical gems used in ceremonies to determine tribes, exclusive to Quadling Country.

Seraphina's Magic Wand – A relic tied to Seraphina, The Forsaken Witch.

Sunspell Stone – A rare and precious, expensive stone used in jewellery.

Wither-Swan Carriage – A shimmering white and silver carriage.

Chronoglint Gilded Dial – The National Clock of Oz that measures Oz's passage of time and used as the reference for logs made in the Book of Records.

Ozian Traditions & Events

Born-Day – The Ozian equivalent of a birthday celebration.

Day Songbird Melody – A sacred song used in worship in Quadling Country, believed to purify even the darkest souls.

Moonshine Coronation – A rite of passage where a magical gem is chosen for a newborn.

Ozma's Eve – A celebration of the birth of the Ozmas, celebrated in the winter.

Time

Sun-Moon - A year.

Oz'moons - A month.

Oz'min - A minute.

Suns - A day.

Moons - A day or poetic term (used interchangeably with "Sun" in some regions).

Morn-mid Oz' Clock – Midday.

New-Oz'Moon – The Ozian New Year.

HourZ - Hours (stylised spelling).

Unique Terms

Byke –A bicycle.

Ryde – A journey by use of a moving vehicle.

Plodsnail – A metaphor for something extremely slow-moving.

Kindling – A young child. (Often used affectionately.)

Yungling – A teenager.

Pryzm Road – A crystal-paved road that refracts light into rainbow hues. Reserved for aristocrats and highborn travellers, it provides faster, exclusive route through Oz.

Middies – Middle Class.

Poorling – Poor people.

Gohd – Ozian equivalence of God.

Make-Do – Make-up/Cosmetics.

Hel/Ell – Hell.

Heahven – Heaven.

Ummi/Sirrah – Mentors assigned to students at university (female/male respectively).

Elphebet – The Ozian alphabet.

Magicore – The Magical Core that exists within magic wielders.

Tod – Slang for male genitalia.

Twiddle – Slang for female genitalia.

Flatheads – small, strange creatures with flat skulls that reside in the enchanted forest.

Wholly – Holy or typically referencing The One Gohd, Ozma, Lurline or Ozian spirituality.

ALTHEBA – A title which translates to: *'The Sorceress Supreme'*. She is the prophesied saviour and most powerful magic wielder Oz has ever known.

Currency

Brz – Bronze
Slv – Silver
Gld – Gold

Exchange Rate

10 Bronze (brz) = 1 Silver (slv)
10 Silver = 1 Gold (gld)

Author's Note

When I first set out to write *GLINDA: The GOOD Witch*, I never imagined the emotional path it would take me on. What began as a reimagining of an iconic character became something far more personal—a story of power, betrayal, love, identity, and legacy.

At its heart, this book is not just about witches or magic or prophecy—it's about women who have been misunderstood. It's about the lies we tell to survive, and the truths we fight to protect. It's about how history picks heroes and villains, and how often, it gets the story wrong.

Glinda and Zelphira—two women bound by destiny, but separated by the choices they were forced to make—are mirrors. Of each other. Of all of us.

If you took anything from this novel, I hope it's this: There is power in choosing kindness. There is courage in vulnerability. And sometimes, the most radical thing we can do is tell our own story before someone else writes it for us.

Thank you for walking this path with me.

May you find your own magic,
And protect it well.

—R.W. ADAMS

ACKNOWLEDGEMENTS

First and foremost, I would like to thank God for allowing me to complete this novel. What began as a strike of inspiration turned into one of the most fulfilling journeys of my life thus far, completing my first novel.

When I began writing this story, I felt more like a scribe than a creator, as if I were simply recording something that had already happened, is happening now, and will happen again. The words poured through me like a current I could not control. I can only describe it as spiritual, divine.

And so, in the simplest words I know: thank You.

To the person this novel is dedicated to, my little sister, Ami, thank you. I know it was annoying when I barged in, laptop in hand, and made you sit through chapters with your eyes glazed over, staring at the wall. But you sat through it. You listened, truly listened, because you knew how much this meant to me. And for that, all I can say is: thank you.

To my mother, who has supported every endeavour I've ever pursued, thank you. Your unwavering faith in me gave me the strength never to second-guess myself. I've changed my mind a hundred times, chased dreams, then chased new ones, and every time, you believed in me. I remember telling you, "I'm going to write a book," and you didn't even blink. You simply encouraged me. And no matter how old I get, or how much I pretend I don't need it, I'll always be your little boy. Your words carry weight, and I carry them with me. Thank you for believing, even in the earlier years when I told you I was going to become an astronaut.

To my little brother, thank you for listening to my ideas at midnight and offering your thoughts. You may not realize it, but it helped more than you know.

And finally, to the Father of Oz himself, L. Frank Baum, to whom I paid tribute in this novel through a character named Elfrank. Your imagination gave birth to a world that has endured for generations. I hope, wherever you are, somewhere over the rainbow, you are proud of what I've created from the seeds you planted.

The simplest way I can express my gratitude is to say it plainly and from the heart:

Thank you.
Thank you.
Thank you.

About the Author

R.W. Adams is a night owl by nature — the kind of writer who'll wake at midnight to chase a passing spark of inspiration before it fades. Stories arrive suddenly, insistently, and when they do, he writes.

He was drawn to Oz not by the infamous Wicked Witch, but by the quieter mystery: Glinda. What shaped her? What broke her? And how did she become the woman we thought we knew? *Glinda: The GOOD Witch* is his debut novel — the first in a sweeping saga that seeks to uncover the full, unvarnished truth of Oz.

Though he reads widely across genres — from horror and thrillers to high fantasy — Adams's stories always seek to do one thing: shift your way of seeing the world. He hopes, by the final page, you feel just a little bit changed…

Not for *Good* but for the *Better*.

To connect, visit **www.rwadamsbooks.com**
Social Media: rwadamsbooks

Coming Soon
From the author of GLINDA: The GOOD Witch
If you thought Glinda was the whole story—think again.

A storm is coming.
And her name is just…
The Beginning.

BORNE WICKED

Excerpt from: BORNE WICKED

"Oh, please do tell us about the green one!" Eleanor, the little girl asked as she leaned forward into the fire's warmth.

"Did she really die? What became of her?" Theodore, the tall boy asked.

The Storyteller fitted their hands into their pockets and let out a heavy sigh then scoured the faces of the seven children that sat before them. "Zelphira."

"Yes!" One child added. "Why couldn't the people of Oz see what was right before them?"

"I get so angry thinking about it!" Charles, the big boy added. "If they sat back to think, they could see through the lies the Wizard was telling."

Eleanor picked up a tiny rock in her hands and tossed it into the flame. "Because people only see what they want to see."

"Right you are!" said the Storyteller. "You see, in a world like this and a world like Oz, if you put out signals that you do not want to belong, people are going to make sure that you don't."

"But it wasn't her fault!" said Eleanor "Her signal was being green; she didn't choose that."

"And Glinda's was her weird nose and that wasn't her fault either," said the Theodore.

The wind had now picked up and the children scooted closer to one another once more as the fire that lay at the centre began to dim and the sky had blackened to its darkest.

Theo, the tall boy turned, "There's no way she died. It's obvious."

"She melted under the bucket of water, just like her vision told her, remember?" Eleanor added.

"What is surviving?" asked The Storyteller. "Are we surviving if we lose ourselves and become something else entirely?"

Theo stood up from the log he was sitting on and paced back and forth, pondering. "Maybe, surviving is going through obstacles, being open to change and being born anew. That is survival."

The Storyteller smiled.

"But what we mean is did she truly die by Dorothy's hands?" Charles asked. "When Glinda sealed the Tower, was that truly her end?"

The wind blew again, and for a moment Eleanor saw the fire flicker from orange to green.

Lime.

"Woah," said the little girl.

"What?" asked Theo.

"Did you not see the fire turn green? I think The Fates are listening!"

"Don't be absurd," replied Theo. "It was just a trick of the light or something."

"What light?" asked Charles.

Eleanor looked at The Storyteller, "You saw it too, right?"

The Storyteller just gave a little wink and a smile.

"Tell us the truth," said Theo, "not that I care but…"

"Of course you care!" said Charles, the big boy. "We all do, because this isn't just about a pink witch and a green one. This is about us and the lives we live. Why we're out here in the woods instead of in the village with the other kids. Why the world is split into good and evil."

Tall boy rolled his eyes and began tracing random symbols into the sand with a little stick.

"They ought to know we're just like them, even us orphans are worth just as much even though we eat their garbage and wear their potato sacks," said the frail boy.

The Storyteller remained silent.

Eleanor shrugged, "I just want to know what happened to the *Rosy Slippers*. Does Dorothy ever come back with Toto?"

The Storyteller broke their silence. "I waited to tell you the tale of the Wicked Witch because I wanted you to understand the difference between her title and the person." They paused. "You see, whether you think she was wicked or not is just up to interpretation and what you believe. Eleanor thought she saw the fire turn green and she thinks The Fates are listening and Theodore thought it was the trick of the light."

"Well, are The Fates listening?" asked big boy.

"They are always listening," replied The Storyteller.

"Bollywash!" said Theo. "They don't exist, you're just telling made up stories."

"Everything is made up stories," said Charles, "We never get the story quite right. We only, almost always know half of the story."

The Storyteller laughed. "You're right Charles, but this time we will know the whole story."

"Just like Glinda's?" asked Eleanor.

"Oh yes, by accounts of The Fates who see all and write all destiny… This is the truth, the whole truth and make of it what you will from what I will tell you about the story of The Wicked Witch of the West—the orphan Zelphira, the girl borne wicked."